GEOFFREY VERDEGAST

SOULS OF ERGOS

BOOK ONE:

OF STAVES AND SIGMAS

THIRD EDITION

Please visit the official website at: www.SoulsOfErgos.com
Critique and corrections are graciously received at: gverdegast@gmail.com

"I May Know The Word" written by Natalie Merchant (C) 1995; Indian Love Bride Music (ASCAP) All Rights Reserved; Used By Permission.

Cover Art by Chip Boles; www.chipboles.com

First published by Dog Ear Publishing
4010 W. 86th Street, Ste H
Indianapolis, IN 46268
www.dogearpublishing.net

Third Edition
Published by Geoffrey Verdegast
ISBN: 978-0-9834539-0-1
Library of Congress Control Number: 2007921725

This book is a work of fiction. Places, events, and situations in this book are purely fictional and any resemblance to actual persons, living or dead, is coincidental.

This book is printed on acid-free paper.
Printed and bound in the United States of America

ACKNOWLEDGEMENTS

Many are the good people of past and present who have inspired and encouraged (and sometimes humoured) me in this ambitious project. Some of them—the philosophers, the literary masters, the composers—I know only by the phenomenal legacies that they have left for humanity to enjoy and emulate, works that have delighted the masses and endured the eras. I can only marvel at their tremendous fortitude and insight. As for those of you who have aided and emboldened me directly, you have my deepest affection and my most profound gratitude. Most of you know who you are. For those who may be unsure, please read on:

This work is dedicated, above all, to my parents, Jack and Edith, who sacrificed so much of their free time and family income to ensure that their kids had childhoods filled with a rich abundance of historical and cultural experience. You were the shapers of my imagination.

Thanks also to my crazy, dysfunctional siblings, Dan and Diana, and their families, whose individual quirks and rampant zaniness have been every bit as helpful in my research of abnormal psychology as were the sundry texts and papers that I bought and borrowed (or thieved from unsuspecting psych majors). Maybe more so. A special nod to my brother-in-law, Bob, who so often served as a sounding board for my initial outlines and ideas.

To my best pal, Jeff Zoppetti, who was probably never quite aware of the unearthly realms that I was visiting during my considerable, hermitic periods of introspection, but who nevertheless had faith that I would get it all down on paper...sooner or later. Thanks, *paisano!*

To the Reserve Pallet guys—and I mean the *core group*: Rick, Gary, Dale, Tom, and Pappy—you may not have inspired me one iota book-wise, but you slugs have been some of my staunchest confederates over the years. Thanks for indulging me in my insanity.

And finally, to my three lovely muses, Jenny, Amber, and Ashley, who kept my coffee cup filled, and my heart in race (and not just from the caffeine), during my many weekend editing marathons at the Tradewinds Restaurant. I have no doubt that each of you, in your own way, influenced my comedic and dramatic perspectives, and helped me to bring a richer sense of humanity and adventurousness to my characters. You girls rock!

NEW FOR THE THIRD EDITION

This edition goes to press with a terrific new cover, designed and produced for me by Chip Boles, an extremely talented and internationally admired fellow whose services I had the extreme honour and good fortune to secure. Highly adept in both conventional illustration *and* mixed media, Chip is not only astonishingly disciplined and visionary in his craft, but he exudes a refreshingly rare integrity in his business relationships, he's a pleasure to work with, and he boasts a rapier wit to boot. Therefore, I'll be hoping to negotiate for his continued presence as cover artist for the subsequent instalments in the *Souls of Ergos* saga. Not only is his contribution to this edition of *Of Staves and Sigmas* sure to leave you breathless (go ahead, take another gander at the cover—I'll wait), but you can count on seeing more of Chip's work globally, and maybe even galactically, as his reputation grows. In fact, were I a betting man I would wager all of my...er...*chips* on it. Ouch.

In the technical realm, I haven't altered too much of the *Of Staves and Sigmas* text since the Second Edition. In fact, I think I've corrected exactly five things— three spelling errors and two instances of previously-missed italicisation. Trivial, yes, but a good thing nonetheless, for it tells me that the bugs of the First Edition have pretty much been stomped, sprayed, and/or fed to the grammar spiders (who, with their bellies fattened, will finally scurry off on spindly legs to find sustenance in some other indie writer's comma splices and dangling participles). Although it seems that the old phrase, "third time lucky," has proven true for me in this, my Third Edition, I do hope to maintain a more regimented grammatical and editorial vigilance in the release of my future volumes in the series.

Now, as far as the nuts and bolts of *OSAS* are concerned, I must confess that I did momentarily toy with the notion of changing the opening of the story this time around, only because I'd quite frankly wearied of the critiques of roughly one-half of my readership—they who cried *"foul!"* to me, and who railed that the initial chapters are extremely tough-going. You see, some folks felt unjustly tasked for the double-whammy of having to grapple right off the git-go with my highfalutin style while simultaneously trying to get a bead on the story's challenging expository content. I apologise for this. I really do. But, in the end, I left the text as originally written—partly because the *other* half of my readers think it works, and partly because the introductory sequence in question was actually (get ready) the cleanest and most succinct contrivance that I could come up with for combining Wagner's complicated history with his then-current predicament. Let me tell you straight off that I'm no genius—not even close—and yet *I* don't find the first few chapters difficult to read. Granted, I penned them, and thus I know what they're about in their underlying objective, but it's not like they're in legalise or anything.

I suppose what I'm saying here is that if you're approaching my work with the intent to skim it like a summer beach-read, then yes, you're going to be confused and you're going to miss something vital. Back in my college days, about a hundred years ago, I became similarly frustrated in trying to zoom at Mach 1 speed through my course-load of Stendhal, Fielding, Bellow, Joyce, Dostoyevsky, Hawthorne, Homer and the like. It couldn't be done, no matter how badly I wanted to wrap it all up and get to that dorm party before the keg was down to foam. In the end, like it or not I had to slog my way through said tomes; and, yes, beyond all of my literary anguish (of which there was plenty) I benefitted for having read those works word for word. And although I would never deign for one second to liken myself to any of the aforementioned literary greats, it is nonetheless my desire to produce rich and complex literature that demands more than one sitting to kill. The beauty of it is that if you find something that's too difficult for your taste—and it's not requisite that you read it—drop-kick it to the local book exchange and pick out something more suited to your palate. There are a gazillion other authors in print just waiting for you to discover their work. Someone out there has something for you. And sure, I might mope a bit that you let a little verbosity thwart you from an enjoyable tale; but the fact that people still want to pick up a book these days—*anyone's* book, not only mine—gives me the greater pleasure. For, you see, other writers may at times be my rivals, but they're also my comrades. And comrades have to stick together.

Finally, this edition was actually prompted in the first place by my change in publishers. I owe a great deal to my original advocates at Dog Ear Publishing, LLC, who helped a rube like me blaze my way into print. But, after a few years, the planets aligned and the time finally came for me to move on and assume greater control of my work. To help propel this change, I've taken personal ownership of my website and redesigned it from scratch. I'm very proud of its new—and more casual—look, so please check it out at www.SoulsOfErgos.com and let me know what you think. Many of the web design programs available to consumers these days are touted to be pretty much idiot-proof. I'm happy to report that I am a testament to that claim. But, as always, you be the judge.

Geoffrey Verdegast

July 31, 2011

CHAPTER ONE

Oh, wilt though understand
The turmoil of my soul?
  — ANTON CHEKHOV

He had really big problems now.

Only a few minutes shy of 9:00 A.M. and already word had reached upstairs of the crush of people encamped outside the doors of Psych-Trauma Services. Twenty-two by last count, he could only hope that the day-end tally wouldn't see it an even two-dozen. He felt badly enough as it was, badly the way any thoughtful person would expect to feel upon discovering how some inadvertency on his part brought such strife into the lives of others. It wasn't an easy thing to do, shouldering the responsibility for events that were not of his direct agency, and he feared every day for those around him and for himself. He neither needed nor wanted the heft of any more overwrought psyches piled atop a conscience that already buckled from guilt.

The bystander effect was something that he'd come to rue. Even as these particular bystanders should have been considerably flintier than their off-the-deep-end reactions indicated, he couldn't exactly shrug away the fact that their frazzled convergence on the downstairs offices had more to do with him than with any pressing inclination on their part to brush up on their Freud. Broadsided as they'd been a few hours ago by an apparition that, by rights, should not have existed—and which cocked a snook at scientific precepts by existing *anyway*—each of them now wrestled with some ilk of gradated mental backlash, the morning's raucousness having proved far too taxing even for them. Consummate professionals every one, these usually sensible and unimpressible health care providers, most of whom he knew (if only by sight), now mulled about the first floor passageway like discombobulated bees in hover around a blocked hive entry. Fuelled by their nervous energy, any communicativeness that they demonstrated was limited to short bursts of interlocutory volatility, with no one able to finish a complete statement without having his neighbour chime in with seemingly prattlish testimony of his own. As prattle, however, it begged qualification, since what struck the ear initially as nonsensical blather, even self-important grandstanding, was truly neither; for, tucked amid the cyclical helter-skelter of the "did you sees?" and "can you believes?" flowed recountings articulate and commanding enough on their own so as to have no call for the hyperbole sometimes reserved for duller yarns. Much more than just the remedial venting of overtaxed minds in need of purging, it was as if each witness sought the corroboration of kindred, hoping to confirm the synoptic aspects of their collective astonishment before any of them submitted his testimony to the predictably sceptical counselling staff.

Given the circumstances, nobody with privileged knowledge would have thought to begrudge these people their hysteria, no matter that the nature of their occupations so typically inured them to a profession rife with behavioural unorthodoxy. While their training saw to it that they were mentally inoculated for a vast extreme of such unorthodoxies, against *this* morning's circumstances such training could only fall short. After having foisted on them absolutely the most eye-popping of contradictory inconceivabilities that they were ever in their lives to witness, who among these otherwise reasonable persons could have walked away from the phenomenon unaffected? Who could have discounted a spectacle over which physical reality commanded no influence?

In truth, no one could. No one, that is, except maybe the engenderer himself. For he, long acclimated to the "stranger than fiction" demesnes of existence, could do naught but chalk the morning's ordeal up to business as usual. An accursed business, admittedly, it was one from which he would gladly have walked away had his ailment been so inclined to let him—which it was *not*. Still, despite the radical nature of his affliction, no one could say that he wasn't a reasonable person—providing, of course, that you caught him at the right time. Just because *this* particular pre-dawn sally had brought indisputable validation to weeks of rumours and contrivances once believed too way-out and fanciful to ever be taken seriously, he was no less than that good-natured fellow that personal encounter generally revealed him to be. As for the administration's efforts to suppress the truth for so long, in the end no precautionary measure had been enough to avoid—or, at very least, to minimise—the deluge of gossip and conspiracy swelled of his mystique; nor had it been successful in arresting the tremendous furore of tabloidal humbuggery that ensued once word of it seeped out. Hindsight being what it was, were his inadvertent witnesses to be polled, most would at least understand, and perhaps concede to, the facility's prudence in having kept the whole thing under wraps for as long as it had, despite what their various pre-experiential slants may have been.

As for the subject himself, possessed of his insider's clarity he'd long known that the morning's escapade had been an inevitability that, had it not occurred this day, might easily have manifested that evening or the next day or the next week. The probability itself never in doubt, the only variable had been the timeframe; and with *that* unknown being an unknown no longer, his benefactors hadn't any means left now for shielding him from the world, and certainly none for shielding it from him. Time was slipping away for him at a rate proportionate to that of his own degradation. Fate cranked the hurdy-gurdy with furious portent. Sooner or later the weasel had to go *pop*. And when it did, so would he.

For weeks now he'd been living in the vest pocket of insanity, with only a self-fastened synergy forged of hope, humour, and heedful compliance to make his existence tolerable. At the moment, with all of his faculties currently in his rein, he was amenable and outwardly passive. But because he remained in the immediacy of a watchful eye, his current amble along the hospital corridor bore the tincture of mild defiance. It was a nod, perhaps, to the misunderstood youth that he'd once been, the troubled kid who could stretch—no, *elonggggate*—the one-minute march to the principal's office into a daylong dawdle. Even now, in purposely chirping his rubber soles against the institutional tiling, an informed observer might easily have construed that he was mimicking those resistant ways of old. Once upon a time, this might have been true enough. But not now. Here, it was an erraticism far more subconsciously impelled. Something other than mere indolence saw him conspicuously testing each tile underfoot for corporeity before trusting an ounce of his weight to it. Something beyond neurosis had him treating each square as if it were a slat on some rotting rope bridge that spanned the abyss over impending declivity.

And, certainly, something a lot more serious than one man's dissociative travails was responsible for sending twenty-two seasoned professionals over the brink.

The plump little woman in whose company he strode knew a little of what that something was. Garbed in her soporific whites and wearing a face of such utter prosaicness that it made his own expression seem clown-like by comparison, she was in actuality the unlikeliest of warders for a man of his disruptive potential. They both knew that she would much rather have preferred to remain in the staff lounge, glued to daytime television instead of to him—*especially to him*—en route to his consultation; and really, this would have suited him fine. He disliked being chaperoned, and he liked it even less by this stout little ice queen whose already meagre sympathy for him had ebbed even further in the aftermath of recent incidents. He'd have been perfectly fine on his own, thank you very much. After all, he'd been walking these same drab halls to Jon Mazzio's office with such daily regularity that he could have walked them in absolute darkness if necessary. He simply wasn't in the mood for it today.

Hopeless, he thought. A word he'd only recently started using, it summed up for him the aggregate of everything that he felt the doctors and the consultants and the meds and the miscellany of therapies and treatments and monitoring had accomplished. The medical jury may still have been out, but the court of futile efforts was in full session, and its verdict was that it had all been a big waste of time, a lot of well-intended rigmarole with no payoff.

Entering the last corridor, the nurse kept her pace just behind him and to his right so that she could observe his every move. He wasn't dangerous now—they both knew that. There were always premonitory warnings that presaged his spells. Tremors, disorientation, cold sweats—seldom was there insufficient time in which to summon the whole squadron of white-coats before Mister Hyde came out to play. They'd long ago learned how to handle that part of him—learned how to cope with it anyway, sometimes subdue it. What they hadn't learned was how to cure it.

He suddenly caught himself revisiting the premise of the B-picture that he'd seen at least a half-dozen times on the late and late-*late* shows, a low-budget oater from the 1950's that aired practically every other week on the local Christian channel. Released and then re-released under several easily forgotten titles in its half-century of TV repackagings (he remembered it as *The Sharper and the Shootist*), its plot centred on a formulaic gunslinger hero who'd been ambushed and shot up by a vicious gang of badlanders. Desperate and on the run, said gunslinger gave his stalkers the slip by stashing himself in the back of a medicine show wagon, the placard on which read:

"DOC ADAMS'S CURE-ALL ELIXIRS"

And while he, as the film's gunfighter/protagonist, possessed all the natural charisma of an old wagon wheel with a few spokes gone, it was his colourful con man saviour who stole the show. The film's only saving grace, scruffy ol' Doc Adams braved the inconvenience of harbouring a fugitive by way of wry humour and friendly blackmail, and throughout the picture's running gag of extortive table-turning, he and the gunslinger trundled into Tombstone or Cheyenne or some other clichéd western town, selling his bogus analeptic to a mess of ignorant townsfolk. "Doc Adams's Cure-All Elixir," he hawked, "good fer anything that ails ye."

How luckless, that Doc Adams lived only in bad Celluloid. His "Cure-All" might have been just the ticket here, however dubious its restorative properties. It certainly couldn't have proven any less effective than what the doctors had come up with so far. In truth, it may even have made all of their blasted antipsychotic drugs look like week-old chicken broth.

Veering into the last corridor, the escortee ran a tired hand through his unshowered chestnut hair. How long had he been in this place? Nine, ten months? Sometimes it felt like ten years. Yet, incongruously, thanks to his ever-prevailing blackouts it often seemed more like ten *days*—ten days of accumulated lucidity anyway. With a whole slew of new and disturbing manifestations muscling to the forefront of his long-documented chronicle of psyche-thieving episodes, too frequently did it seem that his coherent self was being looted of more and more precious time. By what he'd been told, this latest foray into *Schizoville* had clocked in at just under three hours, the lengthiest to date. But duration itself wasn't nearly as revelatory as *who* had seen him, *what* they had seen him do, and how entirely bugged out they'd become by it. With no way for the administration to effectively contain him now, unauthorised eyes were bound to see him in all his glorious asininity, just as the orderlies had this morning when they came across him in the laundry—slowed by the transition of his disengaging madness, but naked and animated and flinging powdered detergent over blankets and linen carts as if it were faerie dust, and he, the grand and powerful Merlin himself.

This kind of behaviour not all that surprising to the people who'd been assigned to him, it was more the matter of his lunatical persona's unearthly penchant for thwarting his warders' every means of confinement short of shackles, a gunny sack, and an old Houdini trunk, that prompted the real inquiry. A month ago, snapping back to normality to find that he'd descended two entire floors and travelled completely across the complex without incident or staff intervention would have been quite a feat. Yet, a month ago everything had still been standard Jekyll and Hyde fare. Things had changed a bit since then. The blackouts had taken on abruptly new dimension. Heck, dimension *itself* had taken on new dimension. His *Other*, his *alter*, his *fugue state*, or whatever the doctors were calling it this week—*that* personality now possessed the ability to circumvent restraints and door locks and other security constructs like the filmic *4-D Man* to whom he'd come to be compared.

Such outlandishness was, of course, a stretch and a leap for anyone who didn't know what he knew. And he could hardly deny that, unsettling as the ordeals were, their frequency was on the rise. Their immediate distillate was confusing and short-lived. Worse, their long-term influence was an unyielding dread of being forever sucked into the maw of madness itself. In cumulative measurement, he easily spent one-half of each day as the beast nobody could tame, and still there was nothing at all even marginally upbeat about his prognosis. Well meant as his warders may have been, they were totally ill-equipped and unprepared for his brand of shenanigans. It was quite ludicrous, actually; the doctors and the specialists hadn't a clue, not a single positive lead. Only Doc Adams's magic elixir could cure what ailed him. That, or maybe a well-timed bullet.

They stopped at the fifth door on the left, the familiar door with the metallic plaque that read "Jonathon R. Mazzio, M.D., Director" in engraved Century Gothic. The stumpy woman knocked twice, and without waiting for a reply, firmly turned the knob and pushed the door open.

The room inside appeared at first deserted, the ponderous oak desk boasting no industrious psychiatrist at the helm, paging through numerous forms and case studies. Draping the immense window behind it, vertical Levolors guided slivers of mid-morning light across the desk's leather-framed blotter and onto the undulations of the doctor's rope hoya plant. An odd exotic, its verdant, wandering tendrils suggested the tentacles of some formerly malefic alien octopod that, over time, had possibly become so complacent in the guise of an earthly houseplant that it ultimately chose to countermand its own race's plans of global conquest in favour of a more preferable existence as a pampered desktop accent. To the left of its sculpted peduncles and its pungent clusters of candy-pink blooms lay the east portion of the room, which extended far beyond one's field of vision from the doorway. It was from this area that a man's genteel voice acknowledged his visitors' presence.

"Yes, please join us."

Identifying his doctor's voice, the *4-D Man* followed the nurse into the oblong office.

As always, his eyes were briefly drawn to the triptych of lithographs framed uniformly against the far wall. They were of the type frequently displayed in bank and law firm lobbies and such—geometric landscapes done in strikingly bright hues, stark plateaus of indigo and violet surrounded by fiery orange skies. Each print a carefully aligned continuation of the other two, together they created the effect of some outlandish vista whose purpose was either to soothe the eye or stimulate the imagination, but which the man found was most efficient at filling up blank wall space with a minimum of effort and artistic consideration. On the leather couch below these lithos sat two people in suits, a man and a woman (both doctors—by now he could recognise doctors at a glance); and to their left, in an elegant, high-backed swivel, sat his benefactor, Jon Mazzio.

The nurse announced the patient as she always did—by mispronouncing his name. It was an intentional disparagement, camouflaged as simple forgetfulness.

"Mr. *Wag*ner to see you, doctor."

Mazzio groaned. "That's *Vahg*-ner, Miss Groller," he said, his tone barely masking his perturbation at a slip for which he'd chided several of his staff in the past—and this woman in particular. "Once again, it may *read* like *Wag*ner on his file, but it's pronounced 'Vahgner.' Vahgner. Like the composer? It's essential, Miss Groller, to get our patients' names right if they are to have any confidence in us at all, don't you agree?"

"Yes, doctor."

Needing no vast intuitive powers to see that his instruction had once more fallen on deaf ears, he readjusted his bifocals upon the bridge of his nose, and then quickly smoothed his neatly trimmed moustache, equally as grey as it was black. Could he have discreetly rolled his eyes, he probably would have. "Thank you, Miss Groller. That will be all."

"Yes, thank you, Miss *Growler*," Wagner gnarred.

With a twitch too fleeting for anyone not familiar with her expressive subtleties to catch, Margaret Groller shot Wagner the fish-eye as only a true master of scathing glances could, and then waddled from the room, neatly clicking the door behind her. Jon Mazzio then turned to him and apologised.

"I'm sorry, James," he said politely. "I thought we'd taken care of that once and for all." He turned that he might include his associates. "Ensconced in the field as I am—as *we* are—I suppose I shouldn't be so irked by habitual inconsideration, even by those in my own employ."

"Don't let it bother you," said James Wagner, the man who pronounced his surname classically with a "V" and who also didn't wait for an invitation to seat himself in the empty chair across from Mazzio. "Margaret knows better. But comparative phonetics isn't high on her list of social proprieties—especially whenever it concerns me. Not after all the times I've socked it to her."

"Yes," Mazzio contended, "but the qualities of respect and diplomacy and compassion never go out of fashion, James. And in this profession they are particularly requisite."

Wagner scoffed. "However sour she may have been to start," he said, "I can't deny being at least partially responsible for her attitude. I think everyone needs at least one arch-nemesis in his life. And Margaret Groller is happy to be mine. Our mutual antagonism helps me to sharpen what precious little is left of my wits. In turn, it provides a distraction from all of this weird complication. As for her doggedness with my name, well, I'm sure that most times it's innocent enough." He looked to Mazzio's guests. "We in the Western world like our vowels flat, plain and simple. We like our "W"s to sound like "W"s, don't we? We're single-minded in that respect. We call'em like we see'em. It was only after hearing *Parsifal* for the first time that I had to go and get all pretentious by adopting the fancy-shmancy 'olde-worlde' pronunciation of my name. That was...let me think...about eight years ago. Um, yeah, eight years ago, when I thought a fresh take on things might bolster me a bit in the ol' self-image department." He scratched awkwardly behind his ear, trying to shrug off a sudden rush of discomfort. "It didn't much pan out."

"You are a student of Richard Wagner?" asked the woman, her elocution of the composer's name quite impeccable—the hard "K" in Richard, the Germanic "V" in Wagner. Clearly she trumped Miss Groller in worldliness by an entire solar system. She looked to be in her early to mid-forties, very professional, very smartly dressed. Her legs were neatly crossed and both hands were folded over the crossing knee, itself prudently covered. Beside her on the couch was a tussled stack of papers and three olive folders with clear plastic tabs. Wagner made out his name on one of them.

"I know what you're thinking," he said. "I'm aware that Wagner's opera do tend to be the listening preference of many a classic nutball. But, for some reason I felt an affinity for his work from the very first time that I encountered it."

"Eight years ago." Her voice implied not so much a question as a verification.

Wagner nodded, suddenly embarrassed by her interest. She was pleasant enough, but already she was digging, scrounging hungrily for a plump, juicy turnip in his overpicked mental hotbed.

He stifled a mischievous grin. *Sorry, ma'am. No turnips to turn up. Not anymore. You'll turn up no turnips before your turn's up!*

It would have been devilishly funny, he fancied, to speak this phrase aloud and then watch to see if they'd go scrambling back to their books like so many had at the beginning. *Ah!* they'd say. *Loose associations—how very interesting!* But he knew that such things were for the genuinely ill who had no cognition of their madness. In his rational states, Wagner knew the difference; he'd personally studied the symptoms of sundry illnesses, viewed them in other patients, viewed some of them in himself by means of the videos. He'd seen the results of his earlier episodes from inside and out, and although he couldn't always remember them unaided, nor decipher the ones that he could recall, he'd gotten to where he could slip into the guise of his illness in the same manner that other people slipped into their pyjamas. He simply had no business burying the elusive core of his own malady under the rubble of a frustrated mendacity that he'd already been helping to perpetuate. He had no right to plague his doctors with false leads, especially not Jon Mazzio, who'd taken such a sincere interest in the analysing and diagnosing of his bizarre symptomatology.

"Excuse me," Wagner said, gently breaking into the woman's next question, "but I think you have me at a disadvantage."

Mazzio suddenly jumped in. "Oh, forgive me, James," he said, promptly rising from his chair to commence with behindhand introductions. "This is Dr. Claire O'Connell. She's the clinical and research psychologist I told you about, from the Jefferson Foundation in Ann Arbor."

He paused briefly as Wagner and O'Connell rose to exchange pleasantries. The other man on the couch stood as well. "And this," Mazzio continued, "is Dr. Brian A. Williams from the McNally Institute for Behavioural Medicine. You may remember that he was visiting with us last August when you were admitted."

Wagner smiled courteously. "Good to see you again, sir. Nice to know I can keep some of my fans coming back. Too bad you weren't here a bit earlier this morning—I hear I was a pretty slippery customer. Is there any coffee?"

Williams took Wagner's extended hand and shook it with ritualistic propriety. He was about the same age as Mazzio, early to mid-fifties, though at least thirty pounds heavier and with a touch more grey along the sideburns. He smelled oddly of spices and of tobacco ash, an observation Wagner validated by the crumpled Amphora wrapper and shiny black pipe lying on the coffee table near the doctor's briefcase.

"My colleagues and I thought it imperative that we gather further knowledge on this case," Williams said as he reseated himself, "especially in light of these more recent 'symptoms' you've been experiencing. This alleged *corporeal degradation* for instance—"

"Now, *doctor*," Mazzio interjected from the nearby service, where a restaurant-grade Bunn-O-Matic warmed a nearly depleted carafe. A piping hot diner mug in his grip, he hastened back to the klatch and graciously handed it off to Wagner. "We agreed to first review the entire course of Mr. Wagner's affliction before juxtaposing the documented findings with the dynamics of these—ah—*newer* developments."

Williams eyed Mazzio impatiently, but nonetheless refrained from further questioning. He was a straight-to-the-heart man with a relentless drive for the truth, and the fact that he'd agreed to re-involve himself with this case indicated most emphatically to his distinguished colleagues his desire to demonstrate exactly where it was that they'd failed in diagnosing the patient's medical unorthodoxies. Well researched in Dr. Mazzio's brilliant perusals of previous cases, and initially impressed by the progress with this one, Williams still couldn't fathom how no fraction of conclusive causation had been arrived at thus far in Wagner's situation, and he furthermore questioned how it had been allowed to stray so preposterously from science into science fiction.

"Jon," said Wagner, "I don't mind if he wants to get right to the juicy stuff. After all, Dr. Williams is up to date on my résumé of inexplicables—at least enough so that we don't have to spoon-feed him or Dr. O'Connell with only the things they're prepared to hear."

"Your disposition, sir," said Williams, "seems to indicate a change in your perceptions regarding your condition. On our first encounter, you expressed quite a different attitude."

Wagner chuckled. "That's probably because by all definitions I'm a perfectly healthy man—at least that's what modern science tells me. But I think we know different. That is, unless you still believe I'm an actor, struggling to find notice through headlines?"

Dr. Williams bit on his lip. While granting that Wagner was indeed an exceptional individual, atypical in so many ways from the standard patient exhibiting schizophrenic—and other various and sometimes irreconcilable—tendencies, Williams remained adamant that Wagner's hotchpotch of abstract symptoms was actually as unlikely to be entangled within the brain of a single individual as were philosophical precedents to be expressed by grasshoppers. In his opinion, because Wagner's overall response to the facility's curative measures and procedural regimens were frequently negative—especially from continued lack of success with prescribed treatment—it was very possible and indeed likely that some part of Wagner's mind had devised a means of creating the illusion of the impossible in response to the continuing impotence of the doctors' efforts. For a man with Wagner's cognition, his candidness of thought, his practical insights, and certainly his eagerness in cooperating, to deliberately impede his own progress after he'd stressed so vehemently his wish to be included in a number of the doctors' speculative discussions was such a sharp turnabout that either some other biochemical culprit had come into play—as Mazzio had recently proposed—or the true one had finally surfaced. Yet, if what Wagner purportedly claimed as his "illness" was genuine, it would throw modern psychiatry into a turbulent limbo from where it would take decades to redefine and reclassify previously unrelated symptomatologies and the theories that drove them. Furthermore, with the exception of the newest allegations—which Williams, of course, found absurd at best—everything else had been pretty much textbook, albeit only insofar as the cataloguing of individual symptoms was concerned. What no one had yet been successful in uncovering was the common, physiochemical thread that pulled everything together. But now it had gone even further—too far, in fact. What once bordered on the outlandish had drifted into the realm of the ridiculous, and one way or another Williams would see to its end.

Yet, much to Williams's and Mazzio's chagrin, their elite fellowship of medical professionals was no longer the only group in the know. For weeks now, James Wagner's professed repertoire of incredible theatrics—genuine, contrived, or otherwise—had kindled the interest of several major publications and newspapers throughout the country, not to mention a whole skulk of scandal-seeking tabloids strung through supermarket checkouts nationwide. *Pursuer Weekly* had already jumped on the latest developments, although how such things got out so quickly nobody knew. *Locale transference! Corporeal degradation!* Terms originally coined by Mazzio himself, only laymen and fools could believe in such sensationalistic drivel. Certainly, that it was making its way out of Howsley could only be tied to an insider, yet the fact that even the reputable houses carried their own versions was fantastic in itself. It may indeed have been his colleague's backyard in which this travesty was unfolding, but Williams viewed it as a personal affront. To him, no respectable professional could take seriously the claims of a man who boasted of so many unrelated and hypernormal maladies, yet whose exhaustively scrutinised medical profile revealed absolutely nothing about him that was amiss. Chemically, physically, there had yet to be discovered a discrepancy anomalous enough to merit flagging. The standard battery of tests all having been deemed inconclusive, the monitoring of Wagner's sleep patterns and dream states suggesting no previously overlooked indicative quirk, the absence of any extraordinary nuance of comportment or demeanour during his non-tumultuous states—nothing in Wagner's behavioural ethology pointed to any identifiable catalyst. Williams knew Mazzio's earliest assessment—that whatever affliction Wagner suffered was revolutionary to the field of psychiatry—but because of the broad range of findings, there was little certainty in any kind of diagnosis, for even the scope of the occasionally biblical *Diagnostic and Statistical Manual of Mental Disorders* in all of its appended splendour was much too limited to effectively define and classify the refractory medley of Wagner's indicants into some logically tidy category.

"I find the handling of this entire case quite unusual," said O'Connell. After all, we have an obviously intelligent patient who offers his self-confessed psychological disorder to any and all takers, yet who appears to demonstrate none of the fearful and desperate emotions of those patients whose far more identifiable conditions warrant considerably less involved diagnoses. This same patient's observable symptoms are so fluid in that they do not always manifest themselves according to patterns. They're like pieces from a rogue jigsaw puzzle that have been covertly slipped into the mix of the quite different puzzle that *we've* been trying to assemble. Treatments have yielded poor results. Diligence and advertence only spawn more questions. All this, and the patient seems more agreeable than he has ever been!"

"Claire," said Mazzio, "I'm extremely grateful for your time with us, and I apologise if elements of the media have toyed with Mr. Wagner's case, but I assure you that this will be worth your time."

"That's all right," Wagner added matter-of-factly, nudging his drained coffee mug toward the centre of the table around which they sat. He then dug his hand into his front shirt pocket, fumbling and eventually producing a roll of Tropical Fruits Life-Savers. "I stated long ago that I didn't want to be coddled, that you can blast away if you want, and I'll do my best with the answers." Pushing up on one end of the roll with his thumb, he freed a circle of mango melon candy and, bringing it gingerly to his mouth, paused momentarily. "Sometimes I think it might have been a mistake, but I figured we could help each other more this way. You have to remember, this hasn't exactly been a picnic for me either."

"All right, then," said O'Connell. "I'm familiar with most of what Dr. Mazzio has written about you. I've studied your own statements and I've read the logs you've kept. I've viewed the videotaped interviews as well as the footage of the two episodic incidents that the facility was fortunate enough to have captured on remote. Now, I need to know the man himself. I need to know *you*. I need you to tell me what *you* think of all this."

Wagner crunched on the LifeSaver. "Fair enough," he said. "To start off, I no longer think I'm just another nutcase in the conventional sense, if there even *is* such a thing. I just have these—these—*differences?*—that I used to think were normal in people, normal because I didn't know any better, because mine was the only mind I had access to, you know? But over the years I've discovered that not everybody deals with what I deal with. Damn few I would say. Actually, probably none, but I obviously don't know that for certain, and neither do you. I've never been able to put it all together, but as it seems I've descended into psycho-purgatory as far as I can go without totally losing my mind, I can look back up from my lonely little outcrop and see things I didn't see before."

"What kinds of things?" she asked.

"That most people don't have recurring dreams for the course of some thirty-odd years. That the bulk of folks out there don't suffer blackouts where they actually feel that they've spent time in a jungle or on the ocean or in the midst of cultures that the good society over at *National Geographic* has yet to uncover. That few people would mistake nurse Groller and her lovable goose-steppers in white for a pack of hungry predators or the like, and actually lash out at them, with the intent to kill, while under that misconception."

"I can list for you dozens of case studies of people suffering from those very maladies, Mr. Wagner," argued Williams. "Probably some individuals who exhibit all of what you've stated and more."

"I'm sure that you can, doctor," said Wagner. "I'm sure that you can. But that's not everything. You see, I also hear voices. And not your standard Beelzebubs, mind you, none that seek to coerce me into dismembering the third floor night nurses with a paring knife and intermingling their body parts in some perverted ceremony of atonement, nothing like that, but voices that are sensible and coherent, voices that offer—I don't know—*spiritual* challenge. Voices from far beyond my reckoning, yet from within my own being, within *me*, voices that express words that I comprehend, yet whose idiom is one that I've never learned and couldn't possibly know."

During his discourse, Wagner pried another LifeSaver from the roll—this one, banana—and popped it onto his tongue, where he juggled it from one side of his mouth to the other, producing light percussive sounds against his teeth as he spoke. The remainder of the roll he held upright in his palm, presumably using it as a distraction from the uneasiness of interrogation. Every few seconds, his eyes returned to it as if it were a ladybird that would at any moment take to the air.

"And apparently," he continued, "it seems that I can speak in tongues as well. *That* one was hard to accept, but Dr. Mazzio, here, was lucky enough to have taped an instance of it while I was whacked-out, so there's not much I can do as far as denying it. And yes, I realise, doctor—*doctors*—that these patencies are also nothing that either schizophrenics or DIDers or crazed holy rollers overcome by religious zeal don't exhibit as well. So, I'll bet you reckon you've got me, eh? The only problem is that therapy or medication or hypnosis or reintegration or deprogramming or anything this side of a simple aspirin can diminish, alleviate, or keep in check every one of these conditions in everybody *except* me—*me*, who not only conjures all of these fun-filled peculiarities for you to marvel at, but who has even *more* rabbits left in his hat."

"I assume you're referring to *this*," said Williams, sliding a copy of *Pursuer Weekly* from under his paperwork and dangling it before Wagner's peepers. There, sharing headlines with both a four year-old girl who allegedly survived two days in the belly of a shark, and the enigmatic *Mr. Miracle*—the latest prophetic precursor to the Second Coming—was a most unflattering photograph of Wagner, conterminous to a movie still of Robert Lansing from Universal's 1959 *The 4-D Man* (coincidentally also a lesser staple of late show TV fare). Wagner's photo, apparently snapped with a long-range lens through the gridwork of his third floor window, showed him in early morning dishabille, sporting his bed clothes and an Einsteinian case of hospital bed-head. The abutting photo showed Lansing's character emerging from a brick wall. Overscoring the montage ran the text: *Real Life Imitates Reel Life! Genuine 4-D Man Walks Through Walls!*

"My fifteen minutes of fame," sighed Wagner. "Not exactly the manner in which a guy dreams of achieving celebrity." He re-studied his photograph. "Really bad hair day, too."

"I think you're mistaking celebrity for notoriety," said Williams, using the mouthpiece of his pipe to emphasise Wagner's headline. "Fortunately, most of this kind of drivel is generally forgotten even quicker than the article itself can be read."

"Thank goodness for that," added Mazzio. "Still, we *have* had our share of inquisitive story-hounds at the front doors since this news saw print. It's an inevitability I suppose."

"Disappointing too, I imagine," said Williams, "that the confidential integrity of this facility cannot be ensured."

"Wait a minute, sir!" shot Wagner. "In defence of this very astute gentleman here, his facility's *integrity*—as you put it—is pretty damned good with matters that fall within the everyday spectrum of psychological disorders and whatnot. And the Howsley staff—even ol' stone-faced Groller out there—has been nothing but professional and discreet in regard to all the poor slobs whose popped rivets give them no other option but to be committed here. I'd imagine, however, that when you see with your own two eyes somebody defying the very laws of physics—I don't care what vocation you're in—it's going to be hard to keep quiet about it."

"Assuming that any such laws have been defied," Williams said bluntly.

Wagner focused on the roll of candies in his hand. It had been a while since he'd argued with anyone, even longer since he'd allowed himself to get upset over the absurdities of his predicament. He'd always prided himself in the character it took to be able to joke about it and to accept the fact that few would be persuaded to actually believe his claims, no matter what kind of empirical evidence cried out to be seen.

"Okay," he said. "I really don't care anymore whether you believe me or not. I'm in this place because I choose to be, because I'm no longer certain that I can function for very long on the outside without inadvertently harming someone. Despite what you may think, Dr. Williams, I do not enjoy my life, nor do I relish the fact that the scandal rags are invading my privacy. But I don't really concern myself over it because I'm not cognisant enough of the time to afford myself the luxury of worrying about it. What I do worry about is that my conscious life is slowly being expunged by some phenomenon that nobody can explain, and that no one save Dr. Mazzio and a few other open-minded souls give a fig about. And the fact that you, sir, are sitting here looking for deceit instead of either just walking away or helping me with my problems incites me with a pretty compelling inclination to snatch that pipe outta your hands and stick it where the sun—"

"Whoa, James! Enough!" shouted Mazzio.

An uneasy silence settled over the room, as if some Dickensian Ghost of Christmas Present had strewn the pacifying properties of his torch about the air. Williams even flinched as if he were consciously repelling cheer of any kind.

"Look," said Wagner, a lifetime's worth of weariness in his voice. "Doctors, let's not get off on the wrong foot here. I invite you to stay on and observe for as long as you like. We can spend the day arguing philosophical pretexts, or we can just hang out and catch some *General Hospital* on the tube until it's time for my next flight over the cuckoo's nest. Or, if you want, we could all have a good laugh perusing some of these stories from the *Pursuer*. Let's skip the one about the four year-old, though—I've lived in the belly of my own shark for a whole lot longer than she ever had to." He quickly riffled through the pages, stopped abruptly, and thumbed back to one that caught his eye. "I know—maybe can scrounge up this guy *Miracle's* P.O. Box, and get him out here to lay his hands on me. It might spare us a heap of time and a huff of tempers—what d'ya say?"

No one gave answer.

"Well, then, it's up to you people. But I can't strut my stuff on command. I'm not a performing chimp, at least not in my current state of mind. Maybe later, when Hyde clocks in, he can keep you better amused."

Wagner rose and headed for the door. Yet, after only a step, he halted and swung around.

"By the way, Jon," he said, pointing to the mug in which Mazzio had served him his brew, "you probably ought to leave *that* one in the back of the cupboard from now on. The double entendre thing, you know? Don't get me wrong—*I* don't take offence to it, but it may not project the right kind of message to some of the more sensitive types who visit your happy home, here."

Before anyone could reply, he winked, turned, and made a curt exit.

Befuddled and intrigued, the doctors glanced at the mug, then at each other. Finally, Claire O'Connell reached over and, nudging it by its handle with her ink-pen, slowly rotated it until its logo came into eyeshot. She smiled.

"I picked that up on my last trip to New York," Mazzio explained. "At a coffee house. Funny, I never gave it a second thought."

O'Connell presented it for Williams to see.

It read: *Chock Full O'Nuts*.

CHAPTER TWO

I recognize the walls inside
I recognize them all
I've paced between them
chasing demons down
until they fall
in fitful sleep
enough to keep their strength
enough to crawl
into my head
with tangled threads
they riddle me to solve

again & again & again
   —NATALIE MERCHANT

After about twenty attempts, Wagner called it quits.

Snapping his book shut in frustrated reply to one too many uncomprehended re-readings, he chucked it to the far end of the couch and assumed a quiet glower of capitulation. The triumphs and tragedies of Daedalus and Icarus, of Theseus against the Minotaur, of Otus and Ephialtes—these and other legends of classical antiquity would have to wait. Neither the epic struggles they delineated nor the bold and foolhardy and often tragic adventurers they depicted could bear up against the furore of the rec room's far more disruptive reality.

Divertive as most great literature was, Wagner would have been long immersed in the Greek mythos but for the raucousness unloosed around him, a raucousness that, to his infinite relief, he'd had no part in initiating. In this place, Chaos was a creature of predictable unpredictability; and as there were sundry other hellions in residency whose own antics occasionally took the heat off of Wagner, any time that clamant origins were traceable to one of these characters—and not to him— so much the better. As for the disruptors this time: enter the notorious "Parker Brothers," a pair of masochistic board game fanatics whose real names befitted them far less than did Wagner's inspired moniker for them, and who together had been reprimanded so regularly for their chronic inability to play nice with each other that they were often prohibited from recreating together. Yet, with board games, as with administrative edict, breaking rules was what they did—and usually in no small way—for not even five minutes had elapsed in their current spiel of Monopoly and already they were eructing like a couple of geysers.

Nowhere in the entire wing was there a more contrary—and complementary—pair of charlatans. Each skewed the rules to his own liking; each pilfered from the bank when the other wasn't looking; each faked nonchalance while surreptitiously scooting his token onto some more preferable square than the one on which the dice had landed him. Gender notwithstanding, they were like an old married couple whose conjugality stood—or rather, shook—upon a foundation of bickering and backtalk, and they'd run this routine enough times for Wagner to forecast yet another high-spirited go-round of underhandedness and sore losing that, like all those before it, would climax with an upended game board and a room a-swarm with careening tokens, fluttering play monies, and fast-flying verbal jabs.

Long inured to the very mutable nature of the ward rec room, Wagner's original plan of seeking out a reasonably serene public forum in which to consummate his literary plans really should have steered him clear of it. But he'd been hopeful, perhaps inordinately so; for what had been a passive atmosphere an hour ago had now deteriorated into a zoo, an arena, and no heroic narrative of mere print and binding had a chance in Hades of vying with the vocal mayhem emanating from his crass co-inhabitants.

Even after months of structured living, there were times when he still had to remind himself that the outside world's tactics did not apply here. These weren't normal personalities with whom he was dealing. The Centre's sequestered environment was more an entrepot for factory seconds of the human sort, the only place where hard-cases with specialised mental needs might ever find a sense of community. Polite society had no meaning in these trenches, and neither did its mannerful customs. Anarchy often ran unchecked, sometimes in isolated incident and sometimes in proliferating abundance; and as he was himself more often the problem than the solution, Wagner found it less hypocritical and sometimes even more therapeutic to endure the outward imposition. This way he could direct his anxieties more efficiently toward the impositions from within.

Checking his irritableness, he settled back and allowed the game-mongers to finish the ritual. Ceding in this manner was preferable over interference or interjection, since personal involvement often drew the mediator into the fray (and usually as the transferee of hostilities). Wagner had learned the hard way that it was far more prudent to abide the debacle with distance and detachment, unless his yen was to be pelted with little pewter game-pieces and tiny plastic houses.

Extending his arms high above his head in a sinewy, finger-locked stretch of resignation, he let out a lazy, late morning yawn, groaning gently as he exhaled, craning his head from side to side until he'd coerced a snap or two of audible relief from his cricked ligaments. Then, folding his arms and snuggling deeper into the niche of understuffed bolster, he sat and waited for two huge windbags to blow themselves out.

Wagner's own life had been remarkably void of this sort of useless squabbling. He attributed this in large part to the fact that he'd never had siblings with whom to quarrel and scrap. This—and an affliction that thieved away increasingly larger chunks of his reality—had generally made quibbling over something as trivial as a material possession a non-issue. He supposed that the hard truth of it was that he'd never been instilled with the disposition to care about tangibles all that much.

Toys and games and trinkets, DVDs, iPods, starter jackets, name brands—they were all just things. Things wore out. Things broke. Things got mislaid, destroyed, stolen. Things could almost always be replaced; and as for those that couldn't— well, he saw no sense in fretting over them. It didn't pay to become overly attached to mere *things,* for it was an ineluctable fact that every *thing* a person held dear would one day be lost; and the more object-oriented the person, the more inclination there would be to worry about that eventuality right up until the very day it occurred. He'd always found it so much less complicated to keep material encumbrance at negligible levels—and better still, at non-existent ones. With no desirous concerns to preoccupy one's thoughts and to foster the insidious weakness borne of unwieldy desideration, the mind could be freed for more constructive matters, matters like just how much there remained of one's mind to free—which, of course, was *his* most pressing concern. Anymore, his mind had been so riddled by holes that substance itself came at a premium.

For Wagner, the idea of a "stolen moment" had little in common with popular conception. Rarely anymore did the term evoke in him the notions of a thoughtful interlude, an intimate tryst, or even a transcendent jaunt for the meditatively and spiritually disciplined. His definition, far more explicit than these comparatively pleasing connotations, had undeniable impetus at its core. From his perspective, a stolen moment was exactly that—cognition literally stolen from him, with his essence and his conscious immediacy both plundered as if they were experiential gatherings ripped by the handful from the greater chronicle of his existence. Random clefts in his life for which he couldn't account, mnemonic ravages that he couldn't forestall, by their unchecked depredation they boded for him some not-so-distant dénouement of moribund bleakness, whereby what little he'd managed to retain would ultimately and inevitably be stripped away with the rest.

Had he foresight enough to have maintained a journal over the span of his twenty-eight years, said documentation would have implied a predacious malady that, over several decades of gradual profusion (and the much-accelerated snowballing of the last year), had come to waylay his livelihood. A progressive smattering of hastily sketched pie charts might aptly have illustrated how his mindful continuity dwindled a little more each day, forfeited to a fugue state that swallowed up cognisance like a whale devouring krill. With nothing more than a scatter chart, or an even simpler line graph, he could likewise have plotted his plunge in coherency against the acclivity of his madness, with each coordinate leading him toward a terminus of total relinquishment.

How dispiriting for him that something so complex might so easily be delineated by way of a few scribbled lines or a group of disproportionate wedges. In truth, he needed no graphics to tell him what he already knew, nor was the desire within him to expend any such effort. With a daily thieving of embraceable awareness, with unaccountable time and actions rapidly displacing trackable lucidity, such utilisation of his wakeful hours required more impellent than anything that he in his decremented existence had left to fuel it. Preclusion enough to deter any efforts in that direction, all of this had become his doctor's job.

In the past year alone, with the singularity jacking-in with near geometric progression, so often now did his mind shunt him into some inextricable, chaotic loop that not only had the past ten months at Howsley seen him looted of precious, irretrievable experience, but consequently he'd been divested of all but a jet-laggish recoupment of natural time. His refractory intervals of mental soundness were too much like the dramatic time of Miss Groller's daytime soaps—implied in some manipulated or environal sense, where he inferred passage void of much of the experiential minutiae. Wipes, fades, lap-dissolves, and other such transitional slights, were all gainful techniques in cinematic storytelling; yet, when similar phenomena started abridging one's conscious existence, life became disconcerting at best and terrifying on the whole. Cheated of those seemingly inconsequential titbits of time that healthier minds took for granted, Wagner's missing moments had become the resort of his *Other* self's habitation, discernable to Wagner only after the fact by way of clues, theories, hearsay, and—in lieu of these—hospital documentation. His noesis so often reasserting in the midst of situational benightedness, he likened himself more to the sporadic viewer of those same soap operas who, in tuning-in after a month-long hiatus and discovering a handful of missed intricacies in plot, nevertheless notes how certain generalities have remained surmisable enough to be reconstructed with minimal effort. In effect, inference and assumption were the mortar and bricks with which Wagner restored continuity to his life.

Months ago, he'd learned that such was what people who suffered multiple personalities often experienced. Yet, interestingly enough, he couldn't truly slot himself into said category because his profile was hardly in keeping with that of a multiples-besieged individual. While some of the hysterical symptoms were unquestionably present, they were by no means representative of his total condition. Even in his most expropriated moments, he demonstrated no marked infelicity discrepant from his nominal personality, no idiosyncratic inconsistencies beyond a certain indocility in the face of provocation, and—barring the occasion of his monodramatic babbling—no sudden supplementary skills or abrupt loss of established ones. Granted, a red flag here, a symptomatic beacon there, the evidentiary clues would have made compelling bases for argument had there not existed specific, irreconcilable differentiae that, in the end, suggested truly little indicative of a dissociative identity disorder. In further concurrence, the consensus of every professional who'd confronted his riotousness firsthand was that it always seemed to be the core personality itself—James Wagner, and not some alter—behaving as if it were somewhere other than where it was, reacting to the people around it as if they were other than whom it knew them to be. The observable mannerisms were almost exclusively Wagner's: the essence of character, the body language, even his elocution of the unidentified tongue—all Wagner's. To the trained eye, to the keenest of intellects, it appeared that there wasn't so much a Mister Hyde per se as there was an unrepressed, licentious, and abstrusely diglottic *Wagner.*

As for the indecipherable babble he spouted during some of his non-synchronous states, this revealed another bugaboo for which no one had been prepared. While it wasn't all that uncommon for an alter to demonstrate unaccountable fluency in foreign tongues, the language that the "affected" Wagner commanded was one that nobody—not even the linguistics experts whom Dr. Mazzio had wrangled into viewing the video footage—could ascribe to any known etymon. Consisting not of gibberish, nor of pilfered fragments refashioned out of any number of rudimentary languages (or their cognates or sundry offshoots),

Wagner's mutterings employed a host of phonemic peculiarities in what those of the PhD set deemed as dynamic, logically structured phraseology with "a competent enough infusion of inflective redundancy and syntactical collocation to denote a substantial complexity"—all of which tilted the scales toward dismissing speculation that any of it was a confidence of slick knavery on the subject's part. But then again, who other than Wagner knew for sure; and given his spotty accounting of his conscious life, did *he* really even know?

Furthermore, while dissociative identity disorder was always officially grouped in with the neuroses, schizophrenia typically stuck to the psychosis side of the house. Not that medical science could insist on stringent boundaries for all mental illnesses (given that some of them hovered vexingly about the fringes, where misdiagnosis was often one of the pitfalls), Wagner's condition was so frustratingly generous in that it called upon a semiotic ruck of previously unrelated disorders and, like dissidents planted in a crowd to incite turmoil, charged them to instigate a free-for-all within the delicate chemistry of one man's brain.

Yet, that was Wagner as viewed outwardly. The part of him that nobody could see, the part unavailable and inaccessible to anyone—save, on occasion, Wagner himself—held more wonders and horrors than any of them could imagine. His psyche, as surveyed across the podium of his mind's eye, was more vastly revealing and infinitely less comprehensible than all the scientific jargon he'd assimilated along this institutional portion of his journey. And it had proved much too tough for the medical field's psychoanalytic hardware to cut through.

"James?"

Jon Mazzio's voice suddenly jarred him from his murk of self-absorbed noodling.

Wagner quickly sought his bearing. That the room was no longer in a state of localised uproar—and the fact of his psychiatrist being unexpectedly before him—told him that he'd ventured deeper into personal reflection than he'd intended. So ruminative had he been that the Parker Brothers had long finished and abandoned their ill-fated spiel. One sat in full sulk on a nearby couch, while the other had joined the glassy-eyed, catatonic set across the room in watching *Full House* repeats on the wall-mounted Magnavox. Not to know whether their board game blitzkrieg had played out or petered, he gazed back to Mazzio, who stooped before him a bit more solicitously than usual, and who had in his grip Wagner's discarded *Bullfinch's*, plucked from the armrest crevice and now offered up to Wagner like a calumet.

"Uh-oh," said Wagner. "Peace offering or entreaty?"

"Hmm? Oh, entreaty, I suppose," said Mazzio. "Listen, we're going to have one more go at the videotapes, James, and I wondered if you would join us in the audio-visual room. I know it's old fare, and rather embarrassing for you, but your personal assessments might be helpful to our guests. Strictly voluntary, of course."

Wagner cupped his hands about his mouth and blew into them as if trying to warm himself to the idea. He had a fondness for the exaggeratedly lengthy ponder, especially when he wished to hedge some course of action that was more proper than desirable; and Mazzio—familiar with his shtick—indulged him.

"Have you got the muzzle and restraints for Doc Williams?"

Mazzio chuckled. "I think you two can manage. Anyway, isn't *one* pair of battling tops in this place enough?" He directed a thumb at the jumble of

Monopoly paraphernalia scattered across the vacant table behind them.

At end, Wagner caved. By his own suggestion, months ago, he'd asked always to be involved, and could hardly shirk when request was put to him. Toting both ambivalence and bother, he rose to follow his doctor from the room, pausing halfway to stoop and snap up a stray orange "Chance" card from under a chair some two metres from where the twin terrors had waxed their discord. Flipping it over, he read its caption—GO DIRECTLY TO JAIL—and then wryly tossed it onto the gaming heap on his way out.

He'd been to the A-V room a few times before, at least twice for each of his episodes that active cameras had captured. Not a lounge, no comfortable seats, it was just a stark room with four large tables butted together to create the semblance of an even larger one, some chairs, a monitor, and an older VCR that flashed 12:00 A.M. with less than state-of-the-art efficiency. He was welcomed by the two eminent doctors, each of whom had taken a seat across from the other, perpendicular to the screen, with their respective paperwork spread over the tables like contested poker hands.

Wagner plopped down across from the monitor, closer to Williams than to O'Connell in what was either a gesture of good will or one of defiance—Wagner himself wasn't even sure.

"All right," Mazzio began, forgoing the niceties of the previous meeting. "If you remember, this earlier episode, marked "Twenty-four January," is the more noteworthy of the two. In it, we see some rather key basics of James's personality asserted through the otherwise obfuscative sway of his malady."

Wagner smiled inwardly at his doctor's imaginative—and generous—phrasing. Whenever in the presence of a patient, Mazzio often refrained from using terminology that could inadvertently be construed as too cold or clinical, instead switching to a family of euphemisms that were almost as discommodious in their awkwardness. But Wagner liked the good doctor, and said nothing to discourage the physician from at least making the attempt to treat him with propriety and respect. After all, it was solely due to Mazzio's concern that Wagner had been willing to stay on in Bishop at the Howsley Centre for Mental Health for as long as he had. Otherwise, he may well have lost the rest of what he held dear—his dignity, his health, maybe his life. He'd already been skeetering the downward path long before he'd reached the crossroads of their acquaintance. Truth be known, whenever under the "sway of his malady," the delusion swapped out his brain like a bad circuit board, replacing it with one whose polarities were incompatible with his inborn electrics, putting new arrangement to the spatial world, transposing and transcending the boundaries between reality and the schists that his illness created. In all likelihood, had Mazzio not taken an interest in his case, Wagner surely would have met with tragedy, either by plunging blindly in his madness into an open manhole or darting entranced into the path of an uptown bus. Wagner owed Mazzio a lot—if nothing else, for not giving up on him.

The videotape ran, and Wagner watched the images of someone with his face and body and voice lunging at, and parrying with, Miss Groller and Co. with a broomstick in the very room where Mazzio had enlisted him a few minutes earlier. The space vacated that day of its usual constituency of couch potatoes, board gamers, outcasts, and basic oddities, a handful of orderlies were seen suddenly swarming into frame from stage right, their mission: to minimise by total subdual the havoc unleashed by Wagner's *wild child*.

An easy enough task for seven burly guys with restraints and two of lesser stature with hypos—all mustered by field marshal Groller—they were all, however, to meet with great surprise, for Wagner's body-commandeering *Other* proved highly adept in his borrowed skin. An undeniable scrapper, at times perceptively animated less by inward upheaval than by outright possession, the manner in which he bade the hapless staff into charging him was evidence enough that he was very much at home in the heat of a skirmish that the well-meaning orderlies had themselves incited. In support of this, the camera had gone on to record considerable liveliness before anyone was able to tame (or was that *tan?*) Wagner's "Hyde."

Confounding as it was for him to view this tape again, to see himself so clearly out of control, Wagner nonetheless experienced an unwanted, almost sardonic, amusement in watching Miss Groller's clumsy attempts to evade the fracas sustained by his crazed counterpart. At times, he even found it necessary to physically suppress his outright guffawing at her ordeal. Such response neither intentional nor prehensive—like unexpected flatulence in the midst of a sombre gathering—Wagner offset it with pre-emptive countermeasures of conscience and shame, especially as a furtive glance cast at each of his co-viewers revealed nothing in their expressions beyond iatric sedateness for the entirety of the playback. Drawing, then, on his layman's versing in psychology, he sought to convince himself that it wasn't heartlessness or callosity on his part that spurred his fleering. Nor did he believe the reaction stemmed from any sympathetic lacking attributable to his condition or to some predisposed omission of inherency. In fact, no such propensity had ever taken more than a fleeting liberty with his character in all his years. He instead reckoned it more an involuntary venting for his mortification, a means of dealing with his horror and his embarrassment and perhaps even his guilt over the cunning, industrious, broomstick-wielding entity that he'd been impotent to control.

Still, he couldn't exactly deny that watching Miss Groller bugging out on closed-circuit was the sort of triumph his lucid self could only dream of eliciting. In an unsalutary and roundabout fashion, he indulged a misplaced wistfulness that saw him rooting along with this inimical side. After all, to the best of his knowledge, no one had ever succeeded in getting Margaret so dithered. Wagner would himself have elevated in his esteem anyone who could. It just so happened that the accomplisher of this feat was, essentially, *he*. Yet, such affinity for, and allegiance with, his ungoverned flipside being a perversity that few outsiders would ever understand—much less excuse—he decided that the inclination was better kept to himself.

Regardless, whether heroic or despiteous or both or neither, his doppelganger was no slouch. Always a step ahead of the orderlies, he readily busted their chops whenever the opening was afforded him, which—due either to his mysteriously appropriated skill or to their complete unreadiness—occurred ad nauseam. In fact, the whole contest was too reminiscent of Alan Hale's trouncing of Errol Flynn in the classic log fight from Warner Brothers' *The Adventures of Robin Hood*. Only, in this instance, there were many more opponents to be throttled by Wagner's nutso John Little and his makeshift quarterstaff.

It was true that, in the end, the orderlies had overwhelmed him. But it had been a strictly fortuitous thing. For reasons not fully ascertained, the doppelganger as good as invited it upon himself with behavioural inconsistencies of his own, suddenly choosing to toss his weapon aside and re-route his energies into a rippingly impromptu speech—a rousing, unintelligible soliloquy meant, perhaps, for his more appreciative, apparitional audience than for that provided by Howsley. Flabbergasted by the intentional and all too inviting breach in his defences, the battered and unsympathetic white-coats quickly and with finality availed themselves not only by bulldozing Wagner across two tables and over sundry chairs in a hurly-burly of bodies, but furthermore by driving him completely through the stratum of lathwork to his rear, from where it would take two custodians and a trauma team to extricate him. It was only later, when he was out of danger and under restraint—and reintegrated with his core being—that he'd inquired about the assortment of lumps and bruises whose origins he never would have totally fathomed had he not been bestowed the opportunity to view this video. To this day, remarkably, he remained unbegrudging of the orderlies for their actions, for he still believed they'd suffered the worst of it overall.

Fortunately, the audio record of Wagner's cryptic blether prior to his violent collaring had been permanently preserved. His voicings embellished with a certain exigency of emotion, any objective observer would surely have surmised that Wagner had believed himself mired in some entanglement of pressing urgency against which a mere broomstick did not suffice. And although most of what the video revealed seemed to raise more questions than it solved, the best that anyone could decipher from this 24 January taping was that the B-side Wagner apparently believed himself embroiled in the direst of frontline martialism. Even the coherent Wagner, having had no verifiable, conscious access to the situation, sensed that his *Other* believed himself to be literally enmeshed in the defence of his very life, against whom or what Wagner knew not. His only certainty came by what he saw on film: his Hyde-side expressing obvious anguish during the course of his delusional dust-up, his raving and reproachful shouting, and then, incomprehensibly, his trading of confrontational tactics for heartfelt impetration— whereby he was almost immediately overrun by his ward guardians' last-ditch assault.

Exactly where the core Wagner had been during the fracas was a tale of another sort. As was usually the case—even more so with each recurrent mind-trip (Wagner called them "benders")—any imagery that remained in mental queue at the moment of conscious rebound was either splintered or buried or stripped away completely. Rarely was he left with more than an intimation of where his essence had been while his doppelganger was running amok. Yet, on occasion he did manage to retain a fading, residual imprint of subliminal phantasmagoria that clung to his inward eye like barnacles to a whale's belly. He knew the imagery was there; but, with a single exception, it was nigh unto impossible to retrieve any of it deliberately, not the way he might have years ago. Back then, in adolescence, his recall had been more vivid, more immediate, and the benders themselves, few and far between. How ironic it was that he'd never recognised in the visional jetsam of days past the insight they might have granted him so many years later. Most had faded from his collective memory, or had been written over by years of subsequent experiences. Like dreams forgotten moments after waking, whatever significance they may have bequeathed him had long been lost.

"Do you have any indication at all as to your mindset while you were holding the orderlies at bay?" asked Dr. O'Connell, reasonably certain of what his answer would be.

"No, madam. Not one bit. But there's a pretty common thread that runs through my alternate behaviour, don't you think?"

"How do you mean?"

"Well, in that state I'm capable of demonstrating incredible violence. But it's never for its own sake. It seems more reactive than not, more the act of defence than one of mindless destruction. It's not raw ferocity in any extreme sense."

"Not extreme?" Williams interjected. "My God, man, you meted multiple contusions to five orderlies, sent one man into surgery for partial mandibular reconstruction, fractured another's third and fourth metacarpals—"

"No, doctor," blared Wagner, "I did no such thing. He did—the Other me. And if you were to observe the tape with a little less bias, every action that he executed was in direct reaction to a perceived threat. Rewind it if you don't believe me. He was simply existing in his own little world—at least initially. No one else was even around. It wasn't until the goons arrived en masse that he grabbed the broom and had a go at them."

It was a defence he'd used before. Wagner flat out denied that any of his double's actions were linked to his own intent. His ired tone and his stressed emphasis were bonuses, useful ones if not entirely persuasive. Even Dr. Williams momentarily withdrew, although not so much from being bested as from a need, perhaps, to retool his cynicism.

"Mr. Wagner, any type of violent, destructive behaviour that will not be controlled cannot be said to have a legitimate purpose in these surroundings, whether you think it extreme or not. That you believe the brawl manifested only after the orderlies provoked it is immaterial. You are at this facility voluntarily, and those orderlies are here to see to your well-being."

Wagner shook his head. "Look, doc, I don't have an overwhelming need to keep one-upping this animosity that you and I have had going on ever since your first visit. But, if your goal is to plop a black hat on my noggin, then fine—I'll play the heavy. Maybe then we could at least acknowledge each other from within that framework, and you won't have to keep alluding to the fact that you think I'm running some kind of scam here."

His demeanour unnecessarily unravelling, Wagner felt up his shirt pockets and eventually produced the LifeSavers roll. Fumbling with it upon the hem of the fabric, he lost it, grabbed for it, and came back with empty air as the roll lightly struck the carpet. Muttering self-deprecatorily, he swung down with a manful swoop and still came up with nothing.

"Relax, James," Mazzio said, scootching a leg beneath the table. With the toe of his oxford he manoeuvred the roll until it lay within his reach. A quick bend, an extended snatch, and he was offering the candy for Wagner to take.

His gesture, however, going too long unreciprocated, he instead placed the confection on the tabletop in front of his flummoxed ward. "No need to get yourself in a fluster," he reassured him. "We're all here in your common interest."

But Wagner was far from flustered. He would, in fact, have welcomed flustering. His struggle was on two fronts now. The sensation that had come so precipitately upon him was kilometres from any abrupt rush of anxiety that his outward appearance may have indicated, and was not in the least prompted by his locking horns with the visiting physician. Arguing with Williams was simply unmomentous sparring, like a teenager's row with his father over keg parties and weeknight curfews, certainly nothing capable of unnerving Wagner to the point of disorientation. What he *was* feeling was psychic reverberation—similar, but not identical, to the clangour that presaged another round of madness—and he was mute to relay it to the very people who he'd hoped would recognise the process.

"Let's go on to the second taping, shall we?"

In passive compliance to Mazzio's suggestion, O'Connell scribbled in her notes while Williams dealt silently and maybe even disdainfully with Wagner's apparently convenient flit with anxiety.

Mazzio's intent, of course, to allow Wagner to collect himself, it would in the next few minutes prove to be a grievous error. Tragically and strangely inconsistent, the astute doctor—who was almost always Johnny-on-the-spot when Wagner took a *turn*—discerned nothing now, perhaps mistaking his patient's besetment for perturbation or even plain old nerves. For all of Mazzio's incisive, analytical proximity to this case, even to the recurring orbits of Wagner's spells, the blinders he'd suddenly donned to everything save the mulling over of old video footage blocked him from interpreting the very initiative stage of transition that they'd all so desperately sought to witness.

The March 2nd clip reintroduced the ersatz Wagner, this time sitting cross-legged on the floor of the observation room, calmly mumbling to either himself or to a ready gathering of phantom collaborates. This type of internal projection was nothing new to the staff at Howsley, not for a good number of the patients, and not even for Wagner. What *was* particularly noteworthy of this taping was that Wagner spent forty-two minutes of film time gesticulating a host of mundane, if not unusual, actions—from the preparation of a small fire via imagined kindling and flints, to the meticulousness of making ready an invisible piece of game or meat for roasting over a similarly fancied spit. Immersed the whole while in the broken reciprocation of multi-partied conversation, he even appeared at times to be delegating the assistance rendered by those spirits whom he had apparently invited to sup with him. Unlike the previous video, this episode was serene and pleasant, almost calmingly therapeutic by its mere nature. But it was nothing astoundingly ground-breaking, and, on its own, certainly nothing for the record books.

Remarkable was it then that even several minutes into it, not one of the three doctors present became disinterested enough to hazard a casual glance in Wagner's direction, and thus to discover the metamorphosis in the midst of overtaking him. Each sat oblivious to the fact that what he most wished to document was passing his detection like dawn before a blind man. Familiar with the clues, aware of Wagner's history, they'd not gleaned any relevance from his agitation because he'd not produced any of the stir relatable to a bender's onset.

But James Wagner knew. For a trice, he owned the secrets of the cosmos. An instant later, he was hard-pressed to recall his own name. Within seconds, he ceased to exist at all. And then suddenly he was back. The mindflux effect was gearing up, and there was nothing he could do to stave it.

Not merely a harbinger of the personality shift, the mindflux was a kind of orchestral prelude to the psychical discord to follow, a con brio medley of delirium that signalled Wagner's impending reconsignment to the abyss. Oddly, it was also one prodrome that Wagner had been unable to report to Dr. Mazzio, or to anyone else for that matter, for in its quickening it seemed to trigger some type of exclusive, anterograde amnesia that furtively suppressed Wagner's capacity to encode and store any recollection of its existence. No downloading into the realm of accessible memory, Wagner's conscious mind was benighted of the mindflux's transitional imagery up until the occasion of a subsequent incident, whereby it cued its own retrieval through synaptic routes not normally negotiated. Of course, with each and every such recurrence, he was no better off than before, for the cycle simply repeated, and any frustration he experienced regarding the lapses dissipated along with his evanescent memory, resurfacing only at the next go-round—and circuitously with every one after that.

This was not to say that, once repossessed of his mind and body, he'd never been able to smuggle an eidectic engram or two back from the grander hallucinatory domain where he served his stints of disembodied exile. The mysterious *sigma*, for instance, had long been a ubiquitous fixture of his visions, dating as far back as his youth, when the benders had been only occasional and infinitely less consuming. A symbol so pervasive, so visionally compelling, he'd given over so much of his teen and young adult life—not only to the fuguish spells, but to his own inquisitional agenda—in the hope of divining some measure of significance from its almost flagrant periodicity. Driven by personal fiat, the hours that other young people frittered away in more convivial pursuits he'd filled with exploratory endeavour, schooling himself in areas of study that public education barely even acknowledged. He read. He researched. He'd even rendered, by way of sketches, sculptures and whatnot, a closet-and-a-half and twelve bookcases full of visual and tactile exemplars, all intended to facilitate his understanding. He romanced and propounded, stretching curiosity to obsessive ends. He camped out at the library, poring over books and across cyberspace for insight into iconology, sphragistics, ideography—anything that might tender some new lead or angle. Enslaved by a visional enigma, he worked to create and recreate the *sigma* glyph as many times and in as many ways as it took to demystify it, in effect solemnizing it through nearly every medium receptive to pen, palette, even pargeting, with his diligence matched only by his lack of success.

That the answer never materialised was disappointing but not completely discouraging. He learned of things he might never have known otherwise, and if nothing else he'd broached new ways to make old perspectives fresh. A casual browsing of any of his school notebooks revealed margins a-glut with errant *sigma* doodles in every variant, every technique and angle that he could visualise. His clay phase, fleeting and unsatisfying, had been followed by a laughable, if ambitious, period of soap carvings—not to mention a disastrous attempt at scrimshaw, a flirtation with stained glass, and a gallery's worth of besmirched canvasses on which he'd made pitiful attempt to perennialise the *sigma* in oils, watercolours, even a pawnshop airbrush. There'd even been a crude relief that he'd enchased in a patch of drywall filler in his first flat. Such repetition and variation were his only vehicles with which to better understand the *sigma's* pertinence to him, for in his visions the symbol boasted far too many incarnations to be denied at least some accolade of significance. Yet, for all of his compulsion, not one of these studies merited him any manner of epiphany or enlightenment, and more times than not only prompted greater provocation. Whatever the *sigma's* secrets, they remained locked and inaccessible within his mental vault, and despite his implacable hopes of unriddling its psychological import, Wagner's feebly meted artistry could never truly do justice to his most visited visional graffito.

But there once was someone whose artistry had.

Indeed, once upon a time, one of the few people whom he'd ever allowed himself to get close to had given him a facsimile of the *sigma* that, engendered by her ten dextrous fingers, made his own sophomoric simulacra look like Play-Doh globs and Crayola scribbles by comparison. The gift—a handmade pendant—she'd bestowed unto him, complete with sterling chain and clasp, so that he could always carry upon his person his "symbolic familiar."

The talent behind the industry was, of course, one Sara Higgins, a former roomie-turned-girlfriend, and one of the few lighthouses in his fogbound existence. At a time when he could still pass his affliction off as eccentricity bordered by neurosis, Sara had been an uncommonly understanding and imaginative young woman. Mindful of his peculiarities, she'd appropriated his *sigma* renditions on the sly and, in the midst of a prolific jewellery-making kick (sparked by her enrolment in a few local workshops), had one evening presented Wagner with a hand-crafted bibelot.

No recipient of an intimate's generosity could have been more delighted than Wagner. Floored by her extraordinary artisanship, touched by her creative means of demonstrating his relevance to her, at a time in their relationship when tensions had dialled-up and misunderstandings went hand in hand with the mental incapacitations that he'd fought to keep hidden, only now, in the wane of his third decade, did he truly recognise and appreciate the bridging intent behind her invention. How fatidic, how very much like him, to instead have allowed that trinket to herald the declivity of all they'd ever shared.

Cast fittingly in pewter, the "symbolic familiar" blended perfectly the element of rusticity with the alchemic intimations suggested by the tinctured, rough-hewn qualities inherent to the alloy. She'd done quite a job on it, excelling far beyond her novitiate status, and Wagner wore it religiously, perhaps overzealously—right up until the day that Sara walked out on him for good.

As the pendant itself not-so-coincidentally vanished that very same day, a fruitless rummaging of the apartment suggested that she'd pinched it back, probably as her means of atonement for having unleashed such a monkey's paw of fomentation upon their private world, that no more bad karma might find vent through its periphrastic machinations. It was to be expected. Factors too numerous to list had predicated, even predicted, her departure. Wagner had known it. Deep down, he suspected that she'd known it too, especially as she'd been no simpleton to be appeased by all of the lame explanations he'd offered for his erratic actions and unexplained absences. With his failure to confide, in the end she'd drawn the only rational conclusions she could: that he was either being unfaithful, or was unconfessedly into drugs—particularly of the psychedelic variety. None of her tactics effecting any change in him, not ultimatums, not tough love, not active concern, she took her last option and made for the door. It didn't exactly sit well, knowing that his obsession with the *sigma*—which she'd by then decided had chemically-induced origins—had come to outflank his devotion to her; and she, in all likelihood, probably chided herself for having fuelled that fire with such blind-eyed solicitousness. Presumably, then, she'd either tossed the pendant or nicked off with it, if only to deprive him of his perversely unhealthy infatuation, little to know that he would be driven to seek more drastic and imperishable means.

She'd been in error, of course, but understandably so. How could he have explained what he himself didn't understand? How did one convey that his inner life spontaneously usurped control from his outer existence? It wasn't something that a psychologically troubled young man admitted to with ease or poise. Emotionally he hadn't the wherewithal to overcome the more considerable depths of his greater compulsion—that which, years later, Dr. Mazzio would label "hypercathexis"—and sadly, way back at that point in his life, it was more his preoccupation that defined him than any type of conscious consideration.

Yet, now, nine years later, frozen helpless in a room full of seasoned mental health experts, he realised that this same preoccupation had grown to become its own entity. It stood and breathed on its own. It had teeth. And worse, *its* preoccupation was *him*.

Wagner's psychical chaos suddenly peaked as the mindflux took dominion. Clinging failingly to lucidity by a single, mental handhold, he could yet see Mazzio and the others around him, but it was as if he were peering at them through an aquarium tank whose filtration system had gone haywire, where plastic sea-bottom accessories were uprooted within a maelstrom of coloured pebbles and faux vegetation, of buffeted toy castles, resurrected galleons and pirates' chests, all swirling at a velocity that he in his paralysis couldn't transpierce in order to alert said doctors to his plight.

Then predictably, as if by some contractual hallucinatory obligation, what image should have skirred across his visional field but the *sigma* itself. Cohering out of the swell of phantasised debris and then dissipating within the same, in passing it elicited the usual rush of familiarity tinged with subtle underscorings of foretokening that, after untold years of such revisiting, had Wagner likening it to the Greek letter of its namesake for no other reason than that it had been the first comparative symbol that had come to mind. Akin to a *sigma* in basic symmetry, it was truly not so far from *epsilon* or the Anglican "E"; in fact, even the Hebrew *sin* and *shin* bore equally legitimate consideration for comparison, as would have dozens of letters and characters from written languages he'd had no interest in pursuing further. Such things weren't of tremendous importance, since it was unlikely that his percept truly shared kinship with any of these symbols. *Sigma* was a referencing, no more, for a phasm that boasted a good deal more regalia unique unto itself. Most often centred within a kind of annularity the arc of which came near to fully engirding it but did not, it bore the further augmentation of a vertical stroke that pierced both aureole and icon, so that the consummate image, evoking an air of archaic surrealism, was like none he'd ever seen in any book or database. Just why it should have wheedled through the weave of his madness was something Wagner could not know; his fixation, however, had him convinced that it promised not only some as yet unfathomable significance, but a significance that was *his* alone to uncover. Resurfacing as it did from his adolescence to his adulthood, by simple acclimation had he finally come to trade his wariness of it for something closer to awe; and later, his awe for the growing monomania that Sara had abided for as long as her good nature allowed. Only after her exit did it dawn on him what meagre control he exercised over his own life, and how truly invasive and destructive his prepossession had become. All too late, it would nonetheless compel him down the road, to gather his resolve and to try repelling both the glyph's subversive influence and his changing mental chemistry as a whole—a challenge that almost immediately proved bootless and beyond his means to accomplish.

The disorienting stage of mindflux now faltering—indeed, breaking away like a spent rocket booster—Wagner's undefended ego suddenly stood at the threshold of full-fledged, psychical uncoupling. There fell a brief moment of calm here, a transitory largo tucked between the prestissimo discordances of flux and full-blown bender, where reality reared itself in a sort of mellifluous disconnectedness anticipatory to his doppelganger taking the stage. Though short-lived, in those few sub-seconds of skewed perception Wagner gleaned enough to know that physically he'd not moved from the viewing room's conjoined tables. The banal footage running across the monitor screen had barely progressed at all from where it had been at the spell's onset. The three doctors were just as they'd been, seated around him, watching the screen, occasionally commenting on the insignifica of his *Other's* behaviour. Upright on the tabletop before him stood half a roll of Tropical Fruits LifeSavers.

As always, what had seemed minutes and miles to him had only been a second or two, tops. This was the first of two certainties. The second was the very imminence that loped toward him like a hungry and unstoppable ghoul. He felt eerily lightheaded, weightless, luxated—and indeed, he knew what all of it meant. He wished to speak but was unsure that he even could, with only scant seconds remaining in which to strong-arm some manner of impartation out of a disobliging larynx.

"*D-d-doctors...*"

He heard his own voice as if he were speaking through an elongated funnel. All three professionals turned to him in unison.

"*Doc...tors,*" he continued, his syllables sluggish and strained. "*Believe...me... now...*"

Combating incredible rigour, he managed to uncrook one arm, and slowly, arduously, he stretched it out across the table, halting in percipient pause at full extension. Then, fingers trembling, he lowered it, palm-side down, over the roll of candy.

The doctors gasped.

His hand passed right through it!

Steadied by tremendous will, Wagner's palm maintained its contradictory hover within the candy's physicality, the torn tatters of foil and bright yellow wrap undisturbed by the encroachment of his impalpable knuckle, the roll's cylindrical base only marginally obscured by the simultaneous spatial occupancy of his destabilised extremity.

The doctors jerked in closer, their necks craned beyond cervical comfort, their eyes bulged like hard-boiled eggs with pupils.

"Oh my God—!" uttered O'Connell, her pen slipping from her fingers, her papers fluttering groundward. "Oh my God!" she echoed. "*Oh my God oh my God!*"

His jaw in freefall, Jon Mazzio still managed to fire off an inquiry. "James—are you okay? Are you with us?"

"He's with us all right," spat Williams, who'd waited a very long time for this moment. He reached over and grabbed at Wagner's wrist. "This magic show is now conclude—"

Williams jumped in startle. His hand hadn't connected with Wagner's at all, but rather had passed completely through it, striking the edge of the table and jouncing Wagner's candy to the floor.

"What the deuce—?" He recoiled briefly, bemusedly, then launched again at Wagner's forearm, his bicep, his shoulder, neck, and torso.

Nothing. The only resistance he encountered was that of Wagner's clothing, which he succeeded in pushing completely through Wagner and to the floor with the same effort as knocking sheets off of a clothesline.

Wagner, who hadn't strayed from his chair, was not truly present either. He was there and yet not, visible but translucent, a phantom, a hologram.

"James? James, can you hear me?" Mazzio flailed his arms before Wagner, his tone fluctuating between fear and concern. "*James!*"

Wagner wanted to answer but couldn't. In partial vapour, his mastery over even the least of his faculties was thwarted by influences he could not reckon, influences that routed him over the lip of oblivion and down to the wonted depths of his maddening. No autonomy, no free will, he could do naught but reconcile himself with the fact that it was all happening again. By now, his doctor's voice was little more to him than the distant plea of one man bewailing another who, shackled to a huge and ponderous anchor, had just been heaved into the deepest and darkest of oceans, and whose only means of ascension was a good deal more Dantesque than Mazzio's catalogues and videotapes would suggest.

Within seconds, he'd lost Mazzio's voice, then Mazzio himself, the room, the very authenticity of every earthly boundary that had, moments prior, bordered Wagner's physical being. Chaos quickly rushed in to fill the void, its deluge so distracting in magnitude that Wagner had no option but to give over his last urgencies of the real world for those of more pressing assault. Hallucinatory events bled and blended into a blustery, dramaturgic delirium that saw him cast as both participant and bystander in a nightmarish allegory whose tumultuousness played out like motion picture coming attractions run wiggy. Images and settings rose up and fell away as new and haunting tableaus coalesced in their stead. Vistas clashed with the formative distortions that replaced them; faceless beings were given features and then robbed of conformation; imperfection became paradisiacal only to be put asunder by cataclysmic insurgency.

Over everything else, topography seemed to bear uncommon significance here. Landscapes and seascapes vacillated between catastrophic and benign happenstance. Other *fragmenti* centred on people, on creatures, and occasionally on devices with marked incongruencies to the greater context. Still others incorporated enough inconsistencies, differentiae, and contortions of space and proportion to have sent the likes of Salvador Dali packing.

One such vision, unfolding with an incident of torrential rains thrashing down through the sunderances of some primaeval woodland, was abruptly and horrifically expunged when the muddied terrain itself violently heaved up like a huge and terrible earthen maw and engulfed the entirety of its tree-studded locale. The undergrowth, the rocks, the boles, the forest complete—all was reclaimed in a single event of seismic retaliation that suggested a sentiousness with no bounds and no tolerance even for itself. Then, the pluming dust and ash and steam that spewed skyward in its devastation acted upon the menacing thunderheads at every point of convergence, defusing and dispersing the storm and ushering a calm as the earth settled back with the diastrophic rumblings of a cavernous belly gorged. Then, in an act of revitalisation it unfurled over jag and jut a blanket of new verdancy that swept the land like water crystallizing across a freezing windshield. The clouds then dissipated, and with the dream-daylight nearly gone, the briefest of twilights gave way to a nocturnal blackness that granted no favour to the eyes save a scattering of phosphorescent dots that bespeckled the nighttide like fireflies dancing among sedges. Growing in intensity as Wagner drew close, these dots revealed themselves as campfires around which a vast assemblage of bedraggled humanity was gathered; and Wagner, no longer only phantasmic, suddenly found himself among them in body.

Quickly discovered, all eyes turned in his direction. A young boy and girl scrambled to remove a cloak from an old man at rest on a stump, and this they brought before Wagner, their tiny arms outstretched. The wizened donor—his thick beard grizzled and wild, his body puny and naked—glanced up with opaque, unseeing eyes, his expression demonstrating no perceptible concern over his sudden defrockment. A young woman from nearby suddenly uncloaked herself and, swaddling the old man in her own vestment, pressed herself to him from behind with daughter-like reverence. Wagner's attention suddenly drawn back to the children, he was perplexed at finding not the old man's cloak in their bestowal, but in its stead a slender white cylinder resembling a common fluorescent lamp. Mired in miscomprehension, only with a gingerly hesitation did he opt to accept it; yet, at the very moment of contact, the implement flared with such unexpected brilliance that Wagner inadvertently dashed it to the ground. Blinding fission followed, a tremulous, all-encompassing and strangely unresounding backlash that bowled Wagner over and into a body of water risen from nowhere, a brine of numbing cold that in seconds had switched-out the forested landscape.

With a drowner's thrust and flail he sought everywhere for shore, despairing at finding not even the former campfires to guide him back. The water, then, his only orientation, he ceased his thrashing and commenced to paddle with broader, less consuming strokes, hoping to conserve his energy until some alternative revealed itself to him. Yet here, his hand almost immediately alit upon a streaking, sub-surface projectile, a rough, emery-like node that was nevertheless firm and sleek and conducive to his grip. Initially retracting in fear, he then realised that he'd clamped onto the dorsal of a dolphin-creature who now carried him through the foam with grace and speed quite splendid. Grateful for the save, he closed his eyes and clung fast, letting the rest of his body go limp as the cetacean towed him effortlessly through the choppy surf.

But then, without warning, the mammal leaped from the water and flung Wagner away like a rag doll. Airborne for a moment, with the bluntest of shocks he struck a suddenly re-materialised earth, his lungs forced into expelling the last of his wind.

Sluggish in recovery, when he next opened his eyes he beheld not only daylight, but a new and much-escalated imparter of terror. Standing over Wagner's soppiness hunched a huge chimaera the physical ghastliness of which suggested some unholy conflation of gorilla and grizzly, but whose lineaments likewise incorporated features freely and haphazardly borrowed from a slew of other predatory beasts. With raptorial limbs grasping, it lurched to intercept Wagner, its tusk-packed submaxilla springing wide on malevolent hinges.

Minimised in bearing, Wagner quickly scampered backwards. His menacer, however, pursued so swiftly as to defy its ponderous girth. Tripping, toppling, Wagner pitched and sprawled back into the dirt, pedalling at the soil in a crab-like scurry until he mustered momentum enough to regain his footing. Soaked head to heel, coated with muck and sand like a breadcrumbed fillet, in finally righting himself he found his escape cut off by rock and thicket too severe to climb or to penetrate. Nearly outstripped by the entity, with his last vestige of rationale he bemoaned his end by such horrible means. He had nowhere left to run, no viable resort, while nigh upon him loomed the frothing abomination, easily as swift as he, and four times his bulk. Brandishing its razor-edged claws and its sharp, snaggled incisors, it reared ominously, casting a huge and terrible umbra over Wagner's sheepish cower.

And suddenly it spoke his name.

At that precise moment, a consciousness away, three doctors looked on in astonishment as James Wagner—crazed and naked and wraith-like before them—sprang like a spooked rabbit and charged cleanly and without consequence through the tables, through the video monitor, and then through the wall itself before any of them could choke out a single word. Indisputably spectral had Wagner been; and in his ghostly wake trailed the many scepticisms and scientific precepts that could no longer effectively plague or hinder or preclude the new reality of what the two visiting doctors had just witnessed.

To them, the *4-D Man* may indeed have been a figment, but no longer was he one of the imagination.

CHAPTER THREE

These fragments I have shored against my ruins.
—T. S. ELIOT

If speculation over the most recently professed symptomatology in Wagner's case had been a topic better left to tabloid reporting and to proponents of the supernatural, then the cat was surely out of the bag now. For a staggering and exhaustive ninety-seven minutes, the chase was on. Jon Mazzio and the available staff at the Howsley Centre for Mental Health sprinted halls, vaulted stairwells, burst from meeting rooms to offices to storage facilities to various patients' quarters—even through the pharmacy—in pursuit of a shadowy projection of a man who, unfettered by the physical barriers that affected solid matter, transmigrated from room to room and level to level like the apparition he had become. No longer unsubstantiated, not just the hysterical evincement of susceptible and suggestible minds, the now irrefutable *4-D Man* skirted the periphery of spatial transudation. Uncatchable in this form, and indispensably driven by the madness so apparently upon him, the orderlies who managed to intercept him at one time or another could subsequently do naught but observe him in said state until he vanished through the next wall—or the next floor, as was sometimes the case.

The latter event occurring less frequently, observably it seemed to be accomplished through acute action on Wagner's part—a scramble or dive, a leap or an abrupt lunge—with the conjecture for how a presumably weightless man might come to acquire momentum being the least of his pursuers' concerns. Such propulsive freedom indeed premising some small measure of molecular sway, still the very fact of Wagner's intangibility (in whatever degree) was an outright flouting of physical law. Almost completely uninfluenced by mass or gravity, even in a static state his body was not disposed to remain floorbound, a peculiarity that produced the unsettling contradictive of his sometimes occupying space midair and between stories. This made for a truly startling sight for eyewitnesses on either side of the substratum, and would no doubt spur a foreseeable doubling of caseloads for the already taxed counsellors downstairs.

At one point, Margaret Groller—who, on being apprised of the nature of the commotion, had barricaded herself in the staff lounge—fell victim to the irony of her actions when Wagner phased through the north corner of the lounge's ceiling. Had he been unentranced and corporeal, all one-hundred-seventy pounds of him would have flumped Three Stooges-style smack onto her flinty little head. As it was, she was spared the trauma, and within seconds his diffluent form had bounded through both her and then the floor, unhindered by her physical person and all but deaf to her banshee-like scream—heard by everyone in that wing, and later attested to have reverberated throughout the halls for a full minute.

With his body commandeered and out of control, from deep in sequestration Wagner's consciousness endured the futility of being buffeted almost cyclically from one dioramic predicament to the next. The inundation was relentless and protean; and while filled with many of the permeable images associated with normal dreaming, very little existed to suggest mutuality. Much more a visional plateau, there was no narcissistic privilege here, no indulgence of id and ego, no inclination that wasn't tethered in some manner to his wakeful coherency. Subliminality, while not entirely absent, seemed to not dominate so much as accentuate. Vexing, variable, niggardly in its retentivity, Wagner's mind-state allowed him to clasp onto little more than a few gleanings of cryptic *excerpta*, a sufficient amount to register but less than enough to define. Partial constructs of revelatory significance, bits and pieces of portency placed like mileposts along the out roads of his sanity, at best they were unapplicable clues to an unspecified mystery. As a participant, he was perennially short-changed, the victim of taunt heaped upon taunt within a far grander scurrility. Epiphany followed by agnosia, recognition by forgetfulness, one moment the carrot of clarity dangled and the next it was gone. Even more exasperating was the unsupportable conviction that the answers he sought were somehow extractable from these teasers, if only inferentially—and providing he had the goods to distinguish between relevance and filler. Yet, therein lay his other problem: a hesitation to rely too heavily on a perception that, independent of physical eyesight, was an admittedly fallible agent that fluctuated from one moment to the next.

Contextually, the visionscapes were composed of elements taken, and just as easily mistaken, for allegory within a zigzagging and doubling-backing of fragmagery that seemed forever locked into a continuous state of spatiotemporal convergence and dispersion. They were sometimes peopled, sometimes barren, rarely contemporary but always plaguingly reminiscent. Aside from the disproportionate concentration of geomorphic integrants in their unremitting decimation and regeneration, Wagner encountered a bounty of fleeting, pictographic vignettes that instilled him with what he could only define as latent urgency and premonitory ambiguity. Some seemed sensical and self-contained. Others blended both notions within the same mental state in the way that voices from a television broadcast or a nearby conversation come to infiltrate the reverie of a person in a proximal doze. Whether even marginally aware of the medium's insinuation into his semi-conscious drift, said dozer is nevertheless influenced, and incorporates what he hears into the fanciful jumble of dissociative imagery made accessible by the fact of his pendency between two mental states. In Wagner's head, this may have meant being one moment allied with a citizenship of rustically clad folk against an array of armoured assailants of mediaeval-flavoured origins whose shields bore Howsley's caduceus upon their heraldic fields. An eyeblink later would find him facing down a pack of frothing, quad-rupedal monstrosities with only a tree branch—or that infelicitous fluorescent tube from his earlier sequence—as his defence. One more transition and he'd be riding the torrent of a buckling waterway while situated atop Jon Mazzio's desktop, or trudging through dank, cavernous, torch-lit halls with metal pails in heft, both filled to overflow with replicas of his *sigma* pendant. The elements were legion and they changed as quickly as he could register them. At one point, he even found himself playing pupil to a reverently robed Dr. Williams, who counselled him in unintelligible gibberish while offering him a chalice draughted from a wellspring that miraculously issued from the body of a dark and oblong mineral the size of a refrigerator. One second, everything made perfect sense and Wagner understood none of it; the next, nothing was remotely scrutable and Wagner was wise to it all. Each vision a hybrid of fact and phantasy, a condensed assortment of pleasures and pains, stoicism and strife, mundanity and magic—all in exaggerated pretext—they smacked of vital, deadly seriousness in a framework of the kind of utter ludicrousness found only in the reaches of a deeply disturbed mind or in one whose imagination had gone horribly awry.

All this Wagner saw—no, endured—before the synaptic plug finally yanked itself free. Then, just as it had taken him, it dumped him curbside into the realm of comparative normalcy. Mass, function, essence—all of them recohered like metal filings drawn to a magnet. By grace unrevealed, once more he was put right.

The sudden reclamation of his bodily heft after such a period of weightlessness came as a shock to Wagner's skeleton. The resumptive surge from thousands of sensory receptors all coming instantaneously back online was likewise a vigorous assault to the central nervous system. Wagner's switchboard in overload, he braved the self-diagnostic influx for the few seconds that it lasted. He clenched and unclenched his hands to confirm his solidity for himself. He tested the synthetic of the carpet below him, breathed in the familiar odour of hospital. Then, blinking the focus back into his eyes, he fixed his weary gaze on his surroundings.

Immediately he was grateful to discover no frothing pack of beasties lunging his way, and nothing in the vein of symbolic flagons, subterranean corridors, or hostile assailants anywhere in sight. In fact, he found nothing but a vacant office and an uncustomary perspective of the city through its window, a view that suggested that he was somewhere on the Centre's north side. The room's desk, bearing a helter-skelter of research clutter—not to mention a half-finished cup of Lemon Zinger and an apricot Danish—looked to have been only recently abandoned, its owner/occupant either off in errand or consultation or maybe even a player in the search for Wagner himself. And while definitely not Jon Mazzio's office, it nevertheless sported the same basic lines and decorative ambience of Mazzio's digs. The bookshelving, the tweed carpet, another functionless triptych—there was nothing here any more inspired than the rest of the hospital's drab décor. But once again, Wagner was grateful. He'd seen lively environs aplenty to last him three lifetimes.

Satisfied, indeed relieved, his adrenal edge gave way, and *he* with it. Having braced an exhaustion worthy of Odysseus, he hadn't further need for the biochemically-heightened guardedness that for the past few minutes had served as shoring for waning knees and buckling frame. Without it, collapse was inevitable, and he struck the office floor like the cadaver that he almost wished he was, with any wistful longings for reaching his personal quarters under his own steam both unrealistic and unfulfillable.

The next time Wagner opened his eyes, he was in his own bed. Linens tucked neatly around him, blanket taut and tidy, two hospital-issue pillows had been squarely fluffed and propped to slight elevation behind his head. The window curtains were at half-draw, although less light filtered into the room by way of the sheers than by one of the small fluorescent fixtures mounted near-bedside. The only acting illumination, it cast a familiar, clinical pallor about the room, at times more reminiscent of an autopsy lab than a living space, even with the warmer-toned lamps that Dr. Mazzio had obtained for him. Though often harsh to the eyes, they were conducive enough for a decent read, as Wagner with his ever-growing library could attest.

For a drowsy moment, he lay listening to the almost inaudible buzz emanating from the lamp's ballast. Then, piqued by association, he turned abruptly to view the tube itself, that he might perhaps gain from it some measure of accessibility to its vision-prompted cousin. A predictable disappointment, he found no more and no less than what he'd expected—a conglomerate of gas and glass, white powder and element—and felt foolish for thinking that clues to his hallucinations might be so arbitrarily meted. Purged of this momentary fervidness, he allowed his gaze to drift a few degrees downward, to the nightstand, where what should he see but a tattered roll of Tropical Fruits LifeSavers. Surprised by the discovery, he wondered why anyone would have gone to the trouble to return a half-pillaged roll of candies to his room, especially after the fracas and high inconvenience he'd doubtlessly created during his amok time.

Taking stock, he assumed that he'd only just been laid to bed, the pristine state of his bedding showing no signs of restless or prolonged sleep. But after espying a chair closely adjacent to his bedside, he reconsidered, for on its otherwise vacant cushion he noticed a small pocket-magazine, the cover of which read: *101 BIG PUZZLE CHALLENGES*. Spine in the air and pages downturned to preserve its enthusiast's place, Wagner came to suspect that he'd been asleep and under observation for some incalculable period, with at least one part-time attendant close at hand to maintain eye and ear on his paranormal theatrics.

That this attendant had stepped out briefly—perhaps for a nature call, perhaps to confer with a doctor—was pretty good evidence that Wagner was no longer deemed an immediate threat to hospital welfare. He hated being thought of in that manner, and frequently defended his incorporeal self to his critics, averring that *he* was not truly as menacing as were those bystanders whose own hysteria was more greatly responsible for the commotion and the property damage. Still, he could hardly deny that their reactions to his ghostly traipsings were unwarranted. Much as he hated to admit it, there was no exempting himself from at least an indirect responsibility; after all, had he not opted to remain institutionalised, the counselling offices and the examination rooms and the dispensary would all have been considerably less congested places.

Lacking feedback on the various adversities that he in his unsynchronous state had undoubtedly inflicted on Howsley's cast and crew, Wagner propped himself up on the plump of his pillow and waited, confident that Jon Mazzio or some other advocate would visit him shortly to guilt him with the dismal report. In the interim, however, there was nothing to be done but to rest and to ponder, and while engaging in both he pushed aside all the non-pressing issues in his mind to see what answers he could unearth from his visional sediment.

Excavating for bits of residual imagery not yet superseded by the more immediate priorities of wakefulness, he expected to uncover little more than scant memories of the escapade. For the most part, he was right. Some notional leaders, some associative bridges, a gist or two of larger thematic patterns—workable data all, they were nothing over which he'd not pored before. Yet, in dusting away these yet-undriven sands of mnemonic recency, with a touch of focusing and some fortuitous clemency he managed to reclaim a few grains of pertinence. Such recall truly surprised him, for rarely these days was he ever able to latch onto so much so readily. Granted, none was a true windfall of benderish decryption, but in the unravelling came comparable unriddling, just as retracing begat reconstruction, whereby Wagner succeeded—albeit marginally—in piecing together an admittedly adulterated visual record, hazy though salvageable, and one that proved right ripe for analytical musing.

While dissevered from the *sigma's* high occasion of frequency within the incendiary—and unretained—mindflux, Wagner couldn't help but to note its pervasion within the greater hallucinatory opus. Highly insinuative, it was usually a secondary, cameo-like detail, seldom ever focal or prominently iconographic. Still, as a persistent mainstay it was likewise a historically fascicular one, repetitive enough perhaps to validate, if not justify, his many past fixations. Like a number that randomly turns up throughout the course of one's day—the $1.04 in change returned from the grocer, the wall clock that happens to read 1:04 on a chanced glance, the school bus in the next lane with the fleet number of 104 stamped on its emergency door—all coincidences to be sure, but what person, when witness to such serendipitous prompting, would not be tempted to run out to the nearest lottery kiosk to indulge a compelling hunch? A revealed symbol, an undivested meaning, Wagner had been subjected to the *sigma's* recurrence over the course of his apparitional history; and, rejecting mere battology or obsession or capricious happenstance, he'd chosen to glom onto it, maybe only in an anticipatory capacity, with the hope that somewhere farther along the co-conscious roadside he'd be in a position to steer into that one psychogenic lotto outlet where his faith in the cyclically-present symbol would net him a whole jackpot of solutions.

Another salvageable bender-snippet was one that initially fell short of exceptionality, mostly due to its propensity toward conventional—and therefore, not extremely ambitious—interpretation. This was the incident of the robed sage, the mega-mineral, and the wellspring. Extracted from the context of the otherwise illusory tableau, the clichés epitomised by these symbols were strictly impoverished ones. Hackneyed and formulaic, any kid who'd ever been to Sunday school or who possessed even a solitary die-roll of Dungeons & Dragons know-how could easily assign the holy man and the eucharistic chalice their token relevance, not to mention expound upon the rock-as-church correlation, with its eternal spring whose purifying waters bespoke the gamut of all those ideals for which humans thirsted—fountain of youth, Holy Grail, knowledge of the aeons, et al. Even so, Wagner wasn't about to ignore anything that such eidola might per-chance to convey, no matter how traditional or trite the metaphors. Certainly less impressive than the catastrophic eruptions, or his being shunted from one terrifying predicament to the next, he still believed that he could eventually tap even such throwaway imagery for its basic truth, whereby any number of visual variables could be plugged into the exemplars without obscuring the implication.

Instead of Dr. Williams's visage looming beneath the mage's hood, it could just as easily have been Mahatma Gandhi or Abraham Lincoln or the Dalai Lama (or Obi-Wan Kenobi for that matter)—anyone who might be said to represent authority or wisdom. Wagner interpreted these decodable but comparatively unremarkable sequences as ready-made fillers, products of his subconscious that, not unlike nocturnal dreams, worked here as fanciful entr'actes, cementing the gaps between what he felt were perhaps the more pertinent psionic impartings. They were simply transitional devices in a larger forum of rapidly evolving and dissipating illusions.

"I see that you've come back to us," said nurse Lemanski as she clicked the door shut behind her.

Wagner looked up and smiled with relief. He'd half-expected to see Miss Groller, only he knew better than to think that Margaret would ever pull duty at his bedside, much less engross herself in a puzzle book. Sally Lemanski, on the other hand, was a nurturer—fun-loving, inquisitive, and caring.

A plain, podgy little woman, she possessed a friendly, old-timey demeanour and an inner goodness that radiated strongly enough to cast a few extra lumina over the most curmudgeonly patient's mood. And Wagner—certainly no curmudgeon, but at times equally as taxing as one on Howsley's staff—had been indebted to her on numerous occasions when the disorienting after-effects of a spent bender had left him vulnerable and frightened and in need of a nurse whose dedication was to her patients as well as to their afflictions.

"So, what's the word down in damage control?" he humbly asked.

"Nothing significant," she replied. "No broken bones, no broken walls. Not even a good sliming. A respectable ghost would at least have left a few ectoplasm trails here and there. I don't think the Spooks' Local takes kindly to that brand of inferior scabbing."

He sat up. "Then I was incorporeal the *whole time?*"

"Somewhere around an hour-and-a-half by what I've been told. I don't know—I never saw you. Not once. And I'd never have believed *any* of it if the closed-circuit hadn't caught some of the action. Do you feel like you might want to eat something?" She produced a notepad, ready to take order. "I've been given explicit instructions to feed you, and after seeing you streaking around on tape like a naked string bean, it seems to me that you could stand to fill out a bit."

Wagner flushed red. But instead of answering, he thought for a moment, processing what he'd just heard about his episode. It disheartened him, knowing that what had started ten months earlier as a confidential study of one individual's very unprecedented disorder was surely the talk of every doctor, nurse, orderly, patient, janitor, and visiting attendant in the facility by now.

"What's the general buzz around here?" he asked. "Have you heard anything about what's going to happen next?"

She picked up her crossword magazine, closed it, and set it on the nightstand. "I'm not sure," she said, taking a seat. "They don't know what to make of it—what to make of *you*. As for what's next, I think they're probably expecting you to phone home."

"Phone home?"

She smirked. "You know, *phone home.* That alien—that *E.T. phone home* stuff. They think you're from Mars or something."

His face rippled amusement. "Aren't *all* men supposed to be from Mars?"

"Well, if not," she said, "I know a few that I'd like to send there."

His smile broadened. Her husband, Bruno, and his black sheep brother, Mory, had long been the butts of her personal venting, and Wagner had no doubt that it was them to whom she referred.

"Well, then Mars would finally be able to boast of intelligent life, right?"

"No—it could boast of a couple of loud, uncouth, unshaven couch-potatoes with an exasperating love of football and an aversion to chores."

"You left out power tools and beer."

"Whatever. I actually believe that they could both do with a little time on Mars. They're much too entrenched in their comfort zones. They could both stand a good, hard dose of reality."

"Reality...like *my* reality?"

She sighed. "Well, no. Never in my born days would I ever have believed in *your* kind of reality."

"Are Williams and O'Connell still here?"

"Oh yes," she replied. "Although I think that Dr. Williams about went into cardiac arrest during the whole shebang. I would say that he looks like he saw a ghost, but I suppose he really did. No one knows what to think now, especially him." She paused and averted her eyes. "How about that lunch? Doctor's orders, you know."

"I guess," said Wagner. "What's a-bubblin' in the ol' cauldron today?"

"Swiss steak. That is, the textured vegetable protein version of it. With whipped potatoes, corn, and cherry cobbler, I think."

Wagner grimaced. "What's behind door number two?"

"A lightly-seasoned, skinless chicken breast with steamed veggies and Jell-O salad."

Wagner shivered and grimaced. "*Real* chicken?"

"I think so."

"What's cookin' over at your house? Anything that you could maybe get Big Bruno to sneak in here for me?"

"Well, for tonight I have some pig's knuckles and homemade sauerkraut in the crock, and a load of potatoes for boiling."

Wagner added retching noises to his previous medley of disgusted reactions.

Sally threw her puzzle book at him. "You rat! I'm a good cook! My Nana taught me, and she was from the fatherland, of hardened German-Polish stock."

"Of hardened *arteries* is more like it," said Wagner. "That greasy, fatty peasant stuff will kill you, woman. And sauerkraut gives me—"

"Gas, I know. But it's happy food. Nana always said—"

"*Sauer macht lustig*, I know, I know. But sour doesn't make me cheerful. It just makes my jaws ache."

"So will *this*," she said, waving a menacing fist at him, "if you don't stop bad-mouthing Nana."

Wagner submitted. He voiced his selection, and she scribbled it down. He studied her face as she wrote, wondering how this stout little woman could banter so calmly with him after what she'd seen and heard. More so, he feared the reactions of the rest of the staff. Would they be negative? Unpredictable? Would he be looked upon as a freak, a pariah, a danger to be shunned? Would nobody come near him for fear of contracting whatever damnable affliction he had?

"Sally, is that why *you're* here? Are you the only one not too traumatised or superstitious to come within fifty feet of me?"

She looked at him, chewing the inside of her lip. "A bunch of people are scared, yes. You can't really blame them."

"No," he quietly uttered. "I suppose not."

After she left him, Wagner resumed his backtracking efforts. He culled every amassable memory of his uninhibited mental hooliganism as if he were outlining a college thesis whose culmination would offer some end-all resolution to what his life had become. Shaken by the increased occasion of his madness, by the changing prompters in the composition of that madness, and especially by the ungodly astral metamorphosing so totally disallowed by science and logic and common sense, every argument that he came up with indicated that he was running desperately low on future. Like the counterweights of a fittingly labelled cuckoo clock, he was descending into his own personal chasm with every swing of the pendulum and every hourly cuckoo call. He was nigh to becoming so precariously suspended in the nether realm as to find his predicament absurdly inverted, where his conscious life was imminently becoming the pesky, intrusive sanity that interfered with the greater, everyday normalcy of his lunacy. For all of his reasoning, for all of his extrapolating, in the end it came down to a confirmation of Dr. O'Connell's mixed jigsaw metaphor. But, in Wagner's case, the unplaced pieces were out of reach or were simply missing. Existing, perhaps, somewhere beyond the empirical, they were likely scattered along transcendental, theological, and certainly esoteric, avenues that he had neither the privilege nor the ability to access. And, frankly, this frightened the bejesus out of him—now more than ever.

Yet, quizzically, somewhere in the subterraneity of his being there existed a longing, an almost calming ardour that inconceivably wished for consummation, that desired the end like a broken man who waited for death. A subversiveness born of weariness, it sought to spur on his declension, to get it over with, to simply embrace the inescapable *force majeure* that usurped his essence with such excruciating gradation. It was a feeling that Wagner hoped was but a cathartic whim and no more, one that soon would whither—and not him with it.

Before Sally returned with his meal, Jon Mazzio stopped by. After three docile taps on the door, he entered the room and stepped lightly to Wagner's bedside. Looking a tad more solemn than usual, he smiled warmly and greeted Wagner with the zeal of an old friend.

"How are you doing, James?" he asked, circling the bed and pulling up Sally's vacant chair. "Have you eaten yet?"

Wagner, who'd been nosing through the puzzle book, closed it and lobbed it onto the nightstand. "Nurse Sally just skedaddled down to the cafeteria to rustle me up some of your fine, institutional grub," he said. "She says that she thinks my phasing is resultant of not having enough 'solids' in my diet."

Mazzio chuckled politely. "Well, it's nice to see that there are a few of us left with a sense of humour about this whole thing."

"Oh, I think she's trying to keep an open mind," said Wagner. "At least she's going all out to hide her reservations. Me, if I never laughed about it, you'd probably be prepping one of your more padded vacancies for me right now—not that you'd be able to keep me there."

"I think the last place you should be, James, is in a safety room. To be perfectly candid, I don't believe I've ever met a more sane man in my life than you. To be able to act and react as you do, to confront these impossible circumstances and not slip completely south and around the bend, is much to your credit."

"Don't butter me up too much, Jon. I'm not—" Wagner froze mid-sentence and eyed his physician suspiciously. "Now, why do I get the feeling that you're about to drop a bomb on me?"

"Oh no—*heavens*—no bomb here, James," Mazzio replied, his hands open and entreatful like a man surrendering. "But, I *have* been thinking..."

Wagner gestured for him to continue.

"Explain to me the importance of these *candies*, that you would always have them with you during our sessions."

"Candies—?" The inquiry had taken Wagner unawares. "You mean aside from satisfying my well-documented sweet tooth?"

"You've got no more of a sweet tooth than I do, James. Let me tell you what *I* think."

Feeling larkish, Wagner indulged him.

"Here's my theory. Aside from the obvious symbolism in the product name, I believe it's more the fact of the candy's compactness that makes it useful to you."

"Its 'compactness.' I'm not sure I follow."

"I think you use it as a kind of...portable *locus*—am I right? You utilise it—oh, I don't know—as a makeshift focal point of sorts, something on which you can concentrate, perhaps to test the status of the disengagement between tangibility and the lack thereof."

Wagner shifted position in bed, not from uneasiness, but from amusement and light embarrassment.

"Well, I wouldn't go *that* far, Jon—it's not exactly the friggin' *Eye of Agamotto* or anything. You make it sound very dramatic and all...but you're basically correct. It's probably more the by-product of happenstance than anything else. Just by chance, I was digging into a fresh roll of these babies the very first time I experienced a phasing. In the process of prying a piece out, the whole darned thing slipped through my grasp. As you might expect, I thought nothing of it at the time. But after several successive failures to retrieve it, it struck me that I'd lost the ability to latch onto anything at all."

"Just like yesterday."

"*Exactly* like yesterday."

"So, on subsequent occasions," Mazzio continued, "you've kept a roll with you to fixate on, and thus to warn you of impending reoccurrences. That's why you're seldom without one."

"No. I'm seldom without one because I *like* them. But otherwise, you're right. Hey—you don't think that the LifeSavers are the catalyst, do you? Maybe I should've switched to Twizzlers or—"

"I could kick myself, James. I should have noticed when you became upset and disoriented."

"You're tired, Jon. You're exhausted. We both are."

"Still, I should have sensed it coming on."

"And then you would have done...*what?*"

The psychiatrist had no answer. He'd already warped ahead in their chat.

"This focusing that you do, James—tell me, do you think it would ever be possible to summon an episode intentionally?"

Wagner marvelled at the doctor's assiduity. "I don't know. I'm not sure that I've really considered it, short of fancy. Summon one intentionally?" He sat quiet for a moment. "Under the proper conditions, I suppose that one can never tell until the effort's been made. What I *do* know is that, up until recently, I always believed that I was bound by the waiting game. I'd sit, wonder, wait for the next bender—or, more of late, for one of these phasings—to hit me so that I could put everything I had into fighting it off, into driving it back. But, daunting as they are, I have to confess that there's something very compelling about them. Actually, 'coercive' might be a better word. And...since you brought it up, I really can't be absolutely certain that some remote part of me hasn't toyed with the idea of deliberately conjuring up a bender, if only as a means to reassert some small measure of personal control."

"How do you mean?" Mazzio's countenance, showing wear from one too many jaunts down scientific blind alleys, suddenly perked up in his intrigue.

"Like the person who frets over some imagined medical condition, worrying so much that his mind, in effect, becomes the instrument that brings about that very condition. Only in my case—already having the condition—the side of me that isn't scared spitless of being sucked under its influence wants occasionally to call forth one or more of its traits to prove to people—like Dr. Williams—that I'm not some grandstander with a secret agenda."

"Believe me, James, Dr. Williams can't harbour that sentiment any longer. Your little demonstration has seen to that. I think it may even have prompted him to don the gloves and take up the cause as your new champion."

"Now *that's* something I'll have to see to believe."

Grateful for Mazzio's company and interest, Wagner was of a sudden beset by urgency. Just a sense, he wasn't sure what it meant—maybe just a pang of despair, maybe an intuitive heads-up of the next bender about to initialise—but it forced his notice of how insignificant his conscious life had become. For too long, now, he'd felt like a stone that, hurled by an unknown hand, skipped erratically over uncharted waters, its lift and momentum sapped by each kiss of the surface, its air-life shrinking measurably between successive contacts. He knew that, very soon, he, like that stone, would be unable to keep aloft long enough to successfully bridge the waters on which he alit with such consuming regularity. Then, with his momentum gone, what would be left but to be sucked into the murky depths of madness?

"I have a feeling," he said, his voice muted by the gravity of an overbearing resignation, "that, where I'm concerned, anything you folks come up with will be too little too late."

Mazzio lowered his eyes. It was clear that Wagner's assessment meant something to him, that it voiced a truth that he himself hadn't wished to admit nor share. "As your physician," he replied, "I suppose I would tell you to maintain a positive attitude, to keep pushing for your health, for hope, for good things, for a cure. But, as your friend, I will this one time deviate from my repertoire of standard-issue optimism to tell you—and I feel I must tell you—that I believe you're right. After ten months, I am still in the dark, as totally dumbfounded as I was the day I took up your cause. Maybe more so. *Absolutely* more so. I fought this paranormal angle from the beginning, and now that there seems to be incontestable validity to it, I'm too far behind to make up for that spent time. If I had the words that would bring you encouragement, James, you have to believe that I would use them. God, I wish I could—I wish I could."

Both men sat in silence, each knowing how very close in degree was one's respect for the other, each knowing how incredibly outdistanced they were by predicament. Very soon, one of them would cease to be the man he was, would be wrested from his lucidity, his sanity, and possibly—and impossibly—even his physical being. The other, though it was his profession, his life's dedication and the very objective of his oath, was impotent to stop it from occurring.

Their introspection ended when a knock came to the door, followed by Sally Lemanski poking in her head. "Doctor," she said in a manner more pressing than usual, "you're not going to believe this, but there's a small group of folks downstairs in admissions asking to see Mr. Wagner."

"What's not to believe?" sighed Mazzio. "Reporters have been trying for weeks to get a byline—"

"Oh, they're not reporters, sir," she said, placing Wagner's food tray on the stand beside his bed. "They're 'wayfarers.'"

"They're *what*?"

"I'm not making it up!" she said. "The gentleman referred to himself and his companions as 'wayfarers.'"

"And which gentleman would that be?"

"Well, see, that's the other thing," she said elusively. "I—I did say you weren't going to believe this...but..."

"*C'mon*, Sally," said Wagner. "We're dying from the suspense."

"Nurse?" Mazzio was giving her the eye.

"Okay, you asked for it. One of them is that *Mr. Miracle* fellow from the tabloids."

Wagner nearly choked on his own tongue. "No way! *Gawd*, talk about prophetic!"

"Oh, for crying out loud!" groaned Mazzio. "That's all we needed—some slick parvenu-prophet come to 'save' you and destroy what little privacy you have left."

"This is *too* bizarre," said Wagner, filliping the air with way-out, Krameresque gestures. "Eerie. I suppose it's a good thing that I didn't wish a visit from the three-headed boy from Oswego."

"Dr. Williams was right," said Mazzio. "It was only a matter of time before every crackpot with a quest for fame showed up in our lobby. These kinds of intrusions will do nothing but jeopardise the Centre's reputation."

"Jon, wait," said Wagner, nixing the doctor's storm from the room. "As curious as it sounds, I'm sort of inclined to talk to this guy. Could it really hurt? I mean, granted, he's probably a kook of the highest calibre—but long ago I pretty much gave up on any kind of faith ever getting me out of this. Maybe sending me a cut-rate man o' the cloth is the Almighty's way of teaching me some humility."

"James, I can see that you're amused, and heaven knows that you deserve whatever amusement you can foster. But these kinds of people spell trouble for us. If I allow this *Miracle* fellow in, he'll probably try to set up shop here, raise a furore, upend my entire facility with wild exorcism rituals and such."

"Well, if he does, we'll just sic Miss Groller on him and watch him hightail it back west, or wherever it is he came from."

"Colorado," said Sally.

"Colorado—thank you, Sally. Seriously, Jon, call it a hunch or a last-ditch effort. Heck, go ahead and call it insanity—you know it won't offend me. It's just that I've got this gut feeling. I feel I should meet this screwball face-to-face. What have I really got to lose?"

Mazzio shook his head and left the room. Sally Lemanski followed him out, rolling her eyes at Wagner as she pulled the door shut behind her.

As their footsteps faded down the hall, Wagner slid from his bed. Stepping to the room's only window, through the metal gridwork he gazed out at the big wide world he'd been forced to abandon. Beyond the Chinese elms that shaded his window, he panned far across to the top few floors of the county-city building, the jail, the library. To the east he could see the intersection of Monroe and Fourth streets with its steady parade of commuters and delivery vehicles, florist vans and soft drink trucks. He eyed the mix of business-suited professionals and casual strollers who freely browsed the latest editions at Fogerty's Newsstand, and noted the huddle of smokers idling unproductively outside the phone company's alley entrance, a social fog of blue-grey poison covering their errancy like windborne camouflage. In front of the Latte Joe Café, the neighbourhood blind guy tapped his way past a group of folks waiting for a bus, an ivory cane in one hand and his guide dog's harness in the other. Somewhere in the distance, muted church bells knelled the noon hour, and Wagner wondered whether the gang over at the Filthy Lucre Saloon, his old haunt only a few blocks away, was dishing goulash to the lunch crowd set.

Scratching his chin stubble, he thought how very pleasant the downtown area suddenly seemed, when he'd always found it rather seedy, even squalid, back when he'd been a part of it. His perception had changed, and the reason for this wasn't difficult to fathom. The terminal often viewed the world with gilded eyes.

Righting the sheers, Wagner sighed and turned back to his adopted world of seclusion and sanctuary. Walking around the bed with unusual sure-footedness, he lifted his meal's warming lid to have a look at what Sally had brought for him.

He would never see the city of Bishop again.

CHAPTER FOUR

He is a stranger to me but he is a most remarkable man—
and I am the other one.
—MARK TWAIN

The "wayfarer" whom Jon Mazzio encountered down in reception was a far cry from the heartland-trekking, New Age preacher-man he'd envisioned. In fact, all pre-notion dispelled at the mere sight of the fellow, Mazzio tamped the brakes of his approach so that he might first rake both entry and by-room for some more inviting candidate. Having never read the *Pursuer* stories, nor seen any photos of the man, he'd had no idea of what to expect. However, with only one adult male in sight, he found his options unchanged, and his wary recipience slated for a bloke who looked as much a spiritual visionary as Miss Groller did Gaea the earth goddess.

Brawny and bearded and barely on the presentable side of tously, this thirty-something chap was clad plainly in a hunter green T-shirt and khaki dungarees, both of which bore the crease and pucker of laundry hastily donned. Yet, despite the breezy informality of such attire, the wearer somehow appeared oddly out of place in them. His feet, shod in desert boots so road-worn that they made his garmenture look lofty, paced the lobby floor with a rhythmic determination comprised of equal parts distress and reservedness. He wrung his hands as he strode, his observable sum and substance suggesting an urgency somewhat out of keeping with his media-driven image of humble palliator and conferrer of good will. Still, where he might have been physically imposing, even threatening, he was neither; in fact, he seemed too mired in his exigence to present any great outward danger. Like a jungle cat in a zoo enclave, he was a walking grapple of anxiety and restraint; his movements, simultaneously raw and graceful; his equanimity, a tether he would sooner snap than be led by. And even as it remained undisclosed, the nature of his agitation lent itself more closely to worry than fury; and this, evidenced in his mien, belied one's immediate assumption that his presence here was self-promotive or even commiserative, and instead seemed to denote something much more paramount.

He wore no watch, no jewellery, no ornament of any kind. His hair was thick and black, and his generous itinerant's beard stabbed at the air with two slender points at its tips. He was swarthy in complexion and even more richly nutbrown in the areas of his nape and forehead and upper arms, the pattern of variegation suggesting an individual whose industry, if not elementally subsumed, had him clocking considerable hours in direct sunlight with scant regard for sunblock or protective clothing. A closer proximity, however, alerted Mazzio to a derogation more greatly mystifying than anything that mere exposure may have wrought, this being the curious and copious occasion of keloidal excrescence that marred a good deal of his flesh. Akin to tiny, almost negligible, razor cuts they flecked his arms and neck in a manner not dissimilar to the scarring associated with incidents of shattered glass laceration or barbed wire entanglement, and occasionally upon patients whose occupations put them either at great personal risk or subject to repetitively adverse causality. Alternately, Mazzio's background was such that he'd run across numerous cases of self-mutilative practises—ceremonial and otherwise—where a subject's skin bore cicatrices along the same lines of those encountered here. While historically such practises had rootings in tribal ritual, their contemporary incarnations frequently incorporated everything from simple faddishness all the way to deep-seated mental illness. By its sporadic and largely undemonstrative incidence here, Mazzio's guess—and hope—was that this scarification had been acquired unintentionally, resultant of some unusual personal catastrophe or circumstantial mishap. But, until he could confirm it— indeed, until he could satisfy a burgeoning list of investigative protocols—there would be no talk of granting so unconfirmed a suppliant an audience with Howsley's most troubled of patients. Unconventionality in itself being no crime, Mazzio's experience in such cases had shown him the sagacity in raising the bar a bit, especially before untested strangers.

Epidermal irregularities notwithstanding, constituently the newcomer swanked all the physical fixings of the strapping, outdoorsy type. Someone along the order of a woodsman, an environmentalist, a hinterlander from the most remote reaches of the Great Northwest or the like—there seemed nothing more complex or newsworthy or unwonted about him than that. Hardy and stout in the fashion of a mountaineer, chiselled and robust like an athlete—in truth he was as unlikely a man of his particular repute as Mazzio could imagine; and Mazzio, rarely one to propound by exteriors what another's proclivity or character may or may not have been, dallied in the presupposition that there was very little about this man and his demeanour to suggest ecclesiastical religiosity at all. But again, it was the unconventionality aspect that steered the doctor narrow, and he was loath to allow himself even this modicum of shallowness. One could not militate in his profession and be so quick to judge people, especially by predominantly outward criteria. Still, even as he strove to reassert his objectivity, his banjaxing was compounded anew by the simple act of the stranger's spinning around to receive him. For here, what Mazzio's rearward vantage had not imparted, and what their face-to-face recontré suddenly did reveal, were two of the most striking cerulean eyes that Mazzio had ever seen in his life.

Momentarily transfixed, Mazzio managed to dislodge from his odyle long enough to rattle off a few words of polite welcome, and to extend said greeting to the small entourage of young people whom he took to be the man's companions. A teenage boy and girl and a twenty-something young woman, they'd been standing quietly by, contiguous to—yet prudently beyond—the trample of the man's fretful pacing.

"How may I help you?" he added, scanning the line of faces before swinging back to the bearded man, whose arms parted imploringly and whose mouth erupted with parol no longer containable.

"He is *here?*"

An interrogatory and yet not, the words came across much more as an imperative, as if the stranger somehow believed himself entitled to the information. Yet, as his enunciation bore the essence of what could have been an eastern European distinguishment, it was not inconceivable that his forwardness may have been prompted less by rudeness than by lingual extrinsicality. His deportment, though competent, lacked the expected reciprocity of either nicety or introduction, and instead rent the air with an almost proclamatory bite, even as his countenance exhibited nothing in the way of aggression or arrogance or disrespect—and in fact delineated nothing more suspect than acute concern. Visibly edgy, even brusque, in his concision he did not truly task the bounds of subordination so much as he failed to recognise that such margins existed. No overt posturing, no minatory gesturing, his only true assail came by way of his debilitating gaze, a vortical swell of blue that—spilling like floodwaters into Mazzio's—seemed almost capable of flushing the information he sought from the doctor's very pupils.

Confronted by the visitor's outward brawn, by his persuasive goggle, even by the renown of his questionable celebrity, a doctor less vehement in protecting his patients and the welfare of his facility might well have felt intimidated, even threatened. But Jon Mazzio was cool and unflinching. Had he even recognised the man before him as the much-hyped shaman and salvor of a morally shipwrecked American yokeldom that the tabloids made him out to be, was not *he*, as the head of Howsley, entrusted to protect his own flock, socially outcast and sorely troubled as it might be? Was it not *his* greater duty to protect James Wagner more than any other, not solely from the media blitz resultant of Wagner's leaked pathology, but because Wagner's need for protection was greater than it had ever been? By allowing access to one dissembler, even a well-intended one, he risked opening the way for a hundred more, each with his own specialised agenda, each with eyes a lot hungrier than the stranger's—and this simply could not happen.

"I assume that you're inquiring about Mr. Wagner?" he asked.

"Of course!" cried the man, incredulous that Mazzio might think him there for any other reason. "You are his minder? His man of physic?"

"I'm—his *physician.*"

"Then it is of vital importance, 'physician,' that I speak with him."

"On what matter, may I ask?"

The man bristled. "With all deference, sir, my purpose is my own concern. I only seek direction or conveyance."

"Neither of which will be granted," said Mazzio, "until I am made fully aware of your intentions."

The intruder studied Mazzio's face the way an engineer scans for stress points in a structure. "Be assured," he said, "that my *intentions*, as you define them, are well-meant. More than this you need not know."

With that he lurched forward, brushing past the doctor, who, barely more than two-thirds his heft, moved to bar his way.

"Call security!" shouted Mazzio, his receptionist already punching up the intercom.

"Wait! Please!"

The plea, issuing from behind them, came from the elder of the young women, who suddenly loped forward and insinuated herself between encroacher and encroached.

"Forgive us, doctor," she quickly added, her tone not so much officious as it was tutelary. "Forgive us for barging in here, and for strong-arming our way through a courtesy that you were under no obligation to extend. We didn't set out to impose upon your hospitality. It's just that—well—we've travelled a considerable distance to be here, for reasons even *I'm* still not sure of, all because my friend is convinced that he knows your patient, this *Wagner* person. We realise that we've come here unannounced. We also realise that our expectations are obviously a lot higher than our vagabondish stature probably merits. And, as if two strikes weren't obstacle enough, it seems that we now have to make amends for a really bad start."

Here, she directed an overtly harmless albeit censuring elbow to the traveller's midsection, to which he responded with muttered confoundment.

"And while I concede," she continued, "that the only thing we should expect from you is a collective boot out the door, please don't be too quick to dismiss us. I'm convinced that there's some great import to all this, even if I don't fully understand what it is."

An artful speaker, there was at once a soulfully wholesome quality about her that Mazzio found compelling enough to pre-empt his standard run-through of hospital regulations for contraveners and upstarts. An uncharacteristic moment of vincibility, it found him subsequently drawn into a pitfall considerably more basal than that which his professional persona generally permitted him, her unexpected waylay of outward charm and apple pie muliebrity being something that he didn't often encounter within the bourn of a single individual.

In appearance she was dark—more ethnically so than the man—with delicate Latin features that complemented a lissom, athletic frame. Her smile was warm and winsome and gently extravagant; her eyes, black as espresso, with brows full and natural. A sass of jet ponytail bobbed playfully behind her, trussed high on her head with a bright yellow tieback. Her attire, far less remarkable than she, consisted of an older St. Louis Cardinals jersey (indeterminate in vintage but conceivably pre-dating her) and denim cut-offs with pop 1970's-era peace and ecology patches blazoned across the seat pockets. Hefty, tundra-class hikers begirded her feet, speed-laced over worsted trail socks the downgathering of which betrayed an easy week's-worth of depilatory remissness across the thew of two nicely contoured calves. Unbedecked as she was, unornamented, even unrazored, her practicality nevertheless seemed to suit her, and could easily have been her métier, for she as good as waved it like a banner. Yet, amid the felicitous schmoozl of her parleying, it seemed but a single facet of a more complex individual, one who, despite her tender years, had discovered how humility and courtliness packed a much beefier punch when alloyed with a fetching sense of diplomacy.

"Just who *are* you," asked Mazzio, "and what is the specific nature of your business here?" He eyed her, then the bearded man, and then her again.

"My name is Maggie," she said. "Maggie Escalante. These are my friends, Nettie and Pete." She indicated the two teens behind her who, by Mazzio's accounting, seemed content to remain at the rear of the vestibule.

"And the impertinent guy, here," she continued, "is our good friend, *Miracle*."

She paused for a moment, giving the psychiatrist time to absorb. "I know," she finally added, "I used to think it was a goofy name, too. But it suits him, believe me."

Realising that she'd gone suddenly flush in the face, her gesturing became more erratic, as if to draw Mazzio's eyes from the fact. "Anyway," she continued, "right in the middle of one of our—how shall I put it—more *chaotic* fellowship crusades, *Miracle* happens to catch this Wagner-person's photo in the same tabloid that tried aspersing our campaign as some kind of circus, and he just flips out. He says he knows the guy. He *knows* the guy, and out of nowhere he has us drop everything in order to come and see him."

She paused again, knowing full-well that she had crammed a whole lot into a whole little. Her dark eyes searched Mazzio's face for some portion of her narrative that he might not have understood, and quickly she gleaned that there was much.

"We've hiked halfway across the country to be here," she exclaimed. "Please don't turn us away."

Mazzio stood quiet in his scepticism. This wasn't at all what he'd expected.

"All right," he acknowledged, a hint of bother in his tone, "let me understand this. Your friend, here, claims to know my patient. Can he tell me *how* he knows him, or what he understands about Mr. Wagner's medical condition?"

She made no effort at reply. Rather, she shifted her stance, shuffled, sawed at the air a bit, and it became Mazzio's turn to glean that she herself didn't know.

"He is my comrade-in-arms," *Miracle* suddenly averred.

Gently nudging his gracious admonisher aside, the grim-faced man with the ludicrous name stepped forward to spearhead his own petition. "He is also a friend who once risked much for my sake."

The statement, with its light spicing of Balto-Slavic accidence, was as resonant and intelligible as it was cryptic, delivered with the same priggishness of his initial exchange. Yet, ungrounded as the claim itself may have been, there was a peculiar tenableness in his sentiment that Mazzio could not so easily ignore, an air of quaintly intrinsic nobility that some more savvy charlatan could hardly have feigned—or sustained—with less than earnest conviction.

"Our commutuality was admittedly brief," *Miracle* said, "but he and I have braved the crush of many hardships. We are two who share a bond. This much I know."

"I'm sorry," chortled Mazzio, "but that's extremely vague. I've had extensive sessions with Mr. Wagner, regressive perusings as far back as his childhood, and he's made no mention of you or anything remotely like—"

Miracle signed the *sigma* in the air with his finger. "He bears a marking on his person—one that looks like this. Its significance is his preoccupation. He is prone to recurring fits of lunacy. His mind is assailed by an inner tumult that spirits him elsewhere, away from what you know as demonstrative existence. He speaks in tongues that no one here understands, struggles against persecutors that no eyes save his can detect, and oft-times he takes to floating upon the air, unfettered by substance, as if his very essence were set free to cascade the depths of aethereal bounds between the worlds that only he and I share knowledge of."

Mazzio mammered uncomfortably. He glanced at Maggie Escalante, who shrugged back at him with a half-bemused smile.

"Well," he admitted, "high drama aside, it's plain to see that you've done your homework. However, most of the phenomena that you've stated has already been leaked to the media by one means or another. With the exception of your knowledge of Mr. Wagner's tattoo—which you may easily have come upon in various ways—you're not telling me anything that the average housewife doesn't already know by now."

"Would you but look more closely, sir," *Miracle* retorted, "you would see that I am no *housewife*. Neither did I come by my knowledge through common hearsay or base reporting. You disparage me by taking my words so lightly."

"That isn't my intention," said Mazzio. "It's just that—"

"So much suspicion and mistrust!" snapped *Miracle*. "Time betakes itself and you stay my path with trifles. No more! By your leave or by mine, physician, you will stand aside and let me pass!"

Maggie clamped onto *Miracle's* arm, breaking his advance.

"¡*Calmate!*" she counselled. "This isn't the way. This man doesn't know us. He doesn't know anything *about* us. He's simply looking out for your friend's welfare, the same way that you would if you were in his place."

She turned to the doctor with humble entreaty. "I'm sorry. He's a bit intractable when it comes to bureaucracy. Going through proper channels is definitely not his best thing."

"I notice that *you* certainly seem to have a knack for it," Mazzio noted.

"Well, I would hope so," she said in smirk. "I get more practise than the doggone Secretary of State—and nowhere near the perks."

Miracle shot her an irascible glance. She answered with another vitiating elbow to his gut, which he this time caught and forestalled.

"Well," said the psychiatrist, "while I can most definitely sympathise, you must likewise appreciate my need to screen anyone who comes through these doors— especially lately. Some days it's so hectic down here that you'd think we were hosting a photojournalists' convention." He sighed uncomfortably. "Having said that, I can't help but to feel that your desideratum—whatever it is, and however misplaced it may be—is more aboveboard than I can immediately discern. I'm just not sure what it is that you think you can do."

His words acknowledged, Mazzio watched as the young woman beamed in almost gratulatory fashion at having (once again, perhaps) snatched her companion from the flames of his own conventional obtuseness. That she held *Miracle* in high regard was obvious; that she had the persuasive clout to dulcify his considerable headstrongness signified at least a begrudging mutuality on his part. Unlettered as he seemed in the realm of the social graces, it would have been no stretch to liken him to a blind man who relied on the woman's sight—or insight— to steer him clear of the impediments that his own obstinacy made more obstructive than they really needed to be. Yet, to Mazzio's discriminating eye, the metaphor worked equally well—if not more suitably—when reversed: *Miracle's* annoyance with red tape, his impudence at Mazzio's proscriptive measures, his general boorishness and his apparent unacquaintance with, or blatant disregard for, basic decorum, it was far likelier that he saw *himself* as the one with vision forced to toddle through an aggravating, very punctilious world of the blind. He wouldn't have been the only eccentric to claim this trait; it was a prevalent self-image, even among the relatively sane, and Mazzio confronted it daily in one form or another.

"So," Maggie pleaded, a world-on-her-shoulders supplication in her expression, "do you think we can agree on some sort of compromise here? Will you allow us to speak with Mr. Wagner? Even a few minutes would really be great."

Recalling with guarded indulgence Wagner's similar request, Mazzio took a moment to consider.

"Suppose I tell you," he said, "that Mr. Wagner had already agreed—largely with diversionary intent—to meet with you, once he'd heard of your arrival?"

Miracle bucked up. "He asked that I be brought to him?" His face suddenly shone like a man who had just been given the news on the birth of his child. "Somehow, then, he knows. By all that has passed, he knows."

Sharing *Miracle's* exuberance, Maggie peered inquisitively into the doctor's eyes. "Then you're okaying the visit?"

Jon Mazzio took a long moment. He had no clue as to why he was about to permit exactly what he'd intended to prevent. Somehow it seemed propitious. It seemed safe. Even as *Miracle's* quick ire was itself a cause for concern, even as his idiocrasy annoyed and his longiloquence anaesthetised, his insights had been a good deal more astute than Mazzio had let on. He'd been completely on the mark about time running out, although to what degree his context and the doctor's were aligned was a variable yet to be explored. As for his alleged prophetic repute—such was a dubiosity better left to people who believed in that sort of thing. Mazzio had no real basis for branding *Miracle* or his companions as grifters—certainly not profiteering ones anyway—but they did in fact skirt the very metes and bounds of presumption. For all of their misplaced affectivity and fervency, they offered little by which Mazzio might adduce or dispute their still-unrevealed designs. Throughout his professional career, he'd rarely lent credence to anything that couldn't be documented, tested, diagnosed, or treated by prescriptive means. He was, after all, a man of science. Going strictly on faith was hardly his style, and to simply allow some quirky sectarian and his travelling salvation show the run of his facility would truly be the act of a complete fool or the folly of a desperate man of stellar proportions. He hated to believe that he was either.

So, finally, calmly, he spoke.

"Let me say first that this is completely against my better judgement. However, I'm going to allow you, Ms. Escalante, you and—um—*Miracle*, to pay Mr. Wagner a brief, uncompromising visit. And I do mean brief and uncompromising. Two of my orderlies will conduct you to his room, and both they and I will remain present for the duration of the visit. Any questions that you may have will be simple and to the point. Physical contact will be limited. Theatrics will not be tolerated, and at the first sign of unrest I will ask you to leave. Lastly, and regrettably, I do request that you submit to a non-intrusive personal search prior to the visit. This is not a strictly typical procedure, but neither is Mr. Wagner a typical patient. It's essential that I be certain that you pose no threat to him or to anyone in this complex.

Believe me, I would never approve of such an unannounced, unsubstantiated meeting were it not for certain circumstances that compel me to bend the rules a bit."

Maggie squeezed *Miracle* excitedly, and nodded agreement for the both of them. Then, detaching herself from his ample biceps, she gestured, somewhat comically, submission to be patted down, with *Miracle* awkwardly following suit.

But none of it was meant to be. For, even as Mazzio began arranging for escort, the floor above them welcomed bedlam back to the building.

Old clamour rejuvenated, it grew by fits and starts, by muted shouts and scampering feet, random thumps and crashes, all of which quickly trundled into the continuous peal that was soon roving like a wrecking ball across floor and furnishings and—no doubt—fleeing hospital personnel. Its origins all too calculable, no one who'd gone through this before could dispute or deny the ungodly licentiousness that Wagner's mind-blown shenanigans had taken with the physics of their personal worlds. Those who had yet to witness it would find themselves living a day they would never forget.

"Dr. Mazzio!" The cry came from the administrative corridor. All heads turned to see a shoeless Claire O'Connell scurrying forward amid a largely paralytic staff, each of whom had ceased in whatever task he'd been performing and now stood, eyes glued to the ceiling, anticipating the advent of that which rumour and mental makeready would prove sorely inadequate preparation. Their mouths agape, their arms raised instinctively in self-shielding fashion, they waited for the eruption, waited like passers-by on the street who by chance happened upon the implosion countdown of a condemned building.

"Dr. Mazzio!" O'Connell gasped. "It's happening again! Dr. Williams and I—we stopped in to visit him—he was eating—he—and the fork phased through him! Dr. Williams was trying to help him counter the—"

"*NO!*" howled *Miracle*. "It cannot be—*not yet!*"

Before Mazzio or anyone else could even summon wherewithal enough to react, the stranger had already bolted from the covey. Traversing the corridor with lupine swiftness, he yanked wide the stairwell door and bounded up the steps like a man insane, a man whose sudden volatility likened him to the very wretch he meant to save.

Minutes before, James Wagner had begun to poke inquisitively around his food tray, debating whether to start in on his entrée of mashed potatoes and gravy-slathered patty, or to skip straight to the cherry cobbler. Surprisingly, none of the choices was completely unappealing, something he couldn't always say about Howsley's cuisine. He finally opted to sample the cobbler first—just a nibble—before lunching in the traditional order, but found his repast interrupted when Doctors O'Connell and Williams knocked and entered his room.

"Are we disturbing you?" asked O'Connell, exhibiting the nervous, well-intentioned smile that one typically reserves for lifting the spirits of the destitute and the dying.

"No, not at all," Wagner replied. "I decided to dine in today. The room service here is so accommodating." He peeled a wilted parsley sprig from his plate and dangled it for their approval. "It's the little, elegant touches like these that contribute to the whole culinary experience."

"How are you feeling?" asked Williams in a rare and receptive moment of concern.

"Not bad, doctor, especially now that I'm back on 'solid' food. That other stuff they were giving me just seemed to slip right through me."

Williams raised an eyebrow.

"Sorry," said Wagner. "It was funnier the first time."

"Mr. Wagner," said Williams. "*James*. I must apologise to you. I am completely at a loss for what to say. I'm sure you understand how these things—these impossible manifestations—wreak havoc with everything that my training and my personal philosophy of medicine represent. I...if I was a bit harsh with you—"

"Forgotten," said Wagner. "Who can blame you? Who could imagine that we could sit around and talk about something like this, and not wonder if we're losing our minds?"

"Oh, I'm sure we've each wondered about that," said O'Connell. "Certainly *you* more than any of us."

"Madam, you have no idea. So, what is it that I can do for you?"

"Well, after witnessing these—these praeterhuman symptoms with our own eyes," O'Connell said, "Dr. Williams and I took it upon ourselves to pore over Dr. Mazzio's backlogs with a good deal more sincerity than we had previously. We've been attempting to study the patterns of your phasing, looking for correlations in conditions and periodicity—anything that might lead us to what it is, exactly, that triggers the phenomenon."

"And?" Wagner snuck another bite of the cobbler.

"So far, nothing. To be quite frank, since we are ourselves understandably ill-prepared for something so utterly unprecedented in nature, we've gone ahead and quietly contacted several of our more progressively liberal colleagues, along with one or two rather 'specialised authorities,' all of whom we feel would be better suited in this capacity. Actually, it took a bit of convincing for Dr. Mazzio to open his doors to yet another expanded base of study, but in the end he agreed that a quorum of less provincial thinkers might be able to view your situation from an angle that traditional medicine cannot. It might be the key to telling us whether the phasing follows some chronological pattern, whether it relies on minute fluctuations in either the biochemical or environmental arenas, or whether it's something we are simply ill-equipped to explain."

"That's *my* vote," said Wagner. "But Dr. Mazzio pretty much touched on all that stuff. I'm sure you know that."

"Yes," said Williams, "but because of the unpredictability of these states, you were never once connected to electronic sensors during your critical moments of shifting. We have no readings, no hard data, and therefore no notion as to what goes on within your chemistry as you lose physical integrity."

Wagner conceded with a nod and a shrug. He didn't relish the thought of being wired-up like Frankenstein's monster for the remainder of his stay, but he knew they were hopelessly shy on alternatives. Fluffing his potatoes, he listened passively as the doctors rambled on with one vapid projection after another on how his projected course of treatment should unfold, listened to their personal interpretations of terminology he'd heard a hundred times over, all of which translated into the same old set of hypotheticals and unknown variables. His meal more palatable than the doctors' curative prognostications, he indulged while he still had appetite to sate, at the same time noshing on his own hypothetical, a sudden whimsy that found him wondering about the coincidental arrival of the maverick rector downstairs—and whether it had anything to do with O'Connell's list of "specialised authorities." He rather hoped not.

Then it happened. Like a furnace jolting to life on a frigid winter morning, Wagner's psychoactive thermostat, dormant but a few hours, suddenly re-catapulted into action. The mindflux gathering momentum, he felt the precipitant tingle that, like fuel for the mindflux's consumption, would touch off the degenerative phase. Different this time, however—fiercer—the imagerial cascade hit him full-throttle and all at once, with visional activity unparalleled by any recollectable event of past synaptic splintering. A boding of what would go on to become the most disruptive and out of the blue mega-daddy of benders thus far, so abruptly had it struck, and so intense its upheaval, that Wagner hadn't been sufficiently clued enough to even brace himself. No fragmenting, no cold sweats, he'd felt none of the indications so common to his previous attacks; yet, within seconds it had effectively stripped him of everything save a vacillatingly detached sense of self-awareness, with no ken of whether he was still in his bed, in his room, or even in his own body.

But the two doctors could tell. They heard the falling fork. They noted the ocular twitchings of a man whose vision suddenly extended no farther than the infarcting hallucinatory event that even then must have been occluding his visual field. They watched as his bedclothes floated down like gossamer through his form, coming to rest on the bedside within the spectral bounds of his degradation. And in the midst of their dumbfoundment and terror, they knew this was a remarkable opportunity.

Williams was first to break from his fear. Leaning forward, he extended a hesitant hand, and, like an astonished savage who was seeing fire for the first time, slowly penetrated Wagner's vapour. Wambling his fingers within the apparition, he spoke to Wagner in firm yet calming tone, urging him to fight the effect or to prolong it—whichever might have been in his ability to do—and above all to try relaying in words the sensation of what was consuming him.

Williams's hand, however, may just as well have been in Wagner's mashed potatoes, for Wagner was no longer truly present. Eyes agape but unseeing, his consciousness was a prisoner of the inner realm, locked away by the same key that had incarcerated his substance. Had he even been of a mind to break free of its hold, he lacked the power to do so. Mesmerised by sound and spectacle, he remained entranced in the manner that one is captivated by burbling brookwaters or by campfire flames or by the bursting chromaticity of skyrockets in a summer night's sky—the difference being that his seduction was internally wrought. He was stalled in the sirenic thrall of his own psyche, far beyond the reach of any grounding lifeline that Williams wished to toss at him, and there would be no reaching him until that force relinquished its mental—and now physical—grip over his personal dominion.

Williams and O'Connell gawked helplessly as Wagner slowly drifted from the bed like a ghostly marionette, conveyed in his rigour across the room with the nonchalance of a feather on the waft. His eyes remained open but unseeing. His expression was blank and unfathomable. Then, of a sudden, in what both doctors construed as a self-initialised exertion, Wagner pitched and scrambled and somehow, without measurable fulcrumage, launched himself through the wall of his quarters and into the hall beyond.

"Claire, find Mazzio and alert the staff!" Williams cried as he tugged loose his tie and hauled through the doorway in chase. "Notify everyone in the building! We can't lose him!"

He then jounced down the corridor in his middle-aged-smoker-with-an-acute-instep pursuit, a gross, caricatured precursor to the wolf-like featliness that *Miracle* would demonstrate scant minutes later.

As for the hapless Wagner, already he was two rooms over, his airborne scurry a seeming autonomic reaction to whatever chimaera wrenched at him from within. Infixed by mind-bending strife, by a catechisation of light, shadow, and insubstantiality that melded the familiar with the bedevilling, the sinisterly alluring with the engagingly perilous, in what amounted to his last falter of coherence he sensed a consummate finality of everything he ever was or would be. This was it; this was the capper, the all-consuming last hurrah of a life no longer viable. Madness or death, whichever of the two lay before him, futurity was rearing fast, with no means of staying what would no longer be stayed. This preposterous affliction having stalked him for months, harrying him into exhaustion and social dispossession, despoiling him to the point of ineluctable collapse, here and now it was toppling him like an ape from the fastigium of his own eclectic existence. Trapped in an irretrievable freefall of rifted consciousness, Wagner's descent into oblivion was fast approaching culmination, his twenty-eight short and illimitably troubled years headed for the same expunction that had already siphoned away his matter.

Overwhelmed, emaciated, too far gone with too little of his will left to fight it, Wagner did the only thing he truly could do, the last action that Mazzio or anyone who knew him would have expected him to do. He let go. He gave in. Wearied nearly unto collapse, destitute of hope, he simply surrendered, resignedly and unreservedly, using the last vestige of autonomy that remained his to exercise. Outclassed more than defeated, yet unable and unwilling to combat an enemy that he couldn't see to define, in his final moment he commended to Fate and Providence the life that it seemed had never been fully his anyway.

In his perfusion, Wagner never knew at what point the man known only as *Miracle* managed to intercept his discarnate image. But intercept him *Miracle* did, albeit for barely a trice, at the far west end of the second floor, mere moments before Wagner phased irrevocably through the building's exterior and into the airspace above the grounds. In those few seconds, the stranger never once paused to marvel at Wagner's unthinkable transience, but threw himself in the path of Wagner's incorporeal drift. Attuned, somehow, to the fact that he could provide no physical influence, his efforts suggested some small hopefulness on his part that Wagner's swoon wasn't turned so totally inward that he might not at least intuit another's impending presence. An ineffective gambit, *Miracle* extemporised next with imprecation and gesture, petitioning Wagner verbally, even flailing about in the fashion of a ballyhoo man—a tack with equally debatable results. Desperate, he was not to be dissuaded; with failure behind him, he stood even more staunchly in his resolve to breach the paranormal barrier between him and the man he claimed he'd travelled so far to find. In fortitude alone, it seemed as if he truly believed himself capable of enticing Wagner back from his aphelion state with little more than gesticulation and pseudo-mysticism. Indeed, by his vehemence one might almost have believed him capable of doing just that, of actually connecting to the man-turned-supernatural-agency, not only exciting Wagner's notice but perhaps establishing the very psychometric beachhead that Dr. Williams had sought minutes earlier. In fact, to the onlookers and facility hirelings who, in likened pursuit, stumbled onto the scene, *Miracle's* doggedness in the face of this hugely preponderant manifestation told them that if anyone could reel Wagner back, if anyone possessed the unmitigated spirit to move mountains—and who could actually imbue with credibility the impertinent vagaries of his actions— it would have to be this odd fellow, *Miracle*.

He cursed some unintelligible malediction as the spectral Wagner permeated him and then phased through the exterior wall behind him. Then, vaulting a nearby desk in order to reach the nearest window, he dashed the curtains aside and grimaced at the sight of Wagner's phantasm, just beyond the edifice some six metres above the grass outside. The window's outward security caging deterring a more drastic path of pursuit, *Miracle* took a quick visual fix on Wagner in relation to the building, and then turned and sped from the room, barrelling through a handful of snailish corridor-gawkers in his mad beeline for the stairwell.

"Outside!" he shouted as he burst back onto the main floor, his three completely perplexed companions the only remaining occupants in an otherwise deserted lobby. With Mazzio and O'Connell presumably lending chase elsewhere on the second floor—and the receptionist and clerk scoured off to parts unknown—the indulgent trio had been quite unsure of what to do in their abandonment, and were no less forlorn as they watched their hell-bent compadre go sailing by them and out the main entry as if at the heel of the Devil himself. Dumbfounded, they gazed one to the other in his passing, trading commensurate looks of vacuity, each of them abstracted not only by *Miracle's* tempestuousness, but likewise by the great inclemency that had swept gale-force through the hospital in whole. With such uproar overhead, and with the very man whose insistence had suborned their presence in this place suddenly in hightail on some ridiculous romp, it took little more than a prompting nod from Maggie to persuade the thus-far verecund Nettie and Pete into whisking up their effects and launching out the door behind her.

Like a seasoned runner, *Miracle* gained the western pale of the grounds long ahead of his friends, and in said time had tracked Wagner's gradual declivity through a threesome of European birches to a point where he wafted in virtual diaphaneity only a metre or so overhead. That he'd descended at all—much less in aimless, airy fashion—toward the sward below would have inclined any thoughtful observer to surmise that his body yet possessed some infinitesimal mote of unrelinquished mass, just drag enough to press him groundward beyond his second-story egress. *Miracle* himself, still neither daunted nor even surprised by this, had calculated Wagner's trajectory with a marksman's eye, and was already in wait when Wagner dipped within range.

Spectre converging on man, the latter positioned himself just in front of and under Wagner's astral bearing, apparently hoping for another opportunity to wangle Wagner from his unworldly sopor. For nearly a minute, *Miracle* sidled and pivoted in compensatory fashion, matching Wagner drift for drift and spiral for spiral so as not to lose the face-to-face ubiety that he believed might help to snap Wagner from his overriding vision. In added measure, *Miracle* offered Wagner verbal encouragement via a steadying counsel of low-voiced refrains, spoken predominantly in English, but boasting an occasional joinder from a language not immediately distinguishable. These phonations—perhaps in his mother tongue, perhaps in some sacred or obsequial rhetoric of antiquity—were rich and melodic in their composition, splendidly guttural yet filled with such eloquent inflection that even a man on his deathbed might have momentarily staved the Reaper merely so that he might hear them in full.

By then, Maggie and the others had scampered up, heralding the prospective arrival, minutes later, of not only Doctors Mazzio and O'Connell, but a nearly breathless Dr. Williams, Sally Lemanski, a plethora of orderlies, and several other assorted medical professionals with curious and/or altruistic natures, all of whom halted at perceptively safe distances from the action to observe what some were ultimately to view as the compassionate nature of a well-meaning albeit unconventional holy man—and others, the antics of an audacious upstart whose allegedly ecclesiastical front gave him the license to intervene and the presumption to think that he could simply dance and gesture the evil spirits out of the Morphean Wagner.

Doubters or encouragers, had any of the witnesses moved in close enough to share *Miracle's* vantage, each would have been hard-pressed to affirm whether James Wagner was even minutely aware of anything in the spatial sense. Indeed, Wagner's expression varied moment by moment. His eyes darted wildly in the clinch of semi-wakeful stricture, with scant, if any, infiltration from a world he no longer truly occupied. Had he the faculty to focus on the stranger before him, *Miracle's* features would still have been impossible to isolate amid the barrage of hallucinatory clutter overloading his processes. As with his previous spells, his mind was more than likely imposing alternate images over the objects it saw anyway; only, through the psychotic-like symptoms of his condition, these images were probably flagrant, fanciful interpretations of the reality from which he was breaking, a reality whose inhabitants his mind often reshaped into antagonistic foes—a detail that Nurse Groller could easily confirm were she anywhere to be found at that moment.

Wagner nearly at ground level now, *Miracle* reached for him, hands outstretched and engirdling his periphery as if he were a house of cards in teeter. Closely contraposed yet an eldritch dimension apart, *Miracle* maintained a steady, finger's-breadth grapple about his untouchable quarry; and it was here, in this pendent moment of apposition, that Wagner's aethereality suddenly flared in a seemingly innocuous, pyromagnetic fulguration that—although less than a tenth of a second in duration—sent the frontmost onlookers sprawling backwards in start, some onto the grass and some into the unready arms of their rearward neighbours.

A frightful oddity and a wondrous one, no one save *Miracle* seemed to sense its sequent significance. But when the others saw with their own eyes Wagner's physical body slumping weightily within the pilgrim's grasp, none could deny the redintigrative evidence; somehow, by some unknottable means, Wagner had been given back his substance.

Jon Mazzio, first of the astounded to jostle his way forward, never once averted his eyes from Wagner's enervated frame for fear of losing him again. As far as he could see, the physical restoration seemed indeed genuine, although Wagner's observable behaviour indicated that his intellect had yet to fully exuviate the bender's incapacitating effects. His face hinted at the befuddlement of the newly roused, and his frangibility corresponded to the familiar post-bender wane in vitality. He winced several times, tried shaking himself from the vestigial myopia that, sometimes accompanying the reboot into lucidity, was a temporary condition that most likely barred him from even focusing on the man who'd apparently reined him back in.

"That's remarkable!" cried the jubilant doctor. "I've never seen him regain normalcy so quickly after phasing. I've never known him to respond to outside stimulus either—not like this!"

"Be not fooled," *Miracle* warned. "His essence is here for but a moment. The crossing lies before him now. Would that I had only arrived a day sooner."

Mazzio heard the words but made no reply. Instead he stared grimly at his long-time patient, whose sight had by now concentred enough to barely accord him a disjointed appreciation of his surroundings. Percipient but failing, cognisant but mute, Wagner turned with paling countenance toward the two figures before him, and, with no more than a strabismal glance, managed to impart an embranglement of two perceivable emotions.

The first was easily culled from his expression. It was the familiar meshing of trepidation and reconciliation that had become Wagner's mindset in the last few months whereby, in the vein of Kübler-Ross's seminal work with the dying, he'd come to view the inevitable through embittered but fatalistic eyes. The other, and the more poignant of the gazes, he aimed solely at the doctor in what was unmistakably a bestowal of visceral gratitude, a gratitude that, in uninflicted moments, he'd often stressed he could never recompense. The doctor had served him well—and vice-versa—although neither had truly come away profiting in any curative sense. Their achievement had been in the *bond*, not the *beyond*, and the fact that Wagner could communicate without words such resolute acceptance and appreciative assignation demonstrated invincibility where all else was overrun by flood. Collectively, they were nuances that would etch themselves into Mazzio's memories for a very long time.

As Wagner's head slipped back into droop, Mazzio suddenly drew meaning out of *Miracle's* abstruse cautioning, and it came to him that the outsider had grasped the truth long before any of them—the very same truth that Wagner himself now knew in its epiphanic entirety. This apparent remission wasn't what it had at first seemed. It was illusory and fleeting, a temporary stay that, for whatever reason, either prefaced or prolonged Wagner's final moments. The guard was changing. The magnitude of what would next occur far outstripped Mazzio's already feckless qualifications and wanting hypotheses. The precarious and confounding trail over which man and doctor had stumbled and groped and sifted for clues for nearly one year of their lives would end here, before these Stygian waters of dimensional interphasing across whose depths some as-yet-unrevealed Charon would ferry but one of them.

With laborious effort, Wagner once more struggled to lift his own frame, but found himself mired in retrograde. Asquint, he gaped at his would-be benefactors, trying—and failing—to mouth the merest utterance. Then, upraising himself in a last-ditch futility that Fate would slap down, he up and vanished. Summarily, irretrievably, he simply went out—went out like a movie-projector image vanquished by a yanked plug, went out void of utterance or sign or motion or of any describable causality. Once and over, he was gone.

Miracle's grip suddenly giving in to the collapsed airspace, he blundered ill-balanced into the spot where Wagner had been. Mazzio reached instinctively to bolster him, but withdrew as *Miracle* found his own footing; and then both men just stood idle in their dumbfoundment, each in his private disconcertion, each as sullen as the conspicuously absent afternoon breeze and the eerie silence that enveloped the grounds.

Of the fourteen people who witnessed the passing, not one of them stirred for a very long time. Some with jaws distended and eyes googly and disbelieving, some inwardly disconsolate, others outwardly aghast, they remained collectively encircled about that plot of grass where, in the space of an instant, life had been and life had gone. What on any other day would have been a lovely, idyllic spot in the shady largesse of three beautiful birches, for nearly every one of those fourteen souls, it was now and forever a cordon of unreality.

And for at least two of them it had become the loneliest place on the face of the earth.

CHAPTER FIVE

The fool of nature stood with stupid eyes
And gaping mouth, that testified surprise.
  —JOHN DRYDEN

The passage of time can be a difficult thing to gauge when its measurer finds himself deprived of all benefit of sensorial input, of sight and sound, of the ability to monitor actions, events, the motion of surrounding stimuli. And although time—an abstract concept in itself—is for most purposes constant according to humankind's earthbound, mechanical chronometry, it is alternately mercurial for one who, in lieu of the obligatory timepiece to ogle, has only his intuition or the evidence of external progressivity by which to make his assessment. Hence, time is thought to career with uncanny rapidity when one's desire is to savour it, and to mull within an endless bog of languor when nothing short of its quickening will do. James Wagner, however, no longer even grasped the concept of time's passage, whether hare-swift, snail-like, or otherwise, for his very essence was swathed in the void. He possessed no body to control, nor one whose tactility might put its influence on him. His motoring abilities, his physical senses, his involuntary diagnostics, even his desires—all wrenched out from under him like a parlour-trick tablecloth, there was no relying on the sensations that flesh provided. As near to a nirvanic unfettering as one might ever know, he found his consciousness suddenly on par with infinity, with all manner of reflex and psychological contrivance cast off like so much ballast.

Here, he told himself, *was spirit. Here was freedom.* This was more than just the shedding of the body's physical confines as he had done so often in recent days, for this time he possessed the presence of mind to realise this truth in perfect, peaceful cognisance. Not a care, no fear or preoccupation with dreams, visions, insanity, he was unhindered by bothersome memories and unconcerned with what was yet to be. *This, certainly,* he thought, *was the last, great mystery solved. This was death. And death seemed a pleasant thing.*

Although so uncoupled from flesh and things corporeal—moreover, divested of electrophysiological receptors of any kind—he nonetheless imagined the thrill of acceleration from within his sphere of unsheathing calmness. There was no accounting for it; and, given the rhapsodic indiscernibility of his present state, he yielded no more than a negligible notice toward it, the notion of destination too easily disregarded for the quiescent nothingness that had usurped his earthly existence. Drifting on the tides of a tranquillity like none he had ever known, he entrusted his surviving essence to the all-encompassing sedateness that—

What a cruel and terrible joke!

—forced his sudden resumption of the gravity he hadn't anticipated and never again reckoned he would encounter. Laden with the abrupt heft of what, by contrast, felt utterly pachydermatous to his unwarned frame, he buckled, flopped, and jack-swiftly found himself prone upon a bluntly restored stratum of earth.

Scragged by disorientation, Wagner struggled like a newborn gasping for first breath. Arms and legs sunk in the paralytic numbfire of a circulatory system unready for demand, frantically he kneaded at his extremities to expel the nettling as quickly as he could for fear that some immediate danger might require his even more immediate mobility.

A cursory reconnaissance put him at ease. Recognising at once the familiar distillate of his symptomatology, it seemed that his suppositions of finality had been sorely premature. Tranquillity and eternal bliss out the window, his peaceful detachment traded for paraesthesia—despite all other presumption, that last bender had apparently not been the definitive one he'd anticipated. In fact, its grandest consequence turned out to be nothing more than his reintegration into a rural acreage some considerable distance from Howsley. With no inkling of time and place, and no ken of how long he'd been in his doppelganger's thrall, all he knew was that his resumption found him stranded in that much-bandied place of lore, referred to by the errant and the astray as "the middle of nowhere."

Shaken but recomposing, with the heat of the noonish sun just barely offsetting the perspiratory chill of his nakedness, Wagner summoned the grit to rise and to survey the legacy of yet another bender's rampaging. No spires of a distant downtown Bishop anywhere in sight—indeed, civilisation itself completely insensible—around him unfurled a virginal meadowland of teeming grasses, of bristly weeds and catkinned reeds, of swarming insects and aimlessly wafting pappi and no less than a dozen genera of wildflowers in various stages of colour-spangled efflorescence.

He tightened. Unquestionably a pleasant scene, even a beautiful one, he nevertheless felt his insides besieged by the hot and cold volleys of dread. His chest a steady throb of tom-tom pounding, his mouth had gone abruptly dry and his throat convulsed as if a ping-pong ball had lodged in his trachea. Though nothing around him presented any identifiable threat, his gut was deeply a-twist with foreboding.

In every direction he was bombarded with the overmeasure of new localisation. Bumblebees danced and darted among multi-coloured blooms whose airborne amalgamate jumpstarted his olfactories like a fragrant kayo to the nares. Great haywires of gnats flitted overhead with frantic gregariousness. A good thirty paces distant, several large poplars brooked the tow of a playful breeze, their restless foliage providing venue for the various birds and cicadae whose caws, clicks, and buzzes made for an overture of discordance that seized Wagner's ear for more than just a moment. These were sounds he'd not heard in a long time, natural phenomena that spirited him back to bygone days and wayside years. Indeed, the resplendence in everything before him reminded him of all that had been absent from his life for many a long month.

Alone and vulnerable, he stood clothed in nothing but his awe. Gently debating his next course, he brushed his knees free of dirt and clinging chaff, and then turned a complete revolution in hope that a cautious assessment of his environment might net him greater bearing.

The meadow—perhaps several acres in area—was engirded on three sides by varying degree of forestation. Within the fourth tract lay a miscellany of scattered shrubbery and saplings among more grasses, with a lonely tree here leading to a familial cluster there, until the entire clearing eventually succumbed to the same wooded area that boxed the immediately encircling trends. The sun at meridian, discerning his direction would be an unreliable venture for another hour or so; but as he stood conditionally calmer now, and better inclined to his situation, Wagner chose to edge his way toward the closest vicinage of trees, that he might benefit from the cover and from the security he believed they might provide, at least until he could devise inconspicuous means for getting back to Howsley. A time or two in his pre-incorporeal days he recalled having snapped awake from a bender to find that he'd inadvertently covered several miles in his incapacitation; and although by admitting himself to Howsley he'd initially prevented the further occasion of such wakeful surprise, its effectiveness had found unexpected thwarting by the advent of his sudden penchant for phasing.

Scrutinising both the woodlet in which he travelled and the vastness beyond it, he wondered if he'd blundered onto a private chase or some untouched backwoods of state parkland. Once, long ago, he and Sara had larked away an afternoon on the trails of one such preserve, the largest and most popular one, located just outside of the city's southern limits. If this was somehow that same place, Wagner remembered that its public campground areas had been about ten miles south of town, maybe twelve from Howsley's doors. Such information meaning very little unless he knew in which direction the tourist and information facilities lay, he was largely in the dark outside of the so-so conviction that he actually *was* where he presumed he was. To his speculative eye, it had every indication of being an unblemished, natural sanctuary. He knew of no other sizable, similarly verdant areas in or around Bishop's sprawl, nor of any substantial sylviculture adjacent to its unincorporated townships and a fair number of the county divisions as well. The bulk of those areas was, more than anything, active farmland. Yet, this wasn't to say that an unspoiled haven like this couldn't have existed on the fringes of those broad stretches of land.

Lacking itinerary, and realising that strolling haphazardly through wilderness while so completely *au naturel* would do little to expedite his return to Bishop, Wagner commenced a heedful but steady hike in order to ferret out some small evidence of civilisation. His choice of direction not purely arbitrary, the tract of forest that he occupied was airy, bright, favourable to the cautious traveller, and as good a tack as any to a man who'd lost his way—and his clothes. Whenever the wilds grew denser, as it occasionally did, he sought out the most easily negotiated, nudist-friendly avenues, hoping that the coppice would remain at least marginally accommodating until he happened across some indication of hikers, campers, park personnel, guide markers, maybe even that pair of walking, ownerless trousers from a Dr. Seuss story of long ago—trousers that he could have used right about then.

Deeper into the duskier heart of the woodland, however, he began to sense an escalating uneasiness with his decision, second-guessing that perhaps it might have been a sounder choice to have maintained a route that merely skirted the edge of the timberline rather than penetrated. With every few paces his path had grown in obstruction, with the proliferating vegetation choking out what scant light the forest canopy hadn't itself occluded. As it was, he found it difficult to confirm that he'd even been maintaining a strictly linear path, for at times he'd found it necessary to veer to the right or to the left in order to access a natural easement; and without benefit of compass or the sun's arc of descent, he was forced to correct his course with only a layman's grasp of bearing. Even more vexing, he was made to endure the mounting assault of an intolerably voracious insect population, each species of which possessed its own unique means of laying siege to him for a chance at the nectareous spoils of his lifeblood. At length he slapped at mosquitoes easily the size of hummingbirds, swatted at pesky deer flies who swooped and buzzed his head like Great War dogfighters, flicked away ticks that dive-bombed him en masse from the greenery above—the onslaught at times so annoying that it made Wagner actually long for the intangibility he'd always dreaded.

Soon, the treescape took a downward veer, and Wagner happened across what seemed a path forged by deer or other foraging wildlife. It wound on for a considerable distance in narrow, meandering randomness through an otherwise imperforate underbrush, in places so heavily flourished as to create a labyrinth of thicket that even Theseus would have had difficulty peregrinating. Eventually, however, its invasive flora receded to more manageable proportion, and at one point gave way to a modest yet abundantly bright glade where, in their falling, two sizable oaks had opened a rift in the densely interwoven ceiling. Now decrepit, both trees bore the outward evidence of having over time become fodder for the forest's pulp-devouring denizens who, in their inconspicuously tireless toiling, were converting the once mighty giants into brittle shells of sawdusty nothingness. It was near to these fallen husks that Wagner chose to rest—not chancing to sit or to lean anywhere, but rather utilising the tried and true squatting posture of the ever-cautious nude man in a semi-hostile environment.

He thirsted, but hadn't yet found opportunity for refreshment. He'd come across no running water source in his trek, and hadn't even the most rudimentary know-how for going about in search of one. He imagined that there were ways to extract, even to distil, water from succulents and such; but again, his survivalist skills were subpar. He'd be okay for a while longer; of this he was fairly certain. Still, he hoped it wouldn't be all that long before he barged into someone's family outing, where a parched, naked, uninvited interloper might actually not be taken for a pervert, but rather, offered a cool drink, a chequered tablecloth sarong, and a map back to the city.

To his advantage, when he gazed up through the clearing he could now determine that the sun's position had declined just westwardly enough to provide him with a ballpark indication of direction; the downside, of course, was that he still had no clue as to his whereabouts, nor which heading would be his most expeditious avenue back to the civilised world.

In weighing options, he noted that an easterly route suggested a more prominent notion of open daylight forty metres or so through and beyond a tunnel-like foreground of Grimmesque woodland. This being the most promising of his choices, he picked up and set off anew, his hopes of stumbling across any of the helpful folks in his sundry rescue vignettes spurring him to override the fatigue of two legs so disaccustomed to such unplanned and extended jaunting.

Having appreciated a gradient change in some of the surrounding flora during his last hour or so of wandering, this new heading not only reverted in increment to a more taxing incline, but revealed to him some new visual diversities as well. The insinuation of pines and spruces by far the most dramatic change, their incidence had now come to outreach that of the deciduous species that had so predominated at his point of reintegration. Boscage was also no longer as prevalent as it had been, and for unknown reason he fared considerably better on the insect front as well. Even the diffusion of sunlight was different here, with infiltration not so much apertured as it was columnar—an effect that only added to the forest's already ample majesty.

As for the tract's initial gloominess, it owed much to the phalanx of these newly encountered conifers whose near and steady proximity impressed on Wagner the notion of an encincturing much more cavernous than arboreal. Umbral green, thickly needled at their peaks yet increasingly sparse and ruddy along the scaly furrows of their earth-sprung boles, only the most light-sensitive vegetation and fungi flourished at their bases, making Wagner's tramping a task of relative ease. No obstruction here, nothing to skirt around, his only challenge came by the subtle uphill veer of a terrain consisting of spongy, pungent humus that was itself composed of moulds and pine needles and cone fruit in decay.

The moist air clung damp upon Wagner's flesh and settled heavily within his lungs. Still, this warren of cooler clime was nonetheless enlivening to a man who'd been on the move, sans canteen, during the day's hottest hours. A little eerie and surreal (and at the same time, stirring and invigorating), that a wanderer might be enshrouded in such pocket-twilight when fifteen metres overhead a sweltering sun bathed the land—it almost made Wagner want to dawdle a while in quiet awe.

Within a few dozen paces, however, he would discover a wonder far grander than that provided by simple contrasts of light and shadow. In fact, what confronted Wagner next had him shelving his dendrological perusings quickly and altogether. For, to his utter dismay, the allure of daylight that he'd espied and pursued from back at the fallen oaks now revealed to him a surprise that he could in no way have anticipated or predicted. With his emergence from the woods, it was no mere clearing upon which he happened, no lea or pasturage, nor a common pathway that held the promise of some Yogi Bearish campground unfurling at its terminus. He instead found himself high on the edge of a soft bluff, facing a milieu that resembled nothing of the local geography that selvaged Bishop, and certainly nothing even remotely in liking with the Midwestern United States in whole.

Dropping away before his slung jaw and his bramble-bitten feet sprawled a small valley—a meandering fecundity of lush, green hollow that crevassed the very heart of the woods for kilometres in either direction. Sudden in declination, heavily serried in scrub, its slopes were largely excursive and flexuous, although sheer enough in places to warrant perhaps only the most deliberated of downward ventures. Peppered, too, with shrubs and saplings, only in a handful of spots was the fall so drastic that a careful traveller might not find ample handholds and footing for achieving his prudent descent, and thereafter, find himself able to partake of the supreme reward suddenly noticed at bottom: a pleasant, purling little brooklet of near crystalline purity.

This, the only temptress capable of luring Wagner willingly down a potentially treacherous hillside, he would already have been halfway down the versant had fresh water been the whole of what his eyes beheld. It was instead the conglomerate vista that froze him, that gave his flesh the skitters, that knotted his insides with collywobbles more feazing than any swap of locales ever had.

Given his arguably casual relationship with the unexpected, for him to step out of a bender and into the midst of a vast, unpeopled wilderness was, in itself, hardly a remarkable thing anymore. Unexpected vales and burbling rivulets likewise fell within the boundaries of fuguish happenstance, no different from the sundry back yards and strip-mall parking lots and supermarket dumpsters of his past re-entries into reality. His mind had long ago come to draw upon an array of self-protective measures to aid him in adjusting and adapting to the environmental switches resultant of his blackouts; and, up until now, said measures had been adequately compensatory. But this, here, now, was something that he'd not even considered. This was an evolution of his condition that seemed to have stretched duration and distance to new limits. Even a desperate screwing of his eyes failed to alter the scene before him. For, over and beyond the opposite crest, rearing behind a vast brolly of woodlands, rising amid the nebulous graze of low-hanging clouds, stood two of the most glorious snow-capped mountains he would ever hope in his life to see.

Simultaneously daunted and consumed by his own ilk of psychogenic vertigo, he gave way hard to overwroughtness, and dropped to the lip of the ridge.

How? He wondered. *How is this possible?*

His hand glued to his mouth, his eyes boggling, he could do nothing but stare in disbelief. Stumped, distraught, flushed and trembling, he couldn't begin to consider the protracted manner of mind-tripping necessary to have allowed him to cover such tremendous distance while in an amok state of bodylessness. Were he to have rolled INCREDIBLE and IMPLAUSIBLE into one big UNLIKELY, it would scarcely have begun to explain this. *And just what and where was this, anyway—Wyoming maybe? Montana? British Columbia?*

He didn't budge for a very long time. Seeking out campsites or information centres seemed a rather ludicrous endeavour now. Deliberating a means for short-term wilderness survival appeared the more sensible strategy, although he truly wasn't clear-headed enough even for this.

He realised, now, that in his earlier surmising he'd unearthed only a tiny potsherd of truth, that the increased intensity in his spells had been portending a new facet of his condition, and not the death or oblivion of his previous presumption. Yet, compared to the underdivulged complexity of his lapses, his phasing, his life's anguish over incredible circumstances that defied all known science, a geographical dipsy-doodle like this should have been child's play to figure out. "An amplified bout with the integrity-loss phenomenon," as Mazzio may have claimed, "together with an ultra-extended fugue of displaced consciousness and incorporeal hyperkinesia," and *voila!*—the subject awakens a hundred, maybe a thousand, miles from his previous location. It was as good an explanation as any—just the right amount of verbosity to lend authenticity, and certainly logical enough as far as logic ever pertained to his amorphous bag o'tricks. His spells noticeably augmented over the past week or so, manifesting more often, with lengthier durations and greater mental dishevelment, it all had to be building up to something. And apparently this *something* was the next step in his malady's evolution. Like the incipient flashes of imagery that forever dotted his childhood, like the more intricate mind-trips that plagued his adolescence, these had been but preparatory intrusions for the phasings that would eventually manifest. The phasings themselves, once believed the apex of all inconceivabilities, were now in danger of being upstaged by this new and unsettling transcontinental transcendence. It was all exquisitely patent now, plain as the Arcadian-like paradise that lay before him, and he laughed sardonically at his premature reckoning of how Death had finally taken him. It would seem that things were not to be quite that easy.

Sufficient time spent bemoaning his luck, Wagner finally rose. Charting what he hoped would be his best choice for a path of descent, he clambered boldly over the lip and orchestrated a heedful amble down the shrub-choked slope. Entrusting his heft to only the most tenacious and firmly established vegetation, he found in return enough confidence in grip and rung to deliver him to the valley floor with little more than a minor scotching and the pitchy nuisance of plant resins upon his hands. Along the measure of his decline, he'd watched the distant peaks sinking beyond the faux rearing of the opposite crest, sighing self-delusively once the uprisen versant obscured them entirely, for only then could he play them off for what he wished they'd been—the hallucinatory residue born of drastic thirst or chemical depletion or some other bodily imbalance that his imminent rehydration would surely cure.

Once reaching bottom, he paused to reconnoitre a brief, visual sweep of his surroundings before beelining for the rill's prize. The water he found icy and refreshing, so much that he plunged his head in whole beneath the current, guzzling up great, greedy mouthfuls until his belly surrendered in shock and bloat. Hands cupped then, he plashed glacial rejuvenation over his shoulders, chest, and back, and then plopped himself onto a nearby boulder in order to indulge his scourged feet with a bracing swash. Several hours of trudging over clods and prickles, needles and nettles, had taken an abrasive toll, transforming his tenderfooter's arches into a podiatrist's worst nightmare. A dousing good plunk into such wondrous briskness was exactly the invigoration they needed.

Giving in here to brief recline, he pondered his next course of action. Surely, Mazzio would have alerted the authorities of his escape, hopefully on a national scale. Someone had to be looking for him, whether it be law enforcement, interested parties, or benevolent volunteers; and even with the predictable chaos that his Hyde-side had doubtlessly unleashed along the way, Wagner seriously considered remaining out in the open for a while in the event of a helicopter or a DNR search-and-rescue team happening along. However, the fact that he had yet to encounter any signs of human intrusion within this vast habitat led him to believe that he was deeper in the bush than any assistance-minded Samaritans had chanced to search. Thus, he concluded that it might suit him better to continue seeking out his own path of salvation.

He confirmed the impracticality of continuing in the direction of the mountains, as they presented an impasse far too challenging for him in his novitiate of unaccoutred nakedness. He likewise deemed it similarly unproductive to go back the way he came. This left him with a heading toward the rill's origin or that of its destination. And since the former was, again, probably the very mountains he wished to avoid, it appeared as if his choice was made for him. So, after one final quaff, he set off—reinvigorated but guarded—following the water in its aimless purl through the heart of some of the most intoxicatingly beautiful wilderness that he'd ever seen that side of a PBS travelogue.

Yet, tracking the stream—for it soon swelled in magnitude such that the terms "rill" and "brook" no longer applied—was to be an ambitious endeavour; and after what he imagined had been another hour or so of legwork, Wagner paused once more, not merely for further refreshment, but for a reprieve from the refractory swelter of the sun's heat upon the rocky shoreline. As he wasn't at all acclimated to any lengthy exposure under direct sunlight either, he supposed (perhaps belatedly, but this he excused as a result of his great preoccupation) that it might be more judicious to rescale the ridge and match the stream's course from the protective cover of the forest's edge, despite the increased encumbrance that such a route would surely present. Still, believing the inconvenience of dodging mosquitoes preferable to severe sunburn, he parted from the water in order to work his way back up the valleyside.

At roughly two-thirds up the crest, however, he was pressed by sensitivity to halt, and halt abruptly. Cocking his head, he held fast in mid-ascent, his ear under the fancy that it had caught some odd timbre of reverberation—a sound, possibly vocal, shrill but eerily guttural, unlike anything he'd heard in his entire day's wandering. Regarded within the midst of his upward trudge, he'd not been keen enough in sense to isolate it from the stream's tireless burble and the rustle of the leaves and grasses that he'd disturbed in his tromp. Whatever it had been, real or imagined, its quality had seemed to him an unnatural staple to the surrounding landscape.

He remained frozen, listening intently for a reprise that seemed most determined not to sound. Ten seconds passed without event, twenty seconds—the only audible emissions, exempting the stream's mingling currents, supplied by the ubiquitous insect population.

Feeling conspicuously in the open, Wagner carefully studied the terrain— upstream, downstream, overhead, and cross-valley. Yet, gleaning no further incident of the sound, he dismissed his assumption, chalking it up to the same false impression that prompts a person to think he hears the telephone while having a shower or running the vacuum. Shrugging it off, he resumed his clamber.

Then he heard it again.

Or at least he heard *something*, for this time it was different, different to the degree that he couldn't link it to the source he'd previously imagined. This was more a hullabaloo of sounds, a jumbled intermittency of shouts and bawls whose vector was too skewed by valley's unique acoustics for him to peg.

Hurrying, thrusting himself over the lip and back onto high ground, from there he peered down at the stream, once in either direction.

He saw nothing. Even the insects had stilled, a conspiracy to confound him.

Scanning curiously ahead, he noticed what appeared to be a dry gully, approximately fifty metres downstream, that opened to the watercourse from his side of the ridge. Its appliance apparently dependent on cloudburst and spate—neither of which seemed to have occurred for some time—the influence of even such incidental outflow was nonetheless evident, for just beyond what would have been the point of confluence the stream veered away in a diverted flume, as if coerced over time by the outwash of persuasive storm waters.

Maintaining his high ground along the ridge, Wagner skirted through the underbrush toward this embouchure, not strictly sure of his intention but seeking to at least gain a vantage from where he might pinpoint any further issue of voices. Although faced with no real evidence of humanity other than the brief dissonance that his wishful thinking sought to conjure into a rescue party, he remained open and acute to anything that might offer him a source, and from there, a cautious scrutiny.

While the possibility of finding other people may indeed have stoked his eagerness for rescue, his gut nonetheless bade him caution. Seldom bereft of at least some small sensation of leeriness, he'd learned long ago to heed his intuition. This going double for intuitive foreboding, he recognised the necessary prudence of evaluating any would-be rescuers—if that's what the voices turned out to be—before disclosing himself to any untried faction. After all, if there was an all-points out there with his name on it, the level of partiality in his profile was anyone's guess. If his sheet came off even a modicum short of sympathetic, there would be precious little he'd be able to do to dulcify a posse of potentially misinformed, trigger-happy cops, rangers, mounted police, national guardsmen, or—heaven help him—backwoods bumpkins, who happened across a misunderstood mental ward fugitive in his birthday suit.

Reaching the junction where coulee met waterway revealed nothing but the obvious. One-half as wide as the stream it sometimes fed, the gully wound back and away toward its downpour-prompted beginnings, disappearing behind a crag of scrub-strung pockedness. Yet, from atop the ridge, Wagner quickly found himself privy to the stream's altered heading, and to the subsequence of arboureous territory that it went on to broach.

He paused here to listen for further evidence of voices, footfalls, disturbances in the coppice—anything bearing the potential to twist the picture-postcard vista into something far more lethal. Perched within an indent of natural hedgerow near this pivotal corner between the stream's divergence and the gully's parched yawn, he hid and mulled over the pro and con of re-embarking on his odyssey or remaining cloistered until he felt more confident of his personal welfare.

He hadn't long to wait. The charge and didder of skirmish suddenly flagging his eye, at long last he had physical confirmation of that which he'd refused to dismiss as a mere caprice of the mind.

Across the valley, roughly thirty metres upstream, four figures had erupted from the foliage atop the ridge. Without pause they proceeded down the slope in a furious sputter of spewing dust, skittering rocks, and thrashed vegetation, their unchecked recklessness signalling a common mindset of what could be naught but all-out desperation.

Seizing on their descent, Wagner immediately sensed a deflexure in the drama that wasn't quite right. Not in the breakneck urgency of their movement, nor in the fact that they seemed single-mindedly panicked, what he noted was more an idiosyncratic distinction—and a physical ambivalence—that, because of both their furious pace and his own distanced and downward aspect, hindered any objective attempt at assessment. Gender, race, age, affiliation—nothing other than a uniformity of their outerwear was easily discernable, and colour-coordinated issue alone was hardly a persuading factor by which four light of heel strangers might entice a wary runagate out of hiding.

When they made bottom, they gave no pause but maintained their flight (for it did seem more flight than pursuit) and continued in scramble along the far bank of the stream. Bent, it would seem, on braving the current at its shallowest point, the quartet happened onto a more convenient, if daring, means for crossing, and opted in this new path with execution so fluid that they could almost have been of one mind. Hopscotching the river rock, boulder to boulder, each fleer followed his predecessor in springing over rocky protrusions and natural debris like dancers executing grand jetès, until each of them had safely reached the near bank. Some of the upcroppings a considerable distance, one from the next, Wagner could scarcely believe that all four succeeded in negotiating the course without the slightest slip or stub. Mountain goats could not have been more agile than these daunting, tawny-clad figures who, with momentum undiminished, alit upon the embankment and then put to with even greater speed toward the gully.

Amid the blur of their impressive celerity, Wagner craned forward the better to peer down at his athletic irrupters, only to be struck by a reality most glaring. This—not only an unanticipated validation of his preponderant transmigration, but such in its most extreme and mindfully devastating sense—was a reality check with all the subtlety of a knuckle-sandwich. And like the recipient of said cold-cocking wallop, Wagner was quite nearly rocked from his secret perch.

Sweet reason and logic out the door, his first conviction was that he'd lost his mind. If not, then he'd been gadding about within some new ilk of mind-trip the whole time, his day's excursion through grass and greenwood a phantasy that even sudden self-realisation failed to shatter. This being the case, then once more he'd become the unwitting foil of gall and wormwood and mental infirmity, which in turn made all of the accepted genuineness of the forestial heartland merely another grand delusion of faculty, revealed now by evidence just in. Yet, what other explanation was there but one that saw him mottled by hallucination? It had to be the answer. More so, he *needed* it to be. If it wasn't—and if what he now witnessed was somehow reality irrefutable—then Howsley and Bishop were not merely kilometres off, but forfeited entirely for a completely new and unbidden succedaneum straight out of downtown *Benderville*. And why? Because the figures passing below him were not *people* at all!

No, not people, not even human, it had been purely the foursome's hominal semblance that spurred Wagner's earlier misconception. And Wagner, his eyes popping like two cue balls, wondered how he could have missed what was suddenly so blatant.

Almost lupine in their makeup and movements, the fleers were lanky and sinewy, frightening and magnificent—and now quite unimaginable to Wagner's bestrewed sense of comfort. The nature of their coverture far from the misreckoning of his first impression, what he'd mistaken for matching rigout was instead a complete lack of clothing, the conspicuity of their beige/buff pelts so obvious now that Wagner beat himself up over his perceptive laxity. Their remarkable athletic prowess likewise made absolute sense now, for its basis was rooted in the praeternatural. Bestial yet bipedal, they could well have passed for living lycanthropes, werewolves beyond the calibre of token horror, and Wagner knew as he watched them bolting away—knew by this huge, evidentiary wake-up, knew by his sequatiously altering theories of his surroundings, of the alpine scenery, of the crystalline brookwaters and of skies unmarred by jet-trails, knew by all of the underlying inklings that he'd been suppressing since the very moment that he'd come to—that the earth beneath his feet belonged to a world other than the one on which he'd spent the last twenty-eight years of his life.

Resorting back to insanity, he tried to force coherence along this route, if only because it was the more logical—and comforting—explanation. Still, he couldn't just arbitrarily affirm his out-and-out dottiness, despite the outrageousness of what he'd seen. More than this, he found it curious, even a tad disturbing, that he might experience so sober a reaction to a sight (moreover, a tangible reality!) that should have had him quaking on the level of one of Howsley's jiggly Jell-O salads.

He had little time, however, to ponder his lack of reflex, for new incident forced his attention back to the ridge where the four teratoids had first broken from cover. At the very same point of brushy egress, a second group of beings had emerged, a trio this time; and although these figures differed in appearance from their furry predecessors, the distinction was no more reassuring to Wagner's wanting sense of comfort.

Bipeds also, these three seemed more kindred to Wagner in form; their proportions, their postures, even the quirk of their locomotion—all closer to his own. Yet, as with the wolfish creatures before them, the distance across the breach made it difficult for Wagner to note any true wealth of particulars. While confident in his camouflage, he nevertheless thought better of sidling back to the valley-side vantage for a more obliging view, the draw of even one discrepant rustling from his leafy keep a blunder that might cost him dearly. Instead, he settled for the limitations of his eyeshot, even here observing that, unlike the four ferals who were themselves free of unnatural adornings, each of these new figures was outfitted—"armoured" was perhaps a better word—in an improbability of gear that boasted more mediaeval European influence than Wagner had latitude to appreciate.

A veritable head-to-foot show of antiquity, their costume followed a strict regimental uniformity replete with protective breastplates, codpieces, assorted greaves and vambraces and other accoutrements for which Wagner lacked appellation, all conjoined by gussets of defensive mail and topped by spherical helms that masked each figure's lineaments unto the collar. A single, T-shaped aperture on the face provided for the rudiments of vision, breathing, and intelligible communication—a design that, if even marginally expedient for the wearer, offered Wagner less than a scant hint of countenance outside of a grim aspect of black, lustreless metal.

Exceeding this pageant of Old World lethality was the gratuitous array of barbaric weaponry that each figure carried on his person. One clutched a flail-like variant that consisted of a single, iron ball connected to a club by a pair of chains, while the other two wielded crankable crossbows, cocked and loaded with multiple bolts. Each bore additional armaments as well, an unsavoury variety of strap-on apparatus: swords, daggers, axes, bindings, and several types of side arms that Wagner had never before seen in either text or museum.

A redoubtable bunch, these three, they huddled above the descent, and in a brief and lively brawl of gesture, posit, and argument, their focus inevitably converged on the mouth of the gully. Perhaps tipped by some vestigial wisp of dust stirred up by the creatures' flight, perhaps clued by trackable evidentia that Wagner's untrained eye would have overlooked—it was clear that this was to be their avenue of intent. Indeed, as the two bowmen rechecked the safeguarding mechanisms on their crannequins, the third made ready to lead them down the very route forged by their quarry mere moments earlier.

In that precise instant, however, something occurred that put fateful paid to their foray. Before their point-man could so much as fix a boot heel upon the slope, the very copse around them opened up like the barrel of a cannon and shot forth a streaking juggernaut, a living, thrashing, indistinguishable ferity that, awhirl with razored talons and unremittingly vertiginous fists, lit into the soldiers with an assail so savage that Wagner would have sworn that they'd been overtaken by the gyre of an aircraft propeller. Swift and slaughterous and almost mechanically relentless, this all but invisible raider made quick with the unready trio, systematically targeting only those scant and incapacious areas where their armour did not shield. Mere gapes in their plating almost entirely disregarded, it made their visors its busiest objective, and without conscience or quarter it tore, jabbed, punctured, and ultimately eviscerated their most precious vulnerability, the venom of the ambuscade matched only by the velocity at which the mutilations were delivered. Flail and crossbows sent in tumble down the slope, relinquished by hands too eclamptic to hold them, not one soldier had found time or clarity enough for even the most fundamental of counterattacks.

Wagner cringed at the sight of three ravaged and avulsed hoplites in their ghastly, headlong plummet toward the bedrock below. Like so much scrap metal tossed into a landfill, at end these panoplied brutes—so outwardly formidable only seconds before—struck bottom with three abrupt thuds of life-extinguishing finality.

Clinging to a creeper in wide-eyed silence, Wagner marvelled at the speed with which they'd been dispatched. None had even found voice enough to scream.

Across the vale, he watched as their executioner fleetingly observed the results of her deed. Then, with no more remorse than she'd had mercy, she skirted down the slope in pursuit of what Wagner now realised must have been her young—or, at the very least, her charges. A larger and more greatly matured incarnation of the creatures previously seen, this sanguinary adult was likewise in unadorned state, the exception being seven or eight thin strips of blanched cloth that girded her arms and waist at various intervals in the same fashion that a person might don an accenting array of torque or cincture. She was trim and agile, with lean, powerful limbs, a columnar brawn of shoulders, and a distinctive vertical furrow of musculature that cleaved her torso from high breast to groin. Her neck, slightly more elongated than suited her body, crooked forward as she ran, almost as if nature intended that her frightful snarl reached her adversaries long before her body did.

As she passed below his cover, Wagner was able to garner only slightly more detail, and here noted that her ears and nose were truly more feline than lupine— the former, jutting back in triangular contours across the crown of her head, and the latter, amply sculpted and regal.

Wagner theorised that she had urged the younger ones on while purposely lagging and remaining in wait, her ploy having been to allow the overconfident stalkers to track ahead of her position so that she could ambush them from the rear. This inferred a greater intelligence than presumption was eager to extend, much less even entertain. Not only a shrewd gambit, but an ambitious one— achievable solely by she with the courage and the prowess to execute it without weaponry of her own—Wagner didn't know whether to admire or to reprehend this extraordinary beast who even then made nimbly up the coulee in tail of her long fled clan. Indeed, far after losing sight of her around the bend, Wagner continued to rerun the atrocity in perpetual, visual loop, with his stomach re-churning the whole thing in repulsed reply. Yet, as he cast his eyes once more on the sight of the three unfortunates, each lying entombed within his metalled carapace, each with his infernal instruments strewn before him like jackstones from the Devil's toy box, Wagner silently wondered who, they or she, had truly been the more bestial.

Imbrued in the spectacle, he was suddenly seized by understanding. A belated phenomenon, and not an entirely unexpected one, it broke him from the bystander's rigour that had momentarily grafted him to the very shrubbery that concealed him. Denial and distraction and all manner of mindful suppression no longer feasible, everything bestowed of the last few minutes not only negated all earlier hypotheses, but indeed necessitated an entire day's-worth of revamped perspective, all the way back to the very moment when he'd first uprighted himself amid unfamiliar meadow and woodgrove. His weightiest mystery could no longer be disregarded. Somehow, someway, he had emerged at the far end of his madness—not simply into the nearby public campgrounds of his first suspicions, nor even a remote reach of highlands several states off, but across impossibility itself, to some oblique and anachronistic transmundanity that had both the substantiality of wakefulness and the incarnate absurdity of a dreamstate. Not at all the spatial and temporal hopscotching of his mind-jaunts, this was reintegration with a crabwise skew. It was as if during his sublimation the world he knew had been filched and replaced with a facsimile whose few inexactitudes were a few inexactitudes too many. Post-bender displacement always difficult enough to accept, his hallucinatory divertissement—though disorienting—had always been short-lived in relativistic terms. But what he faced here was not absolute phantasy. Nor was it the product of a brain in short-circuit. Wherever he was, whenever, how and why, this felt real. It felt undeniably, inexplicably, authentically real.

Such reckoning was not an easy notion to grasp. Like a crashing wave of inexorability, it deluged his mental breakwaters. And Wagner, unable to ascribe to fancy what had become irrefutable, caved to the onrush of event and circumstance, his previously passive detachment disintegrating like a sandcastle before the tide. Inconceivability had become truth, while truth itself had skipped out under the veil of Wagner's own befogging. Even the once reliable buttress of insanity was unattributably absent, and with it, his hopes of any moment snapping back to his bed at Howsley.

Like no predicament ever, the fact that he'd not reacted as most men might have under the same circumstances, he could only presume that his mind had been shielding him all along with the very self-protective measures that it had utilised for years to ease the flummox of bender aftermath. Still, such total environmental transposal as *this* proved far too taxing for even his psychical fail-safes. Lackadaisical condonation (deliberate or otherwise) equally unacceptable, his every mental buffer—from objective neutrality to outright denial—had been unseated by evidence more irrefutable than he ever would have believed. It had suddenly become crucial that he synthesise what had been mere visional salmagundi yesterday into the macabre credibility of today, for clearly this neo-reality was not about to coddle him until he found the grit to pull himself together and get with the programme. It existed. It wasn't a choice for him to reject. Neither could he simply quit and go home. No wish would end it; no sensorial delegation would override it; and no amount of resignation and restiveness would spare him from the undiscovered country ahead.

While permissibly much too obliging for one whose already complex existence had been invaded anew by armoured brigands and ferocious bipedal felines, Wagner was not totally without fear—hardly!—but curiously neither were his anxieties revving into the rpm range commensurate to the circumstances. More than an hour earlier, on finding a backdrop of alpine peaks in what he had been presuming was rural, far-northern Indiana, he'd accepted the inordinate switch in venue with far less ordeal than he might have demonstrated had one of the rec room locals at Howsley changed TV stations on him. Something was unquestionably awry in his mental wiring, something more greatly complex than any standard, subconscious defence mechanism; and in this brief and unadulterated moment of clarity, he found his psychical telemetry in serious want.

Snapped from his unguardedness by the onset of distant shouting, Wagner ducked back into the brush. With a darting eye, he uneasily scanned the valley and the trampled copse from where the others had emerged, yet saw nothing indicative of further rovers of either variety. The voices, however, came ever more voluminously, emanating over the slopes with a reverberant choppiness that prohibited any attempts at reliably pinpointing their origin. Such acoustical deceptiveness bringing Wagner no solace, it went that whoever owned the voices could have been a goodly distance away or conceivably as close as the nearest blind. His senses, contrarily, told him that the source was somewhere farther upstream; and although he strained to espy the least of detectable movements, his callow scrutiny proved initially unfruitful.

In wait, he surveyed more diligently, relying less on aural suggestion than on the more faithworthy cullings of sight and intuition. Nothing notable for several near-breathless minutes, it wasn't until he traded raptness for a more general and peripheral approach that he finally caught the glint of motion—upstream, just as he'd first surmised.

Clued, now, to what he'd been seeking, he came to fix upon an ambulation of chary figures inching its way along the bank in loose V-formation. Still some distance removed but creeping steadily forward, one vigilant figure walked point along Wagner's side of the bank, followed by a cautious flanking of peers, one string on each side of the water. Even at this extreme distance, their affiliation with the dead soldiers was all but confirmable.

A new dilemma only minutes removed, Wagner quickly pondered whether to run or remain. It was true that, up until now, his ridge-top camouflage had proved an adequate refuge. But, as one unit of troops generally suggested many more units behind it, once these approaching scouts happened across their fallen comrades—some thirty metres from Wagner's vantage, no less—only a fool would think that they wouldn't scour the area, understandably bereft of affability, in search of the agents of that aggression. Wagner did not want to be the one they found.

Longing for the inuredness that he suddenly found in ebb, Wagner struggled to assuage his sudden trembling. Fear had finally stepped onto the scene, had brought confusion and panic along with it, and all three were having a rave in the pit of his stomach.

Fleetingly he toyed with the idea of doubling back the way he'd come, thinking that it might be possible to slip discreetly past the scouts from high overhead. Reason, however, arguing that while the doomed patrol had indeed emerged from the far ridge, he could not be sure that he wouldn't encounter another such patrol on his side. Without the werecat's claws or fangs, or at least the benefit of some more modern weaponry at his disposal, he was entirely confident that he wouldn't fare quite so well as she. Alternately, any thoughts of proceeding downstream demanded an open descent followed by a scaling of the gully's other side, a tack that, while no significant physical hindrance, was detainment enough for any speedy and clandestine escape in that direction. A third elective was to retreat along the gully lip, in the direction that the ferals had fled, until the terrain levelled out or until he found a substitute route that branched away into some denser obscurity of woods. True, such a course could bring him dangerously close to his furry forerunners, and he'd already seen the distasteful challenge that this might present him. With but a few seconds, then, to weigh options, he nevertheless decided on this last choice. Yet, already he tweaked it slightly, so that his route along the gully would occur a bit more thicket-side than initially imagined—close enough to keep him parallel to the gully but isolated enough to minimise his risk of becoming inadvertent werecat kibble.

Hesitating for but a moment, still on the reluctant side of foregoing his leafy retreat, Wagner leaped into survival mode, his legs engaged and racing him through the coppice almost before he'd even made the decision to run for it. His physiology refining energy from raw terror, the effort expelled by his flight seemed almost negligible to a body suddenly hyper-fuelled by inner fortitude upon instinct.

In rushed and haphazard flight, Wagner was indiscriminate about where, and upon what, his bare feet alit. The thistly underbrush restrictive and unaccommodating, it plagued him with one snagging obstruction after the next, one stickly impediment within the tangle of a dozen others. But on he sped, his mind's singular fiat of survival numbing and overriding his physical distress. For all of the bodily anarchy he endured, his vigour remained strangely undiminished, his adrenal glands pumping propellant as fast as his limbs could expend it. With senses all acutely heightened, his eyes gauged the admissibility of every gape in the shrub-choked fenestration ahead while his ears fell attuned to the sounds at his back. Euphoric and petrified at the same time, he'd never felt so physically energised.

How crushing, then, to find that, less than thirty seconds into his launch, he'd already been discovered.

Dead-on in his hunch, a second unit had indeed been dispatched to his side of the ridge—four or five troops by his glimpse—and they'd been keen enough in their reconnoitring to catch sight of his thrash through the otherwise undisturbed tract. Obscured as he was by colonnade and scattered foliage, he truly hoped to be mistaken for a spooked deer or the like; but the same intuition that portended the soldiers' deployment told him that he was not to be so fortunate. Regardless of the manner in which they'd perceived his fleeing image, upon his sighting they broke into a jubilant chorus of shouts and animated hails that would doubtlessly rally the subsequent scouts from crest and vale and beyond into collectively trading their personae of vigilant stalkers for that of frothing pack-predators—all for the hunting and hounding of one unwitting man unlucky enough to become foot-tangled in the hem of circumstance.

Over-numbered, targeted like quarry, Wagner hied wildly through ramage that would have stymied a timber wolf. Although lacking the provision of deflective clothing and footwear, his nakedness actually made him nimbler than his pursuers, more compact and vastly lighter, and this—his *only* advantage—he utilised by speeding full tilt into the thickest nettlement of the terrain, hoping to discourage even the most determined of his panoplied stalkers. Attempting, too, to broaden his lead, he angled his course dramatically away from the soldiers, eventually to find himself racing directly alongside the gully by twenty paces or so, his intention being to cross it at some upcoming easement—but not until he was suitably to the fore. Only then would he attempt an uncompromised essay; and *this* only if he could be reasonably certain of avoiding the beasties who'd passed said way scant minutes before.

When at last it seemed that he'd managed to outstrip his pursuers, Wagner, still maintaining his pace, strained to listen for even the faintest disturbance behind and around him. To his dismay, he yet detected a pertinence of noises very far off—the thrashing and cursing of the armoured sloggers as they slashed and hacked their way through the lattice that he himself had slipped through like a mouse through briar. Several isolated shouts traded in that same vicinity caused him equal distress, for he'd been dashing flat out for a significance of time, yet had managed to effect but a paltry few minutes' lead.

Ahead of him, he noticed a small clearing where a long-ago mudslide had shifted the ridge's geography in his favour. A convenient declivity where the earth had given way, it offered an unexpectedly ready access to the ravine floor; and, without slowing to ponder fortuity, Wagner took it. Shooting down the crusty edge of the slope, he hit the basin at full gallop, crossed sides, and continued on from within the gully for as long and far as his wind would take him.

Overwhelmingly ill-prepared for such rampant exertion, Wagner wondered from where he drew his stamina, wondered what source other than fear drove him on with no consideration for the fatigue that by then should have been riddling his muscles like a connecting spread of lactic acid tranq-darts. His breathing was solid. His limbs were light and exhilarated. He wasn't running on the brink of collapse, as panic had sometimes made him feel in the past. Masterful was this show of endurance, but how was it possible? And for how long would it last?

He rounded a gradual bend, his strides broader for their lack of hindrance, until he was certain that his original point of descent was long out of sight. Then he began scanning the clough wall for the quickest means of getting topside. Although the grading here was less severe than it had been back along the stream, it still presented a challenge for someone who lacked the leisure of caution and sensible forethought.

Finding no exceptional upward access amid the twisted furrows carved out by runoff and erosion, Wagner grabbed onto those bits of shrubbery and rootage that could accommodate his weight, and commenced at working his way up the incline. To his delight, this worked beautifully—at least at first—the stolons anchored so resiliently between rock and rigid clay that he clambered up with the easy heave and ho of a climber beyond his seasoning. A bit higher up he found better purchase in the stirrup-like quality of tree roots, and, akin to a child on a daunting playground structure, he scaled the remainder of the rise like a schoolyard champ.

At less than a body's length from the top, however, one root slipped unexpectedly free, and he, with it. Robbed of equilibrium, for an immeasurable instant Wagner swung wildly, like a foolhardy squirrel who'd hazarded one backyard baffle too many. Unable to compensate for the precarious shift in his weight, he could do naught but hold fast as his body swooped down pendulum-style across the face of the slope, his anchoring hand barely maintaining its grasp on his corkscrewish lifeline.

Instinctively, Wagner bowed his body outward in his teeter, that he might minimise the abrasion to his exposed extremities. Yet, he didn't escape laceration altogether, the droughty cragginess of the hill-face tagging his knees, his elbows, his toes, with abrupt and excruciating grating. Clamping down on his agony, he waited for his momentum to wane, whereby he locked his stray hand about the other, and simply allowed himself to go lax.

Not an ideal time to be half-dangling, half-clinging, to a lonely versant in such disregarding idle, Wagner could ill-afford to suckle his pain. Flapping his legs about in search of new toeholds with which to regain support, he cursed himself for pushing too hard, for allowing his panic to affect his escape. Now he would pay dearly for that carelessness, for once atop the ridge he would find the chase significantly more arduous with his knees stinging and blood-riven, and his vitality hampered by a diminished confidence.

With a grimace, Wagner suppressed his discomfort and focused on his need to evade detection and confrontation. Ousting all aspects of the analytical as well, he instead plumbed for those latent skills that he knew he possessed, the ones called upon so frequently by his wily *Other*—yet which had ever remained privileged, unavailable for conscious extraction. That survival kit *did* exist. It lay buried within him, submerged somewhere just below the obduracy of his more civilised conditioning. All he needed to do was to crack through twenty-eight years of self-restraint and denial in order to find it.

He never got the chance. Suddenly seized from above and sheared from his mooring, his predicament at once turned fatal.

From the white-knuckled clinch of dangling under his own power, to being abruptly torn away on the fly, all that Wagner could initially think was that the tendrils to which he'd been clinging had somehow come alive in a vengeful fit of prehensile rage; and by that rage he would either be hurled groundward or detained in mid-air for the arrival and the wherewithal of his virulent stalkers.

Hanging like a fox in a springe, his wrist was caught in a pinchcock of almost unbearable striction. His voice failing him, he hadn't the capacity for blurting the simplest expletive, and barely the grist to unclench his eyes for the wince of his crucifixion. His lungs void, his shoulder disjointing like a drumstick in pry from a Christmas goose, he was completely helpless, and he strained through mottling vision to make out who or what it was—sadistic saviour or cruel executioner—who made so unbearably gruff with him. Slow to shake the muddlement from his eyes, once he finally did he found himself wishing that he hadn't, the price for clarity putting him face to snarl with his certain mortality.

Despite her sneer of toothy contempt, the werecat female did not harm him. Ears furled back, pupils no larger than slivers, initially she did nothing more than to sniff at the air about him. A few, torturous seconds of this, she made it all the more creepy by rotating him a partial turn clockwise, then counter-clock, almost as if she were calculating how many of her brood's bellies he might sate.

Baffled or disappointed, it was a reasonable assumption that the creature had expected to find one of the soldiers at the end of her grip, not some puny, naked man. Were she possessed of the intelligence that Wagner prayed she had, she certainly would have recognised by now that he was less than threatening. Still, to the hunted it made sense to view everything and everyone as suspect, even a scrawny being like Wagner, ghostly pallid as he was, and nigh to voiding his bowels over the parched gully basin.

Remarkably, his body bore her little significance as she stood upon the crest that he'd sought so desperately to reach. She sustained her single-handed grasp on him with negligible effort, without so much as a bobble, the sinewy reserve at her disposal so ample that he saw no gain in giving struggle. This wasn't to say that he didn't trifle with the inclination to riffle off a series of defensive, bicycling kicks in order to free himself from her control—he did. But as she failed to inflict on him little more than a ferocious scrutiny, and as he couldn't help but notice the not-inconsiderable airspace beneath the cycling of his struggling legs, he knew that he was in no position to do anything but to hang there in wait of her whim.

Adversity, however, turned even more sour on his catching sight of the younger ferals, each of whom had emerged from the coppice behind the adult and were now inching forward in cautious hesitation.

Immediately Wagner set to squirming. His heart a bass drum pounding within his own ears, he now fought to break free, a lethal plummet of instantaneous death far preferable to the imminence of disembowelment. A single wildcat had been a terrifying enough executioner; a whole pride would literally make mincemeat of him.

The female, uninfluenced by his fitful wriggling, barely even acknowledged his efforts. His fate remained of her choosing, no matter how unmanageable he made himself.

In his throes, Wagner never once averted his eyes from the curious whelps, even though he perceived less in their bearing to regard as hostile than in their alarming appearance. Their ears flat like the female's, their white eyes wide and probing, in their forward creep they bared no incisors, nor did they exhibit the anticipatory frothing of predators before the kill. More the look of guarded wonder, none of them had the smallest gleam of the Reaper in his stare, not like the parent creature in whose clutch Wagner hung like a hooked trout.

Evidently puzzled by the older one's interest in Wagner—or perhaps by her delay in making quick work of him—they eyed Wagner with great fascination, and he, them. When they'd neared to within a few strides of the female's hindquarter, she growled out several curt syllables of guttural parlance, at which all of them immediately halted, and thereafter, remained so still that they could have been carved of stone. Her inspection of Wagner just about at end, the werecat's aggression gradually stood down as she traded ferocity for intrigue. Up close, Wagner could do precious little in his pendency but to reciprocate her eerie scrutiny. And in all, even his discomposure couldn't eclipse the fact that she was an exceptional specimen—lean, long-limbed and powerful, with an impressively chiselled musculature under dense, buttery-tan fur. She stood on foot-paw hybrids, roughly the shape and size of human feet but with both outer toes slightly larger and longer than the inner three, and the additional advantage of an extra phalange per digit—the distinguishment, perhaps, that allowed her to maintain equilibrium on the ridge in spite of Wagner's offsetting weight.

Her claws also boasted the extra joint, but this was only secondary to Wagner's most pertinent find, namely that each claw came equipped by nature with not one, but *two* opposable thumbs! The bonus thumb occupying the pinkie-spot on each hand/claw, it seemed that the female and her kind enjoyed twice the biological superiority of the most vaunted of traits, argued by many a highfalutin theorist as the primatial exaltation over all so-called "lesser" species. Meaningless rhetoric in this light, Wagner could only marvel in astonishment. Had he been of a mind to speculate, he'd have guessed that the discovery of such physical distinction in so base and tameless a being would have silenced even the most arrogant anthropocentric. Yet, all that he could personally affirm by his own experience was that it provided for his adversary's superior dexterity and, more consequentially relevant, her utterly unbustable grip.

Despite the splendidness of her physical specimen, the werecat exuded an extraordinary ferocity—particularly in her lineaments—that Wagner might have been able to treat with greater dispassion had he the leisure of a face-to-face without the imperilment levelled against his person. Her fangs were ever discased in threat, although by this time she'd retracted the snarl to the point where only her canines and the tines of her incisors remained as dissuaders to any sudden foolishness that Wagner might have been considering. Her eyes, entirely void of irises, offered only slices of pupils within a considerable sclera, and the effect promoted an air of diabolism that was perhaps more perceived than genuine (he had, after all, been at her mercy for several minutes and was still drawing breath). Furthering the incongruity, her actions—or, more precisely, her lack of them— revealed less than malevolent underscorings. Her hide, formerly a bristly erection of classic fight-or-flight edginess, had eased back into standby mode along with her ears and whiskers. Even her grasp had notched a gradation looser, just barely enough to remedy the bloodlessness that was making Wagner's hand feel more like a graft of prosthetic flesh. She was a creature in deliberation, a trawler whose dredge turned up a curiosity she'd not expected, and the call was hers as to whether to haul it in or cut it free.

The luxury of deciding would be moot, however, for the air about them suddenly whistled sharp from a volley of arrows—all near-misses save for one dead-eyed bolt that found its mark deep in the fleshy portion of the feline's thigh.

With an ungodly wail she swung protectively toward her young, inadvertently yanking Wagner up to high ground, where his momentum sent him a-sail like an Olympic hammer. Sprawling into the very dangle of vinery from which the female's kits had emerged, its weave of creepers and the light copse behind it eased the jolt of his impact to the extent that he brooked no serious hurt other than an acrobat's disorientation. His faculty sluggish in its reclamation, he was not so addled, however, that he missed the feline's slapdash herding of her brood into the woods; and he knew that to survive he had to follow her lead.

Crouched tortoise-like in his windedness, Wagner summoned back his breath and brought himself about. The arrows, he now surmised, had originated from across the ravine, a mixed band of longbow and crossbow archers positioned at the far ridge. Noises from the gully below likewise suggested the clamber of foot-soldiers scaling the incline in the same manner that he had.

A second spread of missiles whizzed over his head, with yet another fateful bolt finding mark in the least fleet of the retreating brood. The female, having deftly wrenched out the arrow of her own impalement, raced back to the injured one's aid, scooping the adolescent up and coarsely urging the others to flee. Advice he himself took to heart, Wagner put all of his grit into a mad scramble after them, a third rain of arrows riddling the air as he ploughed headlong into the cover and onward through veil after veil of greenery and concealing shadow.

It never dawned on him not to follow the pride, not to hold their course as opposed to choosing his own escape. As kindred quarry, it perhaps made sense to ignore their obvious differences until they could elude the common pursuer. As creatures of the wood, the cats certainly knew the terrain better than he, and this made for one less decision to get in the way of his terror. Yet, the more probable truth was that Wagner didn't think about it at all. Like the rest of the pack, he simply relied on internal facility to wrest him from the situation; by flying on instinct he could more easily by-step the tripwires that conscious debate too often strung across his field of reason. Whatever his prompting, it was born of solitary focus, the pain of his abraded flesh and his battered joints left back at the ridge like so much moult. His retreat was one of a man possessed—a condition that he was not unacquainted with—and in the space of a few seconds he'd actually narrowed the gap to within mere strides of the fugitive ferals who, for a very brief moment, had become his allies by default in a crisis more imminently crucial.

Were he not in the midst of such direness, Wagner might have found the stretch of woodlands over which he hurtled to be particularly lush and verdurous, fragrant with the musty-sweet scent of duff and decaying bark, flagrant with enough varieties of fungi to fill any botanist's day with thoughtful insight. Instead, each tree was suspect; each bush, a potential blind for ambush; every falling acorn, the footfall of an enemy's slinking. A brief glance back through the underwood brought verification that the soldiers were indeed in distant pursuit, their numbers not yet great, but anticipatorily overwhelming. Within minutes, once their brethren had crossed the coulee, the glut of infantry was sure to whittle down Wagner's odds of an escape clean and everlasting.

With the underbrush congested and the tree limbs drooping closely overhead, Wagner suspected that those of his pursuers who hefted bows would find scant opportunity for unobstructed launching. Thus, he knew that as long as he and his unlikely cohorts could at least maintain their lead over those soldiers who carried close-quarter arms—and whose bulky trappings stymied their progress through the thicket—the possibility of evading the whole unit would be greatly enhanced.

With the injured kit still tucked underarm like a duffel, the female trailed the brood, allowing them to blaze the way out while proffering herself as the greater target for any rearward assault. Wagner remained in close proximity, sometimes following, more often paralleling, their course by a few metres so as to insinuate himself only marginally, with no outward presumption or parity or demonstrated insolence toward the matriclan's sense of unity. At times he wished that he'd opted for some other route, for he in fact feared them equally as much as he did the brutish foot soldiers, even to the point of fancying himself more as their lunch-on-the-go than as their fellow hunted. But whatever beef she may or may not have had with him, the foe they fled was common to them both, and—all naïveté aside—such was enough for the present.

Unbeknownst to Wagner, their path had taken an overall crescent trajectory, veering so broadly that it knocked him for a loop when they emerged from cover atop the very ridge that overlooked the stream he'd been following not twenty minutes before. Startled, he skidded to a dirt-strewing halt to contemplate his best interests, leaving the cats to continue on their career down the slope like slalom skiers going for gold. Fifty metres or so back upstream, nearly obscured by the sharp veer of confluence, he could see the mouth of the gully where it had all begun, although no soldiers—other than the three corpses—were anywhere near the juncture.

Here, a critical decision: was he to remain in the company of the felids, or leave them to their private war with the soldiers? True, the pride had tolerated him this far, but his reprieve had been one of time borrowed. He had no guarantee that they would not later turn on him. Yet, if he parted from their company, would that throw the soldiers off of his own trail? Was it honourable to bow out thusly, and allow these creatures to draw the soldiers, draw the whole bloody conflict, as far from him as they possibly could?

Nodding to self-preservation, his survival won the toss. Keeping to the ridge, he silently bade the enemy of his more copious enemy a respectful farewell and hied off in his original downstream heading. Cowardly act or not, this was never his skirmish, and if he found the means to extricate himself from the equation, so much the better.

The pride, on reaching the bottom of the glen, forded the shallows of the waterway, their crossing and subsequent scaling of the opposite side presumably a strategy to tire and discommode their overladen opposition. Two of the adolescents scampered up first, assisted the third in reaching topside, and then all three waited anxiously, arms dangling in bated biddance, to aid the female in gaining ground with their sibling.

Wagner gave over one last glance. The werecat, with her injured kit now draped over her shoulder, climbed the valley's moderate slope like a spider stringing webbing across a familiar cranny. Never doubting that she would reach the top easily, Wagner swung forward toward his own salvation, desperate to put as much distance behind him as he possibly could before the threat of soldiers issuing from the thicket coerced his re-entry into the copse. Yet, in the midst of final adieu, an indismissable distraction to his rear induced him to twirl askance for a final look-see, and it was here that he fixed upon exactly what he'd hoped not to: four archers, newly broken from the woods, all in the midst of targeting the stalled pride across the way.

Conscience forced Wagner to a dead stop.

Darting behind the nearest trunk, he peered back in hope of seeing the female hoisting herself over the ridge and vanishing with her brood into the far thicket without incident. Instead, he witnessed a spritz of arrows cutting across the breach, arcing toward the spot on the incline where she was still in climb. None found its mark, but each struck dangerously close, one only a few decimetres from her shoulder, and Wagner feared that unless she doubled her effort the next volley would bring fatal consequence. Without truly understanding his impellent, Wagner sprang to. Doubling back from just inside the timberline, moving almost independent of thought, he snapped up the sturdiest length of fallen hardwood he could find, and then raced whip and spur in the very direction that better sense forbade him.

Another salvo of missiles spat across the valley airspace. The female was not far from the top, but in transferring the kit from her shoulder to her breast in order to shield him, she'd sorely governed her mobility by forfeiting an arm that could greatly have accelerated her ascent. Indeed, when the arrows hailed, one caught her in the extreme left flank—and, by the spasmodic nature of pain, forced her relinquishment of the incline.

Clods and rocks and uprooted plugs of grass accompanying her plummet, she lost several precious metres before finding a staving handhold, the abruption of which should have been enough to rip her arm from its socket. Unfazed, however—or at least not giving in to what must have been inordinate distress—with her arm still clamped around her stripling she commenced a crazed, all-out blitz for the top before any subsequent launching did her in.

With bows refixed, and with reinforcements closing in, the soldiers made ready for another barrage, the werecat's setback as good as cinching their victory. None of them suspected the unknown quantity in their midst.

Armed only with a bough, James Wagner ploughed into all four soldiers, bowling them headlong over the crest in a clanking, concussive tangle of arms and accoutrements. Wambling and somersaulting like a cut-rate circus act, the once cocksure archers struck the valley basin in a manner mirroring that of their unfortunate counterparts upstream.

Wagner's own momentum took him belly-down to the edge of the slope, arms draping over the declivity, both hands still gripping the limb that he'd used to topple his antagonists from their perch. Below him, said soldiers lay writhing and dazed and infinitely worse for wear. Across the span, a group of furred onlookers gawked dumbfounded at what had just occurred. Even the werecat herself had halted in her efforts, and craned over shoulder and expanse to view in disbelief her divested assailants, and then, he who'd divested them.

Rising to his knees, Wagner realised that he only had moments before the next rush of soldiers broke from the foliage. He further realised that, by acting, he had tossed his freedom to the wind. Willingly, foolishly, for a noble cause, for a futile one—in all possibility he might never know. Bereft of all but one option, to the din and bluster of the fast approaching horde he hurled himself over the ridge. Sliding, skidding, churning up topsoil like a renegade auger, he reached the bottom, raced on bloodied feet past the prostrated soldiers, penetrated the shallows, and was en route up the other side in less than thirty seconds.

The female, nearing the end of her climb and already hoisting her unconscious whelp toward the others, clung with her free claw to a crag just below the lip.

While the hand-off occurred, Wagner scaled his way up to them, unable to truly concern himself with their progress, since newly launched arrows were now pelting the incline around him from across the expanse.

Her wounded kit transferred to its siblings, the arrow-pierced female renewed her grip and heaved herself to within a half-metre of the top. A quick gaze downward, she cast an uninterpretable leer at the virtually hairless figure scurrying up at her heels. She snarled annoyance, and then growled even more contemptuously at the opposite ridge, where tens of figures had begun working their way down while others mated missiles to bowstrings and aimed said barbs and bolts in her direction.

Her debate at end, with blinding swiftness she descended two rungs of previous footholds and swooped down for Wagner. Surprised and grateful, he countered her lead, transcending comfort and overextending his arm until once again she had him by the wrist. Projectile upon projectile pinking the terrain around them, that none found flesh was hardly a saving grace; for, in the end, it took but one shaft's errancy to divest them of success—one shaft that, in striking a rocky protrusion dangerously close to the she-cat, disintegrated on impact and sprayed her anchoring claw with a painful scatter of shivers.

Her grip suddenly compromised, the creature lost her mooring and went into freefall, crashing smack onto Wagner and sweeping them both groundward like a scaffold in collapse. Glancing the many jags along the downward slope, their coupled bodies pitched and tumbled and flounced in helpless embranglement, careering them ever closer to the streambed, ever closer to defeat.

Without leverage or control, Wagner was helpless to protect himself. Pain so far off the chart that his nervous system seized from overload, all he could do was to brace and hang tough. Yet, beyond the fourth or fifth contusive blow, he became too sloppy-headed even for that.

On hitting bottom, he and she were thrown apart, Wagner landing on his back in all but complete oblivion. Too foggy to assess himself—and in no position to effect either his survival or his death—through a fast-encroaching darkness his eyes happened upon the visages of three furred faces, way on high, who for a moment peered down from the ridge-top as if into a chasmal grave. Then they were gone. And Wagner, almost gone himself, gleaned as if through a darkling tunnel the clanging vestments and the gruff laughs of the henchmen who now drew around him like jackals; and sensing a path into unconsciousness he quickly willed himself beyond the veil before they could deliver unto him the quietus that, regardless, would see him into his doom.

CHAPTER SIX

Virtue is like a rich stone, best set plain.
—FRANCIS BACON

Magdelena Escalante leaned forward in her seat, chin resting atop clenched hands. Her dark brown eyes fixed on an indefinable point of reference between where she sat and the room's far wall, she rocked slowly within the muted stillness of the facility's common waiting area, wondering how much more she had to witness before everything was made clear. Beside her, Nettie and Pete "the Pup" lay nestled in mutual doze on the Centre's butternut settee. Conked out, they were the casualties of over three hours of waiting, the powwow in the next room having gone officially into overtime as the doctors continued levelling question after question at *Miracle* on the remote chance that his insight could help them make sense out of the day's impossibility.

To look at the two of them, wrapped in a snoozy snuggle under a pilfered hospital blanket, Maggie was reminded of her poor kitties, Alonso and Bob, and how they too had always found a way of choosing the oddest times and places in which to pile up in nap, oblivious to setting and circumstance.

She smiled at the comparison—a brief and infusive smile. The recollection, no matter how poignant or how fondly cherished, could not be experienced without an indelible bittersweetness. La Junta was a long time ago, and if not by the calendar then by the amount of industry she'd crammed into the last few years. The immediacies of crusade and quest having detruded life's quainter simplicities for the nonce, only now was she coming to recognise that in her vigour she'd brushed aside so many of the things in her life that she genuinely cherished.

It still pained her to think about Alonso and Bob, even as the better part of a decade had elapsed since their passing, one just a week apart from the other. To this day, she would go to her grave believing that poor Bob died solely out of grief for his long time companion and abettor in mischief. Imps they had been, truly incorrigible ones—houseplant maimers, knickknack topplers, bed sheet spelunkers, newspaper wallowers. Too often of one mind, in joint venture they'd been known to nick off with their fair share of hair curlers and cotton swabs, rubber bands and trial-size toiletries—any doodad whose tumble value was deemed worthy of a good pounce. Ordinary kibble being the reigning house favourite, for a general good time they would practice slapshooting individual kernels across the kitchen tiles until Mama screamed bloody murder. No human ever completely appreciating the gravity of the feline obligation, these two lovable mongrels strived daily to satisfy theirs, happily flocking their dander over skirts and blouses with artistic generosity, leaving hairball surprises in Papa's slippers and in other largely uncongenial places, knocking figurines, remotes, and reading glasses off of nightstands. Their hunting instincts they placated in the ravaging of many an unsuspecting brassiere, which, in a household with five women, were in far more abundance than mice in a barn. Two critters so apparently mortised in thought, action, and soul, Maggie often believed that they'd originally been just one cat whose more than ample mischievousness required a second body to contain it. So utterly inseparable in life, in the end it somehow seemed that Death could not take one without the other.

Although Maggie could never suppress the heartbreak she'd felt at losing them both in such abrupt succession, even at fifteen she had already come to understand the monumental power of devotion, and she remembered wishing that one day she, too, might find some kindred for whom she would feel that deeply. Fate, however, would first spur her in other directions, the remainder of her adolescence progressing and passing devoid of any profound or enamouring attachments. History would instead note the expansion of a young woman's consciousness as Maggie grew to confront the world around her, as she came to question the unhealthy avarice and narcissism so prevalent in modern life, as she responded by lobbying for the old-fashioned values of altruism and virtue, inner fortitude and character, that in her estimation too few people utilised to even nominal potential. Not only would these years see her come of age, but they bore witness to the percipient evolution of a spirit that left little room for frivolity, and just as little for structured academics. A firebrand of independence and impetuosity, she was hardly the type to pine away her youth in wait for some phantasy soulmate whom she had yet to encounter. Neither would she allow her life to become a series of mundane eventualities the benignity of which might dull her edges in the manner that aeons of running water erode the sharpest of crags. Rather, she would choose to cultivate on her own the essences and experiences and self-exploration that, by her determination, needed sating before she could subject herself to any extensive commitments of either amorous or academic natures.

Formulated over the span of her busy adolescence, Maggie's approach to life varied considerably from that of her sisters and cousins and peers. Blessed with intelligence and a splendidly recusant unconventionality, she'd always found herself too short on sufferance for the rituals of role-playing and affectation and courtship and such, and far too long on restlessness to fritter several long years away in academic study, preparing, as her oldest sisters had, for the banal or non-existent careers netted them by their college degrees. Never actually disputing the importance of social interaction and education, it was more Maggie's disregard for hackneyed propriety that drove her to be the way she was—a disregard that was excusable in fine because it was an honest and pure one, stemming from youthful exuberance and a candid (and granted, sometimes a naïve) penchant for challenging conformity.

By no means, however, had she ever limited her contraposition to mere dinner table or classroom forum. Quite the social scrapper, she was more the type to deluge the local paper with scathing editorials that criticised the lemmings of society who executed their dronish routines with self-serving complacency while so much of the world stood in need of bettering. She accused the masses of embracing celebrity over philanthropy, profit over charity, charged them with mislaying their humanity—or worse, trading it for dollars in their Grail-like obsession for gratification. Never an outright attack, her method had been more one of shaming people into questioning their destructive myopia. To her, the unproductive practises of self-promotion and acquisitiveness were only for the short-sighted, for those who favoured golden calf over golden rule. Just as severely did she come down on those of the righteous who she felt had fallen asleep at the wheel. Faith, she stressed, was not about dressing up and sitting like robotic dullards through mass; faith was about putting oneself on the line every day amid iniquity. So wearied, in fact, was she by her own congregation's mumbling of the same old versicle responses in church without truly heeding the enlightenment they contained, that she likened them to those whom Jesus accused of stowing lamps under bushels. She blasted people who married for the purpose of staving loneliness or for fitting in, had children for the sake of prestige or to bolster some failing self-worth, amassed estates and automobiles and finery in order to garner status or to seduce. Such things were for hypocrites and for the hedonists who didn't give a plum whether or not their potentials went unrealised. Maggie wasn't one to be taken in by any such allure, nor *would* she be; she wanted none of it. Her manifesto was considerably *muy grande* than that—perhaps more than she herself even knew.

A perspicacious young woman, her interests always leaped beyond her years. Alternately fascinated and disgusted by politics and world affairs, she allied herself with the human condition and set about to rectify life in any small way she could. Burgeoning with youthful ideals and opinions, armed with remedies for to cure the world's shortcomings, by her nineteenth year she was already long inured to bellying-up at life's gaming tables, where only the bold and the innovative had the grit to even dare to circumvent the house rules of precedent and convention. That had truly been a challenging time for her. Rarely ever settling for orthodoxism, she'd thrown herself time and again into the kinds of social and intellectual adversity that force-bloomed one's maturity. On college campuses and in town hall squares she'd lent herself to environmental causes, campaigned for social, political, and religious reform, rallied for human rights, criticised and openly denounced what she coined as a "derailment of the essential nature of religion itself." Wherever the issues were the meatiest, that was where she thrived. Two years she spent thusly, almost three. Eventful times, compelling times, each new cause sustaining her systemically, aiding her growth, enriching her soul, giving rise to the roborant outspokenness that her family sometimes found difficult to accept—and yet none of it ever seemed quite enough to satisfy Maggie's loftier desires. As few people understood her fervour (and even fewer *wanted* to), she recruited experience and perseverance as her best allies, and with time itself still in copious supply, the wheel of her personal destiny turned in steady spin. New opportunity and commitment sprang from each setback and every victory. Girlish dreams became displaced by the sway of discovery and change. And Maggie, a dauntless young advocate for social consciousness, grew to become a remarkable woman who, despite the barriers of geographic limits and demographic apathy, absolutely refused to lead an unremarkable life.

Enter the man called *Miracle*.

He was hardly the dark and mysterious stranger of her sisters' dopey romance novels. Nevertheless, he *was* a dark and mysterious stranger. He was a man who exhibited not only an appealingly unlikely mélange of staunchness, benevolence, and social detachment, but who possessed enough charisma to wed these qualities to one another in the seamless packaging of a single individual. Hopelessly eccentric, innately honourable, often unintentionally goofy, he was in whole far more than could be ignored by a woman whose own complexities were equally unique.

But Maggie was no pushover, even for a man of such fiery good nature and perception. True, it hadn't taken the eerily insightful *Miracle* long to discern her innermost vulnerabilities, but with them he'd also learned that, come the first signs of oppugnancy, here was one woman who could erect an attitudinal carapace capable of withstanding regimental assault. How often would he declare that, once bent on a mindset, Maggie would see her adversary "grow wizened and expire" before she deviated from it. And this part of her he knew, perhaps better than did her own family, knew that if she held the world to such severe standards, she would expect no less from herself. Ever did he witness how she brought herself to task, her unabashed ideals of liberality and livelihood bolstered by a host of structural spot-welds—many of them courtesy of the steadfast teachings lifted from the very same Catholic tradition she'd come to criticise. A spiritual archaeologist, she believed that contemporary worshippers needed to sweep away the years of obfuscating sediment in order to rediscover God in His most pure and basic form, free of ornamentation, free of stained glass and candelabras and palatial churches. And such abnegation being *Miracle's* apparent forte, theirs was an acquaintanceship destined to be struck. After all, their first encounter revealed to her an intensely cerebral eremite who performed unreciprocatory acts of kindness—how much more akin to her in philosophy could someone be?

Still, it couldn't be denied that he differed in myriad ways from every other male Maggie had ever run into. Pleasantly reserved of ego, *Miracle* was yet confident, sensitive, and sensible beyond what seemed proper for a man of his idiosyncratic propensities. There was a surety to his core that easily surmounted what was either a type of mild, cultural ineptitude or an introversion amplified by his apparently intentional withdrawal from greater society. Quite simply, he made her curious in all the best ways. Without even trying, or even wishing it, he'd endeared her from the get-go.

Unlike her sisters—who were a flighty, fickle, materialistic lot—Maggie was never one to dwell much on a person's outward appearance. But here again, *Miracle* was something to behold, as fit a specimen of the masculine metaphor as she had ever seen, yet whose own aesthetically athletic qualities concerned him only minimally, as if he not so much took them for granted, but dismissed them as mere elements constituent to one's overall essence. Likewise, though his constitutional complexities intrigued her, and his avenues of reason came fresh and virtually free of the paradigms that bogged down so many otherwise bright people, the fact that in their year of collaborating—his, some obscure visionquest for righteous understanding; hers, an effort to pry open the eyes of a self-centred populace—*Miracle,* an uncommon man of peculiar drive and ideals, had never once used the intricacies of their friendship to compromise her in any way, not physically, not emotionally, not financially either. And while this should have been a much welcomed rarity to be sure, it was perhaps not quite as welcomed here as she would have wished—his emotional insouciance somehow managing to nudge at her in ways that she would rather have not have been nudged, putting the nature of both their affinity and their sodality at question and suggesting a detachment in him that she might never quite bridge, despite the fastness and depth of their camaraderie. It was something she just wasn't used to. Back home, too often to her unending embarrassment, she'd been considered the most handsome of the Escalante daughters. Unfortunately, she was also the most brooding, and as these two qualities twined within the same woman translated less to most men as an unattainability than as a challenge, the crush of unwanted vying, wooing, and pursuit was given to exponential inflation. Early on she would discover—granted, first to her youthful delight, but then to a more matured dismay—how one's appearance bore such prodigious correlation to the attention heaped upon said person, especially by the disingenuous and the duplicitous. This sort of shallowness quickly became a bore to her, a nuisance; and Maggie—prudish perhaps, but still no iceberg—soon and out of necessity appropriated a considerable amount of cranial real estate in which to house her growing cynicism after fending off so many curious boys (and later, men) who approached her exhibiting the guise of moral integrity, yet whose rather singular interest had been in compromising hers.

Luckily (although no one had thought so at the time), Papa's ultimately fair but hard-nosed fathering had succeeded in holding the local boys at distance from his precious girls through many a full moon and Saturday night mixer during those crazy, hormone-riddled days of high school. But now, at twenty-four and free of Papa's well-intended guardianship, Maggie—a junior college dropout and card-carrying idealist—had never established a really meaningful relationship with anyone; and time and anew she wondered if someone so attuned to the human condition yet so obtuse to the mechanics of the modern age as was *Miracle* even came close to making a match with her gung ho impetuosity, her headstrong opinions, or her penchant for demonstrative radical thought.

Yet, that was before the smoke and mirrors. Only, as things turned out, *Miracle's* abilities were anything but. It was evident to Maggie from the first that the manner in which he perceived and revered the natural world was quite incongruous with coeval life, almost as if in his philosophy he revisited an antiquity when existence seemed considerably more subsumed by the mystical. A back-country benevolist, he demonstrated more than just a compassion for all things living; he had an enigmatic, almost venerable, gift for comforting people, for lifting them up out of their suffering, for melding them with some greater spiritual intrinsicality that might never have manifested but for his gentle manipulations. These traits alone had been enough to intrigue her during a simple flyer-posting stop at that little mission way outside of Las Animas, where his path and hers converged in serendipitous carom. Here had been a man, green and apparently freshly emigrated from Belarus or Ukraine or some other still non-divulged Eastern Bloc nation, a man whose voice rang faintly with the best playful euphonies of classic Boris Badanov, but whose more subtle qualities blended a sage's eloquent charm with a phantast's emotive idealism. Yet, simultaneously here was an individual who rejected both contemporary mores and perhaps even some of his own charismatic potential in order to approach life from a truly Baptistesque perspective, subsisting on the Bent County equivalent of wild locusts and honey and such, while meting aid and compassion to any bedraggled soul whom Fate sent his way.

Maggie remembered thinking how blessed was he to have found his niche in helping those less fortunate, with nary a concern for his own comforts. You just didn't meet people like him every day. His methods mystified her, tweaked at her, stoked some of the inspirational fires that she'd believed had been snuffed out long ago by habitual disappointment or disillusionment. In fact, so refreshing had she found *Miracle* that she'd stayed on at that ramshackle mission for three days just to observe and to exchange ideas—living out of her old '70 Kingswood station wagon, bathing by way of outdoor spigot, even convincing the strange and overdisciplined ascetic that it was okay to nosh on a Milky Way or a Twinkie now and then instead of his usual tumbleweed. This marked the onset of what was to evolve into a uniquely reciprocal bond, and furthermore established the genesis of their considerable—albeit wholly (and perhaps *holy!*) unpredictable—journey. Indeed, having begun as one animal, it was swift to morph into something decidedly different, making theirs a path upon which neither alone might ever have trodden. Yet, for all of the discovery in store, for all of the truly eye-opening, Kleenex-prompting, grab-the-Kodak moments to come, she never really understood how involved, how amazingly convoluted and incredible, was *Miracle's* gift until months later on that chilly, chilling March morning back in La Junta, when tragedy quite nearly shattered a handful of lives. That morning changed everything for her.

"Would you like something to drink? Some juice, or maybe a soda?"

Maggie looked up to find Sally Lemanski leaning warmly into her face.

"No. No thank you." Extending her arms, she locked her fingers and cracked her knuckles in a lengthy, tendinous stretch. "I'm almost tempted to ask for a good stiff drink after seeing what I thought I saw out there."

"Make mine a double! I don't think I'll ever get over that, and I've been associated with Mr. Wagner for the duration of all of his episodic monkeyshines. Some very mind-blowing roller coaster rides they were, too. You'd think I'd have gotten used to it by now." She glanced at the teens. "It's nice to see that somebody can actually *sleep* after witnessing the impossible."

"Hmm? Oh, *these* guys," Maggie boomed as she playfully thumped Petey's comatose shoulder. "Believe me, just give these two slugs a *hamaca* and they could saw logs through Armageddon itself!"

"That's really something. Reality itself splintered before their very eyes, yet they seem to have been largely unaffected by it. How do you explain that?"

"They're *teenagers.*"

The nurse gazed blankly at the two nodders, then back at Maggie. Both women burst out laughing.

"I mean it!" said Maggie. "I don't know what it is—internet overkill or ultra-techno video games, micro-miniaturised gadgetry or movie special effects or that virtual reality stuff that kids are all into these days—but these two hams on rye think that they've seen it all, and what they haven't seen isn't worth knowing about."

"They sound a lot like *my* kids," quipped Sally.

"Actually," Maggie added, "being around *Miracle* for the last few months has really jaded them as far as mystical manifestations go. Me—I've been with him since the beginning, since we started the fellowship, and I still have a hard time with it."

Sally cleared her throat. "Well, to be honest, I would have been highly sceptical of your friend's alleged abilities had I never witnessed the strange goings-on around here this past year. Everyone involved has had to redefine her sense of reality."

They re-ogled the teens for a moment, weathering an awkward pause before Maggie spoke again.

"Can I ask you something, Nurse...*Lemski* is it?"

"Lemanski. Sally. Sure, fire away."

"What are they doing in there—with *Miracle*?"

Sally slowly lowered herself into the chair next to the settee. "I couldn't tell you exactly. I imagine they're trying to put it all together, trying to determine the nature of what occurred out there. Maybe they're trying to figure how your friend fits in—why and how he seemed to have had an influencing effect on Mr. Wagner."

"Just who was this Wagner guy anyway?"

"At times, a very troubled soul. At others, a delightful human being. I can't begin to imagine how to describe him now. Maybe he wasn't a human being at all. I just don't know anymore. But there is one thing I *do* know."

"What's that?"

"I know that every time I look at your friend in there...for a split second...oh, this is going to sound so crazy..."

"What?"

"When I look at your friend...I somehow feel...like I'm seeing James Wagner."

The younger woman stared thoughtfully and intently at the older. Sally returned the stare with equal intensity. Maggie was the first to break the silence.

"You know what?"

"What?"

"I think I will have something after all."

"That stiff drink?"

Maggie dug around in her rucksack and produced a battered journal and an ink pen.

"Coffee. Black and lots of it."

CHAPTER SEVEN

Rousted from unconsciousness, Wagner came to in the midst of renewed savagery against his person. The unwitting focus of numerous drubbings and larrups lodged against him by indiscernible hands, between his mottling and their maul he could only wonder at the despicableness around him, that anyone would find it necessary to pummel an insensate man.

This gruffness actually precipitating his re-entry into cognition, he was quick to attach a sense of conveyance to his mishandling. That he was being moved was patent, but that he was subjected to such deliberate inconsideration gave him insight into how little his bearers valued him. In fact, once he'd recouped the best of his faculty, he found himself facing a scenario that promised far more downside than up.

Inwardly wrung by nausea, racked by widespread distension, it was all he could do not to pass out again, his musculature harrowed beyond limits that even a few rounds with the Incredible Hulk could not have inflicted. Yet, as his consciousness was much too flinty to give anything back to oblivion, he coped with his anguish, funnelling the whole of his resources into the self-preservation that he would surely be needing.

So completely at the mercy of external influence, there was no autonomy to be had, his extremities gripped by more gauntleted hands than he in his stupor-impaired wiriness could confound. Once able to focus, however, he deduced enough to realise that he was being extracted from a crudely wheeled gaol the design of which harked back to constructs of outright antiquity. Four wooden wheels, plated with hammered metal and mortised upon two log-like axles, they shouldered a caged platform that stood chest-high from the ground. With a base of coarse planking topped by serried gridiron fortification and inwardly aimed barbs, it was in all a stalwart and compact portable cell, and clearly one whose design was intended to accommodate far more remarkable prey than he. Evidently, while Wagner had been deemed worthy of at least a short jaunt therein, his new designation as catch-dog to a half-dozen armoured thugs was quite likely a ritualised retribution for his part in the premature deaths of their compeers.

It was equally conceivable, however, that his scourging had less to do with the events back at the gorge than with simple zealotry, anger, frustration, enmity, or any of a hundred retaliatory instigations. Barring the whys and wherefores for his more painful immediacy, all that Wagner had the leisure to assume was that he'd been peeled from the valley basin, transported within the aforementioned contraption for some irretraceable period of time, and now removed for the purpose of extradition, assassination, or what would amount to a generally good roughing up. All things considered, he would rather have been in Philadelphia.

To his relief and chagrin, he was promptly unhanded, only to be thrust forthwith into the press of a pair of shackles. One soldier tasked with abutting them to Wagner's wrists, a second soldier affixed them by means of what appeared to be an old-fangled crimping tool. Once accomplished, said crimper was traded for a straight peen hammer, at which time his ruffian smithies fitted him with a whopping set of leg irons, clasped with double cotters driven neatly through each cuff.

Enduring all, Wagner nevertheless fidgeted uncomfortably within the overbearance of his captors. His breast scarcely able to contain the drumfire of a panicky heart, the mettle of his limbs likewise found itself undermined by an enfeebling dread inpoured of his body's own chemistry. The fact of his nakedness amplified his anxiety, making him feel small and helpless like a mouse in a lair of pit vipers, and his dignity quickly gave way as he huddled comparatively scrawny and pale in his chains among beings outfitted in ebon-metalled prostheses of intimidatingly robust design. His obvious befuddlement seemed an invitation to his captors, for he was bullied into even greater subservience during his induction, persuaded to keep his eyes lowered, finding that if he didn't the soldiers would berate him and slap at his ears like an errant puppy that wouldn't use its papers. To keep such wrath at a minimum, any visual reconnoitring on his part had to be accomplished by means of rapid and disjointed peripherals, each one furtively executed in hopes of discerning to what end his misfortune had truly led him. Such total providence unfortunately not immediately forthcoming, in stealing a few selective glimpses of the areas just beyond the transport and the host of archaically brutal enslavers, he did chance upon two discoveries of unforeseen magnitude.

Twenty or so paces off, he made out a distant entourage of beings not at all unlike himself, a procession of bedraggled people on foot, men and women—a few adolescents as well—garbed in various stages of dishabille and shackled in the same manner as he. They stood silently grim and in neglect, like needy passengers on an invisible bus whose transit had been interrupted in order to take on a new fare. Wagner had little doubt as to who that rider was.

Needless to say, his conception of futurity was not a particularly delightful premise. Yet, somewhere deep in his gut, amid the fracas of unsurety and trepidation and outright panic, he did manage to breathe one pint-sized little sigh of belated relief: he had finally come across beings who were neither felid savages nor panoplied hoodlums, but were instead seemingly ordinary, garden-variety people.

Granted, it didn't speak well for him, his taking solace in having found others who shared in his burden; but given the circumstances he didn't think anyone would seriously begrudge an inclination over which he had no control. So much had occurred since he last swirled a fork around a glob of institutional mashed potatoes, so much that simply didn't fall within the realm of typical bender manifestations. And now, the introduction of congenerous beings within this newest venue of madness-gone-madder suddenly prompted more questions than could easily be squelched. To be sure, Wagner was not without sympathy for their likened status as prisoners—if not already identifying with them, he was well underway—but he quite understandably felt more immediate concern for his own predicament. Selfish perhaps, but not heartless, he nonetheless drew some mote of twice-removed comfort in being shuffled in among his own kind at what may have been the eleventh hour of a very unpromising destiny.

But what, then, of the werecat? Wagner ran a quick eye over the throng, reconfirming that each of the forty to fifty figures was human. He next shot a lateral glance in either direction and, espying several more drays along the forest's narrow roadway, acknowledged the possibility that the female might have been housed within one of these somewhere up or down the line. Yet, with no cart but *his* being emptied of its inhabitants, no prisoner save *he* being made to join the dismal foot-parade, it seemed that his mystery would remain so. Unless somehow through guile or skirmish or blind luck the female had managed to escape capture back at the valley—and judging by the bruising he'd incurred in breaking her fall, this was a fair bet—the possibility existed that she'd been slain at the site. Otherwise, he saw no immediate evidence of her anywhere—no sign of her subjugation by any soldiers ahead or behind, nor any espial of her in those drays whose occupants he could distinguish.

His second discovery came with his occasion to better observe the odd sumpter animals yoked to the travelling hoosegows. Lumbering, appalling creatures in harness, Wagner found their supreme outlandishness no less in keeping with the other incongruities of his new environs. Quadrupedal and roughly the size of large oxen, these burthened beasties were possessed of thickly stout limbs, hoofed yet very paw-like in appearance, more akin to a lion's pad with a horny covering than to anything remotely bovine. They were tailless and hornless, and their hides were composed of swags of loose, leathery skin very much reminiscent of a Shar-Pei's. Yet, where upon the earthly canines this often appeared lazily quaint, perhaps even pathetically cuddly, on these behemoths it was at once ominous and absurd. As gravity would have it, this sagging epidermal excess draped most noticeably at the midsections and underbellies, with the softer collops around the animals' spines and necks noticeably less pronounced, and non-existent forward of the occipita. Their heads, to some degree smaller maybe than they should have been, boasted flexible proboscises not unlike those of earthly tapirs, with ears and mouths that were equally similar. Their eyes, however, differed to greater extent in that they were black and bulbous and round as radishes.

Inaccordant with their voluminous girth, as draught animals they appeared docile and complaisant in their capacity as wagon-jockeys to their militant masters, probably so domesticatedly dumb that they no longer even possessed sense enough to yearn for some more naturally pastoral existence apart from their long-conditioned servitude. A provocative allusion to what his own bondage might come to represent, Wagner vowed to not be quite so all-relinquishing to his capturers—unless, of course, it became highly requisite to his short-term survival. Were he not to snap back to his own reality anytime soon, it was likely that great concession would be inevitable in the coming hours (or days); and no doubt he would need to bend a principle or two if in the end it ransomed a means of acquittal or escape. Clearly, his options hung somewhere between seriously lacking and all but non-existent.

As if to substantiate this last assumption, Wagner suddenly found himself assaulted, struck from behind with vitriol enough to pitch him off-balance. Reflexes whirling him about in what would amount to an unengageable tat, he immediately came to face the business end of an extremely keen poignard, brandished by potentially the twitchiest of his new masters. Spouting unintelligible demands, said sentry pressed the weapon's tine into Wagner's sternum, the promise of puncture only an indiscretion away. And while the man's words were beyond Wagner's ken, their implication that he join the coffle required no translation.

Not daring to risk escalation, Wagner naturally complied, but not before purloining a forbidden glance at his antagonist's visage, partially detectable through the T-slot in his burgonet. Finding the lineaments in loom within to be far less extraordinary than the horrors conjured by his imagination, the discovery nevertheless did little to alleviate Wagner's wariness. Still, up until now all that he'd known about his enslavers had been limited largely to periphery and physical distance—first, at the valley, when events had succeeded one another with such haste, and then here, upon his waking, where staring at anything but one's own feet was curtly discouraged. In venturing this risky descry, the bulk of Wagner's more fearful devisings now succumbed to revelation somewhat more associable and less fantastic. He now had at least a single face by which to demystify one small gradation of his peril.

The soldier's features in many ways mirrored Wagner's and the other prisoners'. His head perhaps a tad more oblong, his jaw less broad and beardless and slightly jutted, his brow squared and generous—the design of his helmet at least allowed for this much scrutiny. One very notable departure, however, was evidenced in his unusual pigmentation—or lack thereof—for his complexion was an unvarying slate-grey. Certainly noteworthy, the trait in itself was not particularly compelling nor so very shocking, especially when set against the infinitely more outlandish werecats. It conveyed no real pallor or sense of morbidity as one might expect, and indeed complemented the features offered by the breach in his appliance. Proud, prominent nose, heavy-lidded charcoal eyes, thin, angular mouth—in combination they granted an unseemly augustness to this member of an otherwise brutish band of marauders whose flagrant disdain for the weak, the passive, and the heterogeneous, made everything else about them repulsive.

In his now-doubled capacity as both witness *and* wretch, Wagner could do naught but bow to the absolute ludicrousness and unreliability of physiognomy as a means of calibrating character. Truly, precious little of what he'd encountered since eructing into this alternate realm jibed at all with his pittance of comparative norms. Yet, with this coup of a partial disclosure of his captor's features, he'd confronted—even deconstructed—at least one of the more ghastly fabrications of his overreaching imagination. Not the hunter gorillas from *Planet of the Apes*, not the misshapen Moorlocks encountered by the Wellsian Time Traveller—these were beings only faintly removed in the physical sense from the humankind he knew, as well as from those who stood manacled across the way.

Revelation or not, it was no great source of comfort. The humankind he knew was more often than not a schismatic mess, often exhibiting no less cruelty nor any more nobility than all that he'd witnessed and been subjected to in the last few hours. Evidently, the capacity for good and evil and every gradation between them existed in all intelligent creatures.

One soldier coercing him into position, a second conjoined Wagner's wristlets to a curbing chain, a common tether drawn through the bracelets of every prisoner in the throng. He stood docile as they linked him in, stood the way a dog stands for the ceremony of the leash, and once integrated he was just as quickly disregarded. With reluctant compliance, then, he bade goodbye to his last vestige of freedom, since there would be no means now of hieing off, no manner of stealing away into some convenient clump of thicket along the trek to come. He had joined the file of the forlorn.

Amazingly, few of his fellow enslaved demonstrated more than a passing interest in him. Most chose to keep their eyes down, focused along the rutted thoroughfare that they stood upon. Those who dared to gamble a glance did so only briefly, perhaps with the expectation of stirring up a recollection of someone they may have known, or perhaps only to interpret some undefined minutia in Wagner's bearing that underscored his very obvious air of displacement. Aside from his complete nakedness, there was actually nothing physically to set him apart. And as for the group, their complexions varied from pale like his to darkly bronzed; tresses, from straight to undulated, and overwhelmingly brown and black in colour; features, from the classically-sculpted to the splendidly multifarious. A true mosaic of humanity, Wagner was but the newest of what, prior to the ponderous dampers of enslavement, was surely once a lively and animated lot.

As far as clothing, all were garbed in varying degree, many only in tatters, the majority of their attire consisting of stiffly woven fabrics and a miscellany of tawed leathers and peltry, with nary a representative of the cottons, the wools, the poly-blends of Wagner's infinitely more modern acquaintance. As for footwear, the great majority of the congregation did its moving about in primitive boots wrapped with taut braids of cloth or rawhide, with a few even infixed with a rudiment of eyeleted lacing. Others boasted a crude facsimile of Coppergate, a wieldy albeit delicate style of booty that, unfortunately, wasn't particularly suited to the kind of prolonged, terraqueous marching suddenly demanded of its occupants. Yet, even clapped-out footwear was an ultra-lavishness to the least of the thrall's have-nots, for this footsore bunch was forced either to make good with ordinary rags wound around the feet and bound with cording, or, like Wagner, to go divested of footgarb altogether.

Most unpalatable about his convergence with the throng was the unavoidably abrupt discovery that none of these people had been permitted to attend to the affairs of personal hygiene for several days at best. A rank displeasure that he had no option but to endure, these poor sad sacks had the smell of the barnyard about them, the grime and sebum that besmudged every neighbouring face suggesting that most of them had spent an unconscionable amount of time in their shackles. Their filth and dejection a dismal portent of his own future—and foulness— Wagner braced himself for the fulsomeness that severe unaccommodation would inevitably bring.

The call to commence sounded via a coarse relay of shouts echoed along the column. In reply, the coffle lurched forward with the collective groanings of an old freighter gearing up for one final run before the scrap yard. A morass of stumbling feet and kinking irons, it took several shuffling steps for everyone to fall into a synchronous gait whereby the chain's inconvenience found even distribution among its bearers.

Although dissension hung thick about the group, everyone took to the march with prompt, if begrudging, steps. Wagner could only imagine the penalty for lollygagging, and so put forth his staunchest effort. That he was the freshest addition to the queue did little to induce his confidence, for he fully anticipated to pay the price for his more sedentary existence of the last ten months, and suspected that in his unaccustomedness he would see his own endurance wane long before fatigue even began to deplete his hardier peers.

The wheeled vehicles appeared fairly evenly situated throughout the greater procession, with groups of soldiers likewise dispatched at various interstices up and down the line. Those of greater rank rode atop some of the wagons; some even sat astride specially accoutred mounts of the same species that drew the drays.

At the rear of the chain gang, Wagner's even graver predicament was that he marched only ten paces or so ahead of roughly thirty troops, each of them heavily armed with spears, poleaxes, halberds and such. Not just for intimidation, these weapons saw occasional, even intermittent, use along the way in the scourging of Wagner and his forehand neighbours for such inferred trifles as straying beyond proper file or lacking verve in one's step. An adverse arrangement that continually placed the prisoners in the direct line of scrutiny, it had the single advantage of permitting Wagner to eavesdrop on the dialectal maffling taking place within the conquering ranks that, although initially alien to Wagner's ears—and therefore inconsiderable—would shortly prove of revelatory consequence.

Had it remained completely foreign to him, a garbled tongue of unknown derivation—like those first words of beration hurled at him by his shackler— Wagner might have been satisfied in concluding that he truly had phased into another reality. Logic may have granted him this, even given the extreme far-fetchedness of the premise. Yet, as the impossible and the farfetched were already regular staples in his life, the manner in which he perceived them was not nearly as important as the means by which they would recreate his ever-changing sense of reality. The many anomalies so representative of his madness had always been component to his particular normalcy, an evolving catalogue of personal oddities, subject to revision at a moment's notice by the never-seen and surreptitious Guardians of Disorder who apparently delighted in invalidating every theory as quickly as he developed one. In keeping, this newest manifestation was almost too convenient to be believed; for Wagner, in lending audience to the prattle behind him, slowly began discerning in the soldiers' dialogue—*dare he suppose it?*—an increasing scintilla of genuine comprehension.

A mere intimation at first (just a word here and there), followed by insinuation (phrases, clauses), until all too soon he found himself grasping simple remarks and expressions with a spontaneous sort of competence that quickly had him unriddling his captors' exchanges in the manner that one recollects snippets of a second language studied long ago yet believed forgotten over too many years of neglected practise. More than partial phrases, more than isolated words scattered within a greater context, somehow Wagner's lingual ear began to extract and to make sense out of what he was hearing, even as there was no conceivable reason that he should possess the history from which to do so, no assonant or associative prompters to ring in the familiar, no means with which to assess recognition of what should rightly have been indecipherable.

But there he was, listening to sound bites of one soldier's griping about insufficient stipend for thankless duties, and then the next's, about his boots not fitting his feet correctly. Still another shared his desires to return to home and family, at which he incurred the hoots and the reproachful machismo of those in the group who clearly favoured wantonness over domesticity. At times, in their manful baseness, they could almost have passed for some of the Filthy Lucre's patrons, so comparable was the sentiment and camaraderie in their perpetual complaint and brazen peacocking. On the other hand, these clods were ages off from Wagner's old regulars. Their vernacular more archaic, they employed an unlikely formality of structure, even amid the bawdiest subject matter. Their commentary, though common to the human condition at its lesser strata, spoke to outmoded and folkloric conventions that only the fringe elements of Wagner's society still embraced—and then usually only as faddish escapism. And although Wagner knew—*knew!*—that the tongue he was hearing was a foreign one, there were dashes here and sprinklings there that nevertheless fell at him with the unequivocal clarity of the very English that he'd been reared on. Not only this, but by some unprecedented means his degree of fluency burgeoned with each kilometre the caravan put behind it.

Using this discovery as criteria, Wagner fixed upon the notion that he'd previously conceived, that the most plausible explanation for all of this had him finally succumbing to the madness that had threatened for so long like a thunderhead on his mind's horizon. The fact of his prior benders and his recurring visions—these had been but brief excursions into a condition that was destined to engulf him entirely, a test of waters into which he was inevitably to plunge. He conceded that perhaps he now dwelled in a world overwhelmingly constructed of subconscious infiltration, where his mind transposed these bizarre events and people and landscapes over the images seen by his eyes and censored by his brain. In essence, what had been captured on Jon Mazzio's videos in their random brevity of the moment was now sticking at full-throttle in Wagner's noggin, miring him in perpetual delusion, maintaining his obliviousness to the true authenticity of his surroundings. Perhaps, then, these beings whom his brain interpreted as soldiers were in truth the hospital attendants who had pursued him in effort to prevent his injuring himself while in a debilitating state. The manacles he wore could easily have been hospital restraints, fitted by the orderlies for his own safety—and for the safety of others—since, within this scenario, the soldiers he'd eliminated at the valley rim could, in wakeful reality, have been unfortunate ward guardians ravaged in the course of his lunacy. The end result: he was now being moved from Howsley to some facility of increased security, the prisoners who shared his shackles being problem inmates from other, various institutions who, for reasons peculiar to their own cases, also required more regimented observation.

What other explanation was more believable? More acceptable? That his life on earth had been the dream, and his true existence was that of a bottom-caste renegade in some unknown, backwards reality? Either way, could a dreamstate feel so tactile? After all, this new environment seemed every bit as textural as it needed to be in order to convince Wagner of its validity. He could feel the cold metal of his chains, could smell the reek of his companions, could taste the grit of the road in his mouth. And he wondered whether any mind was powerful enough to duplicate sensory perception so convincingly and deceptively.

Ironically, experience told him "yes." Everything he'd ever taken away from the dialogues and the written accounts of medical experts verified that such transposition was not impossible. The mind—healthy or not—had the potential to deceive or be deceived in the most minute ways, to puzzle or be puzzled, to perplex or to become perplexed, to create that which is absent and to ignore that which exists. The senses, too, as the input cables to the brain, were tremendously susceptible to manipulation, and easily hornswoggled by numerous means; any illusionist worth his salt, any film editor, any special effects master—even a good confidence man like ol' Doc Adams—could vouch for this. Yet, by fighting the illusion, or merely by letting it run its course, would the whole creation eventually terminate? Fold in on itself? Would it dissolve once the polarities of Wagner's mind flip-flopped into the next configuration? And if so, when? More critical, why was he confined to this impossible scenario in the first place, and to what end would it lead him?

Answers not forthcoming, the caravan rolled onward through the remainder of the day, halting only once near a rivulet where several of the prisoners at the head of the queue were extracted in order to quench the mounts. Buckets were simultaneously distributed throughout the soldiers' ranks, up and down the line, and only after slaking each and every one of them was the water made available to the prisoners.

Wagner waited uncomfortably for the ladle to be passed his way, and when it finally reached him, he took his cue from his fellow captives by guzzling down as much refreshment as the opportunity afforded. His server was a younger woman, equally stalwart as she was sylphish, whose right cheek bore a tiny "X"-shaped scar a few centimetres south of the eye. Her lengthy drape of hair, dark and damp and gritty from travel, fended the breeze like a soggy blanket hung to dry, some of it clinging sluggishly to her jute vest, and some, to the cinnamon sheen of her neck and shoulders. Her expression was intelligent and stolid, and she fixed her eyes almost dutifully upon the tilting ladle for the length of Wagner's quaff, almost as if she were afraid that he might not give it back to her. But give it back he did, realising, then, the nature of her concern—for she, as one of the servers, had yet to partake of the water herself. In gestured reciprocation, Wagner held the pail for her as she dipped her own draught, an unacknowledged appreciation in the hazel-flecked green eyes that briefly glanced back at him across the rim of the utensil before she whisked the bucket out of his hands and hurried it back to the wagon from where she'd obtained it. Wagner then watched as she and the two other trusties were reintegrated into the line just as the command came to resume the march.

At the onset of dusk, the caravan halted for the night. The soldiers—who Wagner learned through his eavesdropping called themselves *NuRacs*—lit up scores of cressets, which they erected in strategic fashion about the perimeter of the temporary camp. Watch-fires were likewise established throughout the line in almost equidistant increments, ignited via flints and touchwood, and fuelled by the dead twigs and bark gathered by the same trusties who'd done the watering. A seeming extravagance of campfire, Wagner could only assume that their primary function was one of simple visibility, that the NuRacs might better keep tabs on their valuable human cargo. Indeed, once said fires reached ready blazes all around, the flames cast a fluctuant luminosity across the commutual disheartenment of Wagner's fellow unfortunates, enough to set him to wondering if the look on his own countenance filled out the flush of mumpish scowls.

Ergosians was what he'd heard the NuRacs call them—*the people of Ergos*. A title bandied about with an ample measure of sarcastic abandon, it no doubt served the soldiers as a means of inflicting some as yet uncomprehended but deprecatory hurt upon their captives without any immoderate damage to the commodity. Whatever the final fate of the prisoners, evidently they were to arrive at destination with as little physical maiming as the operation allowed, the obvious exception being Wagner—and perhaps anyone like him—who, in resisting capture, had quite nearly given as good as he'd gotten, and was therefore fair game for the occasional stray NuRac fist or boot.

The most severe sentiment, authored and sustained en route by an overweening snip of particularly infantile soldiers, had proved progressively difficult for their more temperate and inevitably susceptible comrades to ignore over the day's course. The fatigue and tedium wrought of any long campaign were like predilectory cobbles infixed along the path of even the most thoughtful soul's indiscretion; and though these inciters were few in count, with a little bit of plying they wheedled their more lapsable brethren down into the trench of their own asininity. Sounder judgement yielding to overtiredness, to unreleased aggression, to the base actions of the impudent—apparently such shortcomings were also universal, on Wagner's plane *and* here. In consequence, incivility had no wanting for voice along the entire day's journey, the most venomous lashings delivered not by flagellum but by tongue.

This order of psychological harrying both convenient and uncompromising, the soldiers had for the most part been concurrent in meting it. Given their rationale, most of them even felt justified in doing so. By what Wagner garnered from their taunts, they apparently construed a particular haughtiness in the prisoners' communal designation, which in turn netted NuRac animus above and beyond whatever other disputes the two factions may have had going. *Ergos* being at least one of the names by which this world was known, in calling themselves *Ergosians* these prisoners—according to the NuRacs—presumed themselves its namesakes, a pretension that the soldiers sought to undermine through the aforementioned humiliation. And whether a graver issue of race, or one of economics or geography, the indignities they dispensed were clearly intended as psychological ballast to buoy their own egocentrism. Yet, where their abrasiveness succeeded, Wagner sensed that it didn't impact the Ergosians nearly as much as the NuRacs were hoping, and indeed demonstrated more completely the soldiers' own inanity. Nevertheless, their ridiculing persisted in one incarnation or another for much of the journey, each occasion of it as juvenile, invidious, and bating as the preceding one, and all of it a cyclical perpetuation of intolerance that had no purpose other than the one they tried assigning it.

Despite long hours of close-quarter travelling, Wagner had yet to find a covert means for communicating with any of his fellow prisoners. As few had even chanced looking at him beyond his initial shackling, it seemed that his captors were as consistent in prohibiting fraternisation as they'd thus far been with everything else. Still, with his increasing familiarity with the NuRac idiom, he'd managed to piece together an exiguous and inexact history of the two races, at odds with each other for some thirty years. The NuRacs were the newcomers, the Huns of this region, who evidently felt entitled to expand their regime in any manner that even loosely befit the articles of their manifesto. The Ergosians, understandably less than thrilled by the prospect, had reputedly countered the encroachment with equal pugnacity—although one would not strictly have been able to infer this from the docility demonstrated within the slave train. Of course, hearing history as told only from the NuRac perspective (and not even by a proper NuRac historian), Wagner reckoned that a Texas-sized job of fact-sifting was in order. It was cliché that the NuRacs would view themselves as the vanquishing heroes of their nation, the delusory weave of a conqueror's own propaganda tending to obscure and overwrite the truth in the long run. From the other side of the chains, Wagner simply could not rustle up the unquestioning enthusiasm to oblige them their perspective.

The soldiers supped that evening on jerky and pickled meats, on hardtack and berries and dry cheeses, all chased by generous draughts from their bulging canteen skins. They sat and argued and debased one another as soldiers are wont to do, and it was here that Wagner came to find that equally as many of the NuRacs were female as were male, the subtle, biological differences now made obvious by the doffing of their headgear and by the opportunity to view them during the one welcomed respite of night's falling.

The females appeared slightly more pallid than the men, at least by firelight— their features, more austere yet boasting cleaner chiselling and bony detail. Chins pointed, noses sleek and narrow, facial structures leaning toward a decidedly triangular visage, they seemed suitable complements to their more broad-bodied but not dissimilar counterparts. The lot of them, however, a bevy of heartless militants, they almost assuredly represented a larger, like-minded populace somewhere far beyond that wooded expanse.

With the sun just departed, a dank chill crept like cadaverous fingers across the forest floor. Night would shortly envelop the entire camp. In an effort to combat the sudden chilling, the prisoners huddled themselves at the outskirts of the nearest campfire—largely inutile at three metres distant—and bided quietly and anticipatorily for the sustenance that had yet to be offered them. Wagner, easily the most bruised, the most baffled, certainly the coldest and most self-conscious of his bunch, sat in cross-legged fashion just a few chain links beyond the greater ruck. While unquestionably fagged-out, he exhibited only vague indication of any physical discomfort, his mind too busily at grips with the events of the day. Anxious thoughts surged and ebbed around atolls of speculation and inquiry. His perceptions about the NuRacs, the Ergosians, his physicality, his sanity—these and other perplexities drove him ever inwardly, into mindful debate over the veracity of that which he had little choice but to endure. It was still much beyond his ken to allege whether he'd become a prisoner to his phantasies or whether he'd traded one phantasy-based reality for one of even less desirable circumstances.

He couldn't help but note that since his "arrival" on Ergos, he'd not experienced a single, true, psychopathic episode, nor the merest excursion into incorporeity. Such incongruity puzzled him, for at Howsley he'd come to expect at least three or four good bouts with psychical abduction and intangibility in any twenty-four hour period, with many more brief and less consequential episodes tucked between them. A two minute inability to keep a pencil in his grip, a ten minute fugue where his *Other* bounced around the rec room like a dodge ball before abruptly receding back into Wagner's head—other than his uncharacteristically caustic assault on the soldiers, there'd been no real trace of his alter or his malady since his initial landfall. It was, of course, far too early for conjecture, despite his theory that there had to have been more to the mega-event that ushered him here than he'd originally fathomed. Erroneously perceived as climactic, it somehow seemed more culminant now, as if the crusty overlords of all tarnation had finally noticed his aberration and, deeming it unviable, had tossed him like a tramp from a train, not merely onto the wrong world, but a back-timed one, where no one had any inkling of his true nature or the manner in which he'd come to be integrated into their decades-old grudge match.

"Is it your desire to remain unclothed?"

Wagner snapped to. The trusty who'd watered him down now hunkered before him, a tattered rag of a shawl in her hands.

"The sentry prime has permitted me to deliver this to you—that is, unless you prefer your denudement."

Wagner stared in bewilderment. The woman's voice, just above a whisper, was as crisp and intelligible as was the English he'd spoken all of his life, every word and syllable delightfully graspable. He watched her lips as they formed each word, watched as her tongue rolled across her diminutive, childlike teeth, and he marvelled, because not only was she *not* speaking English, but neither was she speaking in the NuRac tongue that had already become almost totally familiar to him. Strangely, and perhaps in an all-too-convenient accessorising of the insanity that he still could not rule out, he was now and suddenly omniscient of the distinct languages of two of the three races he'd encountered in his whirlwind Ergosian excursion. It was plainly uncanny, given that everything around him had yet to be disproved as some elaborate construct of his mind. Even if it were not—if he had truly experienced a radical locale shift to a whole other sphere in a whole other part of the universe—how on earth, how on *Ergos*, was it that he'd gained full command over two distinct tongues, neither of which he'd ever before heard, tongues that even Charles Berlitz's whole staff couldn't have versed him in so quickly?

"No," he replied, wresting the shawl from her willing hands. "There's a time for 'denudement,' and this is definitely not one of them. Thank you."

He startled himself with the unconscious proficiency of his retort. The words had come so naturally, so comfortably, without so much as a conspicuous wavering over grammatical relationship. That she never once flinched, he could only assume that his enunciation had been passable, and his accent, unobtrusive.

Abruptly, then, she turned and wended her way back to the head of the coffle. His eyes upon her the whole time, he found her tonicity worth a moment's study. Hardly a time for manly reverie, hardly a time for piquancy, he nonetheless bowed to the inconvenience of long neglected stirrings, feelings that he'd forcibly mothballed many a month back for obvious and unfulfillable reasons. He laughed at himself, amused by the fact that amid so much direness he could still think a man's thoughts.

Turning his attention then to the article she'd provided, he deemed it just as well that it lacked sleeving, for the NuRac guards who'd observed the transaction would likely have made no effort at unbinding him so that he might properly don it. Instead, he shrouded himself in it as best he could—and in so doing, dislodged the memory from his earlier vision of the two moppets who'd offered him the grizzled man's robe. Said gesture akin enough to the trusty's that it put the shiver in him, in his outfitting he passed a quick eye over the Ergosian thrall to satisfy himself that there was no naked, bearded old man within it who suddenly lacked for a shawl. Indeed, he found none. Once more, he laughed at himself, this time for allowing his already saddled imagination to run even more amok.

The meal that finally came consisted mainly of the leavings from the soldiers' rations—the gristlier offcasts of their meats, a basket of pawed-over biscuits, even a few handfuls of berries—the latter going to only the fortunates at the head of the line who were lucky enough to partake before the allowance ran out. In all, not exactly a healthy sampling of the food pyramid; but then again, ravenous people were rarely finicky. Wagner, grateful for anything, ground through his hardtack like a carpenter's router and gnawed at his allotment of meat scraps just as rapaciously. Meagre portions all, it was, however, sufficient sustenance to placate a mounting appetite and to permit Wagner and his fellow prisoners to pass the night unbothered by squalling bellies.

Sleeping, Wagner supposed, and moreover, dreaming, were to be the only pleasantries left to him in his fettered state. Yet, here he was in for a new disappointment, for through a restless slumber comprised of what seemed a thousand galling awakenings—each owed either to his unaccustomedness with a campfire's pops and crackles or to the alternating clamour of snoring neighbours and nocturnal woodland denizens—Wagner discovered that never once was he roused from any manner of normal dreamstate. Nary a vignette of symbolically encoded whimsy, no helter-skelter parade of iddish impulses, his subconscious subjected him to nothing but vacuous sleep. It was an odd and unnatural feeling, this inability to dream (or at least to not be aware of one's dreaming) and he wondered why it should have been. Was he no longer in possession of the ability? Did he no longer require it? Had vital brain functioning been overwritten by some tweak of his previous phenomena? Or, more evocative, did the reason he couldn't recall dreaming stem from the fact that this Ergosian-NuRac scenario was itself a dreamstate or an altered plane of consciousness into which he was already paralytically locked? As good an explanation as the others, certainly it was just as conjectural and even a bit more satisfying. Still, all that he would truly know for some time to come was that he'd be continuously unsuccessful in finagling even the tiniest residuum of subconscious rollick out of nap or nod, swoon or knockout.

During his frequent awakenings, Wagner tried lulling himself back to sleep by tracing stars in the night sky. Despite the outshining hindrance of cresset and campfire, the stellar display overhead was still quite spectacular; and on several occasions he attempted to seek out the familiar comforts of the Big Dipper, only to realise once again that in these skies he would see nothing of the constellations he grew up with—at least not from the same earthly vantage. For all he knew, Ergos might have been an inconsequential little orb circling one of the Dipper's stars in Ursa Major itself; and if so, that meant that any of the twinklers overhead could have been old Sol, millions of light years off. A boggling affair, it took him back again and again to the question of which truth was real, and which, the façade. Was he inhabiting another world, or had he withdrawn so far into himself that *his* was the closed realm of a self-contained lunacy?

With the dawn came reveille, followed by the clinkings and clankings of cookware, of weapons inspections, and of soldiers helping one another to suit up to full accoutrement. Amid this activity, a commanding officer inspectively strode the length of the convoy, and then returned to take his place in one of the forward thoraces, two sections ahead of Wagner's. As far as breakfasting was concerned, nothing was as regimented as the evening allowance had been. The soldiers either fended for themselves out of their private stashes, or they prepped in small groups, pooling their rations for perhaps a more diverse meal, given that not all travelled with exactly the same culinary provisions. The sumpter animals, called *vrohdas*, were provided with heaps of fresh vegetation, collected and strewn before them by Wagner's shawl-bestowing acquaintance and the other trusties who likewise quenched the beasts from the stream that the caravan had been paralleling in its journey. Then the camp was struck. Supplies were packed up. Orders were barked. Water-skins were filled. The fires and torches—dutifully maintained throughout the night—were extinguished, as were the low priority thirsts of the Ergosians themselves, just as the call came down the line for disembarking. Ladles and buckets hastily collected, the trusties quickly rejoined the queue in their respective places. Order was established; instruction was given; and the assemblage fell in. Then, with the mist of the early morning still in swim and swirl across the forest floor, the entire entourage groaned to life, lurching forward in resumption of its unflaggingly westward trek.

Necessity prompting adaptation, Wagner had come upon a means of fastening his shawl so that it remained about him throughout the dishevelment of marching. Rolling up each of two corners, he threaded them through his wristcuffs, weaving them in and out and around the links so that they would remain affixed regardless of the swing of his arms. This provided at least partial shielding for his various cuts, gashes, and contusions that might otherwise have been exposed to further aggravation from low hanging ramage or from the dust and dirt raised by his plodding predecessors. Giving said wounds the once-over now and again along the way, it struck him funny that none gave the slightest indication of septicity despite the forfeit of proper lavage and disinfecting. If not a blessing, then perhaps an inexplicable gratuity of biology, for he knew that the threat of imminent peril sometimes inclined one's body to maintain a higher standard of resistance. The past twenty hours having overwhelmed him with hardship and inner conflict—and the night's respite hardly a suitable convalescence—he nevertheless continued to assure himself that he was on the mend. After all, if beasts in the wild could suffer comparable trauma and persevere without the benefit of humankind's ointments, salves, antiseptics, and soaps, then maybe he—with a little fortitude and a peck of headstrongness—could come back from his many detriments without serious corollary. The key was to not dwell on his injuries, but to forge on like the overfleshed vrohdas that hauled the wagons tirelessly and without squawk or self-pity. In just as many instances as not, it was the primal mind—and not the intellect—that was the most effective saving grace.

The forest remained cool during the morning hours, so much that it found Wagner wishing that his bonny trusty would have thrown a pair of trousers into the bargain. At times he would catch himself glancing ahead for her with the regularity of an infatuated schoolboy, at times glomming onto a willowy figure far ahead in the group and fancying it to be she. Yet, with the majority of the Ergosian women outfitted in comparable attire, he couldn't always be certain. The distraction, however, did him well, for the unsavoury nature of his predicament was far too great an onus to remain his sole, mindful fare. To what end the NuRacs led him, to what manner of subservience or depravity they would subject him and his fellow unfortunates—these were questions that would be addressed soon enough.

His goatish dalliance notwithstanding, by the time that morning had gone the way of night, Wagner had strewn behind him a lengthy trail of meditative breadcrumbs, most of them rent from the staleness of hazy and neglected recollection. Desperate for answers, he'd plundered what he could of his sketchy visional abridgement in hopes of finding a missed premonition, anything that might have foreshadowed this leviathan of locale transferences. Within so much phantasmagory, there had to have been clues. There must have been a clarity amid the chaos. He couldn't help but to sense that *somewhere*, perhaps in some untried inversion of perspective or beyond the impenetrability of the mindflux's dampers, was the illumination that would put distinguishment to the heaviest question on his mind: was all of this merely a psychological break from earthly reality, or was it a true, physical break from earthly *realty*?

In deliberate effort to downplay his discomfiture, he peppered much of his overpore with some of the more positive thoughts of the life behind him. From those most recent, like a moment of levity shared with Sally Lemanski over some classical myth that he'd tried equating with his own madness, to the more halcyon days of his old romance or of his raucous nights as a fry cook in a blue collar boozerie—his reverie served to shroud him from approaching imminence much the way that his shawl shrouded him from the elements. He recalled a period, midway between his break with Sara and his admittance to Howsley, when he'd resided solo on Crenshaw Boulevard, in the one-room shoebox that his landlord touted as a studio apartment. Situated just atop the Filthy Lucre tavern—in whose employ Wagner would eventually find himself—he hadn't optioned the lease without first voicing valid concern about flopping one floor over a honky-tonk reputed for its monster grease fires. But, once the responsibility of grill and griddle fell to him, he was able to relegate those concerns to the "back burner" (along with the specialty goulash), leaving him confident enough in his off-hours to press ahead in what, years later, he would call his all-out crusade for medical precedents, scientific antecedents, and sub-psychical internments.

It wasn't uncommon, back then, for him to spend entire days entrenched in reading, voraciously investigating anything even remotely tied to unhealthy psychology, (A)nomie to (Z)ealotry, paranoia to paranormal. Pennies on the dollar bought him remaindered psych texts from mail order houses and rummage sales, the veritable library he amassed in the process precluding any need for interior décor, his increasingly stratified bookshelving ever so much more attractive than the cracked plaster it obscured. Paperbacks, too—he procured stacks of them, many at no personal cost. Once he'd discovered the covers-for-credit process used by most bookstores for recouping investment on overstocked or poorly selling titles, it didn't take him long to start rifling through their dumpsters in search of literary gold gone out with the garbage.

In retrospect, none of it had availed him all that much—except maybe in a preparative manner, that his future discussions with Jon Mazzio wouldn't demarcate him in a brilliant specialist/outmatched layman sort of way. Although nowhere even in the ballpark of Mazzio's credentialed smarts, Wagner brought enough thoughtful intelligence to the table that it excused him his callow grasp of the field more times than not. That he remained amiable and subordinate throughout his Howsley residency went to his frank-hearted desire to be well, with all but the faintest of pretensions left to those whose certification gave them greater license to be smug.

Mazzio, however, being neither smug nor condescending, had from the start been alternately amused and impressed by Wagner's self-schooling, and even missed his livelier input once Wagner, disadvantaged by his outclassing, took himself out of the mix on all but the most relatable bits of theorising. Not that Wagner had ever totally put the brakes to his speculations, it was just that he'd run the race as far as he could with an admittedly limited knowledge; and by sloughing some of his burden onto Mazzio & Co., he'd believed that it had the potential to open him up to a perspective that his former obsessiveness hadn't permitted him.

Assuming his case, Mazzio had given Wagner the safe haven and the peace of mind that he'd so desperately needed. But even as hypothesis after hypothesis failed to pan out, Wagner kept his one-man crusade at a fairly elevated throttle. Obtaining permission to borrow of the facility's books, he likewise insinuated himself among Howsley's other distinguished professionals in order to browse their libraries as well. His delvings often deemed by Nurse Sally as a little too single-focused, she frequently played the absent-minded card whereby she would "accidentally" leave her lighter fare in his room (*People* and *Us Weekly* and a mix of the various tabloids) that her overly fixated patient might take a break from plying himself with such ridiculous intensity, and for once leave the psychiatry to the doctors.

Her strained subtlety wasn't wasted on him. In fact, it was through her periodicals that Wagner first came to know of the man who would one day show up at Howsley so out of the blue: the twenty-first century prophet of supermarket checkouts, the shady but good-natured tough whose soulful, sorrowful gaze was one of the last earthly things that Wagner could remember seeing.

Miracle, he thought. Thinking back, it had all been a *miracle* of sorts, from the advent of his very first symptom to the event that had thrust him into this new phasis. There was, however, no discounting that the man with the *name* had actually come looking for him, regardless of how late in the game it had been. Details still sketchy overall, Wagner's last recollection of that day placed him—not unlike now—amid trees and people, but with a uniquely different slant of vantage and circumstance. Suspended then by unfelt hands, helpless like a snagged parachutist, he recalled first the haunting condolence in the eyes of the man he'd never met, and then, the fear and befuddlement in his doctor's. He remembered a gallery of other faces, too, but none to whom he could assign any defining measure of familiarity. What *had* been clear was the tremendous feeling of drain, the disintegrative wither that, only moments later, had ushered him as close to death as he'd ever been.

How discordantly different he felt now. Trudging along with his ragtag chain gang of Ergosian dregs, something wasn't evident that maybe should have been. For all of his lack of proper rest, of rounded meals, of timely medical attention and holistic control over his environment, Wagner felt incontestably vital—which wasn't at all what he would have expected of himself. To be sure, he experienced the body aching and the cramping and the anxieties of a man thrown into such strenuous happenstance, but at the same time he broached forward with a dogged endurance drawn from unattributable sources, from physical reaches that he never knew existed prior to being drop-kicked into this backwater realm of brutal archaism. It was here where the visions and the benders halted cold, here where his subconscious had let slip the reins of the most basic dreamstate. But it was also here where he never felt more vibrantly whole and alive.

How ironic, then, that with the bequeathal of his newfound freedoms came a set of manacles, a niche in the ranks of dehumanising slavery, and a future crammed with the limiting prospects of torture and death.

For two more days, the caravan rolled on without incident. Then, at some point on day three it emerged from the woods onto a stretch of prairie, which itself gave way gradually to a marshy region from where Wagner could look back and survey the extreme distance they'd covered. The mountains jutting and jagging in the background like the merlons of some ancient battlement, below them lay a rich, rolling blanket of grey-green forest, its sylvan weave virtually unbroken from the point of its foothilled origins, far beyond the lea of Wagner's awakening, past the river valley of his capture, all the way to where his coffle had just parted company with the woodline.

The NuRacs negotiated the marsh via a narrow, well-travelled hummock that bridged dry ground with only marginal accommodation. Here the wagons could file through singly, with barely a wagon wheel's space on either side for unexpected shimmying. It was awkward and slow going for a while, particularly for the tired and the hobbled, for with no more than the slip of a foot would one's peers, fore and aft, be dragged as one into the sump.

A swoop of gulls soared freely overhead, their playful aerobatics serving as unintended taunts to those whose irons kept them mired in the muck of their castigation. Other wildlife, too, abounded in wanton, unsullied prolificacy across the surrounding lowland; and, once back on more stable turf, some of the NuRac archers took opportunity to fell a half-score of ruminant mammals.

Deer-like and yet not, these docile creatures possessed neither the antlers nor the telltale tufts that Wagner associated with deer. Not ungulates either, they exhibited the same distinction of horny pad found on the vrohdas, which in all probability accounted for their less than deer-like swiftness. Yet, unlike their droopy-skinned cousins, their fur was an extraordinary, silver-flecked tawny that, shimmery like frost on autumn pampas, became snowy white around the chin and underbelly.

Extraordinary only in life, however, their arrow-skewered carcasses were promptly tossed into the very wagon that Wagner had occupied, evidently to be butchered later, upon the making of the evening's camp.

It was in the midst of this unscheduled pause for gaming that Wagner's ear pricked to a peculiar sound amid the post-kill brouhaha. Vexing, inscrutable, it was less an incongruity within his captors' pre-festal spiritedness than it was a sudden surfacing of unreclaimed hope. Intent on wedding the sound to its source, Wagner opened himself to the rebuke of any guard who caught him in the act of eyeballing—so certain was he of whom he would espy.

Indeed, far ahead of the weary slog of prisoners, five drays and thirteen vrohdas forward of the medial NuRac rank, he could just make out two soldiers engaged in an odd embranglement before one of the gaol carts. This, he sensed, was the fount he sought.

A closer study revealed that these NuRacs were using one of the dead creatures as bait to twit the cart's occupant. With jerk and judder they dangled the fresh meat before the bars and yanked it back in callous tease. The imprisoned—ravenous, enraged, or both—emitted the most contemptuous of growls at the soldiers' mockery, at times jutting a sinewy arm through the latticework in effort to seize either a joint of meat or a fistful of tormentor.

Wagner knew at once which of the two options would have pleased the occupant most, for at last he knew the fate of the hot-tempered werecat whose path and his had briefly—and fatefully—crossed. Still alive, she had never truly been far away, only caged and subdued some sixty paces ahead of his own group.

He thought it queer that the creature who'd recklessly lit into—and eradicated—three such armoured assailants back at the valley should have seen fit to remain mute and commotionless until this moment; three days was surely an eternity for one such as she to at least not express a little raucous displeasure. His first notion was that she'd been gagged for much of the trek, and had only recently managed to slip free of her baffle. On the other hand, she may just as easily have been indisposed by a fever prompted of her wounds, and within her first stirrings had come to find herself the target of the soldiers' long denied penchant for bullying. Whatever the reason, her harriers continued making sport of her until the time that their commanding officer happened back along the queue. A no-nonsense fellow, full of pomp and posture, he put a curt halt to their asininity, his reproof an order to heap the carcass in with the others lest he force the subordinates to ride out the rest of the journey from within the werecat's dray. This they did, sparing no swiftness, and within minutes the caravan was again in motion, rolling on toward the next tract of wooded acreage that was to be its host and steward for but a single night more—as the next day would bring the whole machine before its destination.

Later, on making camp, the field cooks and the meat cutters took up their knives and hewers and set at butchering the day's kill. A handful of trusties summoned to facilitate the process, they manned the vats and the stoneware into which the entrails and such were placed for later utilisation. Even the blood was collected in these vessels, along with a host of bodily extracts, some of which were—in a curiously macabre fashion—fastidiously collated and messengered up the caravan line. The hides and other non-comestibles were likewise taken away for gainful purposes of their own, the end result being that almost nothing of the esculent ruminants went to waste. The NuRac flayers quite masterful in their efficiency, in no time at all they had the carcasses reduced to a small congeries of foul-smelling offal that was subsequently shovelled into a pit and covered over with soil.

Wagner, seated well within range of this industry, opted to watch as little of the gutting as his unshielded proximity allowed him. Averting his eyes at its onset, he returned to it only intermittently, a second here, a few seconds there, too weak of stomach to observe for very long the barrage of simultaneous eviscerations—yet oddly not so totally appalled that he couldn't bear to look at it at all. Finding these kitcheners, however, a bit too ebullient in their slicing and dicing, he more readily fixed his sights on a subject of greater personal intrigue, that being the far-ahead gaol wagon of his mismatched ally.

But for the quickening twilight, he would have been able to make her out well enough to assess her condition. As it was, he could barely discern the lank of her formidable silhouette perched motionlessly within the dray's gridiron. Sorely enervated or merely brooding, conserving strength or hatching a plan, the werecat didn't once move for the whole time that Wagner watched, not for the slightest shifting of weight between her superiorly dactyllic feet, not even in reaction to the sentries and trusties who'd begun to rush about in their nightly ritual of torch lighting and campfire setting. The same could not be said of Wagner, not when the woman with the "X" scar passed before him, a wisp of lighted tinder in her hand that she used to touch off each of the many cressets within her designation.

"Why the same three of you all the time?" Wagner blurted as she filed back his way.

"Same three?"

"Yeah. You and your two friends, there." He gestured toward her fellow trusties, one male, one female, across the camp, whose duties paralleled hers. "Why is it that you three are the only ones doing the NuRacs' grunt work?"

For a moment she bore such a look of bemusement that he feared he'd unwittingly committed a social faux paus of the worst kind. Yet, with her answer came his realisation that not all colloquialisms translated the same.

"I am not familiar with this expression," she said. "But as to why I do these things—would *you* refuse to obey those who would hack off your feet for your insolence?"

He shook his head. "No. I guess not."

"Nay, you would not need to guess. You would either follow orders or incur punishment. We do these tasks so that we may all of us live to see another morning—including you."

Wagner sensed an unwarranted reproach in her tone, read it in her eyes, and then saw it die just as quickly as it had risen. Remarkably, her flambeau went out at the same time, and as she cupped a hand about the ember and blew forth the flicker of new fire, Wagner paused to study her in profile.

"Why," he asked, "should you care about keeping *me* alive?"

"Not only you," she said. "Everyone. It is imperative that we all remain at least reasonably unimpaired, for our ungracious hosts sometimes choose to leave the bodies of the collapsed and the dead chained to the group for the entire journey. I need not tell you that corpses are unwieldy things to be dragged over the countryside, and they become more untidy by the day. Therefore, the more of us who live, the less burthen on the rest."

Wagner sighed. It wasn't exactly the answer he'd expected. But then again, nothing had been what he'd expected. He therefore tried a different line of inquiry.

"Why the careful spacing of the fires, then? And the torches at every turn?"

"Now you jest," she said curtly. "Do you think the hounds stay away because we entreat them nicely?"

Wagner shrugged in ignorance.

"It will be especially difficult tonight," she elaborated, "with the lure of fresh zalmiir in the air."

Wagner didn't ask, but assumed that her reference was to the NuRacs' venison bounty, even then almost totally expedited by the hewers into its various apportionments. He welcomed this kind of exposition, for to be challenged by undefined terms in a language in which he believed himself proficient was a return to the more explicable and comforting bounds of interactive learning. In fact, the whole lingual accession thing, while advantageous, had been only slightly less unsettling than everything else that he'd been made to endure; and although he'd come by it almost osmotically, its pervasion was now proving considerably less than absolute. Having infused him with adequate enough conversational skills, it seemed now to have been more a kind of abecedarian screen-dump than anything even remotely akin to perfect fluency—a starter kit of sorts whose limitations he was only beginning to appreciate. Matters of topicality, history, nomenclature, they had no inclusion in the complimentary package. This was not to say that there weren't many undesignated words within his head—there *were*, and "zalmiir" had been one of them—but he couldn't associate them with anything until such time that experiential occasion gave them definition. Thus, any knowledge subsequent to the initial bestowal was exactly what it should have been: continuous, intellectual addenda. And despite the primitive superficies of this society, Wagner knew that he still had scads to grasp in both scholarship and acculturation.

Suspecting that his nescience might already be costing him credibility, for the nonce he curbed his pressing desire to interrogate the trusty. He could ill afford to vaunt too much of his ignorance at once, since even the most innocent of conspicuities had a way of arousing unwanted curiosity—curiosity that, already reputed for the premature demise of unheeding cats, was a well known floodgate to suspicion, fear, prejudice, paranoia and worse.

Allowing the woman to continue in her duties, Wagner then turned away from all manner of inquisitive eyes—real or imagined—and, adjusting his poncho snugly about his shoulders, closed his own eyes and immersed himself in a sentient half-doze until time came that he would be fed and watered. An all too brief respite, it nevertheless gave him opportunity enough to pore over much of what the woman had told him, a chance to assimilate her words, to practise mimicking her syntax, so that he might better walk among both races without noticeable distinction.

When mealtime finally came, the foods consisted of the same stringy meats and bread seconds from the previous days. The former was certainly no more appealing than it had been the first evening; the latter proved either stale or rock-hard or freckled with the onset of soon-to-be-rampant mouldiness. Some of the biscuits plagued by all three maladies, the drawing of one's loaf from the basket (by torchlight no less) proved a decidedly hit-or-miss prospect.

The fresh meat the NuRacs kept for themselves, and here they made no effort to shield their regalement from the Ergosians. Great slabs of ribs were spiced and roasted to a delicate turn over the camp's many cooking fires; shanks the size of bludgeons were spun to rotisseried perfection and then pared and meted, slice by succulent slice, to the smacking soldiers. Their unabashed guttling and wine toasting (and their festal riotousness itself, just under bacchanalian in scope) did everything for NuRac morale and nothing for the Ergosians—excepting, perhaps, to emphasise the latter's ostracism. Afterward, what little of the bounty remained undevoured was collected for stewing or jerking or for some other industry that, in the moment, did very little for the clamouring bellies it could have sated.

As night rolled across the encampment, Wagner curled up under his beggar's shawl, commending his weariness once more to the unconforming palliasse of the forest floor. The insects actually less bothersome at night, those that weren't lured into the fires were driven back by the smoke from the occasional misgather of greenery mixed among the faggots. Tired yet sleepless, Wagner took some small amusement in watching the lively play of firelight and shadow upon the perimeter thicket. The surrounding foliage so animated by the writhe of the flames, at times it seemed that the forest had suddenly come alive with the spirits of a thousand, impassioned pixies, each in the sportful throes of flit and waver, each vying for some mortal audience to bewitch and enthral.

Indulging but a while these fays, fairies, and nymphs of the darkwood, Wagner broke from his engrossment to glance about the camp to assure himself that all else was calm. The merriment of the feast having ended hours ago, the caravan almost completely at rest, the only measurable stirrings were in the grunts of his sleeping neighbours, the bickering of a few dice-tossing soldiers far up the line, and the tireless plod of the night patrols. These dark-hour sentries he found worthy of study, for they were in all a much more elitist group than their daytime peers—and were indisputably professional in contrast to their dicing brethren up the file. Sole of purpose, they were as staid and duteous as one might hope one's guardians to be. Resting in the wagons during the day, these NuRac women and men protected the brigade at night and, beyond that, had little observable interaction with anyone. It was rare even to see one conversing with the retiring troops at the start of their tour. There was no fraternising, certainly no partaking of the wines or other impairing imbibition, and—once on duty—no breaking for anything more than sustenance and voiding. Ever sharp in their policing, never straying a pace beyond the influence of the torchlight, each kept his body at hair-trigger tautness, his lance or voulge gripped at white-knuckled ready, and his eyes attuned both to the camp and to the surrounding boscage.

That they could maintain such intensity night after night in so perfunctory a task had impressed Wagner from the first. Yet, only now had he begun to appreciate the full impetus behind it. Woven into the trusty's "hound" reference was an intimation that the woods were absolutely not safe after dark, that they were perhaps filled with some ilk of roving, nocturnal mongrels to whom the camp would fall prey but for the deterring fires that circumscribed it. Wild dogs, jackals, wolves, whatever manner of carnivores these were to be, Wagner's one impression was that they weren't exactly in the "man's best friend" category. Their alleged presence in the midnight woods therefore lent a certain legitimacy to the elect NuRac unit whose commission it had become to repel them. Apparently a graver threat than the nuisance of feral scavengers, more than just a vying between species in the forestal food chain, these night-hound things had to have been almost diabolically predaceous in order to ruffle the NuRacs as they did. Indeed, had they even a fraction of the cunning of the captured werecat, in suitable numbers such creatures might decrement a whole field army while it lay asleep and vulnerable. This made the NuRac night-watchers into Wagner's defenders as well, and as mounting as his abhorrence was for their daytime counterparts, Wagner held this bunch in far more gracious esteem. Like the few warders at Howsley whom he could never get on side—particularly those who'd cajoled the others into jouncing him unnecessarily through the wall—he always knew that, in their own way, they did what they did in the name of protection. He didn't have to like them to profit from their service.

By late afternoon on the following day, the caravan finally cleared the last of the woods and egressed onto a broad field of grain crops. An acreage of no little expanse, its sun-bright skies and its symmetrically rowed frontage was such a drastic departure from the dappled wildwood that Wagner, piqued but not strictly uplifted by the transition, felt obliged to investigate it in every way that his restrictions permitted.

Sweeping waves of kamut dominated the foreground of this new frontier, with a distinction of a least two other cereals crowding the landscape farther off, left and right, all still months shy of maturity, and all far on the needy end of the rainfall scale. Such effectuated agriculture surely presumed farmers, people, a town or a city. Far from good news, however, for if the culture it represented was no more honourable than its army—indeed, if it sanctioned the organised tyranny that the soldiers visited upon the Ergosians—then the prospect of being deposited into so baleful a society was an uninviting one at best.

Struck by this realisation—contemplated much, but only now with such imminence—Wagner shunted his misplaced vim and yielded to a more appropriate betokening. He felt fluttery, squirmy, cold, his every instinct clamouring for the intervention that he in his fettered state couldn't deliver. Anxious, he glinted back to the woods like a child to the mother who bore him, sensing that even the thousand discomfitures of the past three days—the filth, the infestation, the hunger and thirst—would all seem preferable to what awaited him.

The vrohdas, on the other hand, were never more eager. Their gait indisputably livelier, in their wilful eagerness they so taxed their reinsmen that it was all the NuRacs could do to steady the drays, much less steer them. Prevailing scent in the air, familiar spoor on the road, migrative sense of destination—whatever it was that put the sudden pep in the draughters' plod, it signalled their unmistakable proximity to home.

A likened energy reared within the NuRac ranks directly. Accompanied by jubilant murmurs, rising in the headmost file and travelling throughout the lines with the fleetness of small-town gossip, it prompted in the Ergosian body an antithesis of disconsolateness that, cringe for cringe, made Wagner's premonitory jittering seem almost uplifting. Visual confirmation soon cinched these opposing passions into the same impartible inevitability, the scale and scope of the fortress that of a sudden consumed the horizon far outmatching anything Wagner could ever have anticipated.

The northern skyline showed nothing but grandiose structure. An immense, brick-curtained metropolis erected around one monolithic keep and sundry smaller ones—all fashioned of ebon blockstone—by its high-spired obelisks and its many bastions and bartizans it gulled the unready eye with the notion of a dark, mythical behemoth encamped about the stronghold of some undefined, but certainly malefic, contrivance. A fortress/city of impressive magnitude, seeming thousands of metres in circumference, in area it could easily have accommodated Bishop's entire downtown corridor (the commercial grids and the outskirting strip-club district included) within its dual fortification of inner and outer walls, roughly eleven and eight metres in respective height. Interveniently fortified, with a bulwark so lengthy as to challenge one's sense of perspective, Wagner could only imagine the extraordinary labour that went into procuring enough rock with which to quarry and construct it. He was not so challenged, however, in imagining what kinds of indignities went on within it.

Such inauspiciousness ahead, Wagner heaped credence upon his earlier assumption that his capture and subsequent trek through the wilderness would, with all probability, turn out to be the heyday of his subjugation. By all that he'd seen—by the waged threats of his captors, by the fearful whispers of his fellow prisoners—he simply couldn't see any benefit to be had of all this. In fact, the only thing that kept his dread from consuming him was a certain hopeful impudence, a presumptuous pretext of reasoning that dared to posit that the extraneous forces who'd routed him into this world's archaic infrastructure would hardly have made the effort had they known he would be put so quickly asunder. An unusually sober bit of thinking for such a boggling development, Wagner was, of course, long acclimated to rationalising on the fly.

The procession still minutes from reaching the walls, a ponderous portcullis at the base of the southern curtain slowly clanked open its toothy maw and spewed forth an advance of NuRac soldiers. Several score of them, like ants from a razed nest they swarmed out onto the roadway, promptly linking with the caravan. There to assume the duties of escort, they encouraged the commanding officer and his subordinates to break formation and to proceed up the narrow escarpment and into the city. The caravan, however, did not follow. Instead, it continued west along the southern wall for a goodly distance, all under the inordinate scrutiny of the many, curious faces that filled nearly every crenelle and loophole along the battlement above. At end, at the city's far south-western quadrant, the convoy came upon a postern entrance—smaller, yet no less fortified than the main portcullis—through which the file was promptly conducted. Trundling beneath the iron-capped tines of its uplifted gratings, past the great cranking mechanisms and the guards who operated them, once on the inside the wagons were directed onto the sands of a sizable ward that separated the outer and inner curtains. A buffer of ground that likely encircled the fortress for kilometres around, although spacious enough to accept the choke of the drays and the vrohdas and the people, it could easily have become gridlocked chaos had the NuRac coordinators been less precise in their marshalling. As it was, within minutes of arriving, the coffle was ordered to attention while those within the wheeled gaols were readied for disembarking.

"Stand and submit!" shouted the sergeant at arms, a stocky NuRac with an over-the-top swagger and a ready grasp of the Ergosian tongue. "You are now under the governance of the NuRac regime. Your former lives are no longer of consequence. You would do well to strike their memory from your minds, for I promise you that there will be no return or resumption. From this day forward, your livelihoods will be in the service of QieLahr."

With Wagner's recent enlightenment of both the NuRac and Ergosian tongues, here was a NuRac who dictated to his enemy in said enemy's native Ergosian, impeccably delivered, so that no prisoner could possibly misinterpret the bad news of his newly bereaved status. Like bitter medicine, it was to be taken all in one swallow, with no opportunity for questions, debate, anything other than completely silent subservience.

Above the assemblage, several catwalk soldiers crossed the airspace via a slight scaffolding that, hinged at the inner curtain, had been swung sideways to join perpendicularly with the outer wall for a rapid transfer of sentries. Not far from its pivoted moorings, a cluster of presumed officials observed the proceedings from an ornately structured parapet. While the precise nature of their officiating wasn't at all evident, it apparently varied from one individual to the next, as some were clearly high-ranking officers outfitted in their full regalia, and others, politicians or obviously affluent civilians garbed in ritzy attire (including but not limited to fancy headwear, silken shawls, lace-trimmed vestments and such). These onlookers surveyed every body and face new to the courtyard grounds, at times sharing a whisper or a chortle, often pointing, nodding, commenting, critiquing and speculating—on just what, Wagner had no inkling. Neither would he have time to ponder it; for suddenly stamping up before him was none other than the burly sergeant himself, facing Wagner down with his protruding forehead and his coalish eyes as if Wagner were some boot camp yokel fresh off the bus.

"Eyes down, crovik-fodder!" he growled, his command unexpectedly punctuated from behind by a sharp thwack to Wagner's hamstrings, compliments of a NuRac sentry and his surreptitious quarterstaff. Caught unawares, Wagner buckled and pitched groundward like some nebbishy foil in a schoolyard prank, his chain-checked arms unable to stave the sprawl that his link-bearing neighbours were forced to absorb. Yet, with unintentionally blazing reflexes, he sprang back to his feet in furious defiance, his eyes shooting double-barrelled rage at his attacker for so cowardly and unprovoked an assault. A move with predictably tragic consequences, it was fortunate that his rationale hadn't entirely fled him; and with composure he resumed his lowered glance, and thus, resisted the futility of his impulse.

"Good," said the sergeant as if surprised. "Good! You learn quickly. With such tempered instincts, you will go far here."

An incendiary wave of scuttlebutt dinned among the gathering overhead. Wagner did not gamble to look up.

The sergeant moved on, continuing his orientation lecture with well-rehearsed glibness. As he ran through the short list of dos and don'ts—heavy on the don'ts— the NuRac smiths infiltrated the coffle and began extricating the prisoners from their irons.

"You will be allocated to temporary barracks," said the orator, "until your individual potentials can be assessed. Then, depending upon how you are deemed, you will be assigned to work or to train. Abide easily, and you will be rewarded with increased meal allowances and better slotting privileges. Resist, and you will be the first to sample the many 'pleasantries' reserved for the stubborn and the insolent.

"Sentry!" he shouted, his eyes never leaving the line-up. "Dismiss this ruck and usher them through processing. *Now!*"

The airspace of the ward suddenly came alive with the echoing chorus of secondary commands, spouted superior to subordinate, with the prisoners the inevitable underlings for the NuRac hierarchic low-rungers. Freed from the umbilical chain that for days had linked them—and from the hand and foot restraints that limited their motoring—the Ergosians nevertheless huddled even closer than they had when they'd been fettered. Bedraggled and uncertain, in their uneasiness they exposed their most easily exploited vulnerability, and here the NuRacs began herding them at vigorous spearpoint along the bailey and into a tunnelled avenue to a place deeper within the fortress.

On the other side, they were spilled out onto a great courtyard, surrounded on high by a moderately sentried parapet. This new area—whose eastern wall housed a collection of stony troughs, each with an overhead feed of cistern and sluice— contained seven gymnasium-sized structures in its north-eastern quadrant. Two rows of three, with the odd structure set perpendicularly in the forefront, each construct was served by only a single barred entrance, with no other orifices except for a consecution of loopholes situated just below the rooflines on opposite sides for the entire measure of each building.

At the west end of the compound stood one additional structure, nearly as inornate as the others but for the archwayed colonnade encompassing its outer walls. Amassed of noticeably larger blocks, too, than its cousins across the way, by its design—and by its complement of sentries stationed without—it seemed by far the least innocuous of the eight. In fact, Wagner sensed a downright ominousness about it that he felt content in leaving unexplored. All eight buildings, however, stood at roughly two stories tall, and all bore the distinction of indicia over their entries that offered a thus far indecipherable presumption to their purpose. Yet, while the guarded construct and the six aligned buildings presented inscriptions incorporating multiple characters, the perpendicular structure had only a single charge painted along its entrance—two vertical stripes intersected midway by a horizontal stroke.

Rallied once more into an inspection line, the prisoners were made to stand in wait while their captors facilitated the segregation procedures. Stretchers borne upon the shoulders of unfamiliar trusties were hastened across the yard and then ushered back to the charge-marked structure whence they came, laden heavy with the bodies of the wounded. The brutalised, the stabbed, the broken and the incidentally infirm—the most severely injured had occupied the wagons during the journey, many crammed together in far greater number than any sensible prescription would have accorded. By Wagner's evidence, there were several poor devils who hadn't survived the ordeal, and a number of others who rode the brink of demise.

Last to grace the courtyard was the inimical werecat, sole representative of her kind. Coiled in more chains than Marley's ghost and harbouring a rage worthy of Medea, she strained fitfully to overcome the gimp wrought of her pierced leg, a bane made all the worse by the cumbrousness of her trappings. A slavering hotspur of bloodlust, utterly refractory in temperament, no manner of NuRac provocation short of the spearpoints that continuously jabbed at her backside could goad her forward. Her throaty growl a constant, unquellable resonance, within it lay the promise of evisceration to anyone careless enough to stray within range of her deadly appliance, tooth, nail, or otherwise. Her glance alone had the causticity to stop most hearts, and could easily have given any Gorgon a run for her money.

Spurred to the head of the queue, she was presented to a small committee of warders that had bolted anxiously onto the grounds, eager to examine this evidently uncommon prize. Like seasoned appraisers they looked the female up and down, conferred with one another, pointed that way and this, as if discrepant over how best to immure her. Hailing one of the accompanying guards, they invited him over, the specifics of their exchange too low for Wagner to hear. But in the midst of this interaction, the creature saw opportunity, and lit into the soldier from behind.

Bowled over by momentum, the guard literally gushed across the ground, his throat split open like an overripe pomegranate. A single slash from a single claw, the werecat had circumvented the impenetrability of her restraints, erupting in an assail of such horrific animus that no being present—not prisoner, not captor—could believe his eyes. But there she was, a-spray in the jetting lifeblood of a man whom she'd all but delivered into the grave, sneering toothily at any who would be next.

The grounds an immediacy of explosive chaos, soldiers from all ends of the yard charged in to subdue the beast. Her original escorts still addled by disbelief, they jumped to and regripped her chains in a fretful attempt to anchor her to one spot, giving the arriving enforcers opportunity to stab at whatever vulnerability they could exploit. One NuRac even swung at her head with the blunt side of a voulge, only to narrowly miss her and glance the helm of one of his own by zeal and haste. Quickly overwhelmed, the werecat was ultimately brought down. Yet, even saddled by her irons and set upon from every vantage, she wasn't submitting. In fact, she became more resolute than ever. Defying the combined might that kept her groundward, she reared once more, dislodging her antagonists with a torsional sweep and dragging them in train like so many tins strung behind a wedding limousine. Her intended target, however, a female warder with a studded bludgeon, availed herself of the she-cat's hamper and easily by-stepped the lunge, smiting the beast backhandedly across the shoulder in reply.

By now, a veritable detachment of NuRacs had joined in, each wielding spears or clubs or whips, each inflicting upon the beast as much damage as was in his power to exact. She, however, was so completely consumed by rage as to be unaffected by most of their blows, her motoring given over completely to some extreme, primal ferity that actually seemed to feed upon the excruciation that her oppressors doled. While her bloodied aspect foretold her inevitable finality, the fury within her simply would not let her fall.

Wagner would later be pressed to understand what happened next. Sympathy, empathy, anger—whatever it was that flipped his berserker switch—before he realised that he'd even moved, he was already headlong into the fracas. Not only good sense, but *all* sense, out the window, with fists of indeliberate abandon he stowed in the faces of not one, but two loosely accoutred NuRac heavies. As they teetered, he thieved away one's lance, split it over the head of the other, and then turned it back on the first. The sudden sting of a NuRac lash only riling him more, he reeled and charged his scourger, bowling him over and into one of the werecat's chain-bearers whose tumble at once put the beast's securement in serious jeopardy. Four NuRacs scrambling in from all sides to snap up the unmanned tethers, the werecat resumed the struggle and lunged at her other restrainers, each of whose fate depended totally upon his peers' ability to keep their own ends taut. The nearest of these men nigh to becoming Wagner's next unwitting target, within seconds of connecting Wagner was himself blindsided and summarily knocked to the ground by a glancing blow from the very bludgeon used against the werecat, moments before.

Lost in starried ruckle, unable to focus, Wagner made a drunkard's effort to rise, but found his every limb pinned by boot and gauntlet. Little more than a disabled and naked man now, his enemies fell upon him, and fell upon him hard. Sparing no small measure of wrath, they emptied the coffers of their every hostility upon him, beating him down for an impudence that truly had never stood a chance—and which would now serve as the most explicit of object lessons to his fellow prisoners, that they would see retributive dispensation in action.

For Wagner, however, it was more inundation than inculcation. In fact, so virulently did his enemies rain their fists upon his body that his slip into unconsciousness simply couldn't have come fast enough. Their punches and kicks, while collectively severe, were collaborated in purpose to keep him from falling too quickly into senselessness. Even his blacking out—when it finally happened—wasn't itself an immediate assuagement. He would later recall having felt the buffet of their blows well into the veil of his oblivion.

CHAPTER EIGHT

Look beneath the surface;
Let not the several quality of
a thing nor its worth escape thee.
  —MARCUS AURELIUS

On first waking, Wagner found himself a companion to overweening darkness. In truth, so completely Stygian were his surroundings that it took him a few blinks to confirm that his eyes were functioning at all. A rapid and sequent probing of fingers finding nothing ocularly amiss, in the end he could only conclude that, whatever his situation, it had less to do with occluded vision than with his incarceration in some intemperately darkling place.

His eyes passing muster, the same couldn't be said of the rest of him. In fact, had it not been for a great wealth of bodily distress and a truly indescribable noxiousness in the air around him, he might have been able to convince himself that he was back at Howsley, self-roused halfway to morning by a disturbingly detailed incubus of anthropomorphous cats and armoured brigands, of primeval forests and pummelling fists. Unfortunately, this was not the case. His body racked in anguish quite palpable, it was no infirmary bed on which he'd been placed. Hardly a bed at all, its qualities were unmistakeably organic. As for the airborne feculence, not since he'd been called upon to plunge the men's commode after one of the Filthy Lucre's boilermaker marathons had he confronted anything so extraordinarily vile. Incomparably worse than a cesspit, easily miasmal enough to rival the Augean stables themselves, this was a graveolence like no other.

Carefully sitting up in what felt to be a heap of straw, he paused for a moment to check his person, head to extremity, first to assure himself of his wholeness—a residuum, no doubt, of the trusty's feet-hacking allusion—and then to assess the sundry cuts, bruises, knobs and welts, that he'd acquired in his NuRac thrashing. As it turned out, the angry soldiers had been most generous, for he discovered damage and distension to nearly one-half of his body, the most conspicuous of said inflictions exacted across his left face, temple to chin, nostril to ear, that would surely render him black and blue for the better part of a fortnight. Still a far less lethal consequence than he'd anticipated, by his own deeming he was structurally intact, with no severity of internal complaint, and nothing noticeably missing or broken that wouldn't, in time, mend on its own.

In his uprightness, however, he did experience a twinge of vertigo—the consequence, perhaps, of having one's head used for soccer practise—and this, added to the bristle of gooseflesh suddenly upon him in answer to the chamber's cavernous atmosphere, was incentive enough to compel him back into the mow. His arms clenched in rigour, his emaciation symptomatic of mild consumption, any further investigation of his new domain would have to wait until he felt vital enough to try again. It would be a while.

It wasn't until later that he realised he must have slipped back into unconsciousness, for the next time he opened his eyes he was greeted by a weak filtration of daylight stealing in from above. Its geometry telltale, even in the wane of his febrility he at once recognised its source for a trap door, and undoubtedly the means by which he'd come to occupy his oubliette. Yet, with the pervading darkness still prohibiting any accurate reckoning of spatiality, he was unable to immediately gauge its proximity to him. He only knew that, in all probability, it was much too high to reach unaided.

Lying on his back, Wagner gazed up at the sunstreams that framed the hatch and pierced his fetid compartment like a heavenly issue of hope. Tomorrow had arrived without him, this much he deduced. That his initial awakening had occurred during the night was also patent now—and a relief of no little magnitude. Even so scant an offering of daylight as this was sufficient to lift him in his deprival.

With the greater portion of his equilibrium restored, Wagner rolled gingerly to his knees and took himself upright. A moment of lightheadedness notwith-standing, within minutes he'd not only meticulously paced out the cell's dimensions—roughly three strides by four—but had probed its stony composition for the juts and gouges that might facilitate an upward essay. He found nothing of consequence, excepting the one discovery he'd rather not have made, for it was in his rooting about that he turned up the cause of the chamber's ghastly rankness.

In the far reaches of his cell lay the rotting egesta and ejecta of what had surely been a significant rotation of unlucky predecessors. Their legacy now his, in his investigation he'd made the mistake of plunging his hands into a small mire of the stuff, and was afterwards forced to expend several handfuls of his bedding in order to wipe them free of it. Putrefaction too disgusting for words, whether it had been that everyone before him had been overcome by urgency too demanding, or whether they simply had no qualms about defiling their own living space, Wagner was appalled by the flagrancy of the cell's former occupants, especially as he'd already stumbled across the lidded metal pail next to his bedstraw that was conceivably the intended receptacle for such business. And although said receptacle wasn't by any means a versatility for man's most delicate of anatomical gifts (its unchamfered edges alone made it inconvenient to anyone accustomed to voiding in more ergonomic fashion), it existed to facilitate the most rudimentary of rituals for surviving in such limited space, and Wagner could only wonder at the malaise and pestilence that his unthinking precursors had time-capsuled for him.

With nothing in the cell to occupy him, and with little perambulatory leeway within its muck-choked dimensions, Wagner spent most of his isolation burrowed in his provender. Handfuls of it raked over his body to conserve warmth, his mind he immersed in the distinctively colder contemplations of a man condemned. Eyes focused upon the hatch, ears open to any sounds of activity on the platform above, he had time a-plenty to imagine what his fate might have been had he only opted for some other direction in his post-reintegrative wandering. He wondered about the nature of this reality, and whether every choice of path would sooner or later have led him here, into servitude and imprisonment under the boot heels of this cruelly dominant race.

At some point in his meditations he was alerted by the trot of footsteps overhead, footsteps and the intermittent *ke-chunk-ke-chunk* of some rolling contraption on out-of-kilter wheels. Advancing one moment, then halting, each cycle was bridged by a clank, a thud, and an occasional indistinguishment of bawl and bellow that Wagner likened more to a rebuke than to any manner of hail or hierarchal command. The conveyance trundling closer with each circuit, it was easily thirty minutes, however, before it clanked to a halt over his cell.

After an excruciating inexpectancy of silence, Wagner heard spotty conversation, followed by somebody fumbling with the latch. Suddenly, the chamber was flooded with the painful dazzle of day.

Eyes averted, Wagner listened blindly for instruction from above, hoping—and at the same time dreading—that he was about to be sprung from his antre. Instead, he heard the huffing of two increasingly impatient men.

"Take it, or do without!" one suddenly shouted.

Bewildered, Wagner peered up in painful squint to find an object in dangle barely a metre from his face.

Lunging awkwardly for it, his hands encountered a basin, suspended on four hooks and linked to a single braid of cording that fed upwards and disappeared through the trap above. Steadying this swaying prize, Wagner eased it onto his bedstraw; and once down he discovered within it an earthen porringer and a small, bunged jug, also of clay.

Extracting both receptacles, he found within the crock a concoction of gelatinous stew countersunk with what looked to be a wedge of hard pumpernickel. The accompanying jug, its contents sprightly fluent, held the remedial promise of long awaited rehydration. Eager to eat—and even more anxious to irrigate the desert that was his throat—Wagner quickly set his bounty off to the side. Then, giving a firm tug on the cord, he waited for the crude dumbwaiter to be retracted.

Nothing happened. Risking rebuke, he stepped into the light and looked up in quiet expectancy.

"Your chamber pot!" barked a voice. "Make quick with it!"

Wise now, Wagner scrounged for his bedpan and placed it within the empty basin. Watching, then, as his warders drew it up through the hatch, he became increasingly dismayed by the realisation that both repast and refuse—not only his, but that of any neighbouring inmate along the block—were allowed alternating occupancy within the same appliance. An unsavoury practise to be sure, he was hardly in the position to spout health department protocols to lawless Huns. Nevertheless, it dropped quite the discretionary bombshell on his lunchtime zeal.

During this enterprise of catering/waste elimination (and indeed, right up to the moment that the trap swung shut), Wagner found himself privy to what could only be deemed a running lambaste overhead, where the ranking soldier criticised the lesser for a dalliance that, in truth, was far more attributable to Wagner's ignorance. No matter, however, for the rhetoric itself had quickly clued Wagner to the fact that the subordinate was actually no NuRac at all, but a fellow prisoner—probably a trusty—who apparently serviced the isolation block under the constant carp of one or more NuRac turnkeys. That this trusty had taken flak for Wagner's dilatoriness was regrettable, especially given that the derision did not cease with Wagner's re-entombment. Still, Wagner would have gladly suffered that flak himself for but a single lung's-worth of topside air.

When he'd finished with his stew, he set the crock aside and proceeded to drain the jug of two-thirds of its contents. He could easily have consumed it all—and wanted to—but with no indication of how often he'd be fed and watered he felt it best to conserve the remaining third for rationing throughout the day. Any water still on hand at the time of his next replenishment he would promptly ingest so as not to forfeit a precious drop.

Over the morning's passing, he did all that he could to remain thoughtful. At one point utilising some basic meditative techniques and a bit of interpretive licensing, he trawled his memory for correlations between his bender symbolism and some of the subsistent parallels that he'd noted in this reality. Picturesque landscapes, tireless pursuers, unearthly beasts—the premonition of each had dotted his visions with circuitous regularity. He now had only to nod to their substantiality, to admit that they were real and tactile and not merely an intricate trick of his senses, one sensorial phantasy piled atop another. In diversion less exasperating, he rejected pointless cerebration and instead occupied himself by administering to his body, inspecting his wounds, massaging a cramp or stretching an atrophied ligament, careful not to expend more energy than his pittance of nourishment could mete to his musculature. The obstacles in his life too monolithic to ignore, he still had so much to grasp, and no one around whose brain he might pick for answers. Both literally and metaphorically in the dark, he had no doubt that things would remain such until he was released—or, better yet, until he woke up in his proper environment, amid doctors and staff and rubber rooms and good old-fashioned straitjackets. At this point, he'd have kissed nurse Groller smack on the lips if only to be back home again.

Passing time, he talked to himself for the company of a voice, and even hummed a hook or two from his favourite pop tunes in the hope that a few homey glimmers of familiarity might temporarily thwart the darkness and the stench. By afternoon, he managed to fade back into a doze, a nap spurred by boredom and by the pointless taxing of his faculty; and it was from within this most restful of all his slumbers so far— induced, perhaps, by the relaxing effects of the massage—that he lurched awake to the chilling premonition that he was no longer alone in his cell.

How this was possible he couldn't begin to comprehend. He'd always been a light sleeper, and lately even more so, with each day's waking hurling some new peril in his path, quite nearly to the point of routine. Whether now through intuition or by some extraneous amissness half-heard through sleep-shuttered ears, he felt an undeniable presence within his dark confines, even though he knew that his trap door couldn't have been raised, much less unbolted, without squeak, rattle, and clangour enough to jolt him into readiness.

Frozen, not even chancing to breathe, Wagner gazed blankly about, eyes panning left and right and up and around, the meagre diffusion from above proving only marginally helpful to his sleep-bleared peepers. Yet, finding nothing in the foreground whose distinguishment might have hastened greater alarm—no lumbering Minotaur cohering out of the gloom, no multi-headed Hydra about to snap him up into its lethal embrace—he commenced with a careful pivot, turning himself in cautious, almost imperceptible increment that he might, at full revolution, find the peace of mind to dismiss the vaporous outpour of his rampant paranoia. Only, it was here, at just beyond one-half rotation, that he chanced upon what seemed an incongruous shadow in perch near one corner of the chamber, a penumbral vagueness that shouldn't, by his accounting, have existed.

Darker than its stony background and no less immutable, with overdriven imagination Wagner immediately thought to imbue it with the very worst of baneful intents. Compensating for his disadvantaged vision, he quickly directed his gaze a few degrees to the right of the anomaly in order to gain some distinction of form, hoping to find it all for naught, desperate that his bogeyman turn out to be no more than a trick of the darkness. To his dismay, it was neither. His gambit perhaps too fruitful, the resulting outline was a decisively familiar one.

"W-who's there?" he demanded. Then, realising that he'd spouted his interrogative in English, he repeated it in Ergosian.

"Thank the Twain!" came a stoutly baritone voice from out of the void. "I had initially thought you ill or expired, so deathly still had you lain after my first hail."

"Who are you? How did you get in here?"

"You are one of the newly captured, are you not?"

"I'm not going to ask again," said Wagner. "Who *are* you?"

The intruder crept forward, and in so doing he revealed the means of his access into Wagner's cell—a barely discernible gape in the corner where one of the great blocks had been unseated and slid away from its mortar. Through the resulting aperture Wagner could just make out the dim aura of luminosity provided by what he presumed was that cell's hatchway.

"I am Tamek," said the figure. "Formerly of Vishkor, now of this wretched place. By what name are you known?"

Even in the darkness, Wagner was immediately alerted to the newcomer's Samson-like stature, and for a trice it gave him pause for concern. "Wagner," he replied. "I'm Wagner."

"Well, *Voknor*, you must be quite the firebrand to have landed yourself in detention on your first day. I mus— *here, one moment!* Could it be that you are the upstart who came to the scratch in the inception yard—the dropper who attacked the warders for the sake of a Vofspar? Tell me, *Voknor*, tell me that you and he are not one and the same!"

"I'm not sure I know what you're talking about. What's a Vofspar?"

"The Vofspar—the feral warrioress! The female who, e'en heavily injured, maimed a handful of warders before finally being subdued herself. You had a hand in that fracas, did you not?"

"Ah, that," said Wagner. "Yeah, I guess I did."

"Why, *Voknor*? Why would you risk yourself for a savage? Her kind would just as soon have torn *you* asunder as any NuRac."

"I don't really know. I just did it." He stared at his unseeable visitor. "Anyway, how could you even know about that from down in here? Have you got a secret doorway to the *surface* as well?"

Tamek laughed heartily. "Nay, I regret that I do not. But let me assure you that I am no stranger to this place. Verily, I was impounded again only this morning, e'er in keeping with precedent and policy."

"I-I don't understand."

"Because I renew my remonstrations each time these NuRac blackguards invade our lands in their perfervid bent to impress man, woman, and child into the unjustness of servitude and worse. They accuse me of incitation, of creating unrest among the masses. More to the truth, they find me irritating and loud. When my protests become too grating, they simply banish me for a few days. 'Tis indeed a tedious cycle—and, I need not tell you, an unsalutary one."

Warming to the man, Wagner relaxed into his straw and posed the most obvious of his many questions. "From what I gather," he said, "the NuRacs aren't all that shy about doling punishment to troublemakers. How is it, then, that they don't just lop off your head and be done with you? And why wasn't *I* killed for blundering into something I'd have done better to avoid?"

"You are an infidel, are you not?"

"Excuse me?"

"You are a man, yes—but not an Ergosian. You have little or no knowledge of our creed and our lore?"

Wagner became edgy. "What if I don't?"

"Fear not. I have converted many an unbeliever. And I have found worthy opponents in those who could not be convinced."

Edgy turned to antsy. "I'm not sure I like the sound of that. *Opponents?*"

He laughed again. "I speak in many senses, *Voknor*. Opponents on the field of battle—aye, some—although I am e'er loath to do so, e'en in instances when mine own life may be forfeit. I much prefer the dialectic arena, where quietus yields me converts and not corpses."

"Then you're an evangelist?"

"If you wish. In my time I have enjoyed spiritual privilege, which I am in duty bound to minister unto others. Infidels, émigrés, tramontanes—on the whole, they make for the most ready of challenges, for they are a largely unenlightened lot, too oft disposed to the errancy and aberration wrought of their own purposelessness. Long have I prehended this lacking. I have e'en come to appreciate it. 'Tis occasionally my most insidious ally.

"But, to satisfy your most desirous question first—had it been anyone but this Vofspar whose defence you sought to undertake, you would almost certainly have been slain outright for your foolishness. Howe'er, in the while betwixt the slave train's arrival and my re-impoundment to this neighbouring chamber a few, short hours ago, I found opportunity to listen to some of the accounts of the newly arrived. Sifting, as one must, through the inevitable o'ermeasure of lively exaggerations, I was drawn to a particular allegation, one that connected a man— you—in some heathenish manner to the beast. You see, rumour has it that you were captured...*together?*"

Despite the darkness, Wagner felt himself probed by illiberal eyes. "It's true," he said. "I take it that there's some huge problem with that?"

"One of great magnitude, *Voknor*. You see, to an Ergosian, the Vofspar represents the embodiment of the ills and evils within us—our legends are quite explicit in any number of references. They are nefarious creatures with e'en fewer redeeming qualities than the NuRacs themselves. Howe'er, to the NuRacs—"

"I don't believe that."

"Ne'ertheless, to the NuRacs they are rare prizes indeed, for such splendid performers are they in the games that our captors will tolerate considerable loss to their own ranks in order to obtain but a single Vofspar."

"Then you should be happy to know that at least three NuRacs were brutally killed while attempting to capture her, and that a handful more took some fairly heavy hits in the time between that and the squabble in the yard out there."

"That is indeed capital news, my friend. But, tell true, how is it that you came to be paired with the feral?"

Wagner had only seconds in which to spin together a tale that he could relay to the Ergosian without requiring an elucidation of the facts that he himself didn't understand. A finesse in omitting certain details, the careful sidestepping of issues decidedly too delicate to broach—he saw no profit in sharing his lifelong mysteries with a man he'd known but a few minutes. To reveal anything beyond the scope of Tamek's substantial intellection would only jeopardise his credibility, and make of him an outcast and a dangerous influence to a people who were probably already delimited by the prophetic and religious dogma that Tamek held in such regard. He therefore abridged his narrative into what he hoped would be a passable account of a traveller who'd become lost in the woods, a man whom happenstance delivered into the heart of an isolated NuRac-Vofspar skirmish. The incredulity of his former life omitted, the remainder of his account he relayed in faithful progression, from his unlikely teaming with the Vofspar brood, to the reciprocated altruism that ultimately resulted in defeat and capture, and finally to the inception yard business that prefaced his current detention. When Tamek inquired, as was ineluctable, about Wagner's homeland—what it was called, how far distant and such—Wagner shamefastly confessed to a lapse in memory (slickly accredited to the concussive impact of his plummet) that conveniently left his history too sketchy to make for good ink. Not all that difficult a sham, it was, however, a temporarily necessary one, for he thought it essential that he preserve what precious little remained of his anonymity.

The cell's dark environs an unexpected boon to Wagner's subterfuge, it masked any agitation, any flush of countenance or disinclination toward eye contact that might have given the Ergosian reason to suspect him. Never truly comfortable with deception—it had, after all, lost him Sara, years before—Wagner felt put upon by the necessity of having to bamboozle his way through the topical pertinences that he simply couldn't allow to come to light. He wasn't Doc Adams, huckstering snake oil to the uninformed. He was an interloper in an unenlightened and suspicious—and probably superstitious—society, dispensing potentially damning biographical information to a man who, if not a religious zealot, was patently a hardcore fundamentalist. If Wagner couldn't contrive and persuade within the boundaries of whatever passed for acceptable convention, if he couldn't walk that judicious line, he would be forever sunk, branded a liar and a fabricator from this point on. Yet, if he gave over too much, he might never be able to successfully insinuate himself amid the common populace.

Astonishingly, Tamek actually seemed to buy into his charade—this, or he merely chose to let it slide, given that from his side of the blackness he couldn't be completely certain that Wagner wasn't a criminal or a king. Whatever the Ergosian's thoughts, he didn't air them, and he quite graciously allowed Wagner his privacy for the nonce.

Wagner, relieved for the lack of prying, subsequently came to drop much of his initial guardedness and, in result, soon found his narrative accentuated by some of the liveliness that he generally reserved for his recreational raillery with Sally Lemanski. No doubt in part an ostensible stratagem for glossing over what he couldn't reveal to Tamek's undeniably erudite—and sorely unprepared—intellect, it was no less a constitutional of sorts, an assay into Ergosian-speak that Wagner had barely been given opportunity to explore beyond a handful of en route exchanges with the caravan trusty. What a kick it was to hear this spanking new tongue issuing with such proficiency from his untutored, Anglican lips! Obliged by Tamek's company, and even more appreciative of a learned agency from which to gain crucial insight into the culture, Wagner knew that to continue in his pretence he had but to be friendly and open and marginally creative while keeping specifics to a minimum. Only in this fashion could he protect himself from the unpleasant potentialities that fear and ignorance could conceivably foist on him the moment that he was perceived as anyone other than who he professed himself to be.

"'Tis possible that you are being tested," Tamek said after hearing Wagner's story. "A fall such as you describe can indeed muddle a man's memories. The fact that you continue to draw breath, howe'er, is a tribute to your resilience and fortitude. Unfathomable are the powers that one moment propel you headlong into direness, and the next, whisk you post-haste from the brink."

It was Wagner's turn to laugh. "What—you don't think I'm rash and stupid enough on my own?"

"Nay, I have no doubt of that, *Voknor*. But who am I to make a knave of *you* while *I* occupy the neighbouring chamber?"

"What's *your* story, then?"

"Eh? Oh, are you asking how 'tis that the NuRacs continue to tolerate my impudence?"

Wagner affirmed.

"As a stranger to the realm, you would have little notion, *Voknor*. What you do not know is that, in mine own way, I am fancied as somewhat of a prize to our gaolers."

"A prize...like the Vofspar?"

"Nay, not truly. Her kind is revered for its unparalleled ferocity in the arena. She, like other Vofspars before her, will be pitted 'gainst a predictably unbroken consecution of adversaries, tournament upon tournament, until the day that her windedness from too many successive battles briefly opens her to the maul of some undeserving, albeit more greatly energised, opponent. Conversely, I am rarely slated for games of such grim finality. My political value far too commodious to risk in such wasteful extravagance, I have instead been fashioned into a symbol of a conquered race—a toppled figurehead, if you will—to be paraded before his people, that the sight of my ignominy might divest my kind of whate'er pittance of hope they may yet be harbouring. After all," he claimed, his voice suddenly filigreed in NuRac grandiloquence, *"who among your compatriots would not cower before those who have humbled and hobbled the last of the Sentinels to their holy city of Vishkor?"*

He offered up a pause here, as if his words were to have elicited something more from Wagner than mere silence. Wagner, at once feeling dweebishly unhep to things Ergosian, was compelled to dig deeply into pockets of unenlightened solicitousness for some manner of acknowledgement.

"That should probably mean something to me. I'm sorry, but it doesn't."

Tamek chortled. "Am I so daft, *Voknor*, that I make such presumption of your knowledge, e'en as we have already established that you are not of this region? 'Twould seem that but a few hours in this dank dungeon has been enow to leech the light of good sense from my mind!"

He then bade Wagner listen while he expounded for him the most succinct of histories, that he might provide him a functioning knowledge of his culture.

Beginning with geography, Tamek spoke of how, for untold years, his people had dwelled in the much-varied territories between the eastern foot of the Grobian Alps and the western edge of the Motahlon range. Abutting the far northern regions was the Great Sea, with its restless waters and its gently populated islets, while to the south lay the least charted of locales, a region not commonly travelled because of the vast and treacherous divide known as the Leordahn Crevasse that cleaved the realm and made the southlands all but unreachable. This canyon, no mere rift valley to hear the Sentinel describe it, was immense in area, and—as it was with most unplumbed wonders—one whose repute of terraqueous oddities, of eerie emanations and never-to-be-seen-again wayfarers, invited legends of peril both terrestrial and mystical.

Without bothering to winnow fact from superstition, Tamek proffered that it was perhaps this realm beyond Leordahn whence the "amnestic" *Voknor* haled, if only because it was the only territory of which he lacked extensive knowledge. Too, as he'd already noted enough grammatical liberties in Wagner's speech to rule him out as a national, it initially made sense to ascribe his outsider's status to a realm that few actually had ken of. At this untested juncture in their acquaintance, the south appeared the logical, equitable choice; and Wagner, grateful at last for a convenient pretext, feigned some vaguely recollected affinity of possibility, mostly to perpetuate the opportunity for gathering as much intelligence as he could.

Within the abundant verdancy of the Ergosian woodlands, marshes, mountains and grasslands, Tamek's people succeeded in erecting a handful of magnificent cities. Connecting these were the trade routes, which led to the establishment of the many industrious villages, farms, hamlets and hostelries that had over time come to pepper the realm. A commonwealth of small provinces, it prospered through a robust network of commerce, all governed by the adequately benign leadership of the various burgomasters and burgraves who were themselves counselled by the magistrates and by the priests at Vishkor.

"Many years past," said Tamek, "when my parents were yet children, there came word of a new people from the west, an ambitious race whose migratory venturousness came to set them at the periphery of our territories. I say 'ambitious,' *Voknor*, because theirs was a restless culture, one for whom our ideals of simple contentedness would come to symbolise complacency, failure—a surrendering of spirit, if you will. In those years, the most astute of Ergosians called them 'ravagers,' for indeed they were e'er driven by impingement and conquest, and rarely if e'er did they bestow back to the land that which they first wrenched from it. They ensconced themselves in the fringes of countryside previously assumed Ergosian by proxy. Their encroachment was originally tolerated with hopeful interest, that our mutual respect might sustain peaceful cohabitation. Although they remained much to themselves o'erall, 'twas not unheard of for those of our people whose settlements most closely verged upon theirs to indulge in an occasional exchange of goods."

His narrative paused as both men lifted an ear to the sound of footfalls from above. Tamek moved prudently toward the passageway, but halted when the steps continued on beyond his and Wagner's hatches to another oubliette, three or four cells down. Then, a clanking of chains, a few muffled beratings from the NuRac turnkey, and it was apparent that they'd acquired a new neighbour.

"Hmm, most unusual," said the Sentinel. "Quite a spirited lot with whom you arrived, *Voknor*."

"How do you know it's one of the newly captured?" asked Wagner.

"I do not. But most shellbacks are well acquainted with this cesspit, with its rodents, cragworms and scurrying dung beetles, and they are understandably reluctant to do anything that would return them here."

"Shellbacks?"

"Long-timers. Fixtures. 'Tis said that those of us who are veterans, not only of the training whip but of the tournaments for which said whip prepares us, have developed carapace. Most shellbacks have endured a stint down here at least once during their internment. The sensible ones see to it that they do not take their contumacy 'gainst our oppressors quite so far again. Only *I* seem to be *that* foolish."

"Maybe our new guest is the Vofspar."

"Unlikely. She is most assuredly an inhabitant of the menagerie block deep within the Great Arena's infrastructure, along with the Sunderer and the other ferals."

Wagner guffawed. "Sunderer? What the heck is—"

"One explanation at a time," said Tamek. "Allow me first to finish with your earlier inquiry—where was it that we quit?"

"Um—NuRacs infiltrating your lands?"

"Ah, yes. The passage of many years saw little adverse development in their migration. Life continued much as it had. My forebears were a trusting lot, and therefore, unsuspecting of the NuRacs' insidious aims. Mind you, it occurred gradually, inconspicuously, like a kori sloth who you one day discover has traded one tree for another without your e'er noticing. And although there were indeed Ergosians who expressed their concerns, the majority did not distress, for they knew the realm was wide and accommodating. Few would begrudge those who sought a humbler quietude of existence, e'en if they be unfamiliar in aspect. Those Ergosians who opted to depart for newer lands did so in regretful haste. Those who remained, oh, they fared well enow. But 'twas their progeny who paid the cost.

"In the year that my parents mated, the calendar quickly approached the time of Vorshalah; I myself took breath and life during the Vorshalah—an insignificant occasion, my birth, when set within the context of the Bestowal."

Wagner once more felt as if he'd been left hanging, this time as Tamek ceased speaking in order to initiate a gesture in the shadows that Wagner couldn't quite see to interpret.

"The bestowal of *what*?" he finally asked.

Tamek grunted, probably in bemusement at having again glossed past Wagner's inexperience just moments after his last reminder.

"Listen closely, my infidel friend, and perhaps you will spare me the trouble of having to persuade your conversion at some later date."

With that ominous remark, Tamek provided his soon-to-be-illuminated pupil with a good month's-worth of Ergosian Sunday schooling, stuffed with doctrine like a holiday bird is stuffed with oysters, all delivered within the span of the twenty-or-so minutes they had left before unanticipated interruption was to sever their exchange. Interestingly, and not totally unforeseen, Tamek's account wasn't all that divergent from the shared basics of most of the major world religions of Wagner's acquaintance—at least as far as the heart of said religions went. It included the presence of a dynamic and much-awaited Mahdi-figure à la Jesus, Muhammad, Buddha, et al, but with a radically intriguing twist all its own. For, where the earthly prophets had conjecturally appeared in mortal form within a specific timeframe, with their respective lores enduring beyond their bodily deaths by means of tradition entrusted from one generation to the next (Buddha being the possible exception, the reincarnation of whom Wagner once read was sought out in children born on the death of a previous—and allegedly reincarnated—Buddha who had himself been chosen in such fashion at infancy), it seemed that the Bestowal of which Tamek spoke involved a kind of tridecennial roundsman who returned to this plane of existence roughly once every thirty years. Called the "Paraclete," this venerated individual thus appeared in not only one historical context, but regularly—in intervals calculable enough for even the least of the laity to forecast so long as one could read the signs and had a keen eye for celestial periodicity.

Without recollectable fail, this advocate checked in on his flock personally, thereby bolstering an occasionally wavering populace as only a flesh and blood presence could. How, why, and from where, Tamek didn't clarify, his invocation of several abstract deities duly noted by Wagner but not truly understood with quite the all-embraceable relevance that Tamek intended. All that was extractable from the anagogic mumbo-jumbo was that this much-anticipated figure was in fine a rejuvenator, a spiritual crutch for each new age and for the age in wane, a benevolence whose sublimity encompassed and enlightened both the old, the young, the devout, and the would-be faithful—and whose words, because of his frequency, would not be long misquoted by even the most ungrammatic of scribes.

In the context that it was given, Wagner couldn't help but to find the concept of religious faith reduced here to veritable insignificance in the face of a living, breathing—if limitedly accessible—exemplar. This, more than all of Tamek's mysticisms and presagings, proved particularly intriguing, for it begged an issue of efficacy that Wagner dared not raise until he knew for sure that he wouldn't be wandering irretrievably into blasphemous territory. Still, he wondered—what, in fact, becomes of faith that suddenly finds itself saddled with verifiable truth?

The Vorshalah, Tamek explained, was a series of precursory signs—actually a non-specific timeframe of "miraculous indicants" that betokened the Paraclete's re-culmination by anywhere from a few months to a few years. Most proud of the fact that his own birth had occurred during the last Vorshalah, it was with unabashed verve that the Sentinel relayed how his parents had seen enough portentousness in this to prompt a pilgrimage to Vishkor in order that their infant son might receive personal blessing from the Paraclete himself. The ensuing brush with reverence, if not exactly kismetic, nevertheless proved a tremendous influence on Tamek's life's calling, his rearing years thence steeped in ideals and righteous prescription the likes of which, in his twentieth year, had led to his installation as one of the four elite defenders of the holy city itself.

This Paraclete, however, had no monopoly on the Ergosian faith. There were allegedly greater forces that, in some nondescript sense, oversaw and guided the lives of all who dwelled upon Ergos—the NuRacs included—although Wagner deduced from Tamek's impassioned descriptions that these were vague and obscure non-entities assigned to reign over even more abstract and metaphysical phenomena. The Powers Twain—Eternity and Existence—were two such essences, and apparently the keystones of the delicately balanced pale between life, death, the once ago, the now, and the forever. These dual auras were inextricably linked in an infinite chain of binding consanguinity. Existence represented, among other things, life and thought and substance, from the tiniest mote to the grandest heavenly body to the spark of the simplest idea. Eternity, on the other hand, while seemingly greater in scope, relied upon Existence, was both its parent and its progeny, in a kind of indivisible, cyclical symbiosis wherefrom life sprang out of death; growth, out of decay; prosperity, by way of innovation by way of need— which was itself created by the perdition of some previous prosperity. All very recondite, the best that Wagner could do was to liken the whole premise to that of the Hindu Trimurti: the trinity of Brahma, Vishnu, and Shiva who—as Creator, Preserver, and Destroyer within one three-headed body—covered pretty much the same bases back on earth.

The Powers Twain, the Trimurti: while noteworthy concepts both, neither one held particular significance for Wagner. The former, however, meant the world to his new acquaintance. Moreover, they *were* the world to him. They were the explicative framework for how things came to be and for where they were going. As Tamek put it: "Continual rebirthing and renewal fills Eternity's cup with the wines of Existence, all within the bounds of a complementary dependency. After all, a vessel void of contents serves little purpose, and wine with no chalice seeps away into the mud."

"So," Wagner argued, "although this Paraclete is a flesh and blood person who pops in every thirty-or-so years to see that you're all on the right path, these others—these *Powers Twain?*—have never been seen or confirmed?"

"Look around you, *Voknor.* E'en in this cell you are confronted with Existence, with substance irrefutable."

"I'm surrounded by rock and faeces—that doesn't make me want to worship them."

"There is no worship involved, my friend. What exists, exists. You can feel it, mould it, circumvent it, utilise it, be imprisoned by it. But it does not truly go away. In one form or another, it remains. 'Tis eternal."

"I suppose, then, that if the NuRacs were to totally forget about us down here, we'd encounter your Eternity as well?"

Tamek hadn't time to reply. The trample of boots overhead inclined him towards his corner exit where he briefly remained until it seemed indeed that Wagner's trap was being unlatched. Then, sailing off to his own cell, he joggled the slab loosely into place behind him, with Wagner shouldering it flush just as the hatch swung up.

Blinding light suddenly streamed in, a fulgent, heavenly column that was almost climbable in its drama. Searing to the eyes, Wagner clamped down hard and pressed his face to the very stone that he'd just reseated. The silence that accompanied the intrusion would be broken by rebuke.

"What are you waiting for," spat the warder, "the Monarch's personal invitation?"

Wagner quickly swung to, and from a squint he caught sight of a rope in dangle, a knotty snake that writhed mid-chamber before him. Still half-blind, he inched his way toward it and, gingerly taking it in hand, squinched up at the NuRac, five metres overhead.

"Are your eyes *and* ears filled with dung? Get yourself up, mongrel!"

Wagner broke and shinned up the rope as directed, carefully, steadily, finding it remarkably less arduous than similar endeavouring had seemed back in his junior high Phys-Ed days. Reaching topside, and barely winded at all, he was yanked out by his arms and thrust before the poleaxe of a second NuRac.

"Be on guard," said the first to the second. "This whelp is a wily one. He is the malapert from the slave train."

"The Vofspar suckling?" The pikeman quickly brought his weapon to arm, pressing it against the hirsuteness of Wagner's breast. "Phew! He stinks! And he is unclothed! Is it wise to bring him before AuwNiir like this?"

"So, have him scrubbed! Douse him in the cistern for all I care. He is Ergosian, and so just another nuisance. And thankfully he is your charge, KoviKor, not mine."

Wagner gazed at his escort, harking back to Tamek's hopeful conjecture about the great hands that guided him. Could he have shaken his head without seeming impertinent, he would have done so. Instead, he merely sighed and obeyed KoviKor's direction out of the cell block.

His lungs filling up on deliciously untainted air, Wagner shook the rigidity from his underworked limbs, still sluggish and in distress from the beatings he had taken. The floorstone lined with more oubliettes than he cared to number, he wondered how many of them housed kindred wretches, crouched and crestfallen in the morbific filth, below his own momentarily manumitted feet. All along to his left, a brick curtain cordoned the entirety of the block's floor-level interiors (temporary holding cells and interrogation roomlets, according to Tamek); and to the right, an ambitious symmetry of arched window-ways offered a sun-dazzled view of the courtyard where he'd received his many lumps. These long-trampled grounds, unpopulated now by even a single prisoner, boasted only a bare bones detail of NuRacs stationed at various intervals about the compound perimeter, not unlike what he'd observed in the detention block, where only a mere sufficiency of sentries were stationed along the isolation row, with a few others moving about within its handful of arterial corridors.

At the end of the gallery, prisoner and gaoler were joined by two more guards. This pair fell in behind them as KoviKor spurred Wagner across the yard, toward the very grouping of troughs that he'd seen from his introductory perspective the previous day. Risking a gaze to the rear, Wagner verified what he'd already surmised, that the dungeon block was indeed the same, lone, large-stoned structure that had filled him with such misgivings at first espial. Yet, having spent the last few days deep in its foul crawl, its once forbidding exteriors seemed noticeably less rebarbative now, the architecture only mildly indicative of the subterranean unpleasantness beyond the vaunt of its stonecraft.

The yard was a bright blear of sunlight, so removed from the damp chill of the pit that Wagner all but withered from prostration before he'd even covered one-half the distance to the water. The sand around him shimmering in a rippled illusion of fluid heat, he squinted longingly at the troughs, struggling to override his body's directive to haul off and dive straight into one like a man on fire.

One of the new escorts then took the lead and, opening the sluice gate, topped off the nearest trough with a flush of fresh water. Grabbing a pail, she hung it under the spillway until it was filled, and then plopped it at Wagner's smutty feet. At the same time, KoviKor fished around within a small, metal receptacle situated between the basins, and produced a rough chunk of what was to pass for soap. Lobbing it at Wagner, the latter caught it on the fly, eyeballed it, and gazed back mutely at the NuRac.

"Cleanse yourself," ordered KoviKor. "You have only a few moments, so be swift about it." Then he turned to the third soldier. "Go to the toggery and find this one some raiment—preferably something laundered."

With this courier hieing off for the nearest tunnel in the courtyard curtain, Wagner immersed the laving brick into the pail and commenced to bathe, the swash of the water upon his fingers, his wrists, his arms and shoulders, converting dreary fatigue to revitalising élan. Although the soap was crude, and yielded little more than a few milky-grey bubbles, he worked it diligently across his body in order to purge the filth that for days had enveloped him like a second skin. The guards standing silently nearby the whole while, they remained largely unheedful of the process—although not distanced nearly enough for Wagner's sense of comfort in what he considered to be one of the most personal and private of hygienic rituals.

Few other souls graced the yard during the wash-up, none save for a small preoccupation of soldiers seen crossing the north grounds on some task of its own. Too, along the upper ramparts an occasional sentry strolled a solitary patrol, the sight of a naked prisoner rinsing under a sluice barely warranting even a passing notice. By necessity, by circumstance, Wagner's modesty had quite nearly become an instinct disengaged through simple pervasion—first, with his ectoplasmic streaking about the halls at Howsley, and second, by his *au naturel* prancing through both the wilds of the Ergosian countryside and now here, in QieLahr, with the bulk of his garb-free romps having occurred within venues that were considerably less than intimate. In fact, by having led the hospital professionals and other long-acclimated witnesses on a merry chase or three, the still-earthbound Wagner had just about resigned himself to the unintentional exhibitionism that went hand in hand with the fortuitousness of his condition. On some level, he'd perhaps been inclined to treat it as an exercise in bender-imposed vanity; on another, he may simply have dismissed it as a triviality that in no way superseded the greater matter of survival. Regardless, the part of him that still embraced more civilised convention could hardly wait for the NuRac to return with some clothes.

To have read their body language, KoviKor and the female seemed unrelishing of their menial idleness. Neither, however, made issue of said inconvenience, not one to the other, nor to Wagner (upon whom they might easily—and without recourse—have directed their displeasure). Careful not to invite their wrath, Wagner kept scrubbing and rinsing, scrubbing and rinsing, the residue of too many discommodious days soon puddling murkily around his feet, with the final purge leaving him a rosy mottle of pink and purple flesh, of yellow-grey bruises and half-healed cuts. His hair not washing entirely clean, the grit of the soap left it with a course and grainy texture; but at this point, *anything* was preferable to the muddied, matted state that capture and confinement had made of it.

No drying cloth was provided him, although truly he had little need of one, the action of sun and breeze doing well to wick away the saturation. His hair dried the way it did at the beach, slicked back with the aid of a sculpting hand, while the rest of his body went from sopped to beaded to virtually dry within a matter of minutes. Up until this very moment, he hadn't really thought about the tattoo. There hadn't been time enough or reason for it. But now, with his body clean and bare and with little to hide his *sigma* save for his generous bristle of chest hair, he wondered how the folk around him would react to the symbol that he'd had permanently infixed upon his left pectoral.

Thinking back on the history he knew, the pricking of one's skin with pin and ink, or with thread and soot, went way back before the time of Christ. Sometimes a punitive measure—a blatant mark upon the foreheads of prisoners, conquered enemies, or slaves, all of whom would quickly be identified and handed over to authorities should they ever have escaped—tattoos were just as commonly used to beautify, to invoke mystical protection, to proclaim individuality or affiliation, and occasionally, when the use of parchment was too dangerous or impractical, to relay insurgent information beneath the hairline of seemingly innocuous messengers. Surely, even in this antiquated culture of hybrids and humanoids, there was a history of such things—only Wagner was in no great hurry to play show-and-tell with his. Neither would he have to, unless it happened that he was scrutinised too closely, which—given that the most prevalent sentiments exhibited by the NuRacs thus far were contempt and indifference, in that order—was unlikely to occur.

Made brazen by dehydration, Wagner opened the sluice one last time to slake his Hephaestean thirst. He drank unabashedly and then let go the cord, directing the excess into the nearest trough. Hailed then from behind, he spun quickly and was assaulted by a wad of clothing, flung neglectfully at him by the returning guard—none too happy, it seemed, about his temporary valet status. Without ado,

Wagner undid the pile, gave each piece the once-over, and donned them one after the other.

Clad at last, even if in poor fitting, second- and third-hand tunic and trousers and a truly decrepit pair of sandals, Wagner followed the prompt of his NuRac overseers, who marched him through an ingress in the courtyard wall and into a shadowy maze of barren, torchlit halls. Deeper within, they came upon the increasing occasion of other soldiers, and even a few civilian passers-by, none of whom took more than fleeting notice of Wagner and his party.

The excursion culminated at a flight of steps. Inordinately narrow and steep, they topped-out before a stout door of hardwood, heavily hinged and swelled from the dankly cavernous quality of the substructure atmosphere. As the staircase could accommodate but a single body at a time, only the female guard ascended; and, on reaching the top, she rapped twice upon the wood with the studded portion of her armlet. Hearing acknowledgement from the other side, she pushed open the door, and bade Wagner upwards.

Eerily reminiscent of the manner in which Miss Groller had so often directed him to Jon Mazzio's office, Wagner rejected once more the interminably uprising notion that he could be so deeply entrenched in a hallucinatory state that transposed this Ergosian setting over a framework of earthly realities. The facts, the details, the sensory complexity—it was simply too much illusion for a mind to maintain in a singular, closed format without allowing the diversity of other elemental inconsistencies to seep through. Nothing in this new existence had given up an iota of incongruity—not the slightest discordance of unmatched images linking earth to Ergos, nor anything to connect either of them to any dreamscaped allegory of objects and events independent of both, where one variable might clearly overlap, influence, affiliate, or suggest a relation. There was no betrayal, no fraying through which the weave of the other reality could be seen. More immediately, it would have required quite an imaginative mental disorder to make Margaret Groller into this svelte and sinewy NuRac whose only commonality with her Howsley counterpart was her gender.

"Yes? What is it?" A NuRac officer of discernible pomp stood hunched over a lamp-lit table, his face downturned, his hands rummaging, his apparent unconcern with his intruders stemming from a greater preoccupation with the various scraps of parchment and assorted scrolls and codices scattered in Oscar Madison fashion across the planked tabletop.

"The prisoner you requested, Commander," said the guard.

"And which prisoner would that be?" The officer had yet to look up from his work.

"I know not his appellation, sir. I only know him as the one who instigated the riot in the inception yard."

The Commander's head lifted, his eyes fixing on Wagner. "Oh yes, the impetuous one. Leave us."

"Sir?"

"Post yourselves outside the door. Do not worry—he presents no danger to me."

The guards obeyed, albeit reluctantly, leaving Wagner and the officer facing each other like the last men left standing in a free-for-all. The NuRac, his armoured breastplate emblazoned in intricate regalia, remained drawn over the table, his hands flat and outstretched, his eyes measuring Wagner like an undertaker sizing up a gallows bird about to meet his maker.

"After all the ado yesterday," he finally said, "you still have the impertinence to look at me directly?"

Wagner averted his eyes.

"Oh, come now," the NuRac continued. "Do not disappoint me by suddenly turning timid. After all, it was your spirit in the face of unsurety and insurmountable odds that convinced me to secure your battle rights."

Wagner, again locking eyes with the NuRac, cleared his throat. "Battle rights?"

"Of course. You are understandably ignorant of our ways, Ergosian, being newly captured and all. But you will learn quickly enough. And you will adapt. You all do eventually. I tell you now, my kind is not a single-minded race. We do not simply enslave for its own sake. Do you think that your people are here to simply waste away in our dungeons, without the merest benefit to our economy or leisure?"

"I don't know what to think."

"I hardly believe that. What are you called?"

Wagner, weighing inclination, went with Tamek's pronunciation. "*Voknor*."

"Well, *Voknor*, you have been entered into the roster of my personal stable, and will participate in this month's games. I am AuwNiir, fifth in service to his Excellency the Monarch's elite forces. You will call me 'Commander.' I am also your new master and sponsor. As such, you will be reserved the privileges and allowances bestowed of this status, so long as I am able to profit from your successes. The more you achieve in my name, the more enhanced your reward. Conversely, upon each failing, you will endure twice the gruelling hardship until you have reinstated yourself. With excessive failures, you will be pawned to those brokers who are less accommodating than I—and trust me, *Voknor*, this you do not desire. Have you any questions?"

"Yes, Commander. What do you mean by *games*?"

"Do not be obtuse. We are both of warring races, yes? Battle has become our way of life, and skirmish, our livelihood. Combative mêlée is the very pastiche of our aggressively inherent legacies, *Voknor*. You were instructed at disembarking to remand to memory all notions of freedom. Always hold this in mind. Neither you nor those captured with you will perchance to glimpse the outside world again in this lifetime. You, specifically, are fortunate to even be among the living. So understand that, herein, your every breath and bowel movement you owe to me. You are henceforth to serve a new purpose, perhaps one not entirely removed from your previous life, but most certainly an existence that will offer some rather unusual incentives and—make no mistake—some particularly severe penalties.

"Now, you ask about the games. Games are what you will live for from this moment forward. Obviously, I do not speak of bigratto or Kaimbre's Choice, nor any common child's gambol, but games in which you will beard the Spectre for your very life. Like the others of your race, you will train at physical combat and you will help to perpetuate our military education while likewise providing entertainment for the masses through the mortally serious avenues of arena competition."

Explained in full and understood in part, Wagner's future had just been laid coldly before him like an inevitability that couldn't be sidestepped no matter the dazzle of his persuasive footwork. Commander AuwNiir then hailed the guards, instructing them to accompany Wagner to the infirmary where he was to receive treatment for his injuries. After this, he was to spend the remainder of the afternoon in the training yard, a prefatory acclimating to what had all the indications of being an entry-level portal to the vaunted halls shared by Spartacus, Demetrious, and the sundry other assorted fighters of earthly fact and fiction who partook in those bloodthirsty, gladiatorial endeavours of antiquity.

Disconcerted in his ushering from AuwNiir's chamber, spurred by the point of KoviKor's spear and the drub of the female's palm at his shoulder, Wagner stole a parting glimpse of this newest of taskmasters—and in doing, chanced upon a discovery so momentous that, once prehending it, he could not sunder his gaze. An instantaneity of chilling recognition, of joyless guerdon and revelatory dismay over what had suddenly become laughably misread portentousness, he was amazed that he'd not happened across it—*it*, of all things!—during the course of AuwNiir's exhortation. Perhaps had the oil lamp's playful flicker not toyed so with the shadows of the room, something so vital would have impressed him sooner— for surely it hadn't simply manifested out of nowhere, as by magic. No, the lamplight and the angle of the Commander's bearing had temporarily concealed it. His bolder regalia had outshown it. Only fortuity and a departing vantage had exposed it.

Just below centre on AuwNiir's breastplate was a heraldic embossment, a solitary device in high relief. Unaccompanied by armorial achievements, as coats of arms often were, nor by the superfluity of exterior decoration, it was likewise situated far enough from the Commander's insignias as to suggest little or no relation to rank, commendation, or merit. A curious blazonment of keen, sometimes intersecting, geometry encircled by a partial hoop, its significance was nonetheless tenfold over any mere compartment—at least from Wagner's perspective—for the discovery quickly sent his personal harmonics into irrecoverable careen.

Not hallucinated, not imagined—enchased upon his mortal enemy was none other than the glyph of Wagner's preoccupation.

It was the *sigma*.

CHAPTER NINE

It is a true saying that a man must eat a peck of
salt with his friend before he knows him.
  —MIGUEL DE CERVANTES SAAVEDRA

"By Eternity's flowing tresses! What happened to you!"

The man in charge of the prison infirmary, an elderly Ergosian with a short crop of snowy-white whiskers, had only just looked up from the bedside of an ailing patient to find a very contused and sunburned visitor standing dumb before him. Wagner, on entering the infirmary and having encountered no one to direct him one way or another, had instead sought out the only figure whose actions best suggested the gentle forbearance of an attending physician's. In supplement, he'd almost immediately gleaned the elder's identity by composite from Tamek's orienting tutelage, enough to assure him that this man could not have been anyone other than the one they called Papa Olask.

Patriarchal titles in the Ergosian tongue having a plethora of complex connotations, the implication in this instance was a deliberate, imprecisely paternal one, for it was well known that the man had never sired children in his life. A hypocoristic endearment, such was the honour paid the physician by a prison population to whose ailments and complaints he tirelessly ministered—and only by such endorsement did Wagner have an "up" on what to expect from the crag-faced, sawbonesy fellow who'd just addressed him on the nature of his various scotchings.

A glance about the room showed an array of makeshift cots, no less than sixty, roughly one-third of which was occupied by Ergosian injured. Most of these people were wrapped in blood-spotted dressings commensurate with whatever level of atrocity had befallen them, a goodly number being amputees whose fates beyond shock and gangrenous infection were in more delicate falter than most earthly hospitals would ever have permitted without some manner of counteractive agency. Yet, given the crudity of conditions and the hit-and-miss futility of pre-enlightened medicine, Papa Olask and his handful of assistants rendered without demurral all that was in their power to render, that as many as possible could be comforted within the crimp of the hospital's limited resources. Remarkably, more patients than not seemed to be sleeping—some even peacefully—in the very midst of their restless, wallowing, often wailing, brethren for whom there simply weren't enough consoling orderlies available to minify every anguish. Some of the haler recuperators in turn tried their hand at solacing, most in ineptly good-hearted fashion. Greater in number, however, were those who simply lay propped upon their bedding, conversing now and again with an adjacent neighbour. It was by this lot's sudden conspiracy of stares and murmurs that Wagner intuited that it was he who'd become the latest topic in an otherwise mundanity of talked-out subject matter.

"I ask again," said Olask, "what happened to you?"

Wagner turned his attention to the Ergosian. "Sorry. Um, just a bit of pummelling by a few dozen angry guards."

"Indeed! An *unwarranted* beating I am to assume?"

"Um—no," said Wagner, once more distracted, this time by a pair of bedfast but otherwise flush-looking fellows near the back wall who were playing dice on the cobble between their cots. "I'd say that they had overwhelming provocation."

Papa Olask chuckled—something Wagner was to find he didn't often do. "I trust, then, that you have discovered, forcefully and with painful ado, how *not* to behave around our keepers. Are you one of the yeanling? I do not believe I have seen you before."

"If you mean, am I *new*," said Wagner, "then yeah, I'm new all right—new in more ways than I can begin to figure. And I'm guessing that they sent me in here to get a clean bill of health from you, so that I can go right out and get beat up some more."

"By whose request?"

"Commander AuwNiir's?"

Olask nodded. "Come, then, let us have a look at you."

He led Wagner to an uncongested portion of the hall where stood a bench and some cabinetry laden with little vessels and gallipots.

"Have you any extreme complaint other than what I can see?"

"Mostly just the face," said Wagner. "I'm still a little achy overall from being stomped on, but I don't think it's anything that won't go away on its own."

"I see," said the physician as he groped around in one of the cupboards. "You new ones are always the least wanting of patients. Innocence, pride, and unfamiliarity keep you all a bit obdurate. In time, perhaps, you may learn from some of these others—" (here he gestured hitherishly toward the two dice throwers) "—how to bleed a wood sliver or a hangnail to the fullest, and thus fill up my beds with no warrant other than the desire to be exempt and safe." At this point he produced some linens and set them on the bench. "Not that I am taken amiss by it. No one sympathises more than I."

He then began probing at Wagner's limbs, glancing almost insensibly over the lesions and contusions whose ilk he no doubt saw every day in varied abundance. At times manipulating Wagner mechanically, he checked for signs of impaired or painful locomotion, inquiring with each movement and extension whether anything he did prompted distress. Presumably finding nothing too dire, he lifted Wagner's tunic enough to expose his rib cage and, after careful assessment, moved on to the sternum, the clavicles, and finally up to Wagner's neck and face, the latter of which elicited his gravest concern.

"You reckoned well," he confessed at end. "Superficial injuries, most of them, nothing that a mild alleviatory will not assuage. As for the tenderness about your visage, I think a regimen of glohular is in order. Has there been detriment to your vision? Your hearing? Do you have megrim, or pain that travels, or any unbearable distension or discomfort that tactile examination cannot detect?"

"Not really. Just the bruises and cuts. Vision's been okay. Hearing, too. What's glohular?"

"Why, medicinal salve, of course."

Wagner shrugged.

"Come, son, you *must* know of it." He appeared astonished.

"I—I'm not really from around here."

"It is a staple ointment of great potency, a sovereign remedy for a host of dermal maladies. I am certain that you have had occasion for it at some stage. No one who was ever a child has reached adulthood without requiring it at least once. Allow me stay while I obtain a ceramic for you, and perhaps some general embrocation for your lesser wounds."

Wagner sat down on an empty cot while Olask went off in errand. Pulsing his knees for their nervous energy, he glanced around the sizable room, shying from some of the more curious gazes of the bedridden folk whose inordinate scrutiny made him feel awkward, displaced, pressed by a desire to resettle himself somewhere less conspicuous. Oddly, he was struck by the scene's similarity to any of a hundred doctors' lobbies back on earth, where the unwell sat and waited amid far more prospective co-ailers than one might ever believe could be independently stricken on, say, any given Thursday at 1:37 in the afternoon—and it intrigued him that it should be this way, that two distinct cultures, literally worlds and centuries apart, should share much of anything at even their basic levels. But there he was, just another case in a facility where medical restoratives came in the form of poultices and plasters, where a sturdy wood saw was likely the amputating tool of choice, where folk remedies were the *only* remedies, and where ol' Doc Adams might have been seen more as hero than huckster.

"Here we are," said Papa Olask on his return. In his hand he cradled two small containers. The first, a miniature ceramic about the size of a quarter-ounce cosmetic jar, was sealed with a tiny piece of oilskin and a fastening of rawhide lace—an elaborate business, Wagner noted, for so wee a receptacle. The second container, only a tad larger, was a crude but sturdy mortar, long of use by its appearance, with a nesting lid that resembled that of a sugar bowl's.

Olask kneeled before Wagner. He undid the lace from the oilskin seal, and with his middle and index fingers he dipped a dollop of pistachio-green balm from the vessel and gingerly applied it to Wagner's face. The substance tingled upon contact, not unlike the old menthol liniments of Wagner's ken, and yet just as quickly ebbed, leaving only an odd sort of vibrancy where once was tenderness.

"I am going to give you the remainder of this glohular," Olask said, "to take back to the barracks with you. You need apply it only once per day, and most likely only for another two days after that. Faithfully dosed, and barring the pilfering fingers of your stable-mates, by end your cheek will be comparable in quality to that of a newborn babe's."

Wagner laughed. "Don't newborns usually have blotchy skin?"

"Perhaps," said Olask, "but better still than what you presently exhibit. By what name are you called?"

"My name? Well, let's see. So far I've been called an 'infidel,' a 'mongrel,' a 'whelp,' and a 'malapert.' Oh, and 'crovik-fodder,' whatever the hell that is."

"I see. And with which of these colourful titles would you have me address you?"

"Oh, I dunno. I've kind of been getting used to 'infidel,' but I guess you can be different and call me *Voknor*."

"Hmm. It lacks the imagery of the others, but I will abide by your wish, *Voknor*. Myself, I am Olask, a very weary and overworked old man who complains often and whose responsibility it is to turn broken bodies into whole."

"I gathered that," said Wagner, already liking this man more than he'd anticipated he would. "Your name was dropped to me by someone who has a great deal of respect for you."

Olask raised an eyebrow. "Certainly not Commander AuwNiir, I suspect."

"No. Another man. Goes by the name of Tamek."

"*Fie!* Not the Sentinel! Why, AuwNiir would for a certainty belaud me sooner than *that* self-important knave!"

Although immediately sensing more dramatic pretence in Olask's impugnment than any actual protest, Wagner reiterated Tamek's accolade, only to have the doctor scoff once more.

"That thick-pated vrohda must think me twice the dullard to be taken in by this new tact."

"Excuse me?"

"When next you see him, *Voknor*, tell the lofty Tamek of Vishkor that speaking highly of me to strangers is not even nigh to a clever ruse. More so, inform him that I am not so decrepit in faculty that I can be taken in by his messengered flattery, especially after having proved to him time and anew the failings of his inept sophistry and his self-righteous loquacity."

Wagner did his best to shield a grin. "I think that, for my own sake, I'll just leave that little communiqué for *you* to relay to him on your next run-in."

In all, it warmed Wagner to know that sarcasm had made the transitional world-jump with him. Olask's aspersions, such as they were, no better masked the respect that he obviously felt for the Sentinel than did the duplicity of Tamek's alleged tactics, this "adversarialism" in all probability a lively, ongoing contention of counterpointing dialogues, dialectics, and uncompromisable diatribes between two scholarly types of somewhat disparate creeds and hailings. With formal education a virtually peerless extravagance in these barbarous settings, Olask and Tamek each represented a slightly discriminable faction of cageling authority, with Olask and his patronly humaneness sating some deficiency in the prison population that Tamek's spiritual militancy couldn't always satisfy.

By his own account to follow, Olask had been a prisoner for twelve-odd years, as long as—or longer than—anyone else in the camp. His medical skills had, for the most part, exempted him from the trials of the arena, and his advancing years clinched that exemption. He was instead a one-man Mr. Fixit who assumed the varied roles of mentor, surgeon, counsellor, surrogate, to those of his people for whom the trauma of incarceration was too ponderous a burden to shoulder alone. More challenging, his ear was a sympathetic appendage for anyone racked by the insufferable guilt of having slain or maimed a human opponent in the arena. And while the former did not happen often (unlike the Roman games, here in QieLahr an exhausted combatant could yield without risking quietus, with punitive measures varying between a stay in the detention block to a simple rescinding of entitlement within his own stable), tempers were nevertheless too easily flared under a hot sun, and grudges, prone to mount, with overwroughtness sometimes leading to unmediated tragedy. Olask's lot was to rummage through the rubble of the physical and mental aftermaths, repairing and administering to whom and what he could.

Interestingly, it seemed to Wagner that Olask condemned anyone who gave in to such bloodlust, anyone who in the midst of rage could not just fling his sword into the dirt and refuse to fight. Still, he understood the psychology involved. Chances were that one's opponent might entertain no such lofty ideals—ideals that would just as surely perish with said opponent's final blade-thrust. It was this kind of abomination that embittered Olask more than anything else, that his captors could use fear, provocation, and intimidation to pervert one Ergosian into harming another. Such pitting of a people against itself for survival was detestable at best, especially as the onus of piecing together the survivors and lamenting the victims fell overwhelmingly to Olask and his handful of aides. There had yet to be a mauling or amputative horror the likes of which hadn't graced his operating table at least once; and although never formally trained as either surgeon or apothecary, he channelled the rudimentary skills—learned long ago from assisting other surgeons in such practises and interventions—into this, an unintended career of repairing mangled bodies, of stitching gashes and righting dislocations and basically of plucking the next batch of "sons" and "daughters" from off the death-wheel so that each, on recovery, could be routed back into skirmish in a cycle of violence as unbroken as the immutable perpetuity of Tamek's revered Eternity and Existence. That he loathed the paradox of his situation, this was not yet Wagner's privilege to know. Yet, aside from the taking of his own life (the only—and thus far, unacceptable—method for escaping his ordeal), Olask routinely cast out of his head as much anguish as his conscience allowed, and clung instead to the notion that the good he did far outweighed the antinomy that he struggled with. The result was his own sort of private death-wheel, equally spoked by blessing and curse, where his longevity was ransomed through the competent doctoring that in turn kept him strapped with an unebbing flow of injured.

"If you're as much a prisoner as I am," Wagner said, "then who provides all of these ointments and herbs and stuff? And how did you come to know so much about them?"

"My mother was a mendwife, *Voknor*, so there I was exposed to much of her craft. I have been further acquainted with many new substances and techniques through various means, some even by way of the injured themselves, whose individual clans have found success with such-and-such concoction of their own delving. Even the NuRacs have introduced me to remedies from their own dispensaries."

"Oh, that makes a *lot* of sense! Why would they do that if they'd just as soon wipe out Ergosians altogether?"

Lifting Wagner's tunic to expose his ribs, Olask began daubing the liniment over his numerous bruisings. "Different factions, *Voknor*. Many NuRacs—Supreme Commander SyKrahvo being one—seek to conquer the lands, to emaciate other races, and to divide the spoils. Others, like AuwNiir, are less zealous. They seem only to see the profiteering side of aggression, and quickly take to exploiting the conquered for sport and wager. This was, and is, the purpose of the Great Tournament, and is therefore why AuwNiir and his competitors seek to maintain the health and fitness of those whom they recruit into their respective stables. If, as you maintain, you have been inducted into his troupe of fighters, it is his coinage that goes to replenish these salves with which I treat you."

Wagner blew a dismal sigh and mumbled lowly. "Competitive sports, bookmaking, pay-per-view barbarism—even *here*, on this backwater mudball."

At that moment, the invalid whom Olask had been tending upon Wagner's arrival suddenly pitched into a fit of seizure, his body at once a gripping shudder of bulging, paralytic musculature, his face a deep red grimace of apoplectic immobility.

"Lakaar! Ihmatt!" Olask was before the patient in a crack, grasping and steadying him with the grip of a man of half his years. Wagner clumsily joined and assisted until two orderlies dashed up to assume the ministering duties subordinate to Olask. As such, Wagner backed off, observed the ado for several heated seconds, and—realising that the man's spasm would not be easily calmed—asked if he should go and get additional help of some kind.

The three Ergosians either didn't hear him, or were too entrenched in immediacy to respond, so Wagner stayed put. He watched as Olask inserted a small wooden dowel between the patient's teeth, presumably to prevent his biting his own tongue. At the same time, the orderlies flung aside the bed sheet so to better clasp onto the man's legs. Seeing the linens, however, stubbornly snarled about the patient's foot, Wagner prudently stole forward in a move to free them, and, in doing so, interceded on a level he'd neither intended nor anticipated.

Outreached, the fingers of his right hand suddenly came alive like embers before the bellows puff, shooting forth an aura of hoary, plasmatic opalescence that suffused the stricken man's foot, shot up the limb and enveloped—and then just as quickly fled—the patient's body in trice more fleeting than that of an electric arc.

Quick as instant, Wagner yanked his hand back as if in reply to a narrowly missed scalding.

Olask and the orderlies having been less concerned with Wagner than with the spasmodic man, from their vantage they'd witnessed a conflagration a microsecond in duration, one that each in his own mind imagined initially to be a snap sensory rush, limited only to himself. But as the patient immediately went limp, as the beetishness of his complexion waned to its natural olive and his respiration pared to normal, the three Ergosians traded bewildered gazes like dogs whose master had feigned in throwing a ball. On the cot below them, their convulsionary rested comfortably, his brow lax, his expression peaceful, the void of his previous straits now filled to bristle by their own astonishment.

"I—I do not understand!" cried Olask. "What has occurred here?"

"By the huntress, I know not," said the one called Ihmatt. "My sight went brilliant, and then *this!*"

"And mine as well," said Lakaar in squinch at the stars in his eyes.

Wagner backed away, nearly stumbling over another patient's cot. A cursory glance at his hand, he found nothing truly amiss with it. He even looked hurriedly at his left hand, as if by some trick of absent-mindedness he might have been scrutinising the wrong one. But there was no distinguishment. Both appeared normal, healthy, pink, and adroit.

"*Voknor*—by the Twain, look at you!"

Olask rushed up but stopped prudently short, just the way Jon Mazzio had on that fateful day on the grounds outside of Howsley. Then, resuming his approach in deliberation more heedful, he reached out and touched Wagner's face.

"Vanished!" he cried. "All vanished! Each and every wound, *Voknor*, as if they had never been!"

Wagner looked down at his arms. Then he slid up his tunic to examine his torso. In the infirmary's three-quarter light, his body did appear as the physician professed—entirely unscathed. Stroking his face as Olask had, he likewise encountered no tenderness, no protruding bloat, nothing to indicate that he'd even been injured at all. His knees, too, badly strawberried from his plummet at the gorge, no longer galled him beneath the drape of his reach-me-down trousers, and neither did the peripheral smart of his encompassing sunburn. In fact, in the latter case, his return to the hermitic paleness of his normalcy was contemporaneous with a suddenly present rake-off of exuviae, almost as if the aggregate of dead and damaged cells that his body would normally have sloughed over the course of several days had instead been shed in one fell swoop. His flesh outwardly flecked in this manner, with each graze of his hand he sent scurfy residuum wafting about the air like dust blown from the pages of some ancient tome. More remarkable than repellent, it swirled and settled gradually upon the infirmary floor, eventually to be swept underfoot—and with it, the mystery of its why and wherefore.

By all observations, Wagner had been restored to nominal health in the space of an eyeblink. Still forthcoming, however, was another product of said transfiguration, one that, perhaps more evidentially defining than his rejuvenation, seemed to suggest at least one possible wise to the outrageousness of the incident.

Of two minds over the abrupt eradication of his injuries, with a doubting-Thomas incredulity Wagner drew up his hand to re-evaluate the sudden scathelessness of his cheek. Glancing, however, what should have been the stubble of four or five days, his fingers instead registered a beard so out of keeping with his previous scruff that it was all he could do not to cry out in surprise. Unaccountably, the crop upon his chin was three times the whisker of that morning's awakening, nearly two extra weeks of additional growth by his estimate. How this could be, he didn't even bother theorising; too much of even greater ungraspability had preceded it back on earth. But clearly, whatever the catalyst for the regenerative effect in whole, it hadn't afforded without certain exaction. A cut-rate Rip Van Winkle, by Wagner's outward appearance it looked as if he'd misplaced a good fortnight. In his mind, however, and by the evidence around him, he knew this wasn't so. He'd merely acquired a significant bearding in less time than it took a body to sneeze—not to mention as close to a total cellular restoration as his personal once-over could determine—and for a man who'd thought he'd seen just about everything, here was a new skew on an old enigma, neither version of which was in imminence of meeting with resolution any time soon.

Long practised at masking his various oddities from the notice of others, Wagner couldn't be sure that these men around him (and Olask in particular) hadn't acquainted themselves well enough with his earlier lineaments to even register this new distinguishment. Benignly listening to their bewilderment, he sought to gain some anticipatory insight into their mindsets so that he could, if necessary, devise a clever artifice to deflect answerability in some other direction. Indeed, the trio did make mention of him in their speculation, but thankfully no more than they did each other and the recovered patient; and, as a handful of newly ebullient convalescents likewise chimed in with all manner of misinterpreted dramatics and divinations of what each believed he had seen, Wagner was free to slip from the spotlight.

A few paces shy of the brouhaha, he took a moment to clandestinely re-examine his hands. Neither, however, unchanged from his last look-see, with intuitive impetus and whim he focused this time on the minutiae, and in turn came across a phenomenon of equal pertinence to the breakneck beard and the bodily scurf. His fingernails—if not previously chipped from climbing, then bitten to the nub from nerves—now exhibited the rampant discrepancy of runaway keratin, an outgrow of roughly two week's time; and this, along with the whiskers, the recedent cuts and contusions, and doubtlessly an existent but less detectable gain in coiffure, gave rise to the premise that his metabolism had somehow warped ahead, accelerated to a point several weeks hence, when his body would have naturally recovered from its various traumas.

Such speculation brought him little solace. After all, he'd already settled in to the realisation that his bendering days were behind him, that he might possibly never dream again, that intangibility had been but a temporary aberration in a long list of transitional makereadies—then along comes expressway healing to screw up any hope of a deserved and much longed-for normalcy.

Consumed by imperative, he quickly glanced back to the man on the cot. Like most of the Ergosian males in the camp, said fellow had already been sporting a generous facial outgrowth before the incident, so it was decidedly more difficult to determine if he'd undergone a similar metamorphosis. More sleuthfully, Wagner switched his attention to the man's hands and feet.

Nothing. No nail growth. No flaking dander. Not even a dot of eye crust.

By the same token, the patient was no longer seizuring, which Wagner supposed could be interpreted in several different manners, only one of which relied upon a miracle of weirdly refulgent unleashings.

Then at once it struck him—*Miracle!*

Amid the patchy imagery of his final moments at Howsley, he did recall the vibrant permeation of light whose agency had somehow—if fleetingly—delivered him into the shoring brace of the tabloid prophet. Barely mindful of it at the time, the similarity between that event and this bore such uncanny correlation that he did not even try to dispute the affinity. The sensation had been exactly the same;

the mystical savour, the jolting hysteresis, the resultant vivification—all the same. Then, as now, incidence had reared out of nowhere to put the smack on some otherwise uncontrollable urgency, and for his life Wagner couldn't find a proper avenue by which to approach it.

"Never have I seen the likes of this!" Olask proclaimed as he probed and prodded the recovered man. Then, pushing past his orderlies, he made a cursory sweep of those of the bedridden whose general proximity to the former might likewise have exposed them to some measurable, repercussive effect. This would prove bootless.

"Apparently," he said at end, "the prodigy was limited to this man and yourself, *Voknor*. By all that I see, you and he—and *only* you and he—have been disburdened of all perceivable infirmity, and this quite confoundingly so. Have you any notion of how such thaumaturgy might occur?"

"None," said Wagner in complete deadpan. "I'm as much in the dark as the rest of you."

"How do you feel?" He bade Wagner back into the open.

"I feel good. No—scratch that. I feel *remarkable*."

Olask drew closer, meeting him halfway.

"How very extraordinary," he said, his hand gliding over Wagner's bristly jaw as though it were sculptured perfection. "Such things simply do not happen, *Voknor*—not like this, not beyond the pale of Tamek's fusty scriptures and generation upon generation of ever-aggrandised tradition."

"Not even during the Vorshalah?"

The question, wryly asked, had diversionary intent.

Olask scoffed. "I have been about for a full lifetime, son. Two such ages of alleged auspiciousness have I weathered, neither one of which proffered a modicum of wonderwork that could not be upstaged by the marvel found in a mere change of seasons. Would that I could have witnessed some immeasurable rarity in those times—I know that my devotion would be all the stronger for it. Instead, I have been made to wait into my dotage to meet with unnatural magiks— and these, it seems, from the negligence of my unready attention. Truly, if this is to be my testimony at long last, I confess I do not know what to make of it."

"On the other hand," said Wagner, "maybe that last batch of glohular was just a bit more potent than usual."

Olask accepted Wagner's piffle with sober thoughtfulness.

"Mayhap," he sighed. "But unlikely, *Voknor*."

With nothing to keep him there, Wagner was discharged from the infirmary long before the post-event stirrings settled back into a foreseeability of more intimate and speculative chinfests between the bullishly insistent and the newly awakened refuters. Taking with him neither of Olask's salves, Wagner left the structure and its buzzing inhabitants behind, his mood and his body a-twitter with an indescribable robustness that even the resignation to imprisonment couldn't immediately crush.

Standing without were his by-now listless escorts, parched and gritty from the dust they'd kicked about in their idling; and on seeing them he wished for a camera, that he might have recorded their expressions at finding him suddenly more hale than they.

"By the Warlord's cudgel!" cried KoviKor. "The Ergosian—his wounds are no more!"

The others looked Wagner up and down as if he were at auction.

"For as long as we have been waiting," said the female, the least awed—and the least patient—of the three, "it is no wonder that his wounds have faded. Here, you!" she said, redirecting at Wagner. "We instructed you to obtain treatment and return to us promptly. Think you that we have all day to wait for the likes of you?"

"A thousand pardons," said Wagner with a glibness that he could only attribute to his newfound vitality. "Olask seemed to think it was a good time to trial some new healing potion that Commander AuwNiir's funding had recently provided." Spreading his arms, he flaunted his fledgling healthfulness like holy stigmata exhibited to doubting eyes. "Looks like it was money well spent!"

The guards, momentarily dumbstruck by Wagner's sauciness, weighed his fibbery on scales offset by their inability to distinguish between playful insolence and undermining toadyism. Neither was generally tolerated from an inferior, and frequently earned said upstart some ilk of physical reprisal. But here—due either to their astonishment or to their eagerness to move on with their task—they refrained from remand or rebuke, and instead ushered Wagner gruffly to the next and final stop in his scheduled programma.

Beyond the yard and through a broad underpass, their goading soon set Wagner onto another yard, one heavily peopled by Ergosian combatants locked in the mock battles that, according to Tamek, served to ready them for the arena. Here, on this palaestra, he discovered a scene straight out of *Spartacus*, where scores of half-clad men and women were busily immersed in a sweltering, yard-wide imbroglio of swordplay and ersatz bloodsport under the stoical onlookings of what had to have been a full garrison of NuRac authority. Wielding faux, close-quarter weaponry that consisted of blunt wooden swords (called nodgers), quarterstaves, and an odd sort of tractable mace, many of the contenders also employed a small wooden or wicker buckler that, held with the defending hand, deflected (and sometimes actually even snared) an opponent's "blade," and thus provided strategic give and take for those who would avail themselves of the relative uninjuriousness of practise in order to better their technique.

Wagner was at once impressed by the demonstrative finesse in these hand-to-hand embroilments, where each contender vied for mastership while refraining from inflicting any severity of damage upon his opponent. This sentiment, an ethical code engrained in the Ergosian mindset, found its greatest taxing here, where privileges and rations were waxingly offered to those who, at NuRac behest, might on tournament day choose to overstep decency for the trickle-down boodle skimmed from the receipts of a packed amphitheatre. Such venality, however, was at this point far down on Wagner's list of worries. Less disposed than most to unleash the primal animal that lived in all men, he could not deny gaining an immoderate, if unsettling, thrill out of the circus before him, almost as if somewhere within his sorely pregnable id a twist of dreadful yet strangely home-felt longing had suddenly been dislodged from its previously regressive moorings.

With the exception of a bare handful of heavyset prisoners and a few emaciated ones, the majority of the Ergosian populace looked to be in prime condition, or close to it. Many were solid, supple, bulky but not extravagantly muscular—

nothing like the celebrity iron men so familiar to Wagner, nor like the Schwarzeneggers or the Stallones of Hollywood fame. No, these Ergosian Samsons and Heracleses had closer kinship to the earthly "men outta Mac" paragons of the 1940's and 1950's. Their bodies were more Bob Hoffmanesque and Charles Atlassy—broad and barrel-chested but lacking the keener definition and the chiselled sculptedness attained by modern methods of muscular isolation and such.

This held only somewhat less true for the women on the field, their femininity—by Wagner's standards—not truly jeopardised by gratuitous mass, but rather exemplified through the hardiness of form and stature, stamina and simple grace. The rigours of physical adversity having remunerated them with the energy and tensility of seasoned athletes, in Wagner's appreciation of these consummate females it struck him that any one of them very likely possessed the skill and reserve to knock him on his keister with little more exertion than one would use to shoo a fly.

Drawing on what Tamek had told him, only a portion of the prison population was arena-bound at any given time. Some—the frail, the elderly, the physically immature—simply weren't combatant material, and were rightly passed over by the NuRac recruiters and stable-masters who, in the same manner that earthly magnates might collect thoroughbreds or Van Goghs, would readily empty coffer and purse if only to acquire that one fighter whose promise of renown and popular draw would net them a tidy profit. The unqualified and the underfit—a significant reckoning from each slave campaign—were vassalised as blacksmiths, waterers, trusties, cooks and fabricators, and as such, would better serve their capturers by relieving them, at negligible expense, from having to otherwise staff for these lowlier but necessary duties.

Still, this was not to say that the rejected came into a leniency that Wagner and the other draftees did not. On the contrary, each one's service and productivity— from cesspit cleaner to royal robe sempster—was rigidly documented by the administrating NuRacs to whom he answered. These overseers like shop foremen, each had a quota to meet within his respective network of prisoner services, and most were meticulously inexorable with a workforce whose constituency, being exclusively Ergosian, was easily renewed and replaced. No, it was the gladiatorial caste that actually enjoyed what meed there was to be had (a notion that Wagner inferred from his tête-à-tête with AuwNiir), the utmost of this being directly tethered to one's performance. Reward following risk, physical engagement was the most facile means of measuring individual merit, from the laurels earned in the vanquishing of some feral carnivore, to those of besting an outranking favourite from a competing stable, to the most rare of occasions when a human kill resulted. And although recompense was meted according to degree, this latter scenario—if not merely an incidental occurrence in an otherwise honourable bout—typically netted its victor less fame than infamy, and in blatant cases even brought upon him the inevitability of in-house reprisal and assassination. According to Tamek's primer, arena kills were much more part and parcel of the sponsor's wanting financial solvency. All too commonly were they the product of a prearranged pact between competing owners, with the backer of the doomed fighter, unhappy with his man's record, making a deliberate decision to impair him through drugging or other perfidious means, and—with one mismatched battle—prune his stable of an unpromising sprig while simultaneously recouping his loss by sharing in the tainted receipts. In this capacity, survival had at least as much to do with politics as it did with victory and accomplishment.

Looking about in fascination, Wagner at once noted that there seemed to exist on the palaestra no discrimination in terms of gender, for the number of Ergosian females gracing the field closely matched that of the males. The sparring, however, was almost exclusively same-sex, and barring his observance of a few mixed skirmishes across the breadth of the yard, his Vishkorian hermeneut had already informed him that women only battled men for real when such a pairing bore the promise of an equitable match.

While instinctually stirred by the energy on the field, Wagner's immanent pacifist hardly relished the prospect of entering so greenly into a mêlée of seasoned militants, faux swords or not. True, in drawing upon his many bender-inspired encounters with Nurse Groller & Co., and his unpremeditated and surprisingly impassioned defence of the Vofspar clan back at the gorge, he did not doubt that it was *in* him to do battle up close and personal—and to do it relatively well. But rare was the serious brush or brawl that hadn't included the nick of time switch-out of his mercurial *Other*. Barely a week ago, in his earthly madness, the doppelganger had been his *deus ex machina*, his big guns against improbable odds. Here, on Ergos, that fellow was all but gone, economised into a much less drastic kind of transient volatility that popped in just long enough to buck a hesitating Wagner back from fire to frying pan. Now, seeing the calibre of talent on the palaestra before him, only with the boon of such attitude-adjusting cross-circuitry did Wagner see himself faring even marginally against so many veteran combatants.

Centrally situated in the yard was a platform, a dais of sorts, that seemed in its inordinateness rather like a monstrous wine tun laid flat. Upon it stood NuRac Taskmaster GrumTor, known around the yard as "the Dragon" or simply as "Grum." An imposing figure, rotund and stocky and outfitted in more metal trappings than seemed healthfully bearable for so steamy an afternoon, he surveyed his domain with a surliness like no other. Not just an overseer of the training process, but *THE* overseer, he looked to be the darkest imaginable counterpart to a drillmaster that Wagner might ever encounter. A cold, brooding, largely humourless fellow—unless, of course, one counted gallows humour—his commission was of grooming each stable's fighters for the arena, an ambitiousness that he insisted be done concurrently, on this single field, so as to avoid any accusation of favour or furtiveness, one faction from the other. Assuming this responsibility with mortal seriousness, the placement of his observation dais was therefore no accident. By putting himself at the heart of the daily rivalry he gained absolute insight into each prisoner's strengths, failings, and potentials, and thus acquired firsthand the information that he would need to later suggest to the stable-masters and the intendants the most lucrative match-ups and pitting orders.

Despite an appearance that led some to believe him less keen than brutish, Grum reportedly had quite the thorough eye when it came to collating the respective prowesses of his disfranchised charges. Unnecessary to even commit his assessments to parchment, he knew the fighters so intimately that he could compile in his head their patencies and their exploitable latencies, and reel off on demand which of them was suited best to this event or that. Allegedly incorruptible, unsparing in his ratings, nearly always on the mark with his projections, his was the fiducial say-so in a system of prisoner resources that was far more complex than Wagner might have imagined without the benefit of Tamek's oubliettel overview.

His three escorts parting the crowd, Wagner followed them to the base of the Taskmaster's platform. Grum, having immediately noted their entry into the yard, monitored their approach with seeming indifference, the greater role of his eye given to the demands of his palaestra, ever full of incident, ever needy of his critique. Even as Wagner was set before him, Grum continued blithely to focus his attention elsewhere until he'd sufficiently driven home the point that, in his domain, concerns were addressed when and how he desired.

"What have you here, ZebeKir?" he asked after a suitable moment's silence.

"Commander AuwNiir's most recent acquisition, Taskmaster," said the NuRac female.

"Are you certain of this? I was told to expect a man who looked the trample of ten vrohdas. This one has not so much as a mark upon him."

ZebeKir faltered in her response, perhaps debating the wisdom of trying to convey to him the unaccountable matter of Wagner's transfiguration. Prudently, she forewent it. "This is the man, nonetheless."

Grum locked eyes with her. She didn't flinch. He then turned to Wagner. "You are quite the tempest I hear—although one would never suspect it to look at you. By my reckoning, you have not laboured a day in your life. Clearly, you have never felt the lash. Your flesh is smoother than that of my pubescent daughter."

Wagner looked straight ahead and said nothing.

"And you are impertinent as well," Grum added baitfully.

Seeing how he couldn't win either way with these people, Wagner found inducement to respond, and did so in the affirmative.

"Yes, sir—usually to my own disservice."

Grum spat casually into the dirt before Wagner's feet, and, dabbing errant spittle from his lip, took measure of Wagner with disapproving eyes.

"It would behove you not to be insolent with me," he said. "While it is not in my capability to befriend prisoners, know that I will not hesitate to chastise those who show me contempt. You would therefore do well, yeanling, to give me only the information I request—no more, no less."

Heaving abruptly about, he bellowed a name into the scramble of trainees. There, a distant face turned upward, and within dutiful seconds its owner had broken from the crowd to step up and align himself beside Wagner.

A stocky, bronzy Ergosian, he stood only slightly shorter than Wagner, although he easily outmassed him in brawn. Panting and heavily perspired, he stood akimbo in wait of instruction, his right hand clasped around the pommel of a nodger the edges of which bore so many parrying nicks and gouges that it looked more like a saw than a sword.

"Balgor," said Grum, "for purpose beyond all comprehension, your Commander has seen fit to add this man to your stables. Do you know him?"

Balgor glanced at Wagner, then just as quickly returned his gaze to Grum. "Nay, Taskmaster, I do not."

The overseer looked to KoviKor and snapped his stubby fingers. The guard approached and grudgingly offered up his spear, which Grum snatched away and cast underhandedly to Wagner.

"Balgor," he said, "take this yeanling to the dirt and I will double your meat rations for three days."

Balgor looked askant at Wagner, perhaps to size him up, perhaps with self-kept inquiry for why Grum was advantaging the stranger with a true spear against his own veritable toy.

"I am waiting, realmson," said Grum.

"*Triple* the ration," Balgor challenged, "and I will see that he champs the very dust trampled by your own boots."

The Taskmaster squinted in obvious disapprobation at the Ergosian's audacity. Haggling with a superior was, as already stated, a risky venture, and Grum's disdain clung like phlegm in his throat as he eyed the prisoner whose obedience was to have provided Wagner an exemplar. Wagner likewise gave a squint, but his was idiosyncratic, an involuntary response to his mind's rooting through a hastily conceived slapdash of unexecutable options for how he might possibly hightail it out of the yard without being noticed.

"It would appear that contumacy is in the air today," said Grum. "But you, realmson, are in no position to strike bargains."

"Knowing of your occasional magnanimity, Taskmaster, how could I not at least venture to try?"

Grum grinned dryly, well aware that he was being played. He would not, however, be bested.

"Triple rations for *two* days," he said, "or the pair of you will be put to the block *this* day."

With a prudent and finalising nod, the one called Balgor turned and motioned for Wagner to adopt a stance. Reluctantly, Wagner complied, training the spear awkwardly before him while his fingers fumbled for a proper grip. The length of the lance being such that it would scarce allow him the freedom of mobility that he'd have desired, the fact of its most lethal tine was equally dismaying, for he knew that not only did he sorely lack the skill of his opponent, but he also had no true desire to harm the man either. Not that he could, of course, for this Balgor was undoubtedly a seasoned fighter, and one apparently without the scruples of a nobler opponent who surely would never have allowed the promise of extra sustenance to sway his savaging of a fellow man.

Facing off almost immediately, the swordsman swiftly lunged at Wagner, his nodger clapping reboantly against the spear's hardwood. Like a whirling propeller he struck again and again, the vibratory resonance alone nearly enough to disarm Wagner in the midst of his pedestrian attempts to hold the man at distance.

With scant opportunity to make good with the business end of his weapon, Wagner employed it more as a thwarting tool, a tact borrowed from the desperations of his broom-wielding doppelganger in Howsley's videotape files. Lacking, however, the dexterity and the blind confidence of his insanity-driven *Other*, in his need he nevertheless bemoaned *that* Wagner, and actually wished for a means to usher him forth that he might reduce his unrelenting antagonist to the gladiatorial equivalent of Miss Groller. Yet, dispossessed as he was of said supplementary state, rescue of that sort was sadly unrealisable. Any and all back-up would have to spring from his own ingenuity, from some basal gristmill of spirit and instinct. Trouble was, he wasn't feeling tremendously resourceful at the moment.

Within the first ten seconds of the match, Wagner was given personal introduction to the palaestra sands. Balgor's forceful mastery far overmatching his own undriven, unfocused defence, like a lumberjack in a log-chopping contest the Ergosian hacked and hacked with such single-minded fury that the retreating Wagner bumbled over his own feet and fell smack onto his rump.

The contest did not conclude there, however, nor did Wagner lose heart. Sacrificing a measure of dignity instead, he crab-crawled laterally through the dust he'd raised, scrabbling last-ditch on fingers and feet and evading each of Balgor's subsequent sallies by graceless centimetres. At one point uprighting himself and re-appropriating his clumsily towed spear, with only its far sturdier mettle was he able, again and again, to rebuff the Ergosian's omnidirectional assault. The air around them strown with the shrapnel crazed from Balgor's substandard prop, in frustrating the swordsman's every offence Wagner routed him into new and unexpected tactic, and one that very nearly brought the duel to quit. Charging falsely to Wagner's left, the much more artful Balgor stopped short and drove the nodger into the ground behind Wagner's retreating heel, and thus sent him a second time into the sand.

Derailed and discouraged, Wagner could easily have yielded and been done with it. To his credit—and surprise—he sprang up, ever more enlivened, and made ready to engage Balgor's next assail.

Already bested on several counts and somehow still managing to avoid categorical defeat, over the course of the contest's unpredicted protraction Wagner had gradually come to sense a certain inclination in himself that, at times so prominent, soon proved impossible to dismiss as simple fancy: that his durability was not *his* glory alone, but rather owed to some daedal extraneousness that had been gaining in resource from the moment that Balgor first charged him. A few substantially accretive inconsistencies in his spearplay, undeniably less representative of his initiate's status than that of the veterans around him, here and again he realised a competence too closely on par with theirs, his reflexes and his timing and even his confidence all in swell far too brimful for his inaptitude. In the duel's forerunning moments it had been all he could do just to play down his jitters; yet here, with the affray drawing out, he found himself battling on two fronts—the first being that of the Ergosian's physical antagonism, and the other, a burgeoning upload of ultra-zealousness that threatened to make him hold his own against said Ergosian, who by rights should easily have prevailed within seconds of their facing off.

The longer Wagner stayed vital, the longer he staved his defeat, the more consuming did this spirit become, almost as if his long-absconded Hyde had found a subconscious conduit from deep in mental exile through which to feed him experiential how-to. Most blatant in situations of severe check, in a few such extreme instances Wagner actually turned the tables on his far more capable foe, jabbing the spearhead so like a scorpion's tail that he even drove Balgor back into two rearward sparrers, who in turn blundered into a neighbouring pair, thus setting off a brawl that Grum had to dispatch guards to halt.

Ired by the reversal, a fuming, resolute Balgor flew at Wagner with a burst of quick, blazing affronts the intensity of which all but stove in Wagner's newly mounted courage like a cannonball ripping through the belly of a doomed galleon. Resorting quickly to defence, Wagner redeployed his spear to deflect the downsweeping blows, his countering little more than a series of hasty, fitful blocks that served only to prolong the inevitable. Driven back, abandoned by his allying fortitude, Wagner pitched over and across whomever was unfortunate enough not to have given the contest a wide berth. Trampling the unheeding, inadvertently stomping an errancy of hands and feet, flopping over the stooped and the prostrated—at end an exhausted Wagner was toppled like a pagan idol, was felled hard to the ground, was made to lie supine with heaving chest as Balgor's tine dirked uncomfortably at his sternum.

Finally, ultimately, the Ergosian huffed over him in breathless bother. "I...may not be...the finest swordsman...in the realm," he panted, "but clearly...I am better...than *you*."

Painstakingly propping himself upon one elbow, Wagner brushed dusty defeat from his face. Smacking repellently, he raked several granules of grit from his tongue and, with waggish resignation, vaunted his sand-spittled fingers for both his victor and his new Taskmaster to see, so both would know that all conditions of the challenge had been satisfied. Then, after running an expurgatory wrist across his mouth, he guided Balgor's sword from off his chest and rolled himself onto his knees to stand.

The altercation having drawn the eyes of many, Grum suddenly turned on the idled assemblage.

"Did I miss the horn? Did it sound day's end? I think not! Resume your skirmishing, you lot, or I will deliver every last one of you to the Sunderer's lair!"

The prisoners, although promptly picking up the pace, did not seem overly intimidated by Grum's name-dropping. Like threats of the bogeyman relayed to misbehaving children, this one was likely the Taskmaster's caveat of choice, and was therefore an "or else!" that most everyone had learned to oblige with just enough disgruntled submission to squeak below Grum's retributive radar. For Wagner, however, it was the "Sunderer" reference—the second he'd heard in the space of a few hours—that drew his interest, if only due to the fact of his nescience making the allusion sound more ominous to him than his fellow prisoners' reactions reflected.

"Now, pink one," said Grum, "what is it you are called?"

On his feet, Wagner whisked the last of the dust from his tunic. "*Voknor*," he said. "I'm *Voknor*."

"Well, *Voknor*, it seems that you possess some rudimentary skills that even I could not detect. Unrefined skills, of course, but nothing that we cannot enhance through proper regimen." He turned to Wagner's opponent. "Realmson, I want you to finish out the day by showing this one where he went astray in the promising— yet ultimately ill-executed—attempt he had at you. By final horn I want him to be a match for any third-ranker here—understand?"

Balgor performed a courtly half-bow. "Yes, my liege."

Wagner gawped at the Ergosian, unable to reconcile Balgor's subservient stature with the brash mordancy in his manner. His compliance, while consistently absolute, rarely came without some entendre of cleverly conforming impudence, some insuppressible barb cloaked in just the right measure of submission that it either flew past Grum unnoticed or simply wasn't worth his twist to even address. It could have been, too, that baiting of this sort was specific to their indocile relationship, with, as Wagner would learn, Balgor's string of arena successes making him one of AuwNiir's key fighters, and thus a temporary indispensability who knew how to exploit that indispensability at every licentious turn.

Balgor motioning for Wagner to follow him, the latter snapped up the inutile spear and handed it back to KoviKor, who, along with ZebeKir and the third guard, had been standing by all the while in witness to Wagner's trouncing. Meticulously assessing his weapon and finding it none the worse for the ordeal, KoviKor then turned, and, peers in tow, headed off in the direction they had come, only too happy to leave Wagner to the next phase of his acclimation.

"Whence came you, *Voknor*," Balgor asked, making long strides and expecting Wagner to follow suit, "and how did you meet with capture?"

Wagner bought himself a few seconds with an unneeded throat clearing. "Both are simple questions," he answered offhandedly, not entirely at ease with the Ergosian's sudden sociability. "I'm afraid, however, that the answers involve such a mixed bag of circumstances that even *I* can't fully comprehend them. Suffice it to say that I'm a traveller who happened to be in the wrong place at the wrong time."

"Oh? And where and when would that be?"

"Well, how about blundering smack into the middle of a NuRac hunting party's pursuit of a pack of Vofspars?"

Balgor let out a capricious hoot. "Aye, that *is* a conjuncture that one would do best to avoid. Are you, then, the misguided fool who fended the Vofspar from yestermorning's caravan?"

Wagner felt his face grow warm. It had been frustrating enough to justify those actions to Tamek; now, here was another man fixing to beset him with the same damning arguments.

"You wouldn't think of helping someone in chains whom a gang of armoured thugs was beating to death?"

"*Someone*, perhaps. But certainly not a Vofspar."

"Why's that?"

"For sundry reasons."

"Okay. Give me *one*."

Balgor was clearly uneasy. "One is enough. My oldest childhood friend was butchered by Vofspars before his twentieth year. Not merciful enough to kill him first, they dismembered and disembowelled him before his very eyes."

Wagner acknowledged diminishedly, thinking back a few days to the werecat's gruesome handiwork at the gorge. Yet, just as readily recalling that it had been in defence of her brood that she'd reacted thusly, he appended: "Without any provocation?"

Sensing too late the impropriety of the question, given his own experience with the Vofspars he nevertheless deemed it a fair and relevant—if tactless—inquiry.

Balgor thought differently.

"*What*—suggest you that it might have been condign? I say they rent him to pieces! They flayed his skin from his bones and proceeded to drape the blood-sucked strips of it across their bodies like the silken wraps worn by genteel women during festival. Witness that, *traveller*, and then declare to me that you would fret and fume over one's welfare."

Respectfully, Wagner said nothing. Gazing skyward, he caught sight of a bird of prey soaring effortlessly on an updraft, high and beyond the palaestra walls. Wings at full spread, almost frozen in the air, it held there like a portent for what seemed a long time.

"We are there," Balgor said as he halted before an enclosure in the wall's outmost perimeter. Stooping slightly to enter, Wagner followed him inside, and there discovered rack upon rack of nodgers, spears, halberds, quarterstaves, and bludgeons.

"Wherein lies your experience, *Voknor*?"

"Excuse me?"

"With which weapon should we commence?"

Wagner nervously catalogued the breadth of the armoury.

"Actually," he said, "I'm not versed very well in any of these. My...um...past few years were spent in...more literary pursuits. You know, studying, reading—things like that."

"You are a scholar?"

Wagner shrugged. "Well, no, not really—"

"A useless preoccupation these days," said Balgor. "And, in these environs, an aimless fancy better traded for survival skills."

Giving scratch to his beard, with a finical eye the Ergosian inventoried the array of armaments. "As I find no quills, inkwells, or parchment in here, *Voknor*, it seems I must inure you with some more lethal implement."

Self-assured, he drew a pair of quarterstaves from the rack. Each a stout stick, roughly two-and-a-half metres in length, he lobbed one to Wagner for approval. Deemed satisfactory, he then bad Wagner from the enclosure, where, on a less populated spot on the west end of the field, his tutorial began apace.

Quickly, curtly, Wagner was illuminated with some cursory guidelines that, like a gladiatorial credo of conduct, defined the various constraints and taboos of arena contention. Not a dispensation chock-full of disallowances, it did, however, emphasise the importance of maintaining one's combative honour and integrity in the midst of vital struggle—an ethic that immediately made suspect Grum's earlier insistence that Balgor drive Wagner to the ground for ruthlessly demonstrative purposes. Fair play, like many things, was relative—a principle to be embraced whenever it came free of untoward interference.

Despite the fact that Wagner's fleeting prowess had taken Balgor so unawares during their introductory confrontation, the realmson nevertheless started Wagner with rudimentary instruction, the same as he'd undoubtedly done many times over with previous newcomers. A trial of no mere patience at its onset, it quickly became clear that this veteran—this *shellback*—would have preferred the roughhouse of an opponent considerably more seasoned than the weaner he faced, and ideally one of his own calibre. But equally clear, if only by inference, was the unstated cruciality of not taking the Taskmaster's order lightly (a bit of old-fashioned Ergosian impertinence notwithstanding). Temporarily shelving, then, his superior ability in order to coax a marketable competency from a man whose martial knowledge—regardless of his inspired showing before the dais—was in truth subordinate to that of the youngest hobbledehoy in the camp, Balgor could only imagine how tall an order it could potentially be to instil his yeanling trainee with even the basic resourcefulness necessary to endure the inevitability of deadly serious conflict.

Yet, how stunned he was, as the lesson progressed, to find *Voknor* anything but a dullard. Unfacile as Wagner had initially presented himself, he readily absorbed the complexities of Balgor's nimble-footed orchestrations with finesse and aptitude enough to leave the instructor in question as to whether his student was perhaps more artful than he'd wished anyone to know. A deception or not, this forthcoming felicity was welcomed, and not only because it would spare Balgor a great deal of directional effort, but because it suddenly normalised the recruit; in one very critical sense, it dispelled an enormity of suspicion. A man of the times who did not know how to war? Such was cause for immediate misdoubt. But a man who was, because of his newness to imprisonment and all bad things that went with it, understandably mistrustful of everyone (and who ergo kept much about himself unrevealed)—*this* the Ergosian could both understand and respect.

From Wagner's perspective, it was impossible to reconcile his "default constancy" with the derangement that kicked in only at key moments of insurmountability. Whenever cornered or optioned out, he would suddenly engage in some inconceivably bold manoeuvre of evasion or offence, his quarterstaff awhirl before his weaving and bobbing opponent, with each of these flaring little coups d'état of instinct over conscious effort bunkering an unnurtured and furiously expended sustainment that bridged him from one direful moment to the next. Surreal and real at once, the result was likewise twofold in both its dint and its dauntingness, just as it had been when he'd toppled the NuRacs at the gorge, and then later, in his defence of the tormented Vofspar. Yet, a valley for every peak, in ebb it left Wagner vulnerable to the multifariousness of Balgor's less lethal assails—the annoying head-clonks, the chin-butts, the pommels to the belly—the successes of which both exploited the schism in Wagner's inner largesse and underscored how a few good cuts and thrusts were not enough to win the day over tempered consistency.

Balgor, barring certain expletory blurtings, had been all along hard-pushed to offer any criticism at all, for he could never quite determine whether it was a cunning expert with whom he contested or an inconceivably lucky stumblebum. At times it could have been either one, although overall he discerned far more ineptness than callidity in Wagner's moves, and only the most corruptible brilliance in his reversals.

At end, Wagner would learn much about close-quarter combat from his Ergosian peer, and by the evening's supping he would discover a good deal more in terms of character. The horn sounding at roughly an hour before dusk, and the time for the evening meal finally at hand, the NuRacs began excusing the prisoners in staggered groups to re-rack weapons and to make way to the mess. Each of the twenty-or-so men and women per party were allowed back to the barracks field/inception yard for a turn at the wash troughs before lining in queue at a cloistered end of the wall where kitchen trusties ladled out stew and loaves under the eyes of watchful sentries. As Balgor seemed tolerant of his continued company, Wagner stuck with him as they stepped into the meal line, happy for early dibs at sustenance. The realmson, intent on getting the compensatory bounty promised him by Grum, snapped four empty porringers from off the oak table, handed one to Wagner, and then tucked the remaining three into the crook of his arm. When the culinary trusty (evidently informed by his NuRac commissary of the extra helpings) saw Balgor, he motioned for the realmson to present them one by one, whereby he slopped a generosity of stew into each. An unwieldy business for Balgor to balance the brimming trio of bowls on extended hands and wrists, his happy plight was made more ungainly when the bread-doling trusty plunged a rye loaf each into said porringers in successively torpedic fashion.

In juggling his piping hot, aromatic rewards, Balgor suddenly had the temerity to ask Wagner to assist him in conveying his thriced allowance—the very tender from Wagner's defeat—to the spot on the grounds where he meant them to sup. Wagner, taken aback and yet gracious enough to ignore the indignity, indeed relieved him of one bowl, an obliging that, to his ongoing deflation, evoked the smirks and snickers of many surrounding feasters. To be thought of not only as a bumpkinish Johnny-come-lately, but as a pithless go-along, vassalised by he who'd bested him, it wasn't quite the image one wished to project to a yard full of toughs. But here, between the splendidly subjective layers of perspective, nothing was truly as it seemed. Balgor's dicker with Grum, initially and understandably construed as mercenary, would quickly prove to be anything but. Both men having come to rest, as Wagner endeavoured to return to the Ergosian his rightful spoils, he found his initiative curtly refused. Balgor wouldn't have it. Twice rations, he claimed, would sate him finely, and Wagner would simply have to dispose of the excess.

Such unlikely turnabout incongruous with the man's formerly exhibited privatism, it slowly began to dawn on Wagner that this might somehow have been the Ergosian's intention from the start. Indeed, the mirth of those who supped around them gave further credence to some sort of deliberate ploy. Passive accomplices, no longer able to contain their amusement, their contagion was to become too influential for even Balgor to withstand for long, especially in light of Wagner's great perplexity. The Ergosian's deadpan gradually giving way to a smirk that was itself ruptured by irrepressible guffaw, once an ensuing and conspiratorial good laugh had coursed its way through the collective and back to Balgor, there seemed naught to do but to warm Wagner to the time-honoured practise in which he'd unknowingly participated.

"With the NuRacs too often insisting that we humble the recruits," Balgor confessed, "we have devised our own means for to recompense the disadvantaged. If, as always, that pompous clod, Grum, chooses to interpret my chaffering at your expense as self-serving, then so much the better."

"I wouldn't think Grum to be an easy mark for a self-asserting prisoner," said Wagner.

"Oh, he is not. One need only know how to turn his own manipulation back at him."

Wagner tore an ort from his bread. "So you want me to believe that whupping me in front of Grum was for my own benefit?"

"For mine as well. I am hungry today."

Wagner snorted genially, his recollection of Balgor's earlier ostentation now painted over with jubilantly new colours. Watching the Ergosian partaking, he followed suit, dipping his bread into the stew in likened fashion and bolting down mouthful after mouthful with equally unabashed wolfishness. He ate robustly, ate like a blighter who'd not sat for a prepared meal in months, with all memory of past cuisine—of Bishop's five star restaurants, of its downtown bistros and its corner cookhouses (not to mention the Filthy Lucre's grill and the Howsley Centre's bland-o-rama cafeteria)—outridden by the kind of indigent delectability that the immediacy of an empty stomach can make of even the most unpalatable foodstuffs.

His mind was likewise reshaping his perspective. With so many new distractions, he'd been disposed to shunt his older questions to the back of the pile, the inquiries of the here and now far more pressing than any perennial mystery of bendering and intangibility and doppelgangers. These, while no less confounding than before, were already well on to becoming but secondary negligences, indefinitely tabled for the newest phenomena of refulgent, restorative energies, of automatous battle prowess, of sudden and unnerving omniscience of otherworldly languages, and—perhaps most importantly—of his utter, *a posteriori* acceptance of the whole ordeal as reality. A vehicular shift in sentiment that not only suggested that Ergos might be more than an external projection of his delusion, it *insisted* upon it, insisted that every instance and action and intuition and thought either encountered or entertained on this plane was, in fact, genuine, and not some parenthetical, mind-spun layover from which Jon Mazzio's verbal modulations might yet talk him down.

More important, however, than even the cosmic event of bodily transplantation was his realisation that this place and everything in it had possessed, in one form or another, undeniable status and representation in every vision he'd ever experienced. Somehow, Ergos was what it had all been leading up to the entire time. Ergos—not earth, not Bishop—was the true framing for the puzzle. It was the final bourn of his apparitions, the root of the predestinate images that had trifled with him for so long. Ergos was—amazingly, confounding, and apparently—exactly where he belonged.

CHAPTER TEN

Though thou shouldest bray a fool in mortar
Among wheat with a pestle,
Yet will not his foolishness depart from him.
    —PROVERBS 27: 22

By week's end, Wagner had achieved an arguable proficiency in what he'd come to call "Staff-Fighting 101," and had even forged ahead to "Basic Swordplay Theory 099," a skill he found much more arduous in its practical execution than the flashy and ultimately fallacious examples popularised by film and fancy. True warring with a sword, even a wooden one, didn't suffer well the theatrics or clever choreography that Hollywood would have suggested; it was instead a largely parryless, indelicate, heavily consuming offensive that required a full dedication of grit and stamina—or, in lieu of these, at least the thrift of well-timed underhandedness. A captively quick study, Wagner had little choice but to develop these skills as Balgor demonstrated them, for he knew that if he couldn't abide the rigours of sessional practise, there would be absolutely no chance of staying the limit in an all-out confrontation against a shellback with ambition and real armaments.

One day out of eight, the prisoners were allowed a morning of surcease. An opportunity for some to sleep in, it similarly provided others with the meanwhile to consort, to game, or to visit without pretext a member of an opposing stable—some of which were often blood relatives. For those of the more affable set, it was a time to combine socialisation with hygienic intervention in a communal groom-fest staged just outside the infirmary. Parasitic infestation and other skin and hair woes being no squeamish affair to these people, by availing themselves of the dispensary's various unguents and delousing preparations they gaily ministered to one another while engaging in the banter of happier reminiscences and juicy prison scuttlebutt.

Whatever liberties the NuRacs allowed were squeezed into the morning hours of these easement days, for the procedure dictated that the afternoons be surrendered to the prerogative of each stable's respective financier. In Wagner's case, he and those who likewise trained under AuwNiir's banner would be assembled inside the barracks to hear the Commander's address on matters of late policy and of the pending tournament. The first occasion that Wagner would have to observe his *sigma*-bearing sponsor outside of their initial exchange, it was anticipatorily troubling for him, for it re-raised the insolubility of their connection to such degree that even the rarity of a morning's downtime proved insufficiently distracting.

Balgor, however, with no such qualms or secrets, was another story entirely. A natural fondness for trivialities, with a far younger man's impulsivity he insinuated himself amid the glut of storytellers and boasters, listening to what brag they spouted and then offering up an embellishment or two of his own. Old cavortings relived, past battles rehashed, he relished the fraternity as much as anyone, and for the duration he ardently immersed himself in pastimes the fribble of which proved gainfully antithetic to the rigidity that otherwise predominated his life.

For reasons yet to be uncovered, Balgor was more often than not addressed by his "realmson" epithet, a soubriquet that even the dour GrumTor had come to favour for his unprincipled, sometimes-model gladiator. A clipped version, actually, of the more formal appositive, "Son of the Realm," it was perhaps a means of distinguishing Balgor from other men who might have shared his name. Indeed, as more than a few people in the camp bore nearly identical appellation, qualifiers of affiliation, ancestry, region, even vauntable deeds, were often key for differentiating one from the other. Wagner's dungeon pal, Tamek of Vishkor, was another who enjoyed such designation—although by his renown (and the fact that most people simply called him "Sentinel") it was unlikely that he would be confused with anyone else, especially as there was no peer who shared either his name or his hailings.

Lacking introduction to, and therefore somewhat uncomfortable with, the greater Ergosian populace—and more so, unable to relate to them with even a fraction of Balgor's gregariousness—Wagner didn't dally among the masses on his free day. Instead, he staked an early claim at the wash basins, where the rare providence of a morning's unhurried bathing was far more to his liking. And true, although the luxury of a steamy, pulsating shower-massage was one of the earthly pleasures he would forever miss, the travail of long hours on a dusty palaestra had given him new appreciation for the brace of even the coldest of bathwaters.

To a body that seemed perpetually enveloped in filth, the crude cakes of tallow and lye supplied by his warders were a far cry from Howsley's institutional emollients, and generally left the flesh feeling not so much squeaky-clean as abraded away. His need to feel clean, however, was integral to his twenty-first century tetherings; and no matter the coddle that this hardier folk may have seen in it, he knew better the healthful advantages of cleanliness. Too, this time at the tanks likewise allowed him a twink of momentary well being, enough so that even this brief withdrawal from his surroundings and from his reservations over AuwNiir's imminent address served to refresh him on levels beyond the tactile. And by coincidence, it also made him insensible to the approach of a familiar someone, an acquaintance of whom he'd not had occasion to think for several days.

"It seems we are destined to meet whenever you are lacking your galligaskins," came a rearward female voice as he sluiced a cold drizzle across his shoulders.

Swinging around, he found the trusty from the slave coffle standing behind him, her tunic and vest draped over one arm, the tender symmetry of her partially adorned pulchritude staring him in the face.

"My galli—*what?*"

"Galligaskins," she said. "Breeches. It seems that you are intent on shedding them as often as you can."

She took the spot under an adjacent cistern, slipping from her remaining raiment and slinging each article across a wooden rod, just out of watershot, where Wagner had draped his. She glanced once more at Wagner, her lips suppressing what seemed a taut grin of one-upmanship.

"I think the *real* truth," he said, resuming his rinse, "is that you wait to come around until a guy is naked and vulnerable."

She chuckled amusement. "Oh, I think not. Even so, I have always found that a man stripped bare is not without certain...*weaponry.*" Her eyes wandered low. "If only some of them had discipline enough to keep said armament sheathed."

Wagner shifted awkwardly and muttered under his breath. "Tell me about it."

The woman filled her pail. Then, grasping a soap cake, she commenced to bathe herself, initiating with her arms and elbows and slowly working a paltry lather up around her torso. In an uncommon moment of sheepish fluster, Wagner forced himself back to his own affairs.

As if to compound his disaccustomedness with the practical necessitude of unisex bathing, a handful of other men and women began following suit, migrating toward the wash area, evidently taking cue from Wagner's and the trusty's idea while said option stood. Gathering around the troughs, those too late to claim one of the sluices instead sloshed pailfulls from the reservoirs and field-washed themselves with equally unaffected decorum, the wastewater from the volume of bathers soon filling the shallow channel that, set flush in the sand, directed what runoff it could handle into a gravel drainage, three metres removed.

Hastening his business, Wagner released the chain, plucked up his clothes and moved off. Flapping out his trousers on the go, he halted after several strides and promptly re-donned them, struggling briefly with the fit. Prior to showering, he'd stopped by the laundry to swap out the previous day's soilings for fresh toggery, and, while there, had even been fortunate enough acquire a sturdy pair of buskins to replace the tatty sandals that KoviKor had selected for him. Never thinking to inquire with the supply attendant as to the means by which such a sound pair of upgrades had suddenly become available, he'd already learned how such things worked. Somebody, presumably one of Olask's patients, had finally succumbed, and in any such instance where death was not a result of disease the policy of conservation dictated that all usable vestments of the newly deceased be redistributed among the general population.

With the morning sun at his back, Wagner plopped himself down about twenty paces from the wash area, and went to work at fastening the tedium of his new laces. His eyes here and again covertly reverting back to the trusty—still in a demure state of undress—he watched as she coaxed a scanty froth from the abstergent and diligently worked it through the same richly dark undulations that had been so very nappish upon their first encounter on the slave trail. Yanking on the sluice-chain like one of the inveterately immured, she doused herself in a brief but swashing rinse, and then sedately stepped beyond the source and wrung out her hair, scalp to ends, before squilgeeing her body free of sop with a featly sweep of her hands.

In all, she was truly a delicately sculpted creature, comely and contoured, with a quality of subtly reserved vigour about her that Wagner might never have suspected had he no firsthand knowledge of her outward competence. While physically not without a fair number of the chafes, nicks, and assorted ecchymoses associated with one's living life on the rough, anatomically she had such compelling lines that Wagner, catching himself in shameless leer, decided it better to limit his ogling to those occasions when her back was turned, lest he risk overcarrying his appreciation to the point of lechery. Yet, even here, inclination proved most unbiddable, for posteriorly she was as smooth and seamless as a Grecian statue, with a callipygian exquisiteness that more than defied Wagner's half-hearted attempts at renitence. The ripple of descending vertebrae, the playful dimpling in her loins, the unconscious shift of her hips—oodles of feminine charms seemingly lost on everyone save Wagner, the woman herself was so deep into her lavation that whatever allure she exuded was unwitting and almost certainly unintentional.

Forget it, he told himself. *Don't go there, man—don't even think about it.*

His earthly mindset so ingrained, it was tasking for him to relinquish the guardedness that had become mainstay to his last few years in Bishop. Because of the bendering, so arrant in the final months—and so insidiously pervasive in his "Sara period" to have mouldered away their relationship, spell by unexplained spell—there had come a point where he'd deemed it a matter of personal protection and outward consideration to relegate his biology to cold storage rather than risk visiting heartache upon either himself or upon another innocent for whom he might one day have come to care. Ever at odds with the growing mental tumult, any dalliances that he'd permitted himself in the contrail of Sara's skip-out had therefore been deliberately ephemeral ones, usually tapped from the Filthy Lucre's cast of friendly regulars. There, amid the loosings of liquor and licentiousness, amiable women were rarely out of fashion. And, at a time when Wagner had been understandably wary of re-opening himself to any kind of deep and soulful intimacy, he'd been less averse to engage in the superficial variety that, by its own transient nature, never needed to contend with the impendent and unpredictable loom of his futurity.

Of course, now that he'd been ousted from that life, now that he no longer lost conscious control for untold periods of time nor any longer traversed solid matter like Casper the friendly ghost, what was to say that he couldn't potter about Ergos and maybe find the kind of meaningful companionship that his maladied existence had denied him on earth? He was, after all, a man, and a relatively healthy one at that. His desire was a normality, nothing to be shunned, and no longer something to be stifled and subdued. But then again, how could he even consider giving thought to his libidinal piquings when there still existed so many unanswered questions and so much threat to his sense of personal safety in the form of slavery and combative mêlée and just plain uncertainty?

"I will take that, if you please." The trusty's voice jolted him from his reverie. Looking up, he found her standing before him in dishabille, gesturing at the ground to his left.

Gazing about, Wagner was mortified to discover not only his own tunic beside him, but hers as well, apparently appropriated by accident when he'd gathered up his own clothes. A gaffe no doubt wrought of his preoccupation and haste, he nevertheless imagined what the good Dr. Freud might have had to say about it.

"Sorry," he said, overcompensating for his discomfiture with an embarrassed chuckle that, to his dismay, came off sounding more spurious than he'd intended. Separating her tunic from his, he chivalrously shook the sand from it and handed it to her.

"W-what's your name?" he asked in sudden bluntness, hoping that introduction might help to diminish his foozle.

"I am J'nea."

"J'nea... It's good to officially meet you. I'm—"

"*Voknor*—yes, I know." Fixing her grip upon the tunic, she tried wresting it from Wagner's distracted grasp.

"Are you going to relinquish my vestment," she finally said, "or do you intend to remain agog and foolish until assembly?"

Alerted to the fact that he'd indeed failed to release the article, Wagner nevertheless found her new climate perplexing."

"Well, if you're gonna get all snippy about it," he said, "then I think I'm happy to remain agog and foolish."

She flashed him a surprised look—actually, surprise with a dash of leer—her attitude evidently having morphed from witty mordancy to something decidedly graver.

Appreciating, if not entirely understanding, her change in mood, Wagner released the tunic, whereupon she snatched it up and promptly shimmied into it. Yet, even as the jute slid readily about her, in emerging through the scoop of fraying neckline she was quick to find the nettled Wagner already risen and nearly halfway to his barracks.

While largely unrueful over his apparent—and completely unwitting—indiscretion, Wagner had no intention of making matters worse by trampling any more social graces than he had to, especially with someone so frustratingly mercurial as she. While convinced both that his cordiality and his degree of flirtation had been in direct measure to hers, the fact that he'd still managed somehow to offend J'nea was a mystery that he would need to run by the far savvier Balgor if he was to ever understand it. Then, if need be, he would surely set it right. Contrarily, if it turned out to be some trifle of undermention or a foul-up of semantics, or something as petty as his ignorance of convention (gender-based or otherwise) for which she'd not offered him a novitiate's latitude, then he would just as soon leave her to her sourness and go right on being the tactless stranger, thank you very much.

"You—*Voknor!*" Her hail, not entirely cross in tone, seemed in fact tempered with a barely perceptible tincture of entreaty.

Surprised, the once bitten Wagner decided to borrow a page from her playbook, making certain that his backward glance demonstrated an unmistakeable lack of concern.

Eye-to-eye at twelve metres, for a few seconds he watched as her lips sought to form the issue of some unknowable conveyance. To his disappointment, that issue never came. Instead, she clamped her mouth tight, her subsequent expression proffering little more than a cryptic wryness and a quickly erected façade of stoicism.

Waving disregard, she withdrew. Wagner, following suit, resumed his path toward his billet, only momentarily pensive over whatever it had been that she'd thought better of saying.

On passing into his barracks, he was at once struck by the din of conversation most robust. A barrage to his senses, he quickly married the raucousness to its constituent origins within the room, most of it the effluence of his loudly boastful bunk-mates who, amid gesture and embellishment, recycled old glories and deeds for an audience already so abundantly habituated that anyone with a tongue in his mouth could more likely than not have expounded the very same hackneyed tales from hell to breakfast. It was therefore rare to hear any recounting that did not rely at least a little upon the preposterous to zestify its umpteenth retelling. Exaggeration—or, as Balgor called it, the "latter-handed frippery that history surely would have included had it any sympathy for the storyteller"—turned a good yarn into a better one, and was not only expected in this venue but heartily encouraged as standard *modus operandi* for the consummative entertaining of one's dispirited fellow kindred.

Catching snatches of bravado and heroics too outlandish to be taken seriously, Wagner smiled as he skirted each gathering and the tale-spinner it encircled. Narrowly escaped death at the battle of Red Lake, Mirko of Vargath's absurdly successful reconnoitring behind enemy NuRac lines, a mysterious huntress who single-handedly stripped whole battalions of their armaments simply for trespassing through her forestal habitat—these and other legendary prodigalities were like satiating morsels to the hungry and ear-bent Ergosian birdlings who, regardless of the redundancy of the stories, hung open-mouthed on every descriptive detail.

Leaving them to their dramatics, Wagner navigated his way to his bed duffel. Once there, he worked at scrunching his straw into loose order and fluffing the nap of his blanket that he might wangle what little comfort he could for a mid-morning laze. Satisfied, he reclined, closed his eyes, and set at withdrawing as far as he could from the oral beleaguerment that surrounded him.

His respite was not long-lived.

Although he had learned during his time at Howsley the required mental discipline for maintaining meditative composure amid a whole cacophony of rec room regulars, what had once worked for him wasn't so easily applied to this new existence. Removed only a few short weeks from the relative benignity of Howsley's institutional backdrop, the insecurity of living as an Ergosian did heaps to nix Wagner's established habits of quiet contemplation and tranquil theorising. Basic existence now pre-empted all else. Physical well-being proved infinitely more demanding than any wistful abstractions into the wherefores and whys of predicaments whose answers had been chronically unforthcoming anyway. An all-round swotting of facts, figures, and common lore was essential. Thus, rather than retreating (as had always been his wont) from the intrusions that hampered contemplation, he decided for once in his life to close up shop on stuffy introspection and instead open himself to the rich Ergosian gasconade currently filling every corner of the barracks.

Sitting up, he scanned the room for his Ergosian chum, who naturally would have gravitated to the most animated of the conclaves. Gamühr, the current tale-crafter of this group—a woman of years, often called "the Bard" for her imaginative license with even the most commonplace stories—was the narrator whose account of the Red Lake incident Wagner had caught in snippet on his way toward repose. A defining NuRac-Ergosian skirmish, the battle at Red Lake was said to have been so bloody that the wooded hollow in which it was waged purportedly became steeped in such a volume of blood that it remained in fetid pool for days. A notion as repugnant as it was ludicrous, Gamühr recalled it with nothing less than Homeric eloquence, her alloyage of facts with the more malleable particulars of her fabulist's repertoire rounding out a chronicle of compelling contrivance.

Wagner, himself a sucker for a good yarn, saw a bit of his own machinations in Gamühr's style, even as her flamboyance easily made all his earthly dabblings in verse-craft seem as sophomoric dronings by comparison. Indeed, in times past, whenever Sally Lemanski or Jon Mazzio had been patient enough to subject themselves to yet another of his unsolicited relayings of mythopoeic irrelevance, Wagner would often tailor his causeries to appeal to the penchants of whichever of the two had been gracious enough to indulge him. A dose of romanticism to lift the sorely practical nurse from her earthly rut, a shift to classicism to appease the erudite doctor's more meticulous nature—although clearly Wagner didn't possess even a fraction of Gamühr's natural command, whatever he lacked in felicity he compensated for with a healthy dose of individualisation. Lean and unfrilled though his narratives may have been, he'd embroidered as best he could; and as someone whose personal world had been a mixed bag of psychical hopping, spatial permeatings, and outright amok, it was miraculous that he'd retained any literary passion at all.

The Ergosians, he observed, were a sociable folk—hungry for news, eager for exploits both heroic and base, open to anything that could transform the mundane into the wondrous, the underdog into the survivor, gloom into hope. It was a charming, if optimistically naïve, quality whose unvanquishability was nothing short of commendable given the frustration and grief thrust upon them by their captors. Good storytelling, from the haughtiest of epos to the simplest fable, was all but a contagion here; just as surely as it succeeded in desubstantialising their castigation for all of an hour or two, it likewise gilded their manacles with a dispositional unity that undermined the schism that the NuRacs' stratagem of factions and rewards was meant to foster. In splendid irony, what spirit the NuRacs subverted during the week was reconstituted by the very day of leniency that they themselves provided.

At the conclusion of Gamühr's account, Balgor and the others proclaimed their delight and approval with blustery shouts of "Goodly!" and "Well said!"—interjections that Wagner had come to know as Ergosian equivalents of earthly praise and plaudits. The clapping of hands was no compliment among this people, and in fact usually denoted less than approbatory regard for those who received it. One example of this—commonly called the "cuckold's revenge"—was standard comeuppance for any pair of adulterous lovers who, on discovery, were paraded half-clad throughout the village streets to a steady rataplan of handclapping. A second, and far more morbid, instance was the public response to the open scourging of thieves or murderers who, by magistrate's edict, underwent the deliberate scarring or finger-severing that would thereafter brand them as scoundrels. Recompense for any such wrongdoing was swift, decisive, often indelible, and almost always communal; and the idea of appeal or of legal representation was a luxury reserved for more enlightened nations, and perhaps, more liberal ages. Balgor's tutorials on such matters notwithstanding, it still seemed to Wagner that the Ergosian community in juxtaposition had nothing on the NuRacs when it came to the finer points of punishment.

"Who would be next?" came a cry from within the grouping.

"Who has a tale?"

A chatter grew as the people searched around for someone to step up and continue the folly.

Suddenly, Balgor rang out. "*Voknor*—are you not new to the realm? I seem to recall that you have travelled the nether regions, the lands south of Leordahn. Tell us what fascinations lie beyond! Relay to us how a humble reader of scrolls was able to traverse a valley inhabited by deadly krehak, and emerge undamaged upon our fair border!"

Wagner flushed with annoyance and embarrassment. "Um, yeah," he said. "I think I'll pass. I'm really not much of an orator."

"The hell you say!" Not only was Balgor *not* caving, but he was gleefully pushing, as friends often do. "You nearly talk me into my grave every day on the palaestra, trying to unguard me with your endless questions and suppositions. I *know* that you have the muse's voice at your ear!"

The realmson's grandstanding shifting even more attention to his pigeon, Wagner found himself buttonholed on all fronts by a mob of emboldening petitioners.

"The Vofspar!" called another voice. "Tell us how you came to be paired with her, why you defended her at the expense of your own liberty!"

"Deeds!" hollered another. "We wish to hear deeds!"

"Come, *Voknor*," Gamühr herself craved with a whisper at his ear. "Even the least of warriors has one story. Offer it. Gratify your peers with the smallest figment and you will have done your baiting friend one better."

Wagner laughed and shook his head, laughed and begged off the pressing mass, laughed and finally threw up his hands in surrender, soliciting a thought-gathering silence from his hooting and heckling stable-mates.

"All right," he said. "All right. I'll tell you how it was that I was able to reach your land without becoming fodder to these...these *kreoxes* that my *former* friend, Balgor, keeps yapping about."

"*Krehak!*" sniped the realmson. "Krehak! For smiting's sake, *Voknor*, if you wish to be convincing, at least finesse your lies with a smattering of authenticity!"

The gathering erupted in belly laughs and shoulder-slapping, all freely offered up at Wagner's expense.

"That may be what *you* folks call'em," said ol' Doc Wagner, pooh-poohing Balgor the way that his late show elixir sharper might have belittled a badger in the crowd of potential Cure-All vendees. "To the south of the valley, we call them *kreoxes*. And more ghastly creatures you will never meet."

"Oh? And just how do they appear?" The challenge came from a girthy, powerful warrior whom Wagner had come to know as Uthok the Bonecrusher—called so for the calloused enormity of his hands.

Wagner, still struggling to launch beyond the starting gate, paused momentarily, trying to channel his fluster into the nervous edge of some more convincing bluff. Meeting Uthok's self-satisfied stare, he deliberated over whether to sneak around the man's stumping tactics or to face them head on. Ultimately, he gambled on the former.

"Not nearly as huge and lumbering and ugly as you, my amply-fisted friend. When I say *ghastly*, what I'm referring to is their repugnant odour. They reek of—" He stopped and sniffed grandiosely at the air in Uthok's general direction. "Well, maybe they're not so bad after all."

Silence gripped the crowd for the space of one long and terrible moment. Then, suddenly, absolute pandemonium took the room, with every Ergosian within earshot eructing uproariously at Wagner's saucy retort. No one, *no one*, ever insulted Uthok to his face—at least not without first devising some *reculade* of equivocal escape hatch. And yet here was an audacious incomer who matter-of-factly gave Uthok the what-for.

Wagner, gaining notion of his irreversible departure from anonymity, cracked an uneasy grin as he watched Uthok's howling compatriots closing about the man, playfully thumping his shoulders, mussing his hair and tweaking his scowling jowls until finally the man could do naught but guffaw himself. An obliging heart inhabiting that brutish body, the Bonecrusher laughed as lustily as any other there, even as he waved with exaggeration a gigantic—albeit unthreatening—mitt at his insulter.

Wagner, fractionally anxious under a cucumber façade, waited for the mirth to dwindle so that he could gauge whether or not he was irrevocably committed to delivering a story. Finding, however, that his audience would not let him escape the spotlight quite so easily, he acquiesced. Dipping, then, into his vast resource of Greek mythology, he drew forth one of his favourites—the tale of Daedalus—and with a few manipulations, made it into his own:

> "As some of you may have inferred, I hail from the southern territories. And—um—for reasons that aren't all that important to this story, I left my homeland a few weeks back to embark on...I guess you might call it a 'coerced pilgrimage' of sorts.
>
> "In journeying north over very mild terrain, it was on my second day of travel that I happened upon the camp of a wayfaring young fellow named Icarus. Now, Icarus, not totally unlike me, had left his home due to circumstances that forbade his return, at least until he'd made good on some personal deed or goal that he never chose to share with me. He did, however, relay that he had distant kin somewhere in this realm, although I'm not sure who they are or in what region they reside. But, anyway, a coltish young man he was, this Icarus, with a wild flame of red hair and a freckled, boyish face. Exuding the hell-bent enthusiasm of youth, by his words I

could tell that he would never be content to simply farm or fabricate for a living. He ached, like many of us have at one time or another, to sample all of life's wonders—great and small, adventurous to commonplace, lofty to—well—*less* than lofty. Filled, as he was, with some higher ideals—as well as some notions of pretty racy fancy—at times along our way he became so wrapped up in his zestful aspirations that it fell to me to ensure that we incurred no misfortune from the unseen dangers of the territories that we were crossing.

"Not only for the company, but for our mutual safety, we'd agreed to travel on together, and did so for many days, hiking through some of the most beautiful—and often treacherous—countryside I'd ever seen. We passed along the foot of Mount Rushmore, bowing respectfully to the four ancients, way on high, who watch over the land and all who inhabit it. Several days later we reached the Great Pyramid of Cheops, which, of course, we quietly slinked past for fear of stirring the mummified avenger whose duty it is to safeguard the Pharaoh's treasures. Reaching the river Amazon by week's end, we decided to take the long way around, crossing at its most shallow point, two days upstream, and then doubling back to pick up our original heading. By doing this, we avoided having to construct a vessel that, should we not have been careful enough, would've been swept up in the current and dashed upon the deadly banks of Chernobyl, some miles downstream. Once across, and with no further impediment, we were then able to attain the upper lands without too much ordeal.

"When we finally came upon the Leordahn Crevasse, we knew that in order to traverse it we had to be mindful of the inhospitable creatures who dwelled and scavenged on the plains below. However, after much debating, neither Icarus nor I could come up with anything too strategically sound. Neither of us knew much about the kreoxes down below, not how to avoid them, and certainly not how to overcome them. And, as the ridge itself was far from an ungenial spot, we decided to remain encamped there until we could agree on the best, safest course. Not wanting for water or food, a nearby stream provided all the refreshment we needed, and for sustenance we hunted from a ready supply of indigenous ground fowl that moved about in fairly prodigious flocks. I'm not sure what species they were—I'd never seen their kind before.

"On the fourth morning, after breakfast, I was relaxing, picking my teeth with a sliver of bird bone—part of a wing I think. Anyway, I was gazing at this pile of plucked feathers that we'd amassed in our mutual gluttony, and was at once struck with an impossible idea. I quickly roused young Icarus, explained my plan, and soon we were gathering twigs and vines and pithy grasses to weave into the plaiting that would be necessary for my daring emprise to work. Once this was accomplished, we went looking for honeybees—yeah, that's right, *bees*—and on spotting a flit of them among some wildflowers, we hung out a while and watched, and after a lot of painstaking effort we eventually traced them back to their hive. Then, fabricating two pitchy torches—a trick I'd once learned from the all-knowing oracle of PBS—we fanned smoke into the hive's opening, thus disorienting and debilitating the bees just enough for us to break open the hive and make away with some of the comb. It was, however, the wax that we were truly after, not the honey. The wax was vital to our scheme."

Wagner, oddly more comfortable in his role as narrator than he would earlier have believed, had noted only smatterings of scoff and scruple among his audience, and these, mostly at the onset of his tale. Perhaps only an initial disorienting brought on by his personal speaking style—by his colloquialisms and the general foreignness of his terms—it was still a wonder that no one had shut him down for his presumption upon their grammatical largesse. Surprisingly, he seemed to be reaching, and even entertaining, the majority of his adventure-starved peers whose obvious enthrallment (or indulging politeness) with his unusual and untried spinning encouraged him to plod on to its end.

"The gist of my plan was both simple and outrageous. Having plucked enough feathers and gnawed on enough gizzards in the previous days to pretty much make us crack engineers on avian anatomy, we pieced together four light frames out of the most suitable strips of sapling timber that we could find. Each framework a triple arm's-reach in length, we employed our fabricated twine to fasten the pertinent junctures as firmly as their tensility allowed. Then, using our next meal as a template, we affixed row over row of feathers to the constructs, each quill meticulously spot-welded with dollops of softened beeswax. It took us several days of really intricate assembly work to achieve this, to realise the proper layering of coverts and scapulars and such, and another two days to cure them so that we could be confident that the wax would indeed hold, and that these contraptions—when slipped over each of our arms—could be manipulated as makeshift wings without restriction.

"The entire effort, of course, having been a crazy idea from its conception, we wondered if such outlandish gizmos would carry us at all. For the longest time we were hesitant to even test them. If it wasn't our courage waning, it was the hindrance of insufficient winds, or of too much wind, or rain or fog or sleet or gloom of night. And then, when conditions were finally moderate enough to chance it, we ran low on courage again. So, in the end, the biggest impetus to commit ourselves to the air wasn't from spirit or daring at all, but was instead rooted—believe it or not—in Icarus's growing aversion to eating wild fowl. He'd had it with the gamy taste. He was tired of feather-plucking, too, tired of disjointing and de-boning, tired of accidentally chomping down on one too many errant beaks. Even as I'd been varying the recipe with an occasional handful of mushrooms, roots, nuts or berries, my companion was quickly going into poultry overload.

"One afternoon, as I was walking back to camp after foraging, I gradually came to hear the sounds of high-spirited glee. Seeing nothing of Icarus anywhere near the camp, imagine my surprise when I turned my gaze upward to find him soaring across the heavens! Yep, there he was, the impetuous lad who was fed up with being fed up! *There* was the wild-haired kid whose impatience to cross the valley impelled him to give those wings a try. And although his aerodynamics were as choppy and ungraceful as you might expect, he was airborne nonetheless!

"Believe me, you could've knocked me over with a feath— Um, anyway, grabbing up my own wings, I made ready to join him in the great blue yonder. And this I did—almost too easily—with even the lightest breeze wafting me skyward. Within seconds, my once-sagging faith was transformed into some pretty radical delight. And soon, after the initial shock of overcoming the restrictions of my own weight, I signalled to Icarus that we should cross the valley while we had the winds with us. No wing-twisting was necessary. Almost immediately he swooped past me, and off we glided like natural denizens of the air.

"There was, however, one danger that we hadn't considered. You see, the sun was quite intense that day. And now that we were so much higher up, I felt the swelter even more so. This caused me no little concern, and I shouted up to Icarus to maintain a modest altitude, to prevent our waxy bonding agent from weakening from the increase in temperature. Yet, so euphoric was my young friend that he either didn't hear me or he simply ignored me, taking himself higher and higher until, unknown to him, my fears were realised. The wax on his wings became too malleable. The integrity of his harness began to falter. From below, I watched in horror as feather after feather slipped loose from the trusses and fluttered away. Crying at the top of my lungs, I tried desperately to flag his attention. But it was all for nothing. By the time he'd comprehended his plight, his framework had disintegrated and he was plummeting earthward at high velocity. And I was helpless to do anything but watch in horror. I had nowhere near the dexterity to perform a sweeping rescue, and had I even been close enough to try I was in no way certain that my modest set of wings could have bore the weight of two people.

"With profound feelings of guilt and sorrow, I mourned for young Icarus, who by then had been swallowed by the treetops far below. Saddened and appalled, yet hoping beyond hope, I continued to circle the area for a very long time, taking only meagre solace in knowing that he'd relinquished life long before any kreox—or krehak—could get a hold of him.

"Eventually, with the winds rising, I began to tire in my flight. Having just enough reserve to continue on, I was able to touch down—or 'wipe out,' if you will—upon a grassy knoll on the valley's northern ridge. Shaken, scraped, but escaping serious injury, I kissed the earth for its generosity, and then I stood up to unfasten what remained of my now-crumpled harness. And, as it had been irreparably damaged in my graceless landing, I flung it frame and feather from the precipice as both a tribute to my unfortunate friend and as a gesture of thanks to whatever power had seen me safely across.

"I remained on that ridge for the space of a day, contemplating my hollow fortune and cursing young Icarus's fate. Then, once I'd regathered my courage and resolve, I set off, away from the crevice, actually believing the worst of my ordeal to be over. Little did I know that I was only a few weeks shy of crossing paths with NuRacs and Vofspars. That, however, is a story for another time."

Wagner paused there. His fictional ramblings concluded, he looked sombrely to his listeners for their yeas or nays. The last time he'd relayed a story sans interruption had been a few weeks back at Howsley, talking classic film with Sally. Both big fans of Edward G. Robinson—and Wagner, astonished that she'd never seen *The Amazing Doctor Clitterhouse*—he'd tried arguing the merits of that obscure little throw-away above and beyond some of Edward G.'s more acclaimed fare. Sally, as always, had endured with commendable patience not only his play-by-play account of its quirky plot, but his misguided presumption in actually vaunting that film's entertainment value over *Little Caesar* or *Key Largo*. Being the exceptional psychiatric nurse that she was, she'd allowed him his contentions right to the end before setting him straight from *her* side; and Wagner now wondered if the Ergosians, having been no less generous in their sufferance, would now call him out on some flaw in specificity, some point of unforgivable fabrication, or if they would grant him their suspended disbelief in spite of gross inaccuracy, and enjoy the tale for no more than its telling.

To his unexpected delight, the gathering responded with overwhelming support. Assorted cheers, jeers, wails, and hoots rose up from the audience like a Folsom response to a Johnny Cash ditty, with not one of the Ergosians likely believing for a minute a word of Wagner's yarn, but rather saluting the lively and inventive phantasy provided by what they quickly deemed a sharp and understated wit. Even Gamühr paid homage with an earnest nod of approval, one bard to another, while Balgor and his pals beat up on Uthok and each other for no other reason than the demands of mirthful infectiousness. Some excessive fellow even went so far as to tear up a palliasse—someone else's, no doubt—and unleash upon the barracks airspace a great fluttering of straw whose chaffish fallout soon had everyone looking like scarecrows on a frenzy.

"Look!" the scatterer cried. "Here is all that remains of that reckless whelp, Icarus!"

Some of the throng laughed in reply; many more fleered. Two of the latter, a pair of incorrigible brothers whose names were Grandio and Graspa, set upon the jackpudding from behind and, much to his misease, hoisted him precariously over their heads and paraded him around the room, shouting: "Nay! Look now—here comes gentle Icarus himself!" Wagner was even surprised to espy J'nea standing near the doorway—J'nea, who, although not of this billet, had apparently strolled in at some point during his narrative, and was even then slipping out at its finish.

In the aftermath of Wagner's debut, Uthok gradually broke away from his kidders, ambled his way through the crush, and came to place himself before Wagner. With hands the size of catchers' mitts, he first feigned at strangling the newcomer before easing off and jostling Wagner friendly-like at the shoulders for a tale well told. And Wagner, his well-founded apprehension melting into relief, sighed redemption like a man who'd only narrowly escaped being run down by a bus. Even as he expressed gratitude at Uthok's forbearance, he felt positively minikin beneath the Bonecrusher's congratulatory paws. With all of this unmitigated fuss that Uthok and the others were collectively raising over one paltry little story, it was the sort of gesture that made Wagner feel significantly Ergosian for the very first time. While all around him the last of the straw confetti was alighting on people's heads and atop their clothing and even upon the tongues of those who, in their gaiety, may have been loudmouthing with a bit too much gusto, Wagner came to know just how good it felt to find favour in the eyes and hearts of a community, even a gaoled one.

Suddenly, a voice from the fore area bellowed out gruffly: "What form of warrior's welcome is this?"

The crowd turned as one to behold the figure whose ingress into the barracks had gone largely unnoticed.

"A rain of laurels I would understand," the comer continued, "e'en petals of bellwort cast about my feet. But *straw?* Have I, in my absence, fallen so out of esteem?"

In contre-jour a particularly august and princely fellow, he was without peer the tallest and quite nearly the brawniest Ergosian in all the prison. Recollectively unmet to Wagner—despite long and hourful days of inuring himself to the camp's multipartite populace—the latter was certain that he'd never before laid eyes on this man. Such pre-eminence would not have been easily forgotten.

Fresh from a bath, or so it appeared, the entrant stood clothed in tunic and trousers whose soppish blotching suggested a donning straight from the showers; and his hair, a black shock of corkscrewed ringlets, dripped an unsteady errancy of droplets onto shoulders that not even Uthok's ample grasp could encompass. Sturdy and stout of limb, backlit from the gateway, no deliberate contrivance of light and placement could have done more to dramatise his entrance.

"Tamek!" someone cried out.

"By the Twain—it be the Sentinel!"

"Tamek—back from the dungeons!"

Like a crush of autograph hounds in the sudden midst of celebrity, so did the Ergosians all but forget about Wagner, ploughing past him in their mania to greet their revered Sentinel of Vishkor—and Wagner's former neighbour in stir. Tamek fielded their embraces, their fond affections, their kind words, with the same heartfelt eloquence that had made Wagner's transition into the QieLahran dungeons a little less frightful than it needed to have been. Clearly the Ergosians adored their returning hero, and by nothing more than his presence did they realise a barracks-wide bolster of renewed confidence. In assuring his salubrity, they were in effect confirming their own, and what this meant for Wagner was that there was at once a generosity of crow to be consumed for his having misread the incarcerated Sentinel's boasts of influence and authority as pure vainglory. The figurative boots that he'd likewise donned in order to slog through Tamek's now legitimised deluge of self-indulgence back in the pits were suddenly better suited for the kicking of his own backside, not only for his discourtesy, but for clinging so doggedly to his earthly cynicism in an untried world.

In the course of the revelry, Tamek's gaze twice tracked past Wagner's, neither instance with any notable registry. Yet, with a third vetting, it almost seemed as if the Ergosian was narrowing his overview of the room's many faces to a select few. Indeed, *few* finally became *one* as his eyes zeroed in on Wagner's with a pregnant scrutiny that made Wagner wonder whether a man whom he'd met only in the dark could possibly distinguish one yeanling from all the others. Surely, with the scores of newbies in the camp, and with Tamek having never really looked upon Wagner's features with less than mottled clarity, it was unlikely that he could possibly have identified Wagner—not with a mere glance, not without at least having heard him speak.

Still, the Vishkorian gently worked his way, as Uthok had moments before, through the great crush of geniality until he stood contrapositive to one of the few in his midst who maybe had seemed unbefittingly pensive, avoiding all manner of reception—adoring, adulatory, reproachful, or otherwise.

Arms folded, with one hand cradling his chin, Tamek eyed Wagner meticulously, like a clever man come before the sphinx.

"Well met, infidel," he suddenly blurted. "I bring greetings from your beloved cragworms—they who did keep such gentle company with you in stir, and whom you blithely abandoned in your liberation."

"I'm sure they found a worthy replacement in you," said Wagner. "How are you, Tamek?"

"I am well, all things being relevant to having lolled for untold days within a man-sized chamber pot with insufficient food, drink, and breathable air."

"You don't have to tell me," said Wagner. "I was beginning to wonder just how long they were going to keep you there."

"'Twas an intended humbling, as always. And, as always, it has proven ineffective."

"I'd expect nothing less from *you*. Anyway, things just haven't seemed homey here topside without your steady beratings about my pagan ways."

"*That* we will certainly rectify—in due time, of course. You have been acquired by AuwNiir then?"

"Right out of the dungeon. No other takers, I guess."

"On the contrary. Little escapes our calculating Commander. Your display with the Vofspar obviously impressed him enow to bid for your battle rights. His expectations will be great, have no doubts."

That said, Tamek moved on to converse with those whom he'd not yet visited. Wagner watched him mingle, a pastor with his parish, and, feeling increasingly like a fifth wheel, he chose to slip away, retiring toward the entryway for a private moment and a breath of courtyard air.

Leaning against one side of the archway, he propped up a foot and gazed out toward the wash area, where a small cluster of nudes and semi-nudes yet scrubbed away the blood and sweat of the past week. No "tears" to round out said list of lavables, he'd actually observed nothing thus far in the way of outward weeping from anyone, not even from the minim of Ergosian children in the camp. He didn't know why this was, not exactly, but theorised that the conditioned hardship suffered unto these people eventually begat a sort of provisory acceptance—a forced compromise—that hardened them to the undesirable things that befell them day in and out. More plainly, war and enslavement and brutality were no more than facts of life. It was up to each of them to submit or resist as he saw fit, wholly the individual's responsibility to make the best of his personal predicament. How different, then, were the Ergosians from all of the pampered, over-permitted complainers of Wagner's earthly lifeline who had everything these people had not! The whole slew of fad-chasing, money-fixated, remote control-clutching dumbbells who dominated such a humongous chunk of the civilised society he knew, those who routinely assigned blame wherever they might, and as often as they could, for their own laziness and ineptitude and for their failure at achieving their airy-fairy ends—had any of them even a single clue as to what constituted real hardship?

But now he was thinking like a man beyond his years.

Stowing the platitudes, he refocused on the yard. A half-dozen men and women consorted casually around the spot where he and J'nea had exchanged words both honeyed and galled. Beyond the inner walls, the sun was yet climbing fast in the sky, its warmth already infusing the late morning breeze that wafted through the entry. Wagner closed his eyes and, for a few seconds, imagined himself strapped within the Daedalean appendages of his narrative. Living that image for but a moment, the wind in his hair, the sounds of the recreating Ergosians and the hindrance of all other Ergos-bound constraints falling away with the rest of reality, he snapped himself back with Icarian abruptness. Feathers and wax were unreliable options for what had begun to take root in his mind. So were endoskeleton wing-frames, serendipitous updrafts, even Cinjal, the fiery Ergosian sun herself. No, there had to be more viable means for getting beyond QieLahr's walls.

And he intended to find one.

CHAPTER ELEVEN

Ignorance plays the chief part among men,
And the multitude of words;
But opportunity will prevail.
　—DIOGENES LAERTIUS

"Your concern is mine as well, *Voknor*," Tamek said as he crouched upon the cobble, his fingers working diligently to snug his boots by their sorely weathered lacings. "In truth, 'tis—and continues to be—e'eryone's preoccupation, for we have all of us at one time or another entertained the notion of escaping. Indeed, some have e'en taken it beyond idle fancy, and have intrigued elaborate schemes of daring to see their freedom regained. I regret that no plan has yet succeeded."

"None?" Wagner sat in low squat at the base of one of the barracks' rearmost support columns, where he'd lured Balgor and Tamek for a mid-evening conclave. A shadowy, untenanted nook, it was a common spot for all matters covert. "You're telling me that in all the years that this place has existed, way back to Papa Olask's time, nobody has made it past the walls?"

"Not precisely. If I were to palter with semantics, I could say that many *bodies* have indeed slipped the collars of slavedom, only to find too late that they had slipped free of their lifely trappings as well. In the past, a notable few—the fortunate—e'en managed to survive long enow to clear the outer walls ere a barrage of NuRac arrows took them swift and sudden, sending their essences hurtling back to the Sacred Pool. The less fortunate found themselves recaptured and expedited to the dungeons until the day of the games, when they were promptly delivered into the Spectre's embrace by an arena-pitting 'gainst insurmountable odds. A grisly, horrific bloodbath—such was the consequence and consummation of all their efforts. 'Twas also the sole variable in their caper that they had not taken soberly into account. Nay, although I truly wish I could say different, no one to my knowledge has e'er escaped and lived."

"Even Olask concurs here, *Voknor*," said Balgor, his seldom encountered sombreness just as quickly suspended by the sight and sound of Tamek's laces snapping.

"A pox on these miserable things!" Tamek flung one orphaned laceling at the wall and the other at Balgor for his impromptu gut-bust of hysterics. "These pitiable leathers are older than Olask, and twice as vexing!"

"Aye, Tamek," Balgor nettled between spasms, "I believe they are the very laces that Olask sported on the day of his capture, many millennia ago."

"I would not find that at all surprising," said the Sentinel, "the way that goods come to be traded, pilfered, and inherited in this blasphemer's paradise." He yanked angrily at the remnant laces, loosing and extracting and adjusting until he'd reworked a shorter facsimile of rudimentary binding.

"So," Wagner persisted, "you're saying that escape is pretty much impossible?"

"Not at all," said Tamek. "Merely perilous beyond measure."

"Then, you've never attempted it yourself."

Tamek looked squarely at Wagner, eager to move on.

"Oft have I contemplated my freedom, *Voknor*. Daily do I study the tour of duty for e'ery guard who walks a parapet. I have also, on the occasions when my protestings take me there, had the fortune to glimpse the city's outer fortification from within the embrasuring of the NuRac Tribunal's keep. I e'en suspect that out here, 'neath our very noses, there exist hidden accesses in the courtyard curtain through which a sentry, compromised by unready altercation, might flee to safety."

"What, like the one in your oubliette?"

"Aye, the exception being that 'twas I, and not the NuRacs, who created that aperture, and this only after weeks of fumbling blindly with a thousand mites of crumbling mortar. But, on the whole, I know the general strengths of this prison, just as I suspect some of its weaknesses. And e'en as I have in past times abetted those who approached me with their intentions of escaping, I do not endorse any save the most exhaustively formulated plans—and I myself have vowed not to break gaol personally lest I might take e'ery last Ergosian with me."

"Is that even possible?"

"Void of miraculousness, 'tis unlikely. But there are events yet to unfold, *Voknor*, events that will serve to rally our kind as eyes have ne'er witnessed, and souls, ne'er envisioned."

"Let me guess—the Vorshalah, right?" Wagner's spirit folded as any furtherance of a practical dialogue seemed destined for stymieing by Tamek's segue into mysticism.

"The Vorshalah," said the Sentinel, "will, as always, be the dispatch of multifold transpirations, both dire and wondrous—this much is both foregleamed and precedent."

"And this is significant for me...*how?*"

"Keep in mind, *Voknor*, that our situation here, like all things in the world, is transient. Yet, as surely as Fate and futurity are untemptable, whate'er is to unfold will do so in its own time and with its own pace."

Wagner glanced over at Balgor, who shrugged his shoulders unassuringly.

"How is it," Wagner said, "that the realm's greatest religious warrior comes to prescribe passivity?"

"I do no such thing. I remark that the deluge is coming, and counsel that we all prepare to be caught up in it."

"Even if I were swayed to that," said Wagner, "I don't see why I would preclude myself from acting independently of whatever greater imminence might be heading my way. If these rockin' events are really coming like you say, then what will it matter if they find me sitting here on my hands or busy shimmying across the walls?"

"Ne'er did I say that you should not go, *Voknor*—only that you will risk much and forfeit more. Dreadful though the arena may be, it will teach you useful skills, which in turn may be needed one day to help rout this NuRac scourge from our lives."

Wagner stared into Tamek's eyes for a very long time, wondering if the fire he saw there was resident of the Sentinel's spirit or if it was simply some manner of reflective corposant from one of the sconces in the barracks forefront. Regardless, they were the sort of eyes that, like their owner, could not easily be out-steeled.

Later, on his bedsack, Wagner would find his own eyes too unladen for sleep. The moon, even at three-quarter phase, shone so brightly upon the courtyard that the entrygate's gridwork seemed little more than trace before the brilliance. From his darker recess, amid the snores and snorts of those whom the Sandman held in higher favour, Wagner poured over the evening's discourse, pondering his inexplicable reluctance to slough the Sentinel's over-righteous gobbledygook quite as easily and with as much detachment as he had in the dungeon. Back then, he'd been able to dismiss Tamek's pratings as the evangelical mumbo-jumbo of a man too pickled in his own piety to merit much attention beyond the subjective. Still, something in the urgency of his heedings this night had slipped onto Wagner's radar, had tripped one of those touchy, intuitive switches that Wagner had vowed never again to disregard.

Sorting out the facts and phenomena, going way back, there was much that seemed ever askew—and, disturbingly, just as much that seemed eerily in place. As he'd come to understand it, these people were smack at the onset of one of a revolving series of pivotal tridecenniums in Ergosian history: the Vorshalah. A monumental event in whole, its constituent indicants came shrouded in a religious esotericism that Wagner was not privy to. It was additionally inconvenient that Tamek's accounts of it were often abstruse and ambiguous. The reliable timeline, the revisiting Paraclete, an upsurge of sortilege in the realm—as holy credenda, such things weren't strictly an easy swallow. But, then again, they were certainly no less indigestible than the supernatural circuitousness of Wagner's own bizarre happenstance. Forget not also a noted presence, in more Vorshalic ages than not, of expressed evil—a sinister, opposing faction that very neatly and by unsurprising precedent reared to unleash some unprovoked but ultimately correctable havoc in the realm. All of it a very tidy package of scripted scripture to be sure, Wagner reckoned with both cynicism and certainty that any radical extemporariness that rose beyond the pale of traditional prediction was probably conveniently retrofitted to the lore by imaginative priests and scribes in much the way that earthly theologians contended had occurred with many canonical texts. And here, now, among these people, if Wagner wasn't able to keep his unseasonable abilities under wraps, the next batch of scriveners might very well need to add to the mix a wild-card offlander—fluent in all tongues, possessed of gramarye and hidden insights, outwardly Ergosian but "branded" with a NuRac Commander's device— the existence and pertinence of whom would fall to posterity to unriddle.

The subject of the Commander took him back several hours to the afternoon's assembly, where the *sigma*-emblazoned AuwNiir ran through his ponderous list of concerns, informing the stable's constituency of (among other things) its respective slottings for the upcoming games. Line-ups had not yet been finalised, but with the veteran hierarchies already informally established via rank and merit, most of the unconfirmed pittings were the novitiate bouts, the raw rookies whose fortitudes were yet to be fully put to test. For Wagner, the anxiety of not knowing exactly what manner of clash awaited him was matched only by his disinclination to take part in such barbarism at all. Martialism may have been a way of life for the people of this world—and gladiator-style matches, the compliance of those whose grudging acceptance of their newfound roles as arena fighters far exceeded his own—but to Wagner, killing anyone or anything by coercion was unconscionable. That this monthly tournament was creeping fast into reality, it confirmed for him the unwelcomed imminence of meaningless bloodshed that, up until AuwNiir's little pep rally, had seemed far more distant on the calendar than the days truly read. This gruff slap of impending challenge, then, had been the impetus behind Wagner's emergency bull session with the two men he knew best, that they might critique his unready notions of escape.

Although proving less than fruitful, his clandestine huddle did achieve one thing. It re-jiggered his impression of Tamek that their stint together in solitary had belied, a misrendering originally fostered by way of Tamek's brash and unminced frankness. Nothing short of sedulity to cut through all of the Sentinel's crustiness simply to get a better handle on the ideology that drove him, by meeting's end Wagner affirmed what observation and inference had intimated. More exegetic paring was unnecessary; the cultural and moral obstinacies that kept Tamek so pumped all the time were the very ones that Wagner had encountered in much of the prison populace during his short (and Tamek-free) time topside. Discount the melodrama of the Sentinel's grander vision, strip away the haughtiness and the pedantry and the friendly aspersion, and one found the rudiment of Tamek's faith to be far from tyrannous—and nowhere near unpalatable. The orthodoxy itself was fairly benign. Its conventions were propitious and highly reverent of life and nature. It was merely the Sentinel's abrasiveness that seemed to give it bristle.

Not foolish enough to think that he could map out his entire independence in a single evening of scheming, Wagner gave thought to what he could until he realised that the moon had long fallen below the outer curtain. The distinguishment between latest night and earliest morning no longer readily discriminable, it was suddenly important that he rest, else Balgor would have a field day on the next morning's palaestra, inflicting cheap shot after cheap shot against the sloppiness of Wagner's sleep-deprived fending.

Curling into his straw, pulling his threadbare blanket overtop to frustrate the mosquitoes, he guided himself into the drift, hoping perchance for the reprieve of just one brief and lightsome little dream that would allow him to be as free as the wind, as carefree as the hawk, and as confident in Daedalean physics as his narrative counterpart had been.

With the arrival of dawn, however, he woke as he always did of late, unhampered by subconscious muddle. Sitting up and preparing for yet another day of wearying routine—a bland meal followed by several hours of knockabout followed by blander rèchauffè, a cold shower, and sleep—he thought about how fine it would be, just once, to be able to set out a spread of lawn chairs, fire up the barbecue, and crack a few cold ones to the sight of Grum and the guards partaking in some mindless rock'em-sock'em of their own. But he may just as well have wished for Playboy's X-treme Team girls to come abseiling over the walls—in full rescue gear and with direct orders from ol' Hef to bring him back to the mansion for sanctuary—for all the good that wishing did him. Besides, as daydreaming was the only kind of dreaming that still worked for him, he'd just as soon save it for occasions when its fanciful distraction wouldn't net him a good doling of lumps from the business-end of Balgor's quarterstaff.

Yet, it was no longer only Balgor's desserts that he had to anticipate. In order that Wagner not become too versed in any single opponent's style, the realmson had cleverly begun subjecting him to a whole gallery of new sparring mates, each with his own favourite weapon, each with a fighting discipline as diverse from his predecessor as Balgor could arrange, all this to keep Wagner wired and ever on a defensive learning curve. With this recruitment—a liberty that availed the realmson some small illusion of empowerment in a poky undercutting of Grum's authority—Balgor thus weaned himself from the role of Wagner's exclusive trainer, pawning his trainee off to only his most deviously dextrous brethren so that Wagner might sample technique upon technique from a pool of antagonists who hadn't yet developed the esteem for him that Balgor had. Actually a quite gainful strategy on Balgor's part, the results began manifesting within the first day of said diversity. Knowing well that Wagner wasn't nearly as dispassionate about being beat up, shown up, or bested as he'd initially been, it turned out to be a splendid means of pushing his yeanling friend beyond his comfort level, which would in turn compel his growth as a combatant.

Called on to apply himself as never before, Wagner actually came to enjoy the inevitable upside of these gruelling workouts in the way of newly gained strength and endurance. Taxed daily above all convenience, there wasn't a morning come that didn't greet him without an impingement in one muscle group or another. He was a work in progress, a veritable cakes & ale milksop of twenty-first century earthly ease who, through proper tasking and a strategic jockeying of opponents, was en route to becoming a bona fide man of the realm.

With specialised knowledge of how to limit post-workout discomfort, he'd begun implementing a homespun regimen of flexibility-promoting activities prior to, and following, the day's matches. Ergosian sports medicine still a good millennium removed by comparative earthly measure, his oddly-viewed spectacle of hamstring stretches, side bends, back arches and such, prompted some interesting gapes and asides from an immediacy of peers who had no real acquaintance with warm-up. Most even thought him a little bit daffy.

Unheeding of public opinion, and moreover unaverse to anything that held the promise of netting him a few insider's points with his newly extended family, Wagner fielded the many ensuing queries with a buoyancy that surprised even him. Theories explained and demonstrations given, once one Ergosian and then another began boasting of benefit, by their testimonials were the more versatile of their comrades persuaded to seek Wagner out for similar instruction. Even the camp toughs and machos, initially having made game of their converted peers, came around in the long—although most of these approached Wagner only on the wink so as to avoid putting their brutish reputations at risk.

Wagner could not have been more encouraged. Regarded one day as an eccentric, and the next, as fitness guru and personal trainer to the camp, his programme of stretches and isometrics, pseudo-yoga and low impact callisthenics, would soon become the rave of the palaestra. Not strictly because of the aerobic and anaerobic advantages that better flexibility and blood flow promoted, the exercises served in equal degree as a sort of novelty coursed with benefit, a breakout activity that not only relieved the tedium of the knockabout, but which likewise drastically reduced the bane of preventable injuries.

As demand grew, Wagner introduced some of the staples—push-ups, crunches, Russian twists—followed by subtle variations of the same, incorporating into the workouts whichever exercises he could most easily recall from old Phys-Ed classes, television infomercials, and the gazillion fitness DVDs that had glutted Sara's bookcases in the better days of their commitment. These *addita* were also favourably received, especially with the edge-seeking athletes who were ever looking for ways to make greater gains in bulk and power.

Watching all of this, however, with judgement most unsympathetic was Grum the Taskmaster. Bearing witness to what seemed a contagion of non-productive dalliance on the field, he finally summoned the impert Wagner before the dais with the intent of squashing this new frivolity, along with the jackanapes who initiated it. His intolerance and uncongeniality already firmly established, it was inevitable that he take as a personal affront the fact that some flea would dare to introduce such agitational doings to the practise without having first consulted him.

Indeed, it took no pittance of salesmanship for Wagner to sway the closed-minded Grum. Conducted before the NuRac, two spears couched at his back, between interrogation and censure Wagner was barely permitted juncture wherein to provide apologia. Speaking when he could—and sometimes when he shouldn't have—he touted the various welfares that his "introduced frivolity" was meant to bestow upon the trainees' bodies. This won him a chuckle from one of the guards, and growing contempt from Grum. Clearly, championing Ergosian salubrity wasn't the stance to take with this audience. Failing with said approach almost straightaway—and keen to avoid having any more spears sticking his spine—Wagner scrubbed the health-promoting pitch and quickly angled for something less exclusory.

His new tack, then, found him plying Grum where it mattered to him most: reputationally. With feigned matter-of-factness, Wagner baited the Taskmaster by slippery assumption, specifically one that spoke as equally to Grum's self-impressed hauteur as it did to his purse strings. An artifice that garnered promise in the form of one raised eyebrow of interest, Wagner added treacle to his contrivance by hinting at the laudation that Grum would surely enjoy once his latest instalment of fighters proved even more top-of-form than usual. After all, with haler combatants making for more energised bouts—which in turn begat more appreciative audiences—how could there *not* be greater remuneration and gratitude from the stable-owners?

Speaking all the while with meticulously measured surrender, it was Wagner's subtility that he dispel the slightest mote of individual due. His was a resort of sheepskin and subterfuge, the intention of which—aided by some wolfish cajolery à la ol' Doc Adams—was to push dialogue into delineation, and thus exculpate himself by vaunting the long-term good that he claimed would come from his otherwise ill-judged presumption. Only in unexpected bonus was his initiative perceived as a Balgor-styled impudence; and, seeing opportunity here as well, instead of hangdoggedly apologising for it, he finessed to sustain it that it might catapult him out of his yeanling status and into the comparative leniency of Balgor-like favour without overly impressing upon either peer or punisher that he'd catered the least bit for it.

In all, it was a hard sell if ever there was one. Grum was loath to rule against his own policy, and by his progressively escalating impatience it seemed that Wagner would not be able to turn him. But, after going beyond Wagner to solicit attestation from a random sampling of prisoners, many of whom barely knew Wagner well enough to say "hullo," and others who knew him not at all but for their acquaintance with his limbering routines, Grum eventually dialled down his obstinacy enough to grant Wagner a temporary thumbs up—pending, of course, the cornucopian return that Wagner promised come tournament day.

"*Bones and entrails, Voknor!*" Balgor exclaimed as he accompanied Wagner back into the general population. "If only your sword were as swift as your tongue, there would be no man willing to oppose you."

Wagner was already breathing easier. "Yeah, well, that wasn't all *me* there, let me tell you. The smarminess and the appeal to his greed were just my personal spins on classic Balgorisms."

"I am honoured. Permit me, then, to offer one more lesson. Now that you have made yourself conspicuous, Grum will keep three eyes on you at all times. He will very likely increase your inconvenience on the field for no other reason than that he now recognises you over our shrewder kinspeople who sheer from the very order of confrontation that you invited."

"I didn't exactly invite it, Balgor. Chowderhead that I am, I just didn't look far enough ahead to foresee it. Anyway, what's done is done. Big surprise—I'm on Grum's scamp list. I'll just have to try to stay off of anyone else's."

Balgor laughed. "You are singularly unique," he said. "No, strike that—you are dualistically unique, *Voknor*. Like dice in a bigratto toss, I never know what face you will show."

"You can usually count on it being the one that I should've kept hidden."

"That is fact. Only a man conflicted has such difficulty in reconciling his words to his actions."

Wagner skirted a tussle of overenthusiastic sparrers. "What's *that* supposed to mean?"

"That you are your own antithesis. And do not loop your eyes at me, *Voknor*. Try first to see with mine."

Wagner groaned. "Okay, *Doc Williams*, just what do you see?"

"That you exhibit modesty most when it befits you least, and vehemence, when you would do better to beg off. Your inconsistencies are such that they lead you quite nearly to the point of duplicity."

"Examples forthcoming, I suppose?"

"As you wish. You claim ordinariness, and yet out of mob-compelled pressuring you conjure a tale that stirs even Gamühr to peerful awe. Oft on the palaestra do I find you all but undone by your own pitiful swordsmanship, only to see you suddenly become a devil, replete with foaming grin and a lethal home-thrust. Commensurately, I have heard you say how you do all that you can to avoid strife—yet, on your first day here, what do you do but assail a handful of guards for the sake of a Vofspar. Even today, you were only slightly less reckless, bringing unnecessary reprimand upon yourself for not thinking first to beseech Grum with your exertion novelties."

"It's strictly a problem with my wiring," said Wagner. "My shrink could tell you all about it, but seeing as he's—"

"*And*," Balgor continued, "when left without resort, you respond with riddlish words, steeped in snideness, before apologising and making amends with more rational response."

"Sorry. I—hey!"

"Apology received. Elucidation is surely imminent."

Wagner spotted the weapon he'd left behind earlier, and stooped to pick it up. "Okay, wise guy," he said. "It's true. I do run on impulse a lot. That's because I trust my impulses, even the imprudent ones, because somehow—regardless of the resultant jams I get myself into—doing so keeps me on track."

"To borrow your vernacular," said Balgor, "*what is this supposed to mean*?"

"What it means is that when I ignore intuition, when I play it safe, when I hunker myself in a corner to avoid some immediate unpleasantness that my gut tells me to face, while I may have temporarily dodged an arrow I've also deviated from the path that my spontaneous sense told me to follow."

It was Balgor's opportunity for eye-rolling. "You speak as if your fate has already been written."

"Subconsciously—visionally—maybe it has. Sometimes my actions...well... they have this particular feel to them, like lock tumblers tripped by a familiar key. Even should the ensuing consequences be a drag, there's usually a discernable, eventful alignment to the outcome. In my culture, we have a phrase—déjà vu—that denotes a mistaken feeling that you've pre-experienced the immediacy of a given moment. This both *is* and *isn't* applicable to me. While I realise that I haven't lived any of this before, I nevertheless seem privy to certain experiential phenomena the playing out of which has a way of flushing forth a whole bunch of previously disregarded foretokenings."

"My culture also has a phrase: 'none but a fool bolts a door that lacks hinges.'"

"And which am I—the fool or the unhinged door?"

"I am tempted to say *both*, again because of your duality. However, the interpretation I sought was one of latitude. Outlandish as your thinking may seem to me—and you know that I have little use for anything that my lumpskull cannot make scrutable—I have noticed much about you that compels me not to wed myself too hastily to fixed opinion."

Wagner laughed. "Oh, you're going to *humour* me?"

"Aye. But become any more seized by derangement and I may be forced to kill you and thrift those handsome new boots."

"All right. But don't forget to give Tamek first dibs on the laces."

After they separated, Wagner located the specialist under whose tutelage he'd been learning some of the most efficacious manoeuvres he'd ever seen. Bilahdu was his name, a broad-bearded man of even broader girth, who defied his very corpulence by moving about the field with a boy's light-footed verve. Keen on the coadjuvancy of sword and buckler, he'd been trying for days to wean Wagner from the tendency of favouring one implement or the other in moments of extreme distress, tirelessly coaxing the intransigent into embracing an envisagement of synergic give-and-take that he claimed would bestead Wagner even beyond the circumstantial deprivation of either weapon. An unusual advocate of the shield, and more notably, a shield of wood or wicker, Bilahdu maintained that the merest buckler, when confidently employed, could rake as a sweeping weapon of offence or as a stalemating tool of defence, and could in fact prolong a contest long enough for its cunning wielder to retrieve his fallen blade or procure other means of engagement. This notion he banged into Wagner's noggin time and again by facing off against the fully accessorised pupil with no more than a buckler the size of a dinner plate in his own grip.

Every bit the authority on martial combat as was his NuRac counterpart, Grum, Bilahdu was similarly encyclopaedic when it came to assessing the talent in the yard. With one eye on his student and the other eye scanning for this or that doing on the palaestra, he synthesised the day's progressions, the setbacks, the injuries and such, for no other reason than that he had the scrupulosity for it. This was all the more remarkable when one considered that the man hadn't a lick of circumspectness off the field, and far less common sense—and almost non-existent restraint—in his personal affairs. While he may indeed have had the six ready means for eluding ineluctable death in the arena, and while his mind was the camp's AP wire of forthcoming NuRac edicts, of plain old scuttlebutt, or of statistics on which prisoner had won or lost a given bout three tournaments back, he was an unmitigated dysfunctional in conformist society—although perhaps a bit less patently in the relative unhideboundness of a prison atmosphere. In his free life, he may have been just another braggart at the alehouse (not unlike those who frequented the Filthy Lucre), whose true dower had never been tested—much less taken seriously—simply because there had never been call for it. Yet, here, in dire times, Bilahdu was proof that even the most unlikely and unseemly of men might come forth and draw sword from the stone of personage, and thenceforth be looked upon with estimation for qualities that may otherwise have gone unnoticed.

Wagner, however, secretly more socially misfitted than Bilahdu could ever fear being, was easily as intrigued by his mentor's duality as Balgor had claimed to be by his. He'd known people like him, brilliant in one field and hopelessly clueless in all that lay beyond that pale. Pure serendipity that his trainer should also be a walking almanac of strategy, Wagner knew that if he could only navigate Bilahdu's temperament—especially his predisposition to overstress the complete urgency of *everything*—then he would veritably have his goose of the golden eggs by whose inspirations he could hatch his plans of escape.

"Tell me," Wagner said as he repeated a consecution of sidesteppings for Bilahdu's critique, "do the free Ergosians even know about this place—or about this cutthroat competition the NuRacs put us through?"

Not only failing to acknowledge the question, it was possible that Bilahdu hadn't even heard him, so deeply preoccupied had he become by what seemed an awkward, physical duress stemming from—no surprise by now—a general discomfort with his attire. A too frequent idiosyncrasy, overridingly imperative as always, Wagner recognised it immediately and quit his dialogue, watching in a half-amused, half-bemused fashion as Bilahdu thrashed about like a man with a scorpion down his back, turning a simple adjustment of vesture into an ordeal of paramountcy. Some of the men and women in their vicinity likewise eased up long enough in their bouting to nudge each other and sneak sidelong glances at Bilahdu's latest fitfulness.

Actually a legitimate gripe, Bilahdu's vexation was common among those inmates whose builds didn't quite coincide with the standard cut of fabric. One of the few endomorphs in the camp whose body, despite a modest sustenance allowance, threatened to go right on maintaining its rather well-suited ambit, it was no little wonder to Wagner why the prison textilery, staffed with Ergosian drudgers, could not turn out some form of raiment to better suit the camp's more considerable folk. Never suspecting that there was deliberateness behind it—and uxorial deliberateness at that—for only a while longer would Wagner asperse negligence or callousness on the part of his captors for forcing Bilahdu to take potluck from the toggery's wantage in Big & Tall sizes.

By now, Bilahdu's spectacle of public fiddling was setting new precedent for uncouth gaucherie. A tribute to his dexterity, he did manage to retain a precarious grip on his buckler throughout the whole of his many demonstrative tugs, tucks, and repositionings, somehow finding fingers enough to sustain the trouser-fussing that, by anyone's account, now appeared as if a live fish had found its way into his shorts to give company to the arachnids and the centipedes that had been skittering up and down his spine.

"Umph!" he huffed. "Every day the same, *Voknor*—why am I plagued such? What is afoot with these connivant knaves who pass for camp weavers that they cannot fashion a single pair of galligaskins to suit my manliness? After all— humph!—I am not the only portly fellow in this miserable place. Am I too extreme in expecting that I might take breath without fear of bursting my seams?"

Wagner watched with restraint as the man fidged with the plaits of his pantaloons, the stitches of which—unbeknownst to Bilahdu—had separated in more than one section. The hems all but divorcing in a disjuncturing mayhem that, most rampant along the shirring of his abundant backside, it was all Wagner could do to remain composed. Tempted to remark that Bilahdu's problem wasn't so much in taking breath as it was in taking *breadth*, Wagner chose a more prudent response.

"Okay, I'll bite—why can't they fashion you some larger drawers?"

Bilahdu tugged a few more times before giving up completely. "Why, because of wicked Skagra! She punishes me, of course!"

"Skagra? Who's that? Some evil goddess?"

"How I wish it were so! I would fear her less!"

Wagner shrugged ignorance.

"Skagra! My *mate*! Surely you have heard of her! Surely you know that she is the head sempstress in the prison textilery?"

Another shrug.

"By Eternity's sweepingly infinite tail, lad, have you only just crawled out from under some distant purlieu of reality's fringes?"

Wagner chuckled at Bilahdu's coincident precision. "As a matter of fact—"

"She is a virago, young friend, a sorceress who once lured me to her breast with sugared words and sirenic illusion."

Wagner acknowledged half-heartedly, suddenly wondering if another pummelling by the guards wouldn't be preferable to having to endure Bilahdu's histrionics.

"A thousand years ago it was, *Voknor*. I was but a naïve young fool, a servant to my loins and to my own idle folly. And when I first gazed upon the radiance of that she-daemon's outer visage, I was irreversibly smitten by magiks. Beguiled from the start, charmed into her false embrace, Skagra—and the ogress whom she calls 'mother'—gruffly severed the wings of my lusty bachelorhood and shackled my feet from their wandering ways, dooming me forever to a life of spiteful companionship, of niggling, of cold beds, colder meals, and ill-fitting clothing. I thus became one-half the man that I was."

Wagner pictured—and then just as quickly stifled—a mental image of Bilahdu with his "other half" restored. It wasn't a pleasant one.

"Lacking my freedom, *Voknor*, never able to evade Skagra's talons for even a moment, even my enslavement by the NuRacs was doubly cursed, for she saw to it to be seized along with me."

"Wait—she *volunteered?*"

"Aye! Boldly she leaped from the safe cover where I had instructed her to stay, and with a stew ladle she did beat a full twenty NuRac troops over the headpiece until they conceded her the right to accompany me. To this day, I do believe that she fancied they might have been taking me someplace where I would be permitted a little more joyance than she allowed me at home."

Wagner laughed. Bilahdu's melodramatics, his bellyaching, his tongue-painted tableaus of persecution, and his good old-fashioned baseness—these were the counter-balancing staples to his more noble and industrious talents. Dreggish backwash to otherwise prominent riverbeds of erudition, a person needed only brook the former to discover the latter. And, as would always be the case, in the space between one boutade to the next, Bilahdu found composure enough to recommence in his duties of bringing Wagner's tactics up to snuff.

For a man of Bilahdu's stature, he was gifted with remarkable reflexes and an uncommonly centred footing that enabled him to twist around Wagner's most ambitiously swathing advances with phantomesque ease. Wagner, his inertia too often unmet by engagement, only barely avoided tumbling headlong while his mentor stood by with his ever friendly "tsk-tskings" of reproach.

No ignominy, however, Wagner took his being bettered with reasonably good cheer, especially as proper tat was almost always close at hand. This day would be no exception. Bilahdu's trousers having unseamed themselves a little more with each exertion, by drill's end it was only Wagner who was left in stitches, with Bilahdu's pantaloons much wanting for theirs. What made it all the more amusing was that when Bilahdu—a lone fist clenching his plaits in effort to keep the splaying at minimum—requested Grum's permission to leave the field for to seek suitable replacements, the Taskmaster arbitrarily denied him the opportunity. Such dismissal, and the surrounding laughter it drew, predictably ired Bilahdu into such red-faced, teeth-clamped frustration that he dashed his buckler to the dirt and proceeded to stomp on it like Sergeant Snorkle on Beetle Bailey, a tantrum that didn't so much succeed in changing Grum's mind as it did in finishing the job on Bilahdu's trousers. Then, in the only defying gambit left to him, Bilahdu stripped the unravelled tatters completely from his body and paraded about the yard half-garbed, half-crazed, and fully ridiculous—a scene that ultimately compelled an annoyed and unamused Grum to grant him permission to exit.

"Your stealth and agility must have proven too much for him, *Voknor*," Balgor would later say.

"Well, at least I know how to beat him now. Go straight for the basting, feign left, and snip the drawstring!"

"Aye, but perhaps it demonstrates how even the staunchest opponent possesses an exploitable weakness. I just never fathomed inferior weaving to be Bilahdu's! Whatever you learn from him, *Voknor*, you would do best to forget the 'torn trouser artifice.'"

Outside of Bilahdu's wardrobe malfunction, the remainder of the day crept by with the kind of stifling sluggishness that only heat and high humidity can recruit. Kept no less busy than the combatants was the handful of Ergosian youngsters who, with their water buckets, answered the demands of many a dehydrated prisoner across the heat-rippled sands. Even Grum uncharacteristically showed his mortality by fanning himself with his roster—ever too stubborn or prideful to simply remove his heavy accoutrement (and thus betray his ordinariness). The sometimes estimable Bilahdu had long since returned to the field, grimly disgruntled, emasculated by the patchwork muslin that he was made to wear while Skagra presumably refashioned his pants with more breakaway threads. Looking too much like a moody Dom Deluise in drag for Wagner to take seriously, it was with immense gratitude that Wagner responded to Balgor's sympathetic signal to leave Bilahdu to sweat out his aggravations on his own. While unquestionably an expert soldier and a valuable pundit of facts and intrigue, dealing with the man was like prospecting for gold: in order to extract a few valuable flecks of information, one had to first shovel through a great deal of rubbish. And, as Wagner's agenda indeed involved panning a few ingots of Bilahdu's considerable experience, necessity and impatience forced him to reconsider another stab at the two thinkers he knew best.

At mealtime, Tamek made his way over to join Balgor and Wagner in a shaded nook along the south wall, where the realmson had plopped himself and where Wagner had followed suit. To no one's overwhelming surprise, the stew had once again been thinned in order to eke one last serving out of it. The loaves, on the other hand, were newly baked and richly hearty, and without regard for earthly etiquette Wagner tore into his in fashion more vulgar than usual.

"Make easy, *Voknor*," said the Sentinel, amused by the voracity he witnessed. "You will need that hand to wield a weapon. Do not gnaw it away in your ravenous frenzy."

"Why not?" said Wagner, full-mouthed. "My hand might be the only meat I get, seeing how the cooks have been forced to stretch this mulligan."

"No doubt your Vofspar would have the same notion were she here with you, my friend. 'Tis been a long time, I would imagine, since she has sampled human flesh. She will doubtlessly be craving it come tournament time."

Wagner chased his gorgings with a long quaff of water. "Then she'll have to settle for a nice Vishkorian hambone. My shanks will hopefully be on the run by then, far away from this hole."

Tamek rent a bite-sized strip from his loaf and dipped it in his porringer. "So, you persist in your machinations? How fare you thus far?"

"I saw him gathering feathers this morning," said Balgor. "I suspect he will be soaring beyond the walls come dawn."

Wagner flung a crust at him. "Nah—I never escape the same way twice. You and I, pal o' mine, are getting out by other means."

"Nay, not I, *Voknor*. I have not your inclination toward foolhardiness."

"Not yet, you don't. You have to give me some time to perfect my cajolery."

Balgor chuckled dismissively at Wagner's verbal strong-arming. But, in his eyes there sparked an undeniable glint of longing.

At that moment, J'nea passed them at ten paces, followed doggedly by an Ergosian male whom Wagner knew only as Fostoch. Seating herself across the way, she proceeded to partake of her meal as if Fostoch wasn't even there—and clearly wishing that he wasn't. Although in the course of their meal she neither encouraged him nor truly put him off, he tried unsuccessfully to engage her in natter, in attentive discussion, even in what appeared to be semi-amorous close-talk.

"What do you know about *her?*" Wagner asked.

Tamek hadn't even looked up. "Her?"

"The trusty. J'nea."

"J'nea? J'nea is trouble, *Voknor*. She is a blasphemer and a thief."

"A thief?"

"She is branded," said Balgor. "She was a scavenger in her youth. A reaver. It is customary in some provinces to mark a criminal for life."

"Pretty severe punishment for a child's stealing, isn't it?"

"The stigma is punishment ongoing," said Tamek. "'Tis a reminder of the crime, a mark of disrepute, a means thereafter of alerting common folk to one's character."

"What if you never commit another crime?"

"Then it has achieved its purpose."

"But then, even if you've turned your life around, you're still looked upon as a bad person."

Tamek sighed. "The path does exist, *Voknor*, whereby one may attain absolution. J'nea, howe'er, is unconcerned with such things. She therefore remains a pariah to most, kept at spear's length from a society that values hospitality free of the evils wrought by unscrupulous opportunists. The NuRacs are fond of her for just this reason."

"What about *Goober* over there? He seems chummy enough with her."

The Sentinel glanced up at J'nea and her lubricous dinner partner. "The Agile One? He is far o'ermatched, the fool. He vies for her, seeks to solicit her through subterfuge, not realising that her cunning exceeds his a hundredfold."

Oddly, Wagner felt himself bristling.

"Truly, he tasks the bounds of moral regulation," Tamek added.

"What's that mean?"

"As men," Balgor jumped in, "it is foolish and futile to deny manly inclination. Nevertheless, we must all of us—including *that* knave—tether our concupiscence in this place."

"Or else..."

"Or else our females are put at risk of their lives. The NuRacs have no need for Ergosian sucklings, *Voknor*. And any woman who is found to be with child may be put to the block."

"The act of mating is not forbidden us," said Tamek. "But the product of mating *is*. Therefore, that we not place our females at risk, we needs must restrain that portion of our natures which may be subdued and frustrated but ne'er vanquished, and divert our energies into endeavours o'er which we exert greater control."

"And Fostoch didn't read the by-laws?"

Balgor raked back his hair and scratched at a spot behind his ear. "Some men only comprehend their existence a moment at a time. Fostoch is of the ilk who would quench himself in the presence of thirstier men. He thinks only of himself, a luxury that most of us cannot allow. But behold, *Voknor*—J'nea, outcast that she is, outward slip of a girl, she has no interest in the Agile One's transparent aims. I would wager that she has more interest in, say, his vest."

Wagner scrutinised Fostoch. It was true—his vest was indeed of sturdy weave, nicely woollen and unsullied, certainly an item to be coveted by the many prisoners who went about in shabbies. But J'nea's vest he knew was far from a tattered remnant; and, turning his glance toward her, he so happened upon her eye directed his way, a brief and detached squiz from which she just as quickly disengaged, resuming then her noshing amid the insipid susurrus of her hopeful companion. Wagner fixed on her for a few seconds beyond the disconnect before quitting himself.

"Tamek, tell me more about the layout of the prison in relation to the rest of the city."

"You are persistence incarnate—I give you that," said the Sentinel. "On the outside, you might have made a good tax collector. You ask so many questions."

"Just think of it as a tapping of your abundant knowledge. Where I come from, knowledge that isn't shared doesn't do anybody any good."

"Not entirely true," said Tamek. "But no matter. What information specifically do you seek?"

"I'm not sure. Start with the walls—how well they're guarded, how often the patrols walk them, what lies beyond them in every direction. That'd be good to start."

Later that evening, well before headcount, Wagner sat once more in the barracks doorway, gazing out at a courtyard sparingly lit by a low moon. Only a falter of breeze in the air, even then the humidity felt like a wet glove muffled about his face. Alone and yet not, his brain filtered out the drone of his chattering peers, farther within and initially more listless than usual for that time of the night. Only now and then was it given life by someone's buoyant retelling of Bilahdu's "March of Glory" on the palaestra—a story that would likely never grow tired no matter the number of times that it was resuscitated, simply because it was exactly the type of incident that a congregate stalled by routine valued most. That Bilahdu wasn't present to defend his good name against their raillery was regrettable; he would almost certainly have meted his more unrelenting harriers a jolly good larruping, which in itself would have rounded the evening out quite prescriptively. Fortunately for these jokesters, Bilahdu resided in Barracks Two, two structures away, where feathers no doubt were flying for comparable reasons. In Barracks Five, however, anecdotal imagery was all that Wagner's co-inhabitants had to trade, and this they did for considerable time in entertainingly frolicsome doses.

Although in his guardedness Wagner's face let slip the occasional makings of a grin, the desultory joviality behind him danced mostly across the periphery of his preoccupation. Camaraderie may indeed have been something he'd striven to cultivate here, but solitude was still his oldest friend, and retreating to it wasn't so much an unamiability as it was a means of refreshing himself, of refocusing, of revisiting the wellsprings of past sequestrations. Nothing had changed on the explanatory front. His grandest question ever remained his grandest question. Whatever the extreme extraneousness that had tormented him with mega-visioned turmoil, that had destabilised his mind and his molecular structure, that had exiled him from earthly existence, its execution had sorely belied its intent, because Wagner felt little more than like a cosmic castaway without a purpose. Somewhere in all this mess there had to be a shard of sake or construability. There *had* to be. He simply needed to find it.

And then maybe he might come to know why any of it should have involved him in the first place.

CHAPTER TWELVE

Jon Mazzio stood at his office window, staring blankly down at the lawn where his former patient had dematerialised from existence. The exact spot was flagrantly distinguishable, even from one floor up, for the grass most closely exposed to the irradiation now humbled the surrounding turf by a hearty half-metre's growth with no immediate signs of arrest. Its containment limited to the diametral two-metres' of *Miracle's* and James Wagner's praeternatural face-off, the upspurt had commenced quite nearly on the tail of their exchange, and, to the unapprised, would have seemed more the result of a fritz in fertiliser dispersion than anything remotely beyond the cusp of credibility. But to those who had been there, no inadvertent windfall of Scotts Turf Builder was behind this burgeoning, despite what the authorities or the average passerby might have surmised; and, as Mazzio had instructed the groundskeepers to leave the verdancy undisturbed for the moment, the patch had become a kind of lunchtime gazingstock for both the Centre's eyewitnesses and its second-handers alike. Even Margaret Groller had succumbed to its irrepressible lure, stealing past it on the quiet one pre-tour morning so as not to be the lone holdout in only the biggest thing ever to happen at Howsley.

Yet, as for exactly *what* had caused it, the doctor had little notion. While unable to proffer through analysis or speculation even the most half-baked theory regarding a precipitant or the considerable phenomena that had for weeks preceded it, he could hardly deny that in their convergence Wagner and *Miracle* had exteriorised something of a protoplasmic effluvium for which published science had yet to offer transcription, much less the most basic receptivity or indulgence. Even the aftercrop of grass was only one—and perhaps the least remarkable—of a considerable post-event distillate, for residue that hadn't been immediately apparent had begun manifesting like loaves and fishes in the days to follow. A host of incidental outgrow to ponder, already Mazzio had worked to compile the component transpirations into a conjectural complement of causes, effects, actions, and equalising reactions delineating the decanting and redintegrating of energies the likes of which he couldn't begin to identify—all to provide a model of accountability for an event that had left one man temporarily drained, one man missing, and several bystanders exhibiting convalescent reactions that pointed nowhere else but to a localised association with said event. And although comprehensive testing had thus far revealed nothing terribly irregular in *Miracle's* post-experiential chemistry, it was still top of the list that *Miracle's* proximity had somehow either provided the influential conduit for the effusion, or that he had himself been its agency.

Then again, Wagner's condition had been leaning in final direction long before *Miracle* and company had even made the scene. Whatever that day's impetus had truly been, it had for months telegraphed its macabre intent of luring—no, *stealing*—Wagner's essence through incrementally protracted occurrences regardless of whether the newcomer had showed up or not. The only real binding factor was that *Miracle's* presence had seemed to command some modicum of influence over the severity of Wagner's give-and-take between the known world and wherever it was that his atoms had been scattered. But even this, an observation made of the moment, had lost its punch in the weeks following the ordeal; it had become muddled by time and debate and misapprehension until Mazzio and his colleagues found themselves questioning whether the back roads prophet really had any exogenous bearing on what befell Wagner at all.

Granted, *Miracle* had been most forthcoming in producing prompt, if arcanely fanciful, answers for almost every question pertaining to that day. But, despite what had truly gone down out there on that now rampant patch of orchard grass, it remained in every sense troublesome to accept as fact a bunch of conjurations of otherworldly transference by non-physical means; and until all other explanatory avenues had been exhausted, credence to such notions would have to remain the resort of desperate measure—even as Mazzio was already more inclined than most to step through that door.

Too, the fact that little in *Miracle's* expoundings gibed with the creedbound doctrines of his report was another consideration. Not that it mattered to the doctors, for few in the profession hadn't come across a situation where patient devoutness, whatever the persuasion, fell at odds with this or that medical recommendation—and often, science in whole. People being what they were, however, it was a certainty that the greater laity might have cast aspersions on a faith healer who routinely avoided invoking God's name in his handiworks, nor offered the least vestige of divinely based explanation or attribution for either the restorative comforts that he purportedly ministered in the field, or here, to account for one man's very unnatural disappearance. And *this* was something that *Miracle* did not do, not even once. In fact, if not for the tabloid articles and the reports of his sizably diffracted following in the regional southwest, one would hardly suspect him of being the least bit clerically inclined.

With those suspicions, then, settling like fog over both *Miracle's* spiritual and scientific credibility, the cooperation that he'd continued to offer up so freely to Howsley and its visiting specialists seemed now to have passed its constructive apex. Perceptively enough, nobody realised this more soberly than had *Miracle* himself. As upon his first day, his instincts were in level keel, but his forbearance had begun to fray like an overtrodden rug. Even his extraordinarily devoted friends seemed to reflect his restlessness in an expressed eagerness to move on. They had all quite cordially remained in town in order for the investigating teams to record *Miracle's* insights, to check his physiology, to observe any post-phase reactive symptoms that he—and *they*, for that matter—might have developed; and as neither *Miracle's* nor the enchanting Ms. Escalante's finances were anything close to abundant, the four of them had temporarily sandwiched themselves into a single occupancy room at a no-frills motor lodge just off of Interstate-80. Dreary as this must have been for two adults and two restless teens, they had actually shown themselves to be closer knit in their misfitted cohesion than most of the blood families that Mazzio knew, and this fact the director of Howsley could only attribute to a comfortable mix of highly blendable personalities. Were he more free to explore the anthropologic ties that bolstered their relationship and made it thrive, he would anxiously have allocated the time to pursue such a study. But, fascinating cultural interactions of this sort were not the topic of the day, nor could they compare to the questions that he and doctors Williams and O'Connell faced in their impoverished attempts to explain—to the local authorities as equally as to themselves—how a man could just weigh molecular anchor and sail out of corporeal existence.

Moving from the window, Mazzio seated himself briefly at his desk. A few days'-worth of unopened mail, one or two backlogged cases awaiting his look-see, a rope hoya plant in serious need of a drink—for the moment he ignored it all, instead choosing to rummage through a chaotic stack of folders near the telephone. Uncovering the one he sought, in the recall of some belated urgency he rose and started for the door.

Suddenly he halted. Something was askew. Something about the houseplant, some sidelong detail indeliberately glimpsed and only now registering, Mazzio returned the file to the desktop and slowly backtracked his steps around the planter that he might recreate the effect.

Sure enough, as he came around, his eyes squinched at the unmistakeable glint of metallicity. Moving closer, he fixed upon something more substantial. There, tucked amid the hoya's Medusan undulations, sat a small, reflective object that had no reason for being there.

Too piqued for discretion, with thumb and index the doctor reached in and gently extracted what appeared to be an origamic construct crafted from aluminium foil and lemon-yellow paper. On closer inspection, however, he quickly saw that the materials were not just any papers, but the discarded wraps of several Tropical Fruits LifeSavers rolls. No way of telling how long the figurine had been there—nor why it had been placed in the planter—Mazzio waxed confoundment as he studied the all-too-familiar symmetry of the *sigma* design, complete with defining aureole, vertical transpiercing, and opposing *segmenta*.

"Darn you, James," he said, twirling the ornament in the sunlight before positioning it atop his pencil-holder. "I suppose you've got them all, now, don't you? All the answers that I've been scrambling to find. You've got them all—only you're not talking."

His eyes still tracking the design, for a few moments he tried to intuit Wagner's intent in sneaking the infoldment into his office planter. Had it been simple mischievousness? Some drollery of resignation? A kind of beat-the-gun cenotaph from a man suddenly foreconscious of his fate?

Knowing that he could go on guessing indefinitely, void of satisfaction, with a demitting sigh Mazzio scooped up the previously shunted file and resumed his bloodless errand.

Later that morning, on entering the wing that he'd temporarily had vamped into a research station, Mazzio gazed about in marvel at the level of desertion. With all the necessary readings taken, the probes run, the sweeps completed, many of the research collective had cleared out, eager to examine their findings on their respective home turfs, where more extensive batteries could be performed in properly equipped surroundings. The project thus far inconclusive, Mazzio had spent the better part of the previous day seeing those people off, as well as bidding regretful farewell to other eminent colleagues whose previous commitments and more privately funded interests prevented any more than their brief and limited assistance here. In fact, the only associates still in makeshift residence were the mavericks—the parapsychologists, the psychometrists, the ectoplasmics—who, diggers and delvers and crack researchers all, had invaded Howsley in hurried *Ghostbusters* fashion just ahead of their sundry vanloads of hypersensitive gizmos and gadgets all geared to read and register the "bioluminescent residuality in Howsley's sub-spectral aura grid" and other such aberrations of non-mainstream esoterica.

Actually a refreshing eclecticism of paranormal devotees, replete with deadheadish exteriors and their own specialised vernacular, this group hadn't the slightest qualm about batting around a measure of preposterous theories that mainstream scientists would have slammed and scoffed at—and which the more practically trained Dr. Mazzio had insufficient ken to even judge. True votaries to their field, if ever there existed a band of individuals so hungry and so enthusiastic for the kind of inexplicable phenomena that conventional science too often stigmatised, it had to be these ever upbeat and tireless gonzos. And although it frequently seemed that a good many of them were only a hobgoblin away from Howsley patient candidature themselves, they were willing to come out and do what they did on a mere shoestring of financial backing, and an even lesser aglet of consociate respect.

Entrenched at Howsley at Dr. O'Connell's request, their inclusion in the investigation had ultimately set some—make that *all*—of Mazzio's preconceptions into tailspin, for they were nothing like the conspiracy hounds or the counterculture schismatics of their stereotype. And because of their fast professionalism and their easy predisposition to things supernormal (in some ways a religion unto itself), Mazzio had permitted them to convert the emptying portions of the wing into their personal electronics Expo in hopes that the smallest advance might help to define a nebulosity that no one else, barring *Miracle*, had thus far been able to illuminate.

With methods and machinery to beggar description, they seemed happiest when Mazzio involved himself, when he sought elaboration on this process or that array of instruments. Viewed, perhaps, as a vindicative reconciliation between estranged siblings—respectable psychology and its black sheep brother—the fact that Mazzio had not only made his curiosity a priority, but had actually cut his authority with a few parts of biddability, he'd courted and won their respect and was thus bestowed the full compendium of their findings, warts and freckles both, and not just that which conservative science could abide.

In yield, however, the findings so far had proven provocative if not ascertaining, and had yet to provide the necessary physics for Wagner's bolthole escape into oblivion.

In the midst of Mazzio's reflecting, a voice bellowed his name from behind. A familiar hail by now, a familiar manner, there was no question as to its author. Without pause, the doctor turned to meet the man whom the world knew only as "*Miracle*."

"Good morrow, sir," spoke the itinerant, clamping onto the doctor's hand with a grip that could crush walnuts. No time lost in coming from the motel, his hair fell damp about his shoulders; and his clothing—excepting the fifth-hand JanSport pack that, fully stuffed and readied for the trail, clung like a bearcat across his back—was the very same as upon their first encounter.

"As we agreed," he continued, "my comrades and I will depart this day— provided, sir, that you have no further interest in us."

Mazzio chuckled. "Oh, it's not that we're not interested, *Miracle*. It's just that we believe we've put the calliper to you more times than any man should have to endure."

"And was this helpful?"

Mazzio sighed, unsure if candour was the way to go. "Not initially, no. At least not to the extent that I'd hoped."

"Then I am truly sorry."

"Don't be. Much of what we did learn would never have come to light but for your graciousness."

Miracle begged off with a hem. "Then, sir, you are more fully indebted to Maggie. If not for her counsel, it is likely that I would have made away long ago. I do not suffer your large cities all that well."

"Then I'm glad you listened to her. But don't misconstrue—the fact that we haven't any answers doesn't mean that your input was for naught. On the contrary, from a metaphysical standpoint, you've given us much to think about, even if we haven't yet the courage to fully turn our sights in that direction. And as for hard science—well, while your tests have indeed rendered one or two inconsistencies that we can't immediately explain, sadly none of it can be considered truly pivotal, at least not at this stage. Anyway, you've been around enough scientists now to know that we're an obstinate lot. We have this unrelenting need to exhaust all conventional resources before daring to dip even one toe into nonconforming waters."

At that moment, Maggie strolled up to make it a threesome, followed at distance by Nettie and Pete who, engaged in their usual raze of flirty disparaging, would up the count to a diffractive five. Like *Miracle*, all three were revved and trail-ready, albeit strictly per individual interpretation—each having torn what were undeniably disparate pages from the official outfitter's handbook.

Nettie by far the ace infractor of the bunch, as the more unfledged of the group's females she clearly took no lesson from Maggie's inveterate thrift—except maybe to deliberately fly in its face for individuality's sake. Just as on day one, she was a walking kiosk of rings, wristlets, bangles, and beads, each of which was resourcefully hung, slung, or in pendular judder from a finitude of bodily moorings. A Papa Smurf tattoo on her left shoulder blade, a yellow coneflower blazing around her exposed belly-button, she availed herself of the expressive indivisibility that was the franchise of youth, exercising without apology her right to be impractical—and daring not only to revisit, but to trample, a good chunk of early 1980's pop culture to do it.

As for Pete, he was a choirboy by comparison, content to sport his mop of stringy hair, his retro Mr. Natural tee-shirt, and—when he put up with it—the black circle that Nettie often drew around his eye with a grease pencil to better liken him to the Our Gang pooch whose name he shared.

Together, the teens hadn't spent all too much time moping about the visitors' lounge during *Miracle's* flurry of physicals and interviews. Like all the other models of their generational make, they'd come equipped with the full complement of factory standards—including the Lilliputian attention spans that, by warranty, required scheduled tweaking. Sensitive to this, *Miracle* and Maggie had therefore given them the short leash to go off and explore what hidden culture Bishop had to offer. Such leave (as interpreted by two very fertile minds) gave Nettie and Pete a conditional carte blanche to paint the town, an opportunity that they pressed to happy advantage in a scavenger hunt-like perusal of every sidewalk café and bric-a-brac shoppe along Bishop's "renaissance downtown corridor" (verbatim from their motel's nightstand directory). Multi-tasking their spree so as to outpace its ever imminent rescindability, like eleventh hour shoppers they scoured for bargains in more than a few cut-rate music depots, browsed for baubles in every junk jewellery outlet and bead boutique within the city limits, and corked the ritual the same way every afternoon with a cosy-up in some musty entresol coffee grotto. Adventure on the cheap, all legal, clean, and time-targeted, it was like Fiddler's Green without the fiddler *or* the green, like Saturnalia with a curfew—but it sure as stars beat mooching around Howsley all day.

To Mazzio, such trust at first seemed overly permissive given their ages and dispositions. But, with gradual familiarity he'd soon found indicia enough to persuade otherwise. While never doubting that their puerility was genuine, he was gripped to find a remarkably plumbless sense of obligation beneath their teeny-bop façades that was compelling enough to find them actually *wanting* to stick with *Miracle* and Maggie, *wanting* to remain in their good graces, despite how much this fell at odds with their free-spiritedness. The bond in fact nurtured by reciprocity, the elder pair was equally curatorial to the younger's whimsy, even to the point of routinely justifying it to aspersing outsiders. This was no better demonstrated than in a certain late evening improvidence involving Dr. Williams and an offhand fashion critique made in Nettie's and Pete's absence. Without a beat, a suddenly peppery Maggie hopped upon the maternal soapbox in defence of youthful capriciousness, arguing that it was a necessary rite, a last hurrah of adolescence that even "nerdy, pimply-faced, someday-doctors" had to go through before life hardened them into "crusty cadavers of maturity." Taken aback, the rueful Williams had little doubt to whom she was referring, and thereafter made conscious effort never again to allow fatigue to appropriate his tongue.

"Are we outta here, *Ruby*?" Pete asked, his odd address aimed at Maggie.

"Yeah, brat, we're outta here."

Jon Mazzio looked at her, bewildered. "*Ruby*?"

She rolled her eyes. "Ruby is Pete's mom. He tries to get under my skin sometimes by calling me that. Ruby was—well—quite a character, to say the least. Not the greatest role model a kid could ask for."

"The woman was a harpy." *Miracle's* tenor was as blunt and as experientially honest as Mazzio had come to expect.

"I don't know if she was *that* bad," said Maggie. "But she certainly had some unladylike quirks."

"Aye, she did," *Miracle* went on. "Whence I come, she would be pilloried in the village square until she forsook her shrewish ways."

"A charming custom, I'm sure," said Mazzio.

"An effective one nonetheless," countered the palmer.

Maggie latched onto *Miracle's* arm to close out the topic. "Are we pretty much a wrap on our business here?"

"You are," said the doctor. "And thank you again for your cooperation. Um...but before you go, is there any way—well—somewhere down the road, in the event that I wish to contact you, is there some way that you can be reached?"

"Well, we're not exactly the BlackBerry-iPhone crowd," Maggie said. "Nettie's got an old flip-phone in her bag, but it ran out of charge somewhere around—where was it—Jefferson City?"

Miracle nodded.

"And since we do most of our travelling over prairie and back road, we've really got no reliable way to keep it juiced." She paused. "I suppose, though, that if you want us to check in every now and then, we could do that. But we'd probably have to reverse the charges."

"Collect is fine," said Mazzio. "But I think I can go that one better." He excused himself and retreated, returning a few minutes later. "Here, take this. If you can remember to keep good batteries in it, I'll be able to reach out to you when I have questions or updates. You can either call me collect, as we agreed, or you can use it to send me a number where I can reach you."

"Oh, we couldn't," said Maggie. "I mean, this is *yours*. We wouldn't feel right in accepting it."

"Please," said Mazzio. "I've *lost* more of these thingamabobs than any man has a right to *own*. Anyway, don't get too excited—it's an older model. I won't miss it, trust me."

Maggie smiled sweetly and slipped the unit into her bag. Then she extended her hand. "It's been a pleasure knowing you, Dr. Mazzio. Although I still have no clue as to what happened here, nor what repercussions it will ultimately have on my personal philosophies, I'm nevertheless grateful for the courtesies that you've extended to us."

"And I am indebted to the four of you as well," said Mazzio, returning her lively handshake. He began walking with them. "Believe me, I was no less blindsided by this than you were. My perceptions weren't only altered—they were stood on end and dumped on my head. And the ramifications? I can't even begin to predict them. All I really know is that I lost a patient and a friend by impossible and immaterial causes. I owe it to him to find out how it happened—and why." He sighed. "Sooner or later, however, I may have to face the sad truth that it will remain exactly what it is now—a grand mystery that will keep me wondering for the rest of my days."

The teens reached the vestibule first. Maggie broke away to join them, and together they retrieved their rucksacks from behind the reception counter. It was here, while they donned them, that *Miracle* gently took the psychiatrist aside.

"Be not fooled, Jon Mazzio," he said lowly. "In our discussions I revealed to you many things, most of which I, too, might once have found difficult to accept. And I do realise, sir, how my ways and my mannerisms have struck you as queer, perhaps bombastic, certainly wanting by your customary standards. Still, all that I have confided to you on the weaving of fates, of the man you call James Wagner, of the *descent*—do not dismiss any of it. The veil of your mystery may be lifted more summarily than you know."

"I'm not following," said Mazzio. "What haven't you told me?"

"Only that which I, myself, have still to uncover. Listen to me, Jon Mazzio. With all that has occurred, I cannot promise that you will not indeed go on 'wondering for the rest of your days.' I only suggest that, at end, it may be *you*— and not *I*—who comes by the secrets that I am so bent on uprooting. More than this, I cannot tell you."

Mazzio studied him, unsure of what to say. From the start there had existed in *Miracle* no shred of things scientific, nothing in the archaic nature of his beliefs or in his accounting of the Wagner incident that could be put to empirical use. He was so out of touch with the world, such a throwback, and yet his connection to the essentiality of things was stronger than Mazzio had ever seen in anybody ten times as savvy. He was tuned to frequencies profoundly beyond the pragmatic, deep into the mystical bands—places where the doctor's reception was static-plagued and fragmented at best.

"We'll be right out," Maggie called to Nettie and Pete as the restless pair barrelled through the glazed double-doors.

"Yeah, well, tell *Harvey* to step on it already!" Pete shouted as he let the doors swing home. Outside, he adjusted the strap on his backpack before jaunting off after Nettie like a colt into the mid-morning sunlight. Through the glass, the adults watched with wistful amusement as Nettie—out of doors and free to unleash a cornucopia of tomfoolery that could no longer be suppressed—motioned Pete in for a canoodle, and then flicked his nose and dashed off across the grounds in a jangling farrago of charms and chains, with Pete in semi-vengeful pursuit.

"*Harvey?*" said Mazzio. "Wait, don't tell me. Pete's father, right?"

Miracle scowled ever so slightly while Maggie grinned ear-to-ear affirmation. "*Step*father, actually," she said.

"Not the best role model either, I gather?" said Mazzio.

"Just what *is* the male equivalent to a harpy, anyway?" she funned.

"Goodbye, you two," said the doctor. "Good luck in your travels."

"And you in yours," said *Miracle*, bracing to go. "Think on what I have told you, doctor. And worry not about that which cannot be altered."

Maggie aimed a thumb at her companion and smirked. "What *he* said."

Her words, however, along with the smile, were enigmatic and duteously camouflaged. It wasn't as if she knew anything the others didn't. It wasn't as if she were countering the pall of *Miracle's* darker ambiguity with a booster of her own sunnier disposition. Not exactly. Instead, it seemed more a preparative resignation for what lay ahead, like when a child who, dismayed by the sobering wane of summer, resorts to stacking activity upon activity in order to defer the inevitability of back-to-school. One might even have presumed with relative certainty that *Miracle* had already shared with Maggie the same frank "truths" that he'd revealed to Mazzio in shielded asides, she being his most intimate friend, confidante, and— not unsungly—his interference runner. Too, as not everything in the nature of *Miracle's* beliefs pointed to lofty and benevolent conclusions, that Maggie's expressions and her body language denoted the kind of edginess that *Miracle's* deterministic inelasticity might easily have elicited, she doubtlessly struggled with some of the allusions that the far graver *Miracle* accepted as matter of course. It was a glimpse into her character, a litmus of her perdurability. Given the great depth of her optimism and spiritual rooting, Maggie probably, *frequently*, sifted through and kept only the best from the mix, evidenced here by her afflatus in trying to douse unsnuffable portent with splashings tapped from her most hopeful of inner wellsprings. Still, for all her curative machinations, for all of her alleviative artistry, only time and eventuality would bestow the true intractability of *Miracle's* dispensations.

The four transients crossed out of the Bishop city limits at 10:56 AM, hiking east along Route 23. A busier roadway initially—with a rough shoulder that was gritty and peppered with the road-sullied tatters of fast food packaging and cigarette butts—a few miles out it became gradually more rural, a bit cleaner, and scarcely driven at all after a sudden northerly veer deposited them just above the Indiana state line and into southern Michigan. Even so, roughly two hours in they promptly forsook the asphalt—as they always did—for the first set of eastbound rails they happened across.

Skitching en masse down the grassy embankment, like railway tramps of old they impressed the roadbed below into abetting their resumption of a journey whose terminus only *Miracle* seemed to know. The man himself having no actual regard for trains, he'd nevertheless demonstrated a fondness for the old rails, which perhaps either gainsaid the purest of his conservational leanings or further linked him to the antiquation that some people might have claimed was his strong suit. While indeed seen as a prevailing scar upon the natural landscape, there was something in the rails' utile yet insular nature that *Miracle* found at least as engaging as the peaceful symmetry of their unconquerable perspective. As direct as any automobile thoroughfare—and, in his eyes, only occasionally as dangerous—he bade his companions once more to tighten their laces and to prepare to tack additional loggings onto a plod that had already spanned a good third of the country.

The day was sunny and bright, and all indications pointed to the prospect of a sweltering afternoon. Pete had already slid a blood-red bandana over his sandy waywards; Maggie had popped her ponytail through the eye-loop of her Cardinals ball cap. And Nettie, in her immitigable style, had re-donned her ever impractical, Mechlin lace pillbox that, over the months, had taken considerable friendly fire from her more sensibly outfitted pals. "Really lame sun cover" or not, she wasn't one to be strong-armed into ordinariness, and with her usual inirritability she deflected all incoming flak the same way that her stylishly hep shades filtered out unwanted UV. For all of her vast excess of trinkets and other non-essentials, she proved herself as much a trooper as any of them; and in her black granny dress, her army surplus combat boots, and her SPF 30 *inferno-red* lip glow, she kept apace for as far, and with as much verve, as *Miracle* required.

"So, what's the game plan?" said Pete, a great slew of canteens and collapsible dromedary bags slung across his torso like Ed Norton's hot water-bottle get-up from classic *The Honeymooners* shtick.

"Yeah," said Nettie, "I thought we only came this far so that you could try to stop your friend's beam-out. Now that he's history, why are we still heading east?"

Miracle remained quiet for a moment. When he finally did speak, it was with almost augural calm.

"The incident in Bishop...it appears to have...significantly dampened my insight."

"What—you mean you shorted out?"

"Perhaps, Nettie. Regrettably, I momentarily find myself bereft of scant more than a nadir of my natural intuition. Yet, of the propensities that have not fled me, I am now inclined in this direction. I cannot expressly say why. I ask only that you indulge me."

Sufficient argument for Nettie, she bucked up and scurried forward on the railway sleepers to match *Miracle's* pace—she to his left, Maggie to his right.

"You still didn't answer the question," Pete droned as he brought up the foursome's rear. "*Where* are we going?"

Miracle pointed in the direction of their trek, toward the prairie's farthest reach, where the collateral rails illusorily converged into one.

"Forward, my young friend. Always forward."

Back in Howsley's viewing room, Jon Mazzio sat alone, reviewing the only two existing records of James Wagner's substituent life. The playback muted, he'd supplanted Wagner's indecipherable patter with the more recent audio from his "*Miracle* sessions"—interviews that he and Doctors O'Connell and Williams had recorded in recent weeks. The voice-over running synchronously so that, in effect, it laid *Miracle's* own commentary precisely over the video as he himself had viewed them, this set-up permitted Mazzio to more thoroughly evaluate *Miracle's* uniquely derived motivations for Wagner's behaviour. At times bizarrely akin to a sportscaster's play-by-play of critical field strategy, the traveller's reactions to some of the scenes—especially the free-for-alls—had been more apprehending and empathetic than any other viewer's thus far. Even playing tinny, as they did on the deck's monophone, his words resounded in richly mirthful appreciation of Wagner's wiliness.

> "Hah! He is ungainly there, crude and untrained. But his spirit is as I remember it."

The comment was in response to Wagner's holding at bay two of Miss Groller's orderlies.

> "And that consecution—there! Those expedients are the hallmark of no other influence but— Wait—and there again! Do you see how he takes the initiative? How he tasks those unready stumblebums—"

His commentary halted briefly. At the time of the recording, he'd felt sudden abashment at insulting the Howsley staff, and had gone on to state as much.

> "My apologies, doctors... I realise that this is a matter most grave. And believe me, I am truly beholden that you possessed the wherewithal to ensnare these images. While it is true, I have never been comfortable with this wizardry of the electriks, such fortuity in being able to see my friend in this fashion seems to have all but divested me of my manners. I therefore beseech in advance your gentle understanding should my zeal again outflank my good sense."

The real-time Mazzio halted playback. Silently mouthing *Miracle's* words, he took pleasure in their outdated formality. Coming from anyone else, such speech would have seemed cornball, contrived, and awkward, like John Wayne's Genghis Khan from the erroneously miscast *The Conqueror*. But with *Miracle*—whose very name lent itself to haughtiness—it was strangely befitting, and through some manner of unanswerable logic it commandeered its own credibility.

But how did this odd man fit into the James Wagner puzzle? *Miracle* insisted on having befriended Wagner at some point in the past, laid claim to an abundance of off-the-record knowledge regarding Wagner's physiology, his personality, even intricate facets of his bendering that Mazzio himself had only loosely collated. Wagner had dwelled in or around Bishop for all of his life, while *Miracle*, an obvious foreigner, probably couldn't tell the city hall from the city dump without being coached. His teenage friends, familiarised by their touristing, had become his downtown guides, negotiating his point A to point B meanderings within a bustling cityscape that didn't interest him a fraction as much as did the vined arbour on Howsley's rear grounds. Out on the streets of Bishop, he was a lost soul. Conversely, on plain and prairie, in woodlands and along mountain trails, it was said that the navigator's mantle was singularly his to wear. According to Maggie, in the wild *Miracle* could smell an impending downpour before a single cumulonimbus graced the sky, could construct viable shelter out of twigs and fronds faster than the average homemaker could lay dinner settings for eight, could dig more life-sustaining snips, snails, and puppy-tails out of a common pasturage than most late night refrigerator foragers could purloin in the average snack raid. And all of these inconsistencies were tied to a fellow who'd referred to Mazzio as a "man of physic."

Furthermore, *Miracle* had cobbled together the foundations of an elaborate mythos that explained not only where it was that Wagner had phased to, but the manner in which he continued even then to have his being. But never once was it accompanied by any how-and-why, and certainly not by anything remotely provable. Perhaps this was the beauty of it: like the faith that *Miracle* aided a plethora of back roads Americans in sustaining, it had to be accepted in lieu of proof.

Indeed, after studying Wagner firsthand, after witnessing the phase-out itself, Mazzio could truthfully rule out very little. His guidelines, his boundaries, and his understanding of physical law had no bearing now. That playbook was obsolete. It could just as well be discarded forever and replaced by one scribed by the quill of some cosmic anarchist.

Mazzio restarted both the audio deck and the video. He was eager to reach the second programme, the March 2 segment, where the entranced Wagner had submerged himself in the domesticity of campsite cookery with invisible utensils, and conversation with imaginary companions. Having viewed it innumerable times, it was no longer the video's content that Mazzio sought, but rather the reaction that it had prompted in *Miracle*. This was the real stopper, the wake-up call that had finally roused the doctors into taking serious notice of the newcomer.

Initially, as the programme ran, *Miracle* had sat quietly and listened. But after a moment it became evident that something in Wagner's self-absorption was striking a chord of some distant recollection or transferral, for *Miracle* straightened in his chair, his ear bent toward the audio, his eyes devouring the monitor screen. Progressively he leaned in to better hear and to hang on Wagner's words, scrutinising, mentally transcribing each syllable and phrase, and then—in final shocker—anticipating, and actually delivering, Wagner's own dialogue simultaneously and quite nearly verbatim, in the foreign tongue, as it spilled from Wagner's lips!

It was an imperfect mimicry to be sure, but the bulk of dialogue was so overwhelmingly replicated that none of the three doctors could bring himself to comment until the screen had long gone to blue; and even here their goosefleshy astonishment yielded Wagneresque gibberish of their own, at least until one of them could summon the presence of mind to supplicate *Miracle*.

"It is a discourse from a day of long ago, doctors, a time now overlaid by the dust of a hundred tomorrows. The nature of what he enacts on this television glass—although he appears afflicted and swaddled in lunacy—is in actuality the mirroring of a past event, one in which he and I both participated. An insignificant gathering by any onlooker's standards, it was for us a truly momentous occasion, and my mind cannot help but to retain it in vivid memory, in spite of the forfeiture that severed my mortal ties with that sphere."

Williams tut-tutted:

"Oh, that explains a lot! Can you expound, maybe in terms less vague?"

Miracle had seemed entranced by the VCR tuner's blue screen. It was becoming increasingly evident that the answers hadn't been totally in his ability to give.

"We—he and I—had encountered a third party, she who was to become a fast ally. I recall that the three of us were discussing the possibility of a cooperative effort while preparing a repast of spit-roasted hens that she had dispatched just prior to our arrival. By Craxis! How I do miss that exasperating woman. How I miss them both. Truly, I know not if that realm exists within this one, doctors, or if it lies far beyond it. But, I tell you, it is the mother that bore me, it is the home that has expelled me, and it is the world upon which James Wagner now trods. Do not harry me on how this is possible, for I am ill-equipped to provide explanation. I have no ken of the powers that manipulate my life. Still, if there is reason to be found, I have travelled the path in search of it for many months, and nothing short of my death will force my abandonment of the quest."

Williams sighed heavily, frustrated by the ever cryptic dialogue that *Miracle* bandied about so expertly and with so very great eloquence.

"So, what you're telling us, *Miracle*, is that there isn't really much about you that falls within the scope of Judaeo-Christian teaching at all, despite all reports to the contrary."

Miracle responded without flinch or subterfuge:

"You would be correct, sir. It seems that the people of your land are not content with anything or anyone whose origins and intents are not clearly and succinctly established. Never once have I claimed to be a messenger of their Deity, yet by some means I have come to represent whatever they would have me represent. Even my well-intended Maggie would admit to her unpremeditated role in promoting this aspect of my character when first we struck our acquaintance. Presently, she knows better. And although we have hence tried in vain to curtail such assumption, it prevails and flourishes like a living being—at least for the moment. However, I have discovered this American public to be a fickle lot. The day will come when they will tire of me, just as they tire of every other caprice that they so blindly pursue in order to fill yet another imagined—and self-created—deficiency in their lives. I need no soothsayer to tell me this. I already sense darker times beyond night's falling, but I cannot allow trepidation to interfere with what I must do. Wagner's fate and my own spiral along paths disparate yet reconciled in ways I cannot profess to understand, nor even begin to convey to you. And while I brace for my inevitable declension, while I await my dismantling by events yet to come, I pray that his will be an ordeal more exalted in its culmination."

When asked to trim the frilly ambiguities and to speak in a style more accessible and conducive to at least one good interpretation—as opposed to twenty fogbound apologues—*Miracle* traded his cryptic sombreness for even grander metaphor.

"I stand before you a stranger, existing in your realm by what I gather are much the same means by which Wagner has come to stand in my own. I have witnessed events of past and future. I have, at times, sustained myself with the discretionary influence allotted of this knowledge. Yet, by subtle paradox, both past and future are equally denied me. For months I have been as a soul adrift upon waters more vacillating than any ocean's. I have faced the inundation of the masses, the deluge of a people who want yet who are not *in* want, who need but are not needy. Throughout my odyssey, I have at times found safe harbour in the lesser inhabited 'shallows' of your heartland, but only at the price of permanent scuttling upon unshift-able sands. In contrast, the deep and dark depths of your ridiculously grand cities have provided me with the insignificance and anonymity I desire, yet they and their inhabitants are cold and inhospitable. Should a soul go under there, it has far to sink before making bottom, and many hungry predators to repel along the way.

"Still, I am not so different from you, doctors. I continue forward, seeking out the fate that awaits me. Perhaps I do so in greater increment than do you. Perhaps I employ more lore and auspice than suits your comfort. But I sense that if I am to truly explain my ordeal—and moreover, to unmasque whatever power it is that lifts its boot to my backside—I must attempt to maintain my ideals, lest I lose all sight of who I am."

Mazzio switched off both components and studied the notes he'd been scribbling. *Miracle* had clearly been a moral person. He was also an eccentric and a lone wolf. But the one thing that he *wasn't* was the devoutly fundamentalist prophet that the media and the masses made him out to be. Somehow, through his works, through his beneficence with ailing and afflicted people, he'd been pigeonholed by a commonage that apparently couldn't fully accept a spiritual do-gooder unless he was one of theirs, unless he was fitted to the proper hat. Only then, after lending himself to a succession of unscientifically substantiated (but allegedly wondrous) events, did they hale him as a healer, a marvel, a living representation of his very name—which Mazzio now knew was not *Miracle's* true name or identity at all.

Next came Maggie Escalante, a well-meaning truth-seeker whose only error had been one of judgement. It was she who'd been alternately responsible for first promoting *Miracle* within the framework of established tradition, and then for having to shield him from the cascading effects of her innocent blunder—effects that Mazzio sensed she still wasn't entirely prepared to recount for lack of proof either way. And could anybody blame her? Just witnessing Wagner's departure was enough to rout Mazzio into rethinking a healthy chunk of his *own* belief system.

In Maggie's case, she'd merely hammered the prodigious pegs of happenstance into whatever holes—round *or* square—seemed to best suit her cause. And then, like so many of the well-intentioned scribes, metaphrasts, interpreters of scripture and oral tradition before her, she'd simply disregarded or downplayed those of *Miracle's* oddments that didn't quite conform to the desired geometry of his emerging personage.

That was, until it happened that said oddments had begun to significantly outweigh the concordant ones. To no other's chagrin but hers, it had actually been more greatly to *Miracle's* relief. Patently, he'd never sought such entitlement, didn't like it, never wanted it. This hadn't been hard to infer. But, then again, Mazzio's bread and butter was in reading people. He knew the springs and gears that drove behaviour. He knew the pitfalls of expectations and presumption. He knew the resilience and the fragility of the human spirit. And where the wayfarer was concerned, it worried him, for *Miracle* had made no scruple about his distaste for his celebrity. All too anxious, in fact, to break the yoke of his too-tidy designation, in his outwoods naïveté he had little more than an inkling of the fallout that such action, void of pre-emptive measure, might truly invite. Conceivably, he would do better to simply disappear from the public eye at one swoop rather than offer himself up on the block of disillusioned public sentiment. Either way, the dilemma was a dicey one. Furthermore, it bore one grimly ironic twist: Should he misread his adulators, or permit inadvertence to sabotage his intended disclamation, then it might so happen that what he'd professed to Mazzio and the other doctors about his disenabled future might just prove him more prophetic than he knew.

CHAPTER THIRTEEN

But boundless risk must pay for boundless gain.
—WILLIAM MORRIS

Within the space of a few days, Wagner had not only managed to formulate a basic plan of escape, but had quite nearly convinced a stalling and pooh-poohing Balgor that it would be to his benefit to buy in on the potentially lethal caper. A classic hard-sell if ever there was one, it was Balgor's sense of honour that gained Wagner, at the very least, a ruminative bargaining chip in his bid for the realmson's crucial talents. His athletic ability, his familiarity with the lay of the land, his improvisational cunning—Wagner needed the whole mettlesome kitbag to satisfy every requisite of what could at best be deemed a reckless and ill-considered insanity. Balgor would later confess that he'd consented for no other reason than to end Wagner's whining.

Trust, too, was a vital factor, for even among compatriots were acts of perfidy known to arise. Rivals, dissidents, the envious and the wronged—all of these types and more were in lurk within the Ergosian immurement, usually between competing stables, kinspeople or not. It was exactly as the NuRacs would have it. Treachery more often than not was a beast of opportunity poised to spring at even the most trivial of gains, from petty requitals to extra meal allowances to full upgrades in rank. And although Wagner had by necessity pencilled in a third, as yet unsolicited, accomplice for the scheme's best potential success, he'd first needed to lock in the one partner on whom he could rely without reservation.

The far-seeing prudence in Balgor's reluctance, however, had been like the Gordian knot yet to be untied. In subsequence, Wagner's admittedly ruthless recourse had been to appeal to his friend's nationalistic outrage and to his untenanted dreams of regainable freedom. Tendering several desiderative contingencies that only active perpetration could make possible, Wagner topped his pitch with the vision of his and Balgor's triumphant entry through the gates of Vargath—the last strongheld Ergosian capital—as the infamous two imperts who'd bloodied the nose of the NuRac regime on its own ground. Should this tack have failed to completely sway the realmson scheme-side, then Wagner's supplementary lagniappe of their ability as freemen to supply those at Vargath with enough specifics about QieLahr to spur an Ergosian siege-force into infiltrating the usurped territories and besetting—and forever razing—its walls helped nudge

Balgor to righteous action.

Ambitious ideals though they were, *who* truly knew what was possible, and what, not? This, the basis of Wagner's positing, also became his handy riposte for the "privatism" allegation that the staunchly disfavouring Tamek levelled at him as a test of his resolve. Just because no one had ever busted out wasn't argument enough to say that no one ever would. Furthermore, because Wagner was personally spearheading the plan, no counsel that he'd slipped to Balgor's ear was so reprobate as to earn him a spot alongside Ulysses and Diomedes in the ring of hell that Dante reserved for improvident advisors. While admittedly his reasons for wanting out were not totally open-handed ones, his arguments were nonetheless rooted in the obvious injustices—those of undeserved captivity, of dispossession, of indignity, even of foreseeable genocide—and whether a chance for an organised, retaliatory comeuppance might at some date result from their success or not, the risk beat all hell out of continuing on as NuRac puppets.

As for the plan, it was nothing if not innovative. Wagner hadn't merely slapped together a recklessly conceived wall-hop and scurry. As shrewdly deliberated as it was deliberate in shrewdness, the commodity of his designs surprised even himself in novelty. Indeed, a person with but a basic spatial understanding of what to expect between the barracks "launch-pad" and the final drop beyond the outer walls would have deemed Wagner's strategic unorthodoxies as overly barefaced and brazen. Conceived personally, and developed and revised through Balgor's and Tamek's sagely inputs, there was nary a roadblock thus far that had not been anticipated, nor a scenario that could not be somehow circumvented or turned to their advantage—at least in theory. His stable-mates having the more practical bead on eventualities, Wagner drew from earthly medium, adapting and incorporating from his recollection of every prison and military escape story that he could summon to mind, fact or fiction. British P.O.W.s tunnelling under a wooden vaulting horse, Snake Plissken skulking through a decrepit Manhattan nightmare, Henri "Papillon" Charriere's doggedness to win his freedom from the penal colonies of French Guiana, John Carter's flight from a Warhoon gladiator hold on Barsoom—these were the exemplars on Wagner's checklist of consideration, each with the potential of bestowing some scrap of exploitable design beyond any intrinsic quality of circumstance or plot. The unprecedented was essential here, far-fetched or not, and the unprecedented was exactly what resulted.

The scheme itself: Instead of the obvious, instead of the usual attempt upon the prison fortifications—a stagger of two heavily-guarded walls and one ward whose devilish design made this avenue little more than an architecturally bastioned turkey-shoot—Wagner opted for the unthinkable. He sought instead to breach a section of the more redundant barrier on the east end of the courtyard. This route would at first have seemed the most contrary of goals, for it led not to the outside, but right into QieLahr proper—a blunder that even the thickest dullard wouldn't have committed. Yet, its unconsiderability was its true beauty. Two walls here also, it boasted considerably lighter patrols. Working next from Tamek's knowledge of how and where the camp abutted the city, a fortuitous piece of information that may otherwise have been deemed insignificant had come up in passing. A foible, perhaps, in engineering, the Sentinel had espied it casually from out the loopholing of the keep from where the Tribunal typically heard (and rejected) his appeals. As no other Ergosian had ever stood upon the walls that overlooked the camp, nor claimed the aerial vantage bestowed to Tamek by these incidental reconnoitres, the NuRacs probably felt reasonably certain that no prisoner would truly care how, standing directly behind the pairing of walls that Balgor and Wagner now considered, beyond an intersecting juncture where the prison periphery angled sharply from the soldiers' billet on one side and the Great Arena substructure on the other, there lay bedside access to the grand NuRac city herself. Directly beyond that masonry criss-crossing stood a few administrative structures, and contiguous to these was almost a direct passage to the commercial districts, the cultural centres, the very aorta of NuRac commerce. Yet, this so, one would nevertheless have to be daft to aim intent in said direction. Even at midnight, these areas were potentially peopled by late working merchants, cleaning crews, members of the general populace out for strolls—and as such it was an illogical avenue for swift and stealthy flight. No one in his right faculty would ever opt for such folly. It thus became the perfect choice.

The strategy was a complex one, fraught with a bramble of pesky snags that differed categorically from those of the conventionally straight-out escapes. The most logical avenues—the walls to the west and south, with their titillating immediacy of grassy covert just beyond the staggered fortification—were the ones on which the NuRacs banked that all reasonable attempts would focus. The banquettes on each of said walls were patrolled from sun to sun. Each likewise stood in measured succession, one from the other, with a good fifteen metres' width of parade between them that—when not utilised as marching runways or for military drills—saw more sentry activity than any Ergosian on the lam could ever hope to elude without either the benefit of Wagner's now defunct ability to permeate solid stone or at least a sound set of his Daedalean wings. Just the same, all previous attempts had been conceived with—and doomed by—this very blueprint. Even as some of those brave, albeit unimaginative, souls made admirable cat-and-mouse showings with their pursuant NuRacs over battlement and brickface, every venture had ended similarly—with grave consequence.

On the other hand, the idea of wrangling logic by choosing to infiltrate the metropolitan NuRac district, where security was probably lower (and the chance for obscurity perhaps greater) was a piquing notion for all three schemers. Of course, one intrigant acting alone likely had a better chance of slithering unnoticed through QieLahr's shadowy alleyways for a means of egress; but Wagner knew that his climbing skills and his incursionary limitations were much too wanting to go it solo. A trio of light-footed renegades, however, each with his own specialty and responsibility, could potentially take to the shadows and find a means by which to slip through a city whose defences were geared more at keeping undesirables *out* rather than vice-versa. It was just as perilous as any previous attempt, equally as pendent on the unforeseen—still, it had the element of never having been tried. And while less eager to scratch away that claim than to just get free, Wagner pressed for it with all that he had.

"If it be your intent to avoid the tournament, *Voknor*, you have but five days to perfect this plan," Tamek said as the three of them huddled together over evening stew. "For your own benefit, it should be woven more tightly than a lady's corset, and be equally disguised under a gown of unassuming secrecy. And although your mind will toil and race these coming days in preparation for the chosen eve, the attempt itself must be enacted in impromptu fashion so that none will become suspicious until that hour is long spent."

"By Bilahdu's unravelling breeches," said Balgor, "I find that I am liking this more and more."

"Really?" Wagner was incredulous. "How funny! The whole thing is my idea— and I can hardly wait to go—yet, *I'm* the one who's got a gut full of butterflies."

"What!?" cried Balgor. "Would you have us quit the scheme so easily?"

"Not a chance. Reservations aside, it's still infinitely preferable to doing the arena thing. At least for me it is."

Tamek tore a crust of bread and swirled it amid cabbage and fatback. "Interestingly, there is as much in your philosophy that I admire as I reject, *Voknor*. Although you seek to avoid that which all others here face routinely, you have both the possession and the fortitude to act on your own mettle as opposed to kneeling in wait for the axe. Would that I could accompany you myself."

"Well, we still need that *third* man," Wagner hinted.

"Nay, you know my reasons. Too many here rely on me."

Wagner's countenance turned immediately stoical. "I think you should admire your own philosophy, Tamek. I don't envy your position. It's tough enough for me to be responsible for myself, much more, an entire constituency."

"It appears that his constituency is experiencing a bit of a snarl this fair evening," Balgor quipped as he directed their eyes across the yard of previously supping inmates. Indeed, an isolated skirmish was afoot. Voices echoing interjectionally, dust strewing skyward, the curious pressed forward with a cautious conservatism that kept one eye on the guards and the other straining toward the forefront of the ado.

Tamek glanced at the affray, but didn't rise to investigate. Petty squabbles, shoving matches, grab-assing, and the occasional argument-clinching knuckle-sandwich, were trivial, commonplace goings-on in any close-proximity lodging. He'd endured more than his share of them in his tenure, placated a number of them, actually sanctioned some others; and unless the guards took serious enough action to compel his own interference, matters usually settled back on their own just as quickly as they erupted.

This present raucousness falling easily under the latter heading, *who* should come bursting from the crowd's belly in flabbergasted disgust but the Agile One himself, the lecherous Fostoch of Orrd. Full of grunt and bluster, his face a reddened, angry flurry under a drippy dousing of what could have been nothing other than the evening entrée, the Orrdian ploughed his way through several straggling onlookers who hadn't the sense to skirt out of his path. Flinging cabbage from his beard, he knocked two kinsmen to the ground and then stomped furiously toward his barracks, ultimately catapulting himself like a missile through the entry.

Left with no spectacle beyond his withdrawal, all eyes slowly panned back to his point of origin, following the clumps and drabbles of organic detritus spread along the clomp of his retreat. There, at the opposite end, they focused upon a solitary figure seated on the sand.

All too aware of the assemblage around her, the long inured J'nea calmly and dismissively negotiated bannock and cabbage into her mouth. Void of emotion, seemingly uninterested in anything other than the opportunity of concluding her meal in solitude, she obliged none of her onlookers with even the most infinitesimal of acknowledgements, despite the many eyes that, for long minutes, remained fixed upon her inexpressiveness. Instead, she chewed and shovelled, gnawed and slurped, occasionally wiping her mouth free from the dribbles of haste, straying from her ritual but once to shoo a gnat from her ankle. Her boots vacant and slumped at her side, her feet were rooted in the sand, dug-in to betake of the cooler sift only a few centimetres below. Not far from this toeful tilling lay an empty soup crock, upended and askew, like a crown toppled from the head of an ousted tyrant.

"Methinks Fostoch's pathetic attempts at wooing have given way to a particularly unfulfilling epilogue," said Tamek as he soaked up the dregs of his stew.

"*Methinks* he will go hungry this night," added Balgor. "And not merely *belly-wise*."

"*Methinks* a seaweed and cucumber facial would have been more the ticket," said Wagner. "Yon spicy cabbage will surely haveth a right astringent effect on that saucy knave's complexion."

The two natives looked at the outsider like the alien that he was. Earthly humour—though they didn't know it as such—was, as always, lost humour; and they, familiar with Wagner's cultural cross-plying, nodded bonhomously to his face, shrugged to each other in secret aside, and continued on with their bandying until the mealtime drew out and twilight began its descent upon the field. Fostoch's audience, too, had long dispersed—some, back to their meals, and others, to the barracks or into smaller congress for evening gaming, rumour-mongering, common chatter, and such.

Wagner had, throughout the balance of the meal, maintained a slinking eye on J'nea. He was ever intrigued by her pluck, by her understated comeliness, and especially by the sudden up-throttle that she kept ever at the ready for gunning some particularly irksome argument across the confrontational finish line. While remaining at odds himself with the vex of her multi-directional mood-lurchings in their own encounters, he suspected that there were some things in life that, as a man, he would never be privy to. Thus, it was perhaps better that the sundry mysteries of J'nea—like those of earthly Stonehenge, of Roswell and Area 51, of the JFK magic bullet theory, even of the female gender in whole (earth *or* Ergos)—remained forever unexplained if he truly wished to keep his worries at minimum.

When the hour came late, Wagner watched as she laced up her boots, stood up to swat the sand from her rump, and then retrieved Fostoch's crock before heading off to the serving area to return it with her own. For someone who Tamek felt was in cahoots with the NuRacs, Wagner noted that she hardly acted the part, even when she assumed she wasn't being watched. In the same vein, she could not have shown less concern for whatever suspicions arose regarding her loyalty to either side. It was as if she simply didn't care. Wagner suspected that, much like he, she merely looked out for herself as any loner was wont to do, tending to her own welfare through the best means allowed of her circumstances. As a trusty, however, she was empowered, had a wee measure of autonomy, was even given the occasional opportunity to get beyond the walls during some of the caravan round-ups. Yet, did the fact that she played liaison between soldier and captive make J'nea an auxiliary only to the side of the oppressors, or was it possible that she'd mastered the ability to walk that line using a restrained compassion for her people as counterbalance to anything about her that might be construed as self-serving? After all, she was the only one who'd thought to bring Wagner a shawl, who'd watered everyone else before she herself received refreshment, who'd lighted most of the fires for repulsing the roving night-hounds—all this not solely for the NuRacs, but equally for the prisoners. Were any of these deeds more suspect than the others, or were they merely the actions of a reasonable woman whose motives were made ulterior by a suspicious populace that saw nothing about her but a childhood brand for thievery, and what seemed at least a partial leaguing with the enemy? Despite Wagner's impending intent to fly the coop, he believed it worth the effort to find out.

"Finish up, gents," he said as he rose from friendly company and began an extempore pilgrimage in the direction of the serving area. "And don't do anything daring till you hear from me."

Balgor noted Wagner's trajectory and quickly deduced where he was headed. "Fie!" he cried. "Have care, *Voknor,* else you may be the next fool destined for the order of the ceremonious stew crock."

Tamek, certain that he'd been clear on how he regarded the woman whom Wagner now meandered across the yard to intercept, grunted his disapproval but refrained from further hortation. Wagner was out of earshot anyway, and almost upon J'nea, who'd just sunk her dishes to the bottom of the rinse tub and had turned to make her way back to her billet.

"Is it safe to talk to you?" Wagner asked. "Or have you got a spare kebab up your sleeve that I should know about?"

She shot him "the look" and kept walking. "If you would observe more closely, *Voknor,* you would see that I have no sleeves."

"No sense of the metaphorical either, I see."

She didn't react.

"Okay, then, for my protection—and yours—I'll spare you the wisecracks until you're a bit less inclined to throw things."

"That will be fine," she said. "Come see me, then, in the *next* life."

Wagner scampered to keep up with her.

"Yeah, well, that's exactly my problem. Y'see, I'm already *in* my next life! So, I guess that in some convoluted way I'm answering your invitation a bit prematurely for you, and a bit posthumously for me."

"Do you *ever* make sense?"

"I try to not make a habit of it—not very often. I just have a question—a curiosity—that I was hoping you might be able to help me with."

"Fostoch had a 'curiosity' too."

"Yeah, but mine's got nothing to do with that. Besides, cabbage has a way of staying with me all by itself—I don't need to wear it."

She huffed her irritation. "What *is* it then?"

"Okay. How did you come to be a trusty here?"

She halted just short of her barracks entry and spun to face him. "Why would you ask such a thing?" If her stance was any indication of her mindset, she came off like a cat in bristle.

"Why not?"

"Why not! Because in *my* thinking, I am not so certain that *you* are not some manner of trusty yourself! And, if not a trusty, then a scout or a shill. These other jolterheads may not suspect. But I have seen the evidence!"

She may as well have popped Wagner in the chops for as far as his jaw dropped.

"Come now, *Voknor*," she goaded, her tone quickly impressing that she wouldn't be placated by his provincial doublespeak. "Be unyielding if you wish, but do not regard me as a simpleton. You must know that it does not gratify me to be inculpatory. And certainly, I would never lodge such an accusation without sufficient reason."

"Sufficient reason, huh? Let's *hear* your sufficient reason."

She looked him dead in the eye. Then she moved in tight. "Here, on my cheek, I have borne this hot-ironed abomination since I was a girl of eight. When one bears such a marking, *Voknor*, especially from so early an age, she becomes that much more aware of similar distinctions in others. Secondly, as I am a woman, I am thus inclined to partake more than a casual glance at the males around me—particularly those in transient undress. You were in just such a state the other day at the laving post—do you recall?"

"Yeah, so? I've been naked in front of you a lot. That whole slave coffle thing sticks more in *my* mind."

"True," she said. "But it was not until the more recent encounter that I happened upon *this*." She poked a finger at his chest, bulls-eyeing the *sigma* beneath his jute.

"That morning, *Voknor*, as Cinjal ascended the heavens she bestowed me your wraithy little branding. Quite adventitious, I might add, for had she not shone upon you in just the proper intensity and angle, I might have gone on in ignorance—and, no doubt, much more happily so. True to tell, I know not how I could have missed it until then, especially during the campaign, for I have already boasted of a keen eye for minutiae. I can only speculate that you were too muddied from the chase, or perhaps your hirsuteness impedes all but the most advertent of inspections. I have as yet to hear anyone else in camp make mention of it. Such is only to your fortune, *Voknor*, for if your high and mighty Sentinel realised what you hide, he would quarter you with his bare hands."

"He could *try*," said Wagner, the sudden spurt of machismo taking even him by surprise. J'nea shrank momentarily, for this was a Wagner she'd not seen before.

"So, that's it?" he asked. "You think I'm a saboteur? You think I'm here to pull the rug on Ergosian morale, to steal off with purloined secrets, and to ferret out the dissenters for prompt doses of discipline? Do you really believe, because this marking is similar to the one on AuwNiir's armour, that I'm conspiring with the NuRacs?"

J'nea motioned him away from the building so that she would preclude anyone's overhearing them. "Do I not have ears and eyes? No Ergosian in this camp had ever heard of you before your capture. No one, *Voknor*, not even those whose clans claim some small manner of ancestry near the Leordahn province—

your alleged homeland. In this camp, in these times, that *alone* is amply sufficient to render you suspect to any number of things."

"Okay. So maybe I'm not from the southern territories. Big deal. What else have you got?"

Though her perturbation jumped a full point, she kept it in check. "When the trackers first delivered you unconscious before the caravan officers, the rumour of your snaring while allied with Vofspars—this, too, could easily have been NuRac fabrication, used in order to deflect any inquiry from your true nature."

"Sez you."

She eyed him dourly.

"I grant you that, after what occurred at inception, the trackers' report indeed began to prove more coincident than what would at first have seemed reasonable. Your unprecedented pitch in defence of the Vofspar lent exceptional credence to the NuRac account. Yet, no matter the apparent authenticity of those actions, it is not inconceivable that such spectacle might have been a ploy to gain you higher regard in our eyes, since you undoubtedly knew that—as a lowly prisoner, surrounded by more spearpoints than you have teeth in your head—you would accomplish nothing in your captive state."

"And the bulk of my guard buddies sure went all out to make me look good, didn't they? Allowing their throats to be ripped open, stepping up to have their guts scattered around the sands—now *that's* what I call some serious collaboration."

"I dispute their fates no more than I dispute what I witnessed of your spirit," said J'nea, not quite exasperated with Wagner's derision, but close. "Nor can I deny my awe as I watched it occur. But even more mystified was I when I saw that our warders did not slay you on the spot for your impertinence—as they would have any other upstart. Equally puzzling was the exceptional stroke of fortune—or, perhaps, in retrospect, the cosily preconceived arrangement—of your almost immediate expedition into AuwNiir's stable of fighters. Not RoqaVek's, not SiirKah's, but AuwNiir's—the very Commander whose mark you bear. Now, *Voknor*, given this extravagance of ambiguities, I ask you—could you truly reprehend *anyone* for thinking you a NuRac delator?"

Having readied all of the retaliatory fixings for a proper rebuttal, Wagner suddenly chucked his entire defence for the sake of better things. His ego gobbled by inspiration, he gave over to a notion more mutually advantageous than the almost certain rancour that a diatribe with this woman would perpetuate. Promptly centring himself, he dispelled his resentment (in the manner that Howsley's biofeedback gadgetry had taught him to), and smoothed the ruffles of J'nea's insinuations that he might better slip his feet into her metaphorical boots and perhaps deal with her reservations, her perspective, and maybe—through sympathy and appeasement—find the means to get her onside. After all, her concerns were legitimate and syllogistic. They were, in fact, very much like his own ponderings, only refashioned; they were grown out of Ergosian ideology, and not at all undeserving of address. The evidence against him so considerable, her inquisition had been nothing if not an honest one, rooted both in self-preservation and in the spirit of good citizenship, in the need to be aware of the intents and the prejudices and the afflictions of those around her. Welcoming or ostracising, this community was still *her* community.

As she stood batedly for his answer, for whether or not he could blame her for thinking him collusive, he resignedly shook his head in the negative.

J'nea slipped beyond surprise. Clearly, she hadn't anticipated such speedy, uncontested validation. Immediately believing that she'd misread and miscalculated, she broke into an abrupt back-pedal of reassessed trusts, almost as if she saw Wagner's concession as a grappling iron that drew their disparate worlds into kindred-like approximation. Straightway, contrasts became comparisons; conflict gave way to coaptation. She was suddenly more consentient than ever, while Wagner simply felt as if he'd been rail-switched into oncoming confoundment.

"My own status as trusty," said she, "just as often makes me suspect with the camp population. It is an injurious judging that I do not mean to pass on to you without good reason, *Voknor*, and so I apologise. I will further admit to having ventured a handful of social approaches with you in order to better glimpse your character, your motivation, your general aura and such—most of these before discovering this dubious connection to AuwNiir. Overall, I fear that I have only come away perplexed. Whichever you are, whether devious or virtuous, innocent or impostor—you are most uncommon. And although I have thus far sought to assess you through surreptitious means, I feel better now that I might challenge you openly, with forewarning, no matter your complicity or lack thereof."

"I'll tell you straight out," said Wagner. "My loyalties have been foremost to myself, to getting out of this place—*period*. I'm not from around here. I don't *belong* here. And not just in this prison, either. I'm not a part of this whole friggin' scene. All I've ever wanted since day one was to get out, to get back home. Thing is, along the way it's become a little more complicated than my initial displacement and inconvenience. I've made a couple of friends here, and I've found a lot to admire in the rest of these people. *Your* people. And despite my personal objectives, I wouldn't do anything to bring them more grief than they already face on a daily basis."

"Verily" she said. "I, too, care for none of this—the war, the NuRacs, their city, their camp. *And* their infernal games. Yet, I likewise have little love for those of my own people who survive here by profiteering from the weak and the weak-minded. I certainly have no loyalties to the hidebound Tamek, nor to his sanctimonious cronies or to his gloriously hypocritical city of Vishkor—a city, mind you, that will not stay the flattened smoulder that it deserves to be because its cycloptic ethos lives on within the pate of your precious Sentinel. He knows of my sentiment toward him and his on-hangers. He knows that I prefer tending to my own survival. And, when fate allows, I look out for the truly beleaguered of my kinspeople—at least those who are generous enough to disregard my stain and accept my friendship and my aid."

"And Tamek's predominance really gets your goat—is that it?"

"Your Sentinel does not make this wretched life any easier. He has scant use for those who do not follow his direction like meek little vrohdas. And while I would never let my gall overtake me, I cannot be certain that I would not refrain from interfering should some imposturer—as I have admittedly thought you to be— seek to sap under Tamek's pretentious foundation and topple him like the

Bejodethian obelisk. I might even tell him to have at it. For, to see Tamek exposed for the mere mortal that he is, to see him deplumed and discredited before his sycophants, I think I would dance a gavotte atop Grum's dais. But—and I say this with monitory frankness—if such actions served to obtrude on him, or on any of these people, the faintest upstep in hardship, then that same subverter will suffer all the wrath that is within this trusty's ability to inflict."

Wagner had been watching her intently. Her eyes never left his, not once. Her pupils were full and dark to where they all but usurped the hazel-splashed green of her irises. Were this ocular blackness at all symbolic of her inimical side, then the viridity that gradually reclaimed eyeful dominion suggested a return to the far more poised and unflappable personality that she typically projected. Little be known, in revealing her duality as she did, she'd allowed him a rare, underlinenesque glimpse at the more baleful sentiments that she otherwise kept hidden. By wilfully flashing this less felicitous aspect of herself, she simultaneously demonstrated courage and risk; and whether gamble or gambit, she provided Wagner with gainful and comparable perspective into his own dual nature.

How she had even spied his tattoo, however—without knowing what to look for and where—he hadn't a clue. After all, it was a small, unobstrusive, fine-lining of black that, after nine years, was easy even for him to slight, especially since it was buried under a mess of chesty scrub. The accustomed eye of a friend or a lover could always detect it without bother, although at times it seemed as difficult to explicate as the equivocal drawings in Jon Mazzio's perceptual assessment texts, those that intentionally entwined perspectively alternating images within the same doodle. For Wagner, had his tattoo simply been a snake or a spider or Felix the Cat, and not a recurring symbol from his visions, he just might have forgotten that it was there at all (something that hadn't always been possible with Sara's pendant). It likewise wouldn't be the source of his current fix. But, seeing as the symbol now had a secondary relevance as Commander AuwNiir's personal crest, it was not quite so convenient to ignore, for Wagner *or* for J'nea.

Because of this, on the very moment that Wagner had recognised a connection he'd made a point not to go about in daylight without his tunic, even on the most sweltering days. With the exception of showering, where the rinse-water evidently had a way of temporarily devolumising one's body hair, he'd taken all measure to conceal his secret—which, along with his many others, wasn't all so removed from his earthly routine but for this newer element of non-existent privacy that incarceration had introduced. He was similarly confident that Papa Olask hadn't seen anything either, due in large to a dimly lit surgery, elderly eyes, and the fact that he hadn't been made to completely doff his shirt during his examination.

Less comforted was he, or maybe less convinced, by J'nea's little tale of keen perceptions and sun's angle. Not merely dismayed by her privyness, he sensed an unseemly convenience in her account that only aggravated his "fret-o-metre" more than her allegations already had. Yet, he also knew himself, knew how dishy women had a way of weirding out his instrumentation; and so he let the issue drop before he could mull it to death. She having been grazingly close to him on a fistful of occasions, her discovery could indeed have been made just as she'd described it. And intriguingly, like everything else so far, maybe it wasn't only meant to be, but exploitably so.

"I think I might have preferred the dousing with stew to all this third degree," he finally confessed. "But, I must say that I respect your views, J'nea. I respect your reservations. I even respect your honest suspicion that I'm some kind of infiltrator. I'm *not*, you know—at least not in the sense of being some flunky mole of AuwNiir's, sent to stir things up or to fan unrest and betrayal. If I'm infiltrating, it's infiltration of a different nature, of falling ass-backwards into some offshot, retro-historical stage play whose script I've only been able to glimpse in half-drowsed bits and pieces. I don't know my character. I'm not sure whether I'm the lead or the walk-on, the principal or the understudy. I don't know which lines I'm to read. And as for whoever's directing this little farce, he's got a harsher sense of dramatic omnipotence than the NuRacs have evil devices. I'm being danced like a marionette through this absurdist travesty, with no rehearsal, no script, no promptbooks and—as you've already noted—too often with no costume."

"You speak riddles."

"*Yes! Fluently!* And do you know why? Because riddles are my forte. And thanks to you, I have a new one to ponder."

"What do you mean?"

Wagner pinched back a smile whose impetus he was not quite ready to divulge. He instead borrowed from *her* playbook, shifting the topic and hazarding what would become his own demonstration of courage and risk—an unchary, unpremeditated risk at that—by entrusting J'nea with the one piece of information that would reveal *her* colours once and for all.

"Y'know," he said, "my original purpose in talking to you this evening was, coincidentally enough, to draw you out, to get a fix on who *you* really are. From the start, I've found something about you—something other than the obvious— that keeps snagging my attention again and again, despite my best efforts to give you your space."

She laughed, almost scoffingly so. "If this is how you woo a woman, *Voknor*, then I must tell you that—"

"Whoa—hold on. I never said a thing about wooing. And I'm not implying it now, so you can just drop your shields and relax. Hormonal hankerings aren't a really big priority just now. Not with my prison-break right around the corner and all."

Her jaw dropped faster than his intentional slip had.

"What nonsense do you spout?"

"Nonsense in the best sense, I hope," he said. "And the boldest. Y'know, in thinking about it, I reckon I just might be wooing you after all. But it's your assistance that I'm seeking tonight, J'nea, not your affections."

"My assistance! In an escape? Are you mad?"

"Probably. But since when has that stopped me?"

J'nea yanked him even farther and more gruffly away from the barracks. "Away with your fool, *Voknor*, and bid your pragmatist return that I might hear something sensible!"

"You heard me," he said lowly. "I'm planning on taking it over the walls, and I'm asking for your help."

"Aye, help into an untimely grave!"

"Are you kidding? Look around you! *This* is the untimely grave! This camp is a death lottery, and we all know it. *Everyone* knows it, but no one does anything about it. But beyond these walls lies life. *Freedom!* You all may have forgotten that, but I haven't. I'm still fresh. I know the difference, and I want out. And the only way I can even hope to succeed is by getting the full dope on this place from the people who know it best. That's where *you* come in."

"Nay, this is where I walk away."

Wagner blocked her retreat, and for a trice it seemed that she would roughshod it right over him.

"Whoa, whoa—look," he said. "As a trusty, you have valuable insider's knowledge. I need that knowledge. You're also quick on your feet, and even quicker in your thinking. You're not afraid to kick some serious butt when the situation warrants it. I need that, too. Lastly, Tamek is against the whole thing— which, by my thinking, should make you all the more in favour of it. It's kismet, J'nea. It's been staring me in the face all along. You're the perfect choice, the perfect accomplice for a clean, compact, thrifty little launch to freedom— compliments of yours truly."

For a moment, she stared blankly at him, perhaps less dumbfounded by his outrageousness than by the overbleed of his earthly patois. Often did he encounter a varying degree of difficulty in being understood because of it. Idiom was a tricky thing, even with his unaccredited blanket fluency; and although said phenomenon provided for an extensive translation of terms, phrases, and intents—all decidedly twenty-first century terrene in derivation—there existed no comprehensible Ergosian exchange for his all-too-unwieldy complement of colloquialisms. Yet, more often than not excelling beyond his ken and expectations, whenever communication needed to outrank the frippery of his personal idiosyncrasy, he could usually convey his gist through the use of contextual and gesticulatory supplement. Regrettably, this was not one of those times.

Instead, she reacted anew with the lightest of all suspicions, interpreting his pitch now as some kind of elaborate jest.

"An escape, eh? I thank you, no, *Voknor*, for it so happens that I have one of my own set for this very night. Tamek and I are hastening across the walls at midnight so that we might consummate our secret espousal at the wayfarer's shrine along the bonny banks of the Langöde."

Wagner groaned.

"You cannot gull me so easily," she said. "I have heard rumour of your extra-liminal wit, and can now confirm the same. But, tell me, did you feel your earlier conceit of waxen wings and ethereal soaring too trite to include in this phantasy?"

Wagner looked hard at her with a silent, steelish deadpan that did not vary until he'd routed her slowly and unwillingly back into doubt.

"Nay, *Voknor*—nay—you are truly *serious?*"

"You say you've got ears," he said, "so let me try this with a slightly more personal spin. First off, I've come to accept all of your dark suspicions about me as logically deduced—and therefore warranted—concerns. I can deal with that. After all, who am I but a stranger with some weird notions and a suspicious symbol stamped in my flesh? If I weren't *me*, I'd probably have second thoughts about me, too. But, I *am me*, so I don't. Although I can appreciate where you're coming from, I still find your frequent perturbation and distrust unfounded and unfair, maybe in the same way that your facial scarring vilifies you for a bunch of youthful indiscretions that should long ago have been forgiven and forgotten. On the other hand, you've treated me kindly on more than one occasion, and damned if I don't harbour some strange fascination for you, regardless of our differences. In redress, then, for your compassion and for the sake of this rocky cordiality that we seem determined to maintain, I'm trying to square our acquaintanceship by extending to you my absolute trust. And how better to do that than by laying my biggest, baddest secret in your lap?"

One by one, then, Wagner began rattling off the bullets that outlined the scheme thus far. Not quite so liberal with details, however, as he purported to be, he provided J'nea with little more than a purposely calculated abridgement. This way, should his hunch ultimately prove imprudent, neither Balgor nor even Tamek could be irrefutably implicated by name or design. He knew intimately that he was making a massively incautious gamble—and one that Tamek surely would have sprouted smokestacks over once he caught wind of it—but accustomed as he'd become to using his gut as a situational sextant, he extended the offer to the freethinking trusty with barely a qualm, and actually felt as comfortable levelling with her as she had priorly with him.

Omitting the fact, of course, that the scheme would take its players deep into greater QieLahr, he instead substituted this vital detail with a cryptic blurb about a "revolutionary approach to escape" whereby freedom would be won through persevering craftiness rather than through fluke of fortuity. In reply, he sensed a little each of intrigue and resistance in J'nea's audience, and although he sought to play upon the one and assuage the other, it once again became clear that this woman wasn't easily persuadable despite what kinesics might have suggested. She did, however, listen and react and, at times, even demonstrated a comfortable enough posture of receptivity to imply that not everything Wagner had hatched was complete insanity. Taking heart at this, Wagner put the formal pitch to her, and asked whether or not she was open to recruitment as the third conspirator-hopeful.

He could, however, have saved himself the effort, for she was ready with her answer before he even got halfway through. Flat out, she refused.

"Now," she said, "it is your turn to listen to me. If you are in earnest, *Voknor*, then you are madbrained to have revealed all of this to me. For what you know, I may indeed be a direct pathway of treachery straight to the Tribunal's ear. Others already believe this, and I have little doubt that Tamek has endeavoured to jaundice your own thinking in this direction.

"Going fist-in-gauntlet with your imprudence is your audacity in thinking that your plan could ever succeed. I have seen too many such 'infallible underplots' go awry on my watch. Over time, I have helped to drag a veritable graveyard of corpses back through those gates, some riddled with such an overpiercing of bolts and arrows that my hands were made raw in extracting them all. To attempt these walls, *Voknor*, is like a lethal version of the Scrambler's Treasure that we all played as children. The risks are far more insurmountable than the stone and mortar. And you, whencesoever you truly hail, could hardly have studied these NuRacs, this fortress, with thoroughness enough to acquaint yourself with everything you need to know in order to carry such an ambition to success. More abhorrent, you seem possessed of a particularly virulent disregard for the lives you would put in jeopardy in the process. Nay, I say relinquish this folly. I do not wish to grieve for yet another handful of overzealous dolts who believe they need only to scale a few bricks to obtain their freedom. Nor do I wish to mourn for you personally, *Voknor*, not after I have prevailed so for our increased mutuality."

"Oh, is that what you've been doing? I hadn't noticed."

She let Wagner's words roll off of her. "By declaring your plans to me," she said, "you have simultaneously compromised them. As such, if you are indeed the innocent you claim to be, you may have risked your very livelihood with one addleheaded indiscretion."

"What, so now *you're* the saboteur?"

"I could be. But I am not." She studied Wagner's face like a map. Then she glanced over to the place where he'd noshed on stew and bread with his two cohorts, minutes earlier. Although both men had long since vacated and returned to the barracks, she maintained an eye on the locality where they had been, almost as if they'd remained.

"Tell me, *Voknor*. By what you have said it is obvious that Balgor is the unmentioned second member of your little trinity. Is this correct?"

"Well, I more or less told you that it wasn't Tamek. *You* do the math."

"A pity, that. It would almost be worth my own going, if only to be distanced from Tamek's overreaching influence."

"Come on, he's not *that* bad. It should be freedom from the NuRacs that you should be craving, not getting out of earshot of one man's platitudinous preaching. That's not proper reasoning for risking one's life. So what if Tamek is stern and self-righteous? So what if he's pompous and overbearing? Big whoop-de-doo. You've managed to handle it so far."

J'nea glared at him with fitful spark. Were she and he to have just then intersected his favourite mythos, her scalp would surely have sprouted serpents, and her stare surely would have turned him to stone. As it was, he knew not which of his comments had incensed her so, only that the fuse was lit. All he could do was fall silent and brace for the inevitable backlash.

He was nevertheless shocked beyond resource when she lunged at him in the physical, taking clamp of his tunic and uprooting him by force.

"*What would you know?*" she growled through gritted teeth. "Have you stood on the block of public degradation? Have you been shunned, estranged, ousted from the common populace?"

Not strictly an assault in the maiming sense, but neither one of simple intimidation, she'd unbalanced him with leverage and locomotion skilfully plied to both divest him of his equilibrium yet stop him just shy of a backward topple. Keeping him vulnerable this way, in perpetual falter, she drew nigh him—dour and angry and intimate—clamping her gaze onto his so that he'd have no choice but to read in her eyes all that her spoken reproof might fail to convey. The heat of her breath catching against his face, the flush in her cheeks, her sheeny perspiration and the flare of her nostrils—had he not believed that it was all born of ire he might almost have been inclined to interpret the advance with a palatability more exhilaratingly concupiscent than contentious.

"In a roundabout way," he answered, "yes, I have. But it didn't make me bitter enough to loathe the whole world. I learned to deal with it."

With her left clench she knuckled as hard and close on his *sigma* as she could without losing vantage.

"What say we go and show Tamek your branding then?" she asked. "Shall we see how effectively you 'deal with' the scorn and outrage and distrust that will surely empoison his opinion?"

Wagner relaxed his body under her grasp, forcing her to contend with the defiant slump of his full weight. Amazingly, she bore it, if uncomfortably and with a tremulousness of limb and sinew that compounded with each overtaxing second. Here, as she struggled as stubbornly as he knew she would, he craned in closely and whispered his bluff.

"Let's do it."

Moments seeming like minutes under the strain, she didn't flinch, not immediately. But when she realised that neither was Wagner going to, she suddenly gave up her clutch and withdrew.

"I believe you," she finally said.

"Believe what? That I'd come clean to Tamek?"

"No, I believe that you are not a NuRac shill. If I am wrong—if you have fooled me—I can only say that you are the craftiest quisling ever. And if that be the situation, I would just as soon remain at hand to better observe what it is you will do next."

Wagner flattened out the crumpled material of his tunic.

"Not that I don't appreciate that," he said, "but it seems now that I've jeopardised my plan by confiding in somebody who won't herself be at risk."

"You gambled. I told you it was foolish. But you neither won nor lost in this, *Voknor*. What you relinquished in secrecy you have recouped in respect—my respect. Although you must, for your own safeguarding, exercise a greater level of prudence with those whom you choose to trust, it is exactly this same, dangerously naïve faith of yours that has swayed me. In this sense, you are unrivalled. Necessity may have prompted your procuring your third party from within this hornets' nest of industry and potential betrayal, but that you approached *me* is astoundment beyond measure. Not everyone would lay down his armaments before an untried adversary on mere assumption and impression. And precious few would take it upon themselves to be *my* advocate. This is why I felt compelled to test you so."

Wagner, disappointed, conceded with a shrug.

"Well, if you're not up for the adventure, what can I say? I've got to respect that. If nothing else, maybe my 'dangerously naïve faith' helped to get us past a few walls of our own. The question is, can we keep it that way?"

"If you seek my fellowship, *Voknor*, then you have it."

Wagner nodded wholeheartedly, relieved to at least have achieved that much.

"And," she continued, "since a friend is entitled to offer unsolicited advice, here again is my own: Quit this ludicrous fool's errancy that you call an escape. Reject the notion before you find yourself too late in regret."

"Conditions to our friendship already? What's up with that?"

She looked at him like he should have known better. "Of course not. But consider for a moment how awkward it will be for me to converse with only your dissevered head affixed to a pole in the Great Arena—which is likely to be the *least* severe of your punishments once the NuRacs frustrate your designs and drag you and your band of foolhardy go-alongs back here."

"Your faith in my cunning is overwhelming, J'nea. Anyway, what could be more severe than a noggin-skewering in front of a stadium chock-full of bloodthirsty spectators?"

"For one, they could hand you over to Skol."

Skol. It was not an unfamiliar word around the camp. Actually the more common appellation for Tamek's Sunderer—the daemon whom it was said the NuRacs kept vaulted in the Great Arena's substructure—Skol was reportedly so murderous a creature that no one who'd ever come up against him in the ring had lived long enough to provide any reliable account of him. That this wasn't entirely true mattered little to the Ergosians. There existed enough spooky veracity in the Sunderer's mystique to make for excellent legend; and, in a culture of predominantly spoken tradition, such was the stuff of evocative entertainment. Skol's appearance, his size, his savagery—most of what went around the camp was the typical hearsaid mix of overspeculation and embellishment. In fact, as the tendency was to mystify him as more of an entity than a fleshy being, both of Skol's names had evolved into metaphorical catch-alls for anything remotely associated with a looming threat, a punishment, or some particularly painful demise. Bilahdu made occasional use of them; Balgor, equally so, although with him they more often than not served as qualifiers for bawdier topics— gastrointestinal vulgarities and such—that were never lacking amid any plebeian population. Even Tamek reserved Skol's name as garnishment for his most acerbic censurings. With such ubiquity, Wagner now found it curious that he'd not queried all that much about the creature behind the name until this very moment.

"Skol is no evil spectre, *Voknor*," J'nea explained, "and certainly no faceless bugbear of one's imagination run rampant. He is a ruthless predator, an abomination that should never have been allowed to slip from the ungodly womb that spewed him into this world."

"Wow," said Wagner. "Don't take this the wrong way, but for someone who holds such a dim view of a certain Sentinel from Vishkor, your diction and his can be uncannily similar."

She shot him the ired glare again. "Already you seek to try our fellowship?"

"I asked you not to take it the wrong way, didn't I? No need to get all bent out of shape—"

Just then, the horn sounded for general lockdown. Both Wagner and J'nea, jogged by what they assumed was precipitance on the part of the trumpeter, took inventory of their surroundings and were surprised to find that the courtyard had significantly emptied during their apparently rapt intercourse. Gone unnoticed was the scullery crew's clearing of the meal-site vestibule, the changing of the guard along the ramparts overhead, and the very grounds around them succumbing to the sprawl of tall-shadowed twilight. Atop and beyond the western parapets, the departing Cinjal had gathered up the last of her brilliant train while a brooding night roved in unflaggingly from the east.

"I think it's time to vamoose," said Wagner.

"Aye," said J'nea. "Reveille will sound all too soon." She turned to go, but stopped in mid-stride. "Ask Balgor for further elaboration on Skol, if you wish. He can tell you nearly as well as I."

Wagner nodded appreciatively, and set off for his billet. J'nea thoughtfully watched as he disappeared into the torch-flickered interior, the din of its vociferous occupants briefly muffled by his passage through the entry, and resuming as loudly as before with his gradual recession into the foofaraw of gamblers, boasters, boors, and hardcore warriors that, when properly assembled, comprised one of the most durable and successful gladiator stables in the camp.

Turning, then, for her own quarters, she caught sight of one of the evening trusties in the midst of lighting the successive cressets along the inner walls, and the larger ones about every pertinent ingress. Waving acknowledgement to him, day-shifter to night-shifter, the flame-bearer responded phlegmatically, as one might expect a once estimable individual who'd been leeched of his vibrancy to respond. Like most in the camp, he was a man without prospects, a fellow whose best and only comforts lay crumbling in increasingly dusky memory. Quietly and in passing, J'nea observed as he went about the mundanity of his duties, not so very different from her own. Alternately, she thought about Wagner and his nescient hopes and his raw enthusiasm, and how said qualities had yet to be driven out of him as they'd been from this dispassionate trusty—and from so many others in the camp. She looked at the cressets, at the walls, at the strolling sentries overhead, just as she had for week upon week and month upon month. Then, coming before her own barracks, she stepped stoically past the grate and slipped silently and unnoticed through the boisterous throng, toward the little pallet of straw that had been her bed for so very long.

Over in Barracks Five, Wagner had woven his way through the clusters of chatty cohabitants, carefully snaking a path around the tumbling dice and bigratto jackstones tossed by feverish gamesters bent on squeaking in a few more rounds before roll call. Noting Balgor's engagement in the usual braggadocio, and Tamek's immersion in more subtle causerie, Wagner slid without ado onto his bedroll, laced his hands behind his head, and revisited his and J'nea's most telling exchange to date. Staring at the dancing shadows that the torchlight unleashed upon the flurry of overly pantomimic yarners, he found his thoughts animated with equal rampancy, the images of impending escape unloosed in his head like a riotous crowd a-scramble in righteous purpose. For the moment, just getting free of QieLahr would be enough for him. Once liberated and distanced from the camp, then would he fix upon what to do with that freedom, and on which designs to focus in order to gather up the reins of his personal quest.

As energised as he felt, as bright and invigorating as his idea of the future seemed at that moment, he was nonetheless flagged enough by the day's practise to facilitate an unhampered segue into meditative drift. Long accustomed to the nightly Mardis Gras around him, it had become an increasingly more facile process—especially when fatigued—to manoeuvre his mind into the realm of semi-consciousness, to find and to be drawn into the frangible inner calm below all the outward sensory assault, simply because the release of aggression through the free time activities of his peers held but limited attraction for him. The excitations of his scheming, the voltage from his "J'nea encounter"—both of these set aside, he achieved the mild contemplative transcendence that in the past had been so difficult to establish in pervasive proximity. Tamek an old hand in the technique (he used it regularly every morning, every evening, in both raucous surroundings and solemn ones), he'd been too happy to supplement Wagner's earth-based methods with his own. The Sentinel's extreme spirituality making meditation requisite for his ultimate fidelity, certainly a lifetime of such ritual had its advantages.

Novice that Wagner was, however, the drowse of sleep soon beset him like a hungry lioness in sneak upon a straggling rhebok. He'd delayed its overtaking him for as long as he could, evaded it, outfoxed it, hovered along its fringes for as long as was possible without succumbing; and, in so doing, he'd managed beyond inadvertence to trigger a few unexpected visuals. A brusque and unexpected slicing, dicing, and julienned enticing of the same ilk of fragmagery that had cued up so regularly pre-transference, what now flashed before him were more than mere resuscitations of old visions; rather, they were bindings of both canned and new footage, projected like two films, one atop the other, a living montage of his most fruitful periods of bendering juxtaposed by softer, more inveterate idylls that sorely conflicted with the frightful stuff of norm.

Sifting the layers of simultaneousness, he believed himself in the company of strangers who, as indicated by their dress, were earthly and contemporary. A much greater industry of people around him, the closer notables were three in number, unfamiliar of face yet somehow intimate; youthful, and yet oddly attritted as if by overriding ordeal. Two were female: one, swarthy, the other, ashen. There was also a freckled lad, gangly and callow. These three stood approximate to Wagner as he addressed the crowd in unpremeditated dreamspeak, with Wagner feeling more largely in localised hover above his body than actually within it. Yet, as it was all occurring on the cusp of his subconsciousness, there was no purpose in questioning the sensation, nor why he seemed to feel less directly an agent of his words than he did an instrument for them.

Too difficult to eradicate the accompanying stream of visional miscellany, Wagner tarried about the edge of sleep and pre-slumber for a trice longer, and then simply, dissatisfiedly, let the lioness have him, submitting fully to the jaws of dreamless repose.

When AuwNiir's guards entered the barracks a short time after, Wagner lay corpse-like upon his bedstraw, oblivious to the nudge of the tallyman's boot as he was crossed off as number twenty-seven on the headcount parchment. While it wasn't mandatory that one be awake and attentive for the roll, it *was* uncommon for a snoozer not to be roused with a kick or a thump from a spear-butt for no other reason than intimidation and general meanness. But, this sentry leaving Wagner undisturbed for the most part, he finished logging the rest of the occupants (whose dice and bigratto tokens were suddenly conspicuously absent), and officially declared a satisfactory sum to the sentry prime.

Had this NuRac even the most miniscule inkling of how, in the near future, number twenty-seven might be one of three prisoners hied off on his watch, he surely would have done more than merely nudge the sleeping Wagner for all the admonishment and stripping of rank that AuwNiir would mete to him and his fellow guards. But then, there was no cause for such speculation short of unborn premonition. Escape from the prison was nigh unto impossible. Everyone knew that. It had always been so. And as far as this NuRac imagined, it always would be.

FIRST INTERLUDE

Thirty kilometres to the south of QieLahr, on a forestal high ground that overlooked a great circumspection of flickering watch-fires, a lone man shook awake under a weighty grip of manacles. Quickly gazing to the moon for bearing, at catching sight of it through the boughy overheads he soughed relief beneath the champ of soggy rags that gagged his mouth. His wrists raw, worsted by shackles whose chains coerced his frontal enfoldment around the largest and stoutest of the surrounding kekona trees, he tried the irons and found them too ungiving to allow him the merest alleviative slump.

Angling his chin against the bark, he probed for a jag or outcrop that, with industry on his part, might serve to dislodge his muzzle. Finding none, however, he abandoned the notion and instead began searching about, scanning the copse to his right and his left until finally his eyes registered a mannish silhouette, partially reclined against a log not ten paces off.

Detecting no animation from the figure, the captive strained to make his discomfort known, slapping fecklessly at the bole with maddened palms. Once, he tried—twice. Nothing. In his third effort he clapped as jarringly as his pitiable leverage allowed; and here at last he succeeded in his intent, for the shadow not only started, but rose forthwith and made towards the Promethean with gravest dispatch.

"Can you...comport yourself?" the ambulant asked as he slipped the gag from between the man's teeth.

The prisoner grimaced and smacked his gums in order to entice sensation back into his lips. "Aye," he rasped. "Unbind me."

Extracting the pins, the keeper allowed the manacles to spill to the dirt. The freedman, at once vigorously massaging his hands and wrists in order to liaise circulation through his newly uncrimped flesh, suddenly flumped clumsily onto his buttocks from unanticipated wooziness. Not far away, a nested rook offered up a territorial caw—unusual for the late hour, but hardly out of keeping with that species' crabsticky temperament.

"The encampment is nearly abed," said the keeper as he meticulously remarried each pin to its untenanted clevis, and then neatly gathered up the chain. "Once more, they suspect nothing."

"My gratitude, Jotal." The man rose and placed a hand on the other's shoulder. "We have much to do, old friend, and I fear that time is no longer my ally."

Jotal clamped reverently onto the man's hand. "I know, master. I know."

CHAPTER FOURTEEN

A consistent man believes in destiny,
A capricious man in chance.
 —BENJAMIN DISRAELI

Wagner opted not to reveal to his friends the complete nature of his dialogue with J'nea from that evening. Perhaps a mistake, perhaps no mistake at all, if the scheme's culmination required his riding roughshod over one or two regrettable indiscretions, then so be it. After all, seeking out fellow subversives in the camp was a hit-or-miss proposition; nobody wore a sign and no one advertised his availability on the open exchange. On the other hand, going outside Tamek's and Balgor's channels and trying to strong-arm J'nea into his confidence had been an act of intentional recklessness, no matter how perfect a choice he felt she'd have been. That his hunch had failed to pan out in its intended manner was, however, *classic Wagner*, for at no time in his life had anticipatory planning proved any more influential in shaping probability than had good old eleventh-hour improvisation.

The decision to hide his imprudence from his co-conspirators was not an easy one, but certainly he couldn't reveal such rashness to the headstrong Sentinel for fear of having Tamek shut the plan down altogether. Confessing was akin to schemic suicide, the potential ramifications of his divulgement being all that Tamek would need to shelve the escape indefinitely, to resurrect Wagner's "infidel" besmirchment (only recently laid to rest at Balgor's request), and to leave Wagner a reluctant casualty of the very games he plotted to avoid. Not forgetting that Tamek had never truly favoured the plan, nor that he was not himself a risking member of the proposed trio, he had nevertheless gone way beyond the call by devoting a considerable block of his time to the cause for reasons both charitable and personal, and Wagner simply couldn't risk endangering this generous endorsement if, in its success, it might actually deposit him outside the walls. By omitting, then, the pertinent details of his exchange with the trusty, he avoided Tamek's hammer and anvil of sermon and admonishment for disclosing to an "undesirable" the precious itinerary for his and Balgor's potential freedom. Although by all counts a renitent stepfather to the caper, Tamek's had become the task of rearing, shaping, overseeing the fledgling plan until such time that its wings could be tested, taking Wagner, Balgor, and the as-yet unnamed accomplice with it. And if to maintain that assistance Wagner had to ride J'nea's trust-worthiness for a fall, then he would go right on pretending that all of the colluding and the conspiring was still the privilege of three people, not four.

Being a man of conscience, however, the conflict was destined to linger at length within Wagner's multifocal scruple. Compunction, pretence, honour, obligation—while he struggled beyond good faith to remain mum for the nonce, he found it more taxing here than in his previous life to keep the truth secondary to his desperation, especially since there were people's lives in the balance. On earth, he'd lost the love of a woman because of unconfessable goings-on; here, under markedly different circumstances, he was imperilling the only people who'd invested in him, simply because he'd misjudged a woman's inclinations. It was his error—not theirs, not hers—and like a blackguard, like an unfaithful husband, he would agonise over his lapse in judgement for fear of losing the whole megillah. He wasn't proud of the decision. But neither was he perfect.

Sleeping through the night like a babe didn't make him feel any better about himself. He'd awakened more upbeat than he probably had a reason to be, resigned to just this one amorality and no other; and he went about the pre-palaestral routine as if all things were just as they should be. He thought of J'nea as he trudged out to the courtyard. She'd surely been up and about long before the official barracks roustings, carrying out her usual servility of pre-dawn tasks. He likewise rethought some of their exchange—her testing of him, his dumping the unexpected on her—and couldn't help but to maintain a loftier impression of her than either his carelessness or his failure to entice her partnership could drag downward.

"So, what did you say to her?" Balgor asked, inching forward in the breakfast line and addressing what he perceived in Wagner as coyness. "Surely you did not engage her in conversation for to tickle her fancy. Were you attempting to wrest from her some cruciality of tactical information—or were your motives indeed more prurient than you would have me believe?"

"Yeah, that's it," said Wagner, copping to anything but the truth. "But I think she misread my intentions. After Fostoch's big, bad, wolf act, I think she'd had all she could stand for one evening."

"*Wolf*?"

"Yeah. Aggressive, deceitful, rakish—take your pick. That's what we call guys like him in my realm. Actually, though, it's kind of a misnomer, because true wolves—like your night-hounds, I suspect—are far purer in their primal dignity."

"Qualities that Fostoch has yet to embrace."

Wagner grabbed a crock from the stack and held it out for a trusty to slop porridge into.

"I guess maybe I owe the wolves and night-hounds an apology."

"Aye. Fostoch is far better likened to the figari."

"Why's that?" said Wagner, disguising the fact that he hadn't a clue as to what a figari was.

"Because he climbs like one. This is why we call him the Agile One. Trees, ropes, vines—I even once watched him scale a siege tower from the *under*-side of the ladder, simply so he could be the first man across the hoardings atop Prince

Huleor's doomed castle. This was back when he ran and raided with Juthac of Orrd, and I, with Mirko of Vargath."

"Rivals or allies?"

"At the onset, Juthac the Vulgar and Mirko battled the NuRacs independently. Eventually, however, they joined forces. Fighting the common foe—including Prince Huleor, an Ergosian who consorted with the NuRacs—this made Fostoch my ally. A worthy warrior he was, I cannot deny it. But he was also quite unpredictable, and this oft-times made of him a dangerous confrere. He and I were no more than cousins of the sword. To this day, we embrace very differing attitudes on life and war and honour to satisfy a true definition of friendship."

"I hope your methods of soliciting female companionship are a bit more genteel than his, too," said Wagner, snatching bannock from the common basket and plopping it into his rapidly congealing breakfast.

"Ah, my friend, were you to witness my felicity with the maidens, the ease and grace with which I enamour even the most reluctant flowerage, you would do naught but weep for your own mediocrity."

"I'd be weeping, all right—but I suspect that it would be from laughter."

"Perhaps," Balgor said drolly. "But then again, it would be *you* on the outside, *Voknor*, a sword without a sheath—and I, the fortunate blade, oiled proper and tucked away for the night."

"Yeah, yeah, if you say so." Wagner sat down and carefully studied the gobbish contents of his bowl. Farina, fatty bacon, and molasses—he pressed a probing finger into it and watched as the meat renderings seeped into the impression like seawater in an out-scoop of beachfront sand. "Yum," he said. "Done to a turn, just the way I like it."

As he and Balgor ate, they partook of their usual morning routine of ribbing and boasting, and only after the realmson had proven himself beyond doubt as the better braggart and reparteeist did their conversation make the transition into escape chat. Here they continued on with what had become an extensive, preparative checklist. They reviewed the hints and how-tos for eluding NuRac security; they strategised on the safest and fastest modes of traversing uncharted city boroughs; they debated on where and when it would be best to cross the walls to the outside. Each topic, discussed at length yet nowhere near as precise as it needed to be, was subject to endless revision, for only with the perfect tempering of rigidity and flexibility would it ever hope to succeed beyond its first leg.

Not far into the confabulation they were joined by Tamek, who had negotiated his way through the multitude of breakfasters to complete the three-man clique that had become so customary of late. It spoke to the Sentinel's influence around the camp that no one dished too much about these reticent gatherings, even as the three of them tried to make their reclusiveness appear more fraternal than furtive. That they'd been clanking their heads together for the past week or so had not gone unnoticed, and yet the most popularly drawn conclusions ranged anywhere from the friendship that truly existed alongside the projection, to Tamek's presumed interest in the fledgling Wagner for whatever vestige of bruit he may have possessed of current affairs in the free realm. Wagner being an oddity, a man of varied customs and perspectives—and a seeming patron of the Vofspars—most of the Ergosians were happy to let the Sentinel attend to matters of inquisition, and they thus stayed their distance for these reasons. Most were certain that, in good time, they would be apprised anyway.

Across the yard, those prisoners who had been the most dilatory in meeting the new day now filtered from the barracks to claim their stakes in the dwindled mess line. Among them was, of all people, the ineffable Bilahdu, who rarely arrived late to commons but whose reason for it became at once clear. Having apparently been early to the toggery, he now stood in sport of a pair of marvellously fabricated trousers of which he was uncontainably proud. Spacious and accommodating they were, stitched of coarse threading through reinforced welts, lashed with secondary bindings of far sturdier fare than what the camp weavers typically invested. Some small faction of insurgents evidently having finally tired of Bilahdu's high-decibel ravings, they'd evidently gone behind head-sempstress Skagra's back to provide her mate with a premium pair of made-to-orders whose generosity of pleating looked rigorous enough to withstand the dexterous heft it was designed to encompass. Were Skagra indeed the hell-hag of Bilahdu's description, then surely the transgressors would be facing her wrath the very minute that word of their deed got back to her.

Stranded in the meal line with Bilahdu stood an unfortunate handful of captively hungry people, each of whom was already cursing his poor timing in coming to breakfast. Stuck in queue, forced to listen to Bilahdu singing the praises of his comfy new breeches, it was all that these poor souls could do not to forsake nourishment altogether. Feigning interest, nodding deafly to whatever the lusty fanfaron claimed, each centimetre nearer to the food vat was that much closer to a full bowl and wing-footed flight. It was the most tortuous (and torturous) conceit from the most congenial blowhard in all the camp. The worst, however, was in store for those who'd joined the line behind him. To these would Fate be far less pleasant, for their progression was completely dependent upon Bilahdu's lolling idle that moved the file along only by the coincident fits and starts of some new point or topic. His inevitable transition out of pants-chat, while greatly anticipated, proved particularly painful; for, with nary the shame nor the abashedness of the average person, he steered the conversation into overly candid health matters, kicking off with his most recent bout with foot fungus, and from there, moving steadily up his anatomy, affliction by lovely affliction.

Several heads back of Bilahdu's increasingly cataleptic audience stood Fostoch of Orrd. Brooding and visibly perturbed, this was the Agile One's first public appearance since his dousing. Deeply preoccupied, enough even to filter Bilahdu's exuberance out completely, the Orrdian put his biding to use with a series of shifty gazes about the yard. Scanning the access archways, the wash area, the commodes, and the general locale surrounding the detention block and beyond, he was arguably looking for signs of his comely humiliator. But J'nea, being no kitchen trusty, wouldn't have been present here, not yet, and Fostoch surely knew this. While she indeed had occasional doings in the gaol block, her morning duties typically took her one yard over, to the palaestra, where even then she was probably busy raking the sands, sweeping Grum's dais, or weeding the armoury's inventory of any implements requiring repair or replacement.

Up before Cinjal—as always—the trusties routinely claimed the pre-shift plundering rights for the first breads and biscuits of the day, which they spiritedly snatched up hot from the bakers' ovens and slathered with jams or gravies or flavoured oils, long before any gladiator stirred from his straw. This was an extravagance that common prisoners lacked the benefit of, and perhaps rightly so, as it was clearly no easy thing to be a trusty, to operate as the in-betweener for both the capturing *and* captive sides, neither of which showed particular fondness or respect for them or their duties. Some perquisite was therefore necessary (*else why be a trusty?* as Balgor noted).

Serendipitously, this day had brought the trusties the extra recompense of a cutting of praneez, one liberal meting apiece. Praneez, a spice whose savour Wagner likened to a blending of earthly cinnamon and ginger, was the dried stipe of a plant of the same name. A welcomed treat in powdered form for gruels and breads, in stalk it was prized most for its humectant properties, which were substantial. Placed on the tongue, suckled for hours, it was second only to water for staving one's thirst when natural hydration wasn't feasible. It was therefore a precious commodity around the camp, especially in the summer months. As it was with cigarettes in earthly stir, praneez was golden, and many trusties made no qualm about bartering their ration in return for personal favours, information, protection, and such. The more charitable and self-reliant of recipients shared their distribution with friends, kin, the infirm, or potential suitors. Needless to say, when the palaestra trusties returned from their duties on *this* morning, Fostoch would definitely not be sharing in J'nea's allotment.

At breakfast's end, J'nea indeed sauntered in alongside five of her peers, filed through the porridge line, and then split off singly in the direction of the wash area. Setting her food down, she ran her head under the sluice, wrung her hair, and plopped down in the early sun to dine. Most of the population had by now commenced to clearing out, turning in their empty crocks and ladling refreshment from the kilderkins stationed along the meal-site vestibule. Fostoch, however, chose to quench his thirst at the source.

Wending daringly across the yard, he skirted directly behind the trusty. She was settled comfortably, her knees drawn in to help support her bowl and bread, her tousled hair drying in the breeze like streamers in a department store fan. The Orrdian, passing her asquint, seemed expectant of some small measure of acknowledgement—an apology, a demand for *his* apology, anything. He tramped on when she didn't comply.

A woman of perception, however, and keen to her surroundings, J'nea knew exactly who was skulking behind her, knew without having to lift her eyes. Ignoring Fostoch's intentionally noisy guzzles and incessant throat-clearings at the sluice, she continued eating, her gaze on everything save him, her praneez untouched and tucked neatly through her vest's lacing.

Wagner watched their silent drama from on the move, he and Balgor and Tamek in trudge toward the stony corridor that would lead to yet another day of regimented manoeuvres under the uncompromising eye of Grum the Taskmaster. Curious as to whether or not Fostoch's and J'nea's mutual stand-off would conclude with the Agile One having to justify his sobriquet by dodging another flying bowl, Wagner lagged around the exit for as long as he could before the en masse migration to the palaestra swept him through like driftwood in a flood. Whatever the outcome, he would have to hear about it in gossip.

With a single exception, the day's training proved largely unremarkable. Repetitive, taxing, and sweltering, void even of Bilahdu's periodic seam-burstings (the diversionary hilarity of which became all too evidenced by their absence), when the horn sounded at day's end it seemed to most of the prisoners that a full week had passed since the first nodgers were lifted in spar that morning. With an approximate hour of sunlight remaining, the weary Ergosians turned in their weapons and vacated the yard, eager to trade bodily exertions for verbal ones, their natural inclination for ungoverned banter finally given its free rein. Any and all retorting, derision, beefs and curses and general flap-jaw that hadn't been uttered underbreath during the afternoon could now find moderated release, starting with the ever popular go-round of "badmouth the Taskmaster," an insult game that permitted a quick and highly satisfying venting before moving on to more pleasant and constructive topics.

The access tunnel astir with the echoes of lively voices, Wagner found himself in the midst of conversations as diverse as one might ever find. Some prisoners, still immersed in the day's martiality, rambled on about the upcoming tournament. Others talked of games long past. Still others reflected over fallen comrades and argued on the futility of it all. One or two imaginative ones spoke to the bitter Ergosian-NuRac clashes that were surely taking place on the outside, perhaps even at that very moment, whose outcomes would hopefully lead to eventual rescue and to the destruction of QieLahr. As many scoffs as there were "hear, hears" in reply, the patriots had nonetheless spoken from good conscience, unlike some of their detractors who, having kibble for character, were the very loafers who wiled away their time in the overindulgence of dice and cozenages and scurrility—and who, amassed, were scant more than honourless clods, brimming with grasshopper folly and bogged in trifles that kept company with neither future or past. Yet, more influential than these oafs were those few folks who could dispel the common angst with but a reverie, who could dissolve the trials of enslaved life with a single memory, who could sway even the thickest lout with the things that wit and good will and nostalgia could bestow. So close to mealtime, these souls— of whom Gamühr the Bard was one—usurped the conversation with simple food-talk, with nothing more complex than a few descriptions of tempting culinary fare from their former households and regions.

Using vivid description, they soon had almost everyone in swoon for the bounties of home. The most succulent foods, the aromatic, the plentiful—with imagination and wishful thinking did each find means for rekindling images of steaming platters dished out to familial gatherings in the humble and unforgotten simplicity of stony, firelit hovels. Presented with these phantasy table settings, laden with the visual spoils of harvest and hunt, each of the enthused was free to spice and supplement from his own memory. Sauerbraten simmering the day long in sweetened vinegar marinade, wedges cut from wheels of hard cheeses the size of NuRac shields, crusty breads risen high on the oven-brick, and flagons of black plumwine or steaming mugs of praneez cider—these were passions freely doled and distracting enough for the nonce to sway the crowd's mood from one of self-pity and despair to mouth-watering wistfulness. Clearly these people loved good food, but more so, this little game served as a kind of psychological hypo-injection into better times, a fix to make the abuse and deprivation of their present state bearable. The family repast had meant much to them on the outside—*this* Wagner had learned early on. And in thus revisiting their memories, many managed to overcome the frustrating prospects of a camp diet that provided adequate enough sustenance but without the love and care that went into the meals of old. By this reminiscence would they be able to retain their cheer beyond the "lentil & vrohda surprise" that awaited their exorbitantly whetted palates.

Wagner supped on his ragout in his own company. Tamek having been abruptly summoned before the Tribunal just prior to quitting time, it was assumed that he was off representing the infinitesimal Ergosian interest in some new edict or policy that would see ratification whether he objected to it or not. Balgor, too, was otherwise engaged, but his was a deliberate surrender to his rodomontading countrymen whom he'd been neglecting too long in klatch. J'nea was third on the M.I.A. list, as she'd been yanked into service a few hours earlier to aid in the catering of meals to the detention block. Earlier in the afternoon, she'd been seen husbanding some of her free time in combative pursuits, scrimmaging against varied opponents—even Bilahdu himself—so as to hone a very evident fighting prowess. And while trusties were not generally candidates for the arena games, a person never knew when demotion or disfavouring circumstances might land her in the ring. To simply shrug away such possibility was a foolhardiness that no one could afford; to fail to prepare for it was a fast ticket to the Sacred Pool. For J'nea, the advantages of keeping sharp far outweighed the complacence that privilege sometimes instilled in a domestic slave over time. Slothfulness, too, was a pitfall to many whose non-martial duties seemed to all but exempt them from life-threatening ordeal. But to stare a wild crovik in the eye before thousands of bloodthirsty spectators, and further, to be armed against said creature with weapons and tactics of only peripheral acquaintance—there was little on the face of Ergos that was more frighteningly defining than this.

Augmenting her side arms capabilities was of particular importance to J'nea, for her personal expertise fell more in the category of archery, which for obvious reasons was not a branch of warcraft that the NuRacs were eager to make available. Tried once, it had proven too labour-intensive an undertaking. Long-range weapons, even for something so benign as target shooting, made the parapet guards understandably nervous, and the inordinate safety measures ultimately demanded more resources than the stable-owners had been prepared to remit pocket-wise. There was nevertheless a high number of exploitable, wager-worthy toxophilates among the captured, and it pained the more enterprising owners to see such untapped lucrativeness go to waste. J'nea herself, the second-born daughter of an arrowsmith, had on occasion underplayed to Wagner what was, in all probability, an exceptional fortitude with the bow, and as such it owed much to NuRac foresight that she and her kindred dead shots be steered into some other discipline.

In a way, Wagner found it comforting to know that not every Ergosian was versed to unparalleled competence in every weapon of the culture. Brutal circumstances having indeed coerced most of them into upgrading from the pitchforks, the scythes, and the other agricultural implements that, in their free lives, had been handy for on-the-spur adaptation in isolated skirmishes, it was at the same time fascinating to note how some of the nastiest of their contemporary armaments had patent ancestry in basic farm tools. As former croppers, tinkers, and traders who'd been shanghaied and transplanted and then outfitted with more lethal versions of their sickles and whittles, the Ergosians were slowly being made over into fighting machines—and Wagner wondered if the smug NuRacs even suspected the far-reaching consequence of their devisings. In these times of pendency and forced adversity, survival was a wild stallion that every prisoner was made to mount and ride. It wasn't all that inconceivable that one day they might just ride off altogether. J'nea's initiative alone in acquainting herself with the breadth of the armoury's complement was a construable means in Wagner's mind for undermining one's enemy by its own permission. This was true of the entirety of the gladiatorial training itself. Like inmates in federal penitentiaries who are given license to beef themselves up with weights, there comes a reckoning when the gaoled pose serious threat to the gaolers. Wagner coming in later in the game, greener than anyone, maybe it required the knowledge of two worlds to be able to glean the lesson in this.

Dwelling on J'nea's brief exercise on the palaestra, Wagner harked back to breakfast, wondering whether she and Fostoch had ever exchanged words—terse, apologetic, or otherwise. All that Wagner knew for sure was that when the Orrdian finally made his entrance onto the practise field, there'd been nary a flinging of porridge bedraping his sourpussed mug—which wasn't particularly conclusive either way. Having demonstrated no outward indication of anger, humiliation, or disappointment, the Agile One promptly obtained a nodger and shield, and then threw himself headlong into the morning fracas with a man called Minosh—who would himself share incident with Wagner not long after.

Wagner's fighting of late had suffered due to preoccupation. Bilahdu had warned him beyond incessancy to stay sharp, as had Balgor, yet with all of his machinations coming together so quickly it was difficult not to allow future scenarios to override the present ones. That everything had progressed as far as it had on nothing more than an unswerving resignation to get free was sometimes too good to be true—although he knew that ideals and intentions were unrelatable to true actualisation. Fortunately, his distraction befell him little consequence throughout the morning hours, mostly due to his sparring with several regulars whose styles no longer held much surprise for him. But he received his wake-up at just past the noon hour by way of a rather baleful swipe to the forearm, delivered by a faulty nodger whose "blade" had become splintered by a previous impact. The man in wield was none other than the aforementioned Minosh, Wagner's then-current partner of rotation; and although bloodletting was obviously common-place, unavoidable, even excusable given the hazards of combative drills, Wagner couldn't quite shake the feeling that there was relish—if not calculation—at its core here.

What came next was equally disheartening. In breaking off momentarily, both to assess his laceration and to request that Minosh replace his failed implement with one more sound, Wagner suddenly came under incursion by what seemed an unscrupulous knave intent on proving his prowess. With mercenary zeal, the Ergosian launched himself at Wagner without quarter, bullying the unguarded newcomer quite nearly to the ground in an unwarranted act of malice that fast attracted the attention of their immediate neighbours.

Shocked but undaunted, Wagner regained his poise and rebuffed a subsequent advance with the aid of one of Bilahdu's most elementary techniques. Flummoxed by Minosh's motives—*was he put up to it? was he simply a roughneck? did he take issue with the low-key celebrity that Wagner appeared to share with Tamek and Balgor?*—Wagner was forced by distraction to fall back on instinct. Unable in the heatedness to effectively integrate into his defence either of Balgor's or Bilahdu's mantras on the art of mentally disciplined fighting (which he had assured them had become second nature to him), he lashed out in the inimitable, inimical style of his first and last resorting. One part novice gladiator, one greater part madman, it wasn't so much a matter of his *Other* assuming control as it was Wagner reaching inward and drawing from that dormancy, bidding it come hither, and—through such previously inaccessible coagency—retaliating against his honourless assailer with the might and main of a bona fide warrior.

Balgor's and Bilahdu's expert instruction notwithstanding, when it came to squaring up against an underhanded opponent and his tactics, Wagner found Minosh the immediately superior teacher. His opportunism went beyond mere flagrancy; his callousness surpassed the incredible. His teeth so clamped in grimace and his sword arm flailing with such ferocity, one would have thought him a ruddy-faced maestro conducting some particularly treacherous orchestral movement. He barrelled at Wagner, his shard-fraught nodger awhirl, thinking to avail himself of a swordsmanship that from the onset outclassed the fledgling Wagner's by years. Still, it was a demonstration that he was destined to regret, for he could in no way have suspected the unforeseeable complexity of his opposition.

His intent apparently not to rout Wagner utterly, but to thoroughly dust him as Balgor once had, Minosh appeared to be looking for a means to bowl him over and humiliate him before the yard. Wagner likewise recalling his first day, how he'd been supplied a true weapon to counter Balgor's prop, on now seeing himself in an arguably reversed facsimile of that situation, he decided that his best defence be one by his own terms, with a weapon of his own choosing, and preferably one with greater distancing capability so as to avoid further scathing.

Fully over his initial surprise, beyond his distress, he'd graduated now into perturbation, and he aimed to give his enemy proper what-for in the most decisive way possible. Personal grudge or random venting, Minosh had committed a grievous error, and Wagner vowed to show him the magnitude of that error. Swiftly side-stepping the Ergosian's next lunge, with a quick eye and a curt apology Wagner reached over and snatched a quarterstaff from the hands of a skilled young woman whom he knew as Darzah, and in a seamless right-about that defied even the most arresting scrutiny, he swung around and with one solid crack brained Minosh right through his defences, smack-across the skull.

Minosh went down like a sack of yams. The harsh report of wood against bone so sharp as to make Wagner think that he'd shattered the man's head, he would later breathe relief on hearing that the damage was less than it had seemed. Minosh had been stopped *cold*, not *dead*—and arguably as much by his own incredulity as by the concussive physics of the blow. Lying there in sprawled defeat upon the sand, his spectacle was at once morbid and burlesque, the comic stupor in his coma needing only some supplementary bird twitterings to emphasise his foray into la-la-land. More to be heeded, however, was the colossal knot on his head and the blood that trickled circuitously through his choppy scalp.

In the wake, a pitilessly frustrated and visibly ired Wagner loomed over his attacker. Quarterstaff in recoiled readiness, even with Minosh out for the count Wagner stood poised like an avenging fury come down from the heavens to deal a miscreant his deserved deathblow.

Checking his animus, however, Wagner drew deepest breath and expelled all remaining inclination toward retribution. Within seconds he was again himself—cooler, recomposed, relaxed in underpostured sobriety, his rage and anxiety falling away like the perspiration that dripped from his brow. Yet, not without a tinge of malice for the unconscious blackguard at his feet, with judiciousness light and swift he put boot to the man's haunch—a glancingly harmless kick to serve as a crowning postscript to a tale of backfiring perfidy. Turning, then, to Darzah, he begged her indulgence and placed the staff back in her grasp.

The skirmish, while riveting for the front-liners, hadn't drawn the complete field's attention. Such squabbles being common fare in any forum of contesting bodies (and egos), while hardly escaping Grum's notice it seemed to have been little more to him than an errant spark in the greater conflagration, probably undeserving of anything more than a personal notation to see that Minosh received low marks for going south under the simplest and most easily evaded countermeasure. As for the rest of the yard, most had been privy only to the finale—and this unavoidably, given that the blow to Minosh's cranium was not only distinctly audible, but chillingly resonant. Balgor having been one such spectator, from well across the palaestra he'd howled and yowled in delight of his friend's quick solution.

In sum, Wagner's laceration proved superficial, its greatest consequence being that of a reminder of how crucial it was for a warrior never to drop his guard, even in mock battle. Not bothering to visit the infirmary, he'd instead bummed a dab of glohular from a peer and let it go at that. He didn't exactly thrill to the prospect of the infirmary anyhow, his initial experience having manifested enough bizarre phenomena to dispel any notion of setting foot in there again for anything save the most life-threatening happenstance. Besides, the yard trusties had found no other recourse but to drag the semi-conscious Minosh away to Papa Olask for the once-over—and Wagner had no great longing to be there when he finally came to.

Between slurps of his evening stew, Wagner made a casual inspection of his wound, by then hours old. Although the gash lay protected under the pale greenish film, the glohular itself had become contaminated by the day's dust and sand, and was sorely in need of removal and reapplication. Examining the rest of his body, it displeased him to see the innumerable nicks and cuts and scars that flecked his extremities at every exposure. Each one an irremovable badge of skirmishes past, collectively they were testament to all of the instances where, like that afternoon, he'd been unvigilant before an opponent. He felt a bit chagrined that he'd managed to acquire in a few weeks what many of his fellow prisoners had taken a lifetime to amass. On the other hand, in complexion he could now pass for a native Ergosian—even an inveterate fighter—and such induction was not lacking in its advantages. Nothing to be done about it anyway, flawless skin was a vanity better left to his previous culture, for it certainly had no business here.

It was amusing, however, to note that a few of those epidermal souvenirs weren't resultant of his captivity at all. Some of them had in fact been garnered back at the Howsley Centre, during his pre-phase era, when busting pell-mell in trance through a slab of sheetrock or a glass partition had made for some pretty nasty self-inflictions. With no ready stock of glohular in Jon Mazzio's pharmacy, the nurses had instead expended many a yard of gauze, sundry barrels of antiseptic, and countless needles and threads to preserve and ensure Wagner's ability to wreak havoc all over again on the next go-round.

"I see that your friends are too intimidated to sup with you this eve," a voice suddenly rang, front and centre.

Wagner looked up to find J'nea stooped before him. Her nose and cheeks besmirched by dirt, her fragrance far from its most pleasing, clearly she'd been made to toil the last hour or so in some unnameable foulness.

"Yeah," he said. "You step out of character for a second, and all of a sudden you're a crazed lunatic."

"No 'of a sudden' at all," she said. "I told you as much last night."

"Different context, different kind of lunacy."

"Ah." She lowered herself into a squat. "Are you saying that madmen are allowed to selectively define what constitutes their madness?"

Wagner bit down on a splinter of bone. Annoyed, he spat it out to the sand. "Ouch. I think some madmen are. The ones who aren't mad per se, but rather simply obsessive about something."

"Like *escaping*, perhaps?"

"Maybe." He swallowed. "You know your face is dirty?"

"I would hope so," she said. "I had the grand displeasure of descending into a detention cell to confirm the death of an unresponsive offender. It was not the most pleasant chore of the day."

Wagner paused mid-chew. "And...?"

"He was as near to the veil as one can be without passing through. Emaciated by infirmity, he had not even the vigour to respond to the guard's inquiries." She shuddered demonstratively. "Who would not become ill in such a place?"

"You don't have to tell me," Wagner said. "That could easily have been me, and not so very long ago. I'm assuming that you got him out?"

"Aye, but with neither grace nor satisfaction. A noose slipped about his sunken torso, it required the sinew of but one topside man to gather him out."

"And now?"

"He rests under Olask's care. Quenched, fed by force, his wounds dressed, there is still much doubt as to whether he will survive. He was too afflicted, too infected. Why, his lungs alone sounded to me as if he were drowning in his own humours. Do you know, *Voknor*, that he was once as strong as any of us? But he had been down there for a long time, considerably longer than any in my recollection."

"What did he do to warrant that?"

J'nea rose up to leave. "He was overheard talking of escape."

Setting off for a shower, her words remained for Wagner to chew on along with his stew. He knew at once that this had been her intention, and once implanted in his mind he couldn't ignore it. Picturing that poor wretch in the cell, it wasn't too much of a stretch to visualise himself in that position—a rotting, crumbling man in a cavernous oubliette overrun by cragworms and dung beetles and disease. Whatever the big deal that Balgor made out of Skol the Sunderer's ability to dissever and disembowel a man in seconds flat, or how some Ergosians were made to go toe-to-talon with whole packs of froth-spewing carnivores, Wagner couldn't help but to think that as excruciating as dismemberment, beheading, or even the lethal chomp of fangs through one's throat must have been, any one of these was far preferable to the months-long agony of gradual whither and decay.

After J'nea finished laving, she threw on a light but oversized tunic (acquired beforehand from the toggery), snuggled into an equally fresh pair of trousers, and carried her soiled articles back for laundering. The tunic's spaciousness serving to dulcify her, it bedraped her more like a maiden's shift, temporarily belying the tautness of her athletic build. Even with her coarse galligaskins underneath, it was the most conventionally feminine that Wagner had seen her short of complete divestiture. Her favourite vest rounding out the inelegant ensemble, after breezing through the meal line it actually seemed that she intended to sup in Wagner's company. Just shy of intersection, however, she suddenly veered away to connect with some of her trusty friends, sitting twenty paces removed. Not an act of stand-offishness, however, there was prudence behind it that soon became clear: Tamek had entered the compound and was even then in beeline straight for Wagner.

Noting the exigency in the Sentinel's face, Wagner stood to meet him.

"Where is Balgor?" Tamek asked.

Wagner pointed at the machismo fest across the way. "Over there," he said.

The Sentinel turned. Singling out the realmson, he waited until he caught Balgor's eye, and then motioned for him to join them. Uncommunicative until he had both before him, it was here that he hit them with new complication.

"We have grave trouble, my friends. There has been an occurrence on the outside, some ilk of unpropitious incidence that has given our enemy invigoration enow to recall five entire regiments from the field."

"*Five regiments!*" Balgor was astonished. "Could they have conquered us utterly?"

"Nay, I do not believe so. The climate within the Tribunal, howe'er, was far too galvanic for my liking. By their pregnant gloating, they would have me thinking that the power in the realm has shifted e'en more greatly in their favour. But they would not reveal any more to me than this. What I do know is that there is to be a celebratory assemblage, two days hence, upon the Monarch's palatial esplanade. And this brings me to our quandary."

"The escape?"

"It must be executed tonight," he said. "Or not at all."

"We're not ready," said Wagner.

"Then quash it, *Voknor*. For on the morrow will the first of the recalled troops issue into the city. In a matter of days, QieLahr will have swelled like the brood sac of a spit-hornet queen. By then, any chance you may have had will be forfeit."

Trading glances, one man to the next, each searched for resolve in the other one's eyes. Finally, Balgor spoke.

"As it is, because of the potential for treachery, we have yet to recruit a suitable cohort to accompany us. Now, at this late hour—and given the gravity of this new information—I can think of but one whose skill would benefit us, and whose current frame of mind might be receptive to our entreaty."

"Just tell me it's not Minosh," said Wagner.

"Minosh?" cried Balgor. "*Bones and entrails!* He is a knave and a dullard! I would not trust Minosh to drop his own trousers before voiding. No, I speak of Fostoch."

Tamek winced. "The Orrdian? I cannot agree. He is barely more reputable than Minosh. Ne'er have I considered either of them trustworthy."

"We need not trust him with *anything*," said Balgor. "Not if we impress him mere moments before we ourselves commit."

"What!" cried Wagner. "Just spring it on him? What if he declines?"

Balgor shrugged blasély. "Then we do not go. But I do not believe that he would decline, *Voknor*. Forget not, I once fought alongside this man. His lubricity is not limited to his physical proclivity. He is an oily fellow all around. A debauchee, an emotional usurer, a scurvy profligate clearly stultified by NuRac inhibition—as well as by his public derision at the hands of that peppery trusty—can you truly doubt that he would not leap at the chance to escape? I would even wager that, once he hears that *I* am willing to venture the risk, he will all but trample me asunder that he might be first over the walls."

"Sounds like just the kind of guy I'd want watching my back." Wagner, only slightly more convinced than the Sentinel, knew that options were short. "One big problem, though. Fostoch is billeted over in Barracks Two—not with us."

"That can be remedied," said Tamek. "But you must first assure me that you are both in concurrence."

Balgor and Wagner eyed each other. Acquainted for only a few weeks, friends for nearly as long, their camaraderie was nothing if not rich in simple regard. A Dark Ages *Odd Couple* most of the time, on occasion they could just as easily have passed for two scamps grown up in the same village. Even the most diligent observer needn't have taxed fancy too far to imagine them fast in their youth—a pair of hellions conspiring in boyish prank upon the corner costermonger, or as two truants hieing off to the swimming hole when there was manure to be spread or crops to be gathered. But the truth was that their backgrounds were as diverse as they could be. The bridge of their commonality was a construct of their own making, new but surprisingly sound, with slat after slat laid in mutuality and with high latitude, all tethered under one man's extraprovincial insights and the other's contemporarily archaic mores.

"I'm for going," Wagner said. "If it's our best, *only* chance, then I'm taking it."

"And I," said Balgor, "have been pining much too long for one of Lar of Grönborg's finest stouts, for his hostel's glazed caliboar and onioned praties and flötberry torte. I have dreamed of just one morning being roused by the melodious chipping of a coppice warbler rather than the bellow of Uthok's crovik-like snores. And how I have longed to reunite with my gentle Celsira, the fairest maid in all the realm, to feel her willowy tresses upon my chest and to have her desirous gaze mix with mine under a waxing yellow moon. For these experiences would I allow myself to be swayed."

"Charming," groaned Tamek. "But 'tis likely, my idyll-clinging realmson, that the caliboar are sickly and stringy this year, the praties, blighted, and fresh flötberries, far and few. And although the sweetness of the warbler's song may e'er endure, know ye that the ravages of war and want may by now have so sullied and embittered this fair Celsira of yours as to leave her soured to your touch—or long surrendered to another man's."

"Then let the krehak take her!"

Both Tamek and Wagner gazed at him in surprise.

"Oh, she was naught but reverie anyway," said Balgor, waving his hand. "Just a timeworn phantasy who has outlived her purpose. But one thing that you failed to dismiss, my good Sentinel—and why would you even try, eh?—was the surety of how our lusty kinspeople would scarcely forsake their love of a good Lar of Grönborg stout. Hardship or not, I would wager that much of what grain they reaped was reserved for the brew, brew that no doubt flows copiously even now in every surviving inn and alehouse east of the Langöde. And I intend to be hefting a pint of my own before the week is at end!"

"Sounds like a resounding 'yes' to me," said Wagner.

"Aye—it is," Balgor averred, "so let us have a go at recruiting the Orrdian ere the gods return me my good sense."

The next few hours loped by discourteously, a percipience born not only of the angst and haste of their preparative scrambling-about, but of Time's own unchivalrous penchant for oppugnancy whenever some mortal sought to bend it toward his own convenience. Luckily, Wagner had but one task to complete for the team—an unexpected one, and yet perhaps the most basically vital charge of any. A cruciality for which Tamek provided him both the agent and the instruction, it would be up to Wagner to perform it unseen, sans practise, and without any foremeasure of knowing whether he'd executed it correctly. In most circumstances, it was a deed that the Sentinel would surely have carried out himself had he not a bigger fish to fry in Fostoch's persuading. As it was, between the conspirators and their last-minute recruit they would all be running at metabolic overload until sometime early the next morning, when the three fleers would either be long on their way to Vargath or long returned to a dungeon cell— or worse—while Tamek was left to work rumour control and to feign his best ignorance to NuRac inquisition.

Balgor was currently the least occupied of the trio, and rightfully so. Until eventuality saw him and his cohorts afoot and racing for the walls, his duty in the barracks remained one of discretion, for he would be carrying on his person the means by which the group would brazen the walls—means that weren't easily disguised as a staple of common prisoner attire. Days prior, he and Tamek had purloined through subornable trusties the least dilapidated of the detention block ropes; Tamek had also commissioned the fabrication of a makeshift grapnel, fashioned from the unlikeliest of sources—an iron barb from the caravan drays, a blacksmith's holdfast pilfered from who-knew-where, a partial bracket from one of the torch supports—all cobbled together in manner so outwardly ungainly that only someone with the skills of the earthly Batman himself might have success in catching it on anything. When presented to Balgor, his initial response had been uneasy laughter followed by incredulity; yet, in realising that it was the *only* accessory he would be getting, the realmson resigned himself to it, and simply put stock in the smith's say-so that it would endure his roughest abuse. If nothing else, it had improvisatory potential as a hurling weapon or bludgeon.

While Wagner and Balgor were engaged each in his own commission, Fostoch of Orrd found himself yanked into the shadows outside of his barracks by hands intentful and gruff. The yard at the time having yet been a fair bustle of blatherers and grumblers, no one witnessed the abduction, nor did anyone miss the morose Orrdian who, taken aback by the shanghaiing, showed immediate lack of receptivity to the Sentinel's offer, and in fact cut him off mid-pitch—prior to the details of accomplice or device—to let his distaste be known.

"You must be japing!" he cried. "You whisk me into the shadows for to recruit me into some pathetic coterie of your devising? *I* should voluntarily ally myself with your boggle of nincompoop cronies and cheerfully embark upon the most hopelessly doomed of all endeavours? And all this without preparation or design? Are you daft?"

Tamek bit his tongue; ordinarily, for such a comment, he would have taken the man's head off.

"Preparation is complete," he said. "Design is complete. I give you my word that both are viable. But unpredictably, the hour is upon us, and the portal for success, limited. All you need do, if you have any strong desires to be free of this place, is to provide that which limb, stealth, and daring may offer."

Fostoch glared at the Sentinel, his eyebrows raised in wait for the punchline that the larger man had obviously forgotten. Tamek countered with arched brows of his own, and only after a long and loaded moment of nothing save impermeable eye contact, the Orrdian finally understood what he was meant to understand.

"No, no, no," he said. "This is not like you, Sentinel. This is utter nonsense— nay, beyond nonsense. You of all people know that this is not how surreptitiousness is suggested."

"'Tis admittedly an untraditional approach, Orrdian. But, can you deny that such is precisely the quality that makes it unforeseeable to our captors?"

"Gad so! But why come to *me*, Sentinel? We are not friends, you and I. We are not even remotely affined. Your lack of regard for me is all too patent. To my knowledge, we have only conversed a single time—and then only so that you could berate and condemn me for preferring tangible spoils over spiritual. Nay, I do not fit the niche of your usual toadies. So why this? Is your scheme in need of an expendable gudgeon? A lackey?"

"Fine," said Tamek, turning and withdrawing. "I *told* Balgor that you had not the courage to join him. I *told* him that you had lost your nerve long ago. Why, e'en yon slip of a trusty proved as much with the trouncing you took by her wee hand."

"Balgor? So! He and the south-realmer—they are not merely the contributors, but the participants! That is why your three heads have been as one both day and night?"

"It matters no longer, infidel," said Tamek, mustering his every reserve to refrain from swatting the belligerent for the flea he believed him to be. "Go," he commanded, waving backhanded disregard, "go and delight in all of the 'tangible spoils' that NuRac imprisonment heaps upon you."

Fostoch leered at the departing Sentinel. His ire up, he vacillated between providence and acumen, between disdain and simple pride. All the while, Tamek kept walking.

"Hold, Sentinel!"

Tamek halted, the triumph on his face unnoticed by the Orrdian behind him.

"You say that Balgor is one of your—" Fostoch caught himself and peered around nervously, waiting to proceed until he'd closed the distance between them. "He is one of your associates? And it was *he* who nominated me?"

"He advocated you from the start," said Tamek, not moving but rather forcing Fostoch to come to him. "Truly, I know not why. I had dissuaded him thus far because I believe you to be untrustworthy. Yet, when time failed to produce any more reliable ally, again he suggested you. I suspect, howe'er, that he did so only because of his regard for your alleged prowess in battles past. I do not believe he admires your misanthropy any more than I."

"No matter," said Fostoch, "for he himself is a loudmouth and a lickspittle. I do not have to be his brother to conspire with him."

"And I have informed you that the conspiring is complete. We require only a capable body, and if it be not yours, then we will surely find one more suitable. Personally, I feel that e'en a dead body would prove more contributory in the abscond than *you* would."

"Then you sorely underestimate me."

"Not unless mine eyes are failing me of late. By my witness alone I would venture that a dead man surely could have finessed J'nea more artfully than you and all of your honeyed beguiling."

"Enough about that wench! Stow your mockery, Sentinel, and instead relay to me the details of this hastily birthed scheme, that I might consider it more soberly."

Fostoch was a sneering package of ego, irritability, and unscrupulousness wrapped up in largely tatty, unfestive trappings. And while not a man into whose hands it would ever be sage to entrust one's reputation, one's wife, one's purse, he would probably suffice—and most likely excel—as a co-subverter in a secret enterprise whose intricacies just so happened to be tailored to his skills.

In the end, Tamek had to hand it to Balgor. The realmson had so pegged Fostoch's inability to allow his talents to be seconded or put to question, that it left his recruitment a decision impelled by personal vindication rather than by good sense. The leverage seemingly in Tamek's favour, the die was all but cast. However repugnant he found Fostoch, however sceptical he was (and would remain) about the affiliation, however hesitant he was to sign off on the escape itself, he wasted no time in clueing the Orrdian in on the manner of how the affair would unfold. Its projected course taking him and Balgor and Wagner smack through QieLahr itself, its final escalade to occur at some remote end of the city proper (where inside fortification was minimal)—the premise proved no less fantastic to Fostoch's ears than it inevitably would to the NuRac citizenry the following morning.

Divulging the plan in its entirety could do little harm at this late hour, since Wagner and Balgor had agreed that, without a third player, the whole shebang would be scrubbed with no one the wiser. The time factor likewise gave Fostoch no presentable evidence for NuRac intelligence should he have been toying with notions of treachery, the itinerary being so intentionally last-instant that he'd have little more than his own dubious word to offer them. Worse for him, in the wake of any such consorting there would be no escaping the inevitable reprisal at the hands of Tamek's and Balgor's compatriots due to the very belief that none but the Orrdian possessed foreknowledge of the trio's machinations. And Tamek made certain that he knew this.

"How long before I must commit?" asked Fostoch, his early suspicions overrun by all that Tamek had just thrust upon him.

"There is no unreasonable hurry," said Tamek. "The span of—oh—ten broad breaths should be grace enow."

Fostoch guffawed. "Ten breaths! You jest!"

"Pshaw! Now you have only nine remaining. Contemplate with greater care, infidel. The hardier your lungs, the greater time you have for deliberation. Oh, look—yonder goes J'nea! How fortunate that she has not yet retired this vesper, for she is the next among my candidates to—"

"I am in!" Fostoch spat the three words so quickly that they rang as a single syllable. "You are mad, Sentinel. You—all three of you—are irrefutably mad! But, count me in nonetheless."

"Ah, capital!" said Tamek, over-the-top in gloat. "Follow me, then, for we have much to accomplish ere to lockdown."

Setting off toward the barracks with Fostoch in tow, he halted abruptly and pressed the Orrdian back at arm's length.

"Stay thy distance. If the camp thought for one moment that there existed anything common 'twixt us, we would suddenly have a hundred unsloughable scrutinies fixed upon our e'ery action."

Daggers for eyes, Fostoch fell in behind the Sentinel at a distance more discreet, mouthing silent insult the entire time and nigh to the point of rethinking his decision.

Coming through as promised, Tamek had already a solution in mind for the billeting quandary, and this he spared no reserve in implementing. He intended to use a "double" from Barracks Five (his own lodging, as well as Wagner's and Balgor's), who was to slip into the Orrdian's quarters to pose as an early retiring Fostoch, while Fostoch mirrored the switch in said man's bedroll back in Barracks Five. Both men keeping low in the other's straw, blanket overtop, the only real worry would lie in the nightly muster—and whether or not the NuRac tallier's temperament inclined him to provoke a sleeping man or leave him be.

The decoy, named Kadok—who, had he lived on earth, would by Wagner's assessment have been equal to a street punk—was a fiery and naïve young headstrong, just over the cusp of adolescence. Wagner wasn't at all sure how Tamek came to choose him—or how he would have selected *anyone* for that matter—since playing the part of the shill had unavoidable discovery written into it. Not merely a risky caper of immediacy, it was guaranteed to be repercussive the very moment that the NuRacs revisited the headcount in the wake of the trio's bolting. As unpleasant as life in the camp was, it would become even more unliveable for whomever they found out of place. Yet, *there* was Kadok, with his barely passable resemblance to the Orrdian, tossing caution aside and dutifully slipping into Barracks Two ahead of the greater throng, burying himself under Fostoch's bedstraw and feigning oblivion until dicing and dialogue gave way to the final roster—which, by providence, was recorded without a hitch, with the ledgerman taking little notice of the counterfeit Fostoch but for to note another body in the log.

Only slightly earlier, back in Barracks Five, Wagner had haunted the interior entryway like a restless spirit, trying his best to appear unassuming while he waited for the proper moment to accomplish his charge. Nothing out of the ordinary, it wasn't uncommon on the sultrier evenings to find him hanging about in said manner—although admittedly at later hours—to reap what benefit he could from the barracks' limited corridor of cross-ventilation. But it was not the cool zephyr that he waited on this night, not the sweat-dispelling draught that the billet's rearward loopholing sometimes succeeded in luring through, but rather a bluster of another sort—that of a more human windbaggery. It was distraction he was after, the incidental, inadvertent distraction of tempers and quarrels that, in this element, were predictable enough that they required no staging. No different than the Howsley Centre's Parker Brothers, it was a simple matter of probability, of reliability, that someone in the ignominious bigratto crowd would every few minutes erupt in squawk. It was a fact and force of their natures. Cheater or cheated, scammer or scammed, poor sport, poor winner, or plain old loudmouth— any and all were bound to raise a ruckus over some failed gambit or perceived act of skulduggery. And the moment that they did, Wagner would make his move in relative trust that no eye would perchance choose to concern with him.

As anticipated, he hadn't long to wait. When feathers finally flew and the hubbub peaked with raucousness enough to command every ear and eye, he slipped from his tunic the pale, spongy substance that Tamek had given him, and inserted it squarely into the gate's strike. A seemingly organic material, almost cartilaginous, it was slippery and pliant and kind of creepy all in one, and it fit conformingly into the very orifice where, imminently, a NuRac key would shortly seat the deadbolt for the night.

Whether a familiar mainstay of previous escape attempts or something that a camp scrounger had just come upon or devised, Wagner could only hope that the Sentinel knew what he was doing. Although locks and keys on this world were immensely less complex than anything of contemporary earthly utility, a comparable mechanics still applied; and if the foreign matter was meant to obstruct the deadbolt's travel, then Wagner couldn't comprehend how even an inexperienced turnkey was expected not to notice the difference.

No matter, however, for with Tamek only just returning after indenturing Kadok, and the lockdown guards due at any moment, the time for aborting consisted of an increasingly undestractable dwindle of seconds. En route to his bedding, Wagner passed the masquerading Fostoch—doing a better Kadok than *Kadok*—playing dead to the world under a thin veil of chaff and NuRac wool. His face obscured by straw, his future obscured by a straw-in-the-wind's indeterminacy, the next few hours would be the ink and quill to either the legend or last offices of three foolish men. If, in this countdown of moments, he'd considered a change of heart, if he'd grown at all perturbed with himself by his coerced contract with Tamek or with the same's manipulations, he knew he would be angrier had he stayed behind and the others been successful. He hadn't appreciated the last moment invitation and the manner in which his impatience and his ego and his surly unconformity were leveraged so artfully against him. Not to be outdone, however, he would take lesson from Tamek's cunning, and keep a lid on his own penchants until circumstance found him far enough beyond QieLahr to ditch his momentarily indispensable cohorts.

It wasn't clear whether Fostoch's relatively easy coercion was spurred more by his disrelish for other personalities in the camp or by the dangling carrot of escape that had suddenly become graspable. Hesitation being just as frequently one man's downfall as it was another man's saving grace, for Fostoch the Agile One—whose downfall to him was the shrunken facsimile of Ergosian society under a conjunctive NuRac thumb—he'd had his fill of rules and proprieties. The entire realm was meant to be his oyster, not this stunting microcosm of surrenderers and go-alongs. The spoils of the freelands were far more appealing, far more copious; and the accountability for *having* at them, far less compensatory. Without even knowing it, this was what the Orrdian had been waiting for, and he cursed that he'd not been the one to conceive it. Yet, as it seemed to have risen subsequent to the south-realmer's arrival, Fostoch couldn't help but wonder if together the three conspirers were privy to bruit that no one else knew, that perhaps this *Voknor*, as a go-between, had brought some vital news from the outside that mandated a personal and immediate response at any cost.

Regardless of what met the eye and what didn't, four overly anxious hearts drummed staccato discord as the first of AuwNiir's flunkies came passing through the entry. Clutching a halberd, the sharp-featured woman moved to one side and stood sentry while five of her peers filed in behind her—two with swords drawn, two with crossbows, and one with a slate. In what would otherwise have been the typical nightly routine, in watching the recorder proceeding up the aisle, approaching ever nearer to the feigning Fostoch, Wagner finally understood how his old Stretch Armstrong action figure must have felt, elasticised to the limit so many times back in childhood, for he himself felt such extreme torsional wracking in his nerves that it made him briefly sick to his stomach. It was a moment of pendency that he would never forget. He did, however and happily, find all six of the NuRacs considerably less on edge than normal (one might even have said they were bumptious), and odd or not, this was at once a good thing, for the tallier whipped through the roster in the manner that Bilahdu ripped through trouser seams, passing the low-lying Fostoch without ado and wrapping up counts with nary a sidetracking, a berating, or a reason to level the most minute warning at anyone. It could not have been a more benign run-through had Wagner choreographed it himself.

During the pins-and-needles ordeal, Tamek and Balgor had played it coolest. Veterans that they were, the Sentinel sat reclined on his heap, head on hand, observing everything and nothing with his best peripheral disinterest, while across the way the realmson lay convincingly abed, ostensibly drained by the day's grind, even going so far as to offer up the occasional yawn and stretch to suggest that nothing in the world concerned him more than personal recoupment. Wagner, in his diminishment by such staunch professionalism, did his best to disguise a nervous tic and a restless fidget, while Fostoch—arguably the most operatic in his acting—lay facing the shadowy side of the room, fronting just enough grunt and wallow in his prostration to sway his captors into thinking him nowhere near comfortable enough to incur the customary boot to the buttocks that they so enjoyed awarding to the most complacent slumberer on whom they happened. Yet, even as the schemers passed muster, their pounding chests had only scant respite, for the deciding factor was yet to come in the measure of Wagner's little act of entryway sabotage.

Still in doubt over how his door rigging would convince, Wagner bound his faith to Tamek's innovation. If indeed the guard sensed anything unusual, investigation was sure to follow, and such would effectively deep-six their launch to freedom quite literally before they could get out of the gate. Yet, if by some supernal decree it went unnoticed, and the gate appeared firm and fixed by whatever degree, wouldn't the deadbolt still be fractionally embedded in the strike? And Wagner, being fresh out of jimmying credit cards (which were only employable with latch bolts anyway), he wondered how they were going to dislodge the gate at all.

But, to Wagner's great astonishment, the NuRac turnkey passed off his initial—and manifest—difficulty with the slide as a fault with the key itself. It was obvious that the mechanism wasn't tripping properly, for he withdrew the key, searched the ring for another one, tried it, and with little improvement he grasped and rattled the gate's moorage a number of times to ensure security before hustling off to join his withdrawing peers. Tamek quickly glanced at Balgor, who nodded to Wagner, who flung gestured perspiration from his forehead before turning a reverent eye on the Sentinel in homage to his irrefutable cunning. The slippery Fostoch, too, snuck a peek from the guise of his possum-playing to sneer in the face of so-called NuRac superiority.

Still, as planned, no one budged for two solid hours—not an easy task when one's adrenal glands were revving like a couple of hopped-up muscle cars throttling up before the hanky drop. When Tamek finally deemed that ample time had passed, and all but the three escaping members were asleep, he crept thief-like toward the entrance, careful not to disturb the bedded multitude around him.

Peering through the iron latticework, he surveyed the yard as best he could, and stood immobile for an excruciatingly breathless interim before turning finally to signal the conspirers. Like spirits unbound they rose up in summons, and, drifting through the darkness amid sleeping bunkmates and ill-placed bedpots, they congregated in a semicircle about the entrance. It was here that Wagner was delivered his answer.

Tamek procured a small flask from out his tunic. Once uncorked, he squeezed its liquidy contents about the strike, recorked it and handed it to Balgor. The realmson duteously snuck it into his own raiment.

"Dispose of this along your route," Tamek whispered, "where it will not be prone to discovery."

Here, they did nothing but bide for a few moments, waiting for *what* Wagner could merely suppose. Then a creak sounded. It was a chirk of pressure and stress, metallic in nature, and not dissimilar to the emanations produced by furnace ducting in thermodynamic expansion and contraction. Wagner stared at the lock, seeing nothing but undoubting that something was taking place.

Within the minute, Tamek braced himself and took a bar in each hand. Then, like Big John of earthly song, he emitted a groan and a heave, and displaced the gate out-and-out from what had clearly been but a fractional engaging. With calm and precision, he swung the ingress gingerly inward. Looking back to ensure that no Ergosian within had been significantly roused or disturbed, with a miniscule, fishhook-shaped tine he retrieved a vastly increased piece of cartilaginous matter from the strike. This, too, he gave to Balgor with similar instruction.

Wagner was most impressed.

What came next was akin to a blind leap from a precipice. With nothing left to bar their mad dash for freedom, anything beyond the merest footstep outside the barracks was pretty much a commitment, a point of virtual inevitability. Although it was true that Tamek would delay re-engaging the gate until he was certain the trio had ventured a course beyond retreat, at some determinable moment he would need to do it so that the patrols on their rounds would find everything in seeming order. The escapees understood this only too well, and by their unflagging intent they would waive their right to renege.

The breeze in their faces, with a parting gesture to the yet-reluctant Sentinel, Balgor and Wagner lavished upon him all the respect that any mortal, infidel, or friend could bestow for what had been an indispensable role in the scheme. Then, like hounds on a blood hunt, three brash and foolish men up and bolted into the darkness—Balgor with his truss of rope and his grapnel, Fostoch with his baggage of weighty delusions and self-indulgences, and Wagner with his high-minded hopefulness that the world of Ergos had more to hold for him than servility and slavery.

CHAPTER FIFTEEN

We must take the current when it serves,
Or lose our ventures.
  —WILLIAM SHAKESPEARE

Visibility outside Barracks Five and beyond was patchy, and suitably so, the artificial illumination (or lack thereof) in any given recess or alcove due more greatly to inconsistencies in wick-trimming than in actual cresset placement. A boon for the trio, they filed through the darkest nooks in stealthy confidence—Balgor first, then Fostoch, Wagner to the rear—with no exchange of words, and relatively few of glance or gesture. With the realmson concentrating on the strategies of the point position, the others relied on a deliberate, conscious extrusion of every intuitive and interpretive faculty at their disposal, scurrying when Balgor scurried, freezing when he froze, veering direction on a whim like geese in flight. Punning aside, it was indeed just that—an airless flight across grounds that might at any moment erupt in the cries of discovery and the footfalls of a hundred soldiers racing to intercept three foolish and doomed dissenters. But no surprises sprang at them from out of the blackness, no armoured warriors with swords a-gleam and pikes in point; and likewise, their skulking failed to rouse the attention of those guards who so mechanically paced the catwalks or who made small talk with each other on this, another seemingly unremarkable tour of the night watch.

When Wagner and his Ergosian cohorts reached the portion of eastern wall that was most conducive to ascent, they halted for momentary composure, pressing themselves like Greek columns against the stony curtain while diligently examining the area they'd just traversed for signs of trouble. Thus far, Luck had been an amicable chaperone, but she gave no guarantee that the escape route would not suddenly beset them with unwelcomed hazard.

Wagner, in an effort to augment his concentration, had given his biology almost exclusively over to optics, dismissing the remainder of his senses as unreliable in the pall of his generally energised state. His heartbeat, galloping through his eardrums with a rhythmic discordance that falsely mimicked the steps of rapidly encroaching soldiers, was matched only by the rasp of his breathing that, by his own perception, made the scuba-tank whooshing of cinematic villain Darth Vader's respirator seem like little more than a whistling nostril. These vexing phenomena were, of course, limited to exaggeratedly internal impressions; but nothing could convince Wagner of this as long as he himself believed them to be so overwhelmingly intrusive.

Studying then, as he did, the parapet overhead, it became clear that at least one portion of the scheme's theory had proved sound, for little sentry activity existed at this end of the prisoner residency yard. Granted, an occasional NuRac passed them topside every few minutes; but aside from this, only a limit of defensible attention had been assigned to this juncture. Neglected in requisite torchlight and occulted just enough by the jut and indent of its architecture to advance possibility into probability, the wall was in essence their portage between the landlockedness of castigation and their estuary to freedom; and although it was far from the only dangerous milestone in their ordeal to come, crossing it would certainly bolster their resolve to go for broke.

After an insufferably lengthy pause for proper timing and gumption-culling, Balgor finally made his move. With the rope still coiled about his waist and the grapnel tucked handily through it near his tail bone, he began feeling about for grips and footholds in the brickwork. Regrettably, with the night so clement and the city beyond the wall virtually free of the noises of late night industry, the level of audible distraction was insufficient for masking the clumsy clanks of a grappling iron in heave. It therefore became necessary for one of them to scale unaidedly the eight-or-so metres to the nearest corbel. From there, said man could then affix the hook that would permit the others the ease of shinning the rope to the top in relative silence.

But as Balgor jerked himself up to the first hold, Fostoch stopped him. The two of them then exchanged several sharp bursts of hand gesturing in an act of communicative byplay that probably claimed origin in their legionary days with Mirko of Vargath and Juthac of Orrd—where furtiveness commonly demanded the most severe constraints of silence. From Wagner's vantage, it was impossible to distinguish what it was that Fostoch signed or objected to; yet, when Balgor unexpectedly withdrew, permitting the Orrdian to perform the initial ascent, it became apparent that both of their logics deemed Fostoch the more experienced climber. With no true bruising of ego, no sense of stolen limelight, Balgor's evident respect for Fostoch's abilities—if not his character—allowed him the equity of stepping back, even as he'd been fully prepared to lead had the Orrdian not intervened. This truly admirable restraint and presence of mind did nothing if not fatten the respect that Wagner already harboured for his comrade; and, taking stock in the realmson's confidence, Wagner turned to continue his surveillance of the camp while Balgor unravelled rope and hook and passed both of them over to his Orrdian stand-in.

When next Wagner looked around he was amazed, for in the space of a few seconds, Fostoch had achieved the corbel with dispatch sufficient to have done even one's friendly neighbourhood Spider-Man proud. Seemingly defying gravity beneath the soffit, another few seconds saw the grapnel firmly attached and the rope in groundward spiral like an errant spaghetti noodle. Then, as Balgor shinned his way up, Fostoch pretzelled his legs around a portion of the outcrop and, with an abdominal-wrenching upswing, righted himself just enough to grasp the ridge of the catwalk and peer over its edge for NuRac activity.

The walkway apparently free of trouble, Fostoch quickly disappeared over the lip, where he performed a stealthy roll and pressed himself belly-down, waiting for the others to join him topside. Directly beneath, Balgor hefted himself with a gymnast's fortitude, cramming his stockiness deep within the eave, his feet and elbows locking through consecutive supports. Peering down then, he waited for Wagner to complete his own ascent—which he did, if not gracefully or with the finesse demonstrated by his cohorts, then in the steady and largely formless plugging of his novitiate. Balgor extended a hand at the last half-metre, drawing Wagner up and negotiating him like an overstuffed marionette to an adjacent support. It was an action that evoked Wagner's memory of the Vofspar female, whose similar act at a faraway cirque had cost her so dearly. Clinging to the perch in his recovery, he refiled the memory so as to frustrate potential distraction. Any renewed responsibility that he felt for the Vofspar's fate would have to be penitence for another day, as currency demanded his utmost focus.

Across from him in the blackness, Balgor worked deftly to untangle the makeshift iron from its mooring. Extending himself then, as Fostoch had previously, he passed the precious grapnel up and over to the prostrate Orrdian above him.

With a clear avenue atop the parapet, Fostoch rose and affixed the hook to a post and dropped the rope through one of the interior crenels. Balgor and Wagner then scrambling onto the banquette, the former passed the Agile One and rapidly rappelled down the interior side, followed closely by the latter. Once they'd both made ground, Fostoch, still above, loosed the hook, collected the rope, and lowered the iron earthward and back into the realmson's hands. Next, he himself descended the wall just as he'd earlier conquered it—by hand, foot, and grit—for he knew the trio couldn't afford the chance of being unable to jostle the grapnel free should all three have abseiled in like manner.

One monumental and fleeting victory under their belts, they now found before them a single dirt bailey separating the wall they'd just crossed from the more rudimentary barrier that served as the principal curtain between city and prison. Since this was essentially an interior wall—and not at all the eleven-metre obstruction of QieLahr's greater curtain—it was at first reckoned an easier prospect to traverse. But this was before they saw it up close. Although roughly only five or six metres in height—its stonework consisted of a uniformed bond of smoothly hewn blocks mortised with such precision as to present Fostoch with a challenge daunting enough to diminish his last success to sophomoric calibre. The first to scurry across the bailey, on confronting this new hindrance he quickly set at finding the least stymieing means of bare-boned escalade.

But it was not to be—at least not at this periphery of the city limits. Faced, then, with the prospect of scrambling blindly along the shadowy footway for some promise of more accommodating access farther down, Balgor wouldn't allow them to lose heart. Through signing he suggested that, short of panicking, they first try to achieve their empyrean travel here, via pyramidal means. Fostoch wasn't at all keen on this idea, but as their frames—if properly orchestrated—would indeed put one of them at the wall's apex, he agreed to proceed rather than squander valuable time in debate. Prudently then, with the brawny Balgor in squat as the base, Wagner took instruction and clamped himself first onto the realmson's back, and then atop his shoulders. From there, Balgor pressed up like Atlas of old, coming to full stance with little difficulty. This, however, would be kinderspiel compared to the next step; for as Balgor—already taxed—leaned into the stone, the eager Fostoch scrambled up as an ant might scale a bridge fascicled of its horde's conjoined bodies. A sudden and crushing weightiness for Balgor, it was more a battle of stability for Wagner; but he, too, clung to equilibrium by pressing into the wall at an angle commensurate to his friend's, compensating as best he could for the falter produced by Fostoch's upward lurches.

In moments that seemed all of hours, it was at end accomplished. Fostoch found the means for affixing their hook, and as Balgor regained his wind below, Wagner discovered his second one, and clambered up the rope with robust surety.

Within a few minutes, the escapees had straddled the wall and were back on terra firma on the edge of civilian NuRac turf. Balgor—back in full lankness—had this time been the last man down, and with this lesser wall he'd simply unhitched the grapnel, extended himself from the lip, and dropped quietly to the ground. Once assured that its covertness was yet intact, the trio raced a rapid course through dingy back alleys and along dimly lit thoroughfares, all the while scouting for sentries, constables, and ordinary pedestrians—anyone whose presence could jeopardise the success of their *sui generis* departure from their gladiatorial confines. Unversed as they were with the layout of the city, they advanced with only negligible disorientation—their occasional need for backtracking likewise posing no dire inconvenience, as the city's insulae had been engineered in common quadrilateral measure, with sidewalks, alleys, and municipal accesses cross-cutting at regular intervals through each. The streets were unmarked, but a spotty consecution of shoppe indicia and ornamental façades provided the men with identifying markers for their unready invasion of the downtown grid.

The sally went almost exactly as planned—even better—for a considerable distance; and while this might have lent itself to misgivings of some compensatory reversal later, no one had the fool's luxury of overthinking his own predicament. Occupied with their infiltration, darting in and out of back ways, they skirted the mercantile districts—where foggy bakery windows were already aglow from the pre-dawn bustle of doughy-fingered, flour-tossed industry—and then progressed unflaggingly through the bowels of the city, heading with nary a hindrance in search of some lesser guarded portion of the pomerium, where the potential for penetration was optimal.

Emerging at a fortuitous point along the southern wall, they happened upon an opportunity that—while not the most inviting means of egress, then certainly the least *uninviting*—offered an accessible upstep of risers that led to a portico high atop an ornamental balustrade. From there, a facile access to the inner curtain's rampart, an anchoring of the grapnel, and they would be well on their way across the outer ward, with only the shorter curtain left to cross. A series of simple steps, a means directly before them, said route would require little more than their previously established brazenness and a short measure of fortitude, and soon they would be ransoming their shackles for shelterwood.

With prudent restraint, however, they stayed themselves, holding to the shadows, studying the situation like old lip-scarred fishes eyeing a suspect lure. The pattern of sentry activity above and below being far less than they'd expected, it seemed a little too easy, and for several overly calculating moments they could do naught but look to each other for some manner of consensus on whether or not to commit.

Yet, after three sentry passes—each spaced five-or-so minutes apart—they concurred that this was an exploitable fluke, an understandable laxity of interior defences; and, as such, it would likely be the most promising route they would find. Resuming, then, his original role as lead man, Balgor took back the grapnel. Quickly recoiling the rope in expeditious elbow-and-crook-of-thumb fashion, he scanned the pomerium in both directions. Then, like a kid darting streetward for an errant ball, he scurried across the parade and vanished into the shadowed side of the risers. Nothing subsequent, Wagner promptly copied the launch, joining Balgor seconds later in the blackness across the way.

A minute then passed, with Fostoch failing to appear from the alley where all three had made pact. Two minutes went by, two-and-a-half. Balgor and Wagner, bewildered, could only speculate as to the reason. Conceivably, some soldier or townsperson had unexpectedly entered the alley from the far street, forcing the Orrdian to abscond momentarily. On the other hand, he might have found himself overcome by sudden psychological crisis. A loss of nerve, a perforation in confidence—anything was possible. Yet, given the man that Fostoch was, given his exuberance in scaling the onset wall, such notion was incredibly doubtful. Still, a vexing overmeasure of time had passed without his re-emergence, and this left Wagner and Balgor no alternative but to lie in wait for the next sentry sweep before they could even begin to work on an answer.

Just then, however, fracas erupted across the way, followed almost instantaneously by a figure bursting hell-bent from the alley and hurtling eastward along the pomerium with an exertion that even a wing-footed Hermes would have been pressed to match. Indistinguishable at first, all but a-blur in the sweep of his strides, as this phantom sprinter ran the night's gauntlet of flickered torch-glintings and cross-hatched shadows, it seemed implausible for him to be anyone *but* Fostoch of Orrd. Far too swift and mercurial for eyeful confirmation, by all that Balgor and Wagner could see, the subject was arguably Ergosian; and if indeed he *was* the Agile One, then he had just "agiled" himself into big-time strife.

To satisfy causality, two teetering figures came stumbling from the alley in the fleer's wake. Obviously inebriated, raising alarm more boisterous than specific, their shouts reverberated into the night air, hailing unwanted alert to sentry and bystander alike for blocks in every direction. Fostoch was found out. By cruel misfortune he'd been discovered by a pair of garbage-skip sots, and was of a sudden racing for his life like a mouse set loose in a cattery.

No more cursed could he have been than this, than to have reached the absolute foot of the inner curtain—the very edifice of his and Wagner's and Balgor's attainable escape—and to come head-to-head with a wrecking ball in the guise of two late-evening tipplers. Yet, barring desperation and circumstance and failure most heinous, this notorious Orrdian had actually gone counter to his reputational grain by making his fugitation unexpectedly honourable. Resigned to his own possible capture, his deference to the escape itself must have superseded his usual spiteful proclivity, for he'd steered all spectacle away from the ballustrade, away from his cohorts, while in great likelihood dooming himself to the inevitability of omnidirectional assault and nabbing a few blocks up the way. It was something that neither Balgor nor Wagner would have expected; and as they watched every night owl and newly roused NuRac hieing off in the direction of the chase, they sat befuddled on how they might themselves proceed—or whether they should even try.

"We just can't leave him, can we?" Wagner whispered.

Balgor stared off into the night. "Can we not? His fate awaits him as sure as do the beckoning arms of Death herself, the poor bastard. We cannot aid him now."

Wagner craned to see the chaos down the block. Reluctantly, regretfully, he acknowledged Balgor's logic, and by necessity he set his concerns adrift.

"Well, if his goose is cooked, what's next for us? The alert's up now—every NuRac within earshot is yanking up his long johns and reaching for the nearest carving knife or fireplace stoker."

"Opportunity may yet be ours, *Voknor*. It seems that in the throes of his own misfortune, Fostoch may well have purchased our success. His distraction could yet provide prospect to see us over this wall."

"Why would he have done that? He had no regard for us, no affiliation, nothing heartfelt. He said as much."

"Follow me," said Balgor, forsaking their nook and charging up the risers to the portico above. Wagner—cold, hot, sweat-soaked, and yet still intractable—quickly scanned the pomerium and then hastened up after his friend.

From atop the portico they could see activity abounding for several blocks along Fostoch's route. Amid torchlit street corners, people were rushing about like insects swarmed from an upturned rock. Along the parapet, those soldiers who'd allowed curiosity to override dutiful steadfastness were congregating at the eastern reaches of the ramparts, leaving the sections near Balgor and Wagner advantageously sparse in delegation.

Discarding caution like a birdling at nest's edge, Balgor suddenly braced and leaped from the portico to an ascendant support, executing a series of clambers almost identical to those performed by Fostoch back at the first wall. Manoeuvring himself up and over, within a few precarious seconds he'd acquired footing on the temporarily abandoned catwalk, remaining in crouch until well satisfied that he'd not been seen. Then, as he commenced to fasten his iron to the battlement for the descent, Wagner gave his all from below, duplicating as best he could the former's derring-do. Indeed, like Balgor before him, he easily latched onto the support from midair; but in his unaccustomedness he allowed his momentum to carry him bluntly into the rock-face beside the corbel, quite nearly jouncing him beyond acuity and resilience. Shaken, he maintained his grip, and after a moment of recovery he likewise scrambled topside, a little less for wear but unabashedly pleased with himself.

This was it. With the outer curtain but a stone's-throw away, success was no longer far-fetched ambition, but executable; and while Wagner collected himself, Balgor assured the mooring and then tossed the rope over the crenel for their downshin.

He stopped cold.

Wagner, at first thinking him struck by bolt, flew quickly to his side but found him hale and sound, if riveted to the very banquette as though he, too, were of the same granite.

Then Wagner saw it too. Beyond the outer curtain—stouter and more squat than the inner—lay a spectacle imposing enough to cripple the spirit of the most stalwart Ergosian. A wintry moment in the midst of a sultry summer night, neither man could find within himself the resource to draw even a single breath in the face of this new unfolding. Beginning at the glacis and extending considerably into the arable expanse sat regiment over regiment of reposing NuRac might. An encampment to boggle one's noddle, for as far as their eyes could glimpse they beheld countless cook-fires and cressets; neat queues of transports, drays, officers' wagons and tentings; various munitions, fangles of disassembled siege weaponry, and tetherings of vrohdas to rival the grandest livestock exhibit at any earthly county fair. All this obstruction lay in the path of Wagner's and Balgor's escape. All this formidable evil slept with one eye open under the gentle canopy of cloud-quilted darkness, thus far unaware of the small-scale calamity arisen within the city.

When Wagner finally found his voice, he uttered a single expletive in his native tongue.

As for Balgor, at the sound of Wagner's disgust he geared back into the moment, sighing embitterment of his own. "It seems the troops have arrived ahead of report, *Voknor*. Tamek foretold correctly, but his information was less timely than we had hoped."

Wagner stood dumbfounded, looking all like a pyjama-clad man whose house was burning groundward before his very eyes. "Why are they here, *outside* the walls? Why aren't they—"

"I know not. It is likely that they began arriving late in the day, or at dusk. Perhaps accommodation was behindhand, or it was deemed too impractical to wheel so many into the city after nightfall."

Wagner raked his hair wildly. "Man, how much bleaker could this be? Did I say *Fostoch's* goose was cooked? We're *all* cooked. We can't go forward—we can't go back."

"And we lack your glorious wings, my friend, so the ether is likewise not an option." Balgor moved for cover behind a merlon, indicating that Wagner follow suit. Although presenting a calm exterior, the realmson's breathing was rapid and uneven. Hands clasped and pressing at his chin, he tapped a lone finger against the lip of an indurate pout. Undeniably he was in conflict—intuition and rationale, body and mind—his brain weaving the threads of option, and his physiology eager to sever them and flee.

"I can think of but one alternative," he said. "Within moments it will be busy as market day here. It is therefore my counsel that we double back, *Voknor*, to some other end of the city. Say that we were to course inward, and then veer an eastern path. If we stay ahead of the alarum, and finesse a means to the eastern wall before every soul in QieLahr entire is roused to the fact of our existence, we may yet succeed."

"Sounds completely crazy to me," said Wagner. He panned from the impassable encampment outside to the point along the pomerium where they'd last seen Fostoch in hightail. "So, what are we still doing *here*?"

Were ever a volume of impossible deeds to be compiled, James Wagner may well have qualified for a substantial entry all his own. Even suppressing his original transference to Ergos for lack of personal volition, his worthiness nevertheless abounded in largely unsung, unintentional, unimpeachable example. After all, had he not set precedent by trading favours with a pack of Vofspars without once shedding blood through hostility? Hadn't he raced barefoot and naked over jagged, treacherous terrain with no serious detriment to life or limb? And what of surviving plummet steep and impact blunt under several hundredweights of Vofspar female, or the vicious pummelling by a dozen NuRac soldiers, or being relegated to a filthy dungeon with nothing to assuage the festerings of that pummelling? Forget not, too, that he'd held his own—and even sometimes triumphed—in mock warring with little more than a lay knowledge of the day's weaponry and expedients!

No less prominent, of course, was Balgor of the realm, whose deeds—providing that one could substantiate the veracity of his high boasts—earned him equal privilege and perhaps greater mention within the same tome. Already merited—he and Wagner—if both perseverers could only now accomplish this one remarkable feat, then their registry in the Ergosian *Who's Who* was a lock. If not, their names would grace a registry of another, more discomforting sort.

Such renown, however—nonsense that it was—had no fixing in either man's thoughts. Survival did. And survival, even as a recaptured escapee, would be desired and even entreated if the alternative was torturous death over an endeavour that, foiled in the end, had benefited no one and aided no cause. While personal sacrifice in the name of altruism begot honour by its degree, sacrifice for vainglory, impatience, or stupidity was inutile at best; and both men—while well aware that some manner of prolonged execution would be the most certain outcome of their failure—would hardly argue with quarter (over quartering) should it be extended. Was such a prospect improbable? Yes. Was it impossible? Perhaps not. If they were spared at all it would be from the fact that AuwNiir had sunk a good deal of scratch into both men's warrior peerages, and would thus be loath to write them off without an adequate return of tournament receipts to justify it. Should events turn even more sour than they already had, Wagner and Balgor would indeed hope for this. But for the nonce, positivity and fortitude were the only mindsets they could afford.

Back on soil, the surreptitious duo regarded the turmoil up the way as diversion enough for them to brave the alley through which they'd initially come, their intent this time to conduct their flight east and into the very metropolitan district that they'd been conscious to avoid in their earlier sally. Despite the inclination to race at full gait so that they might sooner breach portions of the city as yet unaltered by the ruckus born of Fostoch's misfortune, this first leg of their infiltration necessitated a more stickling prudence, for already was the populace in this sector alerted—and therefore, undoubtedly mindful of every suspect figure and sound. Watch wardens and window sitters potentially at any given position, it was a matter of scrutiny before scurry, of negotiating the open avenues one pitiful stride at a time while alternately racing full gallop through dark arteries and side accesses to recoup precious seconds. In all, it was truly harrowing roving, and it wasn't until they'd slinked farther into the city, where peril was less immediately prominent, that they were able to ramp up their speed and cut loose with greater abandon. Here, then, with compensation critical upon their minds, they commenced with a wild and indiscriminate tramp through many a NuRac hedgerow, garden, and ornamental motif, short-cutting at every turn, sprinting along the walks, the cobblestoned boulevards, and the shadowy back alleys like roaches mere centimetres ahead of the stomp. Increasing their gait as their winds permitted, nimbly and without pause they continued past the storefronts and the darkened residences wherein were the snores and dream-spinnings of a populace that generally loathed them—and whom they had come to disesteem in kind.

Roughly seven blocks into their new vector, the knell of general alarm arose—as predicted—from out of the previous sector. Bells rang out along the insulae from spires that more than likely had been erected for just such purposes, bells whose far-reaching reverberations could only aggravate Balgor's and Wagner's woes. The heads, then, of every NuRac household were certain to come scrambling out of their homes, half-dressed, rusty sabres or kitchen stokers in hand, ignorant of the crisis but vigilant nonetheless for dubious activity, their voices ready to yammer at the first sight of thief, invader, or rabid animal.

The only factor in the escapees' favour was that the exact significance of the clangour would in all likelihood have been unclear to the sleep-stupefied residents. This, of course, only if a distinct ictus of bell ringing wasn't pre-established for distinguishing between the threat of an attacking enemy, a fire, a riot, or simply for a small party of foolish prisoners stepping out across the border for a city-wide romp; there was no way of knowing, and every reason to assume the worst.

Still, it was within the pale of possibility that no one yet knew about the two of them. Fostoch had been the initial focus; and as slippery as he was, he may well have eluded his string of pursuers. Perhaps he was *yet* on the move—else why these new bells? For all that Balgor and Wagner knew, he was yet leading a gallimaufry of drunks and soldiers and townsfolk on quite the merry chase, cutting zigzags and double-backs through their ambushing assails, popping up and disappearing and popping up again in a lethal bout of QieLahran Whack-a-Mole. After all, he'd earned his agility epithet in combat, and it was in the midst of multilayered peril that it would manifest best.

A new and respondent influx of foot traffic along the avenues hampered the pair's flight even more now. Neighbours spilling out onto the street, they began conferring with one another, querying for information, relaying their knowledge or lack of it to the curious who leaned with cupped ears from the windows above. Lamps lit, torches ignited, sector after sector of the city became bathed in the glow of the inquisitive, and Balgor and Wagner soon found that they could safely go no farther. Holing up amid several oaken skips in a reeky service alley, they hunkered in the shadows in temporary stymie.

"Those friggin' bells did us in," said Wagner, chasing breath. "I think this little escapade of ours is all but finished."

"Many times have I been so finished," said Balgor. "Standing on the toes of Death, frustrated on every front by advancing foe, and still did I walk away in triumph. And know you how, *Voknor*?"

Wagner shrugged, although through the darkness Balgor would have needed feline eyes to see it.

"Because I was young and hard of head, ever too lean-witted to even consider my own defeat. Thus, I fought on, hook and scrap, and by the grace of my ignorance I undid my own undoing without twice thinking."

"Got any of that *now*?"

"I am a different man, now, *Voknor*—but also the same. To both our misfortunes, I am far more pragmatic than my former self. And, I fear, I am far less ignorant. I take greater stock in what 'cannot' be done, and such good sense fully halves our options. On the back hand, however, my experience and cunning overmatch anything that my younger fool ever imagined."

"I guess I must've been listening to my *own* younger fool when I dreamed this whole thing up."

"*Bones and entrails!* If escaping were as simple as we led ourselves to believe, the prison would have been long ago deserted. Even the most ingenious plans go awry. And although it may bring you little comfort in your current crouch, it is in just such contingency that one's mettle is duly tested."

Wagner ducked back as several torch-bearing townspeople stormed past the alley's mouth. "Well, let's test it then," he said, "because we sure as hell can't stay here for very long."

Back in Barracks Five, the knelling within the city proper had immediately awakened fully one-half of the stable, with the remainder gradually coming conscious in reply to the growing morass around them. Most were soon afoot, all too many stumbling about with one leg in trousers and one out, more eager for bruit than for personal comportment and equilibrium. Some pressed in piquancy towards the entryway; others hefted their bunkmates up to the upper embrasures for even the most limited look-see.

Tamek, having never left the gate, stood clenching the iron grating that, during the course of his vigil, he had yet to snap completely and irreversibly shut. Delinquent in his own dictate of locking the post-commitment trio out, while it had remained safe to do so he'd given them leeway beyond good measure in the event that the scheme were to have crapped out early on. Even as time had passed with seemingly nothing askew, he'd delayed for no other reason than to provide his friends a speedy reintegration into the barracks should they have suddenly come racing back on the prow of sentried pursuit.

With the advent of the bells, however, his task was clear. Even had he wished to believe the din to be unrelated, his intuition told him it was not.

Policing the entryway, without a word he turned to face the encroaching prisoners and bade them come no closer. In trammelled frustration they obeyed, reluctantly and *only* because it was the Sentinel who commanded them. Anyone less and he would likely have been trampled underfoot for the sake of inquisitiveness. Staring down their curiosity, Tamek knew that it would be his onus to enlighten them at some point; but for the moment, his concerns were much graver than those of elucidation. The far-off noises suddenly welling close, he turned his back on his people and put his face to the gate, scanning for what could be scanned.

Traffic along the catwalks in rise, the sentries were all on heightened alert—almost eagerly so—over this mysterious crisis unfolding within the city. Filtering through the ado, Tamek picked up on bits of their exchanges, but what wasn't muffled or echo-distorted was in large a useless gabble of quip and sardonics, the prison guards evidently making sport of their higher-living brethren in QieLahr, whose most dangerous duties they pictured as giving chase to apple thieves and stray pets and such. Two soldiers, whose banter Tamek was able to extract from the mix, speculated first that the royal chamberlain had been caught prancing around the city streets naked and drunk and sporting the royal jewels, and second, that Grum's visit to a local brothel had prompted the entire harlotry to evacuate the building in unabatable horror. No doubt these happily deprecating sentries would find infinitely more to be concerned about should the unrest be traced back to their own gaoling negligence. Then, after correspondingly appropriate losses of privilege, wages, and per diem allowances, and the castigation by ranking officers—maybe even reassignment to the most undesirable posts imaginable—they could resume their witticisms from a new perspective. But until the truth was revealed, it was fitting that they let horseplay override horse sense.

"Come now, Tamek, give over to us," pled Gamühr the Bard, standing foremost in the crowd. "What is the secret of the bells that even *we* cannot know it?"

"Hush, woman," Tamek chided, never averting his eyes from the catwalks. "Stay thy distance for but a moment more, and I will explain anon."

"Is the city under siege?" came a voice from the rear. Others quickly followed with mutters and murmurs of possibility and prospect.

"Here, Tamek," cried a new voice from the chafe. "We are not children, to be kept in ignorance!"

Tamek suddenly spun about, eyes agleam, even in the void. "Perhaps not," he spat, "but from that ignorance do you behave more childishly than any whelp. Be patient, knave—'twould do you well this night not to provoke me."

Although his visage was dappled heavily in shadow, no lamp or cresset was needed to see that he was in no humour to be challenged.

The gravity of his transgression all too evident, the malcontent—a man named Vonleor—yielded and shrank back into a crowd whose bolster no longer fuelled his courage. Clearly the Sentinel, known to breast most reasonable challenges with grace, would entertain no such exchange this night. Yet, even in his ire, Tamek wasn't totally unperceptive; and seeing the widespread confoundment around him, he moved personal front and barrier aside to address the comment with what artful diplomacy he could muster.

"My behest was not meant to bar you—*any* of you—from the truth, Vonleor, but rather to allow myself time to ascertain. There is much doing outside our walls this night. Lives are at risk, and thus do I seek your gentle policy o'er the folly of news-mongering."

"Forgive us, Sentinel," said Gamühr. As much a mediator as a storyteller, she'd been known to defuse a situation or two in her time; and as she favoured no tiff here—especially in the congestion of these quarters—with downy words and reasoning she went on to ease the rile of the few northerners in the group whose regard for Tamek didn't quite give over with the majority's.

Vonleor was one such north-realmer. Hailing from the Isle of Orlahn, a clannish principality with cultural subtleties not quite in fashion with mainland thought, he was as much an infidel to Tamek as Wagner was. Demonstrating a deal less elasticity than the greater Ergosian populace in any number of matters, and allowing considerably more leeway in an equal number of areas, the Orlahnians were truly no less rootbound and unrelenting in their ways than was the Sentinel. One might even have said that they were in effect a sort of disputatious obversion to Tamek's own orthodoxy. Sectarian grapes transplaced in a traditionalist vineyard and then tossed by the NuRacs into the common press, if nothing else their presence provided a blend of healthy conflict for an otherwise stodgily dominating theism. And although Tamek, in his evangelical assiduity, would joyfully itemise their scriptural digressions and transgressions alike, in the long run he allowed Vonleor and the others their self-imposed damnation if that was what they desired, just as long as they took themselves out of the charge of his own calling.

Temper tucked away, Tamek returned to his vigil. Yet, with the flap and murmur behind him hindering his ability to eavesdrop on the guards outside, the only tool left to him was that of sight—and sight alone was limiting. He'd heard enough, however, in his previous tap, and could see that relatively few guards had broken from their conversive huddles. That they still congregated, alert but derelict of their respective posts, was a reasonable indicator that they had yet to hear of the ado's true nature. This was good. The situation in the city could still have been any of a hundred scenarios, with the escapees' discovery being but one of them. Regardless, with the alarm up, if things had gone poorly for Balgor and the rest, there was little chance of the trio making it back to Barracks Five under a cloak of secrecy, not now.

Resigned to the unalterable, Tamek chocked his footing and heaved hinge-way on the gate until the deadbolt snapped irreversibly into the strike. Behind him, his co-inhabitants traded their mumblings for one grand and collective gasp.

"The Twain be at your sides," Tamek whispered, chin against the bars. Then he turned to face the multitude.

"Tonight," he said, dashing oxidation from his palms, "three of our own have gone o'er the walls. Three men of courage. Three men of idiocy. Three men, undaunted by the audacity—and unready for the gravity—of their endeavour. Verily, I can only pray that the bells we are hearing are not their death knells."

Balgor and Wagner kicked at full gait down a darkened city street. A business district, the prospect of running into any bleary-eyed townies bearing armaments was slight here; and as such, any headway they could make would be smooth and expeditious while it lasted. They had averted discovery back at the alley strictly through Fortune's mercy, the newest bruit shouted from an upstreet news-crier having distracted the local posse long enough to provide the two lammisters with an unexpected window for reaching the opposite curb and an alleyway beyond. It had been non-stop from there, a breathless, all-out slalom of lunges, leaps, ducks, and dodges, an obstacle-ridden race to stay ahead of the stirrings of an early morning populace who, once roused, would register that something or someone was infiltrating the sleepy sanctity of their neighbourhood.

The buildings and thoroughfares mapping along like a labyrinth, Wagner put his faith in Balgor's navigation, following the Ergosian's lead like a running end at the heels of his blocker. Smooth going in this sector, with each stride they noted how the bells to the west rang more distant, without being joined or supplanted by proximate tocsin elsewhere. And although Wagner didn't dwell on it, he assumed that Fostoch had been apprehended, with the NuRacs in that distant sector not only believing him the sole absconder, but the crisis itself at end.

Their flight soon emptied them onto a broad, cobblestoned agora—a town square or marketplace, complete with a central fountain and companion statue, the overstated drama of the latter suggesting its being a representation of some esteemed "titan" of bygone NuRac history. For Wagner and Balgor, such a plaza was more of an inconvenience than even the most incapacious of city streets, for to traverse it openly was as blatant an invitation for espial as they could have offered.

"You would not perchance be thirsty, would you *Voknor*?" Balgor asked as he eyed the fountain.

"Yeah, but not *that* thirsty!" said Wagner, scanning the same from the recess of a tailor shoppe entry, where they'd taken momentary refuge.

"Good." He eyed the deserted plaza. "If this be the market square, then you realise that we are but midway through the city."

"As much running as we've done," said Wagner, "we should be halfway across the continent by now. Have you got any ideas for speeding up the next leg?"

When his Ergosian co-schemer failed to answer, Wagner asked again, similarly without success. He turned then, and found Balgor peering intently into the storefront.

"A fine time for window-shopping!"

"*Tish!* I have conceived a plan, *Voknor*. Tell me, how do you fancy yourself—as lord or vassal?"

Wagner's puzzlement did not last long, for within minutes Balgor had him not only inside the vacant shoppe but fitted with the rummagings of a NuRac squire's attire.

"Here, maintain this upon your pate," he said, passing Wagner a feathered chapeau. "It will conceal your Ergosian traits from afar."

Wagner examined the hat with wincing disapproval. "What, you couldn't pick out a more foppish one?'

"Come, we must hasten," said Balgor, coaxing Wagner through the storefront, the glazing of which they'd shattered in order to gain entry. Exiting then, garbed in the most sensible fashions they could muster, it was their hope that in their continuation they might pass all but the most intimate of night-time scrutinies.

Despite the temptation for a quick quaff at the fount, they forewent the square altogether, and instead proceeded along the darkened arcade with brisk confidence, their senses tuned to full complement. Trouble would surely present itself—of this there was no doubt. Only the whens and the wheres were unknowable, and even these would be split between surmountable confrontation and unnegotiable defeat. Selecting a suitable, easterly passageway in this, their renewed incursion, they proceeded with the kind of light-footed swiftness that only those of motive and mainspring demonstrate in times of adrenergic extreme. Desperation had a way of forcing one to live wholly in the present, and here they were hardly exempt, for all notion of futurity was rooted solely in the next unpremeditated stride, just as the past was equally limited to the previous one. In many ways, it was almost as if their recollection of the prison—just a short jaunt back by the sweep of the moon—had in the midst of their hypergolic vigour been temporarily cleaved from them and replaced by no more than the single-mindedness of survival.

Their course soon deposited them upon a smaller, central roundabout of converging capillaries, many of which fed into dingy, industrial warrens studded with placarded frontages advertising the smithies and cobblers, the woodwrights and weavers and potters, whose skills made contemporary luxuries readily available to the city inhabitants. Vacant and gloomy now, these routes presented no imminent dissuasion. Choosing one, the pair quickly blew through it like tumbleweeds through a ghost town.

Steady on for a few blocks, however, and they would be exposed to quite a different scene, for here they descended upon the only verifiable slum they were to encounter this night. A dilapidated district to be sure, the problem wouldn't be so much in negotiating the isthmian squeeze of its crumbling, cordon-like structures, but rather in the fact that so many of its street people were out and about at that late (or early?) hour. Clearly, it wasn't due to the western—and by now faint—alarm that this miscellany of misfits wandered the grid, for by their untidy dishevelment and by their carriages in general it was presumed that the lot of them couldn't have cared less about the goings-on in the next *hovel* much less those on the far side of the city. Some in aimless loiter, others in busier forage, a few even bickered coarsely with fellow scamps over saleable trinkets or for the soggy orts of someone's dinner leavings. A few of them even had runny-nosed children in tow—toddlers, imps, and frowsy pre-pubescents who should long ago have been abed. Rubbish and potsherds and other discards of daily living lined the gutters around them in an unsavoury juxtaposition to the window planters and neatly swept curbs of the more affluent sectors several neighbourhoods back. Here, any garbage that couldn't be eaten or bartered remained in strew, with the denizens stepping over and around and sometimes through it in oblivious apathy, with the problem of public health and sanitation left for somebody who actually gave a fig.

Forging anonymous passage through such a hive of bedraggled unfriendliness was deterrent enough to route Balgor and Wagner into detour down the first available alleyway, but not before attracting the notice of at least one barmy reprobate who reproached the strangers for encroaching upon his personal square-metre of squalor. They dodged him easily enough, hieing through said alley and emerging onto the next street over. Even so, their situation had not substantially improved, for comparable predicament here awaited their needful avoidance as well.

"I'd never have believed it," whispered Wagner, careful to use the NuRac tongue, "but we live like fat old kings next to these dregs."

"These 'dregs' have no greedy benefactor to sponsor them and to provide for their existence." Balgor's NuRac was actually a bit less refined than Wagner's; but then, he hadn't come by it quite so unnaturally. "Conversely," he continued, "they are not expected to engage for their very lives as are we."

"Could've fooled me," said Wagner.

Ducking into another access, the pair ventured on—the remote western bells and the few trackable stars overhead being Balgor's only directional beacons—and were near to quitting that impoverished sector when they were suddenly confronted from the shadows by a haggard woman in cloak and hood.

"What purpose have you in this part of town?" she crowed. "Gentlemen do not wander here. No, they do not. Not unless they pay duty for the privilege!"

With that she produced a dagger, and, waving it menacingly, she promptly demanded coinage from the astonished pair whose disguises were proving much too convincing for their own liking.

"Away with ye, slattern," Balgor growled. "We have no patience with miscreant old beldams bearing fangs."

"Neh?" She seemed surprised. "What say you to *five* sets of fangs?"

Without notice they were compromised on all sides by four more attackers— three ragged men and another woman, each closing in with knives, clubs, cudgels. The realmson simply glared back at the hag and smiled.

"Come the dawn, woman, I will have strung myself a necklace of all your fangs."

"*Kill them!*" she snarled.

What next occurred was unprecedented. No sooner had she spat the command to her flunkies than did Wagner, previously so silent and guarded, suddenly catapult himself straight at the crone, roundhousing her jaw with such a brutal start that her very immediacy exploded in a hail of teeth, spittle, and blood. Shocked and incredulous, the woman dropped like a hen before the axe, twitching and convulsing on the cobble in a spectacle so sickening as to prompt even her own despicable enforcers to falter at the sight of her. As for Wagner, without remorse or conscience he turned to meet the next foe nearest him.

Balgor, no less awestruck than the attackers, nevertheless had presence enough to intercept the woman's errant blade on the fly. Swapping grips to his dominant hand, he put himself back-to-back with Wagner and made ready to confront two of the hoodlums who had set their sights on outflanking him. With more time, he might have found opportunity to loosen the grapnel from his waist and simply had at them with a few good gyres; as it was, the knife was convenient—and he, an expert—and with it he sliced demonstratively at the air, that his predators might have more gracious warning than they had given him.

Unpersuaded, the male and female both converged—he, wielding a shillelagh, and she, a dagger. Being mere thugs, however, and probably more accustomed to ambushing lone and helpless quarry, neither had anticipated having to match his own nefariousness against seasoned combatants—and Ergosians at that. Their prey fully exposed now (Wagner not only having lost his metaphorical lid during his outburst, but his literal lid as well), when they realised with whom it was they'd crossed, the revelation had certainly surprised, and yet not deterred, the remaining ravagers. Their ringleader pulped and writhing on the ground—and they, knee-deep in their banditry—it seemed that the remaining muggers were either too committed to reconsider their odds or too enthralled by the possibilities in this new development. Indeed, the slaying of a pair of Ergosian spies probably not only carried no legal recompense, but it would almost certainly reap them some réclame of fame and reward.

With no such preoccupation, Balgor moved to dispatch the man first. In brash gambit, he flung his blade, piercing the NuRac's gullet, and then raced in and wrenched the club from the stunned man's tremoring fingers. Sensing treachery to his left, in the nick he swung about to bludgeon the woman's thrusting arm, the groundward clink of her dagger going little noticed against the sharp simultaneity of both her ulna and radius snapping clean through. Renouncing the ambush right there, she cradled the purple dangle of her wrist and wailed for aid and quarter while her blanching cohort slumped to his knees, clutching his seeping throat in an agony that Balgor was in no mood to assuage.

Wagner bobbed and feigned against his own adversary, using a Bilahdu-inspired technique for courting an armed enemy in lieu of one's own armament. He worked to tire his opponent by avoiding the man's swipes and stabs until weariness and anger left said NuRac open to disarming, followed by some old-fashioned punch-up. Behind them, looking all like a malevolent batboy as he took on the fifth blackguard, Balgor shunted his cudgel from left hand to right and back again in a showy effort to further destroy the man's already waning composure. In his element as Balgor was, there was little chance of his being bested—this he knew—and seconds later, when he'd throttled the NuRac and dropped him cold to cobblestone, both he and Wagner stood and briefly basked in their victory.

Wagner, his wind returning, gazed at the hag whose visage he'd all but relocated. Delirious, in the midst of the fracas she'd managed to crawl into a nearby pile of refuse, where she now cradled her injuries amid mumble and whimper.

"Oh, man!" he said. "Did *I* do *that*? I didn't—"

"Save your remorse," said Balgor. "These villains attempted to prey upon us. In the end, what they have reaped is suitable penance."

"Shouldn't we do something, though? Put a compress to that guy's throat or at least—"

"We have no time. Look."

From all around, figures were drawing near. Foragers, tatterdemalions, idle witnesses who had seen or heard the skirmish and had maintained safe distances until its finish—somewhere between twenty and thirty of them now drew forward in pressing curiosity.

"Don your disguise, *Voknor*, and let us away lest they overcome us by multitude alone."

Wagner quickly complied, grabbing up his hat and falling in behind Balgor as he bolted off into the night. Behind them, the flood of tramps washed over the felled muggers, some offering aid and extending comfort while others, remarkably, picked the victims' pockets and purses of whatever bits of booty the evening had netted them. Any of the bloodied five who was destined to survive his injuries *and* his outright divestment by his own ilk, would thereafter retain a painful reminder of the consequences of villainy and ill-gotten profit. Those who wouldn't be seeing the morn, they whom Death would be gathering up forthwith, need only have been concerned with what the hereafter would be meting them. And, for this night at least, the stolen wealth—aggregated from the many, and harboured by a handful—once more enjoyed equilibrium in its distribution among the lowest of the masses.

A goodly distance made, Balgor's and Wagner's flight through the remainder of the city was splendidly uneventful, a fortuitous blur of black alleys and unpeopled streets that wove on in murky, seemingly loop-like refrain, until finally they were deposited onto a continuation of the pomerium somewhere along the eastern pale. Copious serenity at this end of the city, only a few sleepy-eyed pedestrians shuffled here and there along the walks—either industrious types en route to open up a shoppe, or frolickers stumbling home to the neglected bliss of a fire-warmed hearth and feathered bed. The alarum back in the south-western sector having long since ceased, it seemed that security in *these* parts remained at nominal levels, the escapees' greatest danger graciously limited to the final hour of the NuRac nightwatch.

"Look," whispered Wagner, a despairing finger aimed at the bluing skyline. "Can it be that we've been at it all night?"

"Aye, fair Cinjal will awaken anon. We must seize opportunity now, *Voknor*, else resign to find refuge in some vacant spire, storeroom, or cellar, until next subsidence."

"No way are we gonna hold up here. Not only won't my nerves take it, but our friendly caretakers might actually figure out that we're missing by then."

"So be it," said Balgor. "Let us hope, however, that we are not confronted by a duplication of our earlier spectacle beyond *this* brink of wall."

Keeping in shadow, they searched as before for an easy means up, but found no handy cousin to the portico of their first attempt, now long hours ago. Likewise, there wasn't a single postern gate or climbway along the inner curtain that was lax enough in sentrying to offer breachable advantage at minimal risk. Increasingly precipitate as they hied along block and crosswalk in search of the surest opportunity, both men knew they were within the last sands of the hourglass, for with the impending dawn the convenience of their disguises would cease to convince all but the most myopic passers-by.

"See anything?" asked Wagner.

"Every prospect," panted Balgor, "is long of odds and short of promise."

Wagner rechecked the sky. "Then pick the best one, amigo, because we're just about to lose the benefit of darkness."

Balgor reacted to Wagner's spiralling standards with a shine and a lop-sided grin.

"Relent, my friend—oft-times even stupid men are graced by luck."

Wagner raised an eyebrow, Mr. Spock style. "Or luckless men, by grace?"

"We are not beaten, *Voknor*. Not yet. Not while I yet have a dredgeable stratagem or two from my brasher days."

"You'll have to break down and share some of those early tales with me sometime, to give me a proper template for my aspirations."

"No need for that," said Balgor. "What I have seen of you tonight is, to my own conviction, enough to aver that there is little in experience that you require from me."

Wagner shrugged off a disconcerted embarrassment, as if he were receiving praise he didn't wholly deserve. "Yeah, well, let's save the mutual back-slapping until we're well on the road to Vargath."

Short on options, they chose to backtrack a few blocks to revisit a secondary archway, dismissed earlier but suddenly made more attractive through desperate eyes. Recessed slightly in the curtain, suited for only single-filed traffic, its official purpose wasn't strictly clear. It did, however, appear unstaffed for the moment. Watching, then, from the shadows, the duo waited for the sentries to pass overhead before crossing the pomerium and slipping into the indent. A quick scan for witnesses, in no time they were creeping up the risers and into the very throat of the great wall itself.

Within the upper interior, they came into a low corridor whose overheads were heavily charred by the frequent grazings of torchfire. Ginger of step, they crept steadily along through tendrillish singes of cobwebbing that fluttered about their heads like the wizened tresses of desirous old women. A faint illumination at the end of the passage, they arrived at a tiny chamber—vacant, rank, lit by a single lamp. The north and south walls of the room each boasting a claustral stairwell, dark and suspect and not unlike the one Wagner had clambered at his first meeting with AuwNiir, the southerly wall was easily twice as steep in climb. The eastern brickwork sporting several slender embrasures—some on the wall, some in the floor skirting—through them could be seen both a very imminent dawn and a disclosive view of the outer ward below.

The room, Balgor determined, was an inner casemate, a covert from where missiles and other nasty things could be fired or hurled through its loopholes during a siege where the outer curtain had been breached. That this one had several amenities—a small table and stools, a cot, assorted dried foodstuffs, a few water tankards—was indication that some manner of person or persons was at least in transient residence, the best guess being that the room served, in lieu of outright wartime, as a place of respite for the pre- and post-shift guards.

Delighted by a discovery on the entry side of the wall, the escapees at once found themselves facing an armaments rack, replete with old-stock swords, a broken halberd, some belts, a few coils of cording, and a dusty hunting horn. Balgor snatched two bastard swords from their clips, thumbed the edge of one and handed the better-looking blade to Wagner.

"Add this to your inventory," he said wryly, gesturing at the daggers and shillelagh they'd purloined from their would-be robbers.

Wagner, plucking a belt from the rack, wound it around his waist and frogged the blade to his side. Meantime, Balgor grabbed one of the tankards, sniffed its contents, and swigged himself the granddaddy of all water gulps. Wiping a generous spillage from his beard, he passed the stein to his friend and signalled him to keep watch on the north stairwell. Wagner sipped and obliged.

Starting up the southern flight, dagger at point, the realmson crept warily up to the trim oaken trap on high. He could, of course, have simply waited below with

Wagner for some off-duty soldier to swagger down from either rise; but in less than twenty minutes the sun would be cracking the horizon, and he and Wagner needed to be mere memories to that room by then. Attritional assault on *their* terms was the surest, most expedient means of gaining the upper parapet here. Once atop, then would they make strategy for pressing on to the outer curtain.

Below, Wagner polished off the tankard between noshings of bread and jerky pilfered from the tabletop. Catching a vague pitter-patter from somewhere above him, he threw the scraps back and drew his sword, sidling into the south-east corner in ready recoil. Incidental, pertinent, north stairwell or south, he couldn't be sure if it was Balgor he'd heard or someone else. But this was hardly the time to be lax.

It was here that the door atop the north staircase flew abruptly open, followed by a resounding belch, a grunt, and finally by a NuRac soldier in cloddish traipse down the treads. Too preoccupied with the rebuckling of his tassets to notice—or even sense—Wagner's presence, it was suddenly obvious to the latter that the room atop that staircase was a privy, a commode; and the soldier, not of any search party but merely a common fellow returning from relief.

On glimpsing Wagner, the NuRac was awestruck and spooked. Yet, far too dilatory to beat out Wagner's lunge, within seconds he was on the floor with a point pressing at his jugular.

"Spies!" he gasped. "Spies and saboteurs, come to us in our own raiment!"

Nice deduction, Sherlock," said Wagner, digging the blade a tad deeper, just shy of breaking skin. "Now shut up and listen, egghead, and maybe you'll live. We're here. *Thousands* of us. And while your troops are snoozin' like babies outside the southern wall, our armies have breached the city under your very noses. And we're ready to torch and lay waste to everything you NuRacs hold dear."

Balgor, evidently having heard the scuffle, hastened back down the stairway to investigate. "Whence came *he*?" he asked.

"Up there," said Wagner, "straight off the pot. And it's a good thing too— otherwise he'd be needing a fresh pair of shorts right about now."

"Then that route is its own extremity—unless, of course, you fancy a seven-metre drop into a putrid cesspool, followed by a trudge through a month's measure of NuRac muck in search of the emunctory access."

"Done that. I'll go with door number two. What did you find up there?"

"Viable passage."

Suddenly their captive reproached them. "You have lied! You are not an invasion force at all! You are escapees!"

Wagner grabbed up a partial loaf from the table, took a bite, and then stuffed the rest in the NuRac's unready maw. "What'll we do with the professor here? He's far too clever for my hokum."

Balgor eyed the NuRac, the armaments rack, and then Wagner. "I can think of but two options, but in any case we must be quick about it." He turned back to the prisoner. "Which is you preference, knave—death or humiliation?"

The NuRac looked at him, blank and befuddled.

Mere minutes later found Balgor and Wagner alone, ascending the south staircase, with the casemate below conspicuously lacking one NuRac and two lengths of cording. The sunrise ever more pending, it was a true effort of defiance for either man to maintain his reserve. Without choice, however, they forged onward, Balgor lifting the trap and peering out at the rampart onto which it exited.

Espying only one guard, some twenty paces off, they waited until he'd moved along before scrambling onto the walk. A cursory survey of the outer curtain and the darkling land beyond, what they saw smacked of the bittersweet; for although not a single enemy garrison sat encamped anywhere without, daybreak was nigh, creeping like an assassin over the distant treetops.

Had they been vampires racing to reach native soil by sunrise, they could scarcely have moved with greater speed and purpose than they now did, tying off one of the pilfered lengths of cording and abseiling to the parade below. Stygian and still as a graveyard beneath the twilit battlements, it would be the last hurdle that required darkness for a sure crossing. So little and so much before them, the whole night's daring would culminate in the next few moments. One last dispatch of the grappling iron, a quick bob up and over the curtain, and by grace they would be two quicksilvered silhouettes racing into an unfurling dawn that, only minutes prior, had been their greatest bane.

Balgor coiled the line into seven neat loops. Then, with all that he had, he flung the hook up to the most promising mooring. A capricious urgency nipping at both men, with the incumbency more heavily upon the realmson he perhaps felt it most keenly, this being his most pivotal exertion of the night. Sadly, he failed in this first heave, due in equal portion to fatigue, poor visibility, and overcompensation. The hook clanging derelict against unaccommodating stone, it set off a perfidy of reactionary echoes that lingered long after the implement itself had thunked to the ground.

Both men's hearts stopped. The surrounding placidity now shattered, the ensuing reverberation may well have been a bullhorned invitation to every sentry on the circuit. Dratting his failure, Balgor needed no one to tell him that he had just brought irreversible compromise down upon them.

Recoiling the rope, he rushed into a second attempt, possibly the only chance they had left. Truth be told, it would have been a perfect launching but for the tragedy that so quickly unfolded next. For, in the midst of letting fly, there rose around them the sounds of that which they had so long evaded, dreaded, traversed an entire city in defiance of, and their once lofty spirits suddenly plummeted alongside the grapnel as it trajected ungracefully from Balgor's effort and clanked into the brickface, spritzing forth a shower of masonry fragments that, along with the hook and its spiralling cord, rained down in stinging epilogue to what was rapidly evolving from bold endeavour into ill-fated lark.

The distraction had come from above them, a shout from a sentry along the inner curtain. A lone call, granted, it nevertheless struck life into the morning like the swat of a newborn's bottom, setting into motion an intermittent cascade of cries and interrogatories, frenzied yowls and bursts of trumpet calls, that carried across the ramparts, the scaffolds, and reached far along the successive turrets to the more heavily occupied watchtowers beyond. Within seconds, a dozen foot soldiers were racing at them from each end of the runway, with Balgor and Wagner floundering within a shrinking sphere of freedom. Their stances nevertheless bellicose, their swords brandished in anticipatory stand-off, how unfortunate that their vitals were targeted by a half-score of archers, newly assembled on the wall above.

"Surrender!" cried one of the foot soldiers, his polearm jabbing menacingly at the air before them. "Surrender, or you will surely be slain where you stand."

"Either way we are dead," snarled Balgor. "Only, this way, we may go quickly and with honour."

The NuRac laughed. "There is no honour in standing like practise effigies while our archers riddle you with arrow over arrow. Even as spies, you would be better to take your chance with our magistrate and Tribunal."

"And have a limb or two hacked off as our penalty? I would sooner draw fifty arrows to such a fate."

Without warning, a net suddenly enveloped them from above. Then, from all sides, the NuRacs raced in and seized them in their entanglement, clubbing them down with fists and spear-caps until both men relinquished their swords and succumbed to a trouncing that left them groggy and helpless and—most of all—forlorn that Fate had brought them but a hairsbreadth away from their goal only to abandon them in the brevity of an instant.

CHAPTER SIXTEEN

Let us, then, be up and doing,
With a heart for any fate.
  —HENRY WADSWORTH LONGFELLOW

By his internal clock, Wagner would have guessed it to be late afternoon, long past any civilised tea time, yet still a trice too early for the pre-dinner aperitif. The sun no longer beaming her slivered graciousness through the trapdoor seams, a few more hours would see her departing altogether, leaving him downcast and alone in his private, Stygian domain—a bargain-basement Lucifer whose only subjects were the slinking, slithering, parasitical ilk that neither feared, nor swore fealty to, this newly fallen lord.

Sitting weary in his thoughts, he couldn't actually recall ever having sipped an aperitif, not officially anyway, certainly nothing so elegant or cultured as that which earthly bluebloods—at least those who were true to their stereotype—reportedly partook on a daily basis. Never had he savoured a snifter with any kind of genteelism, nor once imbibed same in prudently measured tipples; and he certainly never had a faithful Jeeves or Giles poised solicitously in the background, empty salver balanced atop white-gloved fingers, waiting calmly on the remanent crystal. If one counted the occasional shooter of Jägermeister that he'd knocked back while slapping a sloppy spatula around the Filthy Lucre's griddle, then certainly he'd had aperitifs a-plenty in his time. But none had ever been downed with the quaint intent to stimulate the appetite—only to smooth the roughs of what, at the time, had been a cyclical existence of psychological crashes, burns, and rebuilds.

Beyond their apprehension earlier that morning, Wagner and Balgor had been given the works in retributive long version—first, by their capturers, and then, by every halberd-carrying grunt and junior officer into whose commission they'd fallen on the long way back to immurement. From the initial seizure on, they'd been the cynosures for NuRac boasting, with every next soldier and bureaucrat soon hitching his wagon to the recognition train, seeking to steal even the most miniscule piece of credit for their arrest. All this, too, before it was even confirmed that they were prison escapees and not outside spies. It was only when the casemate sentry's peers finally happened upon him, gagged and suspended like a piñata ten metres down the cesspit well, that the authorities were presented with attestation enough to have them suddenly seeking confirmation from the camp. Disorganisation being the order of the day, the fugitives were shuttled about from vrohda-drawn paddy wagon to local incarceration to yet another detention facility one district removed—back, forth, ad infinitum, until it was finally determined under whose jurisdiction they would be processed, and by which means, dispatched back to the camp's dungeon block. Several grumpy and crag-faced justices had been mustered from their beds (from their graves by the looks of a few), each to render his two-cents worth of legal learnedness, while word was messengered up and down and laterally across the military hierarchy until inevitably plopping down at Commander AuwNiir's front stoop.

AuwNiir, no mere profiteer, was a man long reputed for his sophistry, and therefore quite exceptionally practised in the sister arts of manipulation and diplomacy. Beyond the ire and embarrassment that the incident surely brought him, he was apparently quick to out-debate the magistrates—and later, the members of the Tribunal—who may well have thought to seize this opportunity to saw the legs off of his particularly notorious renown. In fact, so masterfully did AuwNiir wax eloquence before them that his words disjoined theirs like the decisive snips of a charmstruck scissors, reducing most of their criticisms to smithers and stripping the rest into little more than petty affronts against his person. Add to this his deliberately unpunctual arrival and his patent disregard for judicial decorum, upon escalation he'd left the lesser courts so flummoxed that most opted to offset their afternoon dockets simply for purposes of recomposition.

Just how elaborate an artifice AuwNiir employed in his defence Wagner and Balgor knew not, for by the time he'd finally appeared they'd been long remanded to a civilian NuRac gaol, where they'd remained for the whole of the inquiry, squeezed in among cells occupied by common NuRac thieves, drunkards, abettors, cheats, and the like. Yet, what they *did* get out of one or two bytes of eavesdropped persiflage went to the extraordinary litigating of their stable-master. Allegedly admitting to no dereliction of duty or responsibility, AuwNiir not only inverted the incident, but spun it on its axis in the manner of ol' Doc Adams, presenting the Tribunal with a fabrication that only he—and the aforementioned elixir huckster—could have sold with any kind of conviction. Finagling himself away from the accusatory spotlight, AuwNiir argued something to the effect of his "superior regimentation practises within the institution of gladiatorial affairs," essentially claiming that only those Ergosians who trained in *his* stable, under *his* supervision, possessed enough savvy, stamina, and daring to commit—and very nearly carry out—not only an escape, but an escape conducted through the very heart of populated QieLahr herself. His gladiators, he argued, were of the finest calibre, undeniably the best of the five stables, and one had only to look to the caper itself for incontrovertibility. With such a skewed retrofitting of the facts serving as his platform, he gambled on his ability to keep the details in steady shuffle while dealing one point here and one fact there with his standard surliness. By claiming, too, how QieLahran security could do naught but gain from what had suddenly become his fully sanctioned experiment, he hoped in the end to come away as some type of outside-the-bounds thinker upon whom the populace should really be heaping their thanks instead of their indictments. No more audacious could any man have been.

But his fellow stable-owners knew better, knew all too well how his inclinations were set more upon ink and revenue than on civic duty. After all, they were no different than he; and truly, who could recognise opportunism better than other opportunists? Yet, not one waived objection. And why? Because each saw himself gaining out of this as well, and richly at that. Thus, on the wrap of the day's many dialectics, when AuwNiir in fact came away less in detriment than in benefit, his peerage enjoyed more subtle triumph right along with him. The courts all but buckled by his clever juggling, in the end there hadn't been an intellect within the tribuneship who was able to thresh truth from embellishment with any certainty. The matter therefore less resolved than reserved for advisement, only after the news had subsequently reached the city's four corners would its resonance register within public sentiment—and this by the number of bloodthirsty citizens who would turn out on tournament day and plunk down whatever coinage AuwNiir requested to watch his top-notch stable perform. And who would his champions be battling but the other owners' warriors—suddenly the long-odds underdogs, yet truly no less competent than they'd been the previous day.

By no means, however, was AuwNiir going to feel in the slightest degree indebted to either of his recaptured infractors, regardless of how he stood to profit from their actions in the long run. By their escapade they had demonstrated to him a blatant disrespect and an ingratitude for all that he provided them in their life of necessary subservience. As prisoners, Ergosians, insubordinates, they'd suffered him an immensity of inconvenience, sought to make a fool of him before his people, and in the very moment that they were remanded to his custody he stripped them of all privilege in gladiator caste, and tossed them headlong into the detention block, happy to leave them there until it suited him to consider clemency, punishment, or—more likely—a propitiatory chance at redemption in the Great Arena.

In truth, imprisonment was the least of all the evils the two men had anticipated. Yet, they would soon discover that AuwNiir's wangling to save face would yield the unintended distillate of actually providing for their own reprieve. An incidental upshot that surely—and vexingly—stuck in the Commander's craw, in his efforts to extricate himself from the scandal *and* come out of it smelling all rosy he was thence compelled to maintain his contrivance with one very inconvenient concession: his abstention from punishing the offenders to too great an extent lest he set the populace to wondering why a man would reproof the very stalwarts whom he'd defended, praised, and all but encouraged in their foray into QieLahr. In effect, while saving his reputation, AuwNiir's ingenious, yet hastily birthed, subterfuge created a loophole that he was estopped from cinching directly.

For Balgor and Wagner, the slip had saved their lives, perhaps even some cherished body parts—at least for a time. But neither man fooled himself into thinking that AuwNiir was finished with them. Incalculable miseries lay ahead; of this they had no doubt. A combination of toil, drudgery, peril, and inconvenience beyond measure would abound before either man regained even the most rudimentary favour.

While AuwNiir's subordinates worked to settle accounts with those civilians who'd come forward claiming damages—the tailor shoppe proprietor, for one—

Wagner hunkered in his oubliette, retracing the escape in his mind, critiquing the whys and wherefores of a plan gone awry. The greatest mystery, however, was the fact that there had yet to be made any mention of Fostoch. Nothing overheard amid the many gaol rousts, no gossipy snippet purloined during processing, he wondered whether the NuRacs even knew that the Orrdian was missing at all. There had likewise been nothing mentioned to bring scandal upon Commander RoqaVek, Fostoch's stable-master—and this made no sense at all. Surely the NuRacs would have been wise to Kadok's subterfuge by then; for if there was any one thing of which Wagner was certain, it was that the morning roll-call had doubtlessly been a far more scrupulous affair than usual, with poor Kadok probably sweating bolts while standing amid the inhabitants of a barracks in which he had no business being.

In mulling over his sundry misfortunes and twists of fate, Wagner could not fully deny that some praeternatural influence wasn't still playing fast and loose with his livelihood. Undeniably such influence existed. He wouldn't be on Ergos had it not. Fate or deity, seraph or sprite, something beyond even extrasensory perception was still in auric residence here, something that too often put the skids under his autonomy, trifling with free will and determinism, taking them to the canvas time and again in a recapitulatory duke-out that couldn't be resolved by mortal understanding. Whatever this Überforce was, it proved largely dispassionate over right and wrong, justice and injustice, and was instead content to push things along for the sake of some all-important sequentiality.

Doling Wagner just enough leeway to gain him a foothold on some intended goal before confounding him, the thwarting never seemed a cold cruelty so much as it did a prescriptive imposition that merely manifested under cruelty's guise. To date, Wagner had endured trauma that should have crushed his will like old bones underfoot. He'd brooked brutalities that could easily have rendered far more strapping fellows into souse. Yet, instead of a succession of ravages and heartbreak, trial had annealed him, shored him, beefed him up bine to bole. Whether by design or by catalyst, crisis—especially raw and deadly crisis—unlatched a psychical ripcord that he never knew he had, a cord whose yanking could oust conscience in the wink of an eye and supplant it with a vigour and an icy dispatch that his former bibliophilistic, fry-cooking, loner persona had only ever conceived of in the boyish embroidery of suppressed self-image. Predicaments that probably should have left him slain or maimed had instead galvanised him with a ready brawl of last-ditch proclivities—just as it had his doppelganger—and whether latently encoded or newly bestowed, their imbuement was rarely unwelcome or unneeded, and just as rarely in want of horrific thrill and consequent shame. The critical difference was that said actions were inherently more akin to impulse here, not the total appropriation of mind and body as it had been on earth. It was almost as if the strings of his civilised, earthly Wagner and those of his doppelganger had become irremediably entangled at the gateway between realms, and by said interwinding was he gradually becoming an accountable recipient of his *Other's* skills rather than a bound-and-gagged spectator with perforated recollection and no real answerability.

At the time of his and Balgor's sequestering several hours before, it hadn't clicked with Wagner until now that the cell into which he'd been tossed was by coincidence the very one that Tamek had occupied those several weeks back. Blasting his preoccupation for shielding this fact, he jumped up at once and began fumbling at the wall, using the last glimmers of daylight to help him locate the disjunctured block that doorwayed into his former cell. Although not recollecting on which side his friend had been allocated, hunch told him that Balgor would be *here*, and not in the opposing oubliette. One pivot of the stone and he would know for sure.

Serendipity on an otherwise black day, he indeed found the gallant realmson on the other side. And Balgor, not a little startled by the sudden animation of his cell wall, upon hearing the sounds of a granite slab worming laboriously over slurry and sediment, he sprang up and helped to manoeuvre the stone aside, never questioning that the shoulder prompting it belonged to anyone but his ever-mischievous cohort.

"Well, *Ollie*, this is another fine mess I've gotten you into," said Wagner, ceasing effort once they'd opened just enough gap to permit his entry.

"Aye, we *are* in a predicament," said Balgor. "But I am happy for the company, *Voknor*. I gather that one of these splendid flea-pits is our Sentinel's usual lodgement, eh?"

"Yeah, I got the upgrade while you got *my* old digs. Tamek's suite has better accommodation than this one—three coats of dung on the wall to your measly two."

Balgor chuckled and wasted no time in firing back a quip of his own. For several more exchanges, then, they did nothing but trade jibes, in part to draw normalcy out of a difficult situation, and in other, to batten the hatch of their mutual despair. That their friendship had always been capaciously requisite in humour proved advantageous, for in that dungeoned foulness—more than any other place—it was their ability to crack wise that would re-energise them for whatever hardship AuwNiir was busily concocting for them. Yet, even humour ran thin after a while, and in one such lull Wagner took a moment to offer up an apology.

"Listen," he said. "I have to tell you that I'm sorry for dragging you into this fiasco. I admit—I thought it was a really killer plan. But I was too gung-ho on getting free to seriously consider the downside. It was selfish of me to dragoon you into helping, and now that you've forfeited your standing—and maybe even your life—for something so risky and far-fetched...well, it just doesn't sit all that well with me."

"Bah! Nonsense!" said Balgor. "I am a grown man and a warrior, *Voknor*, not a child to be bullied into misdeeds by the older lads. Had I not seen in your plan the possibility of success, I would never have accompanied you. I have been under the whip for a long time—much longer than you—and the notions of freedom that you limned with such fervour reawakened in me the hope that I had forsaken. Life without risk smothers the spirit. This I now know. It leads the soul to the files of the dead, that none may ever to hearken its piquant yearnings unfulfilled. As it stands, we very nearly accomplished what we intended. It was a good game while it lasted, *Voknor*. And understand this—we are not dishonoured in our capture, nor by standing here in faeces, second-guessing our foiled tactics, but in attempting to bargain with our regret. *Bones and entrails*, man! Sheathe your guilt!

As we yet draw breath, we have hope. Did I not tell you that I am too thick to know when I am beaten?"

His words assuaging Wagner, for the balance of the evening they remained in visit, with Balgor parcelling out a third of his bedstraw to Wagner so that same could huddle comfortably near the ingress in case of any unannounced unlatchings from above. With time to spare, they traded stories—many biographical—and queried one another on topics of interest from within those stories. Foremost on Wagner's list of curiosities, however, was not in any tale but in his eagerness to know the name and nature of the substance they'd used in rigging the gate strike. Although Balgor had disposed of both the substance and its liquid agent per Tamek's instructions—in two different hedgerows along their QieLahran escape route—at the time there had been far more cruciality on Wagner's mind than the desire to augment his knowledge of tricky Ergosian physics.

To hear Balgor describe the substance—he called it *korax*—it sounded very much like some odd form of myelin. Specific to the spinal columns of the dray-pulling vrohdas, it was a fairly accessible resource to a kitchen staff whose job it was to turn the occasionally retired sumpter into evening victuals. This vrohdic version apparently having a uniquely employable property in its post-eviscerative state, that said property wasn't always of uniformly suitable grade in every vrohda set Wagner to suspecting that genotype might have played a role. How these people might ever have happened upon such a discovery he couldn't imagine. But like many earthly innovations, it probably came about by luck or accident. Looking back to his own short-order days, too often did he recall how the mother of invention turned out to be no more than the result of simple kitchen horseplay.

The korax with the proper viscoelasticity existed in the sacral portion of the spine. Once extricated and subjected to a tedium of drying processes that gradually extracted all but a trace of cerebrospinal fluid, its mass would be dwindled to roughly one-quarter its saturated state. Exhibiting the stiff pliancy of kneadable rubber, when reintroduced to fresh spinal fluid—in Wagner's case, by way of Tamek's vial—it reverted to its former size and quality. Receptive enough in its shrunken form to have temporarily accepted the impressing deadbolt at lock-up, in the resumption of its natural dimensions, it incrementally exerted its own pressure back on the device, thereby compelling the bolt a few precious centimetres into its internal mechanism. And centimetres was all that Tamek had needed to dislodge the gate. Unlike the modern locks of Wagner's ken that would easily have frustrated and betrayed the sabotage, these simpler versions proved just fallible enough to be useful. What a shame that the escape proved equally fallible.

"While not an invaluable commodity," said Balgor, "it has its uses. We like it best, however, as a lock impeder."

"I can think of another application," said Wagner, "But, as it involves Grum and his backside, we'd need a much larger chunk of it."

"Zounds! Such hostility against the mongrel who ordered his deadliest warrior—that saucy, realmson fellow—to besmirch you on your first day in training. What was it that Grum called you? Pink man? Pink one?"

"Don't remind me. I was pretty intimidated that day. I didn't know *what* to think when the guards first brought me out there, amid so many steel-hardened veterans. Good thing he pitted me against a milksop like you."

"Aye—so say you. But be not ashamed, *Voknor*. Few are not without fear on their first day here. You only have the character to admit yours."

"Then you were scared on your first day?"

"Of course not. I am no mollycoddle."

Wagner laughed, rewinding his thoughts to that same first day of training, how he'd felt almost nancyish in a yard full of ardent fighters. He remembered standing as tall as his cowering allowed while forced to listen to Grum's indignities. How foreign and menacing everything had seemed that day, with the vaunt of necessitated violence all around him, and his own terror over what would be expected of him. Dumped headlong into the lion's den, every bit as pink and scrawny as Grum had proclaimed, if not for Balgor's merciful reserve he might never have found fertile ground for the confidence that took root in him that very afternoon.

"Just how did you get your nickname, anyway?" he asked. "Realmson, Son of the Realm, whichever—you've never told me. Where's it from?"

"From happier days than these," sighed Balgor. "But it is no mere sobriquet, not strictly, and certainly nothing that I ever intended to have accompany me into perpetuity. Rather, it is more of a factual epithet, sprung out of argument and folly."

"You just lost me."

"To enlighten you properly I must regress a number of years, *Voknor*, that you may comprehend more fully overall. You see, my parentage is unknown to me. All that I know is that my mother—for reasons understood only by her—entrusted me in my infancy to an elderly couple's care before vanishing into an obscurity from which she never returned. Perhaps she had been a mere maid, ashamed of the very indiscretion that begot me. Or, perhaps she was fleeing a brutish husband, a whorer, even the magistrate—in all surety I will never know. My rearing parents, Grath and Linert, resided in Könstrom, an insignificant hamlet roughly ten-days' journey east of Vargath. Although a wizened yoking of mates when they assumed me, they nevertheless nurtured me to the extent permitted of their waning vitalities. Still, the toll of their innumerable years eventually rendered them incapable of keeping so spirited and rambunctious a hellion in rein, and somehow it came to be that the entire community itself extended its generosity, relieving Grath and Linert of much responsibility by adopting me outright, collectively seeing to my welfare and allowing me to fledge in unusual fashion, with sundry parents and siblings."

"Must've been that deceptive charm that you exude."

"Indeed. As is customary for a youth reared in these times, I learned early the arts of swording and archery, and I honed those honourable skills throughout my adolescent years. Yet, I also took equal delight in some of the humanities, in artful thinking and creative industry. Truth be told, were you to have searched the town for me on any given day you had equally as much chance of finding me at the sacrarium, engaged by the lively dialogues of priests and philosophers, as you did outside the local alehouse, listening to the even more clamorous boastings of drunken bawdies who—between their belching, their back alley retching, and the inevitable flatus that young boys also delight in—sought to pass off impossible tales of bravado as their own. Thus, my education was one infused with nigh as many perspectives as there were people in Könstrom.

"Yet, as a young man brought up by many, I had not one household to call my home, but a multitude. With numerous fathers—a smith here, a tinker there—I could not decide on which trade to enter. I also found quandary in determining which of my gentle 'sisters' to one day betroth. And so it went. Faced with a domesticity into which I truly did not wish to become mired, and a Bilahdu-sized mantle of responsibility that I was unprepared to assume, I instead fixed upon venturing out, on exploring the outside proximity to its fullest. And thus, I embarked upon a cultural pilgrimage to Vishkor."

"Is that how you met Tamek?"

Balgor hemmed a bit. "I regret to admit that I never made it as far as Vishkor. You see, from Könstrom, the road to the Holy City was also—firstly—the road to Vargath. And, of course, one can never simply pass through Vargath without the inclination to sojourn, not with its sights and sounds and opportunities abounding. I dare say that I spent no insignificant measure of time there in order to slake certain appetites."

"You naughty boy," said Wagner.

"Eh? Ah—you misinterpret, my friend. I was referring to my cultural education."

"*Of course* you were."

"Vargath being the hub of modern thought, I suddenly found myself front and centre to the finest painters and sculptors and inventors in the realm. A host of prolific thinkers debated daily in the forum, the most provocative arguments recorded on scroll and reposited in libraries the size of our barracks. I even had the fortune of meeting—and befriending—Vargath's infamous native son, Mirko, long before he achieved notoriety in his escapades against the NuRacs. In whole, it was all too awing to abandon so hastily for a pilgrimage that would be ever at the ready." Here Balgor paused as if distracted by a flitting memory. "And, aye, I do admit that a wee bit of wenching was not a repugnant notion for a young rake come of age."

"I repeat: You naughty boy."

"Hmm...perhaps. But each man puts his cubbishness behind him in his own time and manner, *Voknor*, just as I have faith that you will—*someday*."

"N'yuk-n'yuk. Get on with the story, Lothario."

"By the following spring, after culling a handful of other interested pilgrims, I finally set off west on the common route, with the Holy City as my goal. Travelling for the better portion of a week, sleeping roadside most nights, we came one fair evening to a hostelry several days out of Vishkor. It was there that Fate grasped me by the scruff and threw me headlong into the path of soldiering. It was a decision I neither deliberated nor even had time to consider, for in the midst of supping on shanks and egged potatoes, a messenger burst through the door with the news that Vishkor—the city entire—had just fallen before a surprise siege perpetrated without provocation by NuRac forces. I tell you, *Voknor*, this was unprecedented! Despite the years of conflict and incursion between our races, there had been nothing in our histories to warrant so shameless an onslaught, and my companions and I each found ourselves immediately in straddle between terror and uncertainty. Within hours, then, we began to hear secondary accounts of how two, then three, and finally all four, of the Holy Sentinels had met their deaths, and the priests along with them. That these reports were both premature and unofficial mattered not at the time, for, although I was so sick at heart that I could scarcely speak, I nonetheless allied with my kinspeople, and enlisted in one of the hastily forming militias debouching in the wake of the incursion.

"With that decision, I passed into true adulthood within the span of a fortnight. In the merest brevity of time did I learn the true ingloriousness of combat, of how little and how much value can be put to a life, dependent upon its affiliation. My many youthful notions of polished rapiers and ceremonial trappings and honourable conflict were abruptly supplanted by the grittiness of chaotic engagement and indiscriminate hack-fests whose barbarity I will never be able to cleanse from my memory. Before my nineteenth year I had seen more limbs severed, and blood let, than a butcher's shambles. And then, what happened but my *own* defeat—a bludgeon to the back—that spurred to an end my first tour of military service."

"How badly were you hurt?"

"Fortunately, the blow fully missed my spine, but severely contused me within and without. It was nigh impossible to stand unaided, and for many days my relief was copious in blood."

"Not the best way to get a vacation. Who, or rather *what,* was responsible—an errant mace on the fly, or some dastardliness of behind-your-back cowardice?"

"In truth, it matters not. If ever you have been ensconced in the harrow of widespread fray, you have no doubt discovered that what defines cowardice in an isolated duel oft-times becomes obscured in the riotousness of a field-wide struggle. So rampantly does confusion overtake all manner of the mêlée—and so thunderous does the warring heart pound—that if one allows his fear to flow unchecked, he may well lash out at any perceived threat beyond the fix of his own eyes. In my case, it is more reassuring to believe that I was felled by an enemy, and was not merely a victim of a projectile launched in haphazard by some panicked compatriot."

"So," said Wagner, "say that this assailant *was* NuRac. Why do you think he didn't finish you?"

"It was not necessary to cut my heart out, *Voknor.* Not only was I eliminated from the battle, but I was in agony as well. To a particularly vicious opponent, sometimes this surpasses a kill. On the other glove, it is possible that one of my kinsmen slew my attacker in kind. Whichever or neither, it was too late for me. Although I suffered little permanent damage, the injury left me unfit for any form of combat until well through harvest. Once I could be moved without damage, I was trundled—along with others like me—back to Vargath, and there, attended by a number of extremely beneficent people. And when I was very nearly on the mend, it was all that these gentle altruists could do to keep me abed, so determined was I to mete comeuppance to the enemy. I had it in my mind that the first NuRac I encountered was going to take the beating deserved of he whose bludgeon had incapacitated me."

"Even though you didn't know *who?*"

"I wished for vengeance. Although I loathed warfare on such massive scale, I loathed the circumstances of my setback even more. And with retributive flames licking at my newly emerged volatility, I reenlisted the very moment I was able, and waited each day thenceforth for my unit to receive its orders to decamp.

"Now, so you do not think I have digressed completely from your original question, there was one frosted autumn evening during this lull that found me at a local alehouse, whiling my time in brood and brew, listening to the latest tidings of war from skirmishers newly returned from this front or that. Serving me was a buxom young barmaid whose name I cannot recall—"

"Not Celsira?"

"Nay, I told you, Celsira was phantasy. This maid was genuine. At least in the flesh she was. In personal quality she was as honey-tongued as any bar-wench, flirting unabashedly with her customers for tips and favours. However, in feigning her buttery interest in us it seemed that she and I appeared a mite more amiable than suited one particular patron. This old charlatan—a burly, smelly sot, direly in need of a good thumping—did not take kindly to my appropriating so much of 'his especial barmaid's' time, and so he sought to verbally provoke me into an altercation."

"And?"

"I ignored him, of course. His liquor's envy was below my concern, and his fetidness was more than my nostrils could withstand—even at two paces off from where he stood swaggering on legs that splayed and wavered, the way mine did with you and Fostoch atop me at the wall. No stranger to drunks, I was not inclined to entertain this one's churlish ravings, delivered upon the worst kind of crovik-breath, no less. As you may guess, however, my indifference only stoked his ire. Yet, still I behaved as if he were unworthy of my slightest notice, and continued my flirtation with the saucy maid. In return, he spouted obscenities the likes of which actually broadened my own repertoire of base vocabulary. His particular fondness for the word 'bastard' he made quite evident, as he tucked it into nearly every slur as verbal mortar for to bond one colourful epithet to the next. Finally, in complete exasperation he grabbed me from behind and demanded why on Ergos I refused to react to his taunting."

"So you beat the tar out of him," said Wagner, certain that some form of fisticuffs would have been inevitable.

"That was my initial impulse. But nay, engulfed in his hirsute clutches, I instead fought a duel of wits. 'My good neighbour,' I said, 'you persist in calling me a bastard, implying over and again that I am a child of questionable lineage. Why should this upset me? I truly *am* a bastard. I cannot deny it!' Then I conjured up my best madman's face—wildly jagged grin, bulging, tic-riddled eyes—and blathered the following: 'But I tell you what I will do. So that I may no longer be stigmatised as you seem to feel I should be, I will gather for myself a nation of fathers, for surely one among them is bound to be he who sired me, no? Thus, I will simultaneously be the son of the woodchopper, son of the farmer, son of the constable, son of the mason, son of the whole blooded realm. I will freely adopt every man past his meridian as my surrogate father, commencing with you, my inebriated fellow, whose sun has set and yet he has no clue. Today and henceforth, I am the son of the village idiot!'

"As the lummox stood dumb, I shouted, 'Father! Teach me the trade! Let us away so that we may stumble like buffoons from pub to pub, and drunkenly annoy each and every patron we encounter!' Abruptly, then, did I lock onto him in a brutally suffocating embrace, after which I drew back swiftly and—aye—*kissed* the arse-ugly blackguard as a lover, straight on the lips!"

Wagner shuddered. "Ugh—you're *kidding!*"

"I only wish that I were, *Voknor*. But, I must admit that my ploy succeeded splendidly, for immediately did he go pale and peel me away from him like the rind of an ogre-fruit. He flung spittle from his mouth as if poisoned, and then shot out of the pub like a man aflame, his raves of mortification all but eclipsed by the resounding hilarity from within the establishment. Oh, it was glorious! And for the remainder of the evening I had no need of purse, for the soldiers, the merchants— even the proprietor himself—supplied me with stein after stein of stout in gratuity for the entertainment I had provided them. And, believe me, I needed plenty of drink to wash away that man's foul taste. From that night on, *Voknor*, I have been called the 'Son of the Realm' by those who know me."

"And here I thought it was a result of distinguishment or some past illustriousness."

"Ah—then you have confused me with our good Sentinel...who I suspect has by now fallen under suspicion for abetting our little frolic."

They bandied this and other probabilities for some time. Foremost, however, was a prefiguring of the possible duration and aftermath of their internment. But they also continued to speculate over Fostoch's fate, and on what action the NuRacs would have taken against Kadok upon finding him out. Might he have been imprisoned nearby? Tamek, likewise? Had Fostoch managed to evade capture and get himself beyond the outer walls, or was he still holing up in some alleyway in QieLahr? Inquest and supposition ongoing, it was suspended only once—by the interruption of the evening meal—whereat Wagner quickly slipped back to his own cell until the food had been lowered and the cart had wheeled well beyond their traps. Afterward, they supped in proximity—chewing the fat both literally and figuratively—before finally retiring, with Balgor sealing the entry stone into place behind Wagner who, skirting muck and mire, crawled into his compost with an easy nonchalance that his previously imprisoned self would never have believed.

Nesting in that wallow of contamination and infestation, he drifted into the empty, purely somatic sleep that had become his normality by default. The veil drawing in on his consciousness, before it could smother all coherency he paused to reflect on a gradient of self-image that he barely recognised now for its evolution. Once predominant, and presently consigned to the demesne of his apprehensions, Wagner marvelled here at its considerable diminishment. The demesne was itself in desuetude, where once had been upsurge enough to defy containment. The incessancy of all of his earthly anxieties, the self-defeating fears, and the cascading unsureties spurred of his bendering and phasing stages—what had been a wriggle of scorpions in the barehanded fumblings of his former self had, in his acclimation, either minified or given over to new and more tenable control. At times containable, subduable, even exploitable, the anxious overswarm had easily been halved, with much of its detriment converted to resource. In essence, he was coming to know the part of himself whom he'd only ever seen by indication and outcome. He'd begun to meld with that being, adjoin it in vital function, affixing that tangle of strings that perhaps should have been in braid at the start. And while the old anxieties would no doubt always loom, with the uncovering of this newly accessible self-stratum he would further supplement the strides he'd already made in confidence and community, and thereby come to be more whole than he had ever been. That he'd acquired resilience in the face of peril was incontestable. Ever less rattled by setback, now interfacing with proclivities that had always lain just ahead of his conscious reach, he was channelling towards a kind of bodily-mindful completion that crossed the patent with the latent to produce a steelier-layered composite. Only by seeing himself, old with new, was the change blatantly evident. Unaccountably inured to the many misfires of his life, largely unbothered by the discomfort and the imprisonment and the constant threat of punishment and torture—not to mention whatever unsavoury business AuwNiir might have been hatching for him and Balgor—there was an invisible carapace about him now that the more fledgling Wagner had lacked.

With the dawn came the morning food-drop, and with the food came unexpected riches. Waiting until guard and trusty had moved on to Balgor's trap before cracking his meal and water bins, Wagner at once found himself recipient to a single stalk of very select praneez imbedded in the congeal of his cereal. Plucking it out with sudden verve, he ran it cigar-like under his nose that he might briefly savour its cinnamon suspicion before setting it aside and digging into breakfast. No accident, this, he immediately guessed that J'nea was behind it, that she herself had been the catering trusty or had at least arranged by favour to have the tin delivered to his particular oubliette. It touched him to think that she would chance to risk him a treat in what was presumably his darkest gloom, especially in light of their erratically undefined friendship. Such a simple gift, such a daring outreach, it was an office and a magnanimity that he would not forget.

An auspicious start to another dreary day's stint, with this meal's last chew and swallow he reclined belly-plump into his straw, and peered at the ceiling, waiting on the first hint of late-morning sunrise to strew across his trapdoor. Energised, sated, and soon too restless to lie idle, he grabbed an empty tin and clanked it lightly upon the pivot block. Receiving the all-clear from Balgor's side, he then slid the stone from position.

"I was thinking last night," said the realmson, "of the irony in our situation."

"How's that?" asked Wagner.

"I thought of how, in all your many efforts to avoid having to do battle in the arena, the result may well find us both at the forefront of the entire tournament."

Wagner sighed. "Well, yeah, I guess if Fate can trifle with *your* livelihood, what's to stop her from screwing around with mine?"

"It seems that she *has*, by association. You may do better not to draw any further parallels between us, *Voknor*, lest she continues to thwart you with vexings intended for me."

"In case you haven't noticed," said Wagner, "Fate has been dabbling in my affairs for a good long time."

"Aye, true, ever since you reputedly soared across the Leordahn Crevice on waxen wings." He sniggered.

"I can't count the number of times since, that I wish I *had* those wings."

Balgor reflected for a moment. "You spun an entrancing tale for the ingathering that day, *Voknor*. You also skirted much personal inquisition with your entertaining narrative. Yet, as I truly know very little of your past—and opportunity is ample now—I should like to hear an account that more closely aligns with actuality."

Wagner stood mute. In the faintness of the cell, he could just barely discern Balgor's visage, intently fixed upon his own. Perhaps, *finally*, the moment had come for disclosure.

"You're right," he said. "For what we've endured together, I owe you that much. You've earned my trust and then some. But, I'm thinking that, by the end, you'll probably find the 'wings' story an easier one to believe."

"Why so?"

"Because, my friend, not only am I not native to this realm—I'm not even a native to this *world*."

"Indeed?" The Ergosian was immediately amused. "And whence came you—Tamek's Portals of Destiny?"

"Not exactly. I don't really know how to equate it with anything within the bounds of your reality—or *my* reality, for that matter. I was born far away, on a whole other planet. An entirely different sphere. Where I'm from, my sun is called Sol, not Cinjal. I think it shines less brightly than yours, and traces the sky a bit faster. The moon that I know is either smaller or more distant, with geographic characteristics more diverse than yours. As for my people, we're pretty numerous. We have a complex coexistence. We've created a technological society, much of it at the expense of our lands and waters, with brilliant advances going hand in hand with over-consumption and detriment. We've developed machinery to ease the toils of work. We have conveniences that I haven't seen duplicated here. Yet, we also still engage in warfare, experience dissent and adversity—just as you do—but in many cases on a vastly different scale."

"*Voknor*, I am starting to believe that the NuRacs pummelled you too harshly on our recapture."

"No argument there. But, my confession has little to do with a few loose marbles. What I'm trying to tell you is that I simply didn't exist on this world until a few months ago. Some phenomenon—something that you might call 'magiks' or 'sorcery'—brought me here. And although past premonition helped me to facilitate the transition, I still don't know the 'whys' of it all."

"Past premonition?"

"Yeah. See, I wasn't quite in touch with reality in my other life. I hadn't been for a long time. I experienced visions of Ergos long before my transference, and was even prescient of a few things that have since come to pass during my time here. No less strange, I assimilated both your language and the NuRacs' almost instantaneously, without ever having been tutored. Unfortunately, as I was captured a few hours after my arrival—and to this day have no clue as to my reason for being here—I'm kind of *on hold* in my sense of purpose."

Balgor took a long moment before responding. "Aye," he finally said, "your parlance is unlike any person's I have encountered—this I will admit. Often do you corrupt your words, elide them, or employ phrasings with which I am unfamiliar. But *Voknor*, this does not mean—"

"Think about it," said Wagner. "I told you yesterday about the unconscious impellent that overtakes me whenever I'm cornered. Look at how I cold-cocked that old harridan for trying to mug us. That wasn't *me*, and yet it was *my* fist, *my* fury. I space out regularly during our practise sessions, only to jolt back to the moment—sometimes with virulent rage—just in time to snag my sorry keister from defeat. It happened the other day with Minosh. It happened our first day of sparring, too—remember? I had no business lasting even a single parry with you. Grum was right—I *was* pink, untried, unskilled, and completely ungrazed by battle scars. How was it, then, that I held my own with you for as long as I did? That I ran with a pack of Vofspars and came away unscathed? Or that the cuts and bruises I suffered by NuRac hands for defending the Vofspar female suddenly vanished in the infirmary on my first day out of these dungeons? There's a force at work here, Balgor, some kind of external puissance that instils me with a dormant slew of ready-made, self-preserving instincts and abilities. Whatever's behind it, it's given me a handle on the languages, a heads-up on certain eventualities, and an endowment of vitality nearly unto that of a spiritual reckoning—I kid you not. It fitted me with some sort of psychological damper too, one that initially prevented my succumbing to total mental shutdown due to massive culture shock. Hell, it's kept me alive and whole throughout all my acts of subordination, defiance, and being in the wrong place at the wrong time. Explain all this to me in sounder terms, and I'll gladly go on professing origins in your southlands."

Balgor sat in the murkiness like a confessor who thought he'd heard it all and was just proven wrong a dozen times over.

"I am distressed," he finally said. "From the start I recognised the foreignness in your mannerisms, *Voknor*, in your naïveté, and more formerly in your ineptitude with many of the skills and rituals related not only to prison existence but to the most basic fabric of our culture. *My* culture. However, I never suspected to hear anything quite like this. You will pardon me if I find your averment more than a trifle unfathomable."

"I can do unfathomable," said Wagner. "I can do impossible too. Unsettling, unreal, insane—plug in any unlikelihood you want. But don't be thinking that I've suddenly become mentally unhinged. Those words may describe my situation, but not my state of mind. Inside, I'm the same old goober you've always known. It's just that now I'm dropping the other shoe."

"Another example of your curious phraseology," said the Ergosian. "And more curious yet is the fact that I so readily comprehend your meaning."

The testimony was a difficult sell for both—one clean-coming attester and one humouring sceptic, whose whirlwind affiliation had suddenly and momentarily been kicked back to Kansan status. A revelation that may have gone too long undisclosed—still, as the realmson was as approachable and spacious of mind as any man could be, once he realised that Wagner was indeed speaking in earnest (no matter if from verity or delusion or some convolution of the two), it became requisite that he pay him the due of his polite audience. Too, as being gaoled in such darkly insufferable quietude typically made for a day that was long on boredom and short on distractions, here was a topic that ran afoul of all the usual precepts of philosophy, religion, and physics—and even if this new, guilefully fey Wagner was fabricating it for the sake of boastful fancy, it surely beat sitting around in wait of the next food-drop.

Keeping prudent rein on his good sense, Balgor leaned far enough beyond rationale to allow, if nothing else, for Wagner's possible bewitching. Suggesting that an occultist, or some vengeful disgrunt who'd perhaps recruited said occultist, had in reply to a perceived indignity cast a shroud of delirium over Wagner that not only marred his recollection but thenceforth mired him in bemusement, Balgor likewise begged Wagner to consider whether he might even be an unwitting (and sparingly amnesiac?) pawn of more ambient phenomena—namely the events surrounding the Vorshalah. A wayward scholar, a noble, a knight errant or an esquire or a mere transmigrant—any of these could have been Wagner's true being, affected residually by mystically charged environs and withheld now by corrupted memory. That he professed otherworldly agency indicated that he may indeed have been inadvertently influenced, and if not by spell or by some slipped glamour of the realm's regenerative machinations, then by the most simple of traumas—blunt or otherwise.

No more than fringed by superstition in his personal codes, Balgor was as intrigued as he was amused by the notion that Wagner might be an ignorant and unassuming vessel of Vorshalic incidence. Through happenstance beyond all ken, had he been swept up like a leaf on shifting winds, deprived of home and hindsight, and made to forage his way through a realm that no longer bore him homely comfort? And if said were true, any reason above randomness could have had within it the seeds of trial—a schemic testing, perhaps, of Wagner's worthiness. Pitted blindly against old adversity, only by his choices, by his actions, would Wagner in the end discover some neglected measurement of his character. Such was one of the reputed collateralities of the Bestowal, whether one chose to abide in them or not.

In all, it was a theory that courted popular Vorshalic convention. And while Balgor himself lacked the fervour of his far more devout kinspeople, he was willing to defer to the tradition that had in one way or another seen him through to adulthood. Granted, although none of his alternatives was all that irrefutably sound, when set against Wagner's insistence of off-worldly abduction—a piffle that the realmson was even less inclined to embrace—the magiks surrounding the Vorshalah actually clinched the more credible slot.

To be sure, Wagner's claim prompted no strains of distrust or curiosity in their friendship. Spells, seizures, visions, and the folklore that ushered them prominently into the normalcy of accepted phenomena, were commonplace anywhere that fear and ignorance travelled upon the ready vehicles of fallacy and fallibility. That Balgor didn't pussyfoot with any vouchsafing counsel for sparing his cohort's feelings was simply an extension of the quality that Wagner had always found refreshing about his character. Hypocrisy was not big with most Ergosians, and especially not with Balgor, who spoke his mind and spoke it often. It was a trait that had initially taken Wagner a little bit of time to warm up to and to appreciate during his sequestered coexistence with the Ergosian people as a whole. Hard honesty being an abrasiveness that often required a detached acclimation, for Wagner it was an exclamation mark on the regard and the straightforwardness that he shared with his fellow gaolbird. Acquainted for but a few, short months, they were two utterly varied men who'd found an islet of commonality upon a reckless ocean of diversity. That Wagner seemed to be wading into the shallows of lunacy had little sway over Balgor's judgements. But then again, never did it enter Balgor's mind that what Wagner had relayed to him was the absolute truth.

They remained in solitary until the day of the Great Tournament. Wagner knew that the event had been nearing, knew on the night of their escape exactly how far off it had been, and he and Balgor decremented the days from stir. Before the games were even underway on tournament morning, they'd reclined in their adjoining cells, smacking on halves of Wagner's praneez while waiting for the trumpets to signal the afternoon's onset of bloody carnage. Preliminary bouts having been staged at mid-morning in order to advance eliminations and to solidify line-ups, once Grum and the stable-masters had properly winnowed the second-stringers from the luminaries, they then pitted the pertinent players against whichever sleeper, wild card, or long shot was thought to yield the best spectacle. Then, at the noon hour, the games commenced.

Gauging the crowd by the enormity of its opening roar, Wagner and Balgor imagined the stands in brim-spilt burgeon, a record crowd of NuRac blood-mongers all falling over one another in fervid anticipation of the day's altercations. Indeed, the din reverberated far beyond the forum of the Great Arena stonework. The cries of soldiers, of civilians, the gleeful clamour of the prominent, the bourgeoisie, and especially of the common ruck—as it infiltrated the city's farthest reaches it found those citizens who'd opted against attending the gruesome festivities suddenly realising the scope of the blowout they'd be missing. The thunderousness only slightly diminished by the much more proximate dungeon block hatchways, the commotion lit at Balgor's and Wagner's ears like a portentous death chant, spurring unrest and anxious reflection in both men.

Wagner, leaning within the access, knew that inevitability was about to come calling. Soaked cold and palpitating, he was remarkably less consumed by any worry of death than he was by the means of his dying. To be sliced up or run through by blade, to have one's skull crushed by bludgeon, or to feel one's body disjoined of vital flesh by deliberately starved carnivores—he could think of far more preferable ways to check out. Yet, in counterpoise, he told himself that if he couldn't indulge his own theory of how his latent rage would come through for him at risk's edge, then all the avowing in the world of how remarkably dualistic his mind was would prove no better than side and sham. In the end it would come down to this: if his *Other's* essence indeed still dwelled within him, if it was still plumbing his psychical undercurrents at periscope depth with epinephrine-tipped torpedoes at the ready, then he would go to the Reaper knowing that both body and spirit(s) had fought tooth, nail, and grit for continuance. If, on the other hand, the afternoon found him embroiled in deadly havoc with nothing more augmentative than his own resolve and the skills instilled in him by Bilahdu and his many secondary tutors, then he would sure as fire make a go of it with all the fury and competence of the fighting man that he'd become.

The day was fair and breezy, and the first hour of "gala" saw a slew of initial bouts commence and complete in lively fashion. Historically, the opening skirmishes showcased the most benign talent—the newbies, the yeanlings, the up-and-comers—and it was in this grouping that Wagner would most likely have competed had his training progressed without scandal. Sub-par fighters with good survival instincts, the combatants in this circuit generally made for some of the most ambitious and energetic struggles of the day, even as they were often too easily dismissed by an audience jaded to anything but the headliners and the more grisly and chaotic pittings. Interesting to note, Wagner had learned that in years past it hadn't been unusual for the NuRacs to sponsor their own ilk in the games, from QieLahran criminals seeking redemption, to the plebs and muckers throughout the city whose privilege in life was small but for the celebrity they might achieve through victory in the arena. A quick rise to stardom, a fistful of specie regardless of success or trouncing, such was seducement enough for any NuRac convict, street tough, or down-on-his-luck alehouse brawler looking for an out and a ready return. The practise, however, potentially lucrative as it might have become, proved less durable than its conception. In fact, what eventually put the kibosh to it was the national shame and embarrassment that ensued whenever a NuRac contender—no matter how base and mislikable an individual—yielded before an even "lesser" being of the subjugated race. Too, the exuberance in the Ergosian ranks after such an upset left no inconsiderable gall on the NuRac palate, and this by itself was impetus enough to eventually prompt legislation barring any such doings in the future.

The opening bouts, though vigorous, were never lethally charged. More times than not they were nodger scraps that boasted little variance from palaestra sparring. Athleticism and clever feats of arms, they were meant to demonstrate prowess and to prime the audience for the aggravated mayhem further down on the programme. Again nothing to be dismissed; as with earthly boxing, martial arts, and ultimate fighting, even a biocidal audience could not help but appreciate the basic rawness of hard-hitting, albeit kill-free, combat.

These introductory clashes at end, next came more amplified danger from the menagerie. Nodgers were exchanged for steel, and the relative innocuousness of exhibition was traded up for spit and snarl and sharkish rapacity. The nature of the bouts at once notched up in direness, while the human contenders were each permitted the brandish of a single sword or spear, the feral opponents—often released in couplings or trios—boasted manifold snoutfuls of sharp incisors and a pack mentality for harrying and exhausting their prey with an efficiency to be relished. There was, to be sure, a trick or two of resort to be liaised by the human contenders in such besettings—strategy that well-paired combatants of similar mind could swing to advantage dependent on the attacking species. In instance, if the Ergosian side succeeded in wounding just one creature at a precise moment in the pack's fever pitch, its fellow beasties in their bloodlust would on occasion fall upon it for its own weakness—leaving themselves inattentively vulnerable and open to outward assail. Yet, as one never knew with whom one would be allied, nor against what manner of animal, whatever synergy materialised amid the collaborative swivet was always decisive and final, in victory or doom.

With every hour did the contests twist more horrid in scale. And, as would be expected, the more harrowing the event, the more time was needed between stagings to clear the field of corpses and viscera, and for regrading the bloodied sands. So, while the young and the elderly rid the grounds of human casualty and bestial carcass—with the former going to the infirmary, and the latter, off to the kitchen flensers—the redressed sands played host to sundry wrestlers and jugglers, fist-fighters and quarterstaffers, until the next spectacle's players were ready in the wings.

Wagner didn't need Balgor's heads-up to tell him when the heavy-hitters finally squared off, for the row of the crowd was so great as to tremor the very dungeon stone itself. Vibration that disregarded impenetrability, the calamity of cheer and uproar similarly consumed the outward airspace. A sonic booming of shouts, hootings, caterwauls—it did not subside nor even descend a single decibel until well beyond the first headliner's quietus.

A tweak of the memory for Balgor, he was reminded of his sundry tournaments past, where twice before he'd stood adversarial in this highest-tiered challenge. Both times he had triumphed, and both times had he reaped the cumulative perquisite reserved by AuwNiir for his champions. The esteem of one's master always begetting generous recompense for those who made a superior showing, AuwNiir—like the Devil who dispensed ice water to none but the most obsequiously wicked of his flame-wracked minions—preyed upon the Ergosians' wants and desires in order to compel their best efforts. But, privileges of rank, of supplementary meal allowances, of more lenient social hours, and even of sanctioned venery—somehow all these things, once so desired, paled before Balgor's evolving climate. Stripped to yeanling status, clearly he'd forfeited more than had his somewhat gentler cohort. After all, Wagner had already been least of all in the hierarchy to start. This all known, had fame and favour yet been the goals of Balgor's striving, on his return to training he would be forced to go about at rebuilding his standings entirely from scratch, no matter his impressive registry of previous feats and vanquishings.

But only if that was what he *wanted*.

Having sampled freedom again, regardless of degree or brevity, in action he'd inadvertently put rout to a mindset long enforced by conditioning and discipline. His initial imprisonment having necessitated certain concessions, with but his and Wagner's single act of insurgence—shortfallen as it may have been—had all the inclination to concede been obliterated. Those fleet and desperate hours spent in race through a hostile metropolis had flung wide the doors of long suppressed possibility, so much that he now recognised his forced conformity for what it was—not the resignation of a beaten people, not the unquestioned precept of an entire culture inured to hardship and discomfiture, but as an abomination that no enlightened race would ever inflict or permit. Epiphany, however, had not come to him by bolt. It was by Wagner's ethnographic blindness, by his innocence and his ignorance of historicity and norms, that Balgor had re-racked his focus. With thanks to the self-proclaimed offlander, he was no longer astigmatic, no longer willing to excuse the inexcusable by resting on precedent. Most of all, he realised that not only was autonomy the most desirable of all his deprivations, it was amazingly a reattainable one. He and Wagner had quite nearly proved it. Yet, despite what had been nothing less than incredible gumption and commitment, even on falling a hair's breadth short of their goal, the risking itself had put Balgor back at the top of his game. The unconstraint in his flight through QieLahr, the sweet re-exhilaration of individual license and of hope—how could AuwNiir's petty perks and elevated ranking have even vied for his corruption? How could he have allowed them to? Nothing but scraps from a despot's table, thrown to those hounds who best pleased the master—in the end, wasn't upscale prison living still *prison* living? And now, reborn into his innately factious nature, refilling and retrofitting his old skin, the politics of combative exploitation and servitude just didn't seem all that reasonable any more. The Son of the Realm, once far too amenable to NuRac whim and dictate, had reached deep within himself to recover the hope that his captivity had buried.

At roughly an hour into the top-rank bouts did Fate indeed come rapping at their trapdoors. A half-dozen soldiers overhead, the lines were lowered and each offender was hoisted tank to topside for what arguably was going to be the most anticipated event of the day. Gruffly handled, they were filed from the detention block, but not before first being paused atop one of the last oubliettes along the queue where, with four NuRac spears pressing their reserve, they watched expressionless as the auxiliary soldiers unbolted the latch and flipped up the trap.

A lonely line fed downward, the command given, from the depths below an occupant begrudgingly grasped the rope and began a cautious ascent. Balgor turned eye on Wagner. Wagner shrugged befuddlement. In the distance, a cacophony of cheers lauded some unseen ringside atrocity.

Like worming birds, both prisoners pricked to the sounds of sub-level imminence. The rustle of hand-over-hand clamber, the distinct grunting of manly exertion, each had a fair notion of whose visage would materialise from the darkness below. Neither man guessed correctly.

Not Fostoch, not even Tamek, it was Kadok who emerged from the pit. Kadok, the formerly brash hotspur who'd body-doubled for Fostoch, now a smirch-faced jack-in-the-box popping up and into the clutch of a vigorous escort, it seemed that the escape's extenuatory accomplice was in slate to undergo the same ordeal as were its full-fledged instigators.

Nervously, Kadok took his place in line with those whom he and his cavalier improvidence had made into bedfellows. Sour and contemptuous, he did not, however, even brave to glance at the staunch realmson, who by reputation and prior hierarchal standing was irreproachable to one such as he; but to Wagner, an unproven and indictable makebate whom he barely knew, Kadok shot the leer of the ages, as if said were the sole architect of his every woe.

Not discounting their sympathy for the younger man, Balgor and Wagner marvelled at Fostoch's apparent success in avoiding recapture. Somehow having evaded the pursuant mob on the city backstreets, maybe even squeaking over the walls and past the outer perimeter security, as far as they knew he'd gotten clean away, leaving his sorry shill to assume a full one-third of the retributory burden for what was to have been an incidental, if pivotal, role. A travesty from the Ergosian perspective, a fitting justice from the NuRac side, Kadok could only be pitied. The unconsidered folly of his subterfuge had come at a considerable price, and the hour now chimed to remit in full.

Within minutes of Kadok's extraction, they found themselves stepping onto the circus of the Great Arena. Having been whisked through the substructure at breakneck clip, Wagner was astounded at how quickly they'd traversed catacomb and crossway only to be deposited, sans preparation or instruction, onto the inhospitable sands where so many had already fallen.

The whelm of the crowd quite nearly bowling them back, Kadok and Wagner braced against it like palms before the gale. Only the inveterate Balgor stood unaffected, defying the boos, the bellows, the catcalls of ten-thousand bloodlusty spectators. With appetites still unslaked, even after hours spent in gawk at wholesale slaughter and fatuous cruelty, these people sat wedged in the crush of an oversold stadium, waiting to witness the comeuppance of those who had dared to permeate their city. All the afternoon, in shoulder-to-shoulder anticipation had they thrilled to the day's talent, newfound and old. Encouraging the more lively duellists, jeering the uninspired, they wagered and they critiqued and they approved and they disvalued—all beneath a searing and indifferent sun. Because of the oppressive heat, they'd been revived on the hour by wide-scale douching— water sprayed by attendants into the swelter from a host of storage tanks located up near the velaria. The same attendants who performed this dousing were likewise responsible for manipulating the many velarium canvasses so that key portions of the stadium were shaded from Cinjal's indiscriminate scorch.

Wagner bristled to think of the scores of Ergosian men and women who'd suffered trauma this day. He thought of the zoo's-worth of uncomprehending animals who'd been coerced into mauling said Ergosians, and who themselves had been hacked to pieces by defending swordplay. Then he listened to the laughter and the huzzas of the multitude whose every eye was upon him with the foresight of his impending excruciation. It was all he could do to stave off nausea.

Situated a few courtyards beyond the palaestra, the Great Arena was a grand ellipsis of sandy battlefield and encompassing stadium. Directly beneath the stands, hidden from the populace, lay a network of access tunnels that, not unlike the ancient coliseums of earthly Rome, boasted facility and containment for the tournament contenders, both bestial and human. The arena itself had sundry entrances, some gated, some barred by solid doors, through which the new combatants and the depleted ones could enter and exit in respective procession. Other denizens were surely housed here as well, namely Wagner's long unseen Vofspar acquaintance, as well as the entity he knew equally as Skol and Sunderer. The stands overhead had generally copious seating and, for convenience at show's end, a plethora of staircases and ramps, all descending into direct exits to the outside. Higher up in the tiering one could find similar passages; these, however, led to the privies and—for the wealthier patrons—the garderobes, and were easily distinguished from the exits by outward symbol. Finally, at the topmost crest of the structure lay the aforementioned velaria—a network of individually adjustable canvas awnings that extended, by means of poles and pulleys, over the seating for as far as sound engineering would permit. Like a rigging of boat sails, these clever contraptions could be gradually manipulated throughout the day to compensate for the sun's drift or inclement weather.

His awe overreaching the here and now of his predicament, Wagner reverted his attention back to ground level, toward the freshly raked plane that was about to become his battlefield. Barren but for a contrivance of ground-sunk spars at the north end, it was toward these that he and his companions were ushered.

Numbering five, the poles' placement formed a slight one-quarter arc, one to the next. Hardened and pitched, just shy of three metres in height, each bore at its base the indriving of a solitary set of manacles.

Although halted before these fixtures, there came no indication that anyone was to be tethered to them. Indeed, they were spared that encumbrance. Instructed to stand idle, they waited, and within the minute a single trusty scurried onto the arena at ringside. Ungainful in step, arms in clutch of what seemed a load of firewood, he lolloped out to the group and, in prompt and attendant fashion, supplied each combatant with a sturdy, wooden war club. Condoling each contender under his breath as he meted the instruments, a guardly rebuke sent him hieing back whence he'd come.

Taking measure of his only armament, Wagner found the weapon adequate in heft and balance, but otherwise unremarkable. No spikes, nails, or fin-like flanges, no leathers or ribbing to enhance his grip, it was the most primitive of implements, intended for the most primal of conflicts. Exactly how this boded for the yet-to-come was anyone's guess.

With the combatants equipped and in position, the guards likewise withdrew from the field, and this without a word. As much as Wagner despised them he bewailed their departure, for now would the real trial begin. Batedly he watched them duck into the nearest convenience, affixing the gate behind them, leaving him and Balgor and Kadok to tread those sands where the stains of murder and slaughter had been expunged many times over with a hasty till of the rake, and where above them roared a wild multitude of beings who knew them not, but who nevertheless sought to be passive agents to their harming.

In panning the broad concavity before them, Wagner noted something in the far wall that he'd not seen earlier, something situated diametrically across from the trio's vantage, almost as if they'd been deliberately positioned to face it. Set back from the wallfront, isolated by metres on either side from the many smaller and simpler accesses that peppered the surrounding stonework, stood a truly ponderous doorway of black iron. Multi-panelled and filigreed with indiscernible gargoylish imagery, even at a distance it transuded ominousness for no other reason than its composition. Wagner imagined that such a fortification could only be holding terrible promise behind it. Given what he knew and what he'd seen, while all the other accesses provided designated egress not only for the human and bestial combatants, but also for the medical orderlies, the kitcheners, and the groundskeepers, he suspected that this particular outlet could only be barring him from the one entity whose name he knew, but about whom he knew so little. With this in his mind he thereout could not quite impel his eyes to stray from it. Like an ebon portal to the coldest underworld, even more it reminded him of the impenetrable barrier behind which H.G. Welles's Moorlocks had stowed the hapless Time Traveller's machine. And although still some forty metres removed from where Wagner and his compeers stood, there was no place for safe retreat should those iron slabs be separated, nothing to do but to wait and to watch. Indeed, Wagner watched for what internally seemed a very long time, anticipating the precise instant when the iron maw opened to reveal the maleficence incarnate that loomed behind it.

And then suddenly, as if prompted by his fear, the doors indeed began to clank and grind open!

In silent distress, Wagner stiffened against the sparwood to his rear, bracing as he watched the doors mechanically disappear into the pocket partitions concealed within the brickface. The sun being high and south-westerly, even with both hands cupped to his brow he could see no clear aspect beyond the threshold. His breath in waver and exclusively oral, he fought to fill his lungs and to sustain his clarity. Jamming his war club between his knees, he blotted his palms across his tunic and looked aside to his friend.

"Is this what I think it is?" he asked Balgor, his voice cracking for the first time since he was fourteen.

"Aye," said the realmson. "The terrible one wishes to embrace us."

"Well, if they think I'm going *in there*, they've got a few million more 'thinks' coming."

"Worry not. He will meet us halfway."

Wagner efforted a nervous laugh and brought his club to bear. "Are these four-by-fours going to do us any good?"

"Tish! Listen! Even now the capstan is in turn."

Wagner pricked an ear. By what he'd come to understand, the entity Skol was so given to unpredictability that the NuRacs had by necessity fitted him with a yoke of hardest carbon steel. This engirdling was itself tethered to the stoutest metreage of ship-grade chain that was in their smiths' ability to forge, long enough to permit the Sunderer an ambient rein of the arena, but manually governable and retractable by means of a furling mechanism operated by no less than sixteen brawny soldiers. This capstan and its NuRac complement, both safely located in the inward chamber abutting Skol's, regulated the chain's allowance through an eyelet in the dividing wall—and all this according to official instruction communicated through a topside aperture to a redundancy of message-relayers below.

More than just a leash come tournament day, Skol was commonly reeled tight at feeding time—sometimes to the point of complete immobilisation—so that the justifiably timid server could safely deliver sustenance and then vacate the cell without having to feel any more endangered than he already did through his own fear and fancy. For the remainder of the time, Skol was meted slack enough in his restraints to permit him a sufficient amble within the enclosure—although, as Wagner could attest by his own time spent in the pits, even for a loathsome beast, such existence was no existence at all.

With this permanent trussing to chain and wheel, the task of coercing the frothing, blood-crazed Skol back into his lair post-tournament no longer required thirty soldiers with whips and poleaxes, backed by a string of archers. The sixteen toughs in the crank room reeled him back regardless of whether he wished to return or not. That he was so legendarily powerful, this could on occasion take a considerable time. A challenge of sundry repulses and reversals—especially when the brute managed to latch onto one of the moored poles—the crowd found no less sport in this than they did in the carnage events, and indeed even made wager on both how long it took and the number of setbacks.

The rewinding of Skol's chain, however, wasn't Wagner's most pressing concern. Its *unwinding* was. And by Balgor's mention did it seem that this little procedure was in progress. If tradition held true, in moments the three of them would have the misfortune of seeing a magnificently monstrous entity inching his way into the light.

"When he comes to us," said Balgor, "keep to the poles. Shy in and out, lure him within and around them, see if he will not entangle himself. Then bludgeon him skullways for all you are worth. Better still, blind him if you can. Without eyes, his advantage may fall to us."

"Is he fast?" asked Wagner.

Balgor sighed and laughed sardonically. "Likely so. Yet, in sooth I know not. All who have faced him have perished by one means or other, most out on these very sands. The few who survived did so by a bare sinew, only to expire later in the infirmary from the outbleed of their mangling and discerption. Nay, *Voknor*, all that I truly know of Skol's prowess is what AuwNiir and the guards have relayed in threat."

"I should not be here," Kadok suddenly mumbled. "My crime was not so immense that I should share this fate."

Balgor and Wagner traded looks.

"Aye, we are sorry for this," said the realmson. "Our debt to you is great, Kadok, and it is unjust that you find yourself condemned along with us. Regrettably, all that we may offer in gratitude and recompense is to have you stand back and permit us to confront Skol on your behalf."

"That would be cowardly," snapped the youth. Embittered and fearful, yet trying to show a brave front, it was evident in his voice that he would indeed be only too happy to withdraw.

"It need not shame you," said Balgor. "Our kind would understand it. You would not be judged. I will not, however, dictate your actions. You must choose for yourself, my friend. But know one thing—if you opt to fight alongside us, I will demand nothing less than your absolute fortitude. You will strike when I say, and you will not cease your assailing until the brute falls cold. This is no nodgerplay— you cannot up and quit at first scratch and go wailing for your mother's comforting."

"You speak as if we are going to survive this ordeal," said the youth.

"And *you* speak as if we are going to die," countered Balgor. "Where the mind goes, lad, the body will follow. Either stand away and let us defend you, or raise your club with ours and count yourself among the living."

Kadok made no reply. Staring at the ground, he wore his shame like a maiden's frock.

"What's taking so long?" asked Wagner. "The doors are open, the chain's been unwound—where *is* this top-notch killing machine of theirs?"

Balgor studied the orifice in the far wall. "I know not, *Voknor*. Something is amiss here. Truly, the beast should have ventured out by now."

Craning for better sight into the gape, neither man could see a thing from that considerable distance. Above and around them, many in the crowd had given to speculation of their own, with some talking among themselves, some demanding entertainment, some chanting Skol's name. Many leaned beyond the arena ledge for evidence of the delay. All the while, there came no word, nor was there any indication as to why the Sunderer had not emerged. At last, one spectator—a woman whose seat put her one side of the lair—suddenly signalled calm to the audience around her, thus initiating a localised quiet that at its onset crept through her tier in hesitant, resisted increment, but which soon spread to the adjoining levels. A blanketing stillness, as the crowd slowly ceased in whisper and murmur that they might understand the nature of the woman's cueing, they began to glean the sounds of an escalating scuffle below, a gaining, cacophonous brattle accompanied by shouts and growls and one very audible shriek of excruciation emanating from the cavernous den.

"Skol is not cooperating," said Balgor. "This may work to our advantage."

"Or they might rile him all the more," said Wagner. "Ferocious *and* maniacal are not the traits I tend to favour in my enemies."

Kadok pitched to and fro, hurriedly scanning the base of the amphitheatre. "We should avail ourselves of the distraction," he said. "We should flee the field—what say you?"

"And go where, exactly?" said Wagner. "We've only got ten-thousand people gawking at us, and Skol's is the only open exit in the whole arena."

Although logical and somewhat curt, the statement proved incorrect—at least briefly so—for even as Wagner spoke, the latticed gates nearest to Skol's enclosure abruptly ascended, followed by an outpouring of soldiers onto the field, all racing headlong for the maw. What had started as a minor skirmish with an uncooperative brute was in the midst of becoming a full-scale broil to subdue a monster gone mad, and it appeared that the afternoon's grand event was going to be waged by a company of inexpectant warders rather than by the three impertinent Ergosians publicised in the press kit parchments.

The prisoners couldn't have been more grateful. Their execution prorogued, they watched contentedly as their enemies set at confronting what was perhaps an even greater foe. The NuRacs encircling Skol's entryway, a few of the bolder ones elected to actually enter the dwelling—albeit not without falter—their longswords and spears couched for the one task of counteraction they'd neither counted on nor relished.

Fracas emanating from within, it persisted for several long minutes. Wagner could only imagine how an altercation might play out in such cramped and dusky confines. Like walking blind into a room of buzz saws, it was a dust-up of close confusion that would surely produce no winners, and see no one egressing untouched or unscathed. Given the predicament, this would have suited Wagner just fine.

Eventually, however, by some bravery or foolishness beyond the call, the NuRacs succeeded in manoeuvring the Sunderer out into the light, and it was here that Wagner was bestowed his first glimpse of the dreadnought in all his malevolent glory.

Skol was foremost a haltingly squat, bipedal humanoid. Easily five quintals (and probably even six) of tightly bundled muscle, he was so anabolically compact and dense in form that in his single body he could well have comprised the combined masses of all three of the fielded prisoners, perhaps with J'nea thrown in for measure. Hairier than a barbershop floor, his pelage was thick and oiled, with accents of pointed bristle running forearm to elbow and shoulder to spine. Even at that distance, his eyes were immediately comparable to the Vofspar's—shiny, albescent, totally unreadable—while his mouth was so prognathically toothy that it quite nearly usurped consequence from many of his other prominently scrutable features. A reckless, fearless being, as daunting in aspect as Wagner's most chimaeric nightmare, in the repelling of his tormentors Skol as good as validated his legend, his movements exhibiting the kind of spring-loaded tensility and hair-trigger puissance that was usually observed in, and ascribed to, the most feral of predators.

It was easy to see why he was so feared. Awesome and awful, a tameless entity unevidenced by conscience or principle, this slaughterfield was his realm, and upon it he ruled supreme. Even then, assailed on all sides by NuRac steel, the juggernaut exuded a confidence—or an inherent awareness—of his pinnacled place in this little bubbled world that, immediately sensed by Wagner, was probably often misread, dismissed, or disallowed by the provincial and the purblind as anthropomorphic projection.

Strangely, this Sunderer didn't initiate action nearly as deftly as he responded to it. A bit wanting in his offences, his reactions and counter-assails were incredibly sharp and on the money. Innately wired for self-protection, he maintained a fencible sphere about himself with the aid of a most unusual club. Overly long and plated, whether it was his standard implement—or one appropriated from the relinquish of a dispatched soldier—Wagner could only presume. But he wielded it as if it were born to his grip, and never once let any of his attackers slip within bounds.

A purported aberration of nature, really quite an astounding specimen by objective standards, it seemed that this two-legged platoon of a beast could have been a biological amalgam of any number of Ergos's indigenous species. By Wagner's own unaccomplished reckoning, Skol looked much like a hasty gene-splicing of Mighty Joe Young and one of Stephen King's Langoliers, and such being no inconsiderable combination, Wagner was all too grateful for the distance that separated them.

"He still wears his girding," said Kadok. "Why do they not simply reel him in?"

"It appears that their directive to stage our confrontation made no allowance for Skol's particularly sour mood today," said Balgor. "It is possible that the NuRac muscle behind the crank has been appropriated to assist in the brute's subduing."

"Or they just abandoned their post and hightailed it outta there to save their own skins," added Wagner.

"Regardless," said Balgor, "it may be a favourable turn. Although Skol has indeed been driven to the field, he is much too occupied with the vex of NuRac nuisance to even consider us in our passiveness."

"Their nuisance isn't going to be enough," said Wagner. "They're gonna need some archers or something. These guys are falling all over each other like a bunch of Keystone Cops, while Skol is barely breaking a sweat. They can't even outreach him—that club of his is fully as long as their spears. No one can even get in a good prod without risking a wallop in reply. *Look!* See what I'm saying? They ca—"

Wagner suddenly froze in squint as reality knocked him loopwise. Having just watched Skol's weapon connecting with a dilatory soldier—and seeing said NuRac thrown in sprawl, his helmet busting from his head like a New Year's Eve popper—in the catch of an eye Wagner discerned impassable oddity in Skol's weapon.

Simply put, it had buckled. No, even more than buckling, it had flopped. What should have been hardest wood, plated by steel, had flopped like a bolt of fabric, like a ream of tarpaulin caved by indent and longsomeness. Not only this, but closer scrutiny revealed the club to be disintegrating as well, losing extraneous chunks of matter with each backlash—pulpy matter, yet decidedly nothing at all indicative of wood cellulose.

So defying its properties, it was only now, as Wagner refocused on the club's unusual helve, that its composition became horribly, gruesomely clear. What the Sunderer had been swinging in swath like a great, oaken shank was fast proving less oaken and more shank. Seeing it anew, Wagner realised its all-too-macabre semblance to an armoured greave and boot.

"Tell me that's not what I think it is," he said, hoping that he was only tippling fancy. "Tell me that's not a—a—"

"Aye," said Balgor. "It is a leg. The brute staves his attackers with one of their own limbs, *Voknor*. One of their own *limbs*—wrenched like a drumstick from the spit!"

Knowing now that there lay at least one NuRac in Skol's cell whose lifeblood even then gushed from his legless trunk sickened Wagner enough to take him knee-deep to the sand. How odd, he thought as he buckled, that he could so brutally stave in a woman's face a few days earlier, and yet be so repulsed now by the same kind of insensate graphicness. Puzzled, unsure, it took him the longest moment—and a narrowly averted upchuck—to shake away his disgust. Meanwhile, Skol swung hard his "club" in countering fend to the soldiers' advances, despite its evident deterioration and increasing flaccidity as impact after successive impact continued to pulverise femur, fibula, and tibia into smithered flimsy.

Wagner's earlier assessment proved prophetic when an outpour of crossbow archers spilled through the ingresses and fell into semicircle formation around Skol and his poorly failing antagonists. The battling soldiers, heartened by the reinforcement, quickly scurried in retreat, barely making it behind the queue before seven quill-like bolts breached the airspace that the soldiers had only just traversed. Smaller and finer than lethal fare, six of the seven found mark in Skol's extremities—most in his trunky legs—while the seventh strayed erringly into the quartered NuRac shank. The ammunition presumably such that it wouldn't kill the brute so much as weaken and disorient him, Balgor offered that the tips of the quills were steeped in sedatory agent so as to stupefy Skol just enough to make corralling possible. Seven quills, he however noted, tipped the scales of excess, for he'd once seen a bull vrohda felled by a paltry two.

Skol being impossible to control and too valuable to kill, they'd slipped him an airborne Mickey that addled his brain and turned his legs to jelly. Within the minute his flailing and lunging became sloppy and unfocused, and Skol himself sputtered groundward like a helicopter with a snapped prop. Folding on his own legs, his impact released a mushroom of dust that billowed like spirit rent from his body. Then, without comprehension, he succumbed to the commingling drug and ground to a complete stop.

Sprawled there on the sand, but for the heave of his breast it would have been easy to believe him dead. One-half of the crowd cheering, the other half booing, while their hero/nemesis had gone down without a proper battle, to some of the viewers it had still been worthwhile entertainment—even at the expense of some of their own. The soldiers, coming forward like Roman editors, confirmed Skol's paralysis by prod, and simply cast a net of mail about him and let him lie. Superficially impaled by the quills, the man-monster did, however, present evidence of a number of more serious punctures inflicted by sword and spear from the initial roust, and these would need prompt tending before revivification—provided that the NuRacs' intent was to keep Skol alive.

This, indeed, was the question. With Skol prostrate and the soldiers going about at damage control, all five stable-masters, their various associates, and other pertinent officials graced the field and approached the fallen dynamo. Wagner, Balgor, and Kadok all but forgotten, these muckamucks stood around the body and round-tabled over how best to determine Skol's future. One high-ranker, perhaps the officer whose subordinates met death within Skol's cell, bickered more vehemently than the others, pointing and gesturing at Skol, at the disjointed leg, at the enclosure—and in his tirade he seemed very much to be arguing the Sunderer's bother against his worth. The others in the group offered gradated stances. Some expounded thoughtful logic; some argued box office revenue; at least one gave counterpointing tirade back to the first, insisting that Skol was not only a staple, but the main draw of the games, and that it was up to the trainers and orchestrators to devise a better means for showcasing the brute.

"Looks like AuwNiir is plenty steamed that we didn't get to enjoy his little surprise," said Wagner.

"The gods have looked favourably upon us," said Balgor, staring into the gathering and accidentally crossing glances with the ired Commander. "Thus far," he quickly added.

AuwNiir's *sigma*-crested breastplate reflected brightly in the afternoon sunlight, blinding Wagner afresh with each of the Commander's ardent gesticulations. The breastplate and its owner both fodder for Wagner's pondering, he once more speculated on his elusive, could-be connection with the NuRac, and momentarily considered querying Balgor for the emblem's significance. He opted, however, to remain heedfully, thoughtfully, mum—even in this potentially final hour—as both Kadok and the realmson were inexorably glued to the goings-on across the field.

After what had been ten minutes or abouts, the soldiers were regrouped and instructed to help facilitate Skol's refurling back to his hovel. A medical team had since been summoned, and in standing by they'd made ready to either extract the shafts and dress the wounds or to euthanise him—whichever fate the impromptu committee decided. Beheading him outright would not have been an option, for even the barbarous crowd would have considered it unsporting. By instead administering lethality under the pretence of remedy, the payrolled orderlies could later claim that Skol had been too degraded to respond, which in turn would dissever all colluders from responsibility. That this was *not* to be the procedure, it suggested that Skol had indeed been given quarter, and for the next hour or so—until the sedative gave way—he would be purged, nursed, and bandaged to the degree that it was possible.

Once the field had been cleared of all distraction, only the three infractors remained unaddressed. While Skol's event had been a miserable washout, it seemed that their fates would need to be configured anew. Once decided, it wasn't at all long before several trusties rushed out to gather up the clubs and offer an upgrade—a "contender's choice" of either a bastard sword or a poleaxe. The dynamic of the event was clearly changing, and the armaments, turning more lethal. It thus followed that the adversaries would therefore be more numerous.

"Know you with whom or what our battle will be?" Balgor asked the trusty they knew as Rolavor.

"The Beastmaster's Ennead," replied the man.

Wagner looked at Balgor for a simplified translation.

"Nine of the fiercest, swiftest, hungriest croviks you will ever encounter," said Balgor. "Choose the weapon that best suits your skills, *Voknor*—it appears that we have three carcasses apiece to deliver to our overworked kitchen staff."

Wagner examined his dilemma. Squaring off against a human foe was one thing; he was trained for that—if only in the sense of sparring—and in most cases a blade worked nicely. Going against rampaging quadrupeds was another spin entirely, and without experience he could only second-guess his prowess. Relatively unseasoned with a genuine poleaxe per se, he'd nevertheless proven himself fairly dexterous in the use of spears, battleaxes, maces, and staffs. The poleaxe, incorporating the best of all four into one versatile and lengthy weapon, therefore seemed the sensible choice for him. Its apical spike made for easy thrusting, while the opposing blade and hammer made scything or bludgeoning as convenient as a 180° rotation of the shaft. The length advantage, however, was the feature he most sought, for he felt that the farther that he could keep a snapping, four-legged critter at bay, the better were his odds of remaining whole. When compared, then, to a sword—relished mostly by those who preferred the strategic rush and sweep of close-quarter fighting—the poleaxe was the only weapon in town.

Plucking one from Rolovar's grip, Wagner levelled it, plumbed its equilibrium and range, and nodded stiff-lipped affirmation—first to the trusty and then to Balgor. Balgor, of course, went with his namesake, followed by Kadok, who likewise chose a bastard sword. Their selections not escaping Wagner, for a moment he wondered if perhaps they knew something about croviks that he did not. Still, he stuck by his choice. Blade fighting never having been his conscious specialty—despite how his usurping berserker warmed to the rollick of a good swordfight—he elected not to trust his survival to the subconscious *deus ex machina* that may or may not have become a full integrant of his being over the last weeks. Hoping that diversity would benefit the three of them, he turned from his misgivings and positioned himself and his poleaxe alongside his newly retrofitted allies, and together they watched as the trusties raced from the field.

No sooner were they alone in the ring then did a partition on the north-west wall slide away, out of which spewed the hungry croviks, each at the heels of the one before it, rocketing like sepia projectiles onto the sands and straight in the direction of their next intended meal. The crowd above erupted in a volcanic roar of too-long-delayed bloodlust as the nine, bestial eating-machines streaked across the arena in scurry-footed blur, a cyclonic trail of dust streaming up behind them like fiery exhaust fumes. It could not have been more surreal.

In the six-odd seconds that he had before contact, Wagner quickly sized up his remarkable attackers. Looking, as Bilahdu had taught him, for strengths and weaknesses, natural advantages and exploitable shortcomings, he made lightning-fast assessment of what to avoid and what to zero in on. Already he knew that with these beasts he would have to be particularly focused.

Conceivable hybrids of panther and pygmy grizzly, the croviks possessed the vigour, the razored claws, and especially the nasty incisors of the former, with mainly the rounder physiology of the latter. Their compact, ursine bodies by no means undermining their speed and agility, like a living, seething flash flood they descended en masse upon the three men, the leading crovik skirting Balgor and Wagner and hurling itself headlong into the sweep of Kadok's slapdash blade.

The youth got off a good one. His slice sheared the beast's snout clean off to a point just below its eyes. Momentum carrying it groundward, it somersaulted in a spume of dust and blood, flopping and convulsing in short-lived frenzy before succumbing to total somatic shock.

In the same moment, Balgor deftly sidestepped a charging bull so that it slammed full-force into the wooden spar behind him. Two distinct cracks on impact—one of wood, one of bone—the pole would topple seconds later, just as Balgor and Wagner stepped in together to stab the stunned animal's vitals. Swinging back around, Wagner narrowly slipped beneath the next beast's airborne assault. A glancing miss, its claws snagging only the pill of his tunic, Wagner cried warning to Kadok, who, suddenly in harm's way, careened about and split the animal gut-wise.

Balgor spun his sword like a whirligig, hacking and slicing, no single crovik able to penetrate his barrage of cleaving steel. Still, these ravagers were not so completely dull-witted as to keep charging where their brethren had failed. In the wild, croviks hunted in packs, and where outright assault failed they instead wore down their next meal with a nip here, a raking of claws there, a relentless buffeting of tag-team vexing that systematically exhausted and bled out their victim through conspired teamwork. That this host was unable to effectively employ that proclivity stemmed first from the likelihood that few, if any of them, were of the same nurture; and second, the effects of being caged and sustained by regular feedings generally proved detrimental to the basic inclination of any wild animal. Captivity was surely one adulterant of many that helped to close the odds between the croviks and their human quarry.

Sensing the unyielding ferocity of the figure who frustrated their every charge, three croviks made mindset to blitz Balgor from as many directions, compelling him to tweak his strategy by ducking around the four remaining poles. Not nearly a safe-guarding comfort, he zigzagged as dexterity permitted, thrusting when he could, slicing when convenient, careful all the while to keep his two companions in his peripheral concern.

A few metres away, Wagner claimed the good fortune of having to repel but a single crovik to Balgor's three. Even so, dodging said daemon's besetting called for rather drastic gymnastics on his part. Feinting one-side, he briskly withdrew and thumped the misdirected animal hard upon the crown. An awkward affair with his weapon of choice, it convinced him thereafter to rely as much as he could upon its thrusting capabilities, if only to prevent any of the other insidious ferals from sneaking in below his overextension.

The headstruck crovik recovered as if never impinged, charging at Wagner, scampering hither and about as if on a hot smoulder, searching for the smallest negotiant in Wagner's rebuff. Indeed, when it sensed opportunity, it took a chance at his unprotected flank.

Wagner, cursing his failing, extricated himself just in the nick and tilted his spearhead straight into the beast's loins. In yelp and howl, the gored crovik twisted wildly at skewer's end while Wagner pinned the animal between axe-head and ground, heaving his full weight on the shaft while the creature flipped and flailed about.

The crovik seemingly in last throes, Wagner retracted the spear in order to deliver quietus by way of some more vital organ. To his astonishment, the freed animal righted itself split-second and sprung at him in devious reversal, bowling him back in start. Tangled by his own legs, suddenly pregnable in unstoppable pratfall, his only preservation was in somehow manoeuvring the poleaxe up and between him and the rapidly swooping meat-grinder.

Drawing the shaft near in ever-shortening space, he managed to rear it only partially aloft before the crovik impacted atop him. By miracle, it was all he'd needed. The beast came down hard, its bulk and downplummet driving the spike—and, incredibly, one-half of the axe and hammer assembly—deep into its sternum. Carried over by runaway momentum, the dying, blood-spitting crovik arced over and away from Wagner, snapping the overstrained implement in its passing, leaving Wagner up-faced and intact but with little more than a sliverish spear for defence.

His grip syrupy with crovik blood, he scrambled to his feet to confront a new pair of assailants who, singling him out, commenced a more cautious stalking than their impetuous cousin before them. Courting Wagner almost in ritual, they threatened him simultaneously from opposing directions, snapping, spitting, careful to keep shy of even the paltry, partial lance in his brandish.

Vacillating between fronts, wishing desperately for another pair of eyes, stood James Wagner the warrior. Holding his ground—and *amazed* that he was holding his ground—he could not help but pay heed to a queer and extraordinary exhilaration that surged like a groundswell upon his mind. Undetracting—in fact, augmentative—it settled on him like a vervish buoyancy that by pure euphoria almost had him now enjoying the fray, despicable as it was. In nearly every way this was less the usurping persona of his past experience than it was the feeling of suddenly finding his elemental zone in something that had priorly instilled distress and fear and uncertainty in whelming degree. All three sensations he still felt; only now he saw them not as deterrents but as incorporants to be absorbed without flinch into his psyche, each one administering to a particular wantage in much the same way that the allying of one warring faction with its enemies against a greater evil infuses the resulting cooperative with the composure of equivalence. His bedevilments suddenly made into adjuncts, his so-so confidence suddenly elevated to ultra—it bolstered him and propelled him to a new and gainful stratum. As the animals continued at him, fangs in bare like horrible, hungry grins, Wagner defended himself in coolly expert fashion, meeting every charge with nulled emotions and unreasonably high resolve.

While Kadok was now happily bereft of any tormentors of his own, Balgor was yet laden with triple duty. Neatly piercing one she-devil through the sternum, he booted a second one across the snout for attempting to squeak in under his guard. The third crovik, a girthy bull, made no matter of the realmson's adroitness, nor of the glinting, alloyed "tusk" that his bipedal prey wielded so vehemently. Barring injury and charging at him full-freight, he mauled the disbelieving man and ploughed him to the ground.

Twisting frantically beneath the bull's enormous heft, the realmson felt his shoulder perforated by pitchforkish incisors. Too late in struggle, he sought hold of his blade and attempted blindly—and through discommodity—to gouge the beast wheresoever he could. An awkward trial, it was worsened when the second crovik re-entered the skirmish, clamping onto Balgor's boot and attempting to chew leather and flesh as one.

Realising the futility in manipulating his blade, Balgor did the one thing that he was loath to do: he relinquished it. Only a single recourse coming to mind, in struggling against his own savaging he wriggled a hand down between his own abdomen and the beast's, and in base but tactical desperation took hold of the bull's ample scrotum. This, his only precipitate means of equalising the struggle, from within his constriction he wrenched the pouch like an immature ogre-fruit, prompting such a yowl of excruciation from the brute that it momentarily compelled the attention of every other crovik on the field. Bucking violently into the air, its reaction allowed the realmson all of two seconds to fumble up his sword and run the wailing beast straight through the breast.

Scrambling out from beneath the faltering behemoth, Balgor rolled to his knees and managed to likewise thwart the inrushing foot-gnawer with a frontal slice that severed both of its forelegs just below the second joint. Cut down thusly in mid-leap, the hobbled crovik collided unavoidably with Balgor, but quickly dismissed him beyond impact for the anguish of its sudden crippling. Terrified by extreme agony and by its inability to put itself upright, the pathetic gimpling was easily, mercifully, slain. Liberating its head from its neck in one clean stroke, the realmson spun and finished off the expiring bull with equal dispatch.

At the point in Balgor's reversal when his bull had let go in shriek, Wagner had been no less curious about the source of the ado than had his startled attackers. Chancing a squiz in the realmson's direction and noting his friend's despair, he'd deserted his own battle to race to Balgor's aid. Midway over, however, when he saw that Balgor was turning the tables all by himself, he'd abandoned his rescue and swung back around, only to be struck down in buffet by one of the combatants he'd forsaken. Slammed violently onto his back, he lost his wind nigh to the point of blackout. A critical error, turning tail on one's enemy, he'd known it at the onset—and lo, how he knew it now. An act that would have surely garnered him a good lathering from Bilahdu for its foolhardiness, Wagner's true comeuppance would be far worse. Feeling faint and fuzzy, barely able to summon a struggle from beneath the beast's sprawl, with his air expelled and no capacity to draw anew he felt his vision begin to blotch around the edges. Not only inconvenient, it was a lethal inaffordability. Beckoned by sweet unconsciousness, he knew that if he gave it sway he might never wake up again.

He did not, in fact, go under. Nor did he find himself rent to pieces. By pure and provident chance did it happen that the piledriving crovik had impaled itself on Wagner's poleaxe remnant, and that nothing more than its most unwieldy corpse lay between Wagner and his much needed gasp of air.

Like being pinned beneath a grand piano wrapped in bearskin, Wagner had no leverage, and therefore, no out. Not, however, an entirely woesome predicament, the dead crovik actually served him better than he knew. As with a bone that must be cracked and opened in order to sample the tasty marrow within, so did the animal's carcass hinder the last surviving crovik from reaching the vulnerable Wagner below it. Even in helpless flounder, Wagner would at end appreciate the crush and smother that facilitated his salvation.

Two things happened next. Balgor, having witnessed Wagner's distress, raced in to repel the prying crovik, attempting between assail and retreat to rescue Wagner from his underpin. At the same time, across the arena, another panel swung away to loose three additional beasties onto the field. Croviks, yes; but these were different from those of the Ennead—larger, more lumbering, less crazed perhaps but no less dangerous than those of the first batch. An unprecedented departure from tournament procedure, a complete overstepping of trust, it seemed that the NuRacs in oversee evidently couldn't abide the upset in progress—not to mention Kadok's ongoing idleness—when there was a money-plunking, blood-lusty multitude to be sated. This fresh infusion, then, to prolong the battle, to end it, or to offset its current leanings for a more desired outcome, there was undoubtedly attached to it equal impetus to address the pulse of the crowd and to assure its full and utter entertainment—and convention be damned.

Freed at last, but sadly not unscathed, in stumbling to gain his footing Wagner realised the worst—that his burdening crovik had not been alone in its impaling. His fingers leading him to a tender spot beneath a rive in his tunic, he found that he'd been equally and incidentally skewered, and this by the *blunt end* of his implement! The butt-cap having punched its way like a signet into his obliques, this unfortunate subsequence of the crovik's deathfall had saddled him with a wound that was neither through nor clean—which would have been bad enough—but had instead wreaked him a gruesome mash of freebleeding trauma that, only by the beloved grace of adrenaline, caused Wagner far less pain than it did dismay and horror.

Not far off, Kadok's struggle had aggravated to the full. The three additional—and much fresher—aggressors beelining directly for him, Balgor was too busied by the last of the original croviks to intercept any of the recent. That neither he nor Wagner had fully defended Kadok as planned hadn't been entirely due to the unpredictability of the skirmish—which was considerable—but had in large instance come about through the youth's own penchants. While it was true enough that Balgor had allowed the Ennead's headmost crovik to slip into Kadok's offence at the onset, there'd been far less negligence than gambit behind what initially seemed a breach of his protective commitment. Come to know, Balgor had improvised a clever three-in-one ploy intended to busy the lad straight off, to separate the alpha crovik from the pack, and to present Wagner and himself as more attractive targets for the ensuing eight. For the most part he had succeeded. Yet, as Kadok so bitterly resented his condemnation for his trifling role in their escape, his dourness, his fear, and his nervousness all worked to amplify his preoccupation, which in turn made him all the more a target.

While Wagner scrambled about in scrounge of anything to replace his want for weaponry, Balgor hacked and sliced until his brutalised beast had no gumption left. Running it through, he then hurtled past Wagner to put himself front and centre amid Kadok's distress. Wagner, by his own device, took to the broken spar that Balgor's first attacker had felled through impact, thinking to adapt it as some manner of bludgeon. Regretfully, he found it far too weighty and cumbersome for this. But the chains and manacles dangling in half-rivet from their splintered moorings—*these* he could use.

Balgor, successful in luring one of the croviks away from Kadok, was in the midst of altercation when he saw the youth buffeted in combination by the undistractable two. One charging in low, the other lunging at Kadok's throat, in his feckless defence of both fronts Kadok was bowled over and savaged like a papier mâché effigy.

Unable to swiftly dispatch his own opponent, Balgor simply abandoned the crovik altogether and raced to Kadok's aid. Faring no better, however, than Wagner had previously with similar tactic, Balgor found his adversary decidedly uncooperative. Not accepting disregard, in full gallop the creature raced to intercept him, its claws suddenly like pincers about his legs, its fangs sinking deep into his thigh, and before Balgor knew it he was in toss like a rag doll through the air.

Leaving grip of his sword, through sting and smart he pushed his way free of the beast's jagged gnashers. Careering groundward, he landed as solidly as his wounds permitted and scrambled to regain his blade before further assail. The crovik bearing down fast, Balgor braced for the impending maul with a tensile, hunkering stance, calculating inevitability down to the second before suddenly vaulting the animal as one would a pommel horse, and plunging carbon steel down through its spine. The beast's hindquarters immediately seizing, with its motor control severed it dashed the ground in ungainly tumble, its rear half slumped, its forebody in convulsive writhe, its agony ready and beyond for the quietus that would have followed but for Balgor's wrenching outcry for the younger peer whom he'd not reached in time.

Wagner, scuttling forward too late with his gritted teeth and his fistings of chains, could likewise scarce believe his eyes.

Kadok had perished. There was no doubt. He'd died the worst sort of death, his throat ripped out in the midst of his own reckoning, his fluids spilled while he'd looked on in helpless disbelief. The excruciation of his rent flesh and the memory of his subsequent disembowelment would be his most viscerally vivid accompaniment back to the Sacred Pool. And although his enduring companions would never accept it, although Balgor and Wagner would ever feel the shame of their unmet oath no matter what consolation the future held, all of the fleetness that they might have coaxed from wearied legs and battered bodies to forestall this eventuality would still not have guaranteed Kadok's continuance, nor precluded some equally tragic end by divers circumstances. Still, to philosophise such was cold and passionless and ill-considered. It meant little in the wake of the young man's loss. It meant even less when there were murderous croviks on the field ravaging his remains.

Setting sight on them that gnawed and tore at Kadok's body, each man flew to the spot from his own vantage—Balgor afire with blood-drizzled sword, Wagner with naught but knuckles and chains and a mid-section in heavy bleed. The former reaching the scene first, he hurled himself atop the largest of the pair and sank his blade so deeply into its backside that not even Arthur Pendragon himself might have removed it. The outraged crovik, vitally wounded, nevertheless jounced him off and came at him, snapping at the fast-scrabbling Ergosian with incisors laced stringy with the flesh of the fallen comrade. Wagner, reaching the fray just as the second crovik had joined its brother in overrunning Balgor, flung himself onto said creature's shoulders, and with twisty-turny arms, engirded its throat with his scavenged fetters. The ends of the chain in deliberate coil around his wrists, he was there to stay, good or bad. His knees digging hard at the crovik's flanks, his fixity more precipitous than he even dared to think, as the creature tried bucking him into tomorrow he yanked with tautest force in hopes of crimping its airflow. Yet, as the beast barely gave flinch, with no time to rethink his tactics Wagner tried again. Narrowly avoiding being thrown off, and barely evading an angry backswipe, he wriggled the cinch down along what seemed the crovik's windpipe. Then, with grimace and gleaming eye he jerked the garrotte as mightily as his sinew allowed, and somehow, with just the right impetus and leverage, impaired the creature enough to compel its fullest alarm.

Had anyone been close enough to peer into Wagner's eyes as he brought that lumbering behemoth to a halt, there would have been no detectable intellect behind them, no rationale, no trace of right or wrong, inconsideration or emotion, compassion or conscience. In fact, there was nothing at all driving James Wagner at that moment other than instinct—pure, undistilled, uncivilised instinct. Feral instinct. Uncompromised by morality or immorality, if he was thinking at all it was strictly from within an icy and emotionless framework. And if what he was feeling could have been conveyed with the slimmest measure of coherency, his thoughts were surely, undebatably, primal. Killing, crushing, strangling, quashing—this was *Voknor*, and he wanted the battle over *now*.

To the crowd's astonishment, the gagging quadruped gurgled its last and slumped over dead. In its downpitch, the amok Wagner made capital on its vulnerability by snapping its neck, and after shaking himself from the daze of his great exertion he quickly set at disintricating his battered wrists. It was a tedious business, for the torsion had grated his flesh to tatters. Yet, he didn't once flag, not even after pulling free. Swinging away from the corpse, he bolted to his friend's aid, leaping like a crazed trapezer onto the shoulders of the last of twelve rampaging croviks.

This specimen, still fiercely altercating, had nevertheless dialled down its more reckless assailing after the artful realmson managed to retrieve Kadok's fallen blade and initiate a bold reversal. And now, with Wagner not only astride, but his arms hammerlocking the crovik's throat, Balgor found all the opening he needed. Ramming his sword upward, he neatly spitted the beast's head—oesophagus to crown—and dropped the crovik blankly in its tracks.

Then, on the field where a dozen croviks and one man lay dead, the two remaining warriors—the victors—staggered like bomb-blast survivors near the brink of their own mortality. Sluggish in footing, their carriages a comparable fumble of exhaustion and anaemic stupor, through refocusing and readjusting eyes they surveyed the bloody debacle before them, hoping above all that no more animals would be released through treacherously raised partitions. Up and around them, reverberating throughout the overpacked amphitheatre, the NuRac crowd roared in thunderous, vehement approval. So resounding as to nearly strike an unready man deaf, in truth the weary partnership heard none of it. There was only one sound in their heads: the echoed replay of Kadok's last shrieks, the final cries of the youth they'd sworn—and failed—to protect. Physically they felt nothing but the drain and languidness so common to warfare aftermath. Once recognisably out of danger, their bodies had begun doling sensation back to them while siphoning away the adrenaline that they no longer needed. Like a pair of faltering tops, then, with the loss of biochemical bolstering and the suspension of the immediate danger that had summoned it, they bobbled, buckled, and finally collapsed, their bodies bleeding out, their minds in dark regret, their egos unheeding of the chants and cheers of the new celebrity that ten-thousand of their bitterest enemies suddenly foisted upon them for the morbidity of mindless slaughter, of harrowing folly, and of vicissitudinous interplay—all in the name of entertainment.

CHAPTER SEVENTEEN

After the event even a fool is wise.
—HOMER

Wagner was long accustomed to waking up in odd places. For years, in fact, it was such a predominant wont in his life that the exception had actually come to be on the rare morning when he popped open his peepers to find himself unresettled from the scene of his previous conk-out. Coming round in some unfamiliar space at Howsley, some dingy janitor's closet or the admissions floor lavatory or even on the grounds outside—this had heretofore been his normal state of affairs, with each day bringing new surprises and new mysteries for his befuddled resolving. More recently—and sans the now-defunct influence of mind-tripping roulette— there'd been the grassy purlieu of his Ergosian landfall and the caravan dray following his capture. And how could he forget the handful of disoriented dawns, deep within a murky oubliette, awakening to the dreadful smell of sewage and the busy skitter of dung beetles across his flesh?

That such time-honoured tradition would not fall neglected, here would be one more instance—and one more locale—to add to his burgeoning list. And although he was initially reluctant to leave the easy serenity of semi-consciousness in order to do so, Wagner began to gradually register the periphery of his new environs, starting with the torch-flickered hall that housed him and the tottery cot that supported him.

The surrounding airspace was astir with noise, and the air itself, barely breathable due to a pungency that would not be ignored. In some ways more foul than the dungeon, here was yet another fetid mingling of some of the most nose-cringing excreta imaginable—odours of open bowel and viscera, many of which he'd never had quite such displeasure of sampling at this close range. Given his druthers, he'd have preferred remaining unacquainted by a good kilometre or so.

Soon resumptive enough in focus to attempt a look around, he confirmed that he was far from alone. On the contrary, the hall was all but choked with bedridden people whose pain and confusion eclipsed his a hundredfold. The in-wedging of poor souls to his left and right quite nearly as serried as the Great Arena stands had been in healthy audience, the only real difference seemed the switch of venue—one of brutality and bloodlust for that of its consequence. As ever, the Ergosians were the expendable means of sating the NuRacs' darkest natures; they were the pit bulls, the gamecocks, the subservients whose anguish in the ring provided insight for savvier NuRac wagering on the go-round, and whose anguish here, in the infirmary, was beneath anyone's fast concern excepting their own and Papa Olask's.

This cold, echoey place that Wagner once visited for his first health assessment had been transformed into a combination triage/O.R.—and a damned impressive one at that. Despite the relative barbarism of this culture's medical state, Wagner now observed a host of remarkably competent orderlies and volunteers going about in busied purpose—sponging, dressing, poulticing, stitching, condoling— with no less concern for their kinspeople than Jon Mazzio's staff had shown for its own resident charges. It was, in fact, a scene of such distinctive parallelism that it effectively spiked some of the unresolved issues of credulity that Wagner had been toying with since his transference, specifically the old and undiminished nettle that premised that he was yet a mental ward patient, completely withdrawn and superimposing all of this Ergosian incidence over earthly reality. So much sensory evidentiality and interactive complexity to suggest otherwise, it was nevertheless a notion that cropped up whenever objectivity and situational comparativeness told him that this existence simply couldn't be real.

The tournament had taken its toll on the prison populace; of this there was no doubt. Glohular and other salves and antiseptics were dispensed by the bucketful. Washcloths mopped the foreheads of the feverish. Human comfort—a hand holding, a stroking of hair, a kiss bestowed in sympathetic kindliness—was administered without bias by any number of compeers, even those belonging to competing stables and disparate clans. In this place, in this aftermath, everyone was family. Sewing needles sutured catgut through the bloodied gapings of those who'd escaped most critical injury, while heavy-handled blades lay at the ready for those unfortunates whose limbs proved unsalvageable. Olask being the fierce practitioner that he was, he would course any possible avenue to keep the wounded physically whole; but as he was not omnipotent—and given the unenlightened latitudes of mediaeval medicine—his hands were too often as bound as were those of the poor wretches who required forced restraint for their regrettable amputations.

In truth, the maimed, the riven, and the limbless were no unsizable subgroup in the prison. Their presence was legion long before Wagner ever arrived. In a livelihood embellished by unprotected warfare, how could they not be? That they weren't overwhelmingly numerous, however, was due largely to the rampancy of septicity and post-operative infections and such. Olask often capable of working wonders, he had little sway over microbiological—or human—proclivity; and all the care and cleaning and embrocating in the world couldn't compete with insufficient sterilisation, excessive blood loss, and an amputee's disinclination to live. As for those who pulled through their harrowing ordeals—although no longer physically whole, most of them persevered by finding new purpose in the kitchen or the textilery or in a variety of other duties, all dependent on the nature and severity of their impediments. Ability permitting, the toughest ones sometimes even returned to the palaestra, more determined than ever to prove that a missing eye or arm did not detract from their prowess. Tamek, and sometimes Olask, bargained on a regular basis with AuwNiir and the other Commanders for at least the opportunity for those who wished it to demonstrate their utility in whatever capacity they desired.

In times so harsh, in an age where survival was ever pendent—and leisure, incremental at best—Wagner couldn't help but note the great prevalence of affliction that existed in the camp, and presumably throughout the realm in whole. Not only wrought of warfare, but naturally occurring—from ordinary boils to lameness, and probably right up to congenital malformation—everything that his twenty-first century culture felt compelled to label as unsightly, disabling, or abominable, this culture abided with unblinking eye. Damaged people weren't pariahs here. Neither were they the gazingstocks that they surely would have been in Wagner's society, where revulsion at the merest pimple, the slightest ripple of cellulite, had huge numbers of contemporary Americans disregarding anyone who didn't exhibit the flawlessness of magazine cover perfection. Missing limbs, missing digits, these were the facts and the risks of Ergosian life. Sometimes, as with J'nea's stigma, they were even inflicted by judicatory decree. And as for inborn deformity, Wagner wasn't qualified to offer an assessment, for he had yet to observe any extreme instance. Knowing that nature wasn't foolproof, knowing that deviation must have reared on occasion, he attributed its limitedness here to wanting technology. There were no incubators in these darker ages, no artificial life support. The mortality rate in aberrant newborns was surely and understandably high. Too, as this culture was far from demystified, he imagined that some small portent (or even greater totemism) might find unfortunate application in situations of human malformation whenever it did occur, where interpretative forecasting of ill bodings or of unbidden providence in matters of harvest, weather, prosperity, et al, might lead to lethally barbaric countermeasures. Again, he could not be sure. He simply hadn't had the opportunity or the reason to explore the issue.

Of the physically impaired prisoners of Wagner's acquaintance, he'd found them far more accepting of their various decrements than he'd ever have expected. As there was little to be done about their conditions anyway, without a society that pointed fingers and stared, many of the stauncher survivors treated their new hardship no differently than if they'd bottomed out on a poor roll at bigratto. They recognised the immutability of their lot, resigned themselves to it, brooked it as a setback to be overcome and mastered lest the NuRacs devise some alternative in response to their diminishment in utility. With careful retraining, whether in some prison craft or service—or back in the arena in hybridic warfare—most of them adapted, and adapted quickly.

While this forbearance against the ravages of physical happenstance was indeed impressive, Wagner could not discount the anguish and bitterness that accompanied, and often undermined, the retooling process. Yet, such emotional reactions were nowhere near the calibre of what he'd seen in his former existence, again because survival was key. Continuation was more important than all of the petty styles, fashions, prestiges, and gratifications that Wagner's culture strained to maintain above all else. After living among the Ergosian people, even with some of their comparable shortcomings, he was embarrassed for his own kind's juvenility, especially when he knew that his so-called "enlightened society" had no good excuse for allowing the perpetuation of prejudice or snobbery in any form—

race, creed, gender, age, ability, acquisition, even mental illness—when so many brilliant thinkers and dreamers had posited any number of means for rising beyond it all.

Filing away his judgements, he braced an arm and tried sitting up. Racked, however, by abdominal anguish, he sank back into his pillow and promptly peeled away his fraying sheet to find a large bandage affixed to his side. He recalled, then, the ordeal with the croviks, the wild butchery of the field, and the events that had yielded his injury. Rifling recollection for more particulars, he managed to net a jumbled few—a goring, an individual kill, an isolated fear, an exhilaration—and, stringing one memory upon another like laundry on a line, he eventually amassed a piecemeal recap of the fateful day, right up to his and Balgor's narrow, albeit consummate, victory. One unintended image, however, saw him downgrading that victory to only a partial win, the image of Kadok's horrible defeat suffusing him with remorse quite unexpungeable. Death, it seemed, had been the grandest winner by far. Charon's ferry had crossed the River Styx overladen in steerage; Valhalla's tables were stacked to surfeit for many a warrior's feast. And the Sacred Pool of Ergosian lore?—it was doubtlessly steeped with indeliberate souls, human and otherwise, all waiting for rebirth into happier times.

Beyond the senselessness of it all, Wagner shrank in his bed, seized by ever-worsening scenario: He had no idea how his best friend had fared past their mutual collapse!

Looking around, bed to bed, with such a sea of sheets and pillows and dressings, all under such poor illumination, he had no easy task of locating one face amid so many. Craning one way, then another, he eventually switched tacks and instead looked about for Olask or any handy orderly whom he might query.

"Must you thrash so?" The chide came from the cot to his left. "We were told to rest comfortably, and here your wallow is five jounces in excess."

Twisting about to confront the snide neighbour, Wagner forgot about his injury and wrenched himself to piercing result. Cringing, gnashing, groaning, he grabbed hold of his side and fought through clench and wince to face the fellow.

"*Gently*, brave warrior! Think you that your next arena challenge awaits you so soon?" Clearly the voice's owner was more amused than concerned.

"My next *challenge*," Wagner grumbled, "will be to jam my fist down your throat if you don't nix it with the badgering."

The man chuckled in his bed. "Such sauciness from a fellow who cannot even bend to fasten his own trousers! Were I to lop off your head in this instant, no doubt it would go right on acting the tough."

Wagner looked up with familiar suspicion and found himself grimace to grin with Balgor of the Realm. Similarly bedridden—and right next to Wagner no less—Balgor was neither sullen nor self-pitying for his convalescence. He was sharp and corky and ever the rascal, and seemingly quite content to be the thorn in Wagner's other side.

With a self-depreciatory snicker, Wagner plopped back onto his pillow, and brought his palms to his eyes. "I should've known it was you," he said, pressing hard enough to see stars. "I should have known that I'd not only find you *alive*, but in despicable good humour. Can you possibly—*remotely*—be in as much pain as I am?"

"Oh, that and more, I assure you."

"Oh, really? And how do you figure that?"

Foraging within himself for his best Bilahdu impression, Balgor jumped into the part:

> "Why, you bear but a paltry spear wound, Voknor, a mere child's nick! As for myself, not only am I bruised and battered, but I am covered ear-to-heel with the ghastly perforate of crovik fangs. Legs, arms, shoulders—punctures everywhere! Were they but the impassioned nibbles of my mate, Skagra, from within her sundry throes, well, then I might more easily assuage my great suffering with the knowledge of the immensity of satisfaction that I provide for her. But, as they are the result of a great bale of carnivorous devils who sought to devour my living mass—of which there is ample—I feel justified in overstating the severity of my ordeal."

Wagner shook his head. "Not too convincing."

"Nay?" Balgor looked disappointed. "Well, then, let us hear *your* complaint."

"Me? Oh, nothing more boast-worthy than a whole load of pain from being trephined in the gut by a blunt object. Other than feeling like crap and having to listen to your impossible cheerfulness, I'm just hunky dory."

"Oh? One would think that you were half-laid in your grave, the way you were fussing and churning."

"Yeah, well, maybe it would help if my dressings were a bit sturdier, instead of this slipshod mess. They look like they were slapped together by a blind man."

Suddenly, a voice interjected from behind. "What say you to a *half*-blind woman?"

Wagner turned—more cautiously this time—to behold Ponahr of the Orb, a seamstress from the textilery who indeed had but one good peeper. The other socket devoid of its eyeball, the vacancy she kept occupied with what looked like an earthly child's marble. The other Ergosians referred to it as her "orb," and thus her title. Like other fabric workers, her skill at stitching often lent itself to doubling as suturing assistance in Olask's surgery, a tremendous asset to the medical team during times like these, when the torrential flood of injured so glutted the infirmary.

"I had not yet finished with you," Ponahr said, producing a loosely furled skein of ivory cloth. "I merely needed to procure a lengthier wrap for your midriff than that which the orderlies provided me." Requesting that Wagner relax, she then peeled away his temporary gauzes, revealing a handiwork of fine stitches already completed. "See here," she said proudly, "is this the fashioning of the blind?"

"Oho," said Balgor, admiring from the next bed. "You weave nothing less than grace through a man's flesh, Ponahr."

"Thank you, kind sir," she said, beaming.

"How is it then," he added, "that it took you crafty people months to produce a suitable pair of breeches for Bilahdu?"

"It is not my place to countermand Skagra's wifely precepts, good Balgor. If she wishes to torment her boorish husband, that is entirely her concern. In truth, she yet hunts for the recreant sempstress who fabricated the galligaskins that now adorn him. Daily does she storm through the textilery shouting 'Traitor! Traitor!' It is really all very frightening...in an amusing sort of way."

"I don't get this whole thing," said Wagner. "If they don't love each other, or even *want* to be husband and wife, why do they keep torturing one another?"

Ponahr stopped what she was doing, looked at Wagner, and then gazed over at Balgor. "*This* one does not know much about marriage, does he?"

"He does not know much about *anything*," said Balgor.

Wagner shrank a bit. He glanced at the realmson, who smirked but kept rein over his mirthful tongue.

"He is not from around here," Balgor added.

"I would say not," said Ponahr. "Regardless, I suspect that Skagra will be a trifle more cordial to her man, as he suffered a great scatter of graltor bites in his arena bout."

"Indeed?" Balgor immediately began craning about. "Is he here, in the infirmary?"

"He was, but there was nothing about him so serious that a dose of glohular—and some considerable overpraise of his courage and prowess—could not mend over time. Truthfully, I believe that Papa Olask grew weary of his theatrics, his exaggerated groans and his canvassing for sympathy, and released him beforetime into Skagra's care—along with a bitter herb potion that she is to administer every few hours."

"Aye, to quicken his healing," said Balgor.

"Nay—not at all. I believe Olask typically uses that particular paregoric for stomach upset or hives or whatsoever. Skagra covertly requested something harmless but foul-tasting so that she might prolong Bilahdu's comeuppance."

Wagner threw up his arms. "Here we go again!"

"You may take interest in knowing that he did briefly pay visit to the two of you here on his release. But Skagra—she of the chronic impatience—hurried him along."

"By the ear, no doubt," said Balgor. "Said he anything as he passed?"

"Indeed he did. He told Skagra: 'Confound it, woman! Stop hounding me—I am a wounded hero!'"

The three of them laughed heartily before Ponahr continued.

"He also paused here, and looked upon the two of you with reflection, almost as a man gazing at his slumbering sons—"

"Gods help us!" said Balgor.

"—and he called you 'valiant men of the highest calibre.' I do believe he somehow fancies himself accredited with your survival."

"Aye, and he should," said Balgor, changing his tone. While it was true that Bilahdu was an impossible man, he had taught both Balgor and Wagner a refinement of core manoeuvres, many of which had proved indispensable in negotiating their survival. "But I would not go so far as to liken him to us in any paternal manner. The merest hint of such possibility would be enough to send most men scrambling pre-emptively for the nearest asylum. Even I, a man with a veritable nation of possible 'fathers,' would be averse to allege that he was any more than an eccentric uncle, thrice removed."

"I hadn't considered it before," said Wagner, "but now that I'm hearing it, it does seem that you and Bilahdu have more than just a few mannerisms in common."

The jibes going around, in time—even as Wagner and Ponahr cemented their acquaintanceship—the orbed one was soon compelled to press on to other, more needful, patients. In her departure, however, the two bedfellows continued trading quips, their élan elevated on a multitude of levels, not the least of which was a post-cathartic relief for having braved the awful games for another month. Although the process was soon to begin anew with a period of healing, a gradual resumption of activity, and the inevitable transition into full-fledged training, they would, for the moment, recuperate with no small measure of reserve, like wildebeests in the wake of the hunt that divested the herd of its weak and infirm. Not that either man would have even thought to devalue his fallen comrades with such callous disregard—quite the contrary; both men ached over the loss of those with whom they'd shared quarters, supped, slept, trained, and laughed, even if they had yet to hear the roster of who it was that had been lost. Still, it was neither unbeseeming nor obscene for those who endured, who triumphed, and who carried with them the memories of them that had perished, to bless their own fortune. Indeed, it was both an expected and a necessary thing. Else, why live at all?

As evening descended, an unexpected guest surprised them with the briefest of visits while on his way back to the barracks for lock-up. Tamek of Vishkor was one of the last persons they'd expected to see, at least in a topside encounter, for both men would have wagered that the Sentinel would long have been tossed into detention for some bellicosity before the Tribunal. Looking gaunt and weary, it seemed that incarceration may indeed have been in his recent past. Surely AuwNiir and the others had implicated him as the mastermind and chief abettor of the escape; and if he hadn't been flung into stir for arguing away from those charges, then he'd probably overstepped himself with his unremitting solicitations to rescind all but the merest conspiracy charge against the then-flush and vigorous Kadok.

Tamek confirmed much of their speculation. Without bothering to downplay his contempt for NuRac bureaucracy, he groused about his dealings with the Tribunal, how once again they'd taken offence at his vociferous appeals, and how they simply weren't swallowing his artifice of how Kadok's identity switch with Fostoch had been the latter's misrepresented agreement between himself and the youth as a prank or as a makeway for a night of mixed-barracks trysting—and not as a cover for Fostoch's escape. This, the safest of possible stories (with Fostoch being in absentia, and therefore unable to repudiate the theory), Tamek had insisted that Kadok's charges be reduced to mere connivery and fakement. There was no need to discuss how poorly *that* had gone over.

The ruling to have Kadok share equally in the blame needn't have been his writ of execution. Yet, it unfortunately opened him to the likelihood, and whether by action or by lack of action he had perished just the same. That he could as easily have died in some lesser—and unrelated—bout meant little in consolation to Balgor or Wagner, for the history that played out was a permanent, mnemonic etching that neither man wished to dwell on any more than he had to. Tamek himself suffered no less in guilt than they, for it was *his* counsel that had swayed Kadok into compliance; and it was equally *his* burden to live with the legacy of so frivolous a death.

"Being pitted against the Ennead-plus-three was not strictly a death sentence," argued Balgor. "What happened to Kadok was undeniably tragic, but truly it need not have been. Every one of us is, at some ultimacy, forcibly cast upon the arena sands in dire exigence. And although a victory free and clear may be an unlikelihood, barest survival is always a possibility. Are *Voknor* and I not proof of this? I have personally fought and flailed my own way out of many a dark battle, some of them far more precarious than a ravin of wild croviks. This fray, like any of those former, could have concluded in as many ways, with a diversity of consequence. As it took Kadok by incident from this life, I will mourn for him and pray that he be bestowed a better rebirthing elsewhere. But it is over now. His pain is no more, Tamek, just as yours should be."

"You speak a firm truth, realmson," said the Sentinel. "But to hear the truth is not always to accept it amain. Words—e'en noble ones—can pass easily o'er the lips only to be rebuffed by unready ears or ingrained conviction. Guilt, howe'er, is like mortar upon the soul, and much weathering must occur ere it crumbles."

Artfully changing the topic—and circumventing the poetics—Wagner inquired about Fostoch. He plied Tamek for whatever bruit he may have heard, as well as for any personal speculation that he might offer. But there had yet to be word. The last anyone knew of the wily Orrdian was Wagner's and Balgor's account of his flight from the townspeople along the inner footings of QieLahr's south wall. Whether caught and killed by the mob, or holing up in some dusty storage cellar, or even halfway to Vargath—whatever his status, it was anyone's guess. From deductive lines, as word of his death by overzealous NuRac townsfolk would never have remained mum—and as his lam likewise wouldn't have gone much farther had he indeed attempted to cross the wall at that point, not with the soldier encampment without—the most reasonable choice was that he was in hiding. Yet, what temporary haven could he possibly have found, and for how long would he be safe there?

On an unrelated note, Tamek shared the news that the monstrous Skol was neither dead, nor seemingly all that gravely wounded. After much debate among the stable-owners and the warders, the Tribunal and the military, the NuRacs determined that the resilient brute would be spared the axe and allowed to convalesce without interference, that he might continue to generate receipts and revenue for the promoters and for all of the fillable pockets and greaseable palms responsible for his reinstatement as the main tournament attraction. Even as the trio spoke of it, new measures were being drafted to prevent Skol's unruliness from ever triggering a recreation of the previous fiasco's embarrassment. The games would likely go on as before. The next slave caravan was nigh unto rolling in as well, rife with a new infusion of forlorn souls and gladiatorial templates to fill the vacancies left by these most recent games.

Tamek's visit tasked the prudence of the hour, but after finally saying his goodnights and heading off for his billet, Wagner and Balgor settled in among their kindred injured. The infirmary's cressets and oil lamps continuing to burn throughout the late hours, Olask and his orderlies alternated between making rounds and stealing away in the lull for a few winks of catch-up sleep. Any handy cot generally fit the bill, but there were also several makeshift beds near the dispensary for just such purpose, at least one of which was always occupied in these post-tournament days by a steady revolution of attendants.

Around midnight, a detachment of soldiers showed up with a load of additional medical supplies that Olask, in his providence, must have requested by messenger to the stable-owners. Drugs and dressings and the like, procured at premium through QieLahr's apothecaries, many of the soldiers begrudged the doling of pharmaceuticals to their enemies; but as AuwNiir, RoqaVek, and the other owners purchased the goods with the express intent to see out the revivifying of their investments, there was little that any short-sighted sentry could do about it without inviting unwanted recompense.

Much misery was quelled in the hours before dawn, and Wagner drifted in and out of slumber with frequency enough to note the ongoing fastidiousness of the medical team. Balgor slept even less, for—as revealed in the tale of his origin—he wasn't one to be bedridden for long, no matter the severity of his injuries. He'd ultimately risen during the night in order to calm the fevered ravings of a woman on a neighbouring cot, and after steering her back to rest he'd remained up and about, wandering the floor, assisting when he could, but more often just standing before the entry in wait of whatever breeze veered errant through the structure. Wagner, feeling increasingly selfish in his own idle of choppy sleep and loll, eventually stepped out of bed in kind, and carefully negotiated the disarrange to join his friend in his pre-dawn pensiveness.

"We nearly made it away, *Voknor*," Balgor said softly after noticing his friend beside him. "Behold the east, how its warming hues come to brush away the night. Had we succeeded, we might at this very moment be watching sweet Cinjal lifting her first veil over a horizon of sylvan wood, or shimmering in ripple upon the icy mountain brooklet whence would come our first quaff of the day. Instead, we are blind to the best of her dawning. We bide in her half-light. We wait until she ascends high enough to clear the parapets that keep us in cold captivity. So divorced are we from the light of the world."

"Wow. You're quite the poet. That's something I'd have never figured when we first met."

"I have been here too long," sighed the Ergosian. "We all have. I do not know how I could so easily have forsaken my life on the outside, resigning my livelihood to the travesty that these fiends would have us call 'existence.' Truly, *Voknor*, we must do something to turn this around."

"You know me," said Wagner, "I'm always up for a good caper."

As casual as his response was, in his heart Wagner sensed that Balgor's words were more than empty rhetoric. Somewhere along the way a seed had sprouted, and hope was growing within this Ergosian at beanstalk speed.

"Have you got any ideas on just how to do it?" he added.

Balgor cleared his throat. "Nothing as yet. But are we not clever men?"

"Sez you. Right now I'm just one big pile of hurt and dashed hopes."

Suddenly a voice came low from behind.

"If the guards see you on your feet they will not hesitate to put you back into the healthy population."

Neither man needed to turn to know that Papa Olask had joined them.

"All the less trouble for you then," said Balgor. He smiled and reverently patted Olask on the arm. "By my word, Papa, I am fine. You know well that I have launched into the fray with more extensive injury than this."

"Yes, son, but I am not speaking of your young, caddish days of juggling one too many maiden's hearts and incurring the wrath of all. These were croviks who gashed and tore at you."

Balgor chuckled. "Aye, Papa. And believe me, the croviks were far easier with me than any jilted hopeful *ever* was."

Olask blotted his eyes and forehead with a damp rag, probably in substitute for the morning's bath that he knew he wouldn't find time to have. "And what of you," he said, "um...Voknor was it? You were impaled! I inspected the wound myself. It surely cannot be agreeable to be on your feet so soon."

"I'm dealing with it," said Wagner. "Don't get me wrong—it smarts pretty good. But I'm not going to be outdone by *this* guy. If he can suck up the pain, so can I."

Olask broke into an old man's grin. "What delightful vernacular you have! Your dialect is most uncommon. You are an out-realmer, no? Although we did not find opportunity to better acquaint ourselves on your initial visit, I have since heard that you hail from the south."

Wagner nodded awkwardly.

"Very *much* to the south," added Balgor.

"Do you know, *Voknor*—I still have not been able to solve the riddle of that day's occurrence. Do you remember? The phenomenon with the seized patient and that strange refulgence? And your sudden salubrity as well! Long did I dwell upon it, and ever so often thereafter. Even now I cannot proffer any plausible explanation."

"You sound just like another doctor I know," said Wagner.

"Oh? Am I given to understand, then, that you have witnessed some similar causal sequence on a prior occasion? The same such phenomenon? And in a medical facility?"

"Well, yeah, I guess. You could say that I've seen a number of evolving peculiarities in my time. And for some odd reason I'm pretty much habitually and inextricably in the cross hairs of each one. I'm not sure I could tell you why."

"Indeed?" Olask was well beyond enthrallment, so much that he failed to hear one of his orderlies summoning him for advice with a patient. Balgor nudged his attention and he turned to go his way, but not before latching onto Wagner's arm.

"Delay your next escape," he said, tongue in cheek, "until after we have had opportunity to discuss these 'evolving peculiarities' that you have mentioned. Will you vow to this?"

"Word of honour, Papa. No escapes for at least another few days."

In Olask's off-scurry, Balgor stood a half-pace behind his friend, eyeing him on the sly. So many new things about Wagner had come to light of late, so many layers peeled away to expose even more strata within, that even Wagner's taradiddle about having ridden upon the firmament and entered the realm on a contraption of waxen feathers suddenly seemed less an absurd fabrication than it did a feat that Wagner could actually pull off.

"So," he spoke, "what you told me before was not exaggeration. The convulsing man, your bruises, the flaring of light, the revivescence—all witnessed and accepted as fact by the most sensible and rational man I have ever known."

"Oh, ye of little faith," said Wagner.

"Well, do not gloat too much. You have yet to convince me satisfactorily in your claim of other-sphered origins. This, of course, and your even greater delusion that J'nea—your morose little sylph of thieving and reaving renown—has actually seen fit to bestow you with the rare jewel of her confidence."

"Y'know, that praneez that I found in my food was quite a refreshing treat, wasn't it? Funny, I still find myself wondering where it came from. Don't you?"

"Aye," said Balgor. "As often as I wonder whence *you* came." He paused, and then tacked on Tamek's favourite topper. "*Infidel.*"

"Hey, that's 'crovik-fodder' to you."

"Nay, you proved that sobriquet invalid yesterday by your refusal to be eaten. But be not dismayed. You may yet be fodder for a more dangerous breed—namely your frosty trusty—if you do not see to it to exercise a proper measure of caution."

"Oh?" Wagner mused for a moment, a bit of incorrigibility running rakish through his head. "I think I could probably live with that."

Balgor consoled him with a few sympathetic pats on the arm. "Know you, *Voknor*, that those were the very words that Bilahdu uttered at the onset of his courtship with Skagra?"

Within a few hours, many of the volunteers from the previous evening had returned to the infirmary to resume in the dispensing of dressings, salves, and good cheer to those of their ailing compatriots who required them. Several newcomers donated effort as well, taking direction from their well-practised peers on how to blanket-bathe a patient, where to dispense with the bedpans, and how to concoct a durable poultice. In fact, with palaestra training not to resume for at least another day, so many altruists from all five stables had petitioned to lend a hand in alleviating the workload that it became suddenly convenient for Olask and his troupe of overfrayed orderlies to clock off in bulk and recoup on sleep. Most, however, remained on the premises should complication have demanded their more experienced hands; and Olask, who permanently resided in the infirmary, was always at the ready.

From his bed Wagner watched the rounds being made all about him. He intercepted a friendly wink from the bard, Gamühr, as she administered to one of his neighbours a few fingers of liniment from the various gallipots that she toted about the room. He tuned in (and just as quickly out) on an injured yet insuppressibly garrulous Uthok, who could be heard across the breadth of the infirmary boasting to his attendant about each and every scratch he'd acquired the previous day. He even saw his suture-queen, Ponahr, applying herself down the aisle, redressing the wounds of those whose bandages had either shifted askew or become overly imbrued.

On the cot next to him, a reclined Balgor observed the goings-on through equally restive eyes. Neither man was accustomed to spending so much time so lackadaisically, and despite the fact that they were expected to quietly—*patiently*—convalesce, it wasn't long before both of them came down with an irreversible case of the fidgets. Like cats a-twitch with the wild hair, these were men whose acclimatization to action made it difficult, even in injury, to sit or lie around in prolonged purposelessness. They craved distraction for its own sake— anything to counter the restless decompression that resulted when death-edged immediacy was of a sudden traded for doodlish dawdle.

Exhausting what they had of pithy contrivances and banter, a bored Balgor finally looked at a listless Wagner and said his mind:

"I can endure this no longer. What say you to a bold venture out to the sluice, where we might collect some cool water for these people?"

"I say 'Lay on, Macduff!' I'm going bonkers lying here with nothing to do but eavesdrop on Uthok's annoying self-promotion."

"Eavesdropping is an intentional act, Voknor. You could stuff an entire vrohda, one in each of your ears, and still not shut out that one's gaucherie and petty braggadocio. Truly, he all but makes me long for Bilahdu's long-winded pomposity."

"Truly," said Wagner, shifting up gingerly from his cot. "Now, let's go after that water before your long-windedness makes Uthok's and Bilahdu's seem like mimery."

A scowl in reply, the realmson turned and led the way. Finding several unutilised pails sitting haphazard near the entryway, Balgor snapped up the very best of the lot. Hobbling behind him, Wagner fought to disengage the least banged and buckled of the remaining prospects from their tapered nesting, his difficulty therewith ultimately raising a clangour every bit as interruptive as Uthok the Bonecrusher's aural assaults. Giving cringe and shrug, Wagner waved apology to those whose rest he'd disturbed, and then brattled off behind his friend as quickly as his wounds permitted.

The courtyard without was deserted. Those who had either been fortunate enough to avoid serious injury or who had for other reasons been exempt from the games (and who were not among those currently helping out in the infirmary) were very likely barracks-bound or had gone by volition to the palaestra to engage in informal, self-instigated exercise. And while Grum—having little love for anything in life save his role as Taskmaster—would no doubt have been on hand for those of the latter inclination, Wagner had heard how he was actually less demanding of his charges on this first day beyond the games. A stern and competent trainer, he was remarkably not so totally severe in his directives that he could not permit a day of relative laxity for those who came to the palaestra seeking holistic release through light nodgerplay, nor for those who chose not to leave their billet at all. Thus, if not an actual "free" day per se, it was certainly one of more relaxed regimen, where nearly everyone who'd managed to slip beneath the Reaper's scythe was generally at ease to spend this day unharassed by dictate or fastidious demand.

Reminding himself that the prisoner caravan was due any day, Wagner wondered how many more innocent beings had been uprooted from their homes, their families, their lands; how many were at that moment being clamped into chains and servitude; how many were destined to be dumped into this camp to replenish the status quo and to restore viability to the horrors of full-scale training and NuRac blood sport. Harking back to the day of his own arrival, he recalled too vividly the disembarking and the processing, and how almost immediately he'd defied behest by charging to the Vofspar's defence. That he'd espied no evidence of the female beyond that day meant little either way: her race was understandably unintegrable with the human ranks, and as the games weren't open to Ergosian eyes (save those in topical contention), it stood reasonable that she'd been featured in her own event sometime prior to Wagner's and Balgor's and the ill-starred Kadok's disastrous *piece de resistance*.

Perhaps it didn't matter. Perhaps the brief bond that he and she had shared in their desperation had no real significance beyond the salvation of her brood. That it proved a vehicle both for the kits' escape and for the mother's and Wagner's capture, this may only have been fatidic incidence, an improbable convergence of two beings on disparate, if intersecting, paths. A pivotal moment in juncture, it was a hap and hazard now relegated to the past—unexceptional, unworthy of historical footnote, and only ever to be revisited in fancy upon the "ne'er travelled crossroads" of what might have been.

On their return, Balgor and Wagner delivered water to every patient who requested it, a task that consumed several hours. In many instances they could hardly excuse themselves from certain individuals without feeling obliged to listen heartfully to the complaints or to the trivialities whose simple conveying seemed to distract the imparters from their misery. Who could deny an invalid a moment of harmless chit-chat when so little went so far in easing discomfort? Certainly not Wagner. It pained him to see so many Ergosians—many of only his marginal acquaintance—so slashed up, contused, bone-broken or divested of limb. Just as easily could such have been *his* circumstance, and it continually awed him that he, James Wagner—certified greenhorn, somnambulant warrior, and the most *alien* of illegal aliens, fresh off the intergalactic express—managed once again to escape grievous happenstance in the manner that he had. With but a single thought cast back to Kadok's horrible demise was his astonishment amplified, and his indebtedness to Balgor and Bilahdu, swollen to overflow. Whether by their instruction, whether by his own multifaceted instincts, whether by God's grace or by gods' grace, the accomplishment was nothing if not a remarkable one.

More remarkable, however, was what next occurred—no, what *transpired*—in a bumblish misstep of negotiation between cots. A recurrence of that which had manifested twice before (once on earth, and once in Olask's presence) with the same inconceivability, as Wagner subsequently lurched to save himself and the buckets from a complete forward sprawl, he ultimately did far worse by tearing agape his stitching. A mishap that prudence might certainly have pre-empted, Wagner's zeal to quench the thirsty had overridden his poise of step; and as the mind, ever anxious and determined of the moment, often fudges priority between conscious reflex and bodily preservation, Wagner grappled recklessly with the pails (whose overturn really would have done little harm) and was rewarded for his efforts with an excruciation quite nearly at the level of his original impaling—relived this time sans the lance but feeling all the same like a human kebabbing of the most painful sort.

For those who, from their beds, chanced to behold the minor ruckus, they would later claim to have witnessed an instantaneous flaring of solar magnitude right there in the room—a silent, salient, explosive brilliancy of only a fractioned second's duration. Enigmatic but not so totally nebulous that it could not have been explained away in some inventible fashion, each witness on his own may initially have taken it for the simple glint of skewed sunlight reflecting off of one of the flailed buckets. Some, specifically those with head and facial trauma, may even have regarded it as a kind of residually optical backlash remanent of their injuries. In all likelihood, no more might have been said about it if it were not for the fact that said witnesses all bore combinative testimony to the same incident, each from his own personal vantage and varying state of health.

It was quite different for Wagner. At the first issue of oblique pain, he'd flopped the buckets down in splashy save while moving to clutch his side. His fingers clasping at the gauze, he suddenly felt a tremendous convection emanating from beneath the wick of his bandages. Not the heat of blood-seep, nor the warmth of simple spasm or contraction, the sensation was at once illusory and patent, faux yet palpable, as when a frostbitten hand is plunged into tepid water. Sensorily hot to the point of perceived discomfort, logic assured him that he was in no way aflame. More, through some slipway of intuition he discerned that the fiery prickliness was in itself an uncomfortably benign side effect to a more benevolent end. The effulgence, however, was akin to corposant. It shot from his impalement, bespread his immediacy like flash powder, and then was sucked back into him, all in a trice. His puncture the apparent centre of both its ignition and its extinguishment, when inclination accorded that he lift away his hand, there was no longer any pain, nor even a recent wound, where both certainly should have been.

Amid a commotion stirred like a kettle by those nearest, Wagner sat on his discovery by acting no less baffled than his peers. Rubbing his eyes just as they had, craning about in feigned bemusement, in truth he was searching for the most furtive means of removing himself from the scene before he became its inconvertible clou. Picking himself up, then, he retook hold of the pails and made for the entry gate, and in so doing he became immediately sensible to the inordinate ease and grace of his effort. He'd felt this way only once before, and that circumstance and this one were without distinction.

Bursting from the infirmary, he scurried along its exterior, faking purpose until he was convinced that he'd left all peerful scrutiny behind. Only then did he abandon the buckets and peel away his dressing. Only then did he confirm his suspicions.

Impossible, unsettling, and yet wonderful beyond reckoning, beneath the smear of bloodied bandages he found exactly what he'd guessed—a pallid, fleshy scar of a once-ago impaling, interwoven with a loose-looped corruption of Ponahr's once-taut handiwork. What minutes before had been a neat symmetry of fast stitches was now a ratty old suturing, long overdue for extraction. By an outsider's observation it would seem that a good month had passed since his trauma.

A glimpse at his fingernails found them exactly as they'd been on the earlier occasion—elongated and keen, weeks of growth sprung up in the space of an eyeblink. Without premonition he shuddered, his eyes glued upon his digits, his mind stuck on the coincident truth. A staggering notion it was that the body, his body, *any* body, could be coerced into such an eerie, accelerated convalescence.

And, just as with the previous event, all it had taken was a moment of perceived imperativeness—a flash of panic—to trigger the process. In fact, barring situation and result, the effect had differed little from the way that his ultra-aggressiveness reared in a scrape whenever things got tough. Always had he heard how time healed all wounds; but for him, with such an incredibly equalising handicap, nothing short of mortal injury stood the merest chance against such remedial advantage.

That varying measures of pain and fear and direness seemed catalytic to both types of benefaction, Wagner wondered to what degree these might be harnessed consciously, and if any of them could be short-circuited or circumvented by wilful stolidity or even by something as radical as suicidal intent. He also questioned why the tripping over one's feet—or the fitful seizure of a bedridden patient for that matter—might prompt the effect. Not exactly life and death exigencies, still each had been a kind of cruciality in its own right, an instance of high anxiety and clamour that evoked quick and instinctual response. And here, no different than that rejuvenation of a few weeks back, his metabolism had shot ahead like a cannonball, exclusive of any experiential accompaniment; and he, with no fathom of how and why, had been made whole once more.

"Are you ill?" The voice unexpectedly beside him, Wagner jumped from surprise. He'd not sensed Balgor's approach.

"No," he said, abandoning his self-exam. "In fact, I've never felt more healthy."

The realmson shot him a bewildered glance. "What is all *this*, then?" he asked, swatting at Wagner's arm. "Whence came these millings?"

Wagner looked down and found his skin dusted with a flaky scurf that flittered groundward at his friend's disruptive graze. He smiled confirmedly.

"Do you remember all of the claims and confessions I made back in the brig?"

Balgor nodded disconcertedly.

"And the one regarding the injuries from my NuRac beating—how they just up and vanished in a flash?"

"Aye. Is that it? Have you undergone another such spell? Is this the offscour of that illumination from a moment ago?"

Wagner peeled back his bandages. "Take a gander."

Balgor looked beneath the tatters like a kid gawking at a two-headed calf at the county fair. "*Bones and entrails, Voknor!* What manner of sorcery is in your keeping?"

"Check it out—there's not a single scratch on my body that hasn't healed over. And look here, at my hands—the nails have grown out just like I told you."

"Aye, and I believe your beard is broader and your hair more flowing. It is truly as you professed! *Incomprehensible!*" He skirted around Wagner, giving him a more rigorous once-over. "I confess that I am not only confounded, but genuinely affrighted that such a thing might be. I know not what to think or say."

"Well, *that's* a first, in any case," said Wagner.

"It is almost—" Balgor paused a moment, not certain that he actually wanted to say what he was thinking. He looked at Wagner, looked at his rejuvenation, and began anew. "Although I have ever straddled the mean betwixt reality as I have encountered it, and that which the devout tell me exists beyond the grasp of mortal ken, in this instance I am completely shorn of all explanation—save one.

And as I have so often made light of the credenda that Tamek and his fellow purists so vehemently defend, I suppose it is only fitting that I surmise no source for your miracles other than the Vorshalah itself. It appears that you, by chance or design of the times, have been invested with the gift of thaumaturgy."

Wagner searched his friend's face for any and all sarcastic trace. He found none.

"Come on, you don't really believe that—do you?"

"My belief matters not. The truth shouts to me. I know not whose truth nor which truth, but we stand in evidence of a power that is greater than either of us. And if, as you would claim, it has no rooting in the Ergosian faith, then it must be a sortilege either brought with you from afar or acquired through fortunate happenstance."

"*Fortuitous*, maybe. I'm not so sure about *fortunate*."

"Nay? Then think, *Voknor*. You have lurking within you the wherewithal to cast infirmity from your body—and, it would seem, from the bodies of others. Tempered and properly disciplined, it may prove possible to harness this ability, to one day summon it by necessity. Imagine what you might accomplish."

Wagner laughed. "For somebody so cynical in matters of faith and superstition, I don't understand how you can accept this so soberly when it still scares the bejesus out of me!"

"Cynicism does not belie faith *or* superstition, *Voknor*. It goads them like a good riding crop, compelling them along some manner of credible path or none at all. And although I am indeed among the most disgruntled and disillusioned of my faith, this does not make an unbeliever of me. On those occasions that you hear me provoking Tamek with quip or gentle harangue, it is more often my way of forcing him to refashion his arguments, to render them to their most fluid and basic lessons, so that one day I might have no choice but to embrace them for my inability to counterpoint."

"So, you witness something supernormal like this, and out of nowhere you're waiving perfectly good doubt and query for stuffy scripture and folklore?"

"Nay, I am merely making wider the footbridge of common possibilities. Faith, according to most teachings, is trust in a given foundation, void of proof. In kind, superstition is the acceptance of dubious proof in lieu of foundation. In these contexts, my cynicism is not forfeit but only challenged before a proof that is suddenly neither lacking nor dubious, and a foundation that precedes me by generations yet which just as suddenly has begun to mesh and manifest with present events."

"Well, you believe what you want. The bottom line for me is that whatever this manifestation might be, wherever it comes from, and however long it might last— first and foremost I can't let our friendly neighbourhood NuRacs find out about it."

Balgor agreed, and within minutes both men re-entered the infirmary to continue quenching the bedridden. Wagner having redressed his abdomen in the semblance of its former bandaging, both friends performed the remainder of their good deeding with stoicism and distracted mechanicalness—Wagner attuned to every little byte of effulgence-related chatter going on around him, and the realmson, far more preoccupied with the magiks that he didn't understand.

Later, on having again taken to their cots, they conversed in low-speak about the tumultuousness of the past few days. Always coming back, however, to the topic of Wagner's healing, it was only through intimation and cleverly coded wording that they dared to broach it at all. No one, it seemed, was ever too ailing to pique to a good scandal, and many were the receptive ears that, even in infirmity, sought to glom onto anything enigmatic and engrossing, if only for the diversion. Eventually, then, to avoid the unnecessary tedium, Balgor and Wagner opted to stick with the lighter fare of critiquing the botches and missteps in their escape adventure, or reliving portions of their fateful scramble in the arena. They traded supposition on how their bout with Skol might have gone had the monster been more accommodating; they spoke of Kadok, speculated about what could possibly have happened to Fostoch, wondered how AuwNiir had justified to the NuRac populace his decision to dump at Skol's hirsute feet the very warriors whom he'd only just finished praising before the Tribunal. Yet, when it became obvious that even in whisper their words were the focus of their co-convalescents, they livened up the banter by imaginatively restaging some of the circumstances and outcomes of their escapades purely for the sake of entertainment, using a broad license of fancy and probability to embellish each fabricated likelihood—which proved not only amusing and distracting for their neighbours, but for themselves as well.

At midday, Olask and crew returned afresh and resumed the orchestration of their skilful nurturing, relieving the much-appreciated volunteers from the morning watch. Nearly a full day beyond the games, most of the unfortunates who were going to die of lethal wounds had by now succumbed or lay perilously close to the edge, and those who yet clung to breath found their wills tested anew upon the battlefields of their failing bodies and febrile mindscapes. Orderlies toiled at hefting the dead from the building to the weeping accompaniment of friends and bed mates, with few grieving more than Olask himself—Olask, who could not outwardly afford to show his despair, but rather immersed himself more deeply in his tending to the living, to those whose survival would at best be legacy to this most recent bloodbath.

Not much later, Wagner was delighted to see J'nea enter the infirmary. It amused him that she pretended not to notice him, instead jaunting unveeringly past his cot on some premise of requisitioning medicine from Olask for one of her ailing dungeon denizens. With Olask instructing the dispensary orderly on what remedy to mix up, only in her idle did J'nea feel compelled to acknowledge Wagner and Balgor, even coming round to chat them up with her standard gamut of insults and wry contempt. Even as she upbraided Wagner a good five or six times for coming into so much strife in his short tenure as a prisoner, hers was a welcomed nettling in an otherwise sombre ward environment. In turn, Wagner gave as good as he got by alleging some dire lacking in J'nea's own spirit that barred her from ever flouting NuRac prescript in order to experience all of the illicit fun that he and Balgor so enjoyed. Naturally, J'nea scoffed and criticised him anew, although she was a great deal less successful at concealing the fellowship and admiration she harboured than she might have suspected. Still, she shored up her guard enough to maintain a certain toughness of pretence throughout, with even Balgor failing to escape his fair share of tongue-lashing. Fully a degree or two colder with him, however, than with Wagner, and her pot-shots lodged in a manner that demonstrated a cloaking of incremental contempt—and maybe even a satisfactory notion of justifiable comeuppance—J'nea's attempts at riding the realmson's ego by gloating on his loss of rank, on his and Wagner's potential double-cross at Fostoch's hands, and on their strategic ineptness in general, were all less than sympathetic gibes.

By his resilience, Balgor appeared amply conditioned to her barbs, as if he'd endured this tone before. And, of course, he had. Having habitually weathered the cavility of the very best deriders in his own social circle, listening to the trusty was barely an effort at all. In the end, her flap had about the same effect on his ego, mood, and confidence as a spread of rocks catapulted against QieLahr's outer curtain.

Her sarcasm suddenly dissipated, however, when talk turned to the arena battle, for there was obviously little she could say in sport about heroism and lost life. She in fact confided to having used her position as trusty to wangle a verboten ringside view of their bout through one of the substructure loopholes, her concern and her curiosity having overridden the demands of her other duties. In a brief concession of her usual detachment, she confessed her awe at their fury in meeting and dispatching an enemy against whom they were not intended to prevail. She even had several reverent words for Kadok despite her well-documented disregard for him on many a previous occasion. But mostly she spoke of their unpredictable victory.

"I saw such ferocity on the field," she said. "Ferocity and vile cunning—and it is not solely of the beasts that I speak."

No more eager to open up to J'nea than he would have been to snuggle up to a swarm of bees bearing honeycombed treacle, Balgor remained true to form. "When you have been embroiled in as many pub fights and imbroglios gone amob as I have, you quickly learn the skills for deadly mêlée," he said. "I discovered early on that if one can master one's inebriation enough within the common brawl to retain poise and reflex, then those same skills can be aggrandised to better end on the most sober fields of battle."

"Not me," chimed Wagner. "I just go stark raving mad whenever you set me in the way of danger. So don't you be ruffling my feathers, girlie, or I'll have to put you in your place."

She looked at Wagner with affront and startle, and then busted out in irrepressible laughter.

"Watch it," he warned with a Three Stooges bluster. "I mean it—I'll tear ya' limb from limb if'n I hafta."

"And on the topic of limbs," said Balgor, "tell us, J'nea, what word have you of the Sunderer, other than the fact that he yet lives?"

"Very little," she replied. "The NuRac surgeons extracted the arrows and pottered about in the patching of his wounds, but they quickly had him removed to his cell when he began to emerge from his stupor. If we are fortunate, he will die a miserable death from infection and distension."

Beyond her shoulder, two guards appeared at the entry. The first, Wagner recognised instantly as KoviKor, the spear-happy subordinate who'd delivered him from the detention block a day past his eventful arrival; the other was unfamiliar to him, possibly a transferee from one of the many returning units that Wagner and Balgor had seen from atop the south wall at their escape's first glitch. On sensing them, J'nea suspended their small talk and scurried off in Olask's direction, leaving Wagner and the realmson to resume with quiet discussion on their own. All the while, however, they kept careful sight on these new visitors, for they surely hadn't entered the infirmary for their own folly.

The NuRacs, scanning the bedridden and watching as the attendants floated busily about the room like lifeboats on shipwrecked waters, finally signalled to one of the orderlies. With many a subsequent gesture and inquiry—and considerable finger-pointing—it became clear that they were interested in the wounded. Many individuals were identified, evaluated, noted or discounted—Wagner and Balgor among them—before both guards turned and briskly left the structure.

"What do you think *that* was all about?" Wagner asked suspiciously.

"They are canvassing for the healthiest among us in an effort to return the able-bodied back to duty as swiftly as possible. It is always thus after the tournament."

"Well, if they're thinning out the slackers I guess that means I'm in trouble— me being so healed up and all."

"No one save you and I know that, *Voknor*. But it will not be long before Ponahr or Olask or some other do-gooder examines your wound and stumbles upon a most startling discovery."

They shared a brief pause, within which they watched J'nea depart as well, a gallipot of salves in each hand.

"To be honest," Wagner admitted, "I'm kind of hankering to get out of here anyway. I can't really explain it. Where I was just fidgety before, I feel too good now to just lie here like a stiff. And get this—I've got this peculiar longing for physical activity, for grabbing a quarterstaff and letting loose. Minosh's skull would do for starters."

"Hah! It sounds to me as if an errant warrior's spirit has taken to nesting in that hollow space that you call a noddle. That, or Bilahdu must have discovered a moment betwixt his endless blathering and his plague of drooping drawers to actually imbue you with the heart of a fighting man. So be it, then! Let us both away from this place."

Wagner stared surprise as Balgor rose up from his cot.

"Although you be most ungenerous, *Voknor*—aye, selfish—with your healing magiks, do not think that a few hundred scratches and incisor punctures will keep me from taking to the field with you."

"If I knew how to harness my 'healing magiks,'" Wagner said, "I'd cure you of that chip on your shoulder. Then maybe I'd gain everyone's gratitude for sparing them any more of your bravado and your tired old yarns."

Both men left their beds and made for the bin near the entry where a limited sum of fresh raiment was stored. Doffing their hospital togs and donning this and that of the newer garments that fit them best, they waved over the nearest orderly, that she would record their departure.

The woman, in fact the very same who had conferred with the guards moments prior, counselled against their leaving, arguing that they should avail themselves of the leisure that was rightfully theirs. After all, she noted, thraldom under Grum's steerage would fall to them soon enough, but sanctioned bed rest was a precious commodity that should not be thrown away. While Balgor's gentle reply embraced the compassion in her reasoning, he insisted that in their recent battle he and Wagner had come much too close to the permanent leisure of the grave; and as opportunity for similar fate would loom again for them soon enough, they would rather rejuvenate through locomotion and liveliness, even if it meant subjecting themselves prematurely to structured martial routine.

Acquiescing, she bade them stay while she inquired into what medication to dispense them. Both, however, refused her offer before she'd gone a single pace. Nothing, they claimed, was needed; and indeed, she stood perplexed in their departure, as only one of them showed any measure of limp and laceration.

Once strolling across the courtyard, Balgor posed Wagner a question. "Did not Olask wish to speak with you upon any recurrence of the healing force?"

"Yeah," sighed Wagner. "I'll bring him up to speed some other time. He's got his hands full right now, and I certainly don't need any more attention foisted on me."

Suddenly a voice harped at them. Turning, they came face to onrush with KoviKor. Alone this time, and armed with his poleaxe, he was anxious to know why they were back in prison issue so soon after he'd seen them abed. Quick on the sly, Balgor fed him a line of baloney, saying that they felt compelled to atone for their gross insurgency by ignoring their pain and dragging themselves onto the practise field as penance. Wagner could hardly listen to said spiel without breaking up, but somehow he was able to muster his best look of sternness, and with this and a sturdy nod of affirmation he backed up Balgor's flam.

"Well," said the NuRac, "it just so happens that Commander AuwNiir has relayed a standing message in your regard, bearing explicit instruction pertaining to your pending release from hospital."

"A grand feast in our honour, no doubt, for defeating the Beastmaster's Ennead?" asked Balgor, suspecting that the true nature of AuwNiir's orders was quite the opposite.

"A feast? Aye, perhaps," said KoviKor. "But not of the sort that you imply. Turn yourselves about, my healthy mongrels, and accompany me into the arena substructure. I have a great surprise in store for you there."

CHAPTER EIGHTEEN

It is best to bear what can't be altered.
—SENECA

"We redeem ourselves in the arena, prove our mettle before thousands, suffer laceration and impalement, and still you cannot leave us unharried for even a single day?"

"Make no mistake, Ergosian—I had no say in it."

KoviKor didn't like being questioned by upstart prisoners. As he didn't much care for Balgor either, it made his orders all the sweeter.

"However," he added, a bit of the churl in his manner, "the more I consider it, the more do I see the justice in it."

Prodding them onward, their backsides not spared the point of his poleaxe, they traversed corridor after stony corridor, guided only by the flickering sconces that kept the passages awash in eerie ambulations of half-light. Close and yet cavernous in quality, the substructure atmosphere actually varied little from the dungeon but for the torches; and these, if not served by the network of venting flues located prominently throughout, would have made for an equally uninhabitable—and poisonous—environment to anyone whose duty or punishment kept them too long in cloister.

"Know you," KoviKor chided, "that my sister and her children were fast abed only a half-block from where you were recaptured in QieLahr, their safety jeopardised by your nefarious rampage?"

"*Nefarious?* There was nothing nef—"

KoviKor jabbed at Wagner's back. "Had it been *my* decision to make, you would have been executed simply for the havoc and the discommodity that you caused. As it is, I must say that Commander AuwNiir's decision to pit you against insurmountable odds was a reasonable substitute. How unfortunate that it did not yield the rightful end."

"It did for *us*," said Wagner.

KoviKor stuck him again.

"Impudence will bring you naught but increased hardship."

That was it for Wagner. The sting of the tine, the irk of his pain, in less than an instant he slipped beyond the spur, swung round, and snatched the weapon clean from KoviKor's grip. Then, levelling it vengefully against KoviKor's breastplate, he drove the wide-eyed NuRac to the wall.

"Speaking of increased hardships, what say we talk about *yours*?"

"*Voknor*! What are you doing?" Balgor lunged forward and took clamp of Wagner's arm. "Stay your hand. If you kill him, we will not survive the day."

"He speaks true!" cried KoviKor, suddenly reduced to school boy stature, replete with cracking voice. "There are soldiers at every turn. You have no hope of escaping. Killing me would—"

Wagner's zeal suddenly diminished like sunlight blocked by cloud. "*Kill* you? I'm not trying to kill you. I'm trying to tell you that I don't take kindly to people poking me with sharp objects—especially when I don't deserve it." He danced the spear point over KoviKor's plating, scoring its thin ebon veneer in a playfully menacing fashion. "Now, you're not gonna stick me again, *are* you?"

"*Voknor*—" Balgor steeped his voice in low and soothing pitch. "Listen to me. Do not invite reprisal. End this amicably."

Wagner ignored him, leaving KoviKor's query standing. "*Are* you?"

The NuRac gulped. "N-no. I will t-treat you fairly."

Wagner stepped back, drawing the poleaxe with him. His eyes fixed upon KoviKor's, he righted the weapon, business-end skyward, and handed it back to the perspiring NuRac. He'd never in his life played the role of a tough, never even knew he had it in him, and now he would gamble that he'd intimidated the substandard soldier enough to continue the escort with a mutuality of understanding.

For a moment it would seem that he would lose that gamble.

"By rights," said KoviKor, his courage waxing, "I could murder you on the mark for your insurrectionary conduct."

"*Murder* would be right. There's not a one of you with the stones to face us on equal terms."

"*Voknor*—"

"By all means," said KoviKor. "Advise your insolent friend to still his tongue or I will be only too happy to forget this disgracing little pact and deliver you both to the morgue instead, with no one the wiser for my humiliation."

"Until they see your calling card," said Wagner, pointing to his breastplate.

Balgor and KoviKor simultaneously glanced to the spot where Wagner had run his doodlish scratch, their faces at once bulging surprise—the NuRac's, in mortification; the realmson's, in flourish.

"You knave!" cried KoviKor. "You calumnious knave!"

Like a man aflame, the NuRac raced to the nearest sconce, and there, began combing soot from the wall and smirching it over his breastwork to fill in what Wagner had burred.

"*Voknor*," Balgor snorted, trying in vain to suppress his unwanted delight. "How could you be so invidious?"

"I take it that's not the kind of symbol a fellow wants to flaunt?"

"Why, *you* etched it—surely *you* must know!"

Wagner shrugged. "Nope. It just popped into my head. What's it mean?"

Balgor took him aside as KoviKor made crazy with the soot.

"It's NuRac for 'catamite.'"

"Yeah, okay. What's that?"

"A catamite, my friend, is a young male kept for—well—less than savoury practises."

Wagner held his hand to his mouth. "Oh. *Oops.*"

"You bastard!" shouted KoviKor, rushing him. "I should kill you for this!"

"Hold up," said Balgor, intercepting the flustery NuRac and disarming him a second time. "*I* am the bastard here. And now I will have my say. Your armour is temporarily restored. And so, I hope, is *Voknor's* good sense. Now, here is what will happen next. You will remain in charge, KoviKor. You will take us to wherever it is that we were going. And we will all arrive as if none of this ever occurred—do you understand?"

"I have been abused by prisoners," blustered the NuRac. "How am I to pretend that nothing has occurred?"

"Because you must. Carry out your orders. Deliver us, forget these things, and your peers need never know."

KoviKor remained fixed in sneer like a little boy bested by older urchins.

"Do it!" said Balgor. "Do it, or I will scour the soot from your plating and take you by the scruff to your fellows so that one and all may make sport of you."

"Look," added Wagner. "I'm sorry, but *you* started this. I was following your lead. I was marching where you told me. You didn't have to keeping pushing it. Hell, we practically just got done mixing it up with a band of wild croviks. You'd be testy, too, if someone started jabbing you after all that."

After a long pause, KoviKor stood down. "Very well. But after this day you had better curb your recalcitrant tendencies."

Before Wagner could mutter hem or haw, Balgor answered for him. "Agreed then!"

His weapon again his own—and he, gripping it more firmly than ever—KoviKor urged them on; and in minutes they came upon a greater doorway of coarse-wooded planking. A series of raps alerted someone on the other side, and after considerable clangs and jangles it swung wide to receive them.

KoviKor then announced his "guests" and beckoned Wagner and Balgor entry into the dimness within. Manhandled at once by the three NuRacs inside, the pair was ushered beneath a low archway and into the presence of a ponderous wheel. Wound fat in thickly-gauged chain, said wheel was stationary—locked into position by a brake and sprocket device. Extending tautly from the heart of its coiling came a corpulence of interlocking steel loops that spanned the room and disappeared through a collared feed in the wall. Two metres to this feed's right stood yet another door, this one fortified with studded billet and reinforced with riveted braces. Vault-like, it boasted two separate locks and a pair of steel slats horizontally run through similarly metalled braces.

"By whose authority do you bring us *here?*" said Balgor. "This is the Sunderer's lair!"

"What?!" cried Wagner. "Skol's cell? Are you kidding?"

KoviKor smirked. "This is AuwNiir's solution."

"To feed us to the beast?"

"No. To *tend* the beast."

Both men looked at him in daze.

"You are to be his new caretakers. Until the daemon is fully recovered, you two are going to attend to him twice per day. You will bring him his meals, water him, clean his foulness—all in addition to your normal martial training, of course."

"Oh, but of course," mocked Balgor. "And are we to perform pantomime for the brute as well, and coo praise at his every bowel movement?"

"If you like," said KoviKor. "Praise him, scold him, taunt him—it is all the same to Skol. Simply stay shy of his great maw. We cannot have him maiming you straight off. Although, with this decision to have Ergosians assume all responsibility for his welfare, I do not foresee any great shortage of replacements."

Balgor bristled at KoviKor's harshness. Glaring hot reply, he let the NuRac see his eyes drift down to his breastplate, to the soot-obscured graffito. He thought of how easy it would be, with only a little spittle and a quick wipe, to sully KoviKor's reputation and win the moment. But, as KoviKor was merely honouring his end of their agreement—acting as if there had been no incident—Balgor held to the sensible and set aside his ire. After all, a pact was a pact.

KoviKor departed forthwith, removing all temptation, leaving the three sentries to itemise for Balgor and Wagner all that their new bane would entail. As Skol had long been served his morning slop, it fell immediately to Balgor and Wagner to venture into the cell to extract the buckets. Tethered to this task would also be the enclosure's occasional "reconditioning" (i.e., shovelling up the Skol-apples), a chore that by the guards' snidely relayed low-down had been seriously neglected for weeks, and probably months. The padlocks removed, then, by way of safeguarded keys, the NuRacs stepped back and with devilish gaiety watched as the unhappy prisoners slid the slats from their moorings, creaked the monolithic door ajar on hinges the size of Oxford dictionaries, and crept into the acrid domain of the most hellish of creatures that either man had ever laid eyes on.

The cell within was squalid and caliginous; add to this the stench that struck them like the open-handed slap of a malodour one gradation short of decomposing flesh, and their old oubliettes suddenly seemed as posh suites by comparison. The room's only discernible light stole in through six narrow slits located high upon the far wall, just beneath the first tier of arena stands; and below these stood the double-doorway that Wagner and Balgor had only seen from its other side, on tournament day. If the capstan in the next room was a workable, if cumbersome, means of manipulating the creature, then these doors had similar function in that they were mounted on a track of primitive cogs and retractable chains that could be partitioned from adjacent rooms to prevent unnecessary contact with the cell's occupant.

Before setting a single toe into that room, Wagner peered meekly beyond the door. There, manacled and immobilised by a custom-crafted steel truss, stood the former dreadnought himself, now stiff and subdued and pressed to the wall as if by a huge electromagnet. Fixing on the sight of his intruder, the beast emitted but a paltry grunt—one-part malevolence and two-parts malaise—and although little more than a barely sustained misfire of a warning, it was enough to send Wagner into prudent retreat.

"What if this is a set-up?" he whispered. "How do we know those guards won't release him once we're inside?"

"We do not. But if you wish, I will keep my eye on them while you go about your business in there."

"Oh-no-you-don't. I think Skol would prefer a meaty Ergosian hors d'oeuvre to the stringy flesh of an outworlder. After *you*, my good man."

Balgor tut-tutted. "Oh no, I insist. You first, *Voknor.*"

A reprimand suddenly bellowing from behind them, both men unwillingly lurched into the cell. Again, Skol glanced up, yet did little save growl at them, a lingering febrility from his many injuries the suspected reason for his unusual lethargy.

The empty buckets that they sought lay not far from the brute, strewn on their rims, with their chum-like dregs dribbling out and mixing with the muck along the floorstone. A third receptacle, that which originally bore his drinking water, they found drained and upended at the far end of the enclosure.

Hopscotching around the biggest piles of excreta, each man hesitantly gathered up the receptacles closest to him, all the while keeping careful vigilance on their near-cataleptic host, a Skol vastly more weakened than the one they remembered. Almost limp beneath his restraints, he looked like a quarter-ton rag doll, a wookie with a glandular problem and leprosy both. His eyelids fluttered between consciousness and coma, while within them his glassy eyeballs roamed their orbits like wearied tigers in a pitfall. His pelage was encrusted with scabby crisps of dried and drying blood, and the arrow gapes themselves were rife with pustulation and looking none too hopeful in their mending. Flies, gnats, and other assorted pests infiltrated the wounds and feasted on the coagulum caked to his coat; and he, like a creature of the wild, did naught to dissuade them beyond the occasional rake and sweep of a spastic claw, which here seemed more impulsive than consciously directed.

"This guy has definitely seen better days," said Wagner.

"So have we all," replied Balgor, edging towards the door. "And if we plan on seeing others, we had best hasten from here."

Surprisingly, the NuRacs allowed them leave with little ado, even locking up behind them, with one guard exiting the crank room with them and escorting them first to the scullery to drop off the pails, and then to the palaestra of their original intent.

Stunned to see two of his prodigals gracing his sparsely peopled field so prematurely, Grum was only too happy to welcome them back. Not counting those who contended voluntarily, most of the prisoners whom KoviKor and his peers had deemed hale enough to leave the infirmary and return to sparring were a largely spiritless, sluggish lot, which had forced Grum to crack his Taskmaster's playbook for a few of his less caustic snarls, insults, and threats for coaxing same to a proper liveliness. Wagner and Balgor, he hoped, might likewise help to goose things up a bit.

Even as they neared him, Grum's eagerness to critique their tournament performance shone in his eyes like the alleged phosphorescence of a night-hound's glare. Quick to commend them on their steadfastness, their fleetness of foot, and their unique resolution to the bout, he did not fail to ride Balgor for having risked—and lost—his elite ranking in their futilely-botched escape. In unexpected turn, however, the realmson scoffed with nonchalance.

"How far can rank elevate one here? A prisoner with full perquisite is still a prisoner—a slave to his captors and a lackey to a couthless gaggle of gamesters and deadpates."

Grum screwed his eyes with goggled fists. "Do my ears and eyes betray me? Is this truly Balgor of the Realm? Or is this some lowly impostor? By Drux, it scarcely even sounds like him! Not that I would expect him to feel compunction for his actions, no. But such bitterness? Such bitterness speaks to one thing—that the company he has been keeping of late must be adversely affecting his wits."

Knowing disparagement when he heard it—and no longer one to take it without at least a measure of reciprocity—Wagner chimed in. "I must confess, Taskmaster. I'm definitely the one you ought to blame. They were *my* ridiculous notions, my outrageous phantasies, that corrupted Balgor with faulty reasoning. Why, the mere suggestion that freedom might somehow be a better alternative to all of these gracious amenities that you and your kind provide—what could I have been thinking?"

Grum squinted contempt. "I have ever noted how strife seems to find you on its own, *Voknor*. Why, then, do you come seeking it from me?"

"Character flaw, I guess."

"Indeed. Mend it or be undone by it. Now go, both of you. Occupy yourselves in whatever capacity your injuries permit, or I will devise something for you."

Even as plunging so precipitately back into bouting seemed less than sagacious—especially for the unrestored realmson—both men nonetheless made way to the weapons enclosure, and there, plucked two sturdy quarterstaves from the rack. Thrilled to have left the infirmary behind them, considerably less thrilled with having to nursemaid what was arguably the most repugnant charge the world had ever produced, they were content to engage in anything that even momentarily supplanted the events of the past day. That neither had given much ear to Grum's initial whitewash of their resource against the croviks, nor to his pursuant gibes and credit-vying (all curtly thwarted by the pair's indifference), it demonstrated a germination of exactly what the NuRacs sought most to squelch: envisagement, hope, possibility. Neither man sought Grum's praises or panning anymore than a husband wished for his wife's nagging. Pleasing the owners, winning the rank upgrades—those were short-sighted ends that led to prospectless futures. All that Wagner, and now Balgor, fixed upon was an end to this dreary way of life. And it was solely their lot to go about in obtaining it.

As aloof as they were to Grum's post-game palaver, they were soon enough inundated with congratulatory rehashings from the Ergosian side. Approached successively by their fellow sparrers, they endured more lauding and back-slapping than they had aplomb to receive, not only for the arena match but for braving the escape. Saluted and hullooed by admirers and well-wishers on the thinly populated field, even thinner was the number that did not claim inspiration simply from having heard of their daring. Somehow in the course of their lock-up, their arena bout, their brief convalescence, the duo had managed to garner something of a cultish celebrity with their kinspeople, a celebrity of deedful achievement. And now, with a surfeit of kudos and affectionate kidding—none of which had anything over Bilahdu's trademark superfluousness—Balgor found reconciliation to that cunning and saucy inner fellow of his earliest days; and Wagner, formerly pegged as a quirkishly insignificant upstart and outsider, had lavished upon him the ilk of approbation long accoutred by Balgor of his own reputation. The eyes and hearts of the people, long opened to their native realmson, were expanding to encompass Wagner as well, with his new éclat less the product of his individual proclivity than of both his co-conspiracy with the savvy Balgor and his previously disregarded confidences with the Sentinel of Vishkor.

In the midst of their eminence—which did not overstay its novelty, but rather, yielded quickly to the matters at hand—the two of them enjoyed a more bracing session of stave-play than either one would have thought possible. Both, in fact, came away with the kind of enlivening holism that such routine rarely inspirited on the most productive of days. To the layperson, it may simply have been deemed as optimism, perhaps even some ilk of post-traumatic elation. After all, everything about their ordeals still cleaved to them in a visceral sense, infusing them with the inrush of invincibility that usually thrives heaviest—and most often, delusionally— in one's adolescence. But it did seem that a heartier admixture of blood now coursed through their veins, invigorated by their having resampled autonomy, however short-lived or conditional. A seductive high of the sort that would have seen any number of persons content to rest upon the laurels of mass adulation, Wagner and Balgor let such sentiment dissipate with the breeze-whipped sands. Celebrity was fleeting and fickle and to be shunned at all cost. Most of the "glory" of their recent acts had been born of desperation, not bravery—and if no one else saw this, then certainly they themselves did. Both were acutely aware that their presence on the practise field that day was largely due to happenstance and nothing more.

As for sparring, given Wagner's haleness and Balgor's detriment, one would have expected the former to be the more vibrantly animated of the pair, the more dextrous, the one who had seemingly outflanked infliction and exhaustion enough to put him at the pinnacle of his prowess. Yet, to Wagner's surprise, the realmson sparkled in occasion, projecting a grace in action so fluid as to override every nick, puncture, and clawing acquired of his recent trials. Although not consciously keeping count, the simultaneously dismayed and delighted Wagner found himself driven into defence fully thrice for each of his own successful charges—thus giving credence to the premise that a wounded creature, whether human or bestial, was always the most formidable of foes.

During their breaks, especially whenever they saw Grum distracted by some new sentry on incidental business, they spun yarns for the water-youths who'd been scurrying about the yard all afternoon with their ladles and pails, albeit with fewer thirsters than usual to sample their refreshment. With high-feathered extravagance, Balgor painted wordful canvasses for them of his encounters with ferals, far fiercer than croviks, whom he'd faced and fought in days long since relinquished to the tomes of Eternity. Most prominent was his boast of how he'd escaped a roving band of night-hounds who'd cornered him upon a precipice by the dark of the moon. With no firmamental illumination to guide him, he'd been forced to fling himself blindly from the bluff and into the chasm, gambling that his end-plummet would see him into the river that he knew serpentined below, but which was impossible to discern. Wagner, in turn, ran some earthly lore through the creative wringer to craft his own encounter about a nomadic pack of "bi-kohrs" who roamed the badlands on snarling, fuming mounts known throughout his realm as the "infernal Hogs of Harley." A story drawn from any and all of a dozen incidents from his Filthy Lucre past, spiced with a selective plunder of the *Mad Max* mythos and contemporised with an infusion of purely Ergosian colloquialisms, what resulted was the same kind of narrative fare that once kept Sally Lemanski obligingly entertained back at Howsley. More importantly, in this milieu it proved intriguing enough to at least rival some of Balgor's own fanciful whoppers. Even as the older kids around them were keen enough to see through the whimsy and to detect the serio-comic varnishing in the narratives, they still grinned and thrilled along with the younger ones—all of them apparently willing to suspend disbelief for the opportunity to stand among the two men who had vanquished the Beastmaster's Ennead.

The fact, too, that the kids were witness to each man's covert scoffing of the other's tale—Wagner's silent, behind-the-back mocking of Balgor's elaborations, and Balgor's mugging foolish behind Wagner's—this had more than a little to do with their glee. The realmson was irrepressibly enamoured of children, especially orphaned ones; and this, for obvious reason. Too, as it pained him that any child should have to live a single day in a prison, day by day he did all he could to scatter little bits of joy in their path. Wagner, barely having seen a child up close in years, almost to the point of estrangement, frequently saw a really big child manifest in his friend whenever some of the real McCoys were present, and somehow it became an appreciation shared. On this occasion, however, the shenanigans wouldn't last too far beyond their quenching; for, with Grum's business wrapped up and his attention back on the field, it took but one shrill whistle to send the youths flying off in tangle-footed dashes towards the next batch of parched and parrying combatants.

The warriors likewise turned back to their own tangle of footwork and clashing of staves, spending the remainder of the afternoon enmeshed in moderate, non-competitive circuit. When quitting time came, and supper with it, it was only then that they noted that Tamek had failed to grace the palaestra at all—and more so, it seemed that he was going to be a no-show for mess as well. With naught to go on but hasty speculation, they quickly feared that he'd gotten himself into strife with the Tribunal again, and had been cast into the dungeon to cool off. Just what else could have kept him away at this hour was difficult to discern.

A pleasant surprise to Wagner, the evening meal (indeed, every meal in the first week following the tournament) was uncommonly delectable and liberal in portion. This, he was told, had canny reasoning behind it. As Balgor explained it, the NuRacs wished all surviving prisoners as healthy as possible, as *soon* as possible. Thus, to lure any fakers, slackers, or cravens from the infirmary—where they could duck from duty and malinger with sanction until deemed or discovered hale—the grub provided for the palaestra sparrers alone was rich and select, had no limit on portions, and even came with a serving of jug wine to wash it down! Most Ergosians being the heartiest of eaters when given the chance, perhaps even heartier imbibers, such enticement was more than even the most unscrupulous goldbrickers could ignore; and thus, by the week's end the fittest would be weeded by salivary compunction from the safer sanctuary of clean cots and comfort.

On this night, at first sight of the meal tables being erected and the dishes and utensils in out-carry by the trusties, Balgor and Wagner found themselves excused early so that they could fulfil their newest obligation before seeing at all to their own appetites. So, while their mouth-watered peers all made for the wash tanks and began forming the cafeterial queue, Skol's reluctant menservants retraced their way through the arena substructure, a single sentry in tow, en route to the one destination that, by its pure repulsiveness, had the potential to obliterate their mealtime cravings, no matter the premium quality of the food that awaited them.

Having procured Skol's food buckets from the rearway of the kitchen (which, one might say, was symbolically appropriate), they found the beast's evening fare as raw sewage when compared to the palaestral fixings being meted out a mere prison block away. Two brimming buckets of witch-cauldron scraps—gristly joints swimming in a rendered, congealing swill of bloodied gravy, vegetable discards, and potatoes long on their way to vining out—this and a single pail of water was Skol's evening allotment. Economical, of course, and not inedible, it was an efficient means of ridding the kitchen of off-cuttings and such; and Skol in his limited scope likely knew no better nor cared. Presentation was a civilised concept; it had little meaning before the rumbling, pancreatic demands of such a primal being. A horrid abomination at his worst, a primitive humanoid at his most reserved, he'd likely have eaten an old sneaker had Wagner one to give him.

The duty guards at Skol's enclosure being of a new tour, it seemed that a revolving constituency of personalities and temperaments was to be a part of the long-term experience. And, as with any cross section of peoples, the general reaction to Wagner's and Balgor's assumption of Skol's caretaking evoked mixed opinions throughout the alternating complement. Encountering everything from banal indifference on one end to the profound sense of relief that someone other than a valued NuRac would be putting his welfare at risk, with the exception of one or two despotic warders the prisoners were to be left largely on their own, with what denigration or harassment they were to encounter being generally reserved for their initial arrival or departure.

On this evening, only the second feeding of many to come, Wagner and Balgor quickly went at delivering the beast's sustenance, the visions of their own scrumptious repast back on the palaestra barely overriding their immense distaste for this duty.

Once confident that Skol was indeed secured, both men stepped into the cell. Careful to maintain a prudent proximity, each of them gingerly edged his apportionment to either side of Skol's bole-like shanks, and then made like thieves for the exit.

Barred, however, from leaving, they were each handed a spade, and here instructed to clear a portion of the cell's mounting ordure by directing it into a small orifice in the centre of the floor, beneath which lay the cesspit. Frustrated, put to rout, irked beyond contempt, they could do nothing but comply.

"Ugh!" Wagner gagged as he dredged. "I'll be lucky to have an appetite left after this."

"Quit shirking," said Balgor, flinging a heap at the drain. "Already I have moved twice the excrement that you have."

"That's because you have a knack for shovelling the stuff. Just ask anyone who's heard your stories."

Balgor flirted with the impulse to send some organic treasure flying in Wagner's direction. Deciding, however, that they could ill afford any nonsense, he instead helped Wagner to channel all that they could, as fast as they could, into the inadequate chute. Then, taking one last look at Skol, at the cell, at each other, they tapped at the door with their spades and waited, pretending to each other that they were going to wallop the doorkeeper at first sliver of light.

After a cursory inspection and approval (more dispatchful than either would have believed), they were on their way back to the yard without further delay. Having accomplished their task within a half-hour, they emerged onto the grounds at the first stage of twilight, with most of their peers still stuffing themselves by Cinjal's very last hurrah. To their joy, they found Tamek present and breaking bread with Bilahdu and several others amid the concourse. A more intentful gaze about the area likewise revealed an infusion of familiar faces, many of whom hadn't been on the palaestra that afternoon—and at least a dozen others newly released from the infirmary. Hustling for the sluice, Wagner and Balgor lathered their filth away in record time, after which they beat it back to the mess line where, like hungry mudlarkers, they waited in partial sop, bowls in hand. Jounced, however, by sudden irruption, they found themselves demoted to second and third spot in line by none other than J'nea who, likely just having completed her own miscellany of duties, snuck in ahead of them and squeezed them out.

"Hey!" Wagner blustered. "Lackeys to the rear!"

She glanced back dispassionately. "Ah, so they are."

Wagner turned to Balgor with a wink. "I'll have you know," he said, strictly for her benefit, "that we have risen well above the rank of 'lackey,' thank you very much."

"Aye," said Balgor. "We have achieved the coveted titles of scapegrace and scofflaw. You would do well, wench, to remember this should you engage us again."

"Oh?" She didn't even look back, but rather snapped up a bowl from the stack. "Which of you is the scofflaw, and which, the scapegrace?"

"Pending the circumstances of our frequent insurrections," said the realmson, "we are interchangeable."

She mused. "I see. Like most men, then."

Wagner cringed under direct hit. "Oww—now *that's* cold."

"As is her heart," said Balgor. "Cold as wintry stone."

"Yeah? I thought you told me her heart was made of gristle."

"Nay, it is her brain that is gristle."

"I don't think so," said Wagner. "Wasn't her brain made of bone, and her heart made of gristle?"

Balgor stroked his beard as a sage might. "Hmm... Perhaps I should speak it through, to refresh myself:

> *Brain of bone,*
> *Heart of stone,*
> *Demeanour of thistle,*
> *ice, and gristle.*

"Aye, *Voknor*, you are one-half correct, and I, one-half in error!"

J'nea did not retort. Instead, she smirked like a school girl long inured to boyish playground taunts. It was to a kitchen staffer, and not to her tormentors, that she gave her reply.

"My usual, Ragalto!" she told her fellow trusty, presenting him her porringer. "Extra gristle and bone. And give these two cretins the oldest loaves you have— stale bread for stale wits!"

"And give 'her highness' the mouldy ones," said Wagner, "for similar reason."

"Stale?" said Balgor, perplexed. "How can this be? Ever in my life have I been accused of being too *fresh*!"

Ragalto stared dumb at the bickering trio, wondering if some strain of lunacy more unmanageable than most had overtaken them. While insulting to and fro was a mainstay between personalities both affectionate *and* at odds, the chemistry between this particular group seemed sulphury at best. He long knew the volatility of J'nea's personality and the upstart cockiness in Balgor's; and even if he had only limited insight into the newcomer's tendencies, he saw potential enough to ignite the entire yard in squabble. Balancing wary indulgence with caution, he promptly served up the woman's ragout, making no extraneous effort to angle the tureen for surplus gristle and bone as per instructions, and subsequently recoiled at seeing a dissatisfied Wagner muscling in and fishing about her bowl with an intruding spoon in quest of them. The realmson, too, bade Ragalto to ladle her portion anew, and to "earnestly endeavour" this time to accord her the offal they'd requested. The hapless J'nea, suddenly in straddle between the seethe of irritation and the lure of juvenile surrender, barked at them, swatting Wagner's hand from her meal and cramming a wholemeal biscuit full into his yelping maw. Leaving him red-faced and gagging, she grabbed another breadling, and this she lobbed straight at the rollicking Balgor. Missing his mouth, the roll pelted him squarely on the forehead and—in a million-to-one shot—careered off of his noggin and sploshed back into her own porringer, splattering her face and hair with the simmer of her evening's pottage.

"You imbeciles!" she cried from beneath slathery daub and drip. "Now see what your foolishness has accomplished!"

"*Fostoch!*" cried Wagner as he dislodged the crusty projectile from his mouth. "It's you! You've come back!"

"Aye, true!" said Balgor, pitching into a laughter so convulsive that he doubled over and quite nearly choked. "It is he! It is the Orrdian! I would recognise those stew-splodged lineaments anywhere!"

J'nea, standing in rigid disbelief, leered at them from within a fume that could almost have boiled the stew on her face. Ragalto, seeing two murders in the making, nervously clamped the lid on the pot and backed away from the servery. The other trusties did the same.

Balgor and Wagner, try as they may, were powerless to contain themselves. More unrestrainable than before, clasping their mid-sections as if to keep precious viscera from spilling out, their laughter consumed them; and whatever retributive fury was mounting within the bedrizzled she-devil before them, they were too impaired by their own hilarity to make any attempt to avoid it. Yet, as mirth was itself a contagion—and unbridled mirth, doubly so—it frequently found a way of infecting the most sourpussed of adversaries, softening and assimilating even the most condemning holdouts with little more than proximity and pique. And so it was with J'nea. Her hyenic antagonists oblivious to everything outside their little bubble of idiocy, she actually paused in her rant, upstaged by the two men whose regression into buffoons proved a more riveting oddity for her than any tirade that she could ever have produced. Sneer turning to pout, and pout morphing into a reluctantly skewed grin, resistance was quickly becoming impractical if not impossible; and before she could thwart it, inevitability saw her besieged by their jubilance as well. Laughing, wailing, and yet still cachinnations shy of Balgor's and Wagner's extreme, she squeegeed gravy from both brow and cheek, and flung it at them along with every hurlable expletive in her repertoire.

Although seeing the fellows suitably strewn and no more or less in gale for it, Ragalto and his co-workers nevertheless sensed that they'd not receded quite far enough. Hieing off now, as if having just uncovered a nest of skunks, they blundered through the archway, leaving any further excitement to their seated and supping kinspeople—Tamek and Bilahdu included—whose intrigue had been unshakeable from the first antic.

The NuRacs, as one might imagine, only tolerated tomfoolery for a generality of moments. This one, because of its stridency and its wanton waste of provisions, would fall short of even that leniency. Compelled from their post along the inner wall, two sentries had broken from their watch at just beyond the point of the first dousing, and now converged on the out-of-control trio.

"I should have suspected *you two*," said the first guard, recognising the male offenders straight off. "I see that no measure of rebuking, no length of imprisonment, and no flirt with death seems to dissuade you from your contemptuous escapades."

"Master, I beg your indulgence," said Balgor, slipping into his best bootlicker's persona. "While we indeed made humour of it, our situation is not as it seems. This woman—the trusty—was in the midst of receiving her repast when, by fatidic whimsy, she became the dalliance of a passing shredder-wasp. Granted, an uncommon visitor given the darkling hour, the bold little devil nevertheless swooped in among us with what we perceived as baleful intent. And we—well—I feel we overreacted. *Voknor*, here, moved before any of us to swat the pest and crush it underfoot. Yet, in his well-intentioned ineptness—which, I might say, is quite within the boundaries of his established penchants—he upended the poor woman's porringer."

The sentry rolled his eyes at Balgor's glozing.

"But I *did* crush that wasp!" said Wagner, triumphantly.

"Aye, he did," chimed Balgor. "And so you see, my esteemed warders, with the crisis averted we commenced to laugh at what it had yielded—the sight of this beleaguered woman, so pathetic and ridiculous under a drabble of stew! And from there I confess that we allowed our joviality to swallow up our good sense."

His remarks not for one moment lost on J'nea, she noted the disparagement that he'd woven so cleverly into his backhanded defence of her. And while clearly deliberating any number of recourses, she—perhaps more clever than her annoyers—muffled herself with prudence until she knew whether or not the NuRacs would be magnanimous enough to actually overlook the incident. Taking Balgor down a peg was something that she could do any time.

The guards, of course, were not so daft that they didn't know a load of vrohda droppings when they heard it. Scrutinising the ingratiating realmson, the goom-erish Wagner, and the choleric J'nea—first individually and then collectively—they conferred for a moment, hardly convinced yet neither too eager to begin meting disciplinary action so close to their shift end.

Then, a saving grace! A lonely dragonfly, not unwasplike in natural design, buzzed lazily and late for home through the heart of their stand-off. Lolling ever so briefly, it hovered in place for all of a trice before zipping off toward sunset.

Every immediate eye distracted by its wispy detour, every tongue silent, in the wake of its fortuitous flit did Balgor and Wagner and J'nea let slip three uncontainable smirks born serendipitously of the wonder and coincidence of that moment.

"Well," said the head guard, "although we already know you two knaves for scoundrels, there remains a negligible probability that your story bears some obscure and infinitesimal truth, at least at its onset. And if not, we still see little behoof in trying to make examples of you yet again. Therefore, while the female tidies herself, you will rake over this mess, procure her a fresh meal, and then you will consume your own comestibles in quietude, without further incident. Do not forget—it is criminal to waste rations, and if we see either of you squandering even the merest crumb in a suspect manner, you will be paying another visit to the detention block. Do you understand?"

"We do, sir," said Balgor, whose simper quickly reverted to disdain the very second that the NuRacs passed out of earshot.

"You hypocrite!" spat J'nea. "Why did you not speak those slurs while the guards stood before you?"

"Someday I will," said Balgor. "But not today. Despite the noddy I played just now, I am no fool. You know as I do, that a mouthy rascal who does not govern his tongue is bound to lose it. I simply do and say what I must in hopes that one day I may face my enemy on equal terms. Does that make me a hypocrite? Aye, perhaps. Maybe even a coward. But it is better to swallow a bit of faeces now and plan for revenge than to choke on an entire mound of it for naught."

J'nea had no immediate response. Instead, she studied him—almost disconcert-edly—as if he'd gone and muddied the waters of her formerly perspicuous preconceptions.

"I must say, Wagner, I am amazed at *this* one," she finally said. "Here is the first instance where he has voiced something that I cannot bring into dispute."

"Don't get used to it," said Wagner. "Personally, I find it easier not to listen to him at all."

"Now *that* is something that *I* cannot bring into dispute," said Balgor. "Would you but listen to me occasionally, *Voknor*, we would save ourselves a wealth of strife."

"And miss out on all the fun?" Wagner looked back at J'nea. "He's never had so much raw, nail-biting adventure in his whole life—not before he hitched his wagon to *my* star."

"No?" she asked. "What of all the emprise of past misdeeds that he spins for all of his noodle-headed barracks friends?"

"Pshaw! You could recount your last latrine visit to those guys and they'd all marvel over it. Now, get outta here. Go wash up while Balgor slops you some new grub, as ordered. Only, I think that this time maybe we'll hold the gristle and bone."

She lobbed her bowl to the realmson, forcefully enough to ensure that some of the leavings blotched onto his tunic, and then headed off for the sluice. The crowd eyeing her no less fixedly than they had Fostoch a few nights back, the feistier J'nea actually met and challenged their stares—grumbling at some, picking quarrel with others, shaming most into keeping their eyes on their porringers and their mouths occupied in chew.

"You have to admit," said Wagner, "she's got pluck."

"Not only does she possess it, *Voknor*—she exudes it."

Wagner was still running a reckless rake over the sands when J'nea returned from laving. Balgor in bide, he promptly snatched up a newly-ladled bowl and two breadlings and shoved them into her hands, and then whistled to Wagner to wrap things up. Behind them, the qualmy Ragalto had finally summoned nerve enough to return to the servery where, from safely behind the tables, he worked to dismantle the evening set-up. Wishing no further surprises, he encouraged the trio to take one of the wine skins with them—anything to keep them from coming back for seconds. And, just enough of the grape sloshing within said skin to slake not only their thirsts but perhaps even the thirsts of those who were quickest to entreat them for refills, they sought a place where they might sit and eat without much bother.

On the way, Balgor nudged Wagner, pointing at the suddenly and miraculously recovered Uthok who, not so very long ago, had been bemoaning his compromised health to anyone in the infirmary who would listen. There he now sat, his beard lightly bedecked by gravy and bread crumbs, his three emptied porringers stacked one atop the other in the sand, a fourth tipped to his mouth, and another bowl—a *bowl*, not a cup—of wine wedged neatly and protectively in his lap as if it were a miser's strongbox.

Wagner likewise saw many other familiars who'd not been on the palaestra earlier, and to the more congenial ones he nodded friendly acknowledgement. Gamühr the Bard waved to him, as did the scrappy brothers, Grandio and Graspa, who'd been so quick to embrace—and sing the praises of—his stretching and callisthenics routines. He even caught a sizable leer levelled at him by the ignoble Minosh, and to this blackguard he returned the sentiment with matching scowl and grimace.

Reaching a suitable spot, the three of them sat together in peaceful gesture to show the ogling NuRacs that their ado in the meal line had indeed been circumstantial and not monkeyshines. At first, when they did converse, they kept their palaver general so as not to arouse their irreconcilable penchants. As time went on, however, and the scrutiny subsided, Wagner finally informed J'nea of their new duties with Skol, at which she shared with them how she, too, had once been impressed into tending him for a two-day period back when his maintenance was fully a NuRac operation.

"He was at highest vigour then," she said, mouth full of bread. "And far from docile. He had just savaged two guards the previous week, after a faulty brake on the wheel suddenly allowed him free in his cell while the NuRacs were within. Knowing of this, I was petrified to be in there with him, even as they assured me that they had repaired the mechanism. In fact, once inside the enclosure, my anxiety had me dashing the buckets and exiting the cell before the guards could even think to amuse themselves at my expense."

"Lucky you," said Wagner. "Not only do we have to feed him, but we get to clean up after him too."

"Not we, *Voknor*—you." Using a bread crust, Balgor sopped stew from his bowl. "The guards informed me in private that, after today, I am to be restricted to watching, while you alone shovel up Skol's daily mess."

"And this little conversation took place *when*?"

"It was in an aside. You could not have heard it."

"How very convenient," said Wagner. He looked at J'nea, who smiled and shrugged. Both then looked at Balgor, who would have successfully maintained his deadpan if Uthok's throaty belch had not erupted right then a few heads beyond them. An expulsion of frat-party calibre, it unhinged Balgor with such an unready fit of laughter that his windpipe fell victim to regurgitated crumbs. Fortunately only a minor convulsion—no need for Wagner to introduce him to the Heimlich manoeuvre—with the exception of some spasmodic coughing, one or two orts of spittled rye, and a few teardrops, he garbled his way to recovery. A bit of wine, then, to clear his gullet, followed by a bit of air to blanch the purple of his cheeks, and the three of them finished out the repast in manner more subdued, interrupted only here and then by a dry neighbour seeking the dregs of the wine.

With the sun fled, and the torchlights ablaze, J'nea excused herself, admitting to feeling her spirits just a little more than she'd intended. Heading off in drowsy gait, she was only one of many to return her crockware and commence a meander toward the barracks and a well-deserved night's rest. Tamek's conclave was likewise breaking up, and as he rose to bid his companions goodnight he caught sight of Balgor and Wagner, and made course for them.

"Ah, my friends," he said, "I fully expected to sup and converse with you on this vesper. Now it seems we needs must carry it over to the dimness of our quarters."

"Has something occurred?" asked Balgor.

"It has."

"And?"

He invited them to walk with him. "It does not bode well for us. It does not bode well at all."

Cryptic though the Sentinel was, Wagner thought little about his statement, nor of the ominousness in it, for rarely did *anything* ever bode well for them. Imprisonment, beatings, coerced battle, imminent death, and now their reduction to zookeepers for a bloodthirsty monster with a fondness for dismemberment—what could bode much worse than that?

Inside the barracks and off for the rear reaches, as removed from their kinspeople as they could steal, the three men found a spot to confabulate. Oddly, however, even upon seating themselves in seclusion, Tamek remained silent—pensive perhaps—for more than just a nominally contemplative moment. This was not at all like him. Nowhere beyond his nightly meditations was the lack of loquacity something that one associated with the Sentinel of Vishkor, even in the midst of his most obstinate brood. And when he finally did open his dialogue with them, he enigmatically skirted crux and cruciality for a depthless digression into trivialities and other matters of inconsequence that seemed inexplicably diversionary from his earlier implication. Inquiring into Balgor's and Wagner's respective health since the tournament, he encouraged them to relay to him the scope and purpose of their post-infirmary duties, the general mood of the guards, even their post-tournament impressions of Taskmaster Grum. Assimilating all that they told him, clearly he was seeking something specific, and whatever it was it wasn't strictly rooted in particulars. Intimation over content, intuition over event, he was sifting their recountings to get an overall fix on the enemy's mindset, foot soldiers on up. Everything else, from his own verbal minutiae to theirs, served as a purging, an exercise to make ready their minds for what he'd put in buffer. Only after this was accomplished did he resume with his earlier presentiment.

"Something is afoot," he said.

A simple phrase of such lowering nature, he'd stated it plainly, soberly, and with dilatory prudence; and, like the masque of a certain opera phantom, it hinted at an indelible unpleasantness behind it. Perhaps in their answers he'd gleaned confirmation of whatever privilege he possessed. On the other hand, their information may have added nothing to spur his suspicions at all. Either way, he was going to offer them the product of his own ruminations, not because he wanted to, but because he *had* to, because there was real gravity here. And Tamek never made light of anything with real gravity.

"Through the ears of our many scouts," he said, "from the scullions to the smiths and fabricators to the launderers, I have been alerted to information that has proved unsettling—although I know not yet what to make of it."

"And what be *it*?" asked Balgor.

"I have come to suspect that the many regiments which of late have returned to QieLahr did not come for the games as we may first have imagined. I believe, rather, that they are here to convene in some indefinite capacity, a gathering of warlords and troops for an express formality that we have thus far been unable to determine, save for—" He paused, leaving Wagner and Balgor hanging upon unspoken revelation while he craned about to insure that no other ears strained nearby. "—save for a smatter of seismicity that occurred this morning, well beyond the walls."

"We heard no rumblings this morning," said Balgor.

"There was din nonetheless. I felt it in the midst of my morning lave, and then again just after breaking fast. Initially I passed it off as distant thunderpeal. Yet, as it did not seem firmamental in nature, I was nagged by instinct to suspect otherwise."

"Some sort of ordnance fire maybe?" asked Wagner.

"I know not this expression," said the Sentinel.

Remembering, then, that rudimentary gunpowder was probably unknown to this period (and perhaps not even chemically viable on Ergos, given the unexplored physics of its ecosphere), Wagner subtly explained its prevalence in his own "land." Offering point and counterpoint on the benefits and horrors that its invention had both bestowed and unleashed upon earthly culture, he treated the topic much as he had his other telluric revelations before it—with a vaguely mystical slant. Tamek, listening with no little enthrallment (and still unapprised of Wagner's true origin), marvelled that he'd never heard tell of any such thing.

Misgiven that so lethal a compound might be available in the realm for casual use, it moved him to ponder how a people might possess such ilk of magiks without ultimately being consumed by zealous misuse. Puzzled or not, upon hearing more of Wagner's careful distillings, at end he could neither confirm nor deny that such explosives, as Wagner claimed existed, might indeed not have been the source of that morning's phenomena.

"At one point beyond these occurrences," Tamek continued, "I was intercepted by several sentries who came with orders to dispatch me from the field. Unyielding to my inquiries, they directed me upon the familiar stairpath to the Tribunal's keep, where unbeknownst to me the NuRac lords would present me with news most unsettling."

"You cannot take anything those caitiffs utter as truth," said Balgor. "They spin their lies and they propagandise in order break our wills. And they attempt to puppet you as their mediating oracle, to beset us with false despair."

"Indeed," said Tamek. "Yet, I cannot deny that their argument today demonstrated an eerie vitality of confidence, quite unlike their typical schemes of strained probabilities and hackneyed polemics. They presented me with evidence too compelling for mine own comfort—evidence of their most recent triumph o'er our outside forces."

"What manner of evidence?" challenged Balgor. "Nothing short of a parade of piked heads would sway my opinion." He locked onto Tamek's grimness. "Nay—tell me it was not this!"

"No, friend. Their proof was not in death tolls. In truth, they insist that when our armies most recently clashed, it took scant seconds for our warriors to realise their discomfiture and to initiate a complete divisional retreat. In essence, nary an Ergosian was captured, nor e'en pursued."

Sorely troubled, Balgor leaned into the huddle, palms wide and upturned, as if the information he sought could be made physical and placed into them.

"What evidence, then? If they have no bodies, no prisoners, no captured officers—and now this unlikely rejoinder of having not even attempted pursuit—then what proof had they to convince you?"

"Armaments," said Tamek.

"*Armaments?*"

"Aye. Ergosian shields, swords, banners—hundreds of them—dropped, relinquished, cast away and abandoned, as if toting them would have hindered what I can only presume was a flight for their very lives."

He perceived the realmson's incredulity and quickly outflanked it. "Take heart, Balgor. At first onset I, too, found their evidence wanting, and their professions, ludicrous. Easily could they have amassed such a cache from scores of previous encounters, and piled them before me as from a single slaughter and despoliation. Only, 'twas instead the peculiar quality of the matériel, and not the quantity, that did put rout to my immediate disputation."

"And that condition being...?"

They waited for the Sentinel to wrestle words from emotion.

"By Existence, they were slag! All of them, Balgor. Melted and warped, blackened with scoria, decimated. One piece after the next, each appeared to have been heated to sorghum-like elasticity. And each, in cooling, had retained the distortion. In all of my years of soldiering, I have ne'er encountered any weapon capable of inflicting such consummate damage to good forging. *Voknor*, could your 'gunpoudre' have caused such a vast measure of heat?"

"Only a yield of big-time magnitude and intensity. But here's the catch—in order to be scared off, I would think that the Ergosian troops would have first had to witness their armaments frying. Why else run? And even if, by some improbable circumstance, they'd already laid them down in surrender, with a force as devastating as you describe I doubt that they would've been able to avoid being fried collaterally. Detonation, meltdown, radiation—whatever it was, it surely would have caused some major *human* casualties."

There was a pause as Balgor sulked over visions of fused weaponry, as Tamek sought to rationalise why so many Ergosians might willingly abandon their arms, as Wagner struggled to make heads or tails out of something that he didn't really understand. Of the three, Wagner was the first to proffer speculation.

"Now, granted, it would be going to a lot of trouble, but couldn't the NuRacs have partially melted—or re-smelted—a bunch of old Ergosian arms, collected from handfuls of past skirmishes, in order to evoke your response?"

"I did consider it," said Tamek. "Yet, what would be the benefit? All that bother, all that subterfuge, simply to squash *my* spirit?"

"What, then, of some natural occurrence?" asked Balgor. "Levin from a particularly wicked storm, perhaps. Days later, the NuRacs came upon the discarded weaponry, and—"

"Again, why bring it here and fabricate a tale for my benefit? And why would our people have abandoned their weapons in a storm?"

"It still comes back to logic," said Wagner. "Soldiers on the march don't toss away their arms. Thus, a lightning storm intense enough to sizzle their weapons would have sizzled some of them as well. So, where are the bodies?"

"We have only the NuRacs' word that there were none," said the realmson. "Too, we pyre our dead, *Voknor*. If there was opportunity, the surviving Ergosians would have returned to retrieve the bodies."

"No explanation truly satisfies in all ways," said Tamek. "Yet, I do have another. Only, 'tis one I do not wish to believe, for it smacks of blasphemy and unspeakable peril."

Balgor and Wagner turned to each other, then back to their ominously speaking friend. "So, let's have it," Wagner urged.

Tamek allowed himself a moment's distraction by glancing about the room, noting those already asleep, those who diced by torchlight, and those who contended in lively storytelling.

"In my revelation," he said, "I confessed that in all my years of soldiering I knew of no weapon awful enow to wreak the level of destruction that I saw today. While my statement was a true one, 'tis common knowledge that my soldiering life is the least of who I am. In my most prominent conviction—my years spent in Vishkor— I became a trusted vessel for matters divers and mystical. There, through my enlightenment, I was bestowed the elders' esoteric knowledge, and with said privilege I gained an awareness of things whose least considerable wonder would make an entire palaestra filled with melted armaments seem as an oven of scorched pastries by comparison. And one of the most intensely harboured amazements—the very one that I am loath to think might have fallen into NuRac hands—regards a source of unfathomable causality and consequence to which all things in this sphere are tethered."

"Come again?"

"There are many things under the sun," said Tamek, "and the world endures. Oft-times because of them, oft-times in spite of them. Regrowth follows e'en the most calamitous upheaval. The rains cleanse and replenish, just as wintry soils gestate the seeds of new greenery. E'er has it been, and e'er was it meant to be."

"What," asked Balgor, "has this to do with the temblor today? Or with melted weaponry?"

"From our brief vantage in these shells, Balgor, we bear testimony to the coexistence of the ethereal and the substantial. We note the visible and the tangible, and by them—and by our scripture—are we able to envision both the imaginable and the inconceivable. In our tradition we are meted bits of legend that speak of talismans and fetishes that, by the Paraclete's will, were imbued with elemental properties and utilised to illumine a faltering people's faith. The history of these implements is unfinished beyond the tales that introduce them. And despite having become the fixation of many a quester o'er the years, said talismans have remained e'er elusive, e'er recalcitrant to allow themselves to fall into human possession. E'en as the diggers and delvers claim benignity as they uproot the realm in their pursuit of them, I can tell you that these instruments are not meant to be found—not e'er. At any worth, most fail to realise that 'tis the quest itself, and not the prize, that usually fulfils one's soul and dispenses meaning. The quickest to learn this lesson are also the ones who can most easily relinquish the obsession and return cleansed of heart.

"Now," he continued, "ere you think me a windbag of sermonising twaddle, allow me to reckon these thoughts amid our present quandary. The suggestion that our warriors fled in apparent panic before a prepotency that could fuse metal or rip it asunder—and conceivably mimic the properties of levin and thunder-clasp—leads me to believe that our captors have either created or uncovered some agent of immeasurable power. That they flaunt their new confidence before my face is one matter to interpret. The fact of so many battalions regathering in QieLahr of late is another. That a force so much like thunder might be unleashed devoid of nature makes it three. Thus, I can only pray that what they have discovered is a weapon akin to *Voknor's* 'ordnance' and not some relic the sacrosanctity of which may doom us all, NuRac and Ergosian alike."

"Is this what you feel it may be?" asked Balgor.

"My vows prevent me from revealing anything else until I know undoubtedly that the NuRacs have happened across the forbidden, and thieved it for their own. I am sorry, my friends. Know that I will not give o'er to sleep tonight in light of these troubling suppositions. Instead, I will retain the vigilance to consult inwardly with those spirits whose benevolent mercies might bestow me the enlightenment to know that my suspicions are groundless."

With that, he bade them good night and moved away, lowering himself onto his bedstraw and assuming a meditative, upright position from where he would, by Wagner's guess, tune his consciousness to whatever megahertz brought him his best spiritual reception.

"Do you have any idea what he just said?" Wagner asked as he and Balgor reached their bed piles.

"A little. He suspects that the NuRacs have found a means to tap into a power that is greater than all of us, and he hopes desperately that he is wrong. As do I."

"Y'know, when I first met him in the dungeons, he rambled on to me about the Vorshalah and a whole slew of supercilious mumbo jumbo. I didn't know what to think of it then. I was pretty much caught within a stasis of culture shock at the time. Come to think of it, Papa Olask went on about strange manifestations and unnatural occurrences too, back when I first ran into him. I do admit that he had reason for it, given the ado with the seizure patient and my sudden improvement in health. And although I've always been somewhat of a spiritual cynic, I can't really discount or dismiss his or Tamek's theories of the unexplained, since it's obvious that some kind of sorcery or divine providence is responsible for *my* being here in the first place. Even if I didn't believe in charms and jujus, in Excaliburs, Arks of the Covenant, or in talismans capable of summoning thunder and lightning, I'd still have to be open to it all. The fact that I'm standing here all healthy and sceptical when this morning I had a gaping hole in my side—that's a trifle strange and unnatural as well, wouldn't you say?"

"More than a trifle, *Voknor*. Would that you could have been generous enough to heal *my* injuries as well."

"Those paltry little nicks?" Wagner gestured at Balgor's collection of scabs, ranging from blade-fine stripes to full-bodied strawberries. "I've had pimples that looked worse than those."

Balgor snorted contestation, calling Wagner stingy for not opening his gift to the man who had done nothing but wet-nurse him through the entire escape attempt. A fabrication of course, it didn't stop the realmson from stepping it up, claiming that it was Wagner who sought to keep him injured because it was the only hope he had of defeating Balgor in spar. In turnabout, Wagner made mock of his whininess, while the sleep-muddled Ergosians around them berated them both and pleaded for quiet.

Abiding out of consideration, they muted themselves, yet continued harassing each other in increasingly antagonistic pantomime until Wagner finally reached over to let Balgor have an errantly glancing backhand.

Before either horseplayer knew, stroboscopic refulgence coursed the barracks. Flaring and subsiding with pulsar-like instantaneity, anyone whose eyes had been exposed at flashpoint was now seeing spots and nothing else. Half-blinded, straining and gazing, the recumbent sprung up in their straw heaps while those who'd been standing now teetered about like tops.

Amid the uproar, Balgor grabbed Wagner's still-extended arm. "*Voknor*—I was jesting!"

"I know! So was I! Are you okay—can you see?"

"All I see is a luminiferous swarm of hornets. And you?"

"I'm okay. I must've blinked at just the right time." He looked around guardedly. "Listen," he whispered, "I don't know who saw what, but I'm gonna sit you back down on your bed. Just keep rubbing your eyes, and I'll do the same. Hopefully, everyone else is just as affected as you are. And, if we're lucky, they're a lot more clueless."

At the edge of the confusion, Tamek now walked about, comforting anyone who seemed distressed. Having been engaged in his meditation—and thus closed-eyed—during the strobe, he'd only sensed the brightness through his membranes, and thus had experienced no more than negligible detriment. Troubled and bemused, however, upon reaching his two friends he fished for any elucidation that they may have had, yet got the same story as relayed by everyone else—that, for a split-second, it seemed as if Cinjal herself had materialised within the barracks, and then slipped away with equal swiftness.

Wagner, despite overwhelming compunction, maintained his standard charade. Loathing the compulsion that had him once again slighting the Sentinel and hiding the truth from him for fear of being ostracised and condemned for manifestations over which he had no control, this particular instance was nothing if not serendipitously opportune. The luminosity wrought of the incident not only coincided splendidly with the storm-like phenomena of their earlier discussion, but it likewise bated the notion that the NuRacs may indeed have just reactivated the mysterious weapon that Tamek so feared.

To say that the Sentinel, bereft of any immediate explanation, bought into said theory with the heart and soul of his righteous bankroll would have been a mild metaphor. To say that Wagner was seeding a future estrangement from the very first friend he'd made on Ergos was an infraction that he conceivably still had time to correct. Were it possible to undo every half-truth and omission that he'd tossed around since his capture (and be forgiven without further suspicion or prejudice), he might have decided then and there to come clean. But it was nowhere near that easy. Tamek, steeped in his tunnel-visioned semi-theocracy, was a patriarch whose sternness demanded the straight and narrow tract. Wagner, not through purposeful deviancy but because he saw greater prudence in operating undercover, travelled alternately upon the high and low roads of basic liberality and discretionary self-service. It was precisely because the Sentinel was so prelatic—and the people, so superstitious—that Wagner couldn't bring himself to spill. His saving grace, then, was in all of the "sons" and "daughters" of the Ergosian congregate who constantly looked to Tamek for guidance and strength, and who, by their need, appropriated so much of the Sentinel's time in the camp. This, in turn, reprieved Wagner from having to empty his deep pockets and own up, at least until first finding a way to uncover the answers that could justify the extraordinary circumstances of his life.

Just as everyone's eyes were readjusting, the night guard happened in for the evening roster. Outraged at seeing everybody up and about as if on market day in the city square, they demanded an end to any high jinks, warning that anyone not swift enough to his bed would take his winks in the detention block. The throng, still bedevilled by Wagner's inadvertent and unattributed gramarye, begrudgingly followed edict and scrambled no-bones to their appropriate heaps. Tamek retired as well, his eyes riveted upon the soldiers who surely, by his suspicions, must have been privy to what he was not.

"By the way," Wagner whispered to Balgor before following suit to his own bed, "you owe me big. You haven't got a scratch, a bite, or even a scrape left on your body—at least not that I can see in this scanty torchlight."

"Aye, I do feel vital and whole, *Voknor*. And I must say, I find it most unsettling. Such sorcerous influence is not something that an ordinary man should possess."

"Tell me about it." Quick, then, to avoid NuRac censure, Wagner quit their conversation and slid back onto his pallet. Edgy, alert, a little bit shaken, a little bit self-important, with his face obscured by columnar shadow he watched as his captors finished out the headcount, his hands running one against the other in secret confirmation of the new centimetre of fingernail growth that hadn't been there five minutes earlier.

CHAPTER NINETEEN

Ill fortune seldom comes alone.
—JOHN DRYDEN

Unsurprisingly, the morntime was nothing short of lively. A night of broken sleep for many, with the dawn and the growing collective wakefulness came the predictable imbroglio of surmisings and ascriptions whose task was to put source, meaning, and portent to the previous evening's pyrotechny. Long on restlessness and short on reassurance, more than a few insomniacs had wended the small hours cobbling credibility out of something that no one could evidence or explain. Many didn't even try. But those who did racked considerable points in creativity. Varied and overfed of imagination, the fruit of their assiduity ranged anywhere from notions of a breaching of the celestial fabric that separated the realm of humans from godly ether, to that of a shared vision the nature of which was incomprehensible to mortal eyes except in the form of some absolute purity that no one was worthy enough to see past. One man even called it a "hiccough from the very throat of Existence."

Conspicuously refraining from adding their two cents each to whichever argument dominated the moment, Wagner and Balgor did nothing but exchange a varied assortment of sidelong looks—from uneasy amusement to bewilderment to absentation. Although they knew more about the phenomenon than anyone, neither could deny that Wagner's unwieldy proclivity for channelling unnatural forces wasn't just as perplexing to them. That they were no less clueless in attributing its source, theirs was a conundrum whose real blessing or bane couldn't be known without the forfeit of anonymity. Wagner certainly wasn't courting the means for his eventual outing; he wasn't laying down buffers, wasn't looking for loopholes in the Ergosian mythos through which to soften the evulgation that was both inevitable and inevitably necessary. He simply couldn't be sure how these people—most notably, Tamek—would take the news once he was exposed. Would he be revered or stoned? Hailed as a favoured vessel or denounced as an abomination? While Balgor's fairly ready acceptance of both his history and his tappable potential had proved encouraging, there was no way to tell how the masses would react to an outsider—no matter how liked and trusted he was—who had a latent and potentially lethal ability tucked away in his psyche.

Tamek's explanation of the flash was far more pragmatic than anything dreamed up by the constituency. Not openly declared, but rather, proffered only to a select few, he logically (and erroneously) linked the incident to the rumblings of the previous morning—and then these, with the enigma of the NuRacs' newfound confidence. He was genuinely worried; and not only did this not fall easy to, nor sit well with, a man of his exalted standing, it clearly prompted considerable anxiety in anyone who continued to look to him for his usually cool vigil. His enlightenment and education had always made him the man to watch and emulate, the man whose smarts and resolve could ransom this ragtag prison populace from total despair, despite his P.O.W. status. But for Wagner, Balgor, Bilahdu, and a handful of other confidents, Tamek's perennial enmity of being the NuRacs' subjugated figurehead was nothing compared to his current inability (or disinclination) to explain what new evils might be hatching or what ancient ones were inadvertently being roused and loosed upon the land. Like the actions of errantly twisted children who knew not the consequences of their forbidden deeds, the NuRacs trod wherever they wished, seized what they desired, and chose not to concern themselves with the lands they despoiled, the prohibitions they found too inconvenient to respect, and the sites, reliquaries, and antiquities that they desecrated in their flagitious quest for dominion.

Conspiracies tabled for the nonce, Balgor and Wagner joined the Sentinel for breakfast while Bilahdu sat on their periphery, fending off the inquisitive so that Tamek might at least enjoy one uninterrupted repast. Clever man that Bilahdu was, he chided the persistent ones for their wanting initiative in seeking the least challenging route to the lore and prophecies that their own oral tradition—as it regarded praeternatural events—could address no less competently than could Tamek.

"Delve your own pitiful memories, you sluggards!" he told one bunch. "Consult your neighbours. Put away your dice and your follies, blow the dust from your scripture, and for once in your miserable existences engage one another in some erudite dialogue, and thus allow our Sentinel a reasonable time to contemplate the truths that he is ever deferring in order to address your besiegement of witless inquiries!"

"There was a similar event in the infirmary, just the other morning," Wagner added with coy connivance. "I saw it. Balgor saw it. So did many of the wounded. You might want to talk to them, maybe hear what they have to say about it."

"And, at the very least," said Balgor, "they would be happy for the visit."

Once the curious had departed, some even to the infirmary as hoped, Tamek had inquiry of his own. "Is this true? Have there been other such occasions so near in time? Why did you not tell me?"

"It was a daylight transpiration," said Balgor. "So much of its intensity giving way to the brighter environs, it was less dramatic than what we all witnessed last evening. And although for a trice we found ourselves equally confounded by its fleet luminosity, upon its dissipation there would not have been a soul among us who could have been certain it had occurred at all were it not for the commonality of experience."

"Too confounding," said Tamek. "Thunder without the city. Dual occurrences of lightning-like effulgence within the prison, with no harm resulting from either occasion. The NuRac armies all reunited here in QieLahr. Clearly a kindred thread weaves through it all, but I hesitate to actually speak to that which mine intuition suggests."

"I say they're unrelated," blurted Wagner, his voice broken by ambiguity. "I— Anyway, it was actually *three* times. The flaring, that is. An earlier incident happened on my first week here, just after my release from the dungeon block."

"*What!* Why did you not tell me?"

"Fear? Stress? I dunno. Maybe sensory overload. I was still pretty shook up from my capture, my beating, my imprisonment. I already had major marks against me for that Vofspar incident. I wasn't keen on calling any more attention to myself than I absolutely had to."

"But the emanations, *Voknor!* Surely—"

"I know, I know. But you see, I'd witnessed some equally bizarre things long before I ever imagined that I was in line for a one-way drop kick to this crazy neck of the woods. Last night's flaring, as well as the ones in the infirmary, seemed to me to be just more of the same."

"And you felt that you could not confide in me? *Voknor*—I befriended you in earnest! And while 'tis true that my manner may oft-times intimidate, I would not begrudge a man his creeds, nor his experiential professions, e'en should I find them lacking."

"Yeah, well, I was still a stranger, an 'infidel' if you recall, and had no way of knowing whether I'd be treated as some kind of nutso pariah if I started making all these weird claims right off the bat."

"Then there is more?"

Wagner laughed. "You have no idea."

Suddenly they were assaulted by rearward shouting.

"You pair! This is not fraternity hour on the esplanade! Return your earthenware and report for your duties!"

The voice belonged to the guard who'd escorted them from Skol's enclosure the previous morning, not the sort of character who would ask twice.

"Don't make any assumptions," Wagner told Tamek as he and Balgor shot to their feet, "until you've heard the whole story."

"I fully expect you to apprise me later, upon the palaestra," said the Sentinel.

"Just as soon as we've delivered big-boy his vittles."

Although well-intended, Wagner would not fulfil that commitment in the time and the manner of his word. Little known to him or his friend, this—only their second morning of impressment—was to be the very one that he and Balgor had dreaded, dreaded even more than a rematch with croviks. Ordered at the completion of their delivery to leave Skol to his fodder, they were curtly derailed to the supply room, where they were requisitioned two large rakes, two spades, and some chipping and scouring instruments, the whole unwieldy lot of which they were instructed to schlep back to Skol's enclosure for an unscheduled work detail.

Arriving back in soured frame, Wagner set down his tangled armload and peered inside the Sunderer's cell, noting that the living garbage disposer had already made quick work of his entrail entrée. Unrestrained and gulping water from his pail, the brute paid no mind to Wagner's reconnoitre, although with the bucket engulfing his head and the rumbles of his own guzzling resounding from within it, nothing shy of drumfire would likely have drawn his attention.

At the sound of the bucket's discarding, Balgor entreated the guards to retract Skol securely to the wall. This they did without too much menace, and within minutes the two prisoners were locked in and busy scaling the barnacle-like build-up from the corners of the cell.

Wagner was the first to comment on the futility. "There's not enough Pine-Sol in the world to do this job," he said, seeing the lack of accomplishment in five minutes of intensive scrubbing.

"Aye," groaned Balgor. "But I anticipate that piping above us will expedite our task."

He satisfied Wagner's pucker by indicating the open end of a vertical conduit that protruded twenty centimetres or so from the ceiling, almost dead-centre of the room. Edge to edge, it was about the same diameter as the PVC found typically in an earthly residence for waste conveyance. Suspended a few finger-widths beneath it, affixed by a sturdy ilk of bracketed baffle, was a corroded metal disk—a diffuser perhaps, or some similar contrivance.

Piqued that he hadn't noticed it before, Wagner asked what it was.

"It is but one of the many arteries that lead from the cisterns above these enclosures. If I correctly recall, it can, by directive means, be manipulated to permit a flow of water into a particular cell to facilitate the laving of the occupant or to flush the cell of its disgusting contents—or both, I suppose."

"Bring it on, then! I—wait—aren't the stadium seats right above these cells?"

"Aye, they are. Somewhere nigh to five metres above. The reservoirs, however, are situated between, and are fed by a system of piping that requires human exertion to maintain—and often, pump. I know this, for in my earliest days here it was one of my duties to assist in keeping the cisterns full, shortly before I was ever bestowed combat status. Now the task is largely left to our youngest."

"Well, how do we get it to work? And where does it run off to? Not down this piddly little drain grate, I hope."

"I know not exactly," said Balgor. "But, at the risk of iring our captors, I shall effort to inquire."

"Suit yourself. I'll stay here and keep 'Baby Huey' company."

Bowing to his friend's untranslatable wit, the realmson nevertheless cautioned Wagner against any vagaries of sensible restraint in his absence. While visibly weakened and shackled, their bestial charge was not to be disregarded for any reason. Too many had made that mistake in the brute's prime; and, as Skol was insensate and without conscience, even on his worst day he was more lethal than anything in the camp.

Wagner abided Balgor's warnings, careful to keep one eye on his work and the other on his ward. Without his comrade there to help draw off his nervousness with idle banter, his senses quickly opened to the true affront of the cell—its eerie darkness, the skitter of a million foraging creepy-crawlies, and the stifle of swampy malodour. The latter, no different in essence than what one might breathe through a sewage-soaked rag, was enough to make a man ill if he dwelled too much upon it. Nor did it lend itself the least bit to acclimation over time. And whether repulsive in a funny sort of way, or funny in a disgusting one, there was an undeniable quality about it that was a bit too reminiscent of the gent's head back at the Filthy Lucre.

Hearing a postprandial grunt from behind, Wagner took a moment to give his host the once-over, noting even in the half-light how Skol's wounds were still looking none too good. He suspected that his own limbs would long ago have succumbed to gangrene from the level of infection that Skol's system was battling; and for want of purpose he continued to observe, not knowing whether to pity the hairy monstrosity or to rejoice in the justice of Skol's rightful suffering. But certainly, he was awed by the brute's ability to endure what must have been excruciating misery without so much as a peep.

"Pal, you're just one, big, nasty wad of pus," Wagner said, wincing at a particularly abhorrent canker that looked like a month-old cheese Danish. "Just what is it that's keeping you kickin'? You live in a toilet. Your quality of life sucks. So what's the incentive for hanging around? Are you just too stupid to keel over?"

He paused a moment to decipher what he could of the muffled conversation from the other room—Balgor trying to convince the NuRacs to flush out the cell, the NuRacs informing him how this wasn't his concern and suggesting that he resume his duty if he knew what was good for him.

"*Mgomphhh...Tooostooopid...*"

Wagner dropped his scraper. For an eternity of seconds he stood frozen in his third-hand boots. Then slowly, gingerly, he came about to face the unlikely source of an uttering that he couldn't possibly have heard correctly.

Through the murkiness he studied this other being—part humanoid, part abomination, trussed and stuck fast to the stone by ponderous restraint. The distillate of daylight from the loopholes of the opposite wall revealed too little of the behemoth's grizzly countenance to be of note, nothing beyond the weird opaqueness of his eyes, the blood-caked whiskering, and the ridiculously massive prognathic maw that dripped continuous ooze like the cinematic xenomorph in *Alien*. In every sense, he was a wretched, feral beast on the edge of expiration.

Still, had it been Wagner's imagination? Or had this mindless daemon-spawn just mimicked a phrase?

"Did we just...hear something...from the gallery?"

Skol did not answer, did not grunt, did not even appear to be breathing until he suddenly swiped at a pesky flit of gnats performing air manoeuvres about his brow.

"Our hosts choose to be unaccommodating," said Balgor in abrupt re-entry. "We must first deliver the cell of as much solid waste as possible, and only then will they purge it."

He gazed at the unresponsive Wagner, still preoccupied with Skol.

"*Voknor? Voknor?*" He paused a moment, arms akimbo. "*Voknor*, allow me to introduce you to the voracious, heinously insane monster, Skol. Skol, this be *Voknor*, your gentle nursemaid for today."

"He spoke," said Wagner.

"He *what?*"

"He spoke. He aped two of my words."

Balgor looked to the brute. "Nay, *Voknor*. The sewage fumes have overrun your brain. You heard a belch, a grunt, a digestive rumbling, or a—"

"No. I didn't. He actually, *truly*, said something. Like a baby, he heard it, and then he said it."

Balgor looked to Skol a second time. "Aye, well, perhaps." He drew back. "I have learned not to discount anything that you aver, my friend, no matter how improbable. And accept my word—*this* is most improbable."

"Maybe. But it happened."

"Very well, enjoy your delusion. Although I was absent, and thus, *conveniently* unable to substantiate, for the moment I will take you at your word. More presently, however, it seems that we are to lose the best portion of the day to this dismal task—time abundant for you and your student to satisfy my doubt. If he has anything more to expound, then certainly I will be witness to it." He paused and took one more look at Skol. "And if he does indeed utter anything even vaguely resembling human speech, I warn you not to bar my way to the door, for I will be exiting on legs even swifter than yours whereon you run to swoon over J'nea."

"Get outta here—I don't swoon over anybody!"

"Aye, no *body* save hers. Not that I discommend you, *Voknor*. She is a fireball, that one. And well-crafted."

"Yeah, yeah. Keep your bawdy phantasies to yourself."

With that, they dug in, using the rakes to gather the muck from out of the corners and into several heaps. The older refuse along the walls being more dense and compacted than the centralised slime, it required a good deal of chipping and shovelling before much of it could be loosened and reduced to manageable clods. Siccant, slimy, or a combination of both, it was all of it a nasty business, a struggle to organise a roomful of rot without succumbing to any number of sensory offendings or uprooted microbial nastiness.

A great help, however, soon came to them not long into the toil, this being the retraction of the ebon partitions that separated the cell from the stadium. Not truly a measure intended to facilitate light (or the splendid breath of day) to two stifled prisoners, the greater purpose awaited without in the form of a vrohda-drawn cart. A pair of sludge tanks on the back, a dangle of shovels, pails, and ropes along the railings, it appeared that this was the NuRac equivalent of a septic truck, the manner by which considerable quantities of waste solids were eliminated from the animal blocks.

An Ergosian trusty seated low upon the rig, reins at the ready, this operator quickly alit and bade Wagner and Balgor from the cell so that she could help them reeve a pulley for shucking bucket-loads of sewage into the tanks.

"Come, brave warriors," she said with mocking affection. "Tame the flux and bring to me the spoils."

The two men, asquint from the blitz of mid-morning sunlight, stumbled out obligingly, using their arms as visors. Once past the point of foulness, both sucked at the arena air like newborns in slap.

"Ah, this smells *too* good!" Wagner exclaimed.

"Gather those pails," said Balgor. "Let us expedite this business before asphyxia wins the day."

For several hours, then, they shovelled and relayed buckets to the cart, where the trusty—called Hidessel—was gracious enough to dump the rankness into the tanks. Although this was the only function she performed, she had barely an idle moment, so briskly and untiringly did the two men sling their horrid mixture of dung, dirt, and debris into pails heaped to overflowing.

By early afternoon, far beyond the point where their weary limbs were pleading for respite, did they finally clear the cell of all the detritus that mere shovels could finesse. The enclosure, of course, was still far from in order, for the build-up in some of the corners was all but petrified, with nothing short of a pickaxe capable of splitting or shifting it. It was, however, much less inhospitable than it had been, and after waving Hidessel on her way, Balgor rapped the door for the guard.

"I bet I know where they dump all that stuff," said Wagner, standing smudge-faced in the archway between cell and arena. "In the detention block. They probably have a sluice and pipeline rigged so that they can pour it right down, probably into the very oubliette that I'll end up in next."

"At least you would be comforted by familiarity, *Voknor*." Balgor rapped once more. "Do you not agree, Skol?"

The brute was oblivious. Balgor turned to Wagner with a triumphant glow. "He had the whole morning's opportunity to speak, *Voknor*, and his silence was most eloquent."

Wagner hid his defeat. "Yeah, yeah. You probably wouldn't feel much like talking, either, if you were ravaged by infection and covered with maggots and caked blood."

Balgor struck at the door with the shovel. "No? I am wearing the beast's own faeces atop and across my raiment, *Voknor*. How is it that *I* feel like talking?"

"Because you're a loudmouth by nature?"

Before Balgor could think to retort, the door threw open to reveal one very perturbed guard.

"What!" he bawled. "Think you we are out here idle and at your whim?"

Balgor glimpsed the coinage clenched firmly in the NuRac's left grip, an indication of the dicing going on without. "Nay, sir," he replied. "Never idle, and certainly not at our whim! In our undeliberated audacity we thought that you might wish to know our progress."

Although his manner niggled, Balgor's words were vexingly proper, and the guard could do naught but stow his ire behind him—along with his purse—and poke his head into the cell.

A brief surrendering of pretence as he scanned the much improved dwelling, the NuRac quickly redonned his caustic aspect in order to properly huff on how long it had taken the two of them merely to upgrade the cell to its present state. And even this miracle of purging, it seemed, would not be enough; for, despite Balgor's and Wagner's compliance, despite their drudgery and all their vigour in heaving-ho, their task was hardly completed.

"Gather your rakes and stand ready," said the NuRac, exiting the cell and barring them once more within.

Disappointed, both men thumbed disgust at the absent NuRac as the ebon arena partitions likewise clanged shut. Wagner spat and chuckled. "I've gotta tell you," he said, "when it comes to double-talking these clowns, you are the prince of pettifoggers."

Balgor scoffed. "It is a refinement that bemoans my honour, *Voknor*. Such abidance, so taxing and distasteful, serves only to ransom another day for me—and perchance, a morrow's opportunity to not only dole these blackguards a thorough comeuppance, but to free ourselves from this hell."

"Now there's an idea. How's tomorrow sound?"

Balgor chortled delight. "No redress would be more sweet, *Voknor*. Might it be within your resource to have a wide-scale revolt underway by then?"

Wagner scratched his beard, unintentionally dislodging a few crusties of unmentionable matter. "Well, the notice is a bit short," he said. "What say we shoot for the day *after* tomorrow?"

"If you can provide," Balgor joked, "then I am with you."

From above them came the squeaks and squeals of the cistern valves working open. Nothing beyond that at first, the ensuing seconds witnessed a few ruddy dribbles—like the wring of a dirty dishrag—plinking from the contrivance above. A few more squeaks, however, and the pipe abruptly exploded to life, gushing a brown column of influx that struck the deflector just so, and drenched the entire cell with a fountainesque symmetry of deluge.

Straightway the two men went to action, lashing at the floor and the walls, their rakes clawing at the mung and the munch that clenched at the brick every bit as firmly as the mortar beneath it.

Resilient at first, under the water's steady douse the encrustation began giving way to sludge, great gobs of which splattered both prisoners and beast with baleful liberality. The inner downthrow quickly washing off one lamina only to uncover another beneath it, this insalubrious cycle repeated for the duration of the task, with splutter and sordes flying like the pie-filling in some old two-reeler comedy. Although Balgor and Wagner quickly learned when and where to duck, total evasion was unachievable amid so much confusion, the prime concern being to keep one's face down and one's mouth zipped.

In the midst of it all, Skol was showing the first bit of life since tournament day. Invigorated by the tumultuousness, he took to it like a child to an opened summer hydrant. He grunted; he heaved; he bobbed and craned and struggled from within his constraints to catch the mercurial refreshment that must have seemed to him a most remarkable thing. Despite having been continually and reticently aware of the two intruders in his domicile, he was enthralled enough by the inpour that he didn't once move to swipe at the flurrying rakes, nor at their implementers, carding the walls around him. Distracted, displaced of his venom, or quite simply recognising no threat, it was almost as if Balgor and Wagner weren't there at all—only this marvellous spray of rain; and beneath it he was momentarily content to favour sensorial pleasure over savagery.

The shower ushered certain benefit to Skol as well. It flushed his festerings of parasitical scourge, purged scab and pustule of lingering discharge, coldly stung and yet soothed his innumerable lesions to the point of giving his uncanny metabolism better lease at shoring a path to recovery. The cascade, becoming warmer as the tepid top-water funnelled low within the cisterns, soon swelled to ankle-depth across the cell floor, with Balgor and Wagner working to the measure of Skol's stamp—a macabre parody of a toddler's joyful romp—to keep the drain cleared of debris.

After several minutes the guards checked their progress, and shortly thereafter the valves were closed. With the spray thinned to a drunken trickle, Wagner directed the last of the loamy liquid into the grate whose subterranean burbling and gurgles indicated a grudgingness to accept any more volume from this unbidden force-feeding. The cell, while still decades away from tidy, was up to farm-stall tolerance, even if Wagner and Balgor were themselves more residually offending than they'd been even during their last detention block stint.

Finishing up, both men took a moment to observe the suddenly disenchanted Skol. His arms still in skyward stretch, he beckoned towards the diffuser, wondering what had interrupted the glorious flow. Waiting, waiting, and then gradually resigning to its complete suspension, he lowered his limbs and stood glumly still, nothing left for him but to study with curiosity the beading water as it clung to his hirsuteness like a thousand glittering baubles.

"I scarce believe it," said Balgor, wiping his forehead. "Shackled and ailing as he is, I never dreamed that he could be so childlike. Not when I know of all the life he has wrenched from so many souls."

Wagner swept the droplets from his own brow. "So, you've seen a lot of his kills up close and in person?"

"Twelve in all. Generally, however, unless you are a trusty or a combatant slated for the event immediately following Skol's, you have little, if any, opportunity to observe the brute at his business. You watch as your peers are plucked from the ranks to face him, and—minutes later—you watch as their corpses are dragged back. But few are we who have actually witnessed with full eye what the bulk of the Ergosian congregate knows only by legend."

"Well, I guess we were lucky to get off so easy with our paltry pack of croviks."

Although Balgor might have deemed Wagner's words callous in what seemed a flagrant disregard for Kadok, he did not. Kadok had been a virtual innocent caught up in circumstantial cross hairs, and there was no shield strong enough to completely soften the brunt of hard reality. Both men knew this, and both men had made their peace with it. Pragmatism was key here, stronger than remorse or regret, stronger than any intimacy or injustice, even stronger at times than love and hate.

They were deep into late afternoon when the NuRacs finally interceded, bringing to a close the day's distasteful industry. In being dismissed, Wagner tried his hand at Balgor's obsequiousness with the guards, confessing to them that this had been the most refreshing day's work he'd yet experienced in the camp. Further, he noted that by ignoring the stench of "a few turds," he and his co-worker were able to reap the benefit of a dousingly cool payout. The NuRacs, weary and too obtuse to realise that his dig was as much about them as it was the sludge, muscled both men through the passageways without acknowledging Wagner's comments nor expressing any particular disdain.

Remarkably, the eight hours spent at rehabbing Skol's cell would not go down as the most eventful occurrence of their day. In fact, a topping spectacle was already in progress, unfolding upon the palaestra—or rather, above it—even as Wagner and Balgor emerged onto the field. Both men expecting to be met straightway with the ribbing and jibes of their peers who, close to wrapping up the day's training, would normally have spilled forward in unquellable razz of their sullied state, what they instead stumbled upon was a convocation—and not just any convocation, but one that was decidedly more unusual and more sinister than common circumstance would have suggested.

An eerie aura of moribundity hovering about the field, the nodgers and the bucklers and the other various items of the sparring trade lay strewn upon the sands like the forgotten toys of absconded children. Gathered beyond said implements stood the Ergosian congregate—men and women, young and old, gladiators and gladiatorial support—in loose and localised assembly, most of them looking much like scolded puppies, and yet all of them fixed upon the machinations of a broad, backlit tirader upon the catwalk whose verbal besieging spumed over them like the bitter gavage of a sadistic master.

Wagner looked to Balgor, who was uncharacteristically awestruck with the sea of coerced stoicism that permeated the yard in increment rarely seen beyond that of new prisoners on their day of disembarkment. Tamek, perhaps the highest of head both in physical stature and tenacity, was one of the few who stood out among the lot, flanked on either side by Bilahdu and Uthok, neither of whom Wagner had ever seen so wan. J'nea, too, was present, just outside the weapons enclosure, mingled among her compatriot trusties as if their privilege might lend her some sparingly greater measure of innocuousness from the raining causticities. Whatever the purpose of the cat-plank diatribe, it appeared a gearing to the gladiator-based sect alone, for no outsiders stood present—no hospital orderly, none of the ambulatory wounded, and not a single soul from either the textilery, the kitchen, or the laundry.

"What's going on?" Wagner whispered. "Who's the bigwig up there?"

"He is SyKrahvo," said Balgor, under his breath. "One of the three Supreme Commanders."

"Uh-huh. And who are the other goons?"

Suddenly reticent, Balgor shushed Wagner and signalled him to listen. Wagner complied well enough, yet at the same time he could not shake a peculiar feeling of undecipherable familiarity. Some may have called it an intuition; others, an oddly intimate foreboding. Had Wagner been more finely attuned to the particular resection of megacosm that had opened him to so much inconceivability, he might have defined it as a flash of psychical pre-occurrence. As it was, he simply felt caught in the tumult of unbefallen re-experience. Like the pulse-jumping twitter of the mindflux, like the cold sweat that forecasted imminent incorporeity, he may not have understood the nature of this spotty premonition/recollection that suddenly evoked the most harrowing of his old bendering days, but he certainly recognised the subsidiary processes.

Former visions once fuzzied and turbulent began locking into place like Lego blocks. He'd stood like this before, in this place, in a dream, among his fellow prisoners, amid strangers, presided over by this same censorious overman who was dispensing to the crowd a discomforting revelation that Wagner had somehow heard before and already knew.

SyKrahvo's point at issue, while still unclear, was delivered in eloquent yet antagonistic fustian, spoken down to the Ergosians truly in both senses—the first, stemming of his physical vantage, and the second, of his authoritative station. At times on the edge of ranting, and then demonstratively reserved in the very next moment, his manner was such that it rivalled that of a certain, charismatically evil führer at the pinnacle of his own execrable reign. Adorned in his battle regalia, this Supreme Commander strutted about the planking like a man with no limits, a man who'd amassed venom enough to cripple a nation, and who now stood on the eve of using it. That to which Tamek had alluded in his hearing before the Tribunal was now becoming more clear than anyone wanted to see. There was something about this NuRac's air, his brimming confidence, his uncompassionate surety, that projected the convictions of one who commanded the genie, and who might indeed have possessed the wherewithal to literally rape an entire realm.

"You stand there gawking at me," he taunted, "thinking me long-winded and perverse, a cockalorum with high rank who thinks that decoration and position give him the right to spew hateful declarations at a beaten people. Were it even true, such opining would be of miniscule concern to me. What any of you think is hardly important to the NuRac order.

"Six short days ago our regiments returned from their campaigns amid the fanfare of glorious victory. I am testimony to that, for the battalions fighting under my command were those that cut the greatest swaths through the very heart of your people's defences. Three hidden encampments have been flushed and obliterated, and the survivors, en route and eager to join you here. They could not stand against us. No army can repel us now. Through NarVuk's divine providence we have been bequeathed that which will insure not only our predominance in the realm, but our total and unquestionable right to crush or control any living beings inhabiting its boundaries—as we see fit!"

"The realm is not some jewelled diadem for a single race to don and flaunt in the face of others!" shouted Tamek, striding boldly to the foreground of the populace. "The realm is no more yours than 'tis ours. We belong to *it*, and not *it* to *us!*"

"Pious buffoon! Your holy city has long been vanquished. Your kinspeople scatter and retreat eastward with our every advance. Vargath, your allegedly impregnable stronghold, will be next to fall. And you, Sentinel, stand there barking at me like a fangless hound. The realm already *is ours*—just as every one of *you* is ours. All that is left for us to do is to assume ownership."

With that he extended his hand to one of his nearby aides, who produced a wooden box. An elongated, rectangular shell, to Wagner it looked about the size and shape of the pool cue cases toted by some of his old Filthy Lucre patrons. Its contents, however, he suspected would be far from such benignity.

Gently springing the hasp, SyKrahvo flipped open the lid and produced a piece of cloth—or rather an object swathed in a cloth protectant—which he proceeded to unwrap one fold at a time.

Below, the crowd stood stilled in confusion, each prisoner fathoming a guess as to what would be revealed from beneath the fabric. Perhaps another sceptre of some Ergosian prince whose province the NuRacs had just overrun, or the crozier of a priestess whom Tamek, at one time, may have served, or maybe the ancestral dagger of a slain Ergosian officer—the NuRacs were ever fond of flaunting captured artefacts to help in further sinking the prisoners' spirits. All of these familiar possibilities were surmised, all of these and more, up until the very moment that SyKrahvo offered up nothing more remarkable than a simple baton.

Smooth and colourless and unassuming, roughly three decimetres long, with a slight peppery speckling at either end—its value as some mysterious symbol or impressive relic was lost on the crowd; and SyKrahvo, sensing this as he displayed it, smiled knowingly.

Slowly he took the baton into both of his hands and lowered it as if giving accolade to some invisible knight before him. As his arms dropped to just below the point where the dub might have occurred, there arose an almost imperceptible tremor that, sounding and feeling kilometres off, nevertheless grew to encompass the entire palaestra from inside its very walls like some old Sensurround movie that Wagner may once have trembled through long ago at the local Cineplex. Racking up decibels exponentially, the whole seismic affair suddenly broke loose in a rousing thunderclap, with the baton going nova in SyKrahvo's grip and subsequentially launching forth such a jagging splinter of energy that the sands and gravels literally imploded before the crowd, slapping everyone back and over each other like playing cards in a windstorm.

Tamek, closest to the blast, was swept headlong into his flock and was lost among the flailing bodies. Wagner and Balgor, by chance the farthest from the eruption, were thrown back into the vaulted thoroughfare from which they'd just come. Everyone else found themselves caught in varying degree in the brunt of a cascading blast that oddly took no lives but left scores bruised, battered, and uncontrollably shaken.

A cloud of dust swirled about the yard as legacy to the modest plot of ground now replaced by a four metres-wide crater. Like a thousand ghostly tendrils, the airborne debris spiralled up from well below ground zero to far above the catwalks, and was quick to dissipate in the early evening breeze. As it did, the figures of SyKrahvo and his right-handers gradually reappeared and became more recognisable, their gazes turned downward as they eagerly waited to see just how effectively the demonstration had proved.

Below them they found bedlam, a writhing mass attempting to disengage itself without amplifying injury to brother or sister. Cries and wails underscored the anguish like chorused requiem throughout the prolonged process of disentanglement and reconstituting; and once Tamek had salvaged himself and assuaged those whom he'd inadvertently toppled, he stamped once more to the foreground to survey the execrable product of SyKrahvo's dishonourable and unprovoked assault.

A huge void in the earth, there was strangely no solid matter strewn about the yard, no sediment of soil or gravel blanketing the felled prisoners, nothing to represent that which was ousted from the crater—not clay, not a shard of rock or a clump of marl, no earthen dunnage of any sort. Only the lazy tasslings of dust dispersing in the waft gave indication of where at least some of the soil had gone, yet the level of breeze required to carry off such an abundance of the crater's missing bulk would have needed to be a vortex several hundred times greater than this that Tamek saw thinning away before his eyes.

"Why did you this?" he shouted to SyKrahvo, an undeniable cracking of emotion in his voice. "These people here pose no menace to QieLahr. Neither are they a danger to your stranglehold on the realm itself. And ne'er were they a threat to you personally, *Commander*—not ere you came upon the instrument that resonates in your grasp, and most certainly not now that you have come to hold it."

"Have you any idea," challenged the NuRac, "of just what this 'instrument' is, oh fallen Sentinel?"

"A knowledge more substantial than yours—this much is obvious."

SyKrahvo leered at Tamek with a contempt infinitesimally shy of retributive action. "Perhaps. And perhaps not. Yet, what a pity for you that it is in my possession and not yours."

"I recommend that you relinquish it quickly, villain, and beg your gods for your life. For it seems that you know nothing of the consequences of wielding a staffling for iniquitous purposes."

"I know exactly the consequences," he said, bringing the baton again into a threatening angle. "Shall I demonstrate once more?"

The recomposing crowd backed off en masse, screams and havoc abounding. Only Tamek remained entrenched. "You are a base fiend, a blasphemer, and a coward!" he cried, bold accusations to be levelled when his own mortality hung pendent. "How nefariously you do employ forbidden glamour to brutalise a helpless assembly and then liken yourself to a godling in your treachery!"

SyKrahvo's gaze became grinding. "I am so glad to hear you say these things, Sentinel. For you must know that your transgression is a crime punishable by death."

"You are the transgressor—not I. 'Tis therefore imperative that you heed what I say while time permits. Stay from this present path, SyKrahvo. Return the staffling whence it came, or your death will be an agonising one—this much I can foresee."

In the course of Tamek's outcry against SyKrahvo, Wagner had risen and recomposed, and was even then creeping warily forward, driven by curiosity toward the cusp of the David-and-Goliath confrontation. Balgor, too, had exited the passageway; but, unlike his friend, he hastened to the aid of those of his comrades who'd not fared as well as he, a few of whom had met with laceration, loosened teeth, even fracture. Yet, despite his immersion in said meting of comfort, he and every other conscious prisoner kept a roving eye on the drama unfolding near the crater, and each knew that although the Sentinel braved bitter peril on their behalf, his courage could not hope to prevail against the ablative forces that SyKrahvo had mysteriously come to possess.

Wagner was disinclined to deal with individual humanitarian issues when there existed one of such ominous scale transpiring at the wall. Balgor and the others could reset every broken bone sustained of the blast, stave the haemorrhaging in the nastiest of gashes, dump an entire cartload of compassion onto the distressed and the overwrought if that was what they were wont to do; but none of it would mean a thing if SyKrahvo let loose with another bazooka-blast intended to wipe everyone in the yard out of existence forever. Seeing the NuRac gravid in his rage, Wagner sensed that it wouldn't take much antagonising to accomplish just that, and he wondered why Tamek continued to provoke someone who obviously had the upper hand a thousand times over. Was the Sentinel being methodic? Was he manufacturing some secret strategy to be enacted at the last possible moment? Did he truly believe it possible to fire-and-brimstone the clearly warped SyKrahvo into some shame-inspired penitence?

In the three-odd minutes that comprised Wagner's initial impression of the Commander, it was hugely evident that the NuRac might callously raze the palaestra on nothing more than a whim. Even had Grum and his guards still have been present and on the dais, it was likely—and maybe even understood—that

SyKrahvo wouldn't have thought twice about detonating everything in sight, merely to prove a point. An ascertaining of claims and deeds thus far indicated that half the realm charred and obliterated might even have fallen under the category of acceptable losses in this Supreme Commander's eyes, so long as a few NuRacs stood triumphant once the smoke had cleared. How lucky for Grum that he and the sentries had indeed evacuated on cue, apparently having been ordered from the palaestra before Balgor and Wagner were able to join SyKrahvo's little programme-already-in-progress. The resulting, solidly Ergosian audience made the Commander's option to utilise the rod a second time that much less complex. It took no genius to predict that the yard was ripe for becoming one humongous divot at any second.

The baton weapon itself had immediately intrigued Wagner—and not merely because he'd been persuaded into respecting its downright wicked potential. The piquing here went deeper, felt more connectedly relevant; for, up until this very moment in his unplanned tenure on this primitive world, he'd known of only one vessel that embodied anything even remotely supernatural.

And now he'd found another.

The first source was, of course, himself. And, up until this moment, any physics-challenging phenomena on his new world had occurred within his own private sphere. Long could he boast of abilities where none had existed previously—who else here could make such a claim? Since his moment of transference, he'd enjoyed a commanding fluency in languages that he'd never studied, while the two indigenous factions with whom he interacted had achieved their own bilingualism initially through bartering, and then later, from diplomatic and adversarial interaction. In second point, despite Wagner's ranking as a mediocre swordsman, under duress he sacrificed autonomy for instinct, and wielded a weapon as few hardened warriors could. Conversely, the Ergosians' martial abilities were painstakingly developed through years of tutelage and individual experience; for them, combative augmentation came naturally, in response to circumstantial and experiential factors. Lastly, Wagner possessed a spontaneous—although incrementally controllable—ability to heal injury by either conscious or subconscious prompters. For everyone else, healing was achieved the old-fashioned way, with the benefit of time, rest, and pharmaceutical assistance. With all due regard, some of the local salves and folk remedies produced miraculous results, but none demonstrated anything akin to what lay within the scope of Wagner's peculiar metabolic abilities. Amassed or individualised, the wonders in his repertoire were far from ordinary gifts by *any* standard, earthly or Ergosian.

The baton held a second allure for him as well, since something very akin to it had, at times, manifested in facsimile within the seeming abandon of his old hallucinatory states. Mind-trip references in general had become incrementally accessible of late, given the proper catalyst (a prompting event, an associated locus or procedure), subsequently granting Wagner expanded, mnemonic entry into depositories of recollection that, months prior, had been denied him. The baton image itself—variably interpreted in the visions as anything from a simple, fluorescent tube, to an opalescent shower rod, to the dismembered leg of a Filthy Lucre bar stool—was among the longest running, most frequently cycled symbols he'd experienced, and only now did it come anywhere near the threshold of decryption. Often the size and proportion of SyKrahvo's implement, in other mind-trips the "staffling" had appeared lengthier; yet, regardless of its dimensions, it always ended up transfiguring from a mundane object into something far loftier, something that bore special albeit elusive significance, however limited its pattern in Wagner's greater hallucinatory fabric. Frequently depicted as a weapon, equally, as something more sacrosanct, and sometimes, as an obscure gift delivered into Wagner's hands by well-intended spirits (each of the common mind that he actually possessed the wisdom of what to do with it), Wagner was seldom able to maintain more than a precarious grip on the staffling—another detail that he might have considered dredging for its latent symbolism. In the instances when the object didn't abruptly dissipate into the surrounding ether before his baffled gaze, it flared so intensely that he could no longer see it to grip it, and sometimes spread an unholy pitch over his hands and wrists, one that continued like plague up his arms, his shoulders, his torso and neck, until his putrefying astral body either reintegrated into Howsley's physicality or was ushered off to yet the next hallucinatory environment. And although there was little chance of that happening here, what irony for him that it might finally, amazingly, be within his ken to affix some ilk of definitive import to the object mere seconds before it vaporised him into obscurity.

The dust finally in settle about the palaestra sands, more and more of the fissure became visible to those who were only now regathering enough of their senses to register its scale. Wagner, armed only with his curiosity, continued to edge his way through the living mass to observe the smoking crater for himself. At the same time, Tamek and SyKrahvo had reached the impasse in their verbal horn-locking, where chances of a second assailing had just crossed beyond probability and deep into inevitability. Within moments, it seemed that the Supreme Commander would make an example of the Sentinel's impertinence, quite possibly blasting the entire yard's populace along with him.

Although bent on divining the staffling's consequence to him and his visions, Wagner realised that his knowledge-quest was about to be thwarted by this enraged, raving psychopath a few metres above him. Yet, even as he anticipated imminent obliteration, he attempted no mad dash back to the tunnel, made no effort to flee, nor to pray or prostrate himself, nor to scream in terror; neither did he call out to the two adversaries with any mediating distraction or plea for civility, both of which would probably have gone unrequited anyway. All of these things he wanted to do and could not. Instead, he watched as SyKrahvo brought the inscrutable weapon into position. And he could think of only one action that might save Tamek and the lives of everyone around him.

Once more placing his faith in that most elemental of his convictions—that he hadn't come all this way only to perish before even knowing why—he succeeded in squeaking far enough beyond his anxiety to take the only route open to him: to plunge headlong into his psyche and attempt a proactive summoning of the abstractions that had typically been inexorably reactive by their nature. With only a scant few seconds to accomplish this, he propelled himself inwardly, far and deep into his seldom-visited reaches, hoping not only to invoke both the berserker *and* the miracle worker hidden within him, but to actually ally them, alloy them, align them in a twining of the zealous fury of self-preservation and the facility of cellular regeneration that, together, might alchemise something far greater than either could offer on its own. It was a tact he'd not taken before, an unprecedentedly conscious requisition of seemingly subconscious and elusively ungoverned entities. Faceless inhabitants of his deepest recesses, they were like the shiftiest and least convivial of a landlord's tenants, those whose presence might have been questioned were it not for the fact that their mail and their newspapers were always taken in, that the laundry room strong-boxes filled up with spent quarters, that the rent money materialised in spot-on fashion. Only, in Wagner's case, he equated the paid rent with his keister being saved more than once in battle, or with the sudden mending of his body's damaged tissue. And, eremitic tendencies notwithstanding, he would not begrudge his tenants their habitat in his noggin, especially now that they were tenants whom he needed—and, indeed, who needed him—to rescue the habitat from the wrecking ball.

Attempting to incorporate what he'd retained of his Howsley bio-feedback experiences—especially of not focusing too rigorously on the prize—he guided his mind into concentrating not so much on the mutable and unwieldy flow of energies that accompanied the healing phenomenon, but rather, on the way that his body felt whenever the manifestation had occurred. The unusually easy accessibility demonstrated in his mending of Balgor indicated an increasing comfort and dexterity with the gift, and such was diagnostic for the mindset now needed. Less easily summoned was the all-important survivalist response, the warrior, and for this he could do no more than to feed himself the primal and very present fear of life-threatening circumstance, which took all of a miniscule of effort. Pulling it together mentally, he heaved a quick breath and projected a single command—a desperate *"NO!"*—into the void of psychic airspace, praying that his one, measly, telepathic Scud would prove more compelling than the potency of SyKrahvo's rage and delusion.

Whether the Commander's true intention had been intimidation or annihilation, it mattered not; for, within the space of a single blink, a concussive force rocked the ramparts—indeed, shook the entire yard—so that neither Ergosian nor NuRac was able to stand unsupported. Tamek toppled onto his rump; Wagner, likewise; and SyKrahvo's officers all lurched wildly for the hand railings, their arms flailing and their fingers wild and grasping. SyKrahvo himself teetered, but maintained a precarious balance and (of utmost importance to him) the semblance of dignity by unlocking his knees, adopting a distributive stance, and employing the staffling to equalise his sway. Appearing surprised and unsettled, it was obvious that he believed the quake had been of his own doing, an accidental misfire, set off by his surging anger; and, for a moment, so did everyone else, Wagner included. No real damage had come of the event; a few bruises, perhaps, a mortar joint or two shaken loose from the brickset, but no deaths, no burns or gashes, and no comeuppance for the mouthy Sentinel who everyone thought would have bore the brunt of any serious assault. The prisoners, rising cautiously to their feet, found the relatively benign tremor inconsistent with SyKrahvo's threats and boasts, especially as the Commander's own people had come so hazardously close to tumbling from their perches. They were, however, grateful for their lives, and had no desire to press the issue, Bilahdu even going so far as to venture forward with a firm but friendly hand to Tamek's shoulder, to persuade him to withdraw for the nonce, lest his defiance get everyone killed.

Wagner wasn't sure what had happened, not exactly. Barring what it was he'd intended, he had no real evidence of anything manifesting of, from, or by his personal effort. Thus, it was difficult to discern whether he had actually succeeded in somehow muting the Commander's blast, or whether the shock wave was totally of *his* making, of SyKrahvo's, or some kind of reaction forged of both impetuses. Still, he was fine with it either way; crisis averted. If it had been the Commander's intent to quick-fry Tamek like a batch of Filthy Lucre onion rings, then Wagner had amazingly squelched said intent, and would therefore need to come to terms with the magnitude of what this meant. Alternately, if it had been but a milder reprimand by SyKrahvo's whim—with Wagner deluding himself into thinking that his self-important theatrics could have made any kind of difference—then, hopefully, this still would be the end of it. If, however, by some extraordinarily extra-sensory means, the incident was *totally* Wagner's creation—and despite the obvious possibilities, he hoped that it wasn't—then he had some serious introspection awaiting him. If, in fact, he had actually, *truly*, headed off SyKrahvo's malevolence with an extramundane blockbuster of his own devising, then he had blown open the door of relativity between a lifetime of presentiment and one, patently pertinent object of his visions beyond which held the potential for answering everything that he most sought.

"I suggest that you refrain from iring me with distraction," spoke SyKrahvo, visibly confounded but doing his utmost to shield the fact. "For, as you see, within this implement rests the power to vanquish the lot of you, and sufficiently more to gain me the entire realm. In the morning, reassembled and rebriefed, our troops return to the field in a final campaign to systematically destroy all resistance, up to and through the very gates of Vargath herself."

"You underestimate our people," cried Balgor, stepping forward to prevent Tamek from solely incensing the Commander any further. "You are but one NuRac brandishing a vile and terrible weapon, while our resisting forces are as much at home in the grasslands and boscage as you are in your personal bedchamber. Aye, you may currently possess the means to send Vargath the way of Vishkor, but no force on Ergos will ever flush our people from the terrain."

"Your contumelious attitude may be the only attribute that you will take with you to the next life," said SyKrahvo, renewing his menacing gestures with the staffling. "But, I believe I will allow you to continue, *all* of you, that you may witness the immense overcrowding that this prison will be experiencing very soon."

As the disgruntled crowd murmured from within a gallimaufry of forcibly subdued outrage and hushed epithets, Wagner began noticing a particularly unsettling sensation in his body, a vague, unattributable tugging of sorts, as if he were within the gravitational wake of some greater influential body. At first hint, he likened it to his being in the proximity of some mega-electrical field—the bristling hair, the supercharged airspace, and the oddly euphoric dread that often accompanies close and imminent danger—and he quickly assumed that it had something to do with the harnessing dynamics of the staffling's undefined power base. Indiscriminate swirls of ions or random emissions of residual energies—his knowledge of the sciences was sadly lacking. But whatever compelled him, he sensed its draw like the tether of a trail-hot bloodhound, and his first thought was to remove himself from its gravitating sway by cautiously withdrawing from the crater area.

To the astonishment of everybody present, the staffling suddenly broke free of SyKrahvo's grip and launched a slow and tenuous trajectory away from the rampart under its own power. Wagner, having maintained prudent visual contact with the catwalk during his retreat, witnessed the oddity, but did not immediately sense a correlation. Equally as surprised as his peers, as he halted in order observe, the object curiously followed suit, floating motionless roughly one metre beyond the railing.

The NuRac Commander gasped. His officers stood gob-smacked and pale, and the Ergosians below gazed dumbfounded at the sight, some shrinking back, others frozen, each uncertain as to whether this was but a prelude to another violent outburst, a blessing of fortune decidedly ambiguous in its unfolding, or some means of cautioning from an authority greater than any of them.

Wingedly, SyKrahvo plastered himself across the railing and snatched back the staffling, as a starving man might seize a proffered frankfurter. Unresisting, the weapon easily became his once more, his with which to evoke more fear, his to misuse against the realm as intended. The exhaustion of urgency besetting the Commander, he blotted perspiration from his brow, straightened his regalia, and sighed in nick-of-time relief.

If it hadn't been obvious to everyone below that SyKrahvo had truly lost ownership of the rod and had panicked because of it, it most certainly was now. In fact, because of it, hue and cry suddenly ripped through the formerly cringing Ergosian files. Bruit of an ineptness in his mastery over the object spilled across hopeful lips, and enlivened where mere moments before had been despair, for such a fallibility in the NuRac's supposed despotic dominion promoted at least some sliver of prospect for inconvenience in SyKrahvo's grand plans. If, in meting his sorcerous evil, he could not claim complete and total influence over the destructive talisman, the free Ergosians to the south-east might yet discover the leeway needed to retain their liberty.

The hardcore patriots in the crowd availed themselves of this notion and rallied each other for legitimacy in their theory. Others—the wounded and the understandably fearful—encircled Tamek for reassurance, while some of the more incorrigible upstarts worked at kindling an uplifting mirth, and thereby courted trouble, by way of burlesquing the Commander's foolish sprawl to reclaim the staffling. By no means safe nor exempt from further assault from above, these lusty, reckless, wonderful madcaps, whose freedoms had long been revoked, were determined to have their laugh at SyKrahvo's expense, even if it was to be their last one.

"Silence!" shouted the Commander. "*Silence!* You will be stilled by your own accord, or by *mine!*"

Although the sniggering indeed tapered off accordingly, once successfully demonstrated it would not subside completely nor easily—not with this lot, not with the occasional hoots and whoops of the anonymously brazen mocking the NuRac whose dominance over them was unravelling.

SyKrahvo, past the edge of seething and needing to renew his point, brandished the staffling once more with the threat of reprimand. Immediately sobered, the crowd receded—Wagner within it—and here, once again, the opalescent rod tore itself from the Commander's grasp in apparent, synchronous, spatial unison with the mass below.

"By NarVuk's fury, what transpires here?" The frustrated SyKrahvo lunged forward and retrieved it again from the air. Disobliging in his grasp, however, the staffling resisted its retrieval like a waterlogged boot at the lakebed end of some good 20-pound test.

Confused, distraught, humiliated by what he had no choice but to assume was some unanticipated, backlashing effect of the implement that he hadn't before encountered, with perseverance and no small measure of exertion the hapless Commander managed to clamp both hands around it and wrestle it back over the railing.

On the ground, the Ergosians halted in their withdrawal to observe SyKrahvo's undignified grapple. The cockiest of them once more breaking into uproarious laughter, their outbursts again emboldened some of the other prisoners as well, the result being an unheedful heckling of the "high and mighty" NuRac. They called out for him to sing songs, to dance a gavotte, or to turn flip-flops like a proper harlequin. Bilahdu's legendarily hearty guffaws, easily distinguishable within the din, were so comically infectious that they prompted even the most guarded of prisoners to succumb to frolic of their own. At end, the ensuing contagion became the prisoners' weapon of defiance, and how much more shrill and lively did it become when a rabidly furious SyKrahvo, attempting to wield the staffling yet *another* time, was nearly pulled off the catwalk like a prospector with a quirky dowser.

"Descend to the field, oh mighty conqueror!" cried Uthok from the anonymity of the mob. "I will show you where you might anchor that thing!"

The prisoners watched SyKrahvo fumbling, witnessed his aides sailing hither and about in effort to assist him in maintaining a grasp. What had begun as a pernicious abuse of force had ended in farce, and although Tamek—the only prisoner other than Wagner who hadn't given in to some degree of hilarity— reminded those nearest him not to be lured into false comfort, many discovered that, in allowing themselves the barefaced audacity of belittling this high-ranking NuRac, they fulfilled a long neglected need that even their dread of him and his baneful weapon could not discourage.

Tamek therefore assumed the weight of his foreboding alone, as no one else present fully understood the crisis they faced. Clearly a formidably nasty little business by anyone's assessment, only he seemed to recognise the NuRac's disruptor for what it was—unstable, unstoppable, and potentially cataclysmic far beyond anyone's ken, even its wielder's. For those who knew Tamek best, they would marvel at the accuracy of his suspicions were they to survive into the evening, when these events would surely be opened up to critique more objective. Sorcery, from trite parlour tricks all the way up to spiritual summonings, was not unheard of in the realm. Miracles, tokens, mediumistic experiences, curses, visions—it all went with the territory of superstitious peoples, unexplained phenomena, and the splendid mysteries of life, death, purpose, meaning, and the multi-facetted, inexplicable, natural world itself. Outlandishness was no stranger to these contemporary times, but it had been a considerable while since anything of this magnitude had reared in the presence of such mass audience, and thus offered legitimacy over the invention of industrious imaginations or the out-and-out fabrication of notoriety-seeking knaves. Where the most common legends and lore of the people generally accommodated such magiks and gave them credibility in history (and occasionally in the more scrupulously screened hearsay of the day), there had always been speculation on the existence of certain privileged knowledge that was shared only by the highest of priests and dignitaries and their ordained protectors—of which Tamek was the only one remaining. This being the case, the signs had been portentous to the Sentinel's schooled eye and no other, and his assumption, more dead-on than anyone knew.

The crowd watched as SyKrahvo stormed across the catwalk, staffling tucked tight against his breast, and sped into the sentry corridor in order to place himself at as great a distance from his humiliation as was within his gait to do. His officers followed, and were immediately replaced on the ramparts by a corresponding number of guards, who repositioned themselves at their appropriate posts. Grum and his own complement of soldiers soon re-entered the open as well, and, taking up their respective stations on and around the dais, ordered the prisoners to resume in their training.

Many in the crowd chortled, grunted, or offered menial truckle as they reluctantly dispersed and went about retrieving their weapons from the sands. With what had just gone down, a training mindset would be a difficult one to re-establish, much less sustain, but the Taskmaster was not one to be kept waiting.

A handful of concerned prisoners approached and beseeched Grum into allowing them to assist the hobbled and ailing Ergosians to the infirmary. Annoyed that SyKrahvo had robbed him of even more able bodies, Grum accompanied the prisoners to where the wounded lay, to assess their request. Here, he designated which Ergosian merited treatment and which did not, and yammered at the rest to get back to practise.

Despite the reactivation of the business-as-usual mode, Tamek dared to stand silent and motionless at the rim of the crater, staring intently, but not seeing anything that wasn't a product of his mind's eye. Much thinking was going on within his head, and with Grum's attention elsewhere, Balgor, Wagner, and Bilahdu took opportunity to approach their friend from behind.

"Barring the spiritedly jocular outcome, we are all of us unsettled with what we witnessed here," said Bilahdu. "Quite remarkable it was...and quite damnable." He paused for a moment to gaze down into a cavity easily the size of an earthly garbage truck.

"As you well know," he continued, "I often find pride in being sought out as a wellspring of pilfered information and newsworthy morsels in the camp—but I am completely and absolutely at a loss to explain this day's horrors. Can you, Sentinel?"

"I can," replied Tamek, so low that it was almost a whisper. "And 'tis more dire than any of you know."

"You were right, weren't you?" said Wagner, kneeling and peering into the small chasm. "About the NuRacs, about their getting a hold of something sacred—you knew, didn't you?"

"I suspected, *Voknor*. Now I have confirmed. These devils have committed a grievous malfeasance without e'en realising their wrongdoing." He cleared his throat and looked up to the catwalk where the NuRac had stood. "Or, it could very well be that they are aware of the blasphemy and heed it not."

"Tell me, do you allege blasphemy in that they, by some means, implored dark forces to instil this rod with noxious properties?" Bilahdu was more curious than any of them had ever seen him.

"'Twas no need for that. No conjuring or ritualism was required, no blood-pacts with NarVuk or any of their other heathenish deities. The staffling is in itself no appliance of perversion, Bilahdu. Rather, 'tis a Soork."

"A Soork?"

"Yes. In the ancient tongue, the word from which 'tis said to originate—*Sooerkatek*—can describe either 'harmony' or 'equilibrium,' although some scholars have suggested that 'tis more likely derived from a word of action—*Soorhokahlem*—which means 'to govern' or simply 'to maintain.'"

"Nothing about annihilation?" asked Wagner.

"Not in a lingual sense. Yet, I have studied holy parchments describing the existence of physical relics, reputedly birthed and risen out of the Creation, whose mystic properties are unlimited, and whose purpose on Ergos is to nurture the land and all who live upon it. Some were called Vorki, some, Bujavii, and some, Soork. By the descriptions detailed in the sacred texts, that which SyKrahvo possesses is Soork."

"And he is aware of this?" asked Balgor.

"I cannot be certain. Our parchments at Vishkor were solely for the eyes of the ecclesiastic echelon, and that I e'en breathe of their existence to you would, under normal circumstances, be considered a breach of inviolable trust. Most of the common parchments were destroyed along with the city, although I would venture to assume that the priests in Vargath possess certain facsimiles. As for the NuRacs—years ago, I had the opportunity to peruse the available tomes of the NuRacs' Holy Writ and found no mention of such talismans. In lieu of any supplemental NuRac scripture, I am unable to discern whether these paynims understand with what forces they toy. I would, howe'er, wager generously that at least SyKrahvo himself does not."

"Why would you say this?" asked Bilahdu.

Before Tamek could answer, they found themselves assailed by the ever-domineering Grum, who ordered them away at once unless they wanted the task of filling in the crater. They obliged him, and promptly too, although he detained the Sentinel at the pit, for what purpose they were unable to determine.

To Tamek's bewilderment, the NuRac initiated a dialogue, a rare and peculiar as-equals tête-à-tête that harboured no rebuke and no gloat, delivered in a manner most contrary to that of Grum's Taskmaster reputation.

"This smoke-spiralled hollow foreshadows the end of our present state of affairs, Sentinel. Never in all my days have I seen the likes of such power. I can but imagine your feelings of disgust and dread in thinking about it. Believe me when I say I find my thoughts of it just as distasteful."

"I truly doubt that, Taskmaster."

Grum laughed in his own acknowledgement of the absurd. "I suppose that I do sound patronising—I doubt that *I* would believe me either. But there is truth in what I say. You think me a crass and cruel man, Tamek—aye, with good reason. Heartless, depraved, sanguinary—all these I can also live with. I am aware of my 'dragon' epithet among you lot, and although it is, of course, meant to be disrespectful, I cannot help but to think how really it does suit me. It is fact—I am far from a charming man. Born into warfare, I was weaned on vice, reared on avarice. I know little else. Strife—in one form or other—has ever been my sustenance. You might even say that, to me, contention is the teat whose milk strengthened me to make the best of a sorry life."

"With respect, GrumTor—why do you talk to me as a man and not as a slave? Is it out of condolence? The only strife *you* know of is that with which you burden us."

"Now I see from whom Balgor truly has been acquiring his recent surliness. Listen, Sentinel—you and I were both soldiers long before it came to this. In the wars we fought, some rules were followed, some were broken, and some, made to be broken. What you saw today, however, was in keeping with no accord I have ever encountered. The spoils thus far reaped of the NuRac-Ergosian clash, well, they have been my livelihood. However, the total subjugation of your race—or worse, its destruction—will forever change our worlds. This new weapon may just see to that. For this, I do not envy your people."

"Do you not see, Grum, how this makes you worse than SyKrahvo? Yes—*worse!* For within your admission of tangled conscience, you perceive a distinction 'twixt what is just and what is not."

"And this makes me more villainous?"

"Undeniably. You see, SyKrahvo, in his warped manner, believes that his actions are just. His delusional self-image is that of a hero. But *you!* You sense the wrongness, and yet you go along with what he preaches because you are on the side of the conquerors—and because you fear retribution should you e'er raise your voice in protest. Thus, although your sense of morality is less at odds with mine than 'tis with SyKrahvo's, you whore your conscience to him, and to others like him, in order to maintain the comfortable existence that you so enjoy."

"I am no traitor to my race."

"You are a traitor to yourself."

"My sphere is not the same as SyKrahvo's. My only power to wield is over prisoners of the war."

"Then go on exercising that power. But do not come to me with your misplaced guilt. I am your prisoner, not your confessor."

"So be it," said the NuRac. "Away with you then! Retrieve your sword and resume your training. A good hour yet remains before the evening mess."

As Tamek marched away, Grum remained and turned again to stare down into the crater. He mumbled to himself in a maddened, inconvenienced, unappreciated manner, but it wasn't clear even to him whether they were invectives aimed at the Sentinel, at SyKrahvo, at himself, or merely at the malevolent surrealism in the day's evolution. Change was in the air—massive, revolutionary change—and he didn't want it to be. The balance of power, already having lain well in the NuRacs' favour for so many months, had in a single day tipped completely into the ravening grasp of QieLahr—or rather, its military. Soon, a great stain would seep deep into the land, a stain of blood spilled at this newly invigorated army's every passing. It would leave only despair and decimation and uninhabitable territory in its wake. Nothing in the world could prevent it.

And Grum's foremost hope was that the blood it spilled would not come flooding back to QieLahr.

CHAPTER TWENTY

'Tis true that we are in great danger;
The greater therefore should our courage be.
  —WILLIAM SHAKESPEARE

At the evening meal it became evident that the levity risen out of SyKrahvo's ungainliness had all but succumbed to a grim reality that would not be dismissed. As a result, many people couldn't stomach any supper, although the viands actually included meat loaf for a change—formed and roasted, with a side of boiled kale and two summer pippins apiece for dessert. Wagner never questioned the source of the meat anymore, if only because in the long weeks on Ergos he'd come to know his hunger like a clutch of newly hatched starlings—always begging, nagging, chirping, and crying, never truly sated. He'd trained himself to ignore it because he couldn't always assuage it. Like everyone else in the prison—barring his peers' behaviour this particular night—he accepted sustenance whenever it was offered, and he wasn't going to let this uncommon treat go to waste. Ashamedly, he could hearken back to a time when he'd actually refused Howsley's Jell-O for being too runny, or forewent an endive salad because of brown-edged leaves, even sent back a glass of milk for having dishwasher gunk on the rim. Now, if he could have, he'd have joyfully devoured it all, wilted parsley garnish included, orange rinds, even the paper napkin if it was besmeared with a drop or two of pan-fried gravy. Like his assessment of Skol earlier in the day, he would have considered eating an old sneaker if there was nourishment to be had from it.

As he ate, he watched how the bulk of prisoners moped around the yard, cursing their fortune, prophesying doom and lifetime servitude, surrendering spirit and hope to a small, white baton that housed enough raw might to move mountains. He couldn't blame them, for it all seemed so much more bleak now, even as their lives had been nothing short of horrendous already. Gnawing on one of his apples, he backtracked his way through the afternoon's events, halting at the scene of his own involvement, where he'd attempted to defuse SyKrahvo's intent. The mental commands, the desperation, the lack of clarity in what it was that he'd hoped to accomplish at the time—he wondered whether his presence, physical or psychical, had truly bore any relevance to SyKrahvo's woes at all. It was brash and pompous to think that he'd even fractionally influenced the incident; but, as he couldn't easily deny the feats to his credit so far, it made little sense to start hunting along side-trails when this path was so wide and promising. Still, rather than focusing too much on himself, he considered other incidence as well, namely that eerie, magnetic drag that he'd experienced in the midst of all the chaos. Surely, it belonged somewhere on the shortlist of possible instigants responsible for defrocking the otherwise brash Commander. Yet, had Wagner affected it? Had he unleashed it? After all, analysis via memory indicated that the Soork had performed just as SyKrahvo intended it to, up until the moment of Wagner's little essay to stave further destruction. At that moment, and no other, did SyKrahvo's control fluctuate, deteriorate. By all witnesses, the instrument seemed to have acquired its own will, and a stubborn one at that. And this was precisely when Wagner had begun to contend with gravity.

He suspected no autonomous quality in the Soork's animation, however, for it had idled only when the crowd was idle, and moved only when *they* moved, all in very direct proportion to the action. Yet, the chemistry linking the Soork to the crowd below was such that the instrument could be overpowered by proximate physical effort. SyKrahvo ultimately proved this much. Had Wagner been pressed to saddle the peculiar affair with some hasty, sci-fi, mumbo jumbo explanation, he'd have guessed that somehow—maybe in answer to his telepathic strong-arming and maybe not—the Soork had absorbed the crowd's conglomerate aura, and either drew energy from it, or temporarily imprinted that energy onto its own. Suspended within its own little spatial field, the Soork demonstrated a convincing, albeit deceptive, ability for independent travel, which in truth occurred only when the crowd itself initiated the prefatory motion. However, like magnets that could be separated through physical intervention, the attraction was an unsubstantial one, and was quite possibly a characteristic or a residual side effect inherent to an object so thoroughly laced with mystical (or undiscovered scientific) elements.

"So, *Voknor*, what is your stand on today's horror?" J'nea asked as she plopped down beside him. He'd been sitting alone, Balgor having this evening supped with some of his braggart chums whom he'd been depriving too long of his boastful one-uppings.

"Definitely not something you see every day," said Wagner, lips puckered by the apple's tart core. He thought for a second and then added: "or *do* you?"

"When I was a girl, I once saw lightning lash the forest near my home. After the worst of the storm had passed, my older sister took me to see how the strike had rent a kekona tree straightway down its trunk. I remember the charred splinters scattered about, some of them still ablaze, even in the rain. The bole itself smouldered for days after. Until this afternoon, I have not seen anything with so much destructive power."

"Hmm... I have."

She looked at him inquisitively.

"Usually second-hand," he said, "but close enough to home to make me know real fear."

"How do you mean, 'second-hand'?"

Wagner thought back on 9/11, on Oklahoma City, on Hiroshima and Nagasaki and a hundred-and-one other human tragedies. She already knew of hatred and fanaticism, but how could he possibly explain fertiliser bombs, improvised commercial jet missiles, or plutonium? He couldn't even adequately explain *himself* to her.

"What I witnessed in my own land," he said, "was mostly through evidence after the fact. I may not have been there personally when disaster struck, but the aftermaths were undisputable."

"Then, today, you bore *first-hand* witness—true or not?"

He laughed. "True. The difference is that the origins of most of the destructive weaponry in my culture are explainable to the point where anybody with ample curiosity can understand them. That rod-thingy of SyKrahvo's—I haven't a clue as to what generates its high-calibre kick."

"You are in good company then." She bolted down a slice of the meat loaf and chased it with a mouthful of kale; no dainty lady here—she knew the importance of sustenance, just as Wagner did.

"Most people misplaced their appetites tonight," he said, listening as she smacked another gob of the cabbage. "How is it that you didn't?"

"The fools," she muttered in chew. "They overreact. Eating or fasting, neither will alter that which is."

"They're missing out anyway. The grub tonight is actually even tastier than last night's bonus banquet. Do you reckon the kitchen screwed up and gave us the guards' meals?"

"If they did, do not say anything until I have had my fill." Here she finished off her last wedge of meat, and inspected the two apples she'd plucked from the baskets. Apparently less than pleased with her choices, she bit into the plumper of the pair and winced to its sharpness.

Wagner laughed. "*Sauer macht lustig,*" he said, enjoying the variety in her contorted expressions.

It clearly pained her jaws just to chew the acerbic pulp, but she managed a swallow, choking back her own laugh as she did. "*What?* What gibberish do you speak?"

"*Sauer macht lustig.* Loosely translated, it means 'sour makes for merriment.' It's a phrase that my nurse—that my *friend*—used to say to me. Her grandmother was from the old country, and taught it to her when she was a child. She, in turn, would say it to me whenever I did what you just did—bite into something super-sour."

"What tongue is it?"

"Um, we call it German, an old root language in my realm."

"'Sour makes for merriment.' A strange adage, but a good one. I do feel slightly jocund in a...*shivery* sort of manner."

"Let's see you eat the other one."

"Oh, no," she said, pocketing the apple in her vest, perhaps for a nibble of late night *lustigkeit.* "You will need to seek further entertainment elsewhere."

The meal period nearly spent, Wagner saw that he would need to forcibly break up Balgor's machismo-fest, and shanghai him into helping to cater Skol's evening fare. The day's unusual events having put their duty schedule in twist, they'd been permitted a later delivery window for the brute, one that they needed to honour promptly. Before returning his crockware, however, he responded to J'nea's initial ice-breaker, inviting her to share in some quick conjecture over their respective takes on the most discussed topic in camp. Each curious about what the other thought of SyKrahvo's struggle on the rampart, their individual forensics revealed understandably differing conclusions. While her guess dealt with ineptness, unfamiliarity, even overconfidence on the Commander's part, she became enthralled with Wagner's theory—prudently abridged, of course—that the energy contained within the Soork might have exhibited some manner of kindred, organic attraction to the Ergosian aggregate, of which she had been a constituent.

"Now that I do think about it," she said, "the baton did lunge as we shrunk in our apprehension. But, how could that...why would...I do not fathom how this could be. It prompts me to wonder what may have happened had we receded another step."

"SyKrahvo probably would have thrashed a bit beyond his limit, and found himself in an unexpected nose-dive into the crater he'd just created. And if the fall didn't do him in, we could have entombed him under all the sewage that Balgor and I cleared from Skol's cell today."

"And pelted him with a bushel or two of these dwarf pippins, while he bobbed for air within the putrid froth."

"Nice touch," said Wagner. "Would that make it '*sewer macht lustig*'?"

To his chagrin, she didn't quite get his word-spiel. After all, the dragging of a pun through two or three different lingual terrains was an ambition that had little chance at fruitfulness. Even after dissecting it for her, in the end she simply nodded and displayed a quaint smile of half-genuine and half-polite humouring. Wagner, unable to clarify his unappreciated witticism any better than he had, deemed this as good a time as any to make his exit; so, with a shrug, a chuckle, and a hasty "g'night," he excused himself and headed across the compound to rustle the realmson free for duty.

Balgor didn't have a lot to say as they made for the kitchen to fetch Skol's takeaway. In fact, he was downright sullen, and uncommonly so. When cornered on it, he replied that the braggadocio had been exceptionally stunted among his friends, even with those who were typically most boisterous, since everyone yet brooded over the day's terrible revelation. Total domination, servitude, genocide— all were ponderous weights for a national to bear. And although he was hesitant to admit it without being prodded, the realmson managed a confession of how deeply it troubled him as well.

Wagner wasn't certain if his friend, so mired in his funk, would be receptive to hearing any of his theories about the Soork, or if Balgor's misgivings about Wagner's significance on Ergos would escalate at the suggestion that his crovik-battling comrade might inadvertently have had some small sway in the outcome of SyKrahvo's demonstration. Balgor had given a good chew to everything else that Wagner had fed him thus far, but this wasn't to say that he'd swallowed one-hundred percent of it. There was a plethora of impossibility to accept in those tales, and although suspending disbelief really did aid in answering an equally ominous heap of questions—including his own healing at Wagner's hands—the *Voknor* he knew was much too normal a man to be a vessel for such supernal favour. On the other hand, he read Wagner better than anyone. Pensive and witty, tolerant and compassionate, steadfast and full of hidden valour—any sortilege endowed to him might readily have been squandered or exploited for personal gain by men less honourable than he. Why, then, wouldn't the gods bestow such a gift onto an unsuspecting but basically decent man, who in turn must come to learn its administering in the manner that a wee child learns to crawl?

Shattering the contemplative silence, Wagner opted to go for broke and share his insights with Balgor just the same, waiting till the two of them were locked in with Skol before coming clean. There, he had a few minutes of relative privacy in which to provide Balgor with the major bullets of his theory, saving the embellishment for later.

If nothing else, his hypothesis stirred the level-headed realmson into re-examining the incident from an angle no one but Wagner seemed to have noticed.

"Let me understand this," said Balgor. "You attempted to extend your 'mystic faculties' outwardly, and you think that this may have been what unnerved SyKrahvo?"

"Wow—I guess I must explain hocus-pocus better than I do puns," said Wagner, setting the buckets before Skol, "because that, my friend, is *exactly* what I mean."

With a grunt, Skol turned his head to observe Wagner, and then Balgor, through ratty, sheepdog tresses. His wounds, purged by the curative cleansing he'd received, appeared somewhat less septic for the moment; the flies and gnats, however, already buzzed around the resumed putrescence, and it wouldn't be long before the sores would again become life-threatening. Wagner actually recalled several earthly medical studies where researchers reconsidered the old (and repugnant) practise of utilising maggots as a topical restorative, placing them directly on infected flesh, where they would actually consume the bad tissue and promote a more rapid and successful healing. He couldn't imagine anyone volunteering for such a repulsive study—but if ever a candidate existed, Skol could easily have been one for their journals.

"Can you fathom any reason," asked Balgor, "why *you* would be the nave for so much mystical manifestation?"

"Reason? No. Logic, maybe. Although I get the willies sometimes from trying to understand it all, in a way it does make sense that I've become a kind of vehicle for weird phenomena, if only due to the years of being plagued by the visions that foreran my being spirited here to Ergos."

"You are a seer turned sorcerer, my friend. In my life, I have encountered many of the former, even a notable few who were not charlatans. I have met but one of the latter, and that which you have accomplished in my presence has served to inspire me, *Voknor*. But I confess that you unsettle me in equal measure."

"That makes two of us. Now tell me, should I finish what I started and come clean with Tamek? He's the only one who seems to have any insight into this kind of stuff."

"It is a difficult decision," said Balgor. "Despite his claim of an impartial ear, the severity of his traditionalism limits his capacity for accommodating anything that conflicts with his beliefs. That he already trusts you is a mark in your favour. But he will likely require a demonstration, so that he may assess from what causality you ply your gift."

"Proof? I have to prove myself to someone whose own life is steeped in religious abstraction?"

"The Soork is real enough, would you not agree? And, apparently, only Tamek seems to know its composition—what it is, what it can do, whence it originates. If the secret texts told him this much, perhaps they likewise offer explanation for the sortilege that has manifested in you."

Wagner walked to the door and pounded. "Things will never be the same," he said. "All else aside, I'm an outsider to him, an infidel. I—"

"*Things*, as you put them, are already not the same. Time can be our ally *or* our enemy here. With SyKrahvo's might, the walls of Vargath cannot hope to prevail. Yet, if you can be instrumental in stopping—or even just slowing—him, you must try. *We* must try. Tamek will undoubtedly be troubled by what you tell him—aye, and suspicious as well. He may hail you as a hero, or he may brand you an aberration. But to gamble one man's approval against a possible avenue that may spare countless Ergosian lives? *Voknor*, it must be done. And whatever the outcome, whether you have the potential to make a difference or not, know that I will not abandon you, my friend. This I vow."

The NuRac sentry flung open the door at last.

"Well," said the much flattered Wagner, staring Balgor straight in the eye, "with a testimonial like that, how can I go wrong?" He then turned to face the warder. "What do *you* think, sentry?"

"Shut your mouth, worm, and move along."

Wagner passed humbly into the crank-room, stowing his smirk while the guard followed them out into the passageway. On their tramp down the hall, they heard behind them the grinding of the great capstan as Skol was allowed more reasonable access to his food that, unlike their own meals that evening, was ever of the same swillish composition. Leaving all notion of the brute behind him, Wagner suddenly bristled at the thought of approaching Tamek as he and Balgor had discussed. He anticipated Tamek's anger and resentment at not having Wagner's confidence from the start, at being thought of as untrustworthy, unapproachable, biased, narrow-minded, self-righteous. Still—and hopefully better late than not at all—come the morning, Wagner would take the chance, unburden himself, reveal to the Sentinel what he'd already sprung on Balgor; and maybe thereafter he would have that much less of a secret to protect, and that much less guilt to wrestle with. Perhaps, too, through Tamek's vast knowledge he might learn something more about how his energy manipulations manifested. Who knew? Once relieved of the onus of having to constantly conceal his true nature, he and Tamek and Balgor might even be able to derive meaning from this huge mystery, and perhaps provide him with a clue as to what brought him to Ergos in the first place.

SyKrahvo had not lied. The NuRac army departed at dawn from outside the city's eastern ingress, and was joined at the far southern perimeter by those troops who had been billeted in the military complex adjacent to the prison camp. Three regiments in all, six battalions, each in formation and marching behind its respective banner, they escorted the high procession of vrohda-mounted officers who rode at the tail of the fore battalions and at the head of the aft. Tucked between the second and third regiments rolled the massive, ironclad wagon that housed SyKrahvo, GarMogg, and KroenDek—the Supreme Commanders, who had only the Tribunal and the Monarch himself to answer to in authority. Officially combining their divisions for the first time as a single invasion force, this warlord triumvirate settled on a course intended to decimate as many Ergosian outposts and alliances along the way as an army of its size could physically negotiate. The forest far too dense in some areas, and the roadways often too narrow to permit such a convoy, it would become SyKrahvo's call to either channel their forces over some secondary route or to "excavate" portions of the sylvan terrain as only *he* could in order to maintain minimal deviation in course.

Bottlenecking the troops into a leaner column, to more easily traverse the old caravan paths, was essential at times, although it theoretically invited insurgent ambush. The vulnerability of a thin phalanx within the darkwood while the greater body idled without—this was something that even the cocksure SyKrahvo was trained to avoid, even as it seemed that such matters no longer needed to concern him. Still, he and his peers conferred readily on these issues from inside their command vehicle, studying the plotting boards, the maps, the histories, so that when inconvenience reared they would already have relayed their decision to the forward scouts. Such a system was in place, with runners and go-betweens, that entire strategies could be planned, and enemies, engaged, without any Commander ever needing to leave the confines of this mobile headquarters—if that was what he chose.

But this campaign was to bear a slightly different twist, since SyKrahvo fully intended to stand at the forefront of every assault, blasting the Ergosian forces until they fell or scattered in retreat. Then he would advance alongside his NuRac war machine as it ploughed through the next defensive stand, and drove the enemy clear back to Vargath, which itself would topple in the end.

But Vargath was several sennights away for an army on foot, perhaps even more, depending on the number of incidents and the severity of the resistance encountered. Not that the NuRacs would be troubled by resistance—their confidence was tall. And although SyKrahvo would be vanguarding the brunt of the campaign, he would not win, nor even fight, these battles by himself. His purpose was one of intimidation, of providing access through blockades, and of sending the opposition scrambling in terror to regroup and to ultimately succumb. The NuRac army's task was to fight and secure, to pass through the forested apertures that SyKrahvo opened and readied for them. And there was no longer one single door that his "key" could not unlock.

This in itself, however, was leavening for a predictable contention already clearly in the works. GarMogg and KroenDek, suddenly of less authoritative import than denoted of their ranking, had begun to witness a gradual change in their fellow Commander that pressed them to no small degree of reservation. Contrary to what might be imagined with the theories of ambition and unchecked power and such, proprietary concern over the strange new weapon was not strictly the crux of their uneasiness so much as it was the effect of how the weapon's utilisation had acted to alter their peer himself. Granted, the Soork was first unearthed by SyKrahvo's subordinates, and had thus been allowed—by the Tribunal's edict and by right of discovery—to remain solely in his possession. He was, after all, the only NuRac who had learned to tap its latent potential, and his deportment and presence of mind had still been holistically typical at the time of that decision. Yet, SyKrahvo's sanctioned right to flaunt such a mysterious, unintuitive device, virtually without restraint, had since stirred in him an escalating, irrepressible penchant for aggressiveness that had not existed priorly in such amplitude, and which now demanded prudent and thorough observation lest it consume him so completely that drastic alternatives needed to be considered. It wasn't as if he were a servant who suddenly realised that he had the means to usurp his master and rule his house; if this had been the case, no one in QieLahr could have fared against him. Instead, it was more that his soul had become choked with soot; his inner being, daubed with the tiniest splash of venom; everything about him, shaded one gradation darker. And whether it was residuum of the rod's energy or merely a fervour borne of his anticipation of winning the realm for the NuRac race, it was certainly worthy of their cautious scrutiny.

Wagner abandoned his bedding at the first hint of morning twilight. Quietly manoeuvring through the shadows, he seated himself near the barracks' entrance, wishing in vain for the charity of some pitying guard to allow him out to roam the grounds while the yard lay cool and serene below the gently retreating night. He'd noticed that many of his fellow prisoners, like he, had been insomnious as well, some having taken to whispering among themselves, others staring blankly at the ceiling or at the faltering torches, all no doubt wondering about a future that had suddenly gone from uncertain to unsurvivable. At the same time, a great clatter of industry emanated from beyond the walls—odd for that hour—and it wasn't long before the prisoners reasoned the source as the NuRac army preparing to depart. At sunrise, a fanfare of trumpets broke the morning disquiet—some, far distant, and others, more local and to the south—and suddenly every Ergosian felt a morbid, sympathetic dread for their unsuspecting kinsfolk, scattered throughout the land, who would shortly be in for the ordeal of their lives.

Due to the unrest in the barracks throughout the night, that of the bemoaners and of the questioners who vied for Tamek's reassurance, Wagner had refrained from insinuating himself into the Sentinel's company. A private discussion simply not feasible, he'd decided instead to stick with his initial intent of waiting until breakfast to come clean. By then, he'd have rehearsed what he was going to say in the order that he wished to say it, with Balgor running offence for him with the thrall of support-seekers whose requests, though situationally righteous and deserved of Tamek's counsel, would intrude upon and rout the very revelation that might have pertinent bearing on all of their futures. Yet, after the long night of laboured reflection, Wagner found that he'd actually second-guessed himself into a clumsy about-face. In an act of liberality spurred by the logic of a restless mind, he gradually re-evaluated his dilemma and concluded that it may have been unfair and extreme to expect any reaction other than an understandably distrustful scepticism from the Sentinel (perhaps annoyance and resentment as well) at a story whose unaccountable gramarye would be difficult to push, and nigh impossible to prove as inadvertent happenstance. Although legendarily uncompromising in his own credo, Tamek had never shown himself to be unreasonable, and the knowledge of anything mystical or portentous or just plain extraordinary was unquestionably his field of expertise more than anyone's among this sampling of humanity. Surely, all that Wagner couldn't explain, all that he couldn't distinguish either as an unexplored niche of science or as a hackneyed theory in science phantasy, might have found clarity under Tamek's schooled, albeit less than pliant, theology. Wagner's troubled, empirical pragmatism would require obligatory shelving once the Sentinel began to spout his own presumptions, if only because no more plausible premise had been forthcoming. Tamek, after all, was the first person on Ergos with whom Wagner had shared lengthy, episodic dialogue, and from whom he'd acquired his primer of Ergosian philosophy and history, learned the nature of the people's plight, and gained enough expository insight to make it possible for him to muddle by as a bona fide national. Maybe Wagner, in the angst of his culture-swapping transition, had misread their fated, first encounter for mere happenstance. *Who* was to say that, on their meeting, Tamek couldn't indeed have provided certain insight into the visions and the world-hopping from a conceptual slant that Wagner hadn't been willing—or daring enough—to consider at the time? Maybe all that had ever been necessary was for Wagner to have performed a clean rebooting of his own methodology. Wipe away every preconceived notion and paradigm, every earthly frame of reference, every dangling inquiry that choked his progress like an impenetrable thicket, and there may have been revealed a pathway to a completely new set of values—Ergosian values—that held promise in ways he'd simply not considered.

Or maybe not. Perhaps Tamek's reaction would have been something more reminiscent of the early churches of Europe, who took incredible strides to squash any ideas that conflicted with established dogma—thus perpetuating misinformation, suppressing creativity, punishing originality, and shackling imagination in general, for the sake of maintaining its struggling grasp on the indomitably fickle human spirit. Tamek was rigid like this in his piety. He was a father who guided his family with an inelastic leniency that encouraged thought, but ultimately directed all errant ideas back onto the religious mainframe. And it was because of this authority that Wagner, who'd never known his own father, flinched at the idea of demonstrating his considerable differences after so long a time. For, although chronologically the Sentinel had no more than a few years on Wagner, his charisma and his imposing presence were such that he could easily have worn the paternal mantle for most of the prison population, and the nature of this mentor/flock relationship made Wagner's self-revelation all the more difficult.

The information already in circulation about Wagner was mottled at best. Balgor had certain knowledge of everything save the *sigma* tattoo; conversely, J'nea knew of nothing *but* the tattoo, and yet she still had befriended Wagner in spite of his dubious association with AuwNiir's device. The general prison populace thought of Wagner only as an immigrant from the southern regions, whose generally undistinguished combat skills somehow failed to hinder his success against the Beastmaster's Ennead—and had consequently elevated his reputation to well within the ranking of the admired. Lastly, Tamek believed him to be an intelligent if unenlightened man, guarded yet amicable, whose pagan nature deemed him nothing if not a salvageable soul. Once it was discovered, however, that Wagner was not exactly who he seemed to be, it was anyone's guess how Tamek would react. Secrets, of course, were necessary in every person's life, if only to have a safe and central exchange for those rudimentary notions that drift incessantly in and out of one's mind—the urges and aspirations, the jealousies, the hapless desires, and the shame. Too, secrets kept locked the cages on all the monsters, big and small, from those Godzilla-sized crimes committed by the few true deviants against humanity, nature, and spirit, to the thousands of insignificant little sins more common to any given individual's past that, although influential in defining the course of one's evolution, are often better left hidden, buried, or more subtly camouflaged, like a handful of off-colour threads spaced throughout the greater historical tapestry. Yet, so it was that Wagner breakfasted with the Sentinel, to offer him his services as both simple man and unlikely Übermensch, in the name of truth, friendship, and now—with this new development—desperation.

Tamek was initially in brood when Wagner approached him, but he opened up cordially in the latter's presence. His visage one of despondence, it seemed that he was undergoing a metamorphosis of conviction much as Balgor had, where he may have been coming to realise how much of his life had been forfeited to his imprisonment, and how he'd so easily accepted his derailment from warrior of the holy order to some ridiculous parody of a figurehead, a voice crying in the vast wilderness of NuRac disregard. All of his incessant protestations before the Tribunal, all of his stints in the dungeons on his constituency's behalf, even his proctorial function among a common people made adversarial by gladiatorial division—he may well have seen it now as but the pomposity and ego of a powerfully impotent man who never should have allowed himself to be taken alive in the first place.

Wagner, seating himself before him, smiled reassuringly, offered a few niceties, and then—when he could no longer refrain—bluntly petitioned the Sentinel for a dialogue of his own jurisdiction, uninterrupted by comment, query, interjection, objurgation, or judgement. And Tamek, recalling their unfinished business of the previous morning, tidied away his contemplative self-flagellation to honour that request. How surprised he was, however, when what he heard from out of Wagner's mouth was more confession and plea for mentoring than the continuation of their earlier fare. Here was instead an accounting of a great riddle, a line of thought that Tamek would have been quick to discount as the product of a bedevilled mind if not for his promise to hear Wagner out. In fact, sundry times in the course of Wagner's tale did he feel the urge to respond, rebut, rebuke, *condemn*—but in the purposeful bridling of his argumentative nature, he would, in the end, find himself at a complete loss for words.

"So," said Wagner, nearly breathless from condensing a lifetime into the span of a hurried breakfast, "I'm more of a stranger to your land than anyone knows. I'm an unwitting apprentice to forces I don't understand, a guy with a presaged itinerary but no mission. And I've kept mum about it for this long because, quite frankly, it's intimidating—even scary—to live with everything I've endured. To have revealed myself to people with whom I wasn't familiar would have been risky. Where I come from, in an age comparable to yours—and probably even the one I was born into—I'd probably have been burned alive for being some sort of freak or hobgoblin. Furthermore, since I'd gone and marked myself with a symbol that turns out to be—of all things—the crest of my enemy, I couldn't chance coming out until I was reasonably sure that I could do it without disastrous recourse. Yesterday made that possible. On the palaestra, I witnessed the first supernatural oddity around here other than my own shtick. And, horrifying as it was, I came away feeling...well...less isolated. Furthermore, the fact that you, Tamek, never even batted an eye at the staffling's potential told me something about *you*, for that's when I suspected that you'd encountered this kind of stuff before. That's why I'm here now, in an appeal to your obvious erudition in things mystical, to find a means of explaining what the heck I'm doing here."

Tamek took his porringer, scantly touched and now swarmed by gnats, and set it gently in the sand before him. "Come with me," he said, rising and gesturing for Wagner to follow.

Crossing the field, they latched onto Balgor, and strode straight into the infirmary. Searching the premises, Tamek's gaze fell upon a particular patient whose prognosis was far less than promising, and barely a lick above hopeless. Wagner recognised the man as Lahki, a quiet fellow and a fair warrior who he assumed had gotten himself gored in the tournament games. He didn't look at all well, and it truly surprised Wagner that he'd clung to his life for this long. A few accumulative metres of cross-stitched suture holding his belly and obliques together, he appeared feverish, gaunt, probably nearer to death than to life. All too likely, he'd suffered internal injuries that were far beyond Olask's abilities to detect and mend. Looking at what could very well have been Lahki's last moments, Wagner felt a notion of what Tamek wanted here.

"Demonstrate," was all the holy man said.

Wagner stood insensible.

"*Demonstrate!*"

Wagner hemmed. He considered for a moment. He knew what was expected, and he knew had to try.

"Okay," he said, nervously. "Okay, step back. Step back and shield your eyes."

Placing the fingertips of his right hand on Lahki's sternum, and those of his left on the man's pelvic bone, Wagner closed his eyes and set himself to concentrating on what was expected of him. He wasn't at all certain that it would work, wasn't at all certain that he could conjure the effect in such a forced environment of pressure and scrutiny. Only, to his abrupt and unready surprise, his hands spat flaring salubrity almost immediately, prematurely, before he'd even cast a line into the proper mind-realm to summon it. And instantaneously the patient's body became like an ember under the bellows.

In the fraction of an already fractioned second, the deed was done. Lahki lay calm and swarthy, like a gentle fellow in the midst of his afternoon nap.

Balgor and Tamek vigorously rubbed their flashcubed eyeballs. Olask, newly alerted (and ever the last to know), came racing over from the dispensary.

Wagner, on the other hand, staggered back from the cot with the blood-rush of a man who'd launched too quickly to his feet. "Whoa," he muttered. "I—I've never felt *that* before." He took a moment, shook himself out, let the dizziness ebb, and within a few seconds he'd regained enough of his composure to re-approach the cot.

"What are you three doing, fooling about here?" scolded Olask. "Can you not see this poor soul is terribly—" He stopped. He looked. There, before him, lay a man whose colouring was olive-tinged—not pale or jaundiced or slate—but a *healthy* olive. "Here—what is this?" he uttered. "What have you—"

Intrigued, the physician nudged them all aside and carefully lifted the bandage from Lahki's flesh. Underneath lay a lengthy, pink, serpentine scar and two shorter ones, each riddled by a mess of loosely looped twine.

"Hullo! What sorcery is this?"

Tamek's eyes steered Olask's toward Wagner, who said nothing.

Locking stares for a moment, Wagner wavered on precipitous assumption as he waited for comment that was not immediately offered. No tacitness in the Sentinel's eyes, no means of knowing what judgements coursed behind them, Wagner felt the twinge of discomfort, and was therefore the first to break off. Fluidly he traded his focus for one of self-inspection, examining his hands for the telltale runaway keratin that typically succeeded the restorative expenditure. Indeed, he discovered the sprouting of a good centimetre of new growth, a manifestation mirrored in Lahki, whose fingers and toes could now have stood the benefit of clipper and file. Hair and whisker accretion, however, was again less evident, both men already sporting shoulder-length locks and full beards the voluminousness of which would have merited little noticeable contrast.

With his last few acts of healing falling within days of each other, Wagner had come to discern other, less-obvious fallout that seemed—oddly—to vary from case to case. Arid, clogged nasal passages was one; a ravenous appetite, another. An excess of waxy cerumen in the ear canals was a third (although he generally didn't notice this effect until later, usually when chancing to poke a finger in his ear to scratch an itch). And last, there was the powdery residue on his skin, the scurf that he'd already theorised to be no more than the dead cells one would normally have sloughed in several weeks' time—which, interestingly enough, was arguably the time it would have taken Lahki, under optimum conditions, to heal to the point that he had. One of Wagner's original theories, then, was bearing out. These were no miracles of the messianic type; he was no conduit for God or gods or any other benevolent entities who might have chosen to reveal themselves through him. He wasn't channelling elemental energies or refashioning auric ones. Instead, the healing appeared absolutely to be coming from *him*, out of *him*, and perhaps at his own incremental expense. It was as if the holistic core of his very being was unwittingly pawning off small chunks of itself—bits of his own life force?—as packaged doses of energies that lent themselves to an ailing subject's physiology, thus initiating, augmenting, and expediting the metabolic process in said recipient. If a week of time would have been the required period for a particular malady to properly heal, both Wagner and the patient apparently aged a week in the flash of an eye—with the boost of convalescing vigour siphoned straight out of Wagner's body in what seemed a trade-off of involuntarily altruistic sacrifice.

Such a notion made as much sense as anything else he'd so far imagined. Energy, in whatever form, had to come from *somewhere*—it couldn't just be plucked out of nothingness. And despite his inability to explain why, weeks ago, the seizuring man had not experienced this boosted hair or nail growth in the way that Lahki exhibited it, the hypothesis was otherwise of initial soundness. Most of all, it brought to light one very grim notion: if Wagner employed these abilities too generously, might he literally age himself by entire years before he knew it? And, if so, why would he be made to pay so dearly for a few acts of selflessness?

"This is preposterous!" cried Olask. "Was it the effulgence that did this? Sentinel, what can it mean?"

"'Tis a miracle," said Tamek, sans emotion. "A true miracle. There was—ah—certain indication that Lahki would receive prodigy. And so he has. Now tend to him well, Olask, for we must away to the palaestra."

Urging Wagner and Balgor from the infirmary, Tamek waited until they'd reached his and Wagner's abandoned porringers before speaking up.

"*Voknor*, knowing that you do possess these abilities, how can you so callously allow the wounded and dying to suffer?"

Wagner bristled. "Well, for one, I'm still new to the whole thing. Being an inadvertent medium for such unbelievable energy is a hard thing to get used to, let alone to master. It's also a real challenge to pull it off unnoticed in a room full of onlookers. But the biggest factor is one that I've only just discovered. Y'see, each time I use it, I seem to forfeit a little more of myself—a little more of my essence."

When asked how so, Wagner showed both his friends the demonstrable after-effects, explaining the time acceleration theory as if it were fact. And even as Balgor confirmed similar characteristics from his own healing, it was still difficult to interpret Tamek's overall acceptance of the revelation. The Sentinel's temperament was, of course, fiery to begin with, and his moral expectations were as demanding as Grum's day-long calls for swordful engagement. Yet, rather than stay on the defensive, Wagner opted to cut and thrust.

"Listen, Tamek, I'll try to mend everybody in the whole infirmary if that's what you really want of me—side effects be damned. But we really need to get back to my original reason for coming clean. Do you have the vaguest idea of where this power comes from? Even more, is there any way to use it—while it still resides in me—to either stop SyKrahvo or to get us out of here in time to warn Vargath?"

"The new campaign *has* left the prison end of QieLahr more sparsely guarded than ever before," added Balgor. "SyKrahvo has taken every available NuRac into the field. If ever opportunity unbolted its gate, that moment is upon us."

"You two are daft. To aim your sights in such direction will surely get one-half of these people killed. And that does not account for the one, the two, or the twenty treacherous infidels within the other half who might betray us to their stable-masters for favour ere we e'er glimpse the other side of these walls."

"So," said Wagner, "we do it just like the escape. We don't tell anybody until the plan's in motion. Those who want their precious favour can have it—and an empty camp—all to themselves."

Balgor laughed. "Would not that be grand!"

The idea played like a joke without a punchline, for within it loomed the stalwart desire to make it real. In his own way, each had entertained such thoughts, numerous times—dreamed of revolt, imagined breaching or even toppling the walls and making off under both a hail of arrows and a cacophony of NuRac alarum and outrage. The reality of it, however, was hardly obtainable; it was more an inspirational caprice, a hopeless impossibility and no more. Still, all three men knew that it was often by the very hopelessness of a cause that success finds a way, especially when non-believing obstructors allow for no such contingency.

In the end, the troubled Tamek failed to offer his take on Wagner's unique magiks, not solely because of his unwillingness to offer rash assumptions, but also due to the fact that their little jaunt to the infirmary had made them somewhat less than punctual for their respective responsibilities. So, while the Sentinel beelined for the palaestra, Balgor and Wagner set off for the kitchen and for Skol.

There was an effortless float to Wagner's gait as they sped through the passageways, buckets in hand. He'd finally resigned himself to what was sportingly the last recourse for his gender (at least as far as the *earthly* male was concerned)—that of opening up and asking for direction. Granted, it wasn't a surrender from obstinacy, as with the stereotypical male in stubborn denial of a missed exit ramp, who'd too long refused aid either by way of solicitation or by the much slighted roadmap. Wagner's reasons for shouldering his particular cross had been prudent ones, not vain. At stake was his livelihood—whether he would be accepted or suspect—not some paltry matter of pride; and it had felt remarkably splendid to unload. Maybe Jon Mazzio had been right all along with his psycho-analysis gig. Maybe confession was indeed as good for the soul as the old platitude touted.

Balgor opined that Tamek would evidently require time to digest the news, stating that, unlike his own inquisitive, matter-of-fact acceptance of inexplicable curiosities, the Sentinel "strove ever to find prophecy and meaning in all things."

"If two grackles skirmish in mid-air," he said, "and one flies off to the southwest and the other does not pursue, you can wager confidently that Tamek will prognosticate some small symbolism from it."

Skol's condition hadn't noticeably improved. Slumped in his chains against the wall, wounds again crusting over, his was a slow crucifixion at the hands of uncaring centurions who gambled and palavered in the room without. Had he been killed outright at the time of the arena debacle, even promptly euthanised afterwards, it would have spared him a great deal of senseless torment. Instead, bureaucratically blithe in just what it was they wished to do with him, the NuRacs' sentence had become a kind of living death for Skol, an opportunity for survival void of active interference beyond food and drink and voiding, with nothing more than his formidable immune system bridging the abyss of death while he waged a perpetually stalemated battle against infections that would by now have engulfed and squelched any human shell.

"Looks like yesterday's bath wasn't really all that effective," said Wagner, eyeballing the resuming discharge that seeped anew from Skol's wounds. "He has to be suffering something fierce."

"There is naught we can do for him," said Balgor, setting the buckets before the brute's taloned feet. "Remember, *Voknor*—he is a ruthless killer. You cannot let pity or curiosity soften you."

"Can I let inclemency and contempt harden me? *Look* at him. He's a junkyard dog—beaten, abused, neglected since he was a pup. It's no wonder he's brutal. He should've been put down long ago."

"The NuRacs nurtured his brutality, *Voknor*. He is just as they wished him to be. Carnage is all that he knows in this life. His only redemption will be in his death."

Wagner set his water pail next to Balgor's and backed off. Skol looked down at the food and wriggled restlessly in his chains.

"*Hungggry,*" he suddenly slurred in a slipshod NuRac tongue.

Both men did classic double-takes.

"See?" Wagner was elated. "I told you!"

"*Bones and entrails!*" Balgor exclaimed. "I never thought...never *believed* there to be any faculty other than instinct in the beast. Yet..."

"He's got intelligence, Balgor. Somewhere, somehow, there are a couple of Lilliputian lobes in that noggin."

The realmson acknowledged with a hesitant nod. "Aye," he added. "But to what avail? Such a discovery does little to change his nature, nor does it convince me that he is any more than a fiend who can mimic a few, simple words."

Wagner studied the hairy anomaly like an anthropologist who'd found himself face-to-face with a living specimen of Peking man. The ailing brute, already familiar (and seemingly unbothered) with their daily presence, glanced cyclically in his direction, then at the food, at Balgor, down at the chains that bound him, and then back to Wagner.

"I suppose it doesn't mean anything," conceded Wagner, joining his friend and moving towards the door. He took one more look at the cell's lone occupant before knocking for the guard. "On the other hand...it could mean *everything.*"

CHAPTER TWENTY-ONE

Where I am not understood, it shall
be concluded that something very useful
and profound is couched underneath.
 —JONATHAN SWIFT

Tamek had never seen it coming. Nothing could have prepared him for Wagner's sudden disclosure of wizardry, and no one could have made him believe it to be anything other than shrewd artifice or a tasking levelled at him by gods long dissatisfied with his ineffectual dispatching of his people's emancipation. How else might a pagan come to possess such a gift if not in the form of a lesson from beyond, intended as an axiomatic humbling of a holy servant who'd fallen victim to the complacency of his own piety?

Given the magnitude of his scriptural knowledge, his expertise with lore, legend, tradition, Tamek was still far too perceptive a fellow to limit the probability thusly, although spiritually he felt that he deserved to be flagellated with a knout fashioned of his own shortcomings. The truth, however, was that there had been no dereliction or oversight on his part. Thaumaturgy had many agents, many progenitors, and the holy parchments could bear this out. Any number of sources could have engrafted such an ability to the man he knew as *Voknor*, even those lending to some arcane, heretical orthodoxy, or to the minor host of rarely espied goods and evils in the land: the hamadryads of the Chahnuk, the Orlahn naiads, the peris, the undines, the cavern-dwelling kobolds, the oreads of the Grobian Alps, and the various entities who forever toyed with cause and effect under the far-reaching grasps of Eternity and Existence. In the pyramidal pantheon—with the Powers Twain residing at the apex, and the lesser entities gradating down and away to a representative base of innumerably less influential sprites and spirits—the means for *Voknor* to have come by his augmentation was a multifarious lot. Furthermore, distinguishing supernal profundity from pseudo-supernal capriciousness in these types of endowments was ever a befuddling argument, with most querists often choosing to deem them arbitrary whenever scriptural correlation was lacking. Few such manifestations had ever been witnessed and documented by the scholars who might best explain them, whose acumen would ferret out the chicaners and the charlatans, to reveal only those who were truly and authentically blessed, and who could collectively and most competently assess the significance in the endowment, the means by which the individual in question had come to possess it, and the degree of recompense imposed by the gods of its employment.

And yet, therein lay the problem. Tamek had read the signs, had detected them in SyKrahvo's misuse of the Soork. The Soork itself, though incomprehensible, was a sacred artefact, not a weapon, not a conqueror's sceptre, not a telic bane. Certainly it was no toy. Neither was its use free of consequence. In the instant that SyKrahvo first chose to vilify it, he'd ransomed himself to darkness, and out of his newfound malevolence had risen a kind of unseen golem whose essence would gather to itself the evils that the NuRac wrought against land and life. With each blasphemy would its grip tighten, its shadow lengthen, its canker thicken, as it gorged on the fodder that SyKrahvo provided—until the day that its intoxicating influence whelmed that of its Alladinesque sponsor, whereby it would lurch from obscurity to engulf said desecrator in whole. Such was the stave lore of the sacred tomes, that none save the temperate and the worthy might wield such power with relative impunity, and that only the discerning be exempt from the cascade of retributive fallout demanded of those who, like SyKrahvo, mismanaged that which was consecrated, and who unwittingly exposed themselves to the devolution and corruption that would be ultimately attributable to their undoing.

Not so dissimilar, there was inclination to confirm *Voknor's* suspicions that the healing aura that he apparently transferred to his wounded subjects could indeed have been a portion of his own life force leeched away in order for the regenerative process to have a vital fount from which to draw. An eerily analogous account, little known to most, existed on record from more than a century prior, with degenerative consequence ultimately befalling that hapless thaumaturge as well. The lore of the elders taught Tamek of mystical equilibrium, of how miraculous endowments rarely came without even a single string that might not snag or tangle from carelessness in their appropriation. Like the ramifications SyKrahvo was slated to encounter down the road, so fiendishly incremental and cumulative in their nature, the flipside was equally considerable. Even when tapped for benevolent purposes, it seemed that *Voknor's* very longevity was debited with each exercising of magiks—along, perhaps, with the longevity of each of his subjects. The difference, however, was that while the healed forfeited a week to several weeks of their lifespans with a single, restorative flash, *Voknor*—who meted the mending energies and remained the only constant in every incident—was like a wellspring that, in quenching a population, would itself run dry before its time. And although something so uncommon and grotesque would indeed be a phenomenal process to witness, Tamek wouldn't have wished it on anyone, especially somebody whom he had come to call his friend.

The notion of *Voknor's* origins sprouting from a realm beyond Ergos's firmament, though inordinate, was not unthinkable nor even blasphemous, although one would have to wonder how a man might transcend worlds in the manner of spirits and deities. Tamek knew that the gods followed an agenda of their own making, and he was not one to presume what they would or would not do with their discretion. If it was the will of Existence to pluck an outsider from spheres away, or to create a man who believed this of himself, or even merely to allow a deluded soul possessed of healing abilities to live out his being under such assumption, then so be it. None of it fell as threat to the Sentinel's personal creed, nor even to his ego or to his sense of the plausible. He'd seen too much in his limited years to discount anything at first scrutiny. Having studied alongside, and interacted with, an omnium gatherum of gifted individuals at Vishkor—seers, healers, sages, and historians—he might have admitted *Voknor's* pretence, even the indisputable demonstration that followed, as beyond his *own* reckoning, but it was hardly a stretch in celestial largesse for They whom Tamek worshipped. No, it was more the fact that *Voknor* had hidden his secret away that bothered him, that he'd omitted these pertinent and extraordinary facets of his past from their conversations, even long after the two of them had solidified a friendship. This, more than anything else, even more than the symbol branded suspiciously to his chest, brought a tension into their relationship that hence could only serve as an obstacle to whatever mutuality their futures were to share.

As for AuwNiir's device, that which *Voknor* called *sigma*, it bore no immediate symbolism other than the obvious; but Tamek found it disconcerting to think that someone whom he'd considered an ally might voluntarily brand himself with a NuRac Commander's crest, despite *Voknor's* admission that the act had been one of misguided inspiration, carried out during a lull within the otherwise relentless buffeting of his alleged visional tumults. The markings were of an irrelevant design, and were likely AuwNiir's family line or some military means of identification. It was not improbable that a seer—as *Voknor* was apparently turning out to be—might perhaps focus on such a symbol, particularly one that often recurred and would furthermore reveal itself to be the representative device of a man who, one day, would come to literally possess the seer as chattel. That none of AuwNiir's personal assistants, his lackeys, valets, nor any of his private corps, had been observed sporting similar epidermal markings lent credibility to *Voknor's* tale. Yet, this was hardly proof for vindication; *Voknor* had been living and moving among the prison population for months now in varied states of undress, and ostensibly no one had ever once gleaned the iconic distinguishment beneath his hirsuteness. And although he'd never exhibited the erratic behaviour of one with something to hide, even sans tunic, there still could have been explanations for the *sigma* other than the one *Voknor* offered. Who was to say that AuwNiir was not clever enough to strategically mark his spies with his device— with the blatant indicia of their allegiance to him—in order to extort their loyalty and to escalate the difficulty of any potential double-cross? Could there have been others about the camp who had been infixed with the brand, and who, too, would be quick to fabricate some far-fetched yarn in order to finagle justification? It was, after all, quite a thorny bramble from which *Voknor* was trying to emerge, and this for the sake of a clear conscience! No, Tamek sensed that there were other factors at work here apart from those notions of covertness so easily dredged by his paranoia. For one, *Voknor's* beneficent touch could not be denied, nor could the legitimacy of his ignorance and innocence and the propensity toward foreign mannerism that he so commonly demonstrated. His simple earnestness, like a lodestone that generated equal such exudates from those who knew him, was all too influential to be contrivance. His examination of life was like that of an inquisitive child. And the charmingly predictable manner in which his throat and cheeks flushed ruddy whenever he chanced to sit with that comely trusty betrayed an insuppressible and endearing ungainliness that easily exonerated him from possessing a spy's more stolid constitution. These impressions of character, more than anything else, were what championed as Tamek's primary acquitting criteria. A further riffling through *Voknor's* bona fides—his honourable acts, his valour and compassion, his wit and spirit, and undeniably his role in the dispatching of the Ennead (for what NuRac mole would subject himself to this?)—and it became possible for the Sentinel to dissuade himself from aggressive suspicion. That he now faced an objective enormously greater than merely procuring fair treatment for a few hundred prisoners, he needed to be certain of the foundation on which he erected trust; and the fact that *Voknor* had even been willing to offer a sacrificed longevity for the emancipation of a race, then Tamek could do no less than to place a little of his faith in the man.

But still, from this moment on he would maintain a watchful eye over the newly revealed man of miracles; and at the first hint of treachery, he would not hesitate to strike even a friend down for the good of the realm.

Wagner received chiding from the guards outside of Skol's hovel for presuming to advise them of how the brute's condition was again deteriorating. It wasn't Wagner's business, they insisted (perhaps rightly so), for the Tribunal had yet to rule on what measures were needed in order to either eradicate Skol's ailings or to terminate the beast altogether.

"If you are so devoted to the daemon," taunted one NuRac, "then go and obtain the proper unguents from the infirmary, and anoint his seepages yourself!"

Wagner actually contemplated the idea while Balgor waited for him, empties in hand.

"By your leave?" Wagner tested the guard.

"Oh, by all means, flea. I shall enjoy listening as Skol tears you to scraps for your trouble."

"*Voknor*—are you daft?" cried Balgor. "What *is* it with you? Why do you care?"

"I dunno," he said. "Must be the Androcles in me." His answer, though a fitting one for anyone familiar with Aesop, fell here on uncomprehending ears."

They were escorted out as usual, but parted ways after reaching the courtyard, with a sentry accompanying Wagner into the hospital, where Papa Olask and his assistants yet fussed over the wonder of Lahki's accelerated recovery.

"I need a big ol' jug of glohular," Wagner said, catching Olask by the sleeve. "The biggest you can spare."

The elder shot him a puzzled look. "Whatever for?"

Wagner hemmed and hawed and tried to appease his impatient warder by quickly rattling off for Olask the details of the task he was about to undertake. The physician blinked in speechless disbelief, gazing alternately to Wagner and then to the NuRac, before leading them to the dispensary.

"Not to be impertinent," said Olask, addressing the guard, "but will the stable-masters approve of this appropriation of their costly embrocations?"

The NuRac admitted that he and his peers hadn't considered that fact, but assured Olask that it would be satisfactorily worked out among the higher-ups. Wagner noted this sentry's unusual tone with the Ergosian—a respectful answer to a frank question; no expletives, no sarcasm or threat—and stood confused by it, for such was a decency that the NuRac had yet to extend to him or to Balgor after the handful of occasions that he'd been their minder. Of course, their wisecracking, coupled with their deliberate ineptitude with the simplest chore, probably had much to do with that, while Olask had done nothing more during his far lengthier tenure to garner NuRac deference than to have saved a few hundred lives, perhaps some of them even NuRac.

"I suspect," the physician told Wagner, "that the glohular's effect will be marginal if his condition has truly deteriorated as you claim it has. At best it will ease the agony of his inevitable expiring." He tucked the economy-sized ceramic into Wagner's hands, folding Wagner's fingers over it for safekeeping. "As a man of physic," he continued, "and admittedly *only* for that fact, I pity the beast for his prolonged suffering. Perhaps I will even experience a charitable tinge of remorse in his death, for that is my lot as a healer. Yet, as a man who has seen that abomination's handiwork time and again...it shames me to admit that I will more likely rejoice at the final act in his horrid, blood-stained existence."

Wagner nodded sombrely, and vowed to return what portion of the balm he didn't use. Then he was ushered away by his warder, past the cots of those whom Tamek would have him revivify, across the yard, through the dusty catacombs, and finally back to the being who deserved succour least of any, but to whom Wagner had emboldened himself into offering a decisive chance.

"Have at it," said the escorting guard as one of his peers unlocked, and pushed open, Skol's entry. "But be wary. The beast is unpredictable."

"Aye," said the turnkey. "We have made wager on how long into the medicating it will be before he chooses to nip off your arms."

"I *do* love a challenge," quipped Wagner, ducking into the cell before the NuRac booted him for impertinence.

The door quickly barred behind him, Wagner leaned back against it and let slip a sigh. He studied Skol while simultaneously wrestling with a Skol-sized ambivalence driven by his unreasonable empathy for the feral creature. Why *did* he care about this fearsome wrecker? For all of his probing, he wasn't certain—not exactly—yet he couldn't always depend on his rationale anyway. He'd been living on instinct for quite a spell—instinct and the peculiar, superseding, second-consciousness that incidentally and inexplicably ramped and smoothed over his evaluative shortcomings like some steamrolling steward of mental refinement and physical transcendence. Ever since touching down on that faraway Ergosian lea, the path he'd been travelling had been sketchy and portentous and bespeckled with washed-out imagery that somehow had its basis in the old visions. It was instinct that had kept him alive in a violent environment, that had made fruitful many a situation where cognitive decision failed or erred or was perceived by his subconscious as being dangerous, imprudent, or impossible. Now, instinct suddenly impelled him to administer to the scourge of every Ergosian in the camp;

and although enigma hid its purpose in a vast shroud of variables, Wagner put trust in that portion of his mind that so often surrendered itself *to* itself. After all, the faith that Wagner had in *Wagner*—specifically the portion of his psyche that acted of its own accord as sage, oracle, and guardian—was the only faith that had ever delivered him in times of uncertainty. He didn't fully know why Skol was important; he just knew that he was.

He approached the creature slowly, projecting a forced air of confidence that he hoped would muddy any pheromonally-perceived trepidation that Skol may have sensed. In the past few days he'd stood closer to the Sunderer than anyone who'd lived long enough to boast of it, even played Skol as the ignorant straight man to his and Balgor's bantered repartee; but somehow, Wagner had felt less intimidated when the realmson had been right there with him. It was but the two of them now, beast and man, and although Skol was still in tether—and his current demeanour, logy and lifeless—the threat of his unpredictability loomed under link and shackle like great Cerberus dozing at the gates of Hades.

Wagner emitted some gentle, cooing sounds, as if Skol were a spooked horse who required reassurance. He felt foolish in doing so, but with the prospect of dabbing unguent onto a feral being's pustulations, *any* means of garnering trust—even that of aural affectation—was key to coming away unscathed.

The brute, though all along cognisant of Wagner's presence—and indeed comfortable with it due to redundancy—jolted up to re-evaluate the scrawny, bronzy being whose mouth produced noises that he'd never before heard. Pleasing sounds they were, comforting issuances that, because of their foreignness, set Skol a bit on edge and yet simultaneously charmed him enough to goad his attention for more than just a few seconds.

Then Wagner did it. Almost without thought, without fear, he extended a hand toward the beast's shoulder, and softly, delicately, grazed his fur with the mildest of comforting strokes. A risky feat, performed within the space of a single breath, he initiated sensorial contact, and then fluidly retracted his reach, watching all the while to see how this liberty affected Skol.

Far from any animal back in Bishop's petting zoo, Skol nevertheless responded as most warm-blooded mammals do to physical caress: he lifted and leaned into the stimulation in order to procure more of the same. Wagner obliged, but guardedly, for if there was a way of learning how far Skol's toothy maw could extend from his restraints, it involved bidding farewell to four fingers and a thumb, and Wagner was much too fond of his digits to relinquish them so flippantly. His surprise at the brute's reaction was surpassed only by the guttural purr, resonating from Skol's larynx, that sounded like an old farm-shed Briggs and Stratton suddenly being jerked to life after years of sitting idle amid cobwebs and corrosion. Most notable, however, was what occurred shortly thereafter, when a different Skol—one closer to his legend—came abruptly to his senses, falling from his cloud-like ecstasy with the thump of realisation that he'd allowed a strange being to lay hands upon him. In full turnabout, he flinched and snorted a half-growled/half-sputtered warning, torn between the affront to his person and the marvellous atoll of scratchy sweetness amid an ocean of blood-crusted excruciation. Wagner talked to him in melodic tones in order to sway him back over to docility; and, for the most part, he succeeded. But there remained enough unpredictability in Skol's turbulent nature to keep Wagner from denying the all-too-real danger of the undertaking.

When it seemed that Skol appeared a bit more at ease with him in his proximity, Wagner produced the glohular and attempted to course his way through the weave of matted, encrusted fur that obscured each of Skol's many injuries. This, however, proved nothing short of inexpedient. Finding the scabious pelage nearly impossible to breach without having to pry and probe at the ultra-tenderness of the inflictions, an exasperated Wagner soon retreated for an engineer's rethinking, fretting over the realised enormity of the task for which he'd volunteered. With the copiousness of dried coagulum barring his progress like a plague of pruney shells that needed cracking, Wagner knew that he had far too much delicate work to do here before Olask's salve could penetrate to where it might even begin do any good.

Setting the ceramic to the floor, he distanced himself briefly from his bestial host. Although he still sensed it would serve him to help Skol, the procedure—meticulously intricate as it was—would in itself induce such discomfort that Skol might perceive it more as an attack than a treatment. It would hardly behove Wagner's situation to risk jeopardising the tolerance he and Balgor had earned thus far of the brute's otherwise vicious propensity. Yet, on its own, Skol's extraordinarily hardy metabolism seemed capable only of stalemating the infection, not vanquishing it. Wagner was torn. Should he even try? Should he leave Skol be? Would his efforts serve to aid or to aggravate?

In his deliberation, in his search for alternatives, he suddenly found himself toying with the idea of augmenting Skol's overworked antibodies in a manner that only *he* could. Weighing consequence, he stood silent for what seemed a very long time, in a ponder that pitted him against notions of action, necessity, destiny, wrongfulness, negligence, and stupidity. Zeal skirmished with wistfulness; desperation, with allegiance. His mind was unsure. All he had left to him was instinct.

He edged forward once again. Through the vague glimmer of morning light that filtered in from above, he gazed into Skol's pallid eyes. Espying in them only the paired silhouettes of his own reflection, he watched the umbral images as they reached out in unison toward his own hand as he gently touched the monster's shoulder.

"What the hell," he muttered, closing his eyes.

A room away, the handful of sentries—so preoccupied in their frivolity—failed to witness the incredible flash of brilliance that for a split-second flared within the keyhole of the vault door.

Dour was the mood on the palaestra as Wagner stepped from the access tunnel. Although expected to infuse their skirmishes with a proper verve, the populace was clearly bogged in unhappy thoughts; and such preoccupation made itself evident in the sluggishness and ineptitude that had displaced their usually graceful parrying.

Stopping in at the weapons enclosure, Wagner exited just as quickly, quarterstaff in hand, and began a search of the yard for somebody lacking an opponent. In the early days, he'd have stuck to people he knew—Balgor, Bilahdu, sometimes Tamek—but anymore, he preferred to mingle and mesh in the way that Balgor had regimented for him, that he might always be challenged with new tactics from unfamiliar sources.

Surprisingly, J'nea was upon the field, and he paused briefly to watch her juggling nodger and buckler against a stocky woman whom he'd seen around but didn't know by name. Not ever having critiqued J'nea's fighting finesse, he now noted how she gritted her teeth in battle, sometimes in smile, often in sneer, and how she apparently liked to mix it up—slamming buckler against buckler, breaking a deadlocking clinch with a stomp, a trip, or with a surly knee to her adversary's midsection, deftly countering blade with blade, lunge with lunge, as she matched, and sometimes aggravated, whatever assault the woman launched at her. She favoured left-handed battle, which always made duelling against a "righty" a bit tricky for both sides, yet her shield-slinging arm was no less proficient than her left, capable of delivering such staggering dextral blows that the underestimating opponent was forced into spot-calculating the best means of anticipating, and occasionally deflecting, said blows in the rare instance that J'nea might have overtly telegraphed her intent. In physical bulk, the woman outclassed J'nea by about fifteen kilograms; but the trusty's comparative slightness served as a deception for the insuperable menace of her sweep, and for the spring-loaded explosiveness that erupted from legs of tightly bundled sinew. Watching in amazement, Wagner had to wonder from where her prowess came. After all, she'd told him that she'd been the second of three sisters from a humble, non-warring village far to the north-east. But clearly she was no pouting, whining, "Jan Brady" of Bejodeth, and even as her village had long ago been sacked and torched, it boasted the legacy of at least one spirited warrior in the form of this lithe native daughter.

Wagner discovered that he could solicit no permanent partner for himself, as the population on the field that morning fell odd in number. He was, however, able to fill in as substitute in the occasional match where an opponent took a particularly nasty fall or had become too bloodied to soldier on without a precautionary visit to the infirmary. Grateful in these instances, he enjoyed mucking about with the quarterstaff, again having taken to it more naturally, and with less difficulty, than the graver weapons; and although he knew a stave was generally no match for sword or spear except in the most disciplined of hands, he nevertheless favoured the simple weapon, perhaps due to the benignity of his own constitution, and perhaps a little bit because he sought the challenge of besting a foe with this least lethal of armaments.

At midday, the sky turned darkly sour. A cool front bullying through, it drew behind it a violently drenching downpour that proved too dense and diminishing for productive sparring. As was his way, Grum waited until everyone was sufficiently waterlogged and miserable before offering them permission to huddle in the tunnel until the thunderhead waned to the degree that they might resume training without having to slosh around in ankle-deep water. Though there existed ample run-off gratings at the periphery of the yard, a long-discovered flaw in their design rendered them largely unaccommodating to torrential rains, and on occasions like this the Ergosians quietly mouthed their appreciation to the NuRac engineering team's incompetence.

Squatting in the passage, Wagner was joined by Balgor and Tamek. Few words of import, however, were exchanged, due to the mass that pressed in around them. J'nea skirted to the rear of the access to actually join them, striking up a conversation of fancy in order to pass the time.

"Listen," she urged them, pressing a finger to her lip. "Grum is yet out there, blathering to his subordinates—he is too thick to find shelter until the cloudburst draws down."

"Why should he?" said Balgor. "It is the first bath he has had since the rainy season!"

"Aye," said Uthok, chortling. "The filthy mongrel reeks like month-old togs!" As he laughed at his own joke, J'nea squinched at him and sniffed the air about him.

"Should *you* not be out there as well?" she asked. Clearly, Wagner's story-time digs against the once unmockable Uthok had opened a door that would not close anytime soon. Indeed, people began chuckling while the Bonecrusher flustered in grasp of a comeback.

"I *would* be, wench, if you were to offer me your lovely fingers for the lathering of my manly backside!"

"Ugh," she said. "Not even your poor mother was ever *that* kindly."

"That is because his own mother had no hands with which to lather him," came a stray voice from the crowd. "Was she not a vrohda?"

"Nay!" said another. "That is unkind to the vrohdas!"

High-volumed laughter ensuing, Tamek suddenly stepped in. "*Enough of this nonsense!*" he chided. "Have you no understanding of your own fates? Our enemies unleash a heinous terror into the world, and you stand here in folly, insulting each other like undisciplined children! The realm is being devoured, people! 'Tis being eaten away by SyKrahvo and his legions. We are all of us in greater peril than you can imagine!"

"What would you have us do, Sentinel?" asked J'nea. "We are imprisoned, incapable of fighting this war. We are helpless to arrest SyKrahvo's campaign. Should we all just mope about and brood like old men bewailing their youthful virility? Surely you do enough of that for the whole lot of us."

For a stock-still moment, all that could be heard was the rain plashing the ground, sounding incredibly like one of Wagner's old Filthy Lucre griddles in sizzle. Only, the sizzle here was of another source.

"I would not expect one as yourself to comprehend that which motivates me, woman," said Tamek. "You are a reaver, a malefactor, a willing aide to mine enemies. Morally you have nowhere to go save upward. My duty here is as guide, mentor, defender to the Ergosian faithful. Oft-times that mantle e'en extends to protect the ungrateful and the errant, which explains why I tolerate your scathing insult to my character."

J'nea spoke up to defend herself but was overtrumped by the Sentinel's boisterousness.

"Nowhere in my creed will you find more graciousness than that which I have extended to the various kinspeople of our scattered nation. I have gone to the dungeons for you, argued on your behalf before the Tribunal until my very voice gave way. I have efforted myself into exhaustion to provide structure for you, to maintain the faith, to offer counsel and courtesy and a reason to hope in this most wretched of places. Ne'er have I demanded anything in return other than a longevity to your optimism, the trust that somehow—by some means—we will live long enough to effect our emancipation."

"No one denies this," argued J'nea. "But if only you could scratch the scales from out your eyes, you would see that there exists more than melancholy in the sphere of human emotion. For some of us, our wit is all we have left. If it pleases me to tell Uthok he is an oaf and a clodhopper, and he labels me a scamp and a churl in kind, where is the harm?"

This time, it was Tamek's response that was ridden over roughshod.

"That I am imprisoned here has never been enough for you," J'nea continued, indifferent to the many ears around her. "It seems I must forever remain a prisoner to my past indiscretions, and suffer the guilt of my privileges as trusty so that your own haughty reverence might gleam that much brighter by contrast. True, for more than one-half of my life I have been saddled with this condemning brand. Because of crimes committed in childhood, I have been scorned, spoken ill of, judged, *pre*-judged, and kept at distance. Yet, I would be remiss if I did not confess that the stigma has not been without value. Bearing it has taught me more of life than your wizened scholars with all of their dusty scrolls and tomes ever could."

"Doubtful," said the Sentinel, bracing two storms now, nature's and J'nea's.

"Doubt*less*! For ten years, my roguery has undergone a tempering that only humility and victimisation can bestow, enough so that at present I am far more resilient—far more *resistant*—than ever I was as a child. Over those years I was forced into becoming my own mentor, for never did anyone offer me the guidance that you enjoyed. I sought to find spirituality from within myself, since the narrowness of your stodgy, stagnant tradition could never encompass the bitterly varietal bounteousness encountered by one so ostracised by society. What you see before you is a product of Ergosian justice. My inner armour was forged of that justice. I refuse to be made to feel inferior, just as I refuse to be moulded into one of your empty-headed flock who cannot even pick a fleck of cabbage from his teeth without first consulting you and your precious scripture."

"Have care, woman—your venom is dangerously close to provoking the wrath of my 'stodgy tradition.'"

"Splendid!" she cried. "Will further fanning spur it to action, or is dejection your muse of choice?"

While Tamek clenched at a low seethe, Wagner looked to the trusty who never ceased to surprise him. He'd seen this side of her before, and not so long ago. He knew that when bread was cast onto her waters, it was prudent to hightail it inland a ways before the tide tossed back a whole bakery of soggy loaves. J'nea ever a puzzle to him, she was sometimes docile, sometimes rude, often charitable, frequently lippy, and always formidable. Wagner could do naught but to hold her in the esteem of a kindred. In the end, wasn't he also an outcast of sorts? In its own way, wasn't *his* marking as condemning as *hers*?

In such tight proximity, the hesitant crowd added little commentary, but it was a certainty that tongues would be busy come the evening. Admirably—and quite removed of his character—Tamek held rein on the snorting steeds of his ire; and, although not exactly apologising to J'nea, he censured himself openly for his contributive escalation of an argument whose basis had nothing to do with her, and everything to do with his own unchannelled passions. Frustration, anxiety, regret, anger, uncertainty, prophetic ambivalence—together, they formed a thicket that even blades of the keenest fortitude could hack at and only graze. It seemed that even a Holy Sentinel could fall victim to his emotions should he find hope dwindling and faith running a day late.

"I find it to my shame," he said, "that our nation suffers by SyKrahvo's despoliation, and I stand here like a vole hiding from a harmless summer shower. 'Tis neither honourable nor just."

J'nea, deflated from her whinged venting and feeling a tad confounded and abashed in light of Tamek's retraction, nibbled soberly at her inner lip. "Can we truly do nothing...*Sentinel*?" It almost rumpled her public image to hear her utter his title so darned respectfully.

"Always are there courses of action, woma— *J'nea*. Were I a reckless whelp like Juthac the Vulgar—may his madcap spirit be born anew—or the brazen Mirko of Vargath, or e'en our brash and imaginative friend, *Voknor*, here, I would consider many intrepid ventures. But alas, we have kinspeople in the infirmary, wretches in the dungeon block. 'Twould be my duty to salvage e'ery life, not merely the able-bodied."

"Brash?" said Wagner. "Me? I think you have me confused with some other south-realmer."

Balgor could no longer remain passive when the talk turned to escape. "Could we not try once more in freeing a handful who could get message to Vargath? After all, if it was possible for Fostoch to succeed through scoundrel's luck, then surely others might succeed as well."

"*We* couldn't," said Wagner in playful derision.

Balgor shrugged assentingly. "Aye, but at least *I* was not the one sporting a ridiculous squire's hat through most of QieLahr."

"We are not certain that the Agile One e'er reached free soil," said Tamek before Wagner had opportunity to retort. "Long have I known Fostoch. And while he is indeed crafty, regularly have I seen him bollix up the simplest of affairs. 'Twould surprise me little if he yet slinked about within QieLahr's back alleys."

This idea gave rise to a wealth of speculation over Fostoch's mysterious fate, with many in the huddled crowd offering theories of where he might have been and by what means he'd been able to vanish into that night's adumbration of jumbled alarum and confusion. It was a perplexing riddle, one that had long vexed Wagner and Balgor more than anyone else present; yet, despite this new renaissance of debate around them, the Orrdian's soon-to-be-legendary disappearing act occupied a lower tier against the more substantial goings-on in their post-escape existence.

It was not long before the downpour ebbed to mere patter, and the palaestra's floodwaters receded enough to have Grum calling for a general return to the field.

Few were they who weren't chilled, dampened, clammy to the point of discomfort; yet, as discomfort was part and parcel of the convention that they lived by daily, each of the prisoners embraced the chill for as long as it lasted, for soon enough would Cinjal retake the sky with a misery far amplified by the steam and stifle in her ethereal resumption under newly humidified environs. Afternoon showers had been scarce that season, most of the accumulative rainfall occurring during the wee morning hours. Typically, then, with the sands likely to be sere again by midday, training would be accompanied—as always—by a swell of dusty grit that served to encrust one's ears and nostrils like mineral deposits on an old spigot. It would fill boots; it would fill trousers; it would bestrew every anatomical crevice with chafing abrasiveness. It would, in fact, make the mêlée seem like a day at the beach in the *only* sense of the metaphor that was insufferable.

Even so, rain was almost always a welcomed diversion, especially any shower that could force a recess in the routine.

Resuming his nomadic jaunt upon the drizzly field, Wagner was reminded of the artificial cloudburst induced for him and Balgor back in Skol's enclosure the prior day. The association directed his thoughts onto Skol himself, which then disposed him to re-evaluate the scope of his decision of a few hours ago, a decision that did nothing if not validate Tamek's labelling of him as brash and reckless. His vivifying shunt of energies, this time delivered with equal measures of caution and conscious restraint, once more made vital what had been effete. The resulting efflorescence, as always, had been nothing if not phenomenal to behold, despite the potentially nocuous forfeiture of his own perpetuity. More so, one could not discount the tremendous physical risk of Wagner's playing Tyr to Skol's Fenrir. But, unlike that Asgardian god of myth who lost a hand for his troubles, Wagner remained for all purposes intact, and was left free to ponder—and perhaps to second-guess and maybe even to fret—the consequences to be wrought of his compelment. Having watched what they'd presumed had been a crestfallen and frustrated *Voknor* leaving Skol's cell, the barely touched glohular crock tucked in his arm, the small-minded guards hadn't the merest inkling of Skol's metamorphosis, nor of his new prognosis. And if Wagner had them accurately pegged, they were unlikely to have peered into the murky cell with any more than a rushed, obligatory glance now and then, and probably not even that. Balgor, however, would be another matter entirely, for Wagner had little doubt that the realmson would "totally freak" when the two of them paid their visit to the new and improved Skol that evening. Yet, along with the restoration, Wagner had attempted something more novel with Skol as well; and from what he'd observed post-revivification, he'd appeared to have effected the consequences that he'd desired. Where said deed might lead them from there, he had little more than a nascent blueprint. As always, the significance in his actions revealed itself but one veil at a time, in a cryptic guise that was generally periodical, but seldom punctual, and never straightforward. It was much like a ship's view of a coastal vista materialising from out of a fog: first, but an outline rendered vague within the mist; then, the lazy emergence of form and structure, followed by colours, details, intricacies, and finally—hopefully—the utter recognition of locale. But even if he was indeed drawing closer every day to the shores of explanatory reward, Wagner knew that his strange odyssey was fathoms from over—and even farther from making sense.

Fortunately for the sun-scorched gladiator crowd, a light drizzle coolly pelted the palaestra for the remainder of the afternoon. Wagner, continuing to insinuate himself into the various skirmishes upon the field, thought deeply about the content of Tamek's and J'nea's exchange, and he wondered whether the Sentinel may not have had something in mind with his equating Wagner with two of the Ergosians' most celebrated rogues. Juthac of Orrd and Mirko of Vargath—Wagner knew precious little of the former other than the fact of his demise; but as for the wily Vargathian, plenteous were the tales of his exploits. They circulated throughout the camp in vicarious and provocative retellings. Gamühr's versions were by far the best of the lot; in fact, the greatest harvest of camp folklore was seeded by the energy of her spirited narratives. Her take on Mirko evidenced a man with a varied repertoire of valour, forthrightness, insubordinate zeal, and downright bawdiness. He and his ragtag army of insurgents had acted as autonomous agents in this war—much to the bile of the Ergosian military hierarchy—and were unquestionably the greatest bane to the NuRacs, who had lost an immeasurable number of troops by way of some cleverly devised tactics of infiltration and attrition that made any NuRac's venturing about under even a secured forest canopy an often lethal endeavour. A unique and independent unit, the Vargathian's complement consisted almost exclusively of Ergosian victims—those indelibly wronged by the NuRac campaign. Embittered widows, widowers, orphans, the survivors of various massacres, any amputee capable of wielding a bludgeon, and every lusty combatant who had no use for the bureaucracy of the formal military (or *it*, no use for *him*)—these and more accounted for Mirko's followers, Mirko who himself had rejected his one-time officer's rank, declared the military command a "circus of self-indulgent hypocrites," and went on to create a self-contained militia that engaged the enemy free of the grinding wheels of state and commonwealth, while still remaining true to the creeds of the Ergosian people. A bold move it was, frowned upon by some and admired by equally as many. Even Balgor, at the end of his battle-imposed convalescence, ultimately broke rank with the army to seek out and join his old Vargathian boonfellow, participating for many years in Mirko's raids and sorties until his inconvenient capture—and impressment into QieLahr—by NuRac forces.

The bulk of Wagner's peers clearly harboured for Mirko's freedom-fighters the type of respect that would be the envy of any authority-backed command, possibly even the Sentinel's itself—purportedly the most-high authority there was. Bucking the system had particularly undeniable appeal, attributable perhaps to the unbreakable human spirit; and the notion of a band of apparently reckless and undisciplined underdogs, throwing themselves into the fray of unbeatable odds, was one that a group of haggard and wearied prisoners wished to relate to, and identify with, even as insight may have suggested that its appeal stemmed more from the dramatic exemplar than from any conscious inclination towards sedition. To the ordinary national, challenging the NuRac colossus by ungoverned, discretionary assailing was a desirable thing—*regardless*. Any perceived, undermining threat to the more prudent and regimented establishments of Ergosian church and state was a negligible afterthought that seemed hardly relevant.

Yet, to those affected by the consequences of rebellion, it was very real indeed. Revenge had a frightful way of snowballing, with each retributive act on the rebels' part annexing the atrocity of its predecessor. For this reason, Mirko and Juthac—in proclaiming themselves exempt from the red tape of scriptural guidelines and from any passion-dispelling benefit of strategic caucusing—had too often been perceived as mad dogs, as rogue warriors in uncontrolled spin. Their secret raiding parties stoked the wrath of NuRacs who, in finding no means of striking back, revenged themselves on innocent Ergosian villages, which in turn prompted further retaliatory assaults, and thus perpetuated the cycle of violence. And, although Tamek dispraised many of Mirko's tactics (Juthac and a good number of his closest compeers having fallen to a massacre late the previous year), it was all too obvious that the NuRacs had it on their agenda to sack every Ergosian hamlet and shire in the realm anyway, whether possessed of some feebly cited recriminatory excuse or not.

In the end, what it all came down to was methodology. This was what Tamek questioned most, although in his linking of Wagner to these others of unconventional Ergosian ilk did he reveal a methodology of his own, no less exploitative than that of those whom he would condemn. Allowing that he at least understood Wagner's reluctance in revealing his mystical talents, it was possible that Tamek discerned an arguably selfish attitude in that reluctance that, for him, aligned Wagner kindredly with both Juthac and the Vargathian. The same, then, went with their shared impulsiveness. Heroes, outlaws, or merely spirited men in the dregs of their patience—Tamek would surely have conceded that such reckless patriots were needed as much as any other; they were the instigators, the chance takers, those whose backhanded spontaneity touched off the powder kegs of change. And, as change itself was too frequently an expletive in Tamek's "stodgy" canon of traditionalism, Wagner's publicly aired inclusion in the company of these men might very well have been the Sentinel's camouflaged plea for radical action by someone who excelled at it, *from* someone whose moral structure provided few such avenues. Given the level of the Sentinel's intelligence and sacerdotal insight, he knew too well the limitations placed upon him by his faith. His sole duty had been in protecting the priests at Vishkor, a task he'd just barely accomplished as the city itself crumbled. His ethical code was well established within the bounds of scripture. He was guardian to the weak, a stalk among sprigs, his staunchness providing moral foundation to those around him. His fidelity to his deities gave him a means for converting chaos into form, for shaping errant minds and for buttressing those in the midst of falter. Both shrewd and lofty, devoutly narrow yet so very imaginative from within those confines, Tamek remained a man overtly uncorrupted by cowardice; but as his inclination to action was too often curbed at the dogmatic stratum, he'd developed a congenial but puissant flare for manipulative counsel that he managed subjectively to justify. Strewing spiritual seedlings upon fertile ground was easy, but tilling unaccommodating soil required special effort; and had Wagner interpreted the Sentinel's words accordingly, he'd have recognised the plea for what it seemed to be: a request for the same brand of distasteful recklessness that might stretch the limits and help to spur change, implied in the only manner that Tamek's position could allow without a blatant, ethical breach.

Wagner, of course, was way ahead of him in that respect—and perhaps *too* far at that. Where he trod he had neither tether, harness, nor safety net. Yet, were he to be successful in initiating that which Tamek (and his own revisited mind-trips) suggested of him, its consequence might be repercussive enough to compel the Sentinel and the others into measures purely reactive and utilitarian in nature, thereby ushering the Ergosians' last, best shot at freedom while vindicating their Sentinel of direct responsibility. Granted, such a recipe didn't bode well for the "cook," and, in fact, it had the potential for disaster as far as Wagner was concerned, with the likelihood of his being branded as scapegoat and fall guy in the wake of a scheme that could easily collapse into ruin like a bad soufflé. But, with inexplicable gut feelings and mind-trip imagery so disproportionately influential over an ignorance that, in its own defence, was blissfully redeeming if not inconvenient, Wagner was ever game to see what adventure lay beyond the walls of incarceration. And somehow it bothered him that Fostoch might have beaten him to it.

With the evening came quitting time, and after supping came the momentous jaunt through the substructure corridor. Balgor in tow, Wagner had been unsuccessful the entire day in finding the perfect, idle moment in which to prepare the realmson for what he was about to see. With the deed already quite irrevocable and after the fact, however, Wagner deemed it just as well to serve it up cold.

It was a tack that proved evocative if nothing else. Even in the pervading twilight of the cell, Balgor was quick to recognise the change in Skol, in his bearing and in his more galvanic response to their presence.

"*Bones and entrails!*" he cried, stumbling back towards the door. "The brute is whole! By what means—?"

Wagner stood by. "Must've been a really potent batch of glohular, I guess."

Balgor's face demonstrated textbook incredulity. Eyes scanning furiously, he mapped the hairy host from head to arms to heavily fettered torso to oaken legs in shackle at the ankles. Skol was robust and hardy, like Samson, who—his seven locks restored—stood bound between the pillars at Gaza, ready to bring down the house.

"*Voknor*, tell me you did not do this!"

Suddenly, the words, "*I Huungrrry!*" issued simply and matter-of-factly from Skol's maw like a toddler's self-important exigence, catching both men entirely unawares.

Balgor went bug-eyed while Wagner looked as if he wanted to shout *Eureka!* In the rodomontade of a triumphant *I told you so.* Instead of setting the food down— as per routine—and allowing the guards to release the brute once they'd exited, Balgor unthinkingly, almost automatically, suspended his bucket of renderings before the entreating beast, and stepped back as Skol zestfully, almost brutally, devoured of its contents.

"He *speaks*, *Voknor*. And not with mimicry, but with intent! I—I stand confounded."

Although still encrusted and caespitose, Skol's furry hide seemed fuller, almost vibrantly so, and his eyes no longer retained the glassiness so diagnostic of his weakened state. Not quite cover material for a Nice 'n Easy advertisement (unless, of course, Clairol was considering unveiling a line of Halloween products), he appeared to be invigorated and inviolate and extraordinarily on the mend. *This was more the nefarious terror of Balgor's legends*, the intimidatingly crazed powerhouse, slaughterer of countless innocents. Only, somehow, it wasn't really that same being—not exactly, not anymore. Familiarity always had a way of altering perceptions; and, discounting Skol's present robustness, tending him as they had in his enervation had revealed subtle gradations of grey where previously there had been only black and white. Clearly, they'd determined that Skol was no evil marauder from some obscure circle of hell. He was no mindless automaton of teeth and talons. What he *was*, however, was a heinously feral child-thing who somehow transcended the boundaries of genetics, and who seemed more the product of a bizarre melding of entities whose uncommonly brutish and inexorable natures were the stuff of traditional myth. Enkidu crossed with the Windigo of Native American lore, the yeti of the Himalayas merged with the infantile Hulk of comicdom—these and any of a thousand chimaeras and demigods, from a thousand more odes and legends, offered innumerable variables for the composite of Skol's pedigree. In essence, he was an inimitable being whose existence could likely be traced back to origins decidedly mutant in quality. How else to explain away this biological conundrum that stood before them, voraciously gulping swill like a pie gobbler at the county fair?

"By what madness did you come to restore him, *Voknor*?" The realmson had not moved a step since passing the bucket to their savage ward.

"Actually, it was more an experiment in stimulation than one of restoration."

"Oh, indeed," said Balgor, revealing in his tone his inability to distinguish between the two.

"There *is* a difference," Wagner insisted. "Y'see, this morning, right away, I found it next to impossible to smear the glohular where it needed to go. It would have been too tedious, too intricate, too dangerous. So, I kind of toyed with the idea of maybe utilising these creepy abilities of mine to energise Skol's metabolism—just a tad, mind you—to sort of jump-start his system, give it a boost, a crutch, to aid it in getting a one-up on the infection."

"I would say that you surpassed your intentions."

"Yeah, maybe. But give me a break! This was the first time that I ever tried—I don't know—to *temper* the flow. I'm still learning this crazy gimmick, Balgor, and maybe a little more ectoplasm or an extra pinch of psychic joy-juice slipped by than I really wanted to. But, believe me, although what you see may be a healthier Skol, he is definitely not Skol at the top of his form. Healing him whole would have probably wiped me out, and would have made him a lot more scary."

"*Drrrink!*" Skol demanded.

"Already he's starting to sound like his Uncle Balgor at the ale house," said Wagner, springing forward to deliver the water bucket. Skol, lacking any gratitude, promptly upturned the pail, flooded his gullet with a good decilitre of chaser, and followed it all with the customary keg-party belch.

"Does this reanimating of the greatest scourge of my people serve any purpose other than to exercise and define the limits of your fledgling sorcery?" asked Balgor, his drollery only barely veiling a need to probe the unexcavatable dig that was Wagner's mind.

"Skol is a tool," said Wagner. "He's a living weapon, implemented against your people by your true scourge—the NuRacs. And he is one extra-powerful tool—deadly vicious and cruel. But with the advent of SyKrahvo's uncovering of that Soork thingy, our NuRac friends suddenly couldn't care less about him."

"Ah, but not you. You feel pity, and thus have decided to rescue him from a long deserved death, thinking that he will somehow know to be in your debt?"

"Hardly. I told you that he's a tool. And when old tools are discarded for new ones, they often find their way into the hands of desperate people. *We* are desperate people."

"I am not *that* desperate."

"Maybe not. But *I* am."

"And so you would put us all back in jeopardy by snatching this brute from hell's gate?"

"Hopefully not," said Wagner, gathering up the empty buckets. "It's the prison itself that I want in jeopardy—the prison, the guards, the whole of QieLahr."

"And one untameable savage will accomplish all of this for you?"

"Not exactly. He's going to need our help."

The realmson gazed dumbly at his earthling brother.

"That's right," said Wagner, offering up a mischievous grin. "You and me and Baby Huey make three."

CHAPTER TWENTY-TWO

It is through disobedience
that progress has been made.
  —OSCAR WILDE

Word had filtered down that the prison caravan, which normally arrived within the first week after the tournament, had been delayed in the field. Having set off some weeks before—mere days after unloading Wagner's group—with a fresh rotation of soldiers, vrohdas, and trusties, by now the drays would surely have been bloated with backfilling gladiators for replenishing the camp's depleted ranks. Business as usual no longer "usual" in the traditional sense, with SyKrahvo's forces now out on the offensive, the number of free Ergosians to be scattered by siege and severed from their pillaged hamlets in the army's wake was sure to be considerably more whelming than in campaigns past. Marathoner foot-couriers typically keeping the intelligence current between QieLahr and the field, a paucity of privileged communiqués—acquired surreptitiously by Bilahdu's sources—revealed that several additional detachments had been dispatched to the sites of some particularly fruitful vanquishings in order to round up and incarcerate prisoners under temporary cordon until supplementary drays could arrive.

Wagner was glad that J'nea was on the "home" stint of her rotation, and this not strictly due to the contingent nature of the plot that he was hatching. What he felt was personal and selfish. Their exchanges, however curt at times, were always invigorating, and served to ground him in the kind of straight-shooting relevance that engaged his wits—and his chemistry—in healthy exertion. He appreciated this, convinced himself that there existed a friendship somewhere within the tumult of their verbal volleying, an occasional syzygy in the otherwise meteoric clashing of his and her conceptual orbits. The two of them were both dissimilar and alike, dissentient yet just as often in sync. Like the moon, she seemed ever in phase, ever transitory, as if perpetual flux was her only real constant; while Wagner—the former crowning champ of involuntary flux—had always sought the static and the uneventful in an existence unfairly rigged for peril and adventure. And if he was the least bit like the moon, it was purely in the etymological sense, somewhere deep within the derivative link between lunar and lunacy. Granted, he'd once experienced a "phasing" that was all his own, but it was far more likely that corporeal shifting had less to do with things cislunar than it did with the grander cosmic scheme. And as for personal constants, he would no longer have even dared to declare one of any kind. Although permutation was, and had been, the conquering force in his life, over the years it had proven itself too cruel a despot, forever hurling hardship after hardship in his path; and should he ever have presumed to deem instability itself as his constant, right then would the fireworks cease, would the ride come to a gripping halt, would topsy-turvy become upright, and respite overtake turmoil—as if to prove him wrong yet again. He'd been dumped off on Ergos like an unwanted litter-runt, left answerless and abandoned in the remote exile of unfamiliar territory, and sentenced to piece together a new (and no less sorry) existence for himself. He was allowed latitude in discovery and acclimation, but only until his interim of reintegration into what he'd initially perceived to be a realm of more normal physics had sufficiently lulled, appeased, and pacified him into a marginally settled complacence—whereby the next paranormal roundhouse generally clobbered him upside the head, with a new slew of rules and considerably anted stakes.

Balgor had slept the night on Wagner's latest revelation, but found it tricky to fully accept the deliberate recklessness so inherent in Wagner's actions. Recruiting one's enemy to aid in defeating the greater foe was one thing, but enlisting a gargoyle of such unremorseful and unconscionable cruelty as Skol was akin to unleashing a night-hound into one's own village to eliminate an unruly band of brigands. How does a wild predator distinguish between an undesirable ruffian and an honourable citizen? Or an innocent child? Furthermore, just how does one simmer down a rampaging beast once its task is accomplished?

Granted, Balgor's take on Skol had wrestled with unsolicited reconsideration in recent days, for it was increasingly difficult to sustain an intense loathing for an entity after once identifying the external impetuses responsible for said entity's horrid proclivities. Worse still was finding the beast worthy of some tiny mote of sympathy. If it was more Skol's résumé of heinousness—and not the brute himself—that the realmson reviled, then how might Balgor reconcile the callous and malicious slaughter of so many fallen comrades with the discovery that the mighty Sunderer seemed, in actuality, to be more aberrant simpleton than personified evil?

At breakfast, Wagner flagged down J'nea and grilled her for any knowledge that she may have possessed on the caravan's status. Shrugging, she told him that, while seven additional drays had been sent out behind the army's precedence, no supplementary trusties had been approached or impressed into service with them. Beyond this, no one knew rumour from reality, intention from indefiniteness.

Lack of field intelligence wouldn't adversely affect Wagner's machinations. In fact, as he saw it, the lengthier the delay with the caravan, the fewer people there would be to extract from the camp come zero hour. Nothing too unexpected lying in immediate loom, he would nevertheless make effort not to discount any possible contingency. For the moment, then, he occupied himself in the crafting of what he hoped would be the last stratagem that he'd ever need to devise for paving his way to freedom. Here, perhaps, was where his behaviour finally bore acute similarity to J'nea's, albeit not so much in the manner of fluctuations and attitudes as in purpose. One might have described him as result-oriented, but only in the matters that he himself deemed crucial; when a particular notion struck him, whether it hailed from a natural evolution of thought or from a resurging blast of mind-tripping recall, habitually he would abandon any unfinished business in favour of diverting his undivided resources along the new avenue. It was a penchant he'd demonstrated with the business of his and Balgor's first escape attempt, and even earlier with his rejection of the "Ergos-as-juxtaposition-over-reality" concept that he'd theorised during the incipient stages of his displaced life. But even more than a mere measurement of his resolve, he'd often benefited from a quick and dirty accrual of subconscious indicators of which few others could boast. Although the most gainful of these—instinct—may frequently have yanked him from the brink, he could hardly ignore its more subtle sibling—intuition—and the cache of percipient influences existing well beyond the intuitive. Through these he'd come to sense a disparate, pivotal inevitability in his actions, like that of an event horizon long presaged and indivertible in its unfolding. More recently, he'd gained a somewhat natal mastering over the anxieties that these renascent and milder versions of his old mind-trippings might once have stirred in him. Having a bit of the Ergosian experience under his belt, able now to decipher once-bewildering allegory with a more learned eye, psychologically better equipped to grasp and process what he underwent internally—Wagner toyed with the circuitous argument that maybe nothing that he sensed, both presently and months ago, was or had been strictly oracular at all. The mental package, in its formidable entirety, felt oddly more akin to the rekindled memories of actions and incidents previously befallen than it did mere foreshadowing. He knew this was impossible; but the sensation of it existed just the same. In peeling away the borders and barriers, it cast him as a kind of grizzled traveller who unknowingly chances to retrace a pathway once wended in his long ago youth, and who, in responding to the incessant pokes and jabs of mnemonic indicators all clamouring to convey relevance, gradually comes to realise the revisiting. Only, Wagner's memories—alternately magnanimous and miserly in their accommodation—saddled him with an extra, paradoxical step that, in its solving, could conceivably grant him the key to understanding it all. Until that elucidative moment, however, his was the task of unriddling events that chronologically had yet to take place, but which somewhere, *sometime*, had already occurred within a mind whose consciousness retained but a jumbled sampler of its former, prophetic riches.

Shortly after breakfast, having made Skol's gruel delivery, Wagner and Balgor both took a deliberating moment to more deeply scrutinise the convalesced beast at length. Skol ate heartily, drew breath regularly and robustly, stood taller and more ominously potent than any being who'd been in such dire shape a short day prior had the right to. Arrow wounds virtually gone, vitality regained, barring his truss and his shackles he was good to go—free to resume his arena duties of murder and mayhem. What irony, that his days as a NuRac inflictor were at end. Skol's contract was being insidiously acquired by a new party, an enterprising proselyte of desperate measures whose intent it was to fashion a future from the brute's backstairs bourgeon. Skol was a red, ripe pepper, ready to be snapped from the bush and added to Wagner's recipe of revolt. And at full strength, such a pepper would give any revengeful dish real bite.

"So, *Voknor*, what exactly is your scheme *this* time?" Balgor asked as they waited for their bristly protégé to finish his meal.

"Why? Are you thinking of lending a hand?"

Balgor laughed. "It is a certainty that you will coerce me into abetting you, regardless of my intentions. For the nonce, however, I believe a modicum of foresight may be in my best interest."

Wagner concealed his smugness in the shadows. He knew the realmson couldn't have stayed mad at him for long.

"Well, you *do* want out of this camp," he said. "Right?"

"Equally as do you."

"Then, you have to know that it will never happen without some degree of sacrifice. All-inclusive as we may wish it to be, by trying to save everyone we run the risk of dooming ourselves in the process. A comprehensive endeavour like that would be far too complex to pull off without calculated losses. And it's pretty obvious that Tamek thinks the same—isn't that what you got out of his little sermon yesterday?"

"He feels laden by his responsibility."

"Exactly. You see, with SyKrahvo on the loose with that Soork gizmo, Tamek now wants out of here as badly as we do. Maybe more so. Yet, he won't initiate anything himself because, here he is, saddled with a pretty unrelenting ball and chain."

"A *what*?"

Wagner sighed. "Okay, imagine the Ergosian population in camp as this huge iron ball shackled to Tamek's ankle. His people are so precious to him that he's taken on their burden as his own. And as such, they have in a sense become his greatest liability. By caring for them, he's made himself vulnerable. The NuRacs see it, and they play up this angle to the max. They make political sport of him. Whenever he argues for human rights, or for an end to the gladiator franchise, they throw him in the dungeon and continue to do whatever they want. It's been this way for months, probably years. And now, while they're using a mystical relic to declare war on the entire realm, he can't bring himself to abandon the comparative handful to whom he's tethered his loyalties. A man of his character would never willingly take a rasp to that ball and chain of humanity, because he views himself as spiritual mentor to your people. Yet, in turn, he suffers the consequences of limited mobility and almost zero volition. Such crushing responsibility to the prison populace prevents him from being the warrior that he is—and I bet he's a damned good one. But, with this kind of onus hobbling his independence, he can't act rashly or recklessly without putting the flock, and therefore himself, in danger. I have a pretty good idea that this was probably the same dilemma he faced back when Vishkor came under attack, when his duty had been in ushering the high priests to safety. My money says that he would rather have been out there kicking some NuRac butt."

"Perhaps," said Balgor. "Allegiance and duty seldom allow for the latitudes of passion. But, how is it that you interpret the Sentinel's inability to act on his true desires as license to breathe new life into our overly hirsute friend, here? I still fail to understand how restoring an unruly and bloodthirsty child-monster is going to procure our freedom."

"It sounds ludicrous, I know. Let's just say that I've logged a lot of miles by relying on my instincts. What I've got in mind isn't as frivolous as it may seem. You need to look at it *my* way. You need to view Skol as a hopeful piece of leverage—say, a single hazarding of the dice in a realm-sized game of bigratto."

"Ah, but simple dice cannot maim a man."

"Yeah, well, you know what I always say: 'Life without risk smothers the spirit, and leads the soul to the files of the dead—'"

"'—that none may e'er to hearken its piquant yearnings unfulfilled.'" Balgor chimed in resignedly, duly impressed by his friend's levelling of his own words against him.

Wagner, cracking a sly grin, taxied between smugness and semi-humbled modesty for having committed Balgor's little maxim to memory.

"All I'm saying," he said, "is that if nobody—not even Tamek—can initiate a revolt where every Ergosian will emerge intact, why not settle for one with the best odds we can give it? Like Tamek, I empathise with, and *pity*, everyone in this dump. But, I'm savvy enough to realise that I can't save the whole freakin' world. To think *that* way is to be deadlocked in every single choice you want to make. In my thinking, if we come up with a way to free, say, nine out of ten people, I'll feel pretty good about it. Heck, if we can only get one-half of the Ergosians beyond the walls, isn't even *that* worth it if there's a chance that we can help save the rest of your nation?"

"And what if you are not among those who successfully obtain their freedom?"

Wagner gestured reluctant but good-natured humility. "Touché," he said. "I never said there'd be guarantees, not even for me—only an opportunity for as many people as possible. I believe that if we plan this properly, we can at least provide a shot at liberty for just about everyone—those in the infirmary, the kitchens, the textilery, even the detention block—while the NuRacs have their hands full with every distraction that we, and Skol, can provide."

"And what of treachery, *Voknor*? What of the traitors within our own ranks, whose secret allegiances have been purchased with NuRac blood money? The moment that we convey news of a camp-wide uprising, one of these spurious dogs will surely betray us."

"Not to worry, my friend."

"And why not?"

"Because we won't be providing any advance notice."

"*Bones and entrails*! I suppose, then, that one afternoon, in the midst of training, we will simply snap our fingers in unison and everyone will suddenly be of one mind, and commence to scaling the walls. This is not like our little three-man escape, *Voknor*."

"Still, it's the surest way. In *that* caper, by recruiting unproven kinspeople beforehand, we would've increased the chance for perfidy and betrayal, right? With something this much bigger, to bring the camp in on it would multiply the risk of betrayal a hundredfold. Instead of explaining our intent to everyone, instead of trying to organise and prepare them with exact times and coordinates, we may as well just walk ourselves over to the dungeon block and climb down to our cells—the end result would be about the same. Any way you look at it, Balgor, it's gonna be risky. So, what it really comes down to is my faith in our fellow prisoners versus my faith in—well—my *faith*. Y'see, something in my psychical history, or my prescience, or whatever it is that acts as my intuitive compass, tells me that this is possible, that a 'cold-call to arms' can really work, despite how it appears on the drawing board. There's a means to accomplish it, Balgor, and successfully at that. If I can just work with Baby Huey, here, for another day or so, we might just be able to spring this whole shebang on the camp—even onto those who don't wish it—and free a considerable chunk of the population in the process. And since Tamek won't be able to beat himself up over it, his conscience will be clear to confront this situation with SyKrahvo and the resurgence of—of—*what* did he call it?"

"Sortilege?"

"Yeah—and the resurgence of sortilege in the realm, any way that he sees fit."

Balgor stood silently, his face a-twitch with the nervous gesticulating of a man hip-deep in cogitation. "Think you," he finally said, "that this will please Tamek, to launch the entire camp unwarily into a do-or-die recontré?"

"Pleasing him isn't really my priority," said Wagner as he gathered up Skol's empties. The brute, near enough to seize him but astonishingly uninterested, instead worked at preening his pelage for the edible morsels of stew that, in his zeal, he'd drooled and dribbled across his frontage. "I know Tamek likes to be the big cheese in any act of insurgence or escape," he continued, "just as he was with ours. Only, he'd never condone *this* type of scheme. He telegraphed this much to me yesterday. However, I'm convinced that he wants somebody—notably *me*—to initiate something that, once in motion, must be pursued to the end. It's the only way that he can be absolved."

"Why *you* specifically?"

"For one, he lumped me together with Juthac and Mirko—and I didn't interpret the comparison as just a trivial reference. For another, the whole notion of it jibes with what my envisioning persona and my big, bad 'inner warrior' have both been striving to tell me. Somehow, I feel that I've been through it all before. And, conversely, I see myself experiencing it again for the first time in some kind of historical-cum-portent reverie. That, or I've been viewing it through the eyes of someone else, someone who's either already lived it, or has yet to. Granted, it might be a deception, a déjà vu upon which I'm constructing the platform of a fool's salvation...but somehow I don't think so."

Balgor rapped for the guard. "You are a mysterious fellow," he said with a calmness twice removed from misdoubt. "And you become more so the longer that I am in your acquaintance."

"If it's any consolation," said Wagner, "I'm probably more bewildered than you are."

"Aye, perhaps—but the day is yet young."

So it was, that Wagner, in parting with his friend, persuaded the guards to allow him a follow-up to his deceptive nursemaiding of the ever-neglected Sunderer. Indeed, to reinforce his intent, he made sure that the warders saw both the glohular crock *and* the faux finger-scoops that he'd sculpted into the balm in order to give the illusion that he'd been drawing liberally from the gallipot. In fact, he was careful not to waste too much of Olask's precious commodity needlessly.

The handful of sentries on the early shift, though consisting largely of the same revolving faces for days at a time, included a few new but familiar NuRacs upon this morning, and so much the better for Wagner's designs. He absorbed the brunt of their insults with the measure of menial cordiality necessary to shroud his furtiveness; he fielded their boorish digs that portrayed him as Skol's maidservant, his mate, or his next meal; and he allowed himself to be shut away with the creature for the forty minutes or so that the warders felt was reasonable for the task. Fortunately, none paid any great deal of attention to the brute himself. Their lot of being stationed so far from the sublimity of day, and from the hub of regimental limelight—where the odds of one's being noticed and advanced by a superior far outweighed those of serving in this literal obscurity—resulted in attitudes conducive only to the lacklustre and the bellicose. Skol's stench, his grotesque aspect, the redundant nature of guarding a thick-witted monster day after day—each was a factor that, on its own, provided argument enough for their leaving the behemoth to his dark and solitary existence when there was dicing, swaggering, and base storytelling to be enjoyed without. And Skol, who knew no better, was apparently content in not having to endure the perennial sneering and repulsion on the faces of these comparatively weak and hairless and frail beings whom he would crush like brittle twigs if given the briefest of opportunities.

Yet, in fascinating contrast, the brute's perception of Wagner must have fallen into a uniquely challenging category. In the company of *this* frail being, more pallid than the others but far less baleful, Skol may well have accepted said scrawny benefactor within the benignity of a gradually earned tolerance. It was a seemingly unnatural truce between predator and prey, an armistice wrought of reciprocity in a manner not unlike that of the crocodile and the plover, where the huge reptile allows the tiny bird to perch upon its back—and sometimes within its very maw—to feed on its parasites or to work stray foodstuffs from its jagged choppers. Yet, whatever compensation the puny visitor sought to gain from the fraternity, Skol remained unconcerned so long as the viands kept coming. Occasionally, too, when his synapses fired just so, Skol may even have recalled that this fragile being had summoned the "glow" that took away his pain; and through this nod of resurfacing gratitude—if that was a suitable term—the brute's mental chemistry was able to appropriately and astoundingly turn aside his aggressive propensities. Thus, although his harness and his chains limited the degree of any potential violation of their unspoken treaty, while in Wagner's presence Skol failed to demonstrate overwhelming inclination to do him harm.

Furthering his experimentation into gaining Skol's trust, Wagner maintained the pleasing voice tones that seemed to put the Sunderer most at ease—speaking slowly, melodically, solicitously, to better connect and establish a footing in the murky realm of Skol's underrated aptitude. Back at Howsley, he'd seen enough of the psychology in dealing with disadvantaged minds to garner confidence in taking his own stab at it now; but he knew he hadn't the convenience of time to ethically develop, nurture, and coax the results he needed. He sensed instead that he'd be exploiting Skol in much the same way that the NuRacs did, although he truly hoped that his actions would be better justified by the common good that he expected would stem from them. A sin of necessity, he would reserve some future date for his atonement and penance, a kind of "buy now, self-reproof later" promotion whose intent was to save more lives than it doomed. Fate had given him a framework to build upon. His mind-trips had provided the visual mock-ups. Impression and impulse told him which pieces of the puzzle to position, and where to place them. So, if he was to suddenly allow a guilty conscience to assume control, wouldn't he effectively thwart everything that destiny had in store for him? Wouldn't he then simply remain AuwNiir's property, continue to endure abuse from Grum and the guards, and eventually succumb to an untimely demise in the Great Arena under the fangs and claws of some big, bad ugly with a brain the size of a walnut? Worse, what if Skol himself was fated to be his slayer in some imminent tournament beyond the unseeable pall of tomorrow? Would his last living moments be spent in rue of the knowledge that he'd rejected the one, available chance to employ the beast in forcing an end to Ergosian captivity? Was this not for Skol's own good as well?

What he accomplished in that forty minutes time remained strictly between him and the brute. It was a time for discovery, for pressing past boundaries as yet unchallenged, for furthering negotiations between behavioural science and paranormal versatility. Whatever eerie potency had so ensconced itself within Wagner's human shell, it existed for his bidding as equally as *he* did for *its* mystical alchemy; and whatever subliminal tweaking had accompanied the previous day's restoration, he couldn't allow it to be wasted. Yet, despite the recondite Überforce that lay at the root of his magiks, Wagner suspected that his ultimate reward for wielding the unknown might be anything but wondrous in the long run. In every morality tale of the sort, whenever the Devil bargains for a soul, even the cleverest of the inevitably damned discovers that Satan's fiendish contract abounds in inescapable pitfalls. As Wagner stood ignorant, however, of any such covenant of his own—and with ignorance thus completing his trio of attendant genii (of which instinct and intuition were constituent)—he would continue muddling his way through the mental darkwood that so cryptically represented his purpose on Ergos. And, in a roundabout way, that incomprehension, vexing and inconvenient as it was, provided for him a hastily fitted grace of unaccountability should he have chosen to pervert truth in this manner. But, admittedly suspect and sophistic in its justification, he was unable to adopt such a stance. Ignorance was more than just a scurvy boy-child clutching the hem of some Dickensian Spirit's mantle; it was a sign-post pointing to where knowledge was lacking, a means to its very own demise, and Wagner would follow the trail until the knowledge he sought was his, and ignorance itself lay trampled under the muddied footprints of his lifelong inquisition.

On the palaestra, Wagner fought that day like he'd fought on no other, save for that pivotal fray in the ring against the Ennead. As with the advent of his and Balgor's first escape, his zeal and his confidence now soared like a young hawk upon a boding autumnal updraft. But they would not be accipitrine appendages that whisked him beyond QieLahr, nor the waxen feathers of desperate Greeks, but rather, wings fashioned of determination and providence—and just a dash of underhandedness.

Wagner's élan did not go unnoticed. Balgor and Bilahdu paused often in their own doings to observe his improved proficiency and dexterity, skills for which each insisted *his* tutelage be credited, while Uthok the Bonecrusher bided with friendly and mischievous intent for the rare opportunity to spar with a truly ravening opponent for once—and *Voknor* at that—rather than the standard fare of uninspired kinsmen whom he'd properly thrashed over the morning's course. Even

Tamek seized upon a moment where Wagner's signalling for the services of one of the waterers rendered him unoccupied and approachable enough to lend him a greeting and a reconciling stitch for the terseness that so threatened to unseam their affinities of late.

As the Sentinel stepped into Wagner's company, Lischi, a waifish girl of about twelve years whom Wagner and Balgor often entertained with faux bickering and homespun adventures, finished quenching Wagner and darted away to slake the scratch of other parched throats. Before racing off, however, she performed—as was customary for a child—something of a hasty curtsy in reverence to the estimable Sentinel, who in turn smiled approvingly, tousled her mop of dirty blonde hair with a stately hand, and sent her on her way.

"Well met, *Voknor*," he then said, stamping dust from his tunic. "By what I observe of your ferocity today, you appear to have found an ardent means of expelling your anxieties."

Wagner swooshed the last mouthful of water around his palate and swallowed rapidly. "Just honing my offensive skills a bit. It's like you guys taught me—a good defence is enough if the plan is just to stay alive, but an aggressive offence will gain ground and advantage."

"An aggressive *and disciplined* offence, *Voknor*. 'Tis imperative that one have both. Aggression without proper tempering is akin to leaping into the sea while clutching a boulder. The only victory you achieve is your isolation, and the only ground gained, an ocean bed with dooming waters billowing in o'erhead."

"Yeah, well, if I could pile on the imagery like you do, I wouldn't need an offence at all—I could just dazzle my foes with flowery metaphors."

A familiar and long-standing accusation by those closest to him, Tamek could do naught but shrug admittance to verbal festooning. Yet, he was quick to offer mitigating circumstances. "I defy anyone," he said, "to emerge from the seminary after an entire youth spent in study, and *not* show a proclivity towards ornamental phrasing."

Just then, from far across the yard, they caught the ample boisterousness of Grum's berating of some unfortunate gladiator. No day on the palaestra was complete without at least one such reprimanding; after all, quotas needed to be maintained in order for any respectable Taskmaster to retain his nefarious edge. Either too slovenly, too swathed in preoccupation, or deceitfully trying to milk the handicap of some fictitious injury—the errant prisoner had ushered himself straight to the top of Grum's abuse list, where he would assuredly remain throughout the day, much to the relief of the rest of the battling herd.

Wagner, chuckling briefly at the NuRac's usual dosage of clamorous and unreasonable candour, took this moment to ask Tamek if he'd reached any conclusion in regards to all that was bared to him the day before.

"I have given much thought to the entire past week's events," Tamek said, "and, like you, I have concluded that we needs must take action—e'en drastic measures—to save the realm ere SyKrahvo obliterates us all through bloodlust and insensibility."

Wagner was surprised. "Would it interest you to know that I have a plan?"

"'Twould dismay me immensely were I to hear that you had not been concocting at least *one* of your brazen schemes. No doubt this one is as rash and impetuous as those before it?"

"No doubt at all. But then, that kind of tactic worked best for Juthac and Mirko, didn't it?"

Tamek eyed him meticulously, a bit amused, a bit piqued. "Not always, no. But frequently did impetuosity dominate their spirits, while rationale was cast out of the fold. In the end, Juthac the Vulgar paid dearly for the o'erbalance. His demise, howe'er, rendered certain pertinent wisdoms to his surviving peer. The Vargathian has been far more prudent since."

"And less successful, from what I hear."

"Undeniably. Recklessness is a long-odds gamble whose remuneration can be great. Yet, as Juthac too late discovered, one poor gambit can be devastating. Mirko's newer penchant towards caution may indeed stave needless deaths, but I imagine the want of results is less than satisfying to him, along with a diminishment of the glory upon which he has always thrived."

Wagner scoffed. "Glory. Glory's an illusion. There's no glory in any of this."

Tamek smiled. "You speak with the profundity of the dismayed. Verily, at the very moment of our births, we all of us embark on paths of glory—glory in our rebirth, glory of the eternal wilderness, of experience and discovery, of our bindings to this world and to each other. Howe'er, we possess an unfortunate propensity for diminishing that glory o'er time with our actions and with the choices we make. My spirituality aids me in restoring that which I have lost. I have yet to gather what 'tis that aids *you*."

While Tamek pontificated, Wagner had been working to pry a prickling from the grip of his quarterstaff. Finally succeeding in dislodging it, he flicked it to the ground and ran his hand repeatedly over the notch as if he might smooth it. "Instinct," came his answer. "Instinct aids me. Spirituality may work for you— that's fine—that's your gig. But right now, I can't think of being at peace with my inner self while the rest of me is under NuRac lock and key. *You* know my thinking better than that. Spirituality isn't easy for me. I don't have the chip for it. And whatever mote of it I might unwittingly possess, it's got to take a back seat to freedom. Freedom is what needs restoring first."

Adopting a contemplative expression that signalled neither satisfaction nor disappointment, the Sentinel nodded and promised a reconvening of their conspiracy for later that evening. He then withdrew and allowed the bouncingly impatient Uthok an opportunity to spar with Wagner. Clearly, it hadn't been on Tamek's agenda to debate personal philosophies anyway. His visit had been more a referencing of mindsets, a checking-in of sorts with a rather unique comrade who just happened to be harbouring a realm's worth of unrefined magiks within his person. Whether spirituality truly made the hardships of physical bondage any more tolerable, or whether one's obsessing over a single goal was a kind of tunnel-visioned devotion in itself—these were questions to be argued on another day. Tamek's duty to his people had swelled of late to include the additional task of mentoring a fledgling wizard, one who happened to be a friend, and a man of dubious history, but who nevertheless demanded careful observing and a generous amount of structuring.

As for Wagner, Uthok's blinding frontal assault provided him with more challenge than did those of all his other partners that day combined. The scrappy

Ergosian was in every sense a battler, handing Wagner his lumps in the unbridled fashion of a vengeance-seeking barbarian who comes a-calling with the solitary intent of satisfying some ages-old vendetta. Only, with Uthok, there was no malevolent intent to consider or to fear, only a demonstrative outlet for a crude and lusty aptness towards roughhousing. Too, like Wagner and a few others, he possessed a keen predilection for the quarterstaff. Differing from the nodgers—which, to him, were but toyish replicas of *proper* weapons—a stave was a stave no matter how one perceived it. And should he have elected so, this deceivingly lubberish ruffian (with his seemingly innocuous weapon) had a means of besting even the most impressive of opponents who had the misfortune of opposing him.

Agile and evasive enough, but consciously no match for Uthok's powerful blows, Wagner reluctantly drew upon one of Balgor's favourite tactics in order to ransom a win. Undefeated thus far this day against all challengers, rather than risk breaking his streak he contrived to unseat the Bonecrusher by manipulating the strings of his concentration. In unscrupulous, realmson-like fourberie, between parries he began suggesting to Uthok how several of their peers believed, by the nature of J'nea's flirtation with him during the previous day's cloudburst, that she rather fancied Uthok. By so underhandedly engaging the one debility that few men could remain steadfast against—the primal sense of carnality—Wagner launched a loose and desirous cannonball across Uthok's subconscious milieu, enough to momentarily thwart even the staunchest combative impulse, and thus, open an avenue for Wagner's assail.

And he very nearly succeeded. With Uthok in wistful hesitation, Wagner suddenly lashed out with Vofspar-like swiftness, only to have the Ergosian casually sidestep him, thrust his quarterstaff into the hub of Wagner's locomotion, and send the trickster crashing groundward like a drunk from a bicycle.

"Impossible!" Uthok exclaimed as Wagner lay flat. "Fair and gracile though she may be, J'nea of Bejodeth is a saucy wench—and truly too quarrelsome and scrawny for a warrior of my prowess. Your rumour-mongers have misled you, *Voknor.*"

Wagner groaned, and surrendered to his humiliation. "I guess I ought to leave the gossip to Bilahdu," he mumbled as Uthok lent him leverage to get back on his feet. Swatting away the dusty evidence of his sprawl, he tried steering the conversation elsewhere. "Tell me, Uthok—do you have a wife on the outside? Children? Parents, maybe?"

"I...had a mate...*once*," he said, turning suddenly sombre.

"Once?"

"A comely maid, not terribly keen, but gentle, amiable, humble even. She left me for a masquer. She told me that I was cold and gruff, and too passionless in the ways of proper relations." He stood quiet for a moment, his face a slump of chagrin.

"Sorry," Wagner solaced.

"Fie! Who needs her anyway? I do well enough on my own."

"What about family? Do you have any?"

"My mother and father yet lived at the time of my capture. A brother, too. I have no means of knowing how they have fared since." The dialogue had moved on, yet Uthok's eyes continued to betray the lingering regret with his former mate.

"But we are hill people—my clan and I—and thus, very adept at eluding strangers and foes when necessary."

"Let's just hope that your kin are better at it than *you* were," said Wagner. "Tell me something, though—how much would you risk to get back to them?"

The Ergosian guffawed. "Nothing as extreme as what you and the realmson attempted. *That* is certain. Your indenturing to the gods is immense for the many reprieves that you have been meted by their grace. I would not wish to owe anyone so much."

Wagner signalled disregard. "Yeah, but we *do* have fun."

For the remainder of the afternoon, Wagner laced his sparring with bits of brainstorming, visiting and revisiting the dos, the don'ts, and the what ifs of scheming and subterfuge, while Uthok—and later, others—tried lightly to bash his brains in. With the opponents he knew best, he made inquiry similar to that asked of the Bonecrusher, polling, as one might have it, a sample of the population in order to obtain a random measure of camp sentiment since the last tournament and since the Soork demonstration that proceeded it. And for most, the pervading consensus was of their lost hope of ever stepping foot onto free soil again. Such feedback didn't sit well with Wagner. Desperation was what he sought, bitterness and resentment as well. Forlornness and resignation were hardly suited to a proper uprising.

Something more was needed.

Once the day had given up for evening, three men came to meet in the shadowed recesses of Barracks Five. Around them, much of the gladiator community was steeped in its last minutes of bantering and gaming, with an equal number of straw-nestled occupants vying with the stir and scramble for a drowsy escape from the day's drudgery. Few had serious eyes for the trio who had so often, and for so long, converged in that same nook to discuss what common knowledge deemed issues of covert nature. Likewise, few suspected that what the trio discussed might pre-emptively alter their lives without their solicited say-so. But, then again, the NuRacs had dictated their regimen for so long—just which rights were they that yet remained in the prisoners' possession to relinquish?

With Balgor present to verify the incredible, Wagner at first relayed to the Sentinel only the gist of his plan—a crumb here, a titbit there—to sate the pangs of a pressing curiosity. In the past, Tamek had always insisted on being informed of any significant occurrence about to take place within his domain because of its surety to affect those who were to be left behind; yet, despite this newer scheme's objective of not leaving *anyone* back, Wagner still believed that his pious friend would rather have remained ignorant of the ultra-specifics unless they contained actions that he would have considered ethically felonious or blasphemous. And since Wagner couldn't be certain that Tamek wouldn't have labelled his act of augmenting Skol as one or the other, he chose to conceal this particular truth, and instead ran through his spiel like Doc Adams hawking elixir, pitching just the right balance of factual fidelity and deceit, with Balgor nodding or shaking his head in the positive and negative sense of each claim. For the most part, it went over quite well. Omitting those pesky details of the brute's lingual competence and of his liberal convalescence, Wagner propounded his less controversial intentions, point by underplayed point. He intended a simultaneous freeing of the arena's fiercest ferals into the arena substructure. From there, he hoped to route them along the main corridor, away from the prison courtyard, and out onto the northern grounds, where lay the soldiers' billets. There, they would hopefully wreak enough chaos to force the NuRacs into expending the bulk of their available guards into chasing down and defending against the horde of emancipated beasties, leaving the Ergosians under but the most sparing of surveillances—where would lie their best opportunity to: 1) rise up against the few remaining warders; 2) rescue the wretches from the detention holds; 3) gather as many of the infirm as was possible; and 4) scuttle for the walls and the gates.

"And you seek to accomplish this without informing the populace beforehand?" asked Tamek. "Our side would suffer the same chaos encountered by our gaolers."

"With a little bit of manipulation, that chaos can work to our advantage. And that's where you come in. Because of the grave potential for treachery, we need to have as few people in on this as is possible, and *I* don't know who to trust. *You* do."

"How—how many confidants do you require?"

Wagner looked expectantly at the realmson. "Well, Balgor and I will see to the matter of the animals running amok. There are guards we'll need to eliminate, keys we'll need to filch, a host of cells to be opened, and at least one inner portcullis that will require lowering in order to prevent the stampede from heading back our way."

"Such simple matters you cannot perform on your own?" quipped the realmson.

"However," Wagner continued, "back here, in the camp, you'll need to enlist the aid of some runners, Tamek—people who, at the proper time, can alert the prisoners to the uprising in progress. As messengers, whoever you pick will need to be swift and convincing, because not only will they have to alert the kitchen, the textilery, the infirmary, and such, but they'll have to be able to instil everyone with the real possibility—no, the *inevitability*—of total escape."

"And *how* to do this?"

Wagner stammered. "Um...I dunno just yet. We'll work on that. For one, you'll probably be able to hear the ruckus of general alarm over on the NuRac billet side, and see the resulting drain of soldiers from our end to theirs. Oh—before I forget—it would be nice if we could secure some weapons as well. *Real* weapons."

Tamek nearly choked on astonishment. "What! Why not simply ask the gods to whisk us away on the afternoon zephyr?"

"I tried that," said Wagner, trying to defuse him. "But their zephyr machine is booked solid through the autumnal equinox, three years hence."

Encountering nothing but their bewildered gazes, he eighty-sixed the humour in favour of hopeful practicality. "Hey, if all we can get are the practise weapons, they'll do. Sticks 'n' stones, some stray lengths of chain, some of those rock-hard loaves that we get for supper—anything is better than indefensible flesh."

"Agreed," said Tamek. "But 'tis far more prudent to base your scheme on our *inability* to procure e'en those paltry armaments. Then, should we perchance to obtain them, so much the better."

Wagner nodded, glancing from one friend to the other for additional input. An awkward quiet beset them like an invisible tendril of imminence until he gestured the need for some kind of "yea" or "nay" rejoinder to the plan in whole.

"Innovative," offered Balgor. "I would never have imagined unleashing the *entire* menagerie as a diversion."

"'Tis indeed a clever stratagem," added Tamek, ignorant of the realmson's sly non-reference to Skol. "E'en were it to be employed merely for the sake of obstructing, and not to cloak the intent of escape, 'tis still quite capital. The task you have chosen for me, howe'er, will take no little deliberation. 'Twould seem I must select not only the most trustworthy souls, but also fleet-footed and credible messengers as well."

"There must be *somebody*," argued Wagner.

The Sentinel nodded. "And so I shall find them," he said, "for you have demonstrated a sense of honour and gallantry in your calculations, *Voknor*. You have attempted to provide for my requisite that the masses be safeguarded, and with this I am pleased. Let us not, howe'er, fool ourselves into believing that e'en our most intricate orchestrations will circumvent the foreseeable loss of a moiety of our kinspeople. A number of us will surely perish, and that is a tragedy I can scarcely bear. But I can no longer deny that thousands more may unwarily engage SyKrahvo's legions on the morrow, and there, encounter an unearthly power that they have not the most meagre prayer of withstanding. Much as it doth pain me to admit, we have come to face circumstances that demand measures that are decidedly utilitarian in nature. To save our race, we must act. Therefore, if you twain are absolutely convinced of your ability to restrict your feral deluge to the NuRac portion of the substructure, I would say we have the catalyst for an uncommon and moderately achievable revolt."

Wagner exclaimed his triumph with a "Yes!" and a jubilant swish of his fist.

The Sentinel quickly offered chide. "Do not leap too far ahead, my friend. Remember—aggression *and* discipline. Leaving QieLahr behind us will be a child's game in contrast to facing SyKrahvo. Let us first relish in the sound of our footfalls o'er free soil ere we confront that blaspheming madman and the relic he perverts."

Balgor weighed in with his own concurrence, and all three traded regardful glances before adjourning.

Within the coming lockdown hour, Wagner, Balgor, and Tamek could each be found lying supine and alert on his own pallet, the reveries of hopefulness traversing three very emboldened psyches. Buoyant and uncontainable by physical pale, were their aspirations to have permeated the surrounding ether, they might have drawn together in the manner of Jon Mazzio's office triptychs to embody a common, portentous aura of unlikely syncretism. Three men, three vastly different perspectives, each occupied himself within his own private sphere of thought, where subtle variegation in philosophy distinguished the individual being. Beyond the more immediate goal of escape, Wagner's most profound meditation was on the onerous course of one man's destiny sought; Balgor's, on the other hand, was that of a destiny merely to be resumed. And where the former had long wrestled with the ambiguities of purpose, his Ergosian friend had simply to gather up the fumbled reins of a fate temporarily arrested, and recommence on a renascent heading, albeit with deadly new factors to confront. The third conspirer, however, had before him perhaps the most weighty of situations. For, it was through the Sentinel's eyes that destiny seemed at best a desperate pendency. It was through Tamek's soulful presage that the future appeared to be fast careening over doomy cliffs. And somehow he knew that only righteous effort and sacrifice could ever hope to rescue it from the brink of oblivion.

SECOND INTERLUDE

Less than four kilometres to the south of QieLahr, a haggard and weary pair of Ergosian foot soldiers stooped amid the evidence of an incomprehensible event that they'd only barely avoided. Before them, an unnatural issue of fulgurated devastation furrowed through the greenwood. The spiring firs that once flourished here were no more. Charred and pulverised and strewn like so much sooty mulch into the neighbouring—and miraculously untouched—coppice, in their wake lay a tract of desolation a rood or so in width, with a freshly ripped fairway leading off in either direction for as far as the eye could follow. A rough northerly to southerly blazing, the earthen corridor showed signs of recent, heavy tramping—NuRac bootprints mostly—all headed away from QieLahr and on a general bearing toward the southern territories.

It was staggering to these warriors, if only to think of what might have been. Females both, they were scrubby, lean, hardened an unfair decade beyond their years, each of flagging countenance and with spirits trodden no less harshly than the flame-flattened forest before them. With justifiable caution, they studied the caked footprints, the wagon ruts, the vrohda spoor, as if reading the very lifeline of a doomed realm. They considered themselves immediately fortunate, and each relayed as much to the other in laconically guarded utterances. But that which their eyes communicated told more than a modest verbalising ever could. The brutal rape of these woods might easily have included their own extirpation, and that of their sequestered compatriots, had it not been for the shrewd prudence of some unsung strategist back at command. Both scouts blessed their luck for *that* individual, so disposed of faculty and sound generalship, for it was by his call that they had been suddenly ordered into a temporary retreat. Had they received no such forewarning, who knew what tragedy would have befallen them? Already so many lamentable setbacks over the year's course, so much debacle, the effort had been plagued as never before. Juthac the Vulgar was slain and gone, he and fully one-half of his most loyal followers. The remnants of his army, bedraggled and dispirited and divested of all but a minim of their once-regnant insolence and fortitude, had barely made it back to Mirko's side of their alliance. Yet now, with Mirko himself as good as in the grave from trauma recently sustained, only providence and a miracle of propitious contingency had spared his and Juthac's rebels from confronting unawares the NuRacs' hellishly newfound power. Had any of them even suspected the existence of such destructive potential, no Ergosian would have dared to hazard this far north to ambush the NuRac caravan as they had, for it now appeared that that coup had suddenly been upstaged by supernatural authority never witnessed in this generation. Clearly, dark sortilege had reared itself in the realm. This was on all counts irrefutable, and few were they who would not at least consider the notion that it was the impending Vorshalah that made ready the path of its recrudescence. Both of these women, then, in treading upon this unnatural assart of decimation so callously unfurled by their enemy, came upon a common and terrible realisation. If they interpreted this despoilment as a symbolic representation of the infancy of mystical rebirth, then most certainly did grave trial lay before them and before any being who held peace and prosperity dear.

For a while they trudged discreetly about the debris, like survivors of a house-fire rummaging for salvageable possessions. A certain anaesthetised estrangement in their surveying, each was yet necessarily vigilant in keeping her eyes and ears on the battered treescape to either side. Signs of ambulant life, however, were wanting; in fact, neither woman had thus far espied any signs of natural fauna since first stepping out onto the newly blasted tract. Wildlife had fled the area, and apparently had yet to return.

Deeming the threat of combative immediacy as negligible for the nonce, the women soon stood down their apprehension and permitted themselves an exchange on a less reticent scale.

"What hope have we against this measure of might?" said the first, the labouring of her raspy voice less the product of cautious soft-speaking than the legacy of the ribbonish scar that marred an otherwise smooth, olive throat.

"Little, I fear," came her elder companion's reply. "Unless some soul within our faction learns to tame this dragon that our foes have unloosed." She let slip a weighty sigh as she scanned the breadth of razed woodland, only a few days old but seasons away from reconstituting itself. "Pity me," she said, "that, as a maiden, I gave so little heeding to the priests of my village. Had I listened more, and fidged and giggled less, perhaps I might grasp some little insight into exactly what it is we are observing here."

The first one squatted and stroked a curious finger over the talon-like splintering of what was once a hardy conifer, thirty times her height. "I find it too astounding to believe," she said.

"The extent of destruction?"

"That, too. Nay, I was thinking about you, Madya. You once *giggled?*"

For a fleeting moment, the one called Madya fought an uncharacteristic urge to smile. But, like the adversity that had been her life, she took it by the scruff and subdued it, the brevity of the effort passing unnoticed by her younger companion. It had once been said that a person might more readily bend a rod of steel into a grin than to ever goad Madya's lips into a northward curl; and even as the supposition annoyed her, she nevertheless validated it every chance she could.

"In childhood, such things were easy," she said stoically. "Giggles and gambols, absurdity, whim—ignorance in those years is both natural and necessary. And finite. Like the maidenhead of a foolhardy wench—once lost, there is naught to be done but to bequeath it to the next girl-child born, and go forth all the wiser for its unready relinquishing."

"Of that I would not know," said the first.

Madya hesitated, partly amused, partly abashed. "No matter. To answer you, Pelori, yes—I was once a little girl. That was long ago. Regrettably, those of my childhood recollections not obscured by time have found themselves displaced by newer images of war, hatred, and revenge. For me, the road back to my innocence is gone, as obliterated as the greenwood that once stood here."

Pelori, who'd been poking around the ashy rubble, suddenly dislodged a large cockchafer that had flitted onto the clearing for a curious look-see of its own. She tapped its shell lightly with a twig and watched it scurry off with more resolute intent.

"Likely it wonders what happened to its home," she mused, coming to her feet. Madya watched the scarabaeid depart and then gazed around the vicinity one last time, tucking the mace that she'd been clenching into the leather frog at her waist. "Let us hope that *we* will not be wondering the same thought tomorrow."

"Do you anticipate such a—"

"Come," Madya said, heading for the tree line. "There are many who need to know what we have seen."

Pelori following her partner's lead, they made for the edge of coppice, and, without looking back, passed like spirits into the tenebrous curtain of forestation that, directly bordering the despoliation, had remarkably gone untouched by SyKrahvo's passing.

CHAPTER TWENTY-THREE

Wagner would soon become awed by the changes in Tamek. The notion of mass escape like a lien placed against the Sentinel's former principles, over the next two days this more obliging mentor summoned forth such a wealth of industriousness and cunning as to set a discerning person to questioning what had become of the man's stricter ritual and reserve. Demonstrating the sudden wherewithal to effectively survey, plumb, coordinate, and construct from his (allotted) blueprint of Wagner's scheme, Tamek exposed his secret truth of having all along possessed the ability to organise a competent, if not downright superlative, essay—having always chosen *not* to, however, and citing his concern for every last life as his foremost reason. In one sense a philanthropy of the greatest calibre, another perspective argued its equal uncharitableness to those of the masses who, long ago, would have been willing to bank their lives on the slightest chance of surviving the hazards of revolt in order to get free. It proved baffling to Wagner, who pondered whether and why the Sentinel might ever have been resigned—if not content—to forever condemn himself and his flock to gladiatorial servitude had SyKrahvo never have presented, and wreaked havoc with, the mysterious Soork. He supposed, however, that as a mere infidel consigned to the back forty acres of "proper" devoutness, he would likely never know. Still, his intuition clearly signalled that this business with SyKrahvo was even more dire than Tamek had let on.

On his own front, Wagner's two remaining days of bonus time with Skol proved exceptionally advantageous, for with the brute's reconstitution came some noteworthy discoveries in his temperament and his manner that had never before manifested in mixed company. By means of certain undeniable, behavioural indices, Skol appeared to have been undergoing a subtle personality tweaking, stemming perhaps from some unintended facet of the rejuvenation process, or merely—and less likely—as a result of the amicable interaction with Wagner and Balgor. It was assumed by both men that he'd never been treated with even a smidgen of humaneness before they'd been pressed into service as his unofficial nannies; still, it was doubtful that a few days of decency at this point in Skol's miserable life could have sufficiently thawed his brumal virulence to the extent that they now witnessed. Tossing a few frankfurters to a junkyard mongrel would scarcely accord it the disposition of Benji; still, where once had been malevolence and viciousness now stood deportment formerly believed inconceivable. What Skol now presented, more often than not, during the morning and afternoon visits, was conduct that could most closely be characterised as a sort of labile unguardedness, and perhaps even a genuine repose. Pavlovian displays of anticipatory grunting at their arrival, a bit of incidental growling between swills of his muckish ragout, the still-existent yet diminished bloodlust in his glare— indeed, the great bulk of his mannerisms seemed more territorial than hostile. It was as if Skol's titan-sized aggression had been tethered and staked in his febrility by Wagner's more-than-meets-the-eye influence.

But this was not the only new development in store for the unwary caterers. Another one, arising quite unexpectedly and much to the utter delight of Wagner's ornery nature, was the advent of Skol's accruing an unlikely but gradual shining to none other than the hapless realmson himself. It was an unrequited fondness to be sure, and even more certainly, a welcomed one. With no apparent impetus, no intentionally trust-garnering behaviour on Balgor's end, nor any special, ethical treatment above and beyond, the brute had simply taken to studying, even emulating, the realmson with mimery most macabre. Such a development naturally struck loggerheads with the logical, as it was Wagner who'd been Skol's primary benefactor from the first day. But it was simply one of those things. Skol watched and watched the Ergosian like an infant enthralled by a dangled mobile. He goggled Balgor's movements with meticulous regard, listened to his causerie with fascination most curious and devoted. Sometimes he even echoed a fragment of speech or a colourful phrase that had particular verbal pleasure in repeating. Balgor's ubiquitous "bones and entrails" invective became, understandably, the natural favourite, and on any moment that it slipped of habit from the realmson's lips, Skol set right into reiteration, aping it over and over with the ear-grating annoyance of a cracker-craving parrot gone loco.

The whole matter came to horrify Balgor. If it wasn't disconcerting enough to play wet-nurse to an entity once considered his vilest and most brutal enemy, then discovering that he'd suddenly become the focus of said entity's childlike adoration quite reasonably shook him out onto the fringes of comfort. He desired nothing of Skol's infatuation, and rejected outright Wagner's soft-soaping and faux sympathy both. Bonding with the lowly savage, establishing a trust with him— these had been Wagner's ambitions, not his. And whether an inability to balk at the ribbing that his outworlder friend so generously meted him, or simply a new angle in his ongoing forbearance against an often treacherous Happenstance (another of the Fates, no doubt), Balgor resisted any and all encouragement aimed at widening the avenue of Skol's engrossment.

He could have tilted at windmills for all the good it did him.

Wagner, however, plied leverage where he could. "Oh, come on, *Uncle Balgor!* This could prove useful. Your influence might serve to temper his unpredictability—something that would make pulling this whole thing off a lot less tenuous."

"I am *not* this monster's uncle!" argued Balgor. "How befitting do you think it to empower the likes of me with such an unruly, murderous charge?"

"Releasing him is integral to the plan, remember? That you might have some degree of clout in regards to his mental state, it could make all the difference between his aimless rampaging and his receptiveness to our friendly prompting."

Balgor groaned. "My existence was not so very complex before you stumbled arse-rumpward into it, *Voknor*. As callow as you were on your first day—a seeming naïf in a den of cutthroats—my impression of you was cast the moment that Grum summoned me to gaze upon your pitiful tremble. How little, really, did I glean that day."

"Especially considering how close I came to kicking your butt."

"Which, as it seems, you are still hell-bent on accomplishing through your blasted pressuring."

"Just agree to help me with Skol, and I'll shut up. It's as easy as that."

"But I do not wish—"

"Oh, but you *do*."

"I do not."

"I *really* think that you do."

"No, I am certain that I do not."

"Would you, then?"

"I would not."

"Just give it up, man. Say 'uncle' and be done with it."

"Confound it—I told you I am not his unc—"

"Just *say* it."

"I tol—"

"Say it."

It was all friendly egging, but the realmson fought it like a beast in the arena. For a while, in fact, it seemed as if his staunchness would prevail. But Wagner's assail was as unflagging as any crovik's charge, his tongue, as keen as a Vofspar's talons, and his tactics, as beguiling and as galvanising as a child's anticipant beckoning. How could the Ergosian hope to defend against such multifaceted deviousness?

In the end, he could not.

"Oh, *very well*," he conceded. "What is it that you would have me do?"

Wagner grinned victory. "That comes later," he said slyly. "Right now, we probably ought to get out to the palaestra."

"What! And allow me the entire day to regain my senses and change my mind?"

"*Reegayne mye senzzes*," rattled Skol.

Wagner gestured towards Skol as if showcasing a new living room ensemble on "The Price is Right."

"Balgor, I've got such a good feeling about this—I can't even begin to tell you."

He knocked for the guards, leaving the realmson to gaze wondrously at the incorrigible brute.

"Why is it," Balgor grumbled, "that your optimism ever fills me with foreboding?"

At mealtimes, and in the accommodating brevity of one or two asides between bouts, Wagner, Balgor, and Tamek conspired with the same sort of rendezvousing that had ever been characteristic of their cliquish unions. Just the standard head-huddle, none of their peers presumed to speculate on the nature of these commonplace interactions despite the fact that at least one memorable, yet ultimately disastrous, plot had risen out of just such conspicuous trysting. There were instead plenty of other goings-on of far juicier import taxiing the communicative arteries of a bruit-hungry populace. For one, the very latest of Bilahdu's updates suggested that the prisoner caravan may have met with a more unexpected and unspecified delay en route than was previously surmised. And although no one had been able to procure the reason for its few days' tardiness, many of those NuRac administrators whose duties involved prisoner resources were at times seen pacing the periphery of the yard, exhibiting a curious, albeit understated, concern whose readability was ambiguous at best. It seemed conceivable to most that SyKrahvo in his madness might suddenly have seen fit to dispense with the enslaving of a gladiator elect altogether, foregoing the traditional functions of the campaign—indeed defying its considerable influence on the NuRac economy—and had instead opted to simply eradicate the conquered with a few hasty volleys from his infernal device. After all, why bother with the sustained housing and feeding and guarding of one's enemy, when expeditious means existed to eliminate it altogether? A frightening supposition to most; but, to the power-warped Commander, it would have assumed the grandeur of an ethnic cleansing the culmination of which his ego would interpret as the premier intent of a NuRac manifesto too long mired in impeding euphemism. Still, it was hoped that his zeal had not consumed what wavering rationale might yet have remained in his possession.

Although the discovery of the Soork had thrust a terrifying new age upon the realm—pitching the power balance inordinately out of kilter and ramifying the Ergosians' general fear and unrest into near-irrevocable despair—there existed at the same time a glitch in the NuRac primacy, and no insignificant one at that. To listen to Bilahdu, one would have thought it an Achilles heel ripe for some devastating arrow of its own making. And, as it stood that the man of the once-chronic pantaloon woes was seldom wrong, many of the Ergosians desperately clung to his latest augury as if he indeed commanded true second sight, and not merely a bookmaker's feel for probability. Cognoscente, critic, and theorist, Bilahdu felt—as did Tamek—that SyKrahvo's ungoverned passion was a clutch of forbidden keys that bore the means of unlocking every last hindrance that barred him from his dreadful success; yet, equally and foreseeably ancillary would the flinging wide of so many potentially baleful doors accelerate his self-same ruin. Not truly recognising, nor respecting, the Soork for its catastrophic capacity, SyKrahvo was little more than a covetous manservant who fumbled greedily at the keyway to his master's treasures, arrogant and ignorant and unconcerned with the notion that some ingresses might indeed be bolted for good reason. When it so happened that he would overstep his bounds—and, clearly, *that* damnable door was already ajar—Bilahdu and the Sentinel would petition their overseeing powers of Eternity and Existence to insure that only *he* should be made to suffer for it.

Out of respect for Bilahdu, and as an investment in Bilahdu's considerable pool of insight, Tamek persuaded his fellow schemers into enlisting their girthy friend as one of the fraternity. That Bilahdu and Tamek, working together, would come up with a more comprehensive list of trustworthy accomplices than the Sentinel could on his own was, of course, unnecessary hard sell, and both Wagner's and Balgor's confidence in the plan quickly swelled in knowing that the joy of Skagra's life would be along for the ride. And once Bilahdu had overcome his incredulity of what it was that his ears relayed to him, he promptly upshifted into strict left-hemispheric mode and began calculating the types of insurgent strategies that would easily, and in the right setting, have placed him alongside the craftiest of warlording generals. Always one for gathering up even the most trivial shards of knowledge—strewn around him like discarded clues to a puzzle that no one could solve—and utilising those bits, bytes, motes, and mites, in the engineering of palpable methodologies for those who, like himself, were forced to eke an insolvent and undistinguished existence, Bilahdu's real blessing was his gift of practical perspective—the intellectual flipside to his seemingly irreconcilable buffoonery. Fed up long ago with the inhospitalities of life on NuRac soil, his on-board presence would be a resplendent accessorising of Wagner's more crudely conceived machinations.

Adding fortuity to fortune, there came within the day more solid—and completely unreckoned—substantiation of the prison caravan rumour. As the snippets of overheard, thrice-relayed, and admittedly out-of-context NuRac persiflage revealed, not only had the procession met with delay, but moreover it had fallen to marauding Ergosian forces who evidently had evaded SyKrahvo's sweep of those territories most intimate to the NuRac dominion. The densely coppiced forest providing all of the entrenchment required of a seasoned, insurrectionist hit squad, few in the camp doubted that it was Mirko of Vargath and his lusty brigands who were responsible for the raid; and, despite the foreseeable hardship slated to befall the camp denizens for lack of replacement gladiators, most of the populace revelled in this miniscule victory with manner as brash as the one bestowed by that handful of defiers who, days ago, had laughed in the face of SyKrahvo's thwarted demonstration. A few flecks of joy scattered within a greater mélange of despair, any triumph—even one that promised unpleasant recompense—was still cause for elation for those who had little else within their reach.

A providential stroke in itself, Wagner saw in this turn of events a means of stoking the coals of the impending upheaval should he and his co-schemers confront difficulty in marketing their impromptu rebellion to a mass of nerveless, diffident, or stonewalling would-be abettors. If needed, he'd facilitate an inspirational arm-twisting jerked straight from their roguish hero's own reputation. Mirko and his insurgents were the faceless stalwarts, the unflagging, ever-evading, incommunicado resistors whose deeds and doings spawned legend; their generous résumé of anti-NuRac aggression lent sustenance to spirits too emaciated to look past the poleaxe-wielding guards and beyond the mortared walls to a spot outside QieLahr's gates where said captured had been forced to discard their hopes and dreams like overcoats doffed at a dinner party. And if no one else possessed the gumption to pry an entire campful of despondent eyes open to the possibility of redonning those cloaks and mantles of their forsaken aspirations, Wagner surely would. His agenda demanded it, after all. And if he had to falsely bring the Vargathian into it—so be it.

Of more tangible consequence, had the Ergosian rebels indeed infiltrated the

NuRac vicinage, the extent of their presence would prove paramount. With the bulk of the NuRac army somewhere in the field, logic suggested that the ever-cunning Mirko would have dispatched scouts to survey the highly impregnable QieLahr, spotters who would surely relay to him the unlikelihood of successfully besieging a fortress so monumental in scale. As such, it was only a matter of time before he issued the reluctant order to withdraw from the area, his wild card of surprise perhaps having already been played in the caravan coup (and by now shuffled into contemporary epos by way of tongue and testimony). The hopes of liberating his kinspeople from the belly of this sleeping, stony, multi-turreted giant—despite its skeletal complement of defenders—would inevitably seem to him as tantamount to a fool's fancy. So, for Wagner and his fellow conspirators, the time that remained before Mirko's hypothesised withdrawal was a diminishing launch window that halved by every second that they idled in prudence. While it was true enough that the Vargathian's rebel brigands had not been anticipated— nor were they critical to the uprising itself—the speculation of their possible intrusion into these environs held the allure of a deliciously coercing incentive, and more so, it was a manipulatory flashpoint for igniting and channelling the frustration and ebullition that seethed within the prison populace.

"We can do this," said Wagner, most gung ho. "Whether Mirko's raiders are in the area or not, these folks are more apt to rile themselves into a healthy mob state if they believe help is on the outside."

"It is a defensible argument," added Bilahdu. "If we seek to offer our compatriots a convincing route to freedom, it would surely behove us to forge said route through a copse of carefully contrived fabrication and optimism. In truth, it may be the best means available to us."

"Aye," chimed Balgor. "Let them berate us for our deceit as they march alongside us, on the path to Vargath!"

The Sentinel had the final say. In the past, he'd made it known that he was no fan of Mirko's. And now, the thought of invoking the Vargathian's popularity as a chicaning persuasion to achieve their objective?—it soured his stomach.

But, then again, there *was* that nasty business with the Soork. He was helpless to undermine SyKrahvo while he remained under NuRac lock and bolt.

Prior to any condoning, however, Tamek opted instead to dissect and evaluate scenario after scenario with the concordant trio—some that incorporated the subterfuge, others that excluded it—in an attempt to reach concurrence on the most viable method of spurring the incarcerated entirety to action in the shortest possible timeframe, and then in enacting both a rebellion and an escape before alarm brought auxiliary troops racing from all ends of the city. Each of the potential plans hung on precariously pendent threads. Many were far too conditional for plausible consideration, and others, interwoven with the distasteful aspects of sacrifice, outright slaughter, even sacrilege. In the end, once the impossible and the unlikely had been pared from the contending arguments, this deception that utilised Mirko and his brigand liberators survived as the most embraceable choice, and perhaps as the only ruse that could unite not only the fence-sitters, but even the double-tonguers—the secret informers who were given to reaping gains from the NuRac benefactors who bankrolled their treachery.

Tamek knew from which vantage each of his allies sought to orchestrate his own destiny. By no means dullards, said accomplices likewise fathomed something of how the Sentinel perceived their convictions and motivations. Bilahdu and his wife claimed an immensity of family in the free realm, and regardless of the circumstances surrounding Skagra's (alleged) doughty surrender to the NuRacs for her mate's sake, both of them longed to be reunited with their kin. The invitation to facilitate escape, therefore, could not have been any more fortuitous to a still-stunned Bilahdu's sense of priority. Balgor, however—unable to boast of any true blood ties anywhere, while at the same time esteeming an entire realm of appropriated family—found incentive elsewhere, incited and spurred by passions old, innate, and newly rekindled. Dispossessed until recently of the natural furore of his once lusty and headstrong youth, he had, through his association with Wagner, put the torch to the pyre of his resignation, thus re-igniting the zeal for autonomy that had been so nearly extinguished by complaisance. A passionate, indomitable spirit reborn into subordinate surrounds, this enlightened realmson would no longer accept incarceration at any cost.

Wagner's motives were a good deal more discriminative, and Tamek knew these best and least. The *Voknor* persona whom he'd met early on was the least complex of the incarnations that the supposed "outworlder" had since revealed; in *that* scrawny, naked man, Tamek had perceived little more than a stranger who, like everyone else in camp, harboured the singular complaint of having been simply and ungraciously stripped of his freedom. Surviving long enough to regain it had, understandably, been Wagner's most pressingly urgent concern—period. To his detriment, a number of veils had been ripped away since those vestigial days; and, in contravening manner, with every layer pulled aside there was revealed even more convolution than had formerly been apparent. Secrets and half-truths soon abounded like punctures in the craft of Wagner's character. Still, no suspected iniquity could ever quite scuttle him, (A) despite his uncanny propensity for surviving the bleakest of situations, (B) recusant of the denials and the alibis that a less honourable man might have conjured in order to wriggle out from wrongful accusation, and (C) smack-in-the-face of the less than satisfying factual daubery regarding not only his thaumaturgy and his branding, but of the ambiguities between his serendipitous capability and the self-deprecation he finessed in order to shrink conspicuous mountains back into molehills.

Teetering between priority and agenda, Tamek ultimately consented. Accusations and accountability were queries better saved for another day, for on *this* day he hoped to help hatch a surprise that the NuRacs would not soon forget. The three fellows before him rejoiced in as lacklustre a manner as their surroundings permitted them, knowing how Grum and the sentries and the respective Commanders preferred it that smiles and laughter—and pleasure in general—remain absent from prison life. But the question remained as to how to go about it all, how to decide on the proper time, and by what means to gauge the appropriate mood. How does one unleash the great beast of revolt *and* avoid being devoured in its rampage?

Wagner knew. To him, the metaphorical and the literal were more closely related than at least two of his co-schemers could possibly suspect. And Balgor, knowing better than to give Wagner cause for even more inspiration, kept restrainedly and reservedly mum.

Skol was lively that evening, serving up a cacophonous feast to match the sustenance-enriched one that his shushing bucket-bearers delivered to him. Perhaps an unanticipated perk of his continued health, or perhaps stemming from some manner of sympathetic response that compounded what he intuited on a sensory level, he subjected Wagner and the realmson to an extensive run-through of favourite Balgorisms—all delivered in the guttural, infantile manner that stood so at odds with his ominous presence. The realmson, quite hapless, tried rather half-heartedly and ineffectually to admonish the brute, demanding that he instead ply his tongue to the eating of his swill; after all, though only two guards patrolled the crank-room on this evening, they were not complete fools, and likely they had given ear, if not notion, to some of these peculiar noises emanating from within. It was hoped by both men that the warders took the near unintelligible growl-speak for just that, or even concluded that it was Wagner or Balgor themselves in taunt of the beast. As no one had yet opted to investigate, this—at least—they found to be a good thing, and Balgor abruptly donned his best taskmaster's guise to prompt further silence from his rowdy infatuate. It was a tack, however, that met with less than desired success, for he hadn't the wherewithal to convincingly convey authority to a critter who bested him in mass three times over, who wasn't in the habit of taking *anyone's* orders, and who hadn't sense enough to be intimidated should an entire mountain be avalanching his way.

"This would be worthy of my awe were it not so ludicrous!" blurted Balgor, defeated before he started. "I suspect that you mended more than his ailing body with your wizardry, *Voknor*."

"Not *me*," Wagner insisted, pleased and yet designedly undemonstrative. "I just brought him up to snuff. How was I to know he'd come to be such a hardcore fan of yours?"

Balgor harrumphed and re-offered Skol still another chance at his food. This time the brute complied, and commenced at gorging himself, slowly at first, and then increasingly more frenzied, with the realmson sighing like a harried baby-sitter in the exhaustion of his miniscule victory.

"I do not believe it would be wise to make him the crux of your diversionary tactics," the Ergosian said lowly. "Although his demeanour has become more generous toward our presence, we cannot predict his reaction to the pandemonium you intend to foist upon him. Ungirding him may hinder the scheme more than aid it."

"I'm willing to gamble," said Wagner.

"Are you willing to risk the lives of those whom we have sworn to save?"

Wagner gave pause. "It's really the only way, Balgor. If Tamek's going to force his 'everybody goes or no deal' maxim on us, we have to create distractions everywhere, forcing the NuRacs to dispatch what's left of their depleted ranks in order to smother all the fires we light. Baby Huey, here, and the rest of his varmint buddies in this block, are a tremendous resource to aid us in doing just that."

"Aye, but I like it not."

"I like it not *either*. But I'm sure you don't need to be reminded that there's a megalomaniac on the loose, equipped with his magic joystick and about a zillion really badass soldiers, all headed for a little place called Vargath. I'm telling you, it's our last, best chance."

Balgor could find no comfort on either horn of his dilemma. But it was ever clear to him that action needed to be taken, one way or another, and within the space of a single day at that. He'd long reached the point of obsession in regards to getting free, but he did not care at all for this business of Skol's unsettling departure from his former, horrible self. Borrowing a colloquialism from the outworlder, he claimed that it gave him the "willies" to observe the once fearful Sunderer aping him, especially as, only days ago, he'd pooh-poohed Wagner's insistence in point of Skol's special aptitude for speech. Unable, however, to provide an alternative, Balgor supposed that if all went according to plan, by this same time tomorrow he would be spared from ever having to deal with this particular vex again. Emotive detachment was key in what lay ahead, and he vowed to endure just a little while longer.

Having left Tamek and Bilahdu to secure the loyalties of the hand-picked abettors who were to aid in evacuating the various facilities in the compound, Wagner and Balgor stepped up their own low-key emprise to reconnoitre as much of the animal substructure as their inflexible routine permitted. While the realmson possessed extensive knowledge of where nearly every corridor led, he limited his input of assurance to only those passages he'd actually traversed in the past for one duty or another, and hesitated to speculate on the destinations of those he hadn't. He would not risk their lives on untried tunnels for fear of routing the stampede of relinquished beasts up a blind alley and consequently back in the direction of the prison yard. Although politic and conditional, both knew that sticking to the familiar was the wisest choice in what would be an extremely risky operation. But this did not mean that they couldn't improvise.

Preferring a hedging of eventualities that slanted more weightily in their favour, Wagner wasn't about to allow his and Balgor's crucial role in the rebellion to be frustrated by ignorance. He'd already prepared a supplementary plan. He had, in fact, allowed for it from the onset, conceived it and filed it away, pending just such a contingency. And although it would not be a popular course of action, Wagner knew exactly where to find an understructure savant who could provide him with the detailed passageway schematics they required. He needed only to brave her formidable attitude to get them.

Just prior to lockdown, Wagner found J'nea outside of Barracks Three, engaged in light conversation with the woman he remembered as Hidessel, the waste management trusty from Skol's cleaning day. The situation both surprised and pleased him. As trusties shared a bond in the service aspects of their duties, it often—but not always—created a clannish division for them socially, and a necessary one to boot, since many of the non-commissioned prisoners begrudged and sometimes denied trusties any courtesy of confiding interaction. Still, it wasn't terribly common to happen upon J'nea, regularly misdiagnosed as a grumpy loner (during the fraternising hour or any other), actually participating in casual banter with a sister trusty. But there she was, enmeshed in a comparative venting of the chaff, dross, and trumpery of a trusty's life; and Wagner, on beholding this chatty rarity, truly hesitated to shoo Hidessel off merely to ingratiate his way into acquiring a means to his end.

He opted instead to remain about in casual aimlessness, just long enough for J'nea to notice his imminence, and thus to taper and to cordially terminate her conversation so that she might give ear to what his body language declared so pressing. She was, to say little, quite unprepared for what she heard.

"Here, what exactly are you up to?" she asked after hearing his request. With Wagner, she knew that whatever he gave her willingly was usually but one spike on the mace. "Are you and your cheeky cohort already seeking another means of thrusting ill hap upon yourselves? It has not been even a week since your last complot. Are you complete fools?"

Wagner quieted her in mid-admonish. "Though you and I are miles from understanding each other," he said, "we've somehow come to trust one another. I think we proved it with the last caper. Anything I commend to your confidence is certain to stay there—that much I know. I'd even go so far as to say that Tamek himself has warmed up to you a bit after your most recent go-round."

"I would not wager all my specie on that."

"Nor would I," he said, "But I think it was a start. Now, what I'm about to tell you will surely overwhelm you—"

"Is it ever otherwise?"

"—since it's going to make my and Balgor's dash through QieLahr seem like a stroll through the meal line by comparison. No doubt, I'll be breaking any number of trusts by letting you in...but since when did *that* ever stop me? I *need* you, and at the same time, I *owe* it to you to give you the goods."

"Give them then," she said, bracingly cool. "You unload you soul—you may as well unload your burden. How involving, how shattering, can it be?"

As it turned out, it was plenty of both, so much so that even after Wagner had crossed into his own barracks for the night, J'nea yet stood where he'd found and left her, outside Barracks Three, with a walloped look about her that epitomised blatant unpreparedness.

"Where have you been, young friend?" asked Bilahdu, ushering Wagner to the rear of the quarters, where Tamek and Balgor sat in torchlit silhouette. "We have news for you. And, for once, it is pleasant in nature."

Assured and relieved, Wagner seated himself in conclave with his brothers, that he might hear their tidings.

"We have assembled an outfit of twelve men and women to take direction on our cue once this manoeuvre commences," said Tamek, his tone hinting mild disgruntlement on having to repeat the information to the truant Wagner. "Each has been made aware of the circumstances and intent, and, on our signal, each will spread the news of our inward forces welling up to aid and supplement Mirko's fighting legions at the outer wall."

Wagner nodded, waiting for additional information and getting none. "Do these twelve know that the Mirko story is just a ruse?" he asked, curious as to whether Tamek could truly lie outright to his people.

"They do not," said Tamek. Uneasy, he paused, whereupon Bilahdu took over.

"However, we added gilding to the fabrication in order to exploit a resource we had not previously considered."

Intrigued, Wagner assumed a posture eager for enlightenment.

"We explained," continued Bilahdu, "that your previous escape attempt was a ploy to successfully shunt at least one of you beyond the walls, whence that man could then seek out the rebels and confer with the Vargathian on the notion of a full-scale siege and rescue. The day and hour would have been pre-arranged, with only the Sentinel and myself wise to the alleged signal from the emancipating forces. That call to arms is to 'occur' on the morrow, originating in truth from the chaos that you and Balgor intend to unleash within the animal housing structure. Everyone concerned will interpret this din as precedent to rebellion and deliverance from bondage."

"Sounds like a plan," said Wagner, rubbing his palms like a gold-grubbing miser. Yet, before Bilahdu could utter a retorting "indeed," Wagner spat out a sudden realisation.

"Wait just a minute!" he said. "Are you telling me that, in this little fairy tale of yours, *Fostoch* is the one who gets word to the rebels?"

"Aye," said Balgor, smugly. "That was *my* suggestion, *Voknor*—the perfect stroke to explain the Orrdian's disappearance. After all, the suggestion was already in the air during our storm-shelter exchange. All of the gladiators were there to hear it. Why not exploit it?"

"I'll tell you why not! Do you think anyone's going to believe that Fostoch, once free, would give a hoot about us back here?"

"If it involved remuneration, aye," said Bilahdu, brandishing a hoodwinker's grin and glancing slyly at the Sentinel. "What did we say, Tamek? A meed of one-tenth of Vishkor's recovered treasures?"

"One-eighth." Tamek shrugged. "I was feeling uncommonly magnanimous."

"Uh-huh," said Wagner, unaccustomed to anything even faintly humorous coming from the Sentinel. "Let's try this again. Is there *anybody* in camp loopy enough to accept the premise of Tamek's handing over sacred treasure to Fostoch of Orrd?"

Bilahdu gushed with conviction most dramatic. "To ransom the entire camp from NuRac clutches? To save the realm from SyKrahvo's madness? *Of course!* However," he said with flashing eye and shielded lips, "need we mention that there existed no treasure in Vishkor to be meted?"

Wagner huffed confusion. "I don't get it."

"And neither would Fostoch, were all this to be factual," said Balgor. "Vishkor's wealth was not wealth in any material sense. The Ergosian priesthood is an abstemious lot. They do not hoard riches."

"None save an armload of scrolls and parchments," said Tamek, "the rarest and most vital of which the priests and I commandeered on the hour of the NuRacs' damnable assail. You see, *Voknor*, although unfathomably rich in cultural and symposiac regalement, the temple at Vishkor was itself chaste, vericund, and inornate in its material composition. The wealth contained within its walls was not to be found in precious ores or gems or even in architectural finery, but in the oral and penned traditions of our faith."

Wagner stood, paced, sat, and stood again, all the while demonstrating an array of palpable gesturing. "That's all well and good," he finally said, "but let me zero in on the point. Far-fetched stories are generally *my* gig around here—I admit that—but even *I* would have trouble tossing this one out to a crowd. I mean, c'mon—*Fostoch* doing something for the good of his fellow people?"

For a mere moment, Wagner's accomplices sat silent—a monumental task really, given the correspondingly preachy, boastful, and know-it-all natures of the trio before him. Then, stolidly, even quaintly, the Sentinel gave answer, simple and concise.

"How do you know that he would *not*?"

Ambushed by the idea, Wagner stammered.

"W-well, I guess I don't. But—"

"And so neither do we know, *Voknor*. Let that suffice. Most crucially, the conspiring twelve have accepted the premise, and unequivocally at that. So let us continue instigating the remainder of this precarious plot, and not set ourselves astir o'er matters of credulity."

"Aye, and the Fates be our allies!" added a buoyant Balgor, probably wishing he were wending a path through a crowded Vargathian alehouse rather than wading through the crush of Tamek's vernacular.

Well after the adjourning of their huddle—and Bilahdu's jaunt back to his own barracks—the night idled by like a slow freight. What little sleep Wagner managed to nab was episodic and broken, thieved from the pockets of a most ungenerous Somnus; and each time he'd awakened he found himself no more refreshed than when he'd first sought the nestle of his bedstraw. It was still deeply gloomy in the barracks when he finally came to sit up, although beyond QieLahr the dawn had begun to wrest the eastern sky from nocturnal dominion. From his sequester, Wagner may indeed have been denied that first hint of morning, but he sensed it just the same. He could *feel* the dawn. An inexplicable impression, yes, but after so many nights spent in that caliginous structure, daybreak had come to be less an event requisite of physical confirmation than of perceived cognition. To be sure, he knew this may have stemmed from simple biological rhythm risen out of routine; but there was always room in his mind for something else, for the catchall, for the endowment of mystical perception. It was only in the instances when it required neither a lightshow nor a physical avatar that he found it worthy of a good ponder. Either way, such awareness was another child born of his intuition, and one that now superseded his need to crane and peer at the artificially high horizon, beyond the barracks gate and across the towering prison wall, to see that of which he was already keenly aware.

Upon this particular dawn, this very defining juncture of day and night, of things good and things sinister, of freedom and slavery, life and living death, Wagner sat on his bed, taking inventory of the dormant humanity dozing all around him. He pulled off his weathered boots one at a time and upended them, ousting a loose trace of sand and detritus onto the barracks floor, after which he redonned them and snugged them firm with their tired lacing. In the privacy of his distraction, he realised that he no longer pined over modern footwear, or even over sophisticated attire in general, as he once had—not any more, not after so long in want of any kind of accommodative luxury. In his present life, fashion was a frivolity. No need here for physique-enhancing lines or form-fitting comfort, no statements to be made nor statuses to be achieved; all that anyone required were the basics of warmth, protection, and utility. And not everyone acquired even *that* bare minimum with complete success. Too, Wagner continued to wonder how many times his present raiment had been passed down, how many Ergosians had died in the very togs he'd assumed—who they were, how they succumbed, what their aspirations may have been. Had their hopes been even remotely akin to his, then those hopes had likely been struck down with the wearer on some dismally desperate afternoon of tournament carnage, and probably not so long ago. A sobering supposition, he couldn't allow that pattern to repeat. He wouldn't.

On rising, he took a moment to straighten the tousled straw that had served as his bedding for far too many weeks. He plumped it, tidied it, almost as if he were a college-bound teen leaving the bedroom of his adolescence. Absorbed by this preoccupation, on suddenly recognising the mindless mechanics of his actions, he tossed the last handful onto the heap with the finality of intended riddance. Then he rose and made his way toward the entry, where he then sat, eyes fixed upon the purplish morn, until the barracks within began to stir with the incremental rustlings of semi-lucid community.

It signalled the beginnings of what would be a significantly eventful day.

Not only seized of the scheme but truly at its very heart, all through breakfast Wagner found it interesting to note the behaviour of the initiates whom Tamek and Bilahdu had recruited and allied with the cause. He felt as if he were an observer at a convention for rustic double-agents—their exchange of pregnant glances in passing, the affirming nods among one another from within the meal line, the electrification of impending risk and hazard in the bearing of each—with many of the conscripted seemingly vibed more for a lark than for an undertaking most dire. Perhaps, Wagner thought, it was merely imagination on his part. Perhaps he took himself and the cause much too seriously. Perhaps the bent for combativeness coursed the veins of these people naturally, with little in the way of supplementary prompting, instruction, or cautioning required beyond what Tamek and Bilahdu had provided. Sieging, usurping, defeating, succumbing, avenging—these were ever the expectations of, and the everyday flux in, the Ergosians' lives; and the degree in which they chose to acknowledge and act upon such conatus was immaterial so long as, this day, they performed according to plan. There was no sense in Wagner's allowing anything save his own appointed task to occupy the already urgent sense of readiness that so enveloped his being.

It was clear to the four prime schemers that the revolt would be equally structured as it was haphazard. If every detail was planned just so, then one unexpected glitch might cascade into a half-dozen blunders down the line, resulting in more chaos and catastrophe than would be in their ability to improvise around and set right. Alternately, assigning too much to chance would see them thwarted before they ever began. Wagner's reliance on the accrued strategic experience of his comrades was therefore the weightiest of his trusts; for, without the Sentinel, the realmson, and the daedal Bilahdu, he had little sway over the Ergosian populace, and no military how-to on overcoming a race of armed and aggressive subjugators from within the Ergosians' own backyard. Tamek, however, had accompanied—even led—armies before his instalment at Vishkor; Balgor was himself a seasoned veteran of many a skirmish and a handful of very major battles; and Bilahdu, he was both student and historian of sundry campaigns, with a physical stamina that defied his bounteous girth and, trouser hemstitches notwithstanding, set him alongside the deftest of warriors with sword, staff, or spear—most notably in moments when ludicrousness alone was not enough to deter one's foe. Together, with their ties to the remaining kinspeople in the camp, there was no doubt that they would uphold their end. Wagner had only to light the fuse.

"Have the muses of lunacy abandoned you this morrow?" asked J'nea, appearing abruptly with her porringer and snapping him from his mental cog-spinning.

"No," he said bluntly. "Even if they had, the machinery's already geared up. This is our prime opportunity—I told you that."

She plopped down rather forcibly beside him, and remained quiet for only a moment as she commenced a hesitant sampling of the lumpy morning gruel. "I barely slept last night," she said. "What you told me was folly unmitigated."

"Maybe. But that's the kind of logic I'm betting the NuRacs employ too."

She laughed uneasily, nervously clinking her spoon across her incisors. "What the NuRacs employ, *Voknor*, will be razored steel across all your throats. Do not take our captors for fools. SyKrahvo did not march off with only the intelligent warriors, and leave the simpletons in charge."

"I *don't* take them for fools," he argued, "but neither should you take *us* for the same. Just look around—the sentries have never been so lean in number. They're all overworked, haggard, virtual zombies in their fatigue. What more perfect time would there be than this?"

"It is all of it madness, and you know it, *Voknor*." She paused to endure his scoffing, and then put the squeeze to him in return. "As if beseeching me for the passageway schematics on the eve of this foolish gambit is not enough of an indicator, then what of your thinking to incite the entire camp into suddenly rising up and following both their precious Sentinel and that ridiculous, news-mongering jackstraw, Bilahdu, without forewarning? You compound your foolery with such assumptions."

"A mob mentality can be ugly," he said, "but it does wonders for a revolution. If people witness their peers rioting, and see in that violence even a glimmer of success for their cause, they will themselves get caught up in it. We're counting on that. You see, most of the prisoners, Tamek included, have been just barely compliant, because life here—if not productive or rewarding—was at least *possible*. SyKrahvo's little demo put that compliance in jeopardy. His mistake was in showing us that we have to act."

"I see. So, the topping mazzard on this torte of daftness is that your crazed, unstoppable mob intends to counter NuRac weaponry with the trinkets and teetotems afforded by the palaestra's weapons enclosure. What *marvellous* tacticians you are." Never once looking at him as she criticised, she instead appeared content in observing the gregariousness of the courtyard breakfasters while unloading onto him a night's worth of analysis in a softly dulcet rant that took no little effort to keep from escalating into her usual, reproachful fare.

"Does that mean you're going to stand by instead of help?" Wagner asked. "Or are you going to try to squelch the effort before it starts, if only to prove that you're the one person in camp with any common sense?"

"What you call 'common sense' is not so common around here of late," she answered, ever critical but justifiably so in that it was for Wagner's own good. "Since my branding, I have had little choice in this life but to teach myself discretion—a concept that you and your cronies apparently find fit to discard like old bones. I do agree that this death-staff that SyKrahvo carries symbolises all-encompassing atrocity for the Ergosian race. And, of course, I concur with you and your friends in averring that he must be stopped. But with what means? If the lot of you indeed made good your escape from QieLahr and proceeded to face him, how would you hope to defeat him? With *what* can you brave such power, *Voknor*? SyKrahvo has become destruction incarnate. To confront him now is akin to breasting a looming tidal wave of crushing, merciless force. How can such a whelming wall of impendency be thwarted?"

He thought for a moment.

"Sandbags."

"*What?*"

He stated it again, plainly, simply. "Sandbags. Sandbags, levees, dikes, break-waters, jetties—that's how you thwart floodwaters and crushing waves. You pile everything you've got in front of them, heap upon heap of earthen obstruction, made out of anything available—and you let the sea trounce away. Each by itself may only be a meagre, inutile contrivance for battling a greater force of nature. But, get enough of them, and sometimes they do the trick."

J'nea's jaw hung in bafflement. "You have lost me upon a back trail of prattle. You wish the rebels to construct...bags of *sand*?"

"In a manner of speaking, yeah. Y'see, if the Ergosians want to defeat the NuRacs, they're going to have to attack them strategically, from a hundred different fronts, with deterrents placed at every possible point of infiltration."

"And this is *so easily* accomplished," she flouted.

"In order for it to work, they've somehow got to keep SyKrahvo distracted, or otherwise occupied, during any confrontation. Our only chance lies in defeating the people and not the sorcery. Flesh is the key."

"And this is so easily accomplished," she reiterated.

"Flesh bleeds. Muscles fatigue. Nerves frazzle—even NuRac nerves. They're all exploitable weaknesses. The rebels need to make life as uncomfortable as possible for the NuRac soldiers without directly confronting SyKrahvo and the Soork up close and personal. Your people will have to hurl everything they can find in the NuRac army's way, from the grandest rock their catapults can launch to the smallest projectile their slings can propel, calling upon every possible means from every clan in every part of the realm."

"Oh, is this all?" J'nea felt herself summoning every modicum of restraint possessed of her character in order to muzzle the harsher critic within, she who so delighted in lambasting any preposterous notion that happened within range of her tongue and its blazing brusqueness. "*Voknor*, you would be courting a miracle merely for the clans to agree on something so petty as a simple mercantile affair— say, the going rate of rock salt or gingswede or taago root. Yet, you wish them to unite, side by side, in tossing feathers at a gale? You reach for the ungraspable. Truly, you would have a greater chance in making a votary of Skol himself."

Wagner suddenly choked in mid-swallow. He coughed and spat and hacked and grunted until he'd voided his windpipe, his eyes a-flood, his porringer dashed to the sand like Fostoch's of not so long ago. His situation only minimally dire, he declined J'nea's proffered concern, gesturing to her the "please stand by" cueing of a progressing reconstitution; and she, in respect, refrained from intervention, watching as his visage shifted between the rubicund contortions of suppression and the paler ebbing of a peril only marginally avoided. Borderline for a moment, then incrementally settled, his breathing becoming more even and his hands fitfully currying gunk from out of his beard, he rasped a response to J'nea's last remark with all that his besieged larynx had to offer: "Stranger things have been known to happen."

She searched his teary eyes for meaning, oblivious to how the irony in her own words had prompted Wagner's spasm in the first place. She waited for no additional comment. Unsuited as Wagner's voice was for dialogue beyond his cryptic reply, J'nea happily latched onto the opportunity to air her further misgivings in rare and uninterrupted extravagance. Laying into Wagner in the manner in which she was not only wont, but indeed articulately dexterous, she cast an exuberance of argument before him, replete with an illustrative footnoting of the innumerable obstacles to be overcome *and* the documented misery resultant of any past attempts at defying NuRac governing, that she, in her time forfeited to captivity, had witnessed.

Disposed to hear her out, Wagner gradually came to note how, submersed within the body of her grievance, there lurked the essence of a guarded compassion that he'd sensed once or twice before in varying degree. It was an elusive feature of J'nea's personality, like a broaching fluke of concern rearing from deep within enigmatic waters, one that betrayed the existence of an undeniably more complex and resplendent entity below that few others ever saw. Broadly did she indicate in her contestation far less deference for herself—and for him and his co-plotters—than for those in the camp who might not be convalescent enough to withstand the rigours of riotous pandemonium, much more, the considerably arduous exodus from NuRac territory. She feared for those who would be incapable of matching the verve and the prowess of the more stalwart prisoners. She felt that the weak should not be subject to the havoc brought on by those more fit. And here, it again seemed that she shared one more trait with her nemesis of custom—Tamek of Vishkor—although how fortunate for Wagner that he hadn't the voice with which to tell her so, as he may subsequently have suffered a second instance of choking, externally this time, from the clamp of a certain Bejodethian wildcat's fingers.

Of course, she was right. She usually was. But Tamek had vowed to accommodate the infirm and the non-combatants, to make them priority over all else—even over the escape itself—a task that Wagner gratefully, *eagerly*, handed off like a baton to anyone with the legs to run with it.

"They'll be in good hands," said Wagner. "All of them. Tamek insisted that it be that way or no go."

"You are fools," she said sombrely, then adding, "but fools with heroic aspirations. I suppose in your desperation it is the most viable plan that you could devise. But I do not condone it. And I do not share your enthusiasm."

"That's fine," he said. "Just make sure your bags are packed. When the time comes, when you hear the alarm—and witness the ensuing upheaval—then you can decide whether you want to stay or not. My money says you'll be going with us."

She smirked, watching as the bulk of the breakfasters began filtering from the courtyard to the palaestra. "You seem so convinced of succeeding at this," she said. "Whence comes your confidence?"

He reached for his porringer. "From within," he said. "And from afar."

She looked at him askance.

"This 'thing' we're planning," he said. "This mass uprising. I've seen it happen already."

"What do you mean?"

"Visions. From a long time ago." He glanced at her and flushed red at her incredulity. "I know, it sounds pretty nutty. But I've seen pieces of the future, specifically the future as it pertains to me."

She scoffed. "Are you now telling me that you are a seer?"

"Far from it. I'm more what you'd call a reluctant recipient of selective foresight. Or, rather, I *was*. I haven't experienced anything lately. Thus, I can't even say for sure if these images I'm referencing now are linked to my immediate future, or next month's future, or next year's. I can't tell you how our plans will unfold today. I don't know if we'll fail or succeed. But I've seen the machinations in my mind. Skirmish and conflict are going to happen here. And despite an incongruity or two, I'm convinced that the time is now."

"What incongruity? Provide me with a scrap of imagery, that I might associate."

He looked into her green eyes. "Beyond rioting and bloodshed, I remember seeing an overlapping tableau of...siege machines. Outside the walls."

"*Siege machines*?" she asked. "What, wheeled from the distant wood? By our free confederates?"

"I don't know," he said. "I've only been privy to the images themselves, not to their situational logic. But, yeah, I've seen siege machines."

"A vastly unlikely probability."

"Yeah, well, the next time we meet—preferably on the outside—you can grade me on my accuracy."

"I fear there will be more pressing issues to occupy us." She rose with him and they walked together to the dish return. "Last night did I half-heartedly give you the substructure layout. If you proceed, you will surely have the most difficult of tasks, *Voknor*, knowing that your rash actions will spur such calamity and carnage. Your conscience will be laden heavily. I do not envy you. And because there are so many ways to meet with dismal failure, I cannot be a true partner in this madness."

He dumped his bowl into the dishwater. "Then, stand back," he said, his tone at once severe and tolerant, "and let a handful of determined fools confront the tide." Then, he suddenly did something so unforeseeably four-square and unassuming that J'nea had not even the wherewithal to react. He leaned in and planted a kiss on her cheek, firmly, quickly, simply, directly upon the scarified "X" of her past transgressions. A gesture of gratitude, of respect and camaraderie, his lips alit for only a nonce, after which he drew back and said, "Thanks for your help anyway. I won't forget it."

Then they parted, she towards the detention block, and he into the company of a fidgety, solitary Balgor. Gaining but half her distance, the trusty threw back and watched as the two men strode past the Sentinel and Bilahdu, in artful loiter within the palaestra corridor. The four of them exchanging a few nods of taut and resolute assent, they then separated in order to initiate what J'nea knew would be a collision course with destiny. And like it or not, she would be caught in the thick of it.

CHAPTER TWENTY-FOUR

And what he greatly thought, he nobly dared.
—HOMER

There wasn't time enough in the world to accomplish all that Balgor and Wagner were hoping to pull off in the scant minutes of the morning's food run. So much left to chance, such untenable randomness in the manner in which any particular action might play out, still they pressed onward. The whole of the uprising revolved solely around their actions, depended upon their unabated tenacity, insisted on their full and unwavering commitment. They alone would tip the cradle of revolt, and the chaos to follow would be the progeny of their fortitude. It would all start with them.

And just as easily could it end with them. Failure to eliminate even a single guard during "round one" would ensure their ruin. Any oversight—even the tiniest one—would forfeit the already tensive probation that AuwNiir had bestowed them after their last offence, and would no doubt usher prompt closure in the all-conclusive sense. Thwarted and captured, they would surely and swiftly be put to the block, with the whole affair then deemed an isolated incident of insubordination initiated by two well-known dissenters. No one could save them this time; and no one would. It challenged even Wagner's unique sense of the prophetic, for although inherently he'd expected to avoid his premature demise, he took no solace nor found luxury in a foresight so faveolated with variables and uncertainties. Were he even possessed enough of second sight to have envisioned the scheme's outcome in its unequivocal entirety, it would hardly have exempted him from the dread and the suspense, from the catharsis evoked by the events as they were to unfold, or from the infinite number of variants created with even the most infinitesimal decision to act or to not act. There were no guarantees, only assumptions; and regardless of ego or a stowage of old visions, he was far from invincible.

In the crank-room they encountered two sentries on duty—three in total, then, with the inclusion of the guard who'd escorted them through the substructure. Remiss in stricter protocol, these sentries' weapons remained sheathed; their helmets, paired on an oaken tabletop; their expressions, between smug and cocky, almost as if daring the prisoners to step out of line. By all accounts it was a normal day, rife with intimidation and weighty in airs of superiority. As the Ergosian and the outworlder waited for Skol's entry to be made available to them, Balgor flashed his cohort a slyly confident "can do" glance before proceeding into the cell in outwardly typical fashion.

Once inside, they quickly went about offering up sustenance to the frothingly hungry brute, and as he gulped and glutted, they prepared themselves for the point of no return.

"Are you in spirit, friend?" Balgor asked as he limbered himself in ready.

"I'm good," said Wagner, lying. Clenching and unclenching his fists in nervous abandon, he tried distracting himself with the spectacle of Skol's lively voracity. The brute's visage, both horrible and comical, was that of some misshapen toddler plunged headlong into a gallon of strained peas. In less than a minute the pails would be emptied. Wagner's stomach felt hollow. The moment was at hand.

"Are you yet determined to introduce this infantile ogre into the chaos we are nigh to unleashing?" said Balgor, noticing Wagner's edginess.

Eyes still riveted upon Skol, Wagner nodded. "Yeah. Guards first, various beasties second, Skol third—just like we planned."

Balgor sighed. "I pray that you know what you are doing, *Voknor*."

So do I, thought Wagner.

Without ado, they gathered up the empties and, in their last act as scullery thralls, knocked for exit. For several unbearable minutes, then, they bided as the NuRacs dallied without, no doubt enmeshed in some climactic debate or brag-fest that would ultimately fall meaningless against the unanticipated urgency that they would of a sudden be facing. When finally the door swung open, Wagner and Balgor withdrew in normal fashion, and filed staidly toward the two sentries, while the third worked behind them to secure Skol's door.

One second later, both prisoners had slammed their pails upside the chins of the vicinal NuRacs with almost perfectly synchronised, roundhouse swaths that shattered teeth, bones, and cartilage, and sent both guards bloodied and reeling into the great capstan behind them. The third sentry, abruptly careening around and disbelieving of his eyes, fumbled his keys and rushed the prisoners with such panicked fury that his hands could scarcely draw his weapon. With Wagner delivering ancillary assailing to the downed guards, Balgor launched his bucket at the wild-eyed charger, striking him squarely upon his helmet's frontlet and sending him in sprawl against the brickwork in contusive stupor. But it could not end there. They could risk no alarm so early in the game. And so, Balgor swiftly finished the NuRac with the man's own blade before checking on Wagner's situation. Of the remaining foes, it seemed that blunt trauma had permanently eliminated one of them from the struggle; this, however, didn't prevent Balgor from delivering quietus to both, if only to maintain the plan's clandestineness.

"Back to the Sacred Pool with these buggers," he muttered as he stripped them of their armaments, handing off a sword to Wagner, complete with frog and sheathing for to affix over his raiment.

Wagner, eyeballing the corpses with muted ambiguity, grabbled as if with ten thumbs at tethering the weapon fast to his side. In all, their booty consisted of three swords, five daggers of various design, a cudgel, and a smart selection of body armour the donning of which would have proved far too cumbrous for the swiftness required of them for the next phase. Still, they fitted themselves sparingly with metal armlets and vambraces, and strapped to their chests only the breastplates of the sentries' more ungainly accoutrements. Then, recovering the discarded keys from the cell's threshold, they set off to orchestrate the next act in this now-irreversible drama.

The hall outside was momentarily vacant, as hoped. In traversing the corridor in the direction of the NuRac billeting, they made note of every portcullis along the way, and counted the gated ingresses that housed behind them a diverse, lazing menagerie of wild creatures. Skol's cell had been unique in that only *it* boasted the division of rooms whereby his servicing—via crank and chain—could most easily be accomplished. These other, more accessible types of enclosures characterised the greater portion of the animal cells, and would in fact be far more conducive to the wide-scale emancipation requisite of Wagner's plan.

The corridor led on in a wide, gradual arc as it matched the curvature of the arena wall from within, and fully thirty occupied enclosures they passed before encountering the intersecting T-junction that, by J'nea's instruction, would be their point of divarication. It was along this new avenue that passage into the soldiers' habitat could be achieved; and it was also here that the portcullis of the main corridor needed lowering as a detour for the impending stampede to come. While Balgor set about in executing the task, Wagner deviated onto the new avenue, creeping stealthily along the scopic access toward a distant, radiant brightness at the far end that shortly revealed itself to be daylight issuing from beyond the hall's final junction. A cautious peek around this bend presented first a lowered portcullis of considerably grand proportion, and then, the grounds of an unfamiliar courtyard—one peppered with soldiers engaged in regimental activities.

Wagner's expression flared with devilish aim. It was exactly this scene that he and Balgor sought—the perfect venue for their little barnyard surprise party. All it needed were the guests of honour—eighty to one-hundred would do nicely, all furry, feral, and four-legged.

Alerted by the rapidity of footsteps from behind, Wagner jolted from the gateway and glanced back the way he'd come. Balgor was racing toward him, fleetly and with desperation in his stride. Wagner raised a cautioning hand to slow him, to indicate that the goal had been reached. But the realmson would not be stayed.

"Sentries," he rasped, "five of them—approaching from the same direction as that which we ventured."

Wagner's heart quickened. "Did they see inside the crank-room? Do you think they came across the bodies?"

"I do not believe so. I saw no true urgency in their gait. But *that* will quickly change once they set eyes upon the two of *us*."

He stepped forward and peered around the corner at what Wagner had discovered, as if seeking a route of evasion, but instead found only the gate and the hive of NuRacs in the yard beyond.

"*Bones and entrails!*" He clenched to strike at the wall before him, but retracted in the nick out of better judgement. Shifting a calculating gaze from yard to corridor to yard again, his mental millstones all grinding furiously, he grimaced and he glowered and then finally he bolstered himself. Withdrawing the sword of his enemy, he etched at the air with lethal resolve, clutching the weapon's grip as if it were the throat of his mortal foe. In body, he bundled sinew so taut that the drawing of too great a breath might well have cracked the temper of his pilfered breastplate. "Come, *Voknor*," he said, pushing off like a sprinter at the starting pistol. "Rouse thy warrior or thy wizard, afford him with sword or spell, and make ready for either the lengthiest day of your life or the briefest. With blood we have dared to reclaim our autonomy. Now, with more blood we must secure it."

An instant later, they'd retraced half the passageway, frantic to reach the T-junction before the NuRacs did. Wagner matched his friend, step for step, three paces at his heel, his own weapon drawn, poised, and clasped by a hand slightly more clammy but no less resolute than his collaborator's. Although but two men, in heart they suddenly felt like many. Their collective fears likewise seemed strangely less hindrance than auxiliary to their heated scamper. Even the torch-flickered corridors unleashed a chaotic congeries of fetch-like silhouettes in their passing, creating the illusion of ten times their number upon the brickwork, much as if their long-fallen comrades had risen in spirit to join them in retribution.

The NuRacs were near, their voices carrying gruffly from well before the convergence as they noted the lowered portcullis at the T-junction's far side. An oddity on any day that entertained no newly arriving beasties, its distraction played famously to the escapees' advantage, for it was here that Balgor, with the speed of winged Hermes himself, hurtled around the corner and jammed his weapon into the gullet of the closest NuRac. Then, before any of them could even register the impossibility of his assail, he flailed, slashing a second soldier's visage through the minute cleave of his barbute. As the two injured men flounced rearward into the unready arms of their comrades, the unflagging realmson barrelled into the fray like Death's henchman, his face blood-flecked, his teeth in grit, his sword hungrily awhirl.

Wagner enjoyed less the element of surprise, his initial assault deflecting inconveniently off the breastplate of his intended victim. With a second parry, however, he managed to wedge his blade through a joint beneath the thick, leather brigandine of the NuRac's thoracic armour; and although not a fatal strike, it agonised the sentry into buckling over, whereby Wagner wrenched the man's helmet from his head and summarily—and, in truth, quite distastefully—took his life.

It wasn't an act that Wagner relished; rather, he rued it. But neither was it something he had long to endure single-mindedly. In the scant seconds leading up to the confrontation, he'd already been alerted to the strangely piquant influence of his *Other*. He'd felt himself ceding to the familiar inklings of *he* who lurked within those dark reaches of subconscious fringe, where Wagner rarely sought to venture freely, but toward which he was here inclined to shift control. Even as he felt obliged to stand fast and to fight this battle unaided—as did Balgor—he knew that this fragment of himself, this party-crashing Mister Destructo who existed both as a separate, obverse entity *and* as an innate simulacrum of violent predilection, could not have manifested in him so long ago without some specific purpose. The berserker was Wagner's crutch; he was Wagner's shield from the frying mental circuitry wrought of this archaic world's barbarity, a buffer likened to the chrysalid effort of a body's retreating into shock in order to protect its traumatised host, or to the mind's plunging into the depths of insanity to spare its mentally beleaguered core the true harshness of reality. Possessed, then, of this comparable protectorate of his own, why should Wagner not utilise it?

Why not, indeed! In his thinking, if tag-teaming with his alter-ego offered the means to carry him through this day, he would only too happily debate the merits and pitfalls of its emotive numbing, and its once-removed lucidity, come the dénouement. Such things were but a pittance when set against services rendered. As an unbesought subtenant of Wagner's mental habitat, the warrior persona had yanked Wagner from the flame too many times to deny; and if its ruthlessness was *ever* needed, it was on this day, in this hour. And so, in the midst of the sudden skirmish, when the moment of psychical integration flared from potential to inevitable, Wagner cordially besought his *Other* to aid him in the task that he— alone and confidently and with clear conscience—might not otherwise complete.

With three of the soldiers dispatched, Balgor launched at the fourth, Wagner, the fifth, with overbold hopes of snatching the plot back from its potential spiral. The realmson's opponent, a stout female, girded with the ringed armour indicative of the seventh regiment, had briefly availed herself of the time ransomed by the demise of her already fallen peers. Outlasting the initial surprise, she'd found opportunity to draw armament and ready her defence. And now, in engaging Balgor, she deftly matched his swordplay thrust for thrust. Her skill was prodigious, and had Wagner's own opponent not turned and fled in self-serving measure to secure reinforcements, she might even have prevailed. But, on witnessing his retreat, she rebuked him for abandoning the fray, and in the distraction was meted cold NuRac steel by an Ergosian who wasn't about to trifle with martial propriety.

Wagner sped past her collapse, blind to her end, his eyes riveted instead upon the fleeing NuRac already a full ten strides along the passageway. This soldier, though clad in the weighty armour routinised by the guards in the prison complex, nevertheless sprinted the hall like a fox flushed from a hennery, in all losing but a metre or two of his lead to the fleet-footed prisoner so bent on his assassination. In moments, he would pass the Sunderer's cell; then would come the junction to the main corridor and the substructure egress, his imminent emergence into the courtyard certain to usher revelation and summary defeat to Wagner's and Balgor's implacable insubordination.

Unabating, Wagner bounded forward on calves and quadriceps pushed to tensile exhaustion. His focus short-sighted, his mind was void of all save the urgency of pursuit. There was no room for moral dilemma, for regrets or self-abasing, nor was he in the frame to waste resource on how this unwitting NuRac had stumbled into the role of Fate's unready lackey. Yet, in the midst of seemingly unalterable advantage, the sentry unexpectedly snatched a length of chain from a nearby nook and, yanking it hand over hand in phrenetic abandon, dropped a dividing portcullis directly in Wagner's path.

"Hah! You arrant fools!" he cried in near-breathless taunt, quickly cinching the chain to a mooring bracket. "Whatever your intent, I have stolen it from you!"

Wagner jammed his sword violently through the grate, but to no avail. The NuRac, amply beyond the reach of his blade, smirked victoriously. Disaster loomed now, smiling with teeth of black-latticed pig iron.

With a grunt, Wagner gripped and heaved at the anchored barrier, even as he knew that twenty men couldn't have budged it. Indeed, the gate defied his every effort, not ceding the merest millimetre before him. Still, he hadn't entirely depleted his ability to resort. Dredging ingenuity, he once more moved to wangle his sword through the bars, this time in attempt to dislodge the fix of the chain. Predictably, his enemy moved promptly to smite his effort. And here, although awkwardly extended in limb, Wagner managed to graze the man's palm before retracting.

Cursing, the NuRac quickly recoiled, clutching his lacerated hand with his hale one. Bleeding, hedging about in a jig of outmanoeuvred frustration, he backed off one step, then another—bent on fleeing, but not before first vindicating himself. "Go, then, mongrel," he snarled. "Have at it! Even should you manage to free the gate and raise it, I will have returned with a hundred of my compeers!"

He reared, then, to hie in retreat, when inexplicably he startled and shook, his face contorting into a visage of unspeakable horror and surprise. His eyes bulged like eggs in lay, and the whole of his body froze cold except for his arms, which suddenly thrashed up and back in grapple for the unreachable maleficence that had assailed him from blindside.

Gasping with lungs unabiding, he wavered and then fell, first to his knees, then upon the full of his face, his helmet thudding dully on the earthen floor with a final and sub-magnanimous death toll. With but a single convulsion, essence fled, leaving in its wake a lonely corpse and no quick explanation.

Wagner, more than a bit bewildered, lifted his gaze slowly, as if in unconscious pursuit of the man's receding spirit. And then he suddenly held. Twenty paces up the corridor stood J'nea, a freshly-emptied bow in her grip. Its missile, briefly freed, lay half-submerged in the brigandine plating of the NuRac's back.

She looked at Wagner, and he, at her. No words were necessary. What she had just done was irrevocable.

Lowering the bow and advancing, she hurdled the prostrate body and worked to unfix the chain.

"Having a spot of trouble, are we, *Voknor*?" Her manner was almost too dry for the circumstances, yet nonetheless in liking with her established inconsonance of character. And Wagner, noticeably crestfallen of pride, was quick to downplay his gratitude lest she never let him forget it.

"No trouble," he contended. "Just part of the plan. I was merely giving him enough rope to hang himself."

"Uh-huh." Her tone belied the slightest ort of conviction. She motioned for his cooperation, and together they raised the portcullis, seating it on high just as Balgor drew up.

"What passes here?" the realmson huffed, still battle-edgy and now a trifle suspicious at confronting still more unheralded goings-on. "*Voknor*, how did *she* suddenly become part of this?"

"*She* just salvaged this little farce," J'nea snapped. "Do not make her regret it. Truthfully, you two bunglers have the combined foresight of a vrohda—it confounds me that you have cheated your rightful deaths for so long."

Balgor squinted annoyance. "Apparently," he blurted, "in crucial times, the gods send their niggling harpies to give the what-say to misfortunate and misguided men."

J'nea, bristling her intent to respond, found herself pre-empted with rebuff curt and stern.

"Tut-tut!" Balgor chided. "On the morrow I will gladly entertain your assessment of our less than laudatory performance. Presently, however, we are in mortal crisis. Seethe a while longer, woman. Amass your rebuke for some interim less parlous. But I bid you, nock a fresh arrow and prepare to defend this pair of bunglers with your most capable skill."

This seemed to pacify her for the moment, for she stayed her tongue and drew a shaft from the NuRac quiver cinched so tautly to her back. One look at the arrow's uncommon Herculean head—socketed of iron and of yellow-tempered steel—and all question of how she'd managed to penetrate the guard's plating quickly dissipated. This was serious weaponry, even more lethal than what the parapet archers used.

Applying but slight tension on the serving, she assumed the protective stance requested of her, parcelling her attention between the corridor whence she had come and the preparation engaged in by the headstrong and ill-conceiving schemers who'd so easily entrusted her with their custodianship. Daughter of an arrow-maker, and likewise an apprenticed artisan herself, no one but by sheer number would cross the deadline she defended.

Balgor and Wagner raced in a singular fixity of purpose to revisit the portcullis at the edge of the NuRac grounds. Cloaked in the shadows, they inched the egress up until it cleared waist-length, tethered its pulley firmly in place, and then sprinted back to J'nea's position to commence with the seeming folly that had been their plan from the start. The bodies of those slain lay strewn where they had fallen, and expedience demanded that they remain so. Time was a taskmaster long on unpredictability and dreadfully short on lenience.

Collectively they mustered spirit and fortitude. Then Wagner, keys in hand, began migrating down the line, unlocking gate after gate, with Balgor's armed accompaniment an intended deterrent to any creature bent on assailing Wagner through the latticework. Indeed, the pair in their progression became the foci of an abundance of snarls and feral warnings, the first of two particularly brutal offensives coming courtesy of a pack of agitated croviks, who charged recklessly at the bars and then foamed rabid and furious at their own self-inflicted pain. Such untameable ferocity prompted Wagner into postponing the unbolting of this particular enclosure until his return pass for fear that the creatures might jostle the gate ajar prematurely, and thus make Balgor and him the sorry victims of their own snare.

Yet, it was not with the croviks—but at the very next ingress—where calculated ambush lay in wait. Maybe the two subverters had been inordinately unnerved by the crovik encounter, or perhaps they'd been too hasty in skipping over to this next cell; but before either man could usher a syllable of warning to the other, they were besieged through the grid. From out of this blackened enclosure shot a jutting blur of taloned limb, one that clamped onto Wagner's throat and yanked him face-first to the metal grating like an onion to a kitchen dicer. And although the realmson threw himself to Wagner's defence within a second, it was a second too late.

Waffled against criss-crossed iron while his body floundered, Wagner pried unremittingly at the pincers about his neck. Balgor stormed to hack off the attacker's appendage through the lattice, but a second claw struck from the shadows and clamped onto his sword arm in kind, wrenching him likewise to the gridiron. Thrust to the grate, he lost his weapon to excruciation, as both his fist and his forearm were swallowed by the darkness within the cell.

Wagner, with a vice of steely fingers at his throat and an air supply in serious wane, felt unconsciousness crowding out lucidity. Images both true and non-sensical began to bespatter his fuzzying mental tableau, as his mind stepped over and upon itself in its exasperation to relay some minutia of relevance from a jumble of fluidly interlacing scenarios compressed and distorted by encroaching coma. The most prevailing eidolon focused on a human body that lay face up somewhere on the grounds of the Howsley Centre for Mental Health. It was a man's body, a naked one, his own. Jon Mazzio stood over it; Sally Lemanski, too. The O'Connell woman bided nearby, as did Brian Williams, and an incongruous smattering of long-forgotten patrons of the Filthy Lucre. Sara was there, too, statuesque and solemn, sporting a tiny, scarified "X" beneath her right eye. Other figures pressed around in silent gallery, their faces obscured by something that was neither light nor shadow.

Foremost of the entirety was the tabloid holy man, *Mr. Miracle* himself. Garbed in raiment more Ergosian than earthly-contemporary, he was suddenly prominent and close, a pewter *sigma* dangling from his neck by a leather thong. His eyes were bluest blue, and his left eye bore around it the odd ceremony of a soot-like circle. Stepping before Wagner's prostrate form, he genuflected alongside him, a mourner for a stranger. He then took Wagner's limp hand firmly into his own, and, manipulating it like a tool, pressed its middle finger rather mechanically into the lower opisthenar of his own fisted hand, into the small cleft where the back of the hand meets the wrist. Promptly, *Miracle* relaxed his fist, and suddenly did the cadaverous Wagner come alive, his eyes at once seeing the figure above him. Only, the face to whom this Wagner awakened was not as it had been. No longer was it *Miracle's* visage leaning over him. It was the Vofspar female's.

In this precise moment, the physical Wagner, the garrotted Wagner, broke from his vision, jammed his finger reflexively into the opisthenar of his aggressor's contracting claw, and instantly—easily—freed himself of the creature's death hold. His attacker's digits, spasming like limp tendrils of overcooked pasta, retracted into the shadows, but Wagner lashed after them and clamped vehemently onto the withdrawing wrist, using the grate as leverage and yanking the creature bodily into the lattice in the same manner that had been done to him. Balgor, needing no cue, hauled back and wrenched the denizen's other limb through the bars, whereby both men grappled in aggravated brannigan to restrain their revealed assailer—none other than the Vofspar herself.

"Wretched she-devil!" cried Balgor, pivoting his feet and his girth to counter the creature's frenzied locomotion. Her double-thumbed claw, clamped within his arm lock, flounced unimpaired, and it was all that he could do to avoid an unwanted shred-fest.

"Hold fast!" shouted J'nea, now behind them with arrow aimed at the Vofspar's breast. "This one will not go kindly."

"No!" Wagner's voice contended with an escalated pandemonium of snarls and howls from the surrounding cells. "Don't shoot! Don't shoot!"

Both Ergosians protested, Balgor most adamantly. "You would champion such fiendishness?"

Wagner fought to maintain his bracing. "Trust me, Balgor."

The realmson wasn't buying. "Long have I abided and abetted your eccentricities," he said. "And why? Because you are my friend. And true, in the past, your prognosticating has been uncannily sound. But my deference overreaches its limit here and now!"

"Indulge me once more," Wagner pled, his grip yet sturdy. "This Vofspar and I have been linked from the beginning. I can't just let her be killed like this."

"You can, *Voknor*. And you will. Woman, let your arrow fly."

J'nea drew back on the bow.

"J'nea, don't," said Wagner. "This creature is a prisoner like us. She's here against her will! Can you blame her for lashing out?"

"If you could only see your own ravaged throat," said J'nea through her grimace, "you would urge me on."

The Vofspar thrashed and buffeted within their grasps.

"*Now*, woman," said Balgor.

Powerless, Wagner spun reason like a frantic spider. "Balgor, believe me—somehow she's important. Let her live. We can toss her a key just before we let the others out. She's intelligent—she'll figure it out. After that, she can fend for herself."

"You had better decide, you two," warned J'nea. "This ruckus cannot go long without attracting someone's attention."

Wagner locked gazes with his friend. Using his eyes, he begged for the faith that his lips no longer entreated. Balgor, tight-mouthed in contemptuous snarl, knew this ritual all too well. Angrily, unwillingly, resentfully, he grunted assent, and together they released their captive.

The Vofspar immediately made her outrage known to them in a fractious tirade of affront. But without their combativeness to fuel her aggression, she gradually tapered it to something more in keeping with a cautious stand-off between foes who contended under circumstances favourable to neither side. Wagner modelled empty hands before her in a gesture of reassurance; and she, contained of her venom, came to study him and his motions with rising intrigue, much more than she did his two companions, almost as if she were enmeshed in mental rummagings for the answer that might explain the unscratchable inkling induced by Wagner's presence. Seen now through eyes no longer aflame with rage, he evoked in her a stirring of inhostile recency; and although she didn't easily, nor immediately, recognise him, the Vofspar knew that she and he were not without acquaintance either. Appearances may change, but scents never lie.

All three humans left her then, hurrying along in their insurrection before any other ill hap set them further back. Remarkably, they succeeded in unlocking every cell on that side of the T-junction—and this, not a moment too soon. For it so happened that, beyond the corner and down the far end, an observant soldier from the billeting grounds caught casual notice of the half-raised portcullis and, while investigating it, had evidently become piqued by the raucousness within the substructure.

Such could have spelled disaster in no time at all. But, on this occasion, Fortune's pendulum wafted in upswing. Once the yowls and growls dwindled to medial levels in the wake of the Vofspar incident, the guard's curiosity focused back upon the enigma of the portcullis. Here, his inquisitive nature quickly became the prisoners' windfall, for by assuming that the mechanism had been left in partial raise by one of his own—a messenger, perhaps, on a brief undertaking into the substructure—he empowered himself into unhooking the tether, and proudly *raised* the gateway full up!

"Works for me," whispered Wagner as he and Balgor peered around the corner. Speedily, then, they hustled back toward the crovik enclosure, Balgor a few paces to the rear, methodically knocking every gate askew as he went. Wagner then paused until his friend had passed him before cautiously unlocking the crovik cell, careful to suppress the grating's inward draw. Following this, he tossed the entire ring of keys into the Vofspar's cell, and raced away in pursuit of his truest ally. When they'd passed J'nea near the spot where the lone NuRac had thought to hold Wagner hostage, J'nea dropped the barrier behind them; and while she and Balgor watched the animals gradually discovering their liberty, Wagner moved on to the crank-room and to Skol.

The sentries were as they'd been left. Wagner crossed the room and plunged the *one* key that he'd retained into the slot, unbarring the way into Skol's hovel. The brute, having alerted to the ululation both beyond his home and down the outside corridor, looked up almost knowingly, and mutely took in the whole of Wagner's simplistic instruction.

"Skol. Balgor and I are going away. You come too?"

Skol grunted. Whether the concept of "away" meant anything to him was speculation for which Wagner lacked the luxury.

"We go," Wagner repeated. "Bones and entrails—you come too?"

At this, Skol started right up as if Balgor's invective had triggered some post-hypnotic suggestion. "*Bohn'z'n entraylz, bohn'z'n entraylz. Comtu.*"

Wagner flew into the crank-room and unmoored the capstan. "Here goes nothing, Skolsy ol' boy," he muttered to himself. "You're either going to snuff us all within the first minute, or you're gonna be our golden ticket to freedom."

Outside the cell, a glut of animals now choked the corridor. Skirmishing among themselves, some breeds engaged in vicious altercation with one another, while others panicked and stampeded along the only route open to them. Somewhere far up the passage, the NuRac who'd been patting himself on the back for freeing up the lodged egress now stood in absolute horror as a wave of incensed and incisored ferocity gushed like torrential floodwaters around the corner and all too menacingly in his direction. Fumbling for a scrap of wits, he leapt for the pulley apparatus in a hapless effort to redrop the barrier and save himself. Yet, he found his trembling hands quite incapable of manipulating the works as efficiently as they had before. In fact, it was more like trying to fasten one's bootlaces with mittened fingers. He couldn't do it, not calmly, not in time, so he instead made a run for the soldiers' grounds; and, accomplishing this unscathed, he emerged into the open in scream and rave a full octave beyond his normal capability. His words, however, all but unintelligible in his panic, the company of soldiers in the yard had no notion of the deadly issue they were about to encounter within dwindling seconds.

Back on their end, Balgor and J'nea watched until the drove tapered to but a straggler here and there, both Ergosians experiencing the electric perspiration of having instigated such a considerable measure of the bloodbath now occurring in the NuRac compound.

"You *do* know that we are in the thick of subversion and mayhem," said the trusty, "with no path of return?"

"Aye," countered Balgor, his head pressed to the portcullis as he watched the last of the beasts plodding away to join the onslaught. "It is a grand feeling, is it not?"

"Thus far," she replied, "I would say *not*." Turning her attention to a noise behind them, she suddenly blenched at the sight of the most ruthless of behemoths blocking their retreat. Swiftly, she arrowed up and drew her bowstring to full extreme, and was nigh unto releasing when Balgor interceded.

"Nay, woman—he is our ally!" Turning back, he met Skol face-to-face and added: "I hope."

"*Bohn'z'n entraylz,*" proclaimed Skol.

The brute milled about in obvious confusion before turning to the comparatively scrawny Wagner for guidance.

"Oh, tell me this is not madness!" said J'nea. "And you two are far greater lunatics than he. The Sunderer? He is too unpredictable, too demented—"

"Do not tell *me*," Balgor insisted. "Tell *Voknor*. Tell *Skol*."

Inflamed and distressed, J'nea pursed her lips and held her tongue with ill grace. The brute already freed, trying to return him to the wheel would be like a one-armed man trying to flea-dip a crovik. Completely in opposition of their strategy, her mood would be on high simmer until this ordeal reached conclusion. Still, she would go along, if only because the situation now demanded it. Of her own volition she had thrown in with dreamers and risk-mongers, and now was being forced into the mould herself. And anyone who knew J'nea knew that going along on someone else's ride did not come easy to her. Lack of autonomy in a prison camp was one thing, certainly; but to want for control while attempting one's own liberation was quite another.

Her early prognostications were proving accurate: mayhem indeed reigned that morning. Before the four of them even managed to step back upon the prisoner courtyard, full alarum had been raised. Horns blared, bells sounded, shouts reverberated, and racing feet pounded in a magnificently chaotic overture of discord that left guard posts vacated, routines disrupted, and attentions distracted—in all, a gamut of conditions deliciously favourable for revolution.

Minutes into the fracas, when sentries along the palaestra catwalks began disappearing—recalled, no doubt, to aid their hapless peers on the other side of the arena compound—Tamek, Bilahdu, and one-dozen fighting-mad recruits went to work. The word relayed to an already wondering population, only a paltry handful of the newly-enlightened paused in wary hesitation while the zealots and those long on desperation now ate of—and digested—the incendiary bruit like a meal for which they'd too long fasted. Charging the gates, the tunnels, the peripheral sentries, they found that even wooden swords and staffs were effective when wielded by enough bodies, every one of which drew strength in believing that Ergosian liberators warred on their behalf somewhere outside QieLahr's very walls.

Grum, flabbergasted from atop his dais, gathered his bodyguards quickly to him and hastened toward the nearest exit, itself already under siege by rebel dissenters. His henchmen strickled a path for him through the flailing mob, and by their efforts did Grum—so prideful and ominous scant minutes ago—now scurry for his life like a vole unnested by hungry hounds. Tamek, enwreathed by the swayed patriots who would ply their mettle by his order, witnessed the Taskmaster's retreat from afar but could do naught to stop him. It scarcely mattered, however, for the flight of a single foe—even Taskmaster Grum—would weigh insignificantly against that day's agenda. There was entirely too much to accomplish before the advantage of surprise was wrested from Ergosian facility, and Grum in his withdrawal could likely do little to alter this fact.

Confusion fell about the camp like Biblical hail, engulfing routine and regiment with incitive stokings of revolution. The prison's meagre complement of NuRac sentries found itself whelmed by sheer multitude, what alarm they'd succeeded in raising going unnoticed by their congeners, who were themselves the unfortunate hosts to quadrupedal havoc a sturdy javelin's toss beyond the structural division. Never would such full-scale rioting have been predicted. Never would it have been thought possible. And, given what the Ergosian upstarts had accomplished within the first ten minutes, the NuRacs might hence have considered striking that presumptive word, "never," from their list of prison regulatory maxims. Had reinforcements from the great city itself been more precipitate in amassing to the cause of defence, the most critical altercations on all fronts might have been assuaged, and the uprising, defused with the retributive permanence that only flogging, dismemberment, and exemplary execution could deliver. As it was, no timely backup would be issuing through archway or over parapet like some clichéd cavalry of Old West genre cinema—only scads of scampering, wild-eyed Ergosians in unquashable animus.

To the trained eye, the insurgence was undeniably lacking in structure, as the greater portion of this hooting, bellowing mob demonstrated ochlocracy at its most basic and rudimentary levels. True, those representing the gladiator factions were indeed seen to be incorporating some vestige of logical cunning in gaining control of this strategic exit or in vanquishing that cluster of NuRac sentries; but, quite astoundingly, the prisoners who had been emancipated from the textileries and the kitchens—and from other industry where military experience was in limited account—fought tooth and nail in a fashion equally as unpredictable as it was savage. Using sticks, rocks, kitchen ladles, meat cleavers, even treadles and pieces of the harness frames ripped from the hand looms of the weaving halls, they answered the summons in any and all manner fathomable. For the bulk of these folk, their Sentinel and his most trusted aides had, on the spur, ransomed everything for the realm's salvation; and although caught in the wake of this most difficult of decisions, these very people—apprehensive and terrified as they no doubt were—would rally in kind to swell a ripple into a crashing wave, no matter the good or bad that the day's end would bring. In this respect, Wagner had guessed correctly; with revolt already manifesting around them, and the fabrication of Mirko's brigands mobilised without, those who were compelled to hitch themselves to this runaway dray of insurrection hadn't the laxity to dwell on either consequence or discretion, but instead on the once and forever snapping of the loathed NuRac leash.

Ignorant of the coup's progression over on the palaestra, Wagner and his merry band spilled out onto the courtyard grounds and were disheartened by the scene that met them. With the fatter measure of the revolt occurring in Tamek's venue and in the industry beyond, only a handful of the emancipated had found their way back here, where their preliminary duties were to alert Papa Olask and his staff, to make ready to gather up the wounded, and then to move on to the dungeon blocks for further rescuing—all this while simultaneously staving any NuRac opposition that they were to encounter. A tall enough order for armed liberators, it was positively aerial for men and women who brandished little more than sticks and facsimiled blades. Noting their struggle, Balgor raced to add his authentic steel to the fray, while J'nea launched shaft after shaft at every catwalk soldier unfortunate enough to find himself in the sights of her bow and the keen eye behind it. In doomed succession, said sentries pitched groundward like apples felled by blustery storm, with J'nea going nine for nine and all but depleting her quiver in an unflinching run of coolly mechanical volleying. Once expended of arrows, however, she was hardly in want for armaments; prior to leaving the substructure, she'd purloined from Skol's cell the last of the swords and two of the daggers made ownerless by Wagner's and Balgor's butchery, and had additionally tucked the errant cudgel hip-side in her trousers for supplementary peace of mind. Too much was at risk, she'd told her companions, to allow oneself to be caught short in the midst of such fateful upheaval, and any filchable weapon was simply added insurance. Having crossed with them into the realm of no return, she could hardly allow herself to ever be retaken by her hosts, for the punishment for a trusty-turned-traitor was far and above the most agonising of retributions the NuRacs meted. She would sooner perish before letting it come to that, and by her archery she made evident that determination. Within moments, then, the bow— which she'd confessed to have torn that morning from a trophy rack in none other than Grum's private armoury—was rendered useless in its primary function; but briefly did it persevere by way of utility and innovation. Whirling it like a quarterstaff, J'nea thrashed it across a half-dozen helmeted heads until, inevitably, it splintered into kindling, whereby she unsheathed her hand-and-a-half sword and inaugurated its steel in a vitriolic rite of NuRac bloodletting.

In the midst of it all, quietly flanking Wagner, was the mighty Skol. Initially agitated in beholding what, to him, was just another arena battle, he had quite promptly become entranced (and rather vacuously at that) by the sequential plummeting of J'nea's victims as she'd toppled them one before the next from the scaffolding around him. Absorbed at the onset by their graceless sprawling and the ensuing clangour as their armour smacked the earth, his captivation was more with the mushrooming dust clouds jettisoned skyward at their demise; and thus enthralled by this, he paid little heed to the stock skirmishes unfolding immediately before and around him. In turnabout, those at the core of the riot had yet to even notice his presence on the field. If they had, both NuRac and Ergosian alike would have produced dust clouds of their own, risen of their expeditious retreat.

Once evened-up, the courtyard fracas coursed on with no obvious advantage to either side. Eventually, however, it would again favour the NuRacs, for the outer ward portcullis soon ascended and began spewing forth a menacing issue of NuRac reserves. This new inrush, consisting of outer curtain sentries, walk-betweens and messengers, and administrative officers who—alerted to the as-of-then undefined trouble, and banding together procedurally to manage the crisis—were of a sudden to confront the unthinkable. Had they even suspected who and what they would be encountering, they surely would have opted to override procedure with options more prudent and less honourable. To their credit, they strove forward in sublime defence of modality and home soil, for in the end it was all that they possessed.

Glimpsing this eruption of enemy reinforcement, Wagner quickly snapped Skol from his dalliance and coaxed him by entreaty (and with verbal "Balgorisms") into helping to plug the intruders' influx at the source. Incredibly, almost in synergetic reflex to Wagner's forward spring, the brute followed, indeed at a gait vastly more speedy than any established precedent had indicated might lie within his ability. His restricting harness, it seemed, had served in governing more than his inclination to resist incarceration, and here, before the tenth soldier could emerge onto the grounds, they were all of them confronted by a hulking chimaera and the armed prisoner beside him.

Like stepping from a city curb and into the path of an uprushing bus with "OBLIVION" stamped on its route placard—such was how Wagner similised the plight of those luckless sentries who emerged from the tunnel and into the Sunderer's maul. Those who were first to discover their fateful blunder could hardly reverse course once out in the open, while those to the rear kept coming, ploughing into the forerunners who even then were encountering the thresh of Skol's mincemeat-making talons. Overwhelmingly void of emotion, Skol rent their protective armour like a scullion peeling shrimp, and, alternating randomly between his basic MO of maim 'n' mangle and the swifter death by snapped neck or snapped body, he eliminated his luckless opponents faster than J'nea had with her catwalk victims, while Wagner—close to upchucking at Skol's disassembly-line handiwork—lit into those few sentries who'd miraculously squeaked past Skol's snag.

It was no easy thing what they did; and even with Skol's tremendous malice and the collective determination of the entire rebel covey, they only barely succeeded in taking the courtyard for their own. With each foe fallen, his weapon was distributed into eager, upstart hands, and thus the tides of change rose incrementally in Ergosian favour.

In the infirmary, the coup had come as a total surprise to Papa Olask, and it plainly unsettled him. With so many of the weak and afflicted suddenly placed on perilous ground, for all of Olask's misgivings he knew that there was naught to be done to stop a raging juggernaut already in motion—nor would he have thought to try. But neither would he callously cast the bodies of the infirm beneath its wheels, nor let it pass bereft of his actions to safeguard those under his care. And truly, once he'd been appropriately enlightened—and coerced by the incentive of outside liberators—he hurried to prep those in most dire need, and made ready to deliver them into the rescuing arms of a non-existent Ergosian army, the hoax of which he surely would long condemn in an aftermath that Fate had yet to impart.

J'nea, accompanied by the handful of patriots who together had predominated in the initial scrap, scurried on now to the detention block, and there they found the NuRac posts completely deserted from the camp-wide call to arms. Facilely unhitching the queue of trapdoors, the hatches were all swung wide, and the occupants, salvaged with far greater haste than care. With Time herself their most crucial liaison—and the most fickle of allies—the notion of catering to any individual's frailties or impairments was, by necessity, yielded to remissness until the day in its pendency had meted its spoils of disaster or delivery. Gaunt, effete dregs were therefore hoisted from the blackness like malformed babes torn from festering wombs, and were carried away and placed into the arms of newly freed clothiers and textile workers and others whose combatant skills were not on par with their gladiator cousins. Briefly, then, these wretches were to find haven in Olask's entourage of the travel-worthy afflicted. They were dependent upon their kinspeople to get them not only beyond QieLahr, but ultimately to some reasonable place of safety.

Throughout the tumult, Wagner continually entertained the simulacra of revisitation, of having psychically encountered a myriad of comparably constituent situations with an eye and a presence that, though undeniably his own, were conspicuously absent from his sphere of experience. Prognostic and powerfully apocryphal images, their portent now pressed like imprintings over the template of confirmed memory. It seemed almost as if he carried with him some ilk of subliminal blueprint whose end result was yet subject to a host of divergences—each capable of aiding or hindering a solitary, mysterious fruition. Whisking him ever so fleetingly from his current strife, they relegated his consciousness to a place beyond the finite scope of ocular registry, and there he walked the *sui generis* hinterland amid unfamiliar imagery and locales his odd affinity for which he was unqualified to explain. From within his thoughtscape he observed the visages of even more strangers of apparently Ergosian filiation, brothers and sisters unmet and unreputed, yet who nevertheless prompted in him the most inexplicably ardent and steadfast emotive longings. Alongside them he bestrode the surreal grasses of battlefields far removed from (yet undeniably integral to) worldly Ergosian and NuRac skirmishing where, among flailing bodies and violent acts, the inevitability of conflict grappled with the indelibility of hope. At the periphery of these scenes of carnage, Wagner and these companions—like the vagabond children of an alternatively spiteful and nurturing earth mother—bore the flood of this visional chaos as it followed a conformity that, in turn, trailed an antecedent chaos.

Of a hundred such cycles, of the hundred aftermaths that ensued, somewhere amid the ashes and debris of each milieu, Wagner would always espy the Soork, as many times as not a cracked and brittle and sootish facsimile of itself, seemingly spent and discardable as an old shell casing. A talisman, however, in any incarnation, it would survive every cataclysm, if not completely then in part; and in its observable decrepitude, it never failed at some point to commence at radiating inscrutable light—and from said escalation came borne some mode of transformation that undid whatever previously destructive act of infamy had delivered it to that state. Slaughter and devastation gave way to revival; lethality opened anew the gates to life; and suddenly the battlefield and the abstract vista around it teemed with the rejuvenated splendour of nature unspoiled.

Yet, such expectance and upliftment could not remain so for long, not with Wagner's apparitional history. Almost on cue, then, would the vision quite readily re-submerge into unreadable allegory, with one truly vivid—and disturbing—scenario that found the nigrescent figure of Death himself ushering Peace into the world like a debutante, whereby Peace, in an odd and almost instantaneous turnabout, assumed dominance and incongruously set the suddenly eager and obliging lord of finality upon the realm like a hound on the hunt.

Wagner found himself both too obtuse and too intellectually adolescent to either fully comprehend or to reconcile himself to the unwieldy concepts hurtling his way. But of the notions that he *could* grasp—particularly those that flecked his memory's shortcomings with enticing familiarity, and which inferred an undeniable sense of his reliving events that had never occurred—he could not strictly slot them into any one niche of current relevance. Nor could he tag them as déjà vu, for the evidence of faulty or superimposed experiential veracity was lacking all the way around. Many times in the past had his inklings panned out. More often had the visional weavings pulled into a tight-stitched, albeit transient, cohesion of actuality before falling prey to the inevitable mental fraying that kept his senses unhinged and his mind wondering. There was no phrase of which he was aware, and no theory to describe, the circuitous, storybook loop that peregrinated his mind's all too fertile terrain; and in the midst of campwide revolution it was hardly the time to search for one.

Back in the present, Wagner dissuaded Skol from mangling the last of the NuRac bodies that, broken and disjointed like rag dolls thrust into the spokes of speeding bicycles, he'd been flinging about as compensatory release for a bristled aggression still unsated. While the brute distracted easily enough, he couldn't effortlessly be made to appreciate his puny benefactor's intent; indeed, in his bloodlust, Skol very nearly throttled the temporarily unrecognised Wagner in the manner that he had the soldiers—but ultimately retracted his claws by Wagner's timely diktat. For a treacherous instant, however, Wagner had recoiled anticipatorily at Skol's near-walloping roundhouse; and although he couldn't be at all certain, Wagner believed he'd sensed a momentary indication that it was his gift of instinctual sortilege that somehow had either reared invisibly in his defence or, in recognising the imminence of assault, had appealed to—or influenced—Skol's own subconscious impulses on a level more subtle and benign. If true, then perhaps this had been the aggression-dampening governor in his and Skol's unlikely alliance all along, whereby the seed of Wagner's still inextricable manipulation had put forth its shoots amid the monster's volitional pathways, to insinuate and entwine like gentler restraints upon his very soul.

Wagner would have preferred to think this wasn't entirely so.

New furore to his rear prompted Wagner's turnabout, and in his pivot he thrilled to see gladiators filing into the courtyard, far across the way. Likely not having won out on the palaestra, but rather withdrawing on Tamek's command, the strategy would bring the Ergosian mass one step closer to the way out. Seeing the same splendid sight, the always resourceful Balgor stood outside the infirmary, meting pilfered NuRac weaponry to any of the ambulatory wounded who felt confident enough to heft sword, pike, or cudgel. As the threat of NuRac pursuance was surely to plague the courtyard anon, he readied the able-bodied into the do-or-die venture of backing up Tamek's group in its fallback.

Satisfied and assured that events were moving as planned—and anxious to remove Skol from the eyes of those newcomers who would surely be confounded by him—Wagner urged the child-monster through the passage and beyond to the outer ward. Quite a different sight, here, from the one in which, weeks back, he'd been processed from the caravan coffle, it was now a deserted parade of sand and space, unsurveilled in both directions. No NuRacs left to guard it, those whom Wagner and Skol hadn't just ambushed in the courtyard had probably been recalled to aid their compeers in the menagerie ordeal.

Approaching the first of the three massive gates of the outer wall, Wagner implored Skol to help him hoist them skyward. The brute caught on with little prompting. Heartily putting might and muscle into the task, his hirsute and ogre-like frame nevertheless deferred to a barrier that simply would not part from its earthen mooring.

Wagner cursed. Skol echoed the curse, and both beings peered discerningly through the lattice—Wagner, to eye the chains that, fixed by NuRac guards long gone from their posts, frustrated their progress; and Skol, to investigate what manner of beast might be dwelling in what, to his unlearned mind, appeared to be a tunnel-like abode of sorts.

It was clear that, short of scaling the wall and locating the stairwelled descent to the inner alcove, the hope of penetrating here was an unfulfillable lark. And yet, to get the weak and needy beyond the walls, it had to be done.

Within minutes, however, Skol and Wagner were no longer the only escapees upon the ward. The newly freed were rapidly being brought through at the urging—and with the assistance—of Olask, J'nea, and those Ergosian defenders who'd been entrusted with their safety. While another step forward for the uprising, it proved an undeniable hindrance to Wagner's efforts, for there was not a soul entering the ward who did not soon intuit from legend and hearsay just who it was who stood the grounds to Wagner's right. And, as expected, all of them were effectively petrified and declinatory, despite the unified sense of confidence inspired mere moments ago by their escorts and same's newly obtained implements. Few were prepared to observe the sight with objectivity enough to breach the consentient disregard for what was clearly a strange compliance in Skol's carriage and in his manner in general. Knowing the lore, but not the living being, none knew what to make of this relatively becalmed ersatz version poised so nonchalantly at Wagner's flank. The very idea of it shattered their established and eternal verities, creating an impossible sequent that stunk foul like the offal of some deceit of dark sorcery that they were powerless to understand. Their reactions understatedly disconfirmatory, such overwhelming discrepancy between the beast of legend and this exhibitory one launched an armada of verbal confusion and inquiry across a choppy sea of emerging fecklessness. It would have been all that anyone, even Tamek himself, could have done to convince them once and twice and over again that all was truly right—so many spirits, deflated and aghast, did shrink at the sight of the brute.

Wagner took little interest in the people's reaction. His single-minded focus of traversing the passage to the outside overrode the trivialities of reputation or public opinion. He had never been this close before, and he fancied he never would be again. If he felt a peck selfish because of it, he easily shook it off. Nothing else mattered now, save for action. In Greek myth, Perseus once risked wielding the deadly-even-*after*-death head of Medusa to rid Sephiros of a tyrant. Not so utterly dissimilar (and by the grace of some unrevealed deity's irony-loving inventiveness), Skol had become Wagner's own Gorgon's head of utility. Yet, with his long history of unruliness and virulent rage, Skol was at the same time possessed of an unexplored essence of soulful waggery that had, in the brevity of a week's time, endeared itself to two reluctant and totally unprepared gladiators. As it turned out, he was so much more than just a hideous Gorgon, and yet considerably less than Evil personified, and the unforeseen possibilities had begun to nudge Wagner's thinking into new and subversively beguiling avenues. After all, was it conceivable that the mythical Medusa—a repulsive and reclusive creature who dwelled unthreateningly on her remote island, far from humans and their biases—had been equally as misunderstood?

Wagner glanced into the ever-growing multitude. Unable to locate Balgor among the crush, nor Uthok or Bilahdu, he panned across the canvas of visages, and chanced to lock onto J'nea—perhaps not as fully obliging as the others, but far more suited to his needs. Her cheeks smudged with dirt, her hair dishevelled, and her limbs grimy from salvaging souls from the dungeon block, she looked much like she had on the very day that he'd first seen her. Only her expression exhibited deviation from that memory. Now, accompanying Olask at the heart of the overborne multitude, her countenance alternated in brief, almost calculable intervals between steely resolve and indefatigable compassion as she went from comforting this wretch or that ailer, to setting her roving eyes aflutter in cautious vigilance of the unstable surroundings that were ripe for change and new challenge at any given moment. Back and forth it went, two diverse beings in the same body—the succouring ministrant whom she usually hid, and the icebound warrior whom she'd learned to hide behind—and for all of a second it mirrored for Wagner the multifariousness of his own nature.

Meeting his gaze purely by chance, J'nea gleaned from it the imploration unlent by anything he might have shouted to her, and was quick to separate herself from those whom she'd saved so that she might approach him.

"Do you know," he asked, once more putting himself in her debt, "where to find the risers that lead down between these gates?"

She first scrutinised and shook the portcullis as if thinking he'd not made similar attempt to budge it. "Up there," she said, pointing. "The uppermost spire. There is a steep, narrow staircase that—" She paused, stepped back, and surveyed the wall and the corbelling above. "Were I to be hefted to within a handhold of that outcropping," she said, "I, myself, could reach topside with relative ease."

Duteously and mutely, Wagner assented, interlocked his fingers, and offered her a boost. J'nea smirked at his gallantry as she stepped up with her left boot. Then, as Wagner straightened himself, she arched herself in full cat-stretch up toward the corbel some four metres above the ground.

While the trusty evaluated her next move, the captive Wagner glanced out from under the strain to assess the goings-on behind them. There, amid the glut of the freed, he finally caught glimpse of his best friend, hale and energised and accompanied by Uthok and the brothers, Grandio and Graspa, as they escorted the last of the infirm through the passage. Quickly remanding said weak and wounded into the care of the freed kitchen and textilery workers, Balgor wasted not a second in calling for the most seasoned fighters to head back to courtyard to support Tamek's unit, still engaged. Although a handful of adverse contingencies had been factored into the escape, Tamek's group was never meant to manage the full brunt of NuRac reprisal, and it was surely giving Balgor as much cause for runaway concern as it was Wagner. The deputation moving swiftly for the tunnel, Balgor— mid-group—looked back briefly, chancing to intercept Wagner's interest. Their eye-lock lasting only long enough for Wagner to get a general read of concern, it was Balgor who broke off first, integrating with the file and launching into what now was circumstantial necessity within their crazy and unstoppable plan to empty the entire camp of its enthralled.

Before J'nea's stratagem concluded, she had Wagner hefting her far higher and for a good deal longer than he'd anticipated. A foot in each hand, his arms fully extended and in palsied tremor under the strain, he was amazed that he'd actually been able to press her completely upward with so awkward a handhold—although her faith in him was patent in that she hadn't wavered in any extreme, nor needed to check her balance at all. Too, it seemed that his physical strength had, in his weeks of training, come to surpass the genetic limits of his ectomorphic build, and particularly blatantly at that; after all, holding a woman overhead by one's arm strength alone was no fribbling feat. Yet, just as his luck would have it, she entreated him for a little more lift—of which he had none to give—leading to his ultimate recruitment of the curious Skol who, shuffling forward with a certain degree of autistic heedfulness, grasped Wagner harshly by the torso and hefted him gruffly up the rockface, enough to permit J'nea to throw grip to the overhang.

Gasps emanating amid the temporarily halted scurry behind them, none of the prisoners could have been more surprised than Wagner, who, having solicited Skol's assistance while under duress (and without thinking better of it), had once more placed himself in the path of potential peril *and* had come away intact—a few compressed ribs notwithstanding.

J'nea scaled the remainder of the wall nimbly and without incident, and once atop the catwalk she quickly surveyed in all directions before disappearing into the spire. Wagner, again earthbound, turned to his monstrous cohort that he might praise him, but found Skol's attention and purpose already back on the portcullis, which he rattled as a means of rousing the non-existent animal that he believed to be lurking within.

For a pregnant moment, in a different way, Wagner did the same on a psycho-logical scale. Scrutinising the beast, he inaugurated a means of mentally clamber-ing his way down through the endopsychic crags that zagged into Skol's world of isolated ignorance. It was an arduous task, actually, to do so with objectivity; and he wasn't completely sure that he could conquer that stigma. But such insight could certainly prove advantageous. Descending deep into his symbolically created crevasse beneath Skol's external hideousness, beyond the georama of pitchy eschar and lung-stinging acridity that—by means of speculative prejudgement—would typically have been an unenlightened characterisation of the host should one have imagined oneself on the inside looking out, Wagner fancied the area beyond to be more refulgent than anybody's casual assessment would ever have allowed. Past and future had no place here.

They were like old photographs left out carelessly in the sunlight, their images little more than indecipherable phantasms, void of significance, free of sentiment. No concept not easily associated with the immediate claimed any precedence—not regrets, not triumph, not aspirations, not conscience—nothing existed but the here and now. Wagner fancied this aspect of Skol's quiddity as both curse and bliss in the same package; too, it would have been a dereliction were he not to admit to the irreconcilable pangs of pity and envy that he felt as a consequence. An odd cocktail of feelings, he found the sensation not just a little unsettling.

New cries suddenly arose from the compound beyond, and Wagner was compelled to pivot in their direction. The din emanating fatly from within the ward-to-courtyard tunnel, he knew at once that Balgor and the others had met with trouble. Immediately he felt shamefaced and negligent, a shirker who leaves the grisly tasks for others to perform. The sentiment, however, didn't prevail. He himself had cobbled much of this uprising together from scratch; and although originally devised for personal reasons, its success or its failure would, regardless, serve to usher a resounding after-clap throughout the NuRac and Ergosian nations for weeks and months to come. Its message of a people's unified courage would ripple to all corners of the realm. Every role that day was a vital one.

Distracted yet again, the sound of chains skittering over pulleys brought Wagner around. Before him, the portcullis heaved abruptly upward like the gates of hell before the Lamb; and Skol—about the furthest thing from Lamb or lamb—availed himself of the breach and stomped his gleeful way into the shadowed alcove that J'nea, in her expedition, had opened up for them. Hoisting the gate from the inside, J'nea wound the chain firmly around the cleat, careful to maintain a wary eye on the unpredictable beast as she did so. And Wagner, anxious for her safety, followed Skol through, but ultimately found the brute's intent neither with J'nea nor upon the next two gates ahead of them, but rather on unfathomable concerns of the passage's interior itself.

On meeting the trusty, Wagner acknowledged her considerable competence with brief and exaggerated praise. She shook off the homage with a scoffing shrug. Together, they moved on to raise the unsecured second grating, followed by the third, finding all posts deserted, and astonishingly nothing at all between them and the far-reaching lea without.

Wagner was keen to hightail it for the distant woods and never look back; but the grip of something greater than himself held him fast. "Help Papa Olask," he snapped to J'nea. "Help him to get the frail, the wounded, and the kids outta here. Send some of the remaining warriors out first, just in case of an ambush. I'm taking Skol with me, back into the courtyard, so that we won't intimidate anyone unnecessarily."

The trusty looked at him with shadowy, smaragdine eyes of uncertainty. "You are not coming? After all of your tireless babble of wishing for your freedom?"

"Oh, I'm going—you can bank on that," he said, his words coupled with a half-snorted laugh whose expelling seemed to hint at some new but unbrandished significance.

"It would be more prudent to go now," she said. "Freedom beckons. Deny such opportunity, *Voknor*, and you may later be joining hands with regret and remorse in a personal dirge."

He gazed back at her with pithy resilience. "Then I guess I'll just have to take solace in knowing that I'm not as totally unconscionable as we both may have thought."

He turned, then, and headed back into the glare of the ward sun, a sun suddenly even more oppressive than its more magnificent semblance on the free side of the walls. "Go on, J'nea," he called as he went, "gather up your people. We'll hook up with you on the outside. I promise."

He barked a friendly command to Skol, who, ignoring him at first, reluctantly emerged from his inconsequential musings and followed.

J'nea tailed them apace, confused and apprehensive.

"*Voknor!*" she shouted.

Wagner increased his gait. Skol lollygagged, but then closed fast, their deliberate arc of travel steering them away from the crush of Ergosians who, even without J'nea's overseeing, were preparing to evacuate the camp.

"*Voknor!*"

"I've *got* to help them!" he shouted, unflagging. "Without Tamek and Balgor, this scheme would never have flown! I owe it to them—I owe it to *everybody*—to fight alongside them! It wouldn't feel right otherwise!"

Although terrified for him, in the end his loyalty satisfied her. Forsaking an argument that she would not win, she bade him good fortune. Then they parted— J'nea sprinting off to orchestrate the camp-wide efflux, and he, off onto the searing griddle of battle. Skol amazingly still in tow, the two of them made the tunnel and bolted on through it, hardened and resolute and insensible to what might befall them on the other side.

CHAPTER TWENTY-FIVE

Death hath a thousand doors to let out life.
I shall find one.
  —PHILLIP MASSINGER

In the moment that Balgor's detail emerged onto the courtyard, the lusty Bilahdu had been enmeshed in the skirmish of his life. Engulfed by the NuRac reinforcements spilling steadily over the walls from the palaestra and from the city proper, he deftly argued his point for superior swordsmanship, not with words but with the finesse of his whirling blade. Among the first to accessorise himself with the purloined steel of his enemy, he'd been unstoppable in disarming opponent after opponent, then delivering their weapons into the hands of his compatriots and moving on in defence of those not yet so equipped. The blood groove in his sword never lacked for crimson distinction, and his powerful grasp remained taut in spite of a haft literally doused in the commingle of his enemies' fluids.

Tamek fared less well, his penchant for martyrdom leaving him virtually weaponless until long after he'd ensured that the bulk of his kinspeople did not want for armaments of their own. Battling with no more than a practise pike, his procuring of NuRac swords through combat faced much more laborious odds than did the bold, frontal sallies of his stouter brother-in-arms. The target of choice for so many of the rabidly desperate soldiers, he of such stately frame and emboldening presence was viewed as the keystone whose vanquishing the NuRacs hoped might by itself squash the entire uprising.

Efforts in that direction, however, proved futile.

At once strategically acute to Tamek's plight, the realmson remade his company into the Sentinel's defensive guard, wedging itself before Tamek's person like a great anvil of humanity against the greater NuRac hammer. A spare bastard sword opportunely relayed into the Sentinel's hands, Tamek swivelled to bolster the rear of their now-impenetrable nuclear bubble, and together they fended off all challengers.

The field was a cacophonous welter of complete and utter chaos; and although this was exactly as the rebels had wished it in their devising, facilitation had now become their most stubborn snafu. Their extrication from the barracks courtyard to the outer ward to unobstructed freedom was suddenly bogging under the surfeit of NuRacs descending the walls on multiple fronts; and, as dexterously as one wave of them was cleaved asunder, another cohered in its stead and ploughed forward.

Typically, the soldiers in their armour would have been afforded the composure of essaying into the brunt of resistance void of inordinate fear. But *this* day the rebels wore their madness for shielding; and to lock eyes with an adversary whose wide and wild gaze pierced one's soul as sharply as if by tines of steel—this was weaponry unavailable from the NuRacs' armoury. Forged of oppression, of old hates, of perpetuated mistreatment, nothing save a constitution of coolest stone could hope to prevail against it. Precious few soldiers, rattled in their defensive angst, could boast of such unswerving discipline of mind.

The terrible battle raged on, and even with Wagner and Skol finally thrusting themselves into the thick, few could spare the distraction of glancing up to notice the maelstromic scend of bodies suddenly flung like ejecta in Skol's re-ignited glee of unbridled cruelty. It was all Wagner could do to sway Skol in large part from hindering the effort, as his indiscrimination between NuRac and Ergosian manifested in his swatting aside of several prisoners in his attempt to crack the "shells" of the loricated beings whom he fortunately preferred. Though the brute was intrigued by, and drawn to, panoply, Wagner was forced to give him the what-for as far as foe and ally were concerned; and, for the most part, Skol complied, from then on ignoring Ergosian prey—albeit begrudgingly.

Tamek, who at once espied the blood-crazed daemon fighting alongside Wagner, could hardly smother his outrage at what he saw; but so embroiled in swordplay was he that he had no option but to channel his asperity into the affair at hand, seeing every NuRac he felled as bringing him one step closer to being able to blast Wagner for his risk-fraught folly. He couldn't fathom how this could even be; it was infernal and execrable, an affront to honour, an affront to the respected dead and to sound judgement. Yet, conversely and admittedly, he would soon find it difficult to deny how the Sunderer's presence gradually began to alter the dynamic of the mêlée itself. Indeed, it was not long before the gladiator faction had not only truncated the NuRac defences, but had additionally dislodged itself from an unprogressive stalemate and onto a plateau of potential and conditional victory—all influenced by Skol's bestial handiwork and no one else's.

An achievement of volatile fluidity, however, it was nonetheless prone to change with any sizable influx of NuRac reserves. Knowing this, Balgor immediately commenced to ushering the survivors and the wounded through the tunnel, back to where they'd left J'nea and Papa Olask to direct the infirm out from the stony walls that had been their prison for so very long.

Tamek lent his authority to this corralling effort while Uthok and some of the others worked to defeat the very last of the soldiers along the courtyard's only remaining front. Of the later-arriving NuRacs, many were becoming understandingly less vehement in dropping to the yard from above, and for good reason. The sight of their compeers all but whittled away, the pre-eminence of Skol hunched at centre ring in a fit of dismembering elation, neither spectacle provided impetus enough for adding themselves so senselessly to the fray.

Wagner approached the Sentinel out of concern, asking—before Tamek could dish out even a modicum of Skol-inspired berating—about the status of any Ergosian who might still have been housed within the structure somewhere. His people garnering first priority, Tamek relayed that he'd accounted for all of the areas where Ergosians normally performed duties, and that if the infirmary and the detention block had both been evacuated, there was no one left to be concerned about.

"Howe'er," he added, "this dark bond that you have worked with Skol—how do you intend to explain it? And what in the name of the Twain will you do with him now?"

Wagner's face reddened with what the Sentinel perceived as intimidation. In actuality, it fell somewhere closer to ire.

"I'll introduce you to him later," he said, dryly. "Then you can thank him for your life and for the lives of your people."

Tamek scoffed. "Ne'er will you see the day, *Voknor*, when I greet that monstrosity with anything other than a blade to his ebon heart. Be sure that you leave him behind, for he will not be welcome on the hegira homeward."

Wagner could do nothing but stare in disbelief. "His enmity was nurtured by the NuRacs, Tamek. Deep down, he's one of us—a prisoner, a reject, an outsider. He may not have been my first choice in abettors, but I can't just abandon him after all that he's done to help us."

Tamek, suddenly caught up in the desertion as the last of the Ergosians dashed past them en route to freedom, joined the fleet-footed procession—but not before uttering the inconceivable. "Then neither will you be welcome, *Voknor*. Make your decision quickly."

Incredulous, for a moment Wagner watched as the Sentinel worked to reassure, and to coordinate, the anxious who'd accumulated in bottleneck at the tunnel entry. Then, he simply turned away, his eye promptly drawing sight of Skol—who, in the lull, had plopped himself down upon the courtyard grounds like a school kid at recess. There he sat, on a field of strewn bodies and accoutrements, happily crushing gauntlets as if they were empty beer cans, peeling greaves like metaliferous bananas, and snapping backplates of their rivets like great oysters to be plundered for their pearls. Fortunately, there were no NuRacs still inside said appurtenances. Wagner was at least spared that little bit of unnecessary heinousness. That he had to think about the scenario at all made him wonder whether Tamek wasn't right in being paranoid.

Wagner called out to Skol nevertheless. And, as with any child engrossed, only when the request became more sternly delivered did the brute give up his lean-minded pleasures for the grander unrealities of subsistent awareness. The line between his docility and his ferocity was as gracile as a hair—or, more accurately, a hair-*trigger*, the mechanism of which could snap in the flicker of an unheeded second, with consequence both dire and absolute. Whatever the influence that Wagner wielded that permitted this lion to walk among the sheep, he hoped it would never fail him. As horrible as was the fate that Skol meted the NuRacs this day, the knowledge that a handful of prisoners had been buffeted in the midst of Skol's bloodlust sickened Wagner to the heart for what might have been. And although none seemed really to have been seriously hobbled because of it, Wagner still vowed to an intercedence much speedier should any subsequent incident chance to erupt. This, however, meant taking Skol fully into his charge, and such a task was nothing if not titanic. Only a fool would dare to throw his lariat around a barrelling locomotive.

While Skol's presence in the yard certainly impaired NuRac infiltration, the enemy was not content to relinquish authority quite so easily. From the relative safety of the ramparts above, they produced a sparse string of archers who unloosed a stinging rain of death upon the crowd below. In answer, Tamek howled for those at the tunnel maw to hasten through, orderliness be damned; and riotously did they do so, if with a scrap of trampling. Four of five arrows had found their mark, however, with two Ergosians in serious maim, and another pair with skewered extremities. Wagner, Tamek, and those prisoners still in gridlock were helpless to do anything but watch as this lottery of doom descended on them from high overhead.

"We're sitting ducks!" Wagner cried. "What the devil's the hold-up?"

"I know not," said Tamek. "Perhaps the outer ward has been besieged."

An arrow clanked off of Wagner's breastplate, striking from such a steep pitch that it skipped across the metal and deflected to a spot in the earth directly between Tamek's boots. Wagner whooped and threw himself back. "Oh-no-no," he said in splenetic disgust. "This is *not* going to happen. Come on, you people! Get through this passage, and get through it *NOW!*"

The Sentinel, too worried to be irked by Wagner's tone, ushered the last of the prisoners through, latching onto yet another collapsing victim, felled before his eyes.

Wagner looked back for Skol, and found him meandering up, a freshly sunk arrow protruding from his shoulder. Alarmed at first, Wagner realised that Skol seemed unaffected by—even oblivious to—its existence. Indeed, lone and wispish, it looked insignificant against his proportionate brawn, like a porcupine quill lodged in a woolly mammoth. But it wasn't long ago that a handful of such shafts had laid Skol low upon Death's threshold; and, unheeding of Tamek's ultimatum, Wagner made ready to guide the beast through the access way after all the others had passed.

The NuRacs, seeing their salvo about to be thwarted, commenced with a breakneck descent. Shinnying down on hastily flung ropes and clambering over portable stiles, most hit the ground running, while secondaries followed suit, and others pressed forward atop the walls in wait.

Wagner coaxing Skol into the passage, once they were both within, he manoeuvred the chain in rapid, hand-over-hand drags, dropping the gate before the charging host. Hurriedly affixing it about the cleat, he couldn't help but to hone in on a sudden bobbery of high-decibel distress originating from those of the soldiers still stalled upon the far walls. A goodly portion of Wagner's pursuers likewise fetching up in a reflexive glimpse back, through their obstruction Wagner discerned a familiar, rampaging blur tearing across the catwalks. A whirlwind of butterscotch fur and razored talons careening through the NuRac ranks, it was, of course, the Vofspar. And she was being far from beneficent in her passing.

At once encouraged by her incursion into the multitudinous covey, Wagner could do naught but to leave her to her own devices—to the task for which she, by her nature, was so supremely qualified. It struck him that he'd made a noble, and now providential, choice in providing her with the means to escape her cell; and in his own flight he allowed himself to take a dram of pride in this. He truly hoped that the Vofspar could savage her way through the mass and over the walls to freedom. In all probability, he might never know.

But, for some unfathomable reason, he felt the need to.

The tunnel already vacated by Tamek and the others, Wagner routed Skol along until they emptied into a ward that was both free of conflict and almost fully evacuated of Ergosian tenants. There he glimpsed Balgor and Tamek directing the outbound through the final egress. The Sentinel none too cheerful at seeing Wagner emerging with Skol in tow, the realmson hooted a cry of thrilled and profound fellowship at the sight of his outworlder brother still among the living. With gesture he egged them on, that they too might pass into freedom.

Wagner instead waved Balgor cryptically toward him. And when the realmson indeed drew near, it was with an off-the-cuff flare of inspiration that Wagner made his request.

"There's something I've got to do, Balgor. I'm hoping it won't take long, but I'd appreciate it if you'd stick by Skol, and allow me at least a few minutes to get back."

Then, in succinct order, he relayed to his friend the fact of Tamek's displeasure, followed by the reason for this necessary foray; and he bade the realmson to understand, no matter how foolish he thought the plan to be.

Balgor may initially have shaken his head, but he'd resigned himself long ago to indulge his cohort in most of his crazy schemes.

"Aye, you *are* a daft one," he said. "But go, *Voknor*—we appear to be unhindered for the nonce. However, at the first sign of assailment, I will most definitely flee, and if Skol chooses not to follow, so be it."

Wagner laughed. "He'll follow you. He *loves* you."

Before the Ergosian could scoff, Wagner had already bolted. Darting past Tamek and into the escape passage, it wasn't toward the beckoning grassy freedom that he raced, but rather, up the interior stairwell descended by J'nea not long before. Making topside in a trice, he exited the spire and made way for the pivoting scaffold that routinely spanned the two walls during the day—and which had been left extended and latched during the uproar. Running along it like a bridge-worker with hot rivets underfoot, he reached the courtyard curtain in seconds, just above the spot where he'd evaded the archers a few minutes prior. The temptation had been too great. He had to see the Vofspar. He had to know her fate.

Locating her across the way, he found her still fiercely contending with her over-numbering adversaries little more than twenty paces from her starting point. NuRacs a-plenty on the ground below, of those beneath his own position, some were arduously working their polearms and pikes through the iron lattice in their thus-far futile attempts to unseat the chain that Wagner had secured. Other soldiers guarded their backsides, themselves transfixed on the lone and indefatigable she-beast upon the catwalk who was scything through their brethren and sistren like a machete through so much boscage. Still others held bows poised at the ready, but dared not let a single shaft fly for fear of piercing one of their own.

Although an immoderacy of actions permeated the setting, it was an instant frozen in time for Wagner, for so many variables and outcomes had he concocted in the instant before he acted that he almost believed he'd momentarily stopped time itself.

The bulwark upon which he stood was lined with a series of pointy flagstaffs holding the pennons of one heraldic bearing or another, whose significance Wagner neither cared about nor respected. Jerking several from their bracketing, he stripped them of their banners and began hurling them wholesale into the depths of the yard below. He howled curses as he did so, firing off five of his makeshift javelins in rapid, untargeted succession before any one archer could get a fix on his person. If any of said javelins found its mark, so much the better. But it was more for the distraction that he'd initiated the attack.

Spent of projectiles, Wagner swiftly hurdled a divisional merlon, ducked out of sight, and confused the NuRacs below by resurfacing five metres in the other direction. Clearly, his diversion was netting only the most minute of opportunities for the harried Vofspar. But it appeared to be all that she needed. Revitalised by what she saw suddenly as a way out, she ploughed through the distracted tangle of soldiers on the eastern platform—thrusting most of them groundward—and hied single-mindedly along the rampart's gradual arc, amid a briskly fired assault of arrows, spears, and even several of Wagner's recycled flagpoles.

With the female converging on Wagner's position, he cast an anxious glance toward the outer ward. Emptied of all allies save for two, Tamek had successfully ushered the masses out to the faraway woods and to newfound freedom. Balgor and Skol were all who remained. And of these two, only the ever loyal Balgor had done so with purpose. Wagner wondered, as ever, what more honourable friend a man could have.

Calling down to the two of them, Wagner conveyed how it was crucial now that they be off, and that they bring down—and disable—the innermost portcullis behind them. This way, Wagner and the feral could hie across the scaffold, descend, and exit behind said barrier, thereby frustrating any pursuit by similarly sabotaging the two remaining gates in their passing. The realmson more than willing to oblige, he signalled assent and feverishly urged the infantile Skol to accompany him in action.

Moving into position upon the scaffold's bridging, Wagner winced as he watched the Vofspar take an arrow-hit to the forearm. She stumbled, bobbled, and then regained her footing, the situation smacking eerily of their very first encounter. And although Wagner heaved up in sympathetic buttress, the unmistakeable whistle of arrow shafts piercing the air overhead compelled his sidling back to the ward portion of the parapet.

When she had nearly reached him, he shoved off across the scaffold, hoping that she'd intuit his intent for her to follow. But what he saw next all but stopped his heart. Another arrow spiking her from behind, in striking her just so, it triggered a temporary waylaying of her nervous system. Lacking autonomy, losing balance, in involuntary spasm she faltered and went into an eight-metre sprawl to the deserted ward below.

A horrified Wagner dove desperately to latch onto her—so close had she been to him—but his fingers captured only the vacuous rush of her plummet.

The Vofspar, however, would not go passively. Summoning control, and thus, agility, from some unremitting reserve that few other beings would have possessed, she managed to tuck her wiry form and convolute it so that she briefly impacted on all fours before rolling laterally upon the sands. An act of instinct infused with skilful faculty, she'd not only thwarted death, but had evaded driving her impalings deeper through her body.

Groggily, she came to her feet, but then collapsed again, the landing evidently having winded her more than it had first appeared. Shaking, panting, lying in the dirt, she grasped clumsily at the arrows and yanked them out. While the heads were standard issue (nothing at all like the hunting-tipped arrows that J'nea had pilfered earlier), excrucation was still excrucation, and once she'd extracted them she lay there idle, immobilised in semi-consciousness, with only the heave of laboured breathing to impart any hopeful message to Wagner.

The good fortune of her continuation was, however, to become secondary very quickly. On the other side of the wall, at ground level, the unswerving NuRacs had ransomed success from desperation. A persistent few had managed to partially disengage Wagner's mooring below, and were even then attempting to jog open the gate that would bring them before the debilitated Vofspar like jackals to a lamed gazelle.

Unaware of this development, Wagner shouted across the way in the hope that the departed Balgor may still have been within earshot. He was not. But he had done well; his assigned portcullis was down, locked firmly into place. The bad news was that the only means left now for saving the Vofspar was to raise it back up—something that had to be accomplished from the other side. An inconvenience that was just about to turn worse, Wagner saw little alternative.

Speeding along the scaffold, he was nigh unto reaching the outer curtain when he gleaned the unmistakeable cries and whoops of the soldiers, their continued success in jimmying his sabotaged pulley allowing now for a jerky, troubled negotiating of the barrier. A few centimetres of lift here, a few more to follow, each laborious nudge and heft brought them incrementally closer to slipping beneath. The recovering Vofspar noting this inevitability with a foretokening imminently more gravid given her proximity, with every bit of feline sinew still capable of leeching adrenalin, she scrambled to her feet that she might meet her enemy in a final embrace.

Wagner was beset by dilemma. He couldn't possibly raise *his* portcullis now, lest he place Balgor and the just-fled Ergosians in jeopardy as well. Besides, there was no longer any time to reach it. Yet, he was no less keen on descending into the yard and taking on a score and more of warriors with no plan, no means of defending himself, and no way out.

Were he another man, he might have chosen to forsake the Vofspar entirely, and quite possibly have gotten himself down the stairway, out of the camp, and off to the woodlands before a single NuRac spilled from the city and onto the meadowland in long-hindered pursuit. Maybe this was even the direction that Destiny inclined him to take. Maybe it *had* been all along.

Maybe it would come to that yet.

Still, he had to try one last gambit.

Spitting curses, he hunkered near the edge of the parapet and clasped onto the corbel beneath it. Then, reversing J'nea's earlier up-climb, he used the corbels to secure his footing in an unbidden essay downward, light on caution and heavy on speed. Within this precipitous descent, he hailed the Vofspar, bade her in his direction, all but exhausting his communicative repertoire to indicate that she endeavour an upward passage via this means.

She snarled her response. Ferity vying with intellect, it was unclear which would ultimately win. With time in scant supply, necessity would provide the answer. Her ear pricked toward the encroaching footfalls, the war hoots, and the metallic clangings that emanated from the nearby tunnel like birth cries from some vitriolic womb—she needed no pause to decide. Wagner's option was truly no option at all, but a cruciality. The horde suddenly spewing from the gape, she spun and flew across the grounds. The NuRac mass veering after her in kind, spears on the wind, she reached the foot of the wall beneath Wagner's pendency and searched frantically for a means upward.

Were she in prime condition, she surely could have leaped as high as the lowest corbel. As it was, she was barely good for a single effort. Wagner knew this, and he did the only thing he could. Risking all, he locked arm and elbow around the nethermost outcropping, and lowered himself so that his legs dangled just within reach of the female's double-pollexed talons. The rest was up to her and whatever tensility his limbs could offer.

She understood at once. Utilising his body as an instrument of access, she clamped onto Wagner's calves and hoisted herself skyward, relying on his limited brawn to support her considerably weightier bulk. Mercifully swift in her ascent, she scrambled over him like a gibbon. Then, latching onto the first employable stub of masonry, she hauled her body up and away from his charitable discommodity.

The NuRacs were almost under them, swords and battle-axes brandished for massacre. Scattered within their crush, archers plucked from their quivers and made ready to usher dismay and defeat to the only two insurrectionaries left in all the camp. Buffeted, however, by the zeal of their own multitude, none could immediately get off with a steady shot, and fewer could even see beyond the helmets and armaments of their forward peers until the Vofspar had gained conspicuous elevation.

Fagged out by his passively demanding feat, Wagner re-grappled with his hold on the stone. The raucousness below him a compelling cause for concern, he barred it from his mind and crammed every last mote of resolve into chinning up to the protruding corbel. This he managed, but only after tremendous enterprise. Then, locking an arm about the next tier, he boosted himself and finagled a foothold from a node of brickwork, thus achieving the needed leverage for his short but ambitious scale ahead. As he struggled, he lavished silent homage to J'nea for having given her earlier escalade the appearance of breezy effortlessness—although he wondered how she might have fared having first shouldered several hundredweights of Vofspar heft.

Arrows began pelting the rockface, spalling debris in all directions. Panicked, Wagner sensed the figure of Doom tugging at him from within an unfurling shroud of black and nebulous oblivion. And indeed, a clamp of spindly, powerful fingers suddenly locked vicelike about his wrist. But it was no death-wraith that did so. In an almost eerie reprise of the incident at the ravine those many weeks back, the dauntless Vofspar swung low and plucked him out from the lethal hail of bolts. And this time, she did so with the success that had so eluded them in *that* fateful instance.

Once atop the rampart, Wagner was aghast to find soldiers scrambling across the scaffold, straight in their direction. Darting toward the mooring, he fumbled wildly to dislodge it, but was suddenly swept aside. The Vofspar, quite totally brassed off and done with this nonsense, reached in and tore the scaffold free from its latches as if it were a construct of Popsicle sticks, sending it careering off in a wobbly, reckless swath above the ward. As its NuRac occupants teetered and tumbled and plummeted, Wagner directed his justifiably testy accomplice into the spire, and moments later they emerged within the lower alcove. Together, then, with their earlier pursuers working fruitlessly at the curtain's interior gate, they dropped the medial portcullis; and, in seconds, the third and outermost barrier likewise stood nested in semi-permanence within its own rutted mudsill.

The great city of QieLahr was coming alive from within. Like hive insects crazing to an unidentified intrusion, reinforcements from the mercantile districts and from the boroughs immediately adjacent to the camp had come to take up the cause, all quizzical as to why the alarum from the soldiers' grounds had yet to be squelched. None possessed insight of just what it was they would be encountering, nor could they possibly have realised that they were already too late to stop the lifeblood of QieLahr's gladiatorial industry from gushing freely onto the outfields and merging with the darkwood beyond.

Already halfway across the sward, Wagner and his taciturn cohort fled the path of trampled grains and grasses left by the earlier dispersion. A euphoric admixture of terror and elation fuelling Wagner's every stride, it was as if an epinephrine cocktail coursed his veins, delivering natural amphetamine to a voraciously expending anatomy. Easily matching pace with the Vofspar, he surmised that it was the plague of her wounds and the accompanying blood loss that weakened her gait, and he couldn't help but revere the stamina that she continued to demonstrate ever since the day he first watched her break from the underbrush during the NuRac hunt. For all of her vulgar ferocity, she was a noble warrior in her own right.

As they pierced the forest cover, Wagner turned for one last look at the massive, quarried necropolis that they had just toothed and nailed their way out of. He spotted activity now along the upper walls, figures rushing across the ramparts, most of them certainly bogged and boggled in complete disbelief at how a bustling prison had suddenly been transformed into a ghost town. From his new vantage, Wagner could behold the whole of the city's south-west expanse, and although the gateway through which he and the Vofspar had exited remained sedentary, some of the other egresses to the east now opened their iron-latticed maws to expel the first of sundry waves of retribution-seeking NuRacs.

The Vofspar, having steered their flight onto a tract of densely packed pines, slowed her pace upon realising Wagner's dawdle. When he did catch up, however, she suddenly staved his progression, pointing for him a direction more easterly than her own course. Puzzled at first, Wagner came to understand that the route she indicated was that which the Ergosian escapees had opted. And it was then that he understood what she sought to convey—that she could hardly integrate with his group any more than he could with one of hers.

A sad truth, he signalled a comprehension that, laced with regret and rueful of convention's prejudices, he could only express by means of a nod.

Then, in the space of an eye-blink, she sped off. No valedictory gesture, no stolid glance of a camaraderie shared, not even the tiniest acknowledgement of the common weave of their fates did she offer—only a fleeting, fleeing vignette for his mnemonic brush to paint into memory. In seconds, she was swallowed up by the undergrowth as the forest reclaimed one of its lost.

Had Wagner thought of it sooner, he would have happily bestowed upon her the parting gift of rejuvenation; but, as her physiology had proven much more enduring than many, he assured himself that she would mend quite adequately on her own.

Turning toward his own future, he set off as well. Although far from a learned tracker, such skills weren't necessary here. The wholesale trample of several hundred feet over an otherwise pristinely inviolate forest floor was something only a presbyopic could have missed. Despite the considerable number of convalescents requiring guidance and physical assistance in travelling, he marvelled at the expanse that the liberated Ergosians had already covered. Intent on making up for time lost, he alternated between jog and run for a goodly distance before eventually detecting inordinate movement through the woody thicket ahead. Yet, for reasons that he couldn't fully explain, he maintained his wayward position for some time, feeling complacent and comfortable in the buffer between the populace and the lengthily traversed trail to the rear. So long had he pined for his freedom, dreamed of it, schemed for it, initiated it; now, he was suddenly unsure how best to utilise it. Solitude or gregariousness—he'd always been comfortable with one, but he'd gradually come to appreciate the other. It prompted him to dwell upon how very aligned he'd been with the Vofspar and with Skol (and perhaps, in lesser degree, with J'nea) during their prison existence, for they were each of them outcasts, each a complement of one. Yet, the Vofspar was different in that she was clearly no unaffiliated oddity. While peerless among the prison's denizens, she could nevertheless boast of a loyal clan in other parts of the realm. Maybe Skol could too, although it was largely believed that he was somehow a unique mutation. As for Wagner, he'd always been grateful for the company of his Ergosian acquaintances (even the stodgy and hard-headed Tamek), enough to want to be around them, enough to romanticise over their potential as surrogate kinfolk of his own. He did not want to lose that.

But there were more powerful arguments than these for his maintaining a social persona. In fact, the two granddaddies of them all fell within the boundaries of particularly meaningful relevance, especially as they had manifested out of the reliquary of his old mind-trippings. The first of these—the riddle of the *sigma*—linked him in some incomprehensible manner not only to this world but even more closely to his enemy and former stable-master. Yet, wherever AuwNiir may have been at that moment, if *he* knew the connection he certainly had never bent Wagner's ear over it. The second argument, equally enigmatic, had surfaced more recently with the unanticipated advent of the Soork, long a staple of Wagner's visions, and now wielded—quite formidably—by yet another foe, a superior of AuwNiir's, and a genocidal lunatic at that. Both dream symbols had become pertinent; and, as such, Wagner's continuation among his friends, and among the Ergosian people in general, seemed the best means for resolving the mystery of how he fit into it all.

Increasing his gait, he gradually moved to close the gap. Although he'd expected to find Balgor and Skol at the tail of the procession, the first Ergosians he encountered directed him forward until he espied the pair a short way up the column. No one else even dared to walk remotely near to them; for, even should the hesitant have disregarded the lore, the brute still cut a most intimidating figure. Plus, the knowledge that he'd assaulted a handful of Ergosians during the revolt gave those concerned the added incentive to steer shy of him.

"Who are these scurvy dogs on the retreat?" Wagner cried as he pressed up behind them.

Balgor and Skol looked back in almost frightening unison. Immediately the realmson's face waxed jubilation as he blurted Wagner's name and scooped him up in the crush of a hearty warrior's embrace. Not to be ignored, Skol grunted, grabbing both men in a fledgling hug of his own that all but snapped their spines. Both men hollered for release, partially in jocularity and partially from genuine distress, discomfort, and a little bit of fear. Skol relinquished on his own accord; and when he did, the men offered their appreciation by patting his massive shoulders with one hand and probing themselves for broken ribs with the other.

The trailing Ergosians passed most cautiously around the reunion, mistrustful of—and befuddled by—a scene that simply shouldn't have been possible. The arena ravager showing any measure of temperance went against everything they'd ever heard about him, everything of legend, everything gleaned of post-tournament evidence. It meddled with their fundamental sense of reality, even as the impossible incidents of that morning had likewise forever altered their lives. If Skol had been becharmed by sorcery into aiding the revolt, then no sane Ergosian wished to be present when the bedevilment wore off. Each and all were thus glad to leave the trio at the breech of the queue, for the journey ahead would be days, maybe weeks, in length, and treacherous enough without Skol's immediacy to raise hair and hide in unabating alertness.

Wagner noted the concern in the people's passing, and he could do no less than to excuse their ignorance. It was a prudent reaction on their part, understandable, sensible, if not entirely accurate. He himself no longer took much stock in appearances or in reputations or even in what could be learned from any prolonged reticence of observation. Baggage meant nothing without investigation. Until he could open communications with the subject in question, until he could pop the lid off of said being's noggin and slog around for a while in his cerebral mire, there was no way of knowing the depths of that being's psyche, no means of understanding his motivation, and certainly no path for determining whether or not he was an unredeemable monster of his unfortunate repute.

"How did you fare?" Balgor suddenly inquired. "Were you successful in aiding the she-devil? Are any NuRacs in pursuit?"

Wagner laughed at the rapid-fire line of questioning, and was quick to drop hint of several new tales of daring that would put to shame many of the realmson's overtold deeds of slipshod luck and profitable bunglings. He feigned a friendly swipe at Balgor's sardonicism, and then, as they recommenced with their walking, began relaying his ordeal of the Vofspar's rescue, indeed taking greatest measure to employ embellishment enough to make Balgor's bewhiskered tales of daring seem like children's ditties by comparison.

Occasionally, a runner came down the line to check the status of those who may not have been faring well, and each of these chaps Balgor sent back with the assurance that all was in order at their end. In private, however, he confessed to Wagner that it didn't seem quite right that the NuRacs would begin assembling outside the walls—as Wagner claimed they had—and then *not* set forth in an overtaking pursuit.

The explanation came some forty minutes later. By that time, even the most casual of visual reconnoitres could discern the flutter of movement within the sun-speckled breaks in the rearward forest copse. Multiple forms were encroaching over the matted path of Ergosian footfalls; and although still a moderate distance off, both men knew that strife was about to come calling in a big way. Balgor sent word up the line for the warriors to begin shuttling themselves to the rear of the column before the whole procession became its own funeral cortège. Not unexpectedly, feelings of unrest, trepidation, and mild panic rode the wings of his message, even overtaking the message itself before word could reach Tamek near the fore. Soon, no longer just an embryonic stir of anxiety, abject fear swept the ranks of the non-gladiatorial factions, and it became the task of their more militant kinspeople to assuage their concerns and to bolster their mental postures. After all, every one of them had proved his mettle on NuRac soil; armed with no more than sticks, they had risen up and wrested back a freedom once thought lost forever. What being of flesh and fluid dared think he could steal it back from them again?

It was a compelling argument, Wagner thought, but the regiments now in pursuit were prepared where their predecessors had not been. These NuRacs were possessed of guile and resource, and would not be duped by surprise a second time. They were also not only fully armoured and accoutred, but they no doubt acted under the calculated authority of their military hierarchy. In essence, a cliché never spoke truer or more literally: the rebels were definitely not out of the woods yet.

The point of inevitability arrived as everyone knew it would, when the NuRacs, realising they had been spotted, no longer made effort to tread lightly and covertly as they'd been instructed. Assembling en masse, they charged menacingly and boisterously through scrub and thicket, hooting intimidation, flaunting maces, flails, and longswords in their readiness to reap recompense. It seemed that this verdant woodland paradise was to witness the bloodiest encounter since the fabled Red Lake.

With his blade, Wagner hacked expeditiously at a fallen branch, and created a sturdy, if knurly, hardwood club that he hefted and placed into Skol's knurlier claws. The brute's fingers clamped around it quite mechanically, and he brandished it with a swiping dexterity that would have prompted an onlooker to imagine it an appendage newly grown from his body. Then, Balgor pointed him toward the rapidly assailing host, and with an emboldening nod between them, all three broke rearward to meet the brunt of the attack.

It was a fearful picture, seeing tens upon twenties of raving NuRac assailants rushing in one's direction, with scores more spilling out from the more distant darkwood. And, it was true—the propinquity of any unruly multitude could shuck fortitude from the staunchest warrior's backbone, just by their sheer number. Even had the NuRacs been mere, coarse barbarians, unarmed and lacking their ebon armour plating, by their volume alone they were enough to drain the lustiest fighter of his combative aplomb. Just the same, the Ergosians hadn't come this far to simply hand victory back without a bitter fight.

A scenario never included in Wagner's portentous backlog, he found himself oddly cocky, even eager, to take his enemy to final task, despite the enormity of the challenge. Having Skol at his flank may have triggered his sudden flintiness, certainly; but he still housed a beast of his own, down close within himself. And that beast never shied from confrontation.

Although the venue in which they clashed afforded neither side a demonstrable edge, the Ergosians claimed agility and newfound confidence as advantages, and physical vulnerability as their greatest impairment. Alternately, the NuRacs could claim better tactical unification; and this, coupled with their weaponry and carapace, gave them psychological coign. Yet, in proximity fighting, it would ironically denote them the more leadenly encumbered adversary. The odds, then, were not equal so much as they were conjectural. In any conflict there existed the blight and the blessing of unforeseen factors: the curse of perfidy, the providence of dark horses. Anyone ever acquainted with Fate knew her for the fickle gamester she was; conversely, any who denied ever having danced to her manipulative song would receive enlightenment this day.

Skol slammed the NuRac line like a seven-ten strike, leaving the environing NuRacs to the blades of his companions while he cleared a dissilient swath through the middle. Whether drawing from experience or instinct, he knew exactly how to inflict the severest damage on his prey, swinging his club laterally across the soldiers' skulls and snapping their necks clean for the arguable lack of protection provided by their paltry gorgets. In a battle devoid of practical archery, Skol was the undisputed warlord, for none existed who could best him at full strength in close-quartered altercation, especially when he wielded a three-metre war club. Like an icebreaker crunching and cutting through the glacial floes of the Arctic Circle, against his might the NuRacs' plating may as well have been of tin foil.

Balgor and Wagner—both still in NuRac breastplates, both sporting their stolen vambraces and armlets—vaunted the supplementary protection unpossessed by most of their kind. Although other Ergosians had, back in the camp, followed suit in availing themselves of some of the fallen NuRacs' armour, none of these compatriots had yet worked his way to the rear of the column. Of those escapees more immediate, few were so blindly driven as to rush headlong into Death's foyer as had their two obviously possessed brethren and the monster whom they'd welcomed as an equal. In fact, in watching Balgor and Wagner broaching the enemy line, many amended their earlier speculation, and now believed that perhaps it was really the beast who had bewitched the two, and not the other way round.

A man more honourable than he was sensible—and luckily so—Bilahdu was among the first to throw in with the trio. On hearing the report of the NuRac uprush, he'd raced clear from the head of the assemblage to aid his backswept allies in preserving the day's victory. Providing a less unsettling hero to emulate, his actions rousted others into following his lead, and soon everyone whose zeal for freedom extended beyond the walls of QieLahr had added his and her sword to the fray. It seemed that the final stand would be held there, on that lush and unspoiled tract, in the half-light of the arborescent wild.

The NuRacs were diabolical schemers. As their leading forces engaged the Ergosians like rams clashing for dominance, clandestine parties were dispatched from the rear of the regimental thorax to encircle the perimeter from an inscrutable distance. Closing off every avenue of escape, they would then proceed inward for an all-conclusive crush about their prey. Outnumbering the Ergosians four-to-one, adept and efficient and better armed, they likely predicted little complication, followed by a prompt tallying of Ergosian bodies.

Prominently absent from the hub of the clash was Tamek of Vishkor. He was, however, scarcely missed among the plethora of adjuvant compeers suddenly at hand. Uthok the Bonecrusher rushed an advance of NuRacs like a Skol-in-training, his sword slicing aerial figure eights against their equally deft parrying, his pilfered buckler impatiently swatting away any foe who too easily matched his own skill. J'nea of Bejodeth likewise cast reservation aside. Joining Uthok, she scythed the headmost soldiers asunder with a pit fighter's brutality, and intercepted Uthok's cast-offs with competent quietus. A hand-and-a-half sword in her blazing left grip, a steely dirk thrusting from the right, she demonstrated simultaneous forehanded and backhanded ambidexterity the likes of which frustrated any and all who sought to crack her defences. So completely immersed was she that she had no idea that Wagner and Balgor battled just metres away, enmeshed deeper within the scramble. She'd seen neither of them since evacuating the camp, knew nothing of their status, and—fearing them potential casualties—she fought as if avenging their loss and the loss of those who'd likewise succumbed that day.

Had any combatant of either faction encountered lull enough between charge and fend to observe the greater altercation, he would have noticed something most peculiar at the heart of the NuRac phalanx. Perceived through an earthly perspective, one might have supposed that a good dozen NuRac soldiers had abandoned the fray, and had instead taken to bouncing on some ilk of trampoline-like contraption right in the midst of the chaos. One after the other, each flew bodily into the air and off into the brawling crowd, each a missile of unwieldy bulk, bowling over tens of other NuRacs like empty bottles in a carny game. In truth, it was none other than Skol behind it all. Smiting NuRacs left and right and left again with his overtaxed cudgel, he then tossed or batted them in their benumbed swoons upon the body of the mob, and continued on to the next unfortunates. The luckless soldiers who found themselves boxed-in along this front line—so much like Odysseus's crew in the cave of Polyphemus—were easy pickings for the ravaging brute; for Skol, like the Cyclops, offered slaughter as his only hospitality. Just how many bludgeonings his hardwood club could endure before shattering in his grip would be revealed only through his inordinate excesses. Yet, even this would scarcely usher relief. Were it to occur, should his club have turned to dust right then, the terrified NuRacs would discover just where Skol's true, raw capability lay—and this time they would experience it from somewhere other than the relative comfort of the arena stands.

Even with the boon of Skol's ferocity, Wagner's "sandbag" metaphor underwent incredible pounding by the waves of enemy influx. Too many of them there were, too heavily protected, and too encompassing to circumvent. The Ergosians fought gallantly; but with so many of the bedraggled huddled at the core of their defences, the impairment was an obviousness that could not be denied; and the knowing NuRacs gradually closed the pincers of a surrounding vantage that would allow no corridor of retreat. Even Tamek, up front and amid the recoiling wounded whom he'd pledged to protect, felt the tides of reversal rolling in. Postured, resolute, sword bared like an angry tusk—he still would not allow futility to creep in and hinder what could conceivably be their last stand. In an unlikely act of spiritual restitution, he offered up silent pardon to his comrades of good intent whose hasty abandon in orchestrating the escape had brought them, and the upswept masses, to this pivotal crossroads. He himself had been equally to blame—this he knew—and so grim did it suddenly all appear, that simply by the fervent appreciation that he felt for his co-schemers and for his courageous people was he able to reshape his previous adamantness into a heartfelt bestowal of reverence and pride. Even Wagner was not denied at least some iota of gratitude; for although his methods bore the underpinnings of more questionable motive, his nisus had been more misguided than malevolent, even with the impropriety of the Sunderer's recruitment.

Like making one's peace before death, then, it was an odd ambivalence of character that so climactically overtook the Sentinel, even as the NuRac army itself moved to overtake the Ergosian column; for, in cursing the misfire of this ambitious escape that he and his cohorts had thrown together so slapdash, Tamek took solace in knowing that the whole of his kinspeople had rallied flawlessly and cohesively in this, their struggle for their independence. If it were truly to end right there and then, with the realm still enchained, with mystical relics in the hands of blasphemers, and a fanatical SyKrahvo loose upon the land, then Tamek and his doomed Ergosian rebels would perish—not by insufficient fortitude, but by overwhelming numbers. It would befall their spirits, then, to pass through the Sacred Pool and to be meted to a new generation whose legacy it would be to infuse the struggle with renewed vigour.

"Come forth, then!" Tamek shouted as the invading forces impinged. "Come and mingle your blood with that which you would spill!"

In truth hardly the flock's sole defender, Tamek was girdled in the ready company of the staunch and the faithful, who, like he, safeguarded the infirm. Wagner's old sparring nemesis, Minosh, stood at hand, as did the robustious Grandio (who had remained beside the Sentinel while his brother, Graspa, ran to join Bilahdu at the rear). Other valiant men and women barred the way between Papa Olask's mobile medical unit and the oncoming danger. Even Lahki, he whom Wagner had only recently restored to health, was one of these guardians. Not he, and not any of these others, would meet his end idly. Nor would any succumb willingly.

Mounting a charge, the NuRacs assailed the ragtag warriors and their wounded with the callosity of hounds upon hens. This, perhaps, initially deemed the most straightforwardly facile of the conflict's many ordeals, the discovery of the Sentinel among the old, the weak, and the unwhole, was simply an added reward. And as dozens of NuRac soldiers sped forth—each with the intent of being the one to deliver Tamek's death stroke—others fanned out to assault the procession on all sides until swords and pikes and cudgels whirled and stabbed in the awful cataclysm of warfare all along the rebel body.

By now all but bereft of his thoughtful side, the battle-frenzied Wagner joined Balgor in ploughing under the spate of soldiers who'd flooded in through a swath opened by Skol's murderous errantry. Although availed by their minimal armouring, it was critical that the pair adopt a tactic purely and aggressively offensive. In so doing, they hoped to better disarm the NuRacs, not essentially of their weaponry, but in the even more crippling pale of their confidence. It was a gambit that worked swimmingly at first. The NuRacs had seldom faced such savage, unflagging desperation in the guise of two outwardly unremarkable, if hell-bent, Ergosians. But, as zealotry too often sired strategic blindness, the duo in their unallayable fury forged for themselves a path of no return, far into the bowel of enemy clutches.

A predicament as restrictive as it was pregnant with lethality, it failed to elicit even negligible concern from either man. Lashing out in tandem like twins of one mind, cautious not to be separated, they greeted all comers with affronts of sharp, steely bidding, both of them rejecting absolutely their inevitable demise. Perhaps they imagined that if they refused to accept defeat, then such end could not possibly come to be. Proper mindset, after all, could suborn a goodly percentage of any conflict, even an ill-balanced one. More likely, however, was that neither man's concentration could afford the hampering of speculation, not with the existence of so great a calamity on all sides. Yet, whatever it was that evoked their staunchness, they braced within the swarm of onrushing animus as the NuRacs pressed ever forward.

What happened next did not manifest all at once. In fact, the faint reverberation of some new symphony of riotousness had begun to insinuate itself at the battle's periphery only moments after the two factions had engaged. It had started out so low as to merit no regard at all, a distant discordance of muffled shouts barely infiltrating the already raucous din of the forest arena. But it did not remain so. Travelling fleetly from fringe to foreground, blending with—and then challenging—the considerable cacophony of the soldiers and the gladiators at clash, it came to conquer the ear-reach of every contender who matched blade against blade under the lambent coverture of several hundred sublime and magnificent conifers. For those Ergosians still at the more critically protected centre, its origin could have spelled nothing but a far grander multitude of NuRacs than had initially been relayed; and in the grim isolation of that moment, morale could easily have plummeted. Yet, for the bold, for the foolhardy—and for the boldly foolhardy—who'd ventured out to meet the NuRac advance, theirs was a view of quite a different scenario, and few of them could bring themselves to fully trust their own eyes.

Ergosians!

Scores of kindred rogues closing about the NuRac encirclement in a concentred crush of utter surprise, a vigorous new tide had suddenly welled up to supplant the old! Rebels of every shape and stature converged from all directions, drabbled and smutchy in lineaments all, but each in high dudgeon and bellying such audacity as to believe that collectively they might pluck this battle from dismal abyss to even ground. In wanton, headlong hoopla did these yipping infiltrators bound forward, many even sporting NuRac weaponry (no doubt the spoils of previous raids and banditry), and others bearing NuRac armour flagrantly altered with the personalised indicia of the late Juthac's devices.

The chagrined NuRacs, finding their line of attack encumbered by this development, parted their forces in order to rebuff the affront. Their advantage in obvious upset, they themselves—though still not outnumbered—were now the cornered party, and by the fierceness of their counteraction did they make their inconvenience enormously clear.

Wagner and Balgor, lost within a labyrinth of pointy steel and razor edges, dared not avert their focus for more than the trice that it took to recognise the inpour of welcomed support. The deadly contrivance of a dozen hostile swords thrusting at and around them was too direly compelling to risk distraction, even as their hearts billowed new hope. J'nea likewise took on the ballast of augmented confidence, she and Uthok and Bilahdu and Graspa so critically invested in their own gruelling contests of close-quarter butchery. And far within the broil, conscious of nothing save his artisanship of snapped armature, of broken bodies and littered viscera, the mighty Skol rocked the NuRac ranks. His makeshift warclub long fragmented and discarded, he rediscovered utility in his favourite ilk of bludgeon—a soldier's corpse—which he quickly impressed in order to baste and beat back his puny (and, by then, somewhat less ardent) adversaries. Given the off-the-chart readings of his enthusiasm, the unfortunate cadaver in his grasp would enjoy at most a limited longevity in its new application; but while it endured, Skol cleared for himself a commodious corridor through the very hub of his enemy's buttress.

So besieged was the NuRac machine from all sides that it began to collapse like a house of cards. Although expert soldiers all, the breakdown of their formation demanded retreat and regrouping. With trumpets blaring concordantly, they fell back, and as they did the rebels moved in to wreathe their bedraggled kith and kin.

The reunion, however, was brief, and the freedom fighters, necessarily curt in hustling the former prisoners along a path of flight before the NuRacs found the wherewithal to launch a subsequent offensive. Most of the gladiators stood in the wake of their enemy's withdrawal like the perdurable constructs of a post-tsunamic shoreline; the bodies at their feet, NuRac and Ergosian alike, lay like the dismaying jetsam of once vibrant and invaluable intellects. Many of the survivors darted about from one fallen comrade to the next to satisfy themselves that this or that one did not yet endure, despite wounding and prostration. Indeed, a rare few were found to be alive and salvageable, and were thus borne away for Olask's evaluation. A similar number, though maintaining breath—and, in some cases, partial faculty—lay in the agonising throes of decline. Of these pitiable wretches, some required no more than a spot of simple, human comfort to encourage their gentle relinquishment of one world for the next, while those who clearly suffered from their mortal wounding were mercifully relieved by the most steadfast of the living.

Wagner watched in heartfelt astonishment as the usually brash and foulmouthed Uthok delivered compassionate quietus to a warrior with whom they'd both sparred on many an occasion. J'nea knelt behind the man, cradling his head in her bosom, her fingers caressing his blood-matted tresses with the demulcent coddling of a mother. Yet, before Wagner even thought of intervening with a furtive act of hypernormal intervention, Uthok drove J'nea's borrowed dagger high into the man's sternum. In seconds, said man fell limp. Then, together, the pair laid him to rest, both of them stealing a smear from the blade and running a bloodline horizontally across their foreheads in the custom of honouring the clan of any brave soul killed for mercy's sake.

Her dagger J'nea did not wipe entirely clean, but rather she tucked it through her frog as she walked away, the unconcealable snuffling of a weepy nose hindering all serious reparations to the façade of stolid constitution that she forced herself to wear in public. On spotting Wagner for the first time since the camp revolt, she ran a hurried wrist across her upper lip as she approached him, the hint of her little girl smile only partially lifting the sulk of her weighty countenance.

"Your...*lunacy*...proved fruitful," she said, almost hugging Wagner but stopping short. "But the cost has been dear. And it is far from over."

Wagner nodded condolingly. "You're right. On *all* counts." He gazed past her to the sundry bodies strewn across the woodscape. "All those," he said, indicating them. "All of them, dead. And yet, here *I* am, still kicking. I'll be damned if I can figure out why."

"A charm...or a curse. I cannot tell you which."

"Oh, I already *know* which one it is."

She, too, gazed at the dead. "Surely your 'prescience' auspicated great loss of life?"

"No, not really. Loss of life falls more in the realm of probability. I usually only get the 'Reader's Digest' version."

"The *what*?"

He snorted. "However it comes to me, I mostly see a jumble of block images. I envision the 'structure' itself, but not the nuts and bolts. The big picture's all in there, though. I can usually foresee the big picture. I just can't foresee the *whole* picture."

"Well, at any rate, your insight is not infallible."

"How so?"

"There were no siege machines outside QieLahr."

He dwelled for a moment, chewing at his lip. "No. No, there weren't."

Suddenly, one of their Ergosian liberators called out to them to depart with the rest of the ruck. Around them, the battleground had all but been picked clean of employable appurtenances by fellow rebels and comrades, most of whom had already been ushered from the area. Too, a fair number of the Ergosian dead had been located and carried out, some hefted over shoulders, and others, strapped to ramshackle litters and dragged from the scene.

Acknowledging the woman's suggestion, Wagner and J'nea fell in among Uthok, Balgor, and the others. Skol, however, was nowhere to be found. At end it was believed that, crazed by bloodlust, he'd pursued the NuRacs far into their fallback.

Wagner threw a concerned glance in that direction; but, on seeing nothing save for trampled boscage and sun-tinselled forest, he reluctantly diverted himself back to the path ahead, trotting along with his peers as they hurried to leave the carnage behind.

The freedom-fighters soon guided them along pathways that grew incrementally more convoluted and constrictive, and even as they forged through territory too dense for the NuRac army to follow in formation, the Ergosian throng itself became strung out and lean. The thinning, however, was deliberate and of little concern here; for, as they penetrated deeper into the darkwood, the escapees began to distinguish an increasing volume of Ergosian friendlies in lurk within the scrub, behind bushes and boulders, even up in the trees. One of these lookouts Balgor recognised from his brief military stint of long ago—a craggy-faced man with a salt-and-pepper mane and a grizzly white beard. Quickly shielding a mischievous grin upon espying this old comrade-in-arms, Balgor offered up a burlesquing that was certain to unseat the sentry's stolidity.

"I must speak with whoever doles the duties in this command," the realmson barked with noticeable intensity, "to uncover how it is that Gralok of Nogsborg is forever coddled with the least treacherous of assignments!"

Unfooled, the lookout squinted, searching the queue for the agent of those words. A confirmatory smirk then tugged up his beard on one side. "And I," he volleyed, "must discover how Balgor of the Realm has outlasted the inequities of his vapid wit!"

They approached and embraced as old friends do, each jubilant at beholding the other's haleness.

"Tell me, rascal," said Balgor, once they'd exchanged niceties, "what is our destination? Does Mirko intend to lead the troops back to re-engage the NuRacs while our wounded are ushered into some more clandestine camp?"

"I know not, brother." Gralok faltered momentarily. "I fear that Mirko...has not been well."

"Eh?" Balgor cocked back. "I wager, no doubt, from wounds inflicted in battle. Nay? Surely he is not abed by mere sickness?"

"Neither injury nor disease. 'Accursed' is more the report that has swept through the ranks."

"Nay, surely not," Balgor insisted. "After every vengeful malediction spewed at him over the years, what murrain could possibly afflict him now?"

"The curse of a thousand innkeepers, perhaps," blurted Uthok, one of the many who were well acquainted with the Vargathian's roguish repute.

Gralok chuckled uncomfortably. "It seems that he has indeed withstood the worst of it. In truth, Mirko authorised this very foray by his own counsel—we knew not why—but it appears that he sensed a...'weakness' at QieLahr."

"A *weakness*?" asked Balgor.

"Aye. A quite different NuRac regiment passed to our east only days ago—a tremendous assemblage, formicating with a quickening the likes of which I have never witnessed in all my years. Immediately Mirko dispatched scouts to follow them, and others to track whence they had come. Given the news that these runners returned with, it was with little debate that the Vargathian and his advisors concurred that our comparably smaller forces had not the capability to prevail against such an army. Foreboding as it may sound, it is rumoured that our scouts uncovered certain inexplicable evidence of violent and unnatural destruction."

Balgor sighed resignedly. "The Soork."

The others murmured in agreement.

"Soork?" Gralok mouthed the word to himself several times as if trying to unearth a memory.

"An ancient implement of life force," said Bilahdu.

"An instrument of decimation," countered J'nea.

"An exploited holy relic of lost ages," offered Balgor.

"A key to far greater mysteries."

Wagner wasn't prepared for the silence that followed his own personal speculation, one naturally progressed out of those preceding it. But he had spoken the truth—*his* truth.

Gralok studied him for a moment, his eyes augering for a shiver of recognition that never came. Then he continued on with his story.

"Sorely discomfited by the news—and unable to comprehend a force that could raze the land so violently—Mirko instead came to consider the notion of breaching the city itself for its hold of you Ergosian captured. At first a fancy of improbable viability, in the space of a few days it rooted ever more rigidly in his thoughts, quite nearly to the point of obsession. I suppose in the end it was fatidic, for you lot had conspired on a notion of your own."

Wagner listened, struck by the parallels between Gralok's presumptions of the Vargathian's intent and the Mirko-involved fabrications that he and his co-plotters had utilised in goading the camp into rising up. Once again his visions had proven worthy of heedful consideration.

Balgor, too, was noticeably awed by the similarities, and he frequently shifted a glance in Wagner's direction throughout the course of the narrative. Wagner, whose foregleam of intuition seldom failed to baffle the realmson, responded with a modest shrug and an index finger tapped to his temple to let Balgor know that it was all somehow consequential, somehow part of that old jigsaw puzzle that he'd forever been striving to complete. Long before his life with Sara Higgins, long during his association with Jon Mazzio and his antics with Margaret Groller, long after his birthday-suited landfall onto Ergosian soil—the clues had been internally present. Only time and experience had yielded Wagner an occasional cohesion. They were as wink and nod to him; only through them and by them had he discovered the means of combining a thousand obscurities into a handful of usable images, sometimes as climacteric hinges, more often as *post factum* revelations. Enough of these small successes, and he felt that he would eventually have a chance at making sense of it all. But progress had always been a plodding tortoise to the hare-swiftness of his curiosity. Too often did he feel impeded; yet, inherently he knew that everything that had thus far befallen him had occurred according to some pre-cast (if not strictly inelastic) continuity. As frustrating as it was to experience destiny through spontaneous forefeeling, only to have it governed by the incremental gradation of time, it nevertheless helped Wagner to recall that, in retrospect, his sense of tomorrow's history—although discomforting or frequently unjust in its many facets—was ultimately made tenable and sound, if not frighteningly manipulative.

Their coterie moved on through the coppice, the last group in the Ergosian entourage to do so, with no sign of NuRac pursuit anywhere along the circuitous trail to the rear. At one point or another in their passing, a furtive rebel would suddenly materialise from a nearby spinney and proceed to muddle the path behind them and disguise it with loose copse-wood and underbrush. Then, just as spectrally, he would reblend with the wildwood to resume his lone vigil, awaiting any incident of enemy encroachment.

No one quite knew for sure why the NuRacs had yet to embark on retributive chase. False leaders and camouflaged trails would hardly dissuade a resolute army, and the foot traffic of a few hundred escapees was impossible to totally obscure from the eyes of seasoned trackers. As such, many believed that the NuRacs may have overestimated the strength of the liberating Ergosian force, and had opted instead for a more prudent course of relinquishing a senseless hunt in light of the inevitable certainty of SyKrahvo's complete and imminent conquest of the realm. Others thought that, because the forested terrain had itself become the rebel's element, the NuRacs may necessarily have assumed that any advantage of a war waged from within said venue would thus favour the Ergosian faction. Wagner, however, momentarily inclined by romantic mythos, chose to believe that somehow it was Skol who barred the NuRac inroad—Skol, whose over-the-top ferocity frustrated their woodland progression like the pillar of cloud and fire in *Exodus* that blocked Pharaoh's troops.

Truth be said, although no less solid than a pillar, the far more mortal Skol could not have hoped to endure indefinitely against the arsenal at the NuRacs' disposal. Impaled by one arrow going into battle, the company of several additional, well-placed quills would surely have felled him in the manner that they had in the Great Arena; it was only a question of when. Whether the brute had broken off his charge at some point and hied off into the woods, or whether he yet drove himself irrevocably into the heart of his enemy's complement, the question of Skol's fate would—along with that of Fostoch, the *sigma*, and Wagner's sortilege—receive the stamp of unsolved enigmas until the day that the child-monster came galloping up unexpectedly to Wagner or Balgor, like some haggardly way-worn family pet who'd travelled incredible distances in search of its former owners. Of course, his severed head on a pike at the forefront of the NuRac van would provide the more likely answer. But Wagner truly hoped such wouldn't be the case, and until such indisputability presented itself, he steered his speculations along avenues more upbeat.

In the end, the sum of Gralok's recountings quantified much of what Wagner had culled from his own insights and impressions. That Gralok and Balgor shared a history brimming with enough anecdotal copy to fill *The Pursuer Weekly* from cover to cover, their rather sportive reminiscing served to dominate the group's interaction for the remainder of the trek. This freed Wagner to consciously withdraw and to delve more acutely into how his newly acquired freedom might influence the manner in which he interpreted his relevance to the Ergosian conflict, and to Ergos itself. Although busily foraging through the clutter of his private inquest, he made sure to crack the door that linked him with the immediate moment, if only to pick up on the nugacity of some ancient waggishness that had once brought Balgor into strife. Enjoying a quiet chuckle alongside his companions' haler guffaws, he made sure to squirrel away any exploitable incident (for the avail of some future harassment) before again retreating back to questful introspection.

His wish of freedom fulfilled, how ironic that he hadn't the foggiest idea as to what to do next. He likened himself to the gully he'd encountered on his first day—barren, desolate, functionless, waiting for the rains of circumstance to give it purpose. He lacked even the most rudimentary prospectus on life beyond QieLahr. Yet, experience had demonstrated how opportunity seldom knocked when it could just as easily roll a tank over him in his too-thoughtful inanity. Allow but a little time, and it would again; of this he was certain. Gall and wormwood, joy and triumph, supernatural and supernal would continue to besiege his life as they always had, tossed at him like table scraps from the great festal board of providence, each ort signifying some new trial the nature of which he may once have glimpsed while befogged in the transience of his now-distant, psychical experiences. To patiently await his next imperative while biding within the swathing congeniality of friends and newly met compatriots—there were, after all, less appealing distractions than this.

Having covered what seemed kilometres of dense terrain, they finally emerged onto a clearing housed beneath a verdant umbrella of fagaceous giants and royal pines. The forest floor evidently having been defoliated by manually laborious means, it now teemed thick with lean-tos, tents, and other crude structures wrought of haste, and its grounds bulged sorely from the huge inpouring of refugees admitted during the last two hours. What had been a secret rebel camp now served as triage centre and rescue mission, and at the core of it all, Papa Olask and his orderlies continued working frantically with the rebels' medics to save, salvage, and comfort those on whom combat had taken its toll.

J'nea spotted Hidessel and several other trusties clustered together, sharing sustenance and refreshment from a common tureen of mulligan and a water-skin, and she headed over to greet them. Graspa likewise parted off in search of his courageous sibling. Wagner, gazing across a sea of Ergosians both known and new, happened upon Skagra's wearied visage, and pointed her out to Bilahdu. Bilahdu, however, although obviously ecstatic at seeing her alive and well, censured Wagner in typically overstated fashion for heralding the end of his too-brief flirtation with a single man's freedom. Wagner and the others laughed in kind, and as Bilahdu moved off in feigned begrudgement to intercept his mate, Balgor struck out swiftly with his NuRac blade and expertly severed the girdling of Bilahdu's new trousers. Unfixed from his enormous belly, they fell quickly away, collecting flaccidly at his knees in great, floppy folds like a windbag robbed of waft.

Stumbling in mid-gait, Bilahdu yanked them furiously up and cursed his laughter-convulsed gallery of knavish friends with every profaneness that Ergosian vernacular had to offer. Away, then, he hobbled, leaving Balgor and Gralok, Wagner and Uthok, all virtually teary-eyed from the throes of a hilarity that did well to unburden them of the day's weighty ordeal.

Gralok left them shortly thereafter in order to report to his superiors. Reduced, then, to a trio, they mulled about the busy encampment, looking for an uninhabited plot of ground where they might recline and give in full to their fatigue. Open space coming at high premium, they settled at the outskirts between some saplings and a fair-sized berry bush, and collapsed freely on a bed of decomposing leaves.

"We did it, Balgor," Wagner proclaimed in lazy, feather-capped smugness.

From his recline, he stared up toward the tree-tips, his fingers lacing support behind his head. "I don't know *how*, but we did."

"Aye," came the realmson's weary reply. "We did indeed."

Within the minute, all three men were fast asleep.

CHAPTER TWENTY-SIX

Now who will stand on either hand,
And keep the bridge with me?
  —THOMAS BABINGTON MACAULAY

Although still an hour before sunset, the rebels' deep-woods milieu was already undergoing what the Ergosians called *rooksdunkel*—a term for the faux twilight that precedes (and mimics) true dusk in any thickly foliated or low-lying terrain. Wagner had been the first of his companions to awaken in the murky half-light, and this to quite nearly the very sounds of industry that had accompanied him into unconsciousness in the first place.

Beside him lay his out-sprawled comrades, still sawing logs. Oddly, both men's fists were clenched or semi-clenched, even deep in nod. Their bodies, however, were lax, and their visages and clothing were so bespeckled with enemy blood that they resembled a pair of smirchy farmhands after a careless day of barn painting. A trifling of overripe berries relinquished from the bush overhead lay scattered like red gumballs across Uthok's rising and falling torso, and Wagner couldn't help but to chuckle at the sight of one that nested atop the Bonecrusher's cheek like some bulbous witch's wart.

Beyond the short boundary of their flopping, Wagner witnessed the considerable Ergosian membership enmeshed in a variety of social activities. Some chatted and visited. Others rendered or received aid. Still others supped, slept, or gadded about in search of friends or food or a kindly ear.

Wagner stretched his limbs and leaned fully forward, his grogginess all but dissipated, and for a thoughtful moment he studied these ranks of the newly freed. The evidence of their pride he could discern from their enthusiasm alone. He felt a kind of dignity in his own right for having been one of the insurgent architects responsible for inciting the whole *levee en masse*. Casualties aside, the day had been a splendid success as far as big pictures went; and, by the measure of lively animation that he observed, the majority of the escapees would have concurred.

His thoughts then turning to Papa Olask and the wounded, he suddenly guilted up, shamed for having luxuriated in a nap while Olask and the medics almost assuredly had denied themselves similar respite in order to toil over the maimed and the broken. While theirs had not been the same unpalatable hackfest of the warriors, the deliberate amputation of a wounded compeer's extremity or the brandishing of a stoker for the nasty business of cauterisation was arguably the more unsavoury use of steel that day, and the strength of personal resource and competence that was required for performing such remedial atrocity on one's own—this was the measure of character for which no ode had ever been penned. Certainly, it occurred to Wagner, the burden that Olask and his medical team had taken on might be eased by the aid lent of a friendly auxiliary with secret curative skills. And if not, at least he could say that he'd offered.

Stowing his private flagellation for a time when there wasn't purpose to be served, he rose and cut a path through the assiduous community, toward the triage area, leaving his comatose friends to navigate themselves from slumber in their own good time.

As he walked, he noticed many of his old prison-mates intermingling with Mirko's devoted raiders. This prompted him to wonder where the shrewd, albeit reportedly ailing, rebel head man was hiding, that he might get a gander at the Vargathian legend in the flesh. Reputed to be every bit the revered leader, almost to the point of Tamek's calibre, Mirko was—according to Balgor—also and interestingly a far hale from the Sentinel insofar as his methods and mores went. Wagner imagined a roguish Robin of Locksley-type character, a gold-hearted bandit with a big ego and a bigger heart, and this was the image that he would stick with until introductions proved it inaccurate.

Passing near a food prep site, he overheard Gamühr the Bard as she spun tales for those rebels who hungered more for yarns than yams. There wasn't a one, Wagner noted, who wasn't enthralled by her offerings. A day packed with virulent skirmish had done little to diminish the dazzle in her narrative style, and it almost made Wagner want to pause and enjoy her entrancing retelling of a story that he'd already heard a dozen times over. Despite a determination on the edge of waver, he resisted.

Farther on, he glimpsed Lahki seated alongside Minosh, both wiping down their NuRac blades while jawing in the mixed company of former gladiators and newfound acquaintances. To them he paid little heed, but just beyond them he encountered a gazingstock whose dulcet coercing he couldn't resist. Fascinated, he watched as a number of Mirko's more exuberant rebels play-acted, spoofed, and made a fuss in general over the youngest of the prison's freed denizens, with the giggling juveniles and adolescents delighting in their first incident of unaccountable play since their original capture. They were apparently the only youths here, and subsequently were highly prized by the many rebels who obviously cherished—and missed—either the company of their own young ones or of children in general. It was a tender scene that struck Wagner more deeply than the rest.

Almost everything around Wagner sustained and substantiated his push for the prison uprising—*almost*, because he had yet to witness the full degree of the day's consequences. The gaiety he found here surely had its immeasurably darker counterpart elsewhere in the encampment. Yet, whether the end truly proved worthwhile in the grand scheme, whether the means had been too costly, too extreme, or too callous, it truly wouldn't be Wagner's privilege to decide.

The mobile medical unit came next, and it was overall a shamble after bloody shamble of soiled bandages and viscera. By this time, those most critically wounded had been processed and removed to an adjacent area to convalesce, while those who suffered from inflictions that could endure delay were finally invited forward for treatment. Papa Olask and his subordinates looked eerily like the living dead in their fatigue, and at the sight of them Wagner struggled with legs suddenly frozen by the weightiness of answerability.

"You are wounded?" An orderly had come up from behind him.

"Huh? No. No, I'm fine," said Wagner.

"Nay, but you are!" the man insisted, pointing a crimson-stained finger at Wagner's left triceps. Twisting his shoulder, Wagner craned at the spot that the man indicated. A twelve centimetre ribbon of cruor striped the back of his arm, just above his pilfered armlet.

"What, *this?* Pshaw! I've had hangnails worse than this."

"Still, it needs proper attention. And your neck as well."

Wagner ran a quick finger over his throat, raw and inflamed from the Vofspar's savage gripe. He smirked. "There are considerable folk here with injuries far worse than mine," he said. "See to them first. I'm a big boy—I think I can suffer a few scratches."

Well-acquainted with the machismo so often exhibited by fighters, brawlers, and warriors, the orderly simply shrugged and, without ado, proceeded on to the next candidate. Wagner likewise moved on, skirting the busy operational perimeter until he came upon Olask himself.

"Need any help?" he asked lowly after quietly creeping in.

The surgeon being preoccupied and clearly irritable—perhaps from being asked this same question a few dozen times in the past several hours—he quite nearly came back with a snappy, sleep-deprived retort before realising who owned the inquiring tongue.

"*Voknor!* No—no, forgive me—I do not believe that we have anything for you to do here. That is, not unless you possess the wherewithal to banish misery."

"He doth indeed," came a new voice from behind, a voice and an accompanying attitude that Wagner knew only too well. "'Twould have benefited many," it continued, "had his offer come hours earlier."

Demonstrating a familiar involution of displeasure, Tamek of Vishkor intruded between physician and outlander. A gaunter and more pallid facsimile, however, than the robust Sentinel of that morning, for a split second Wagner had to meticulously scrutinise both figure and visage for absolute confirmation. The extremes of tribulation had transformed Tamek into something less than the sturdy linchpin of the Ergosian machine, at least evanescently. His face was a snapshot of the day's losses; his mien, a dour holdall of repressed lamentation; and his shoulders, a declination of sag and slump from upholding both the physical and the spiritual weight of the dead and dying.

"The fighting was tough," Wagner countered. "Once we got *here*, once we found the opportunity to ease up, I guess our exhaustion got the better of us. Balgor, Uthok, and I found an out-of-the-way spot on the edge of the woods and—well—we just collapsed."

"Understandable," said Olask, running one stitch through a patient's laceration and attempting to run another through the estrangement he detected between his two visitors. "You fought hard and well to protect us in our acute unreadiness. I am truly amazed that we outlasted the day."

"Touch and go for a while there, Papa. If it hadn't been for the reinforcements—"

"We would all have perished," said Tamek. He fixed upon Wagner like a principal on a classroom upstart. "Do you now understand the prudence of mine earlier concerns, *Voknor*? Do you not realise how this day might have concluded?"

Wagner nodded unabashedly. "Yeah, I do. You were right to question us."

For possibly the first time ever, Tamek was at a loss for words. He gazed at Wagner, at Olask, and at Wagner again.

"I'll be the first to admit it," said Wagner. "Instead of us standing here, on open soil, under these magnificent trees, with me taking some well-deserved lumps from you, while all around us the survivors of our messy, injudicious revolt are talking or joking, eating or resting, receiving aid or rendering it, you could just as easily be giving me hell back in Barracks Five while we wait for bed check and lockdown and another rotten day of training within yet another more rotten *week* of training, that will eventually culminate in our senselessly brutal deaths for popular NuRac fancy."

Olask cracked a smile and sutured another stitch. Tamek fumed behind cool eyes. Wagner gulped a lungful of air and went on.

"Don't you see, Tamek? We did the impossible. All of us—*together*. We rallied everyone in that prison in what was probably their first-ever act of consequences-be-damned solidarity. Maybe if we'd known that so many of our own would lose their lives in the process, then yeah, maybe we would have scrubbed the whole effort. But now that we're here, within reasonable refuge, within a reasonable sphere of freedom, can you honestly look back and say that it wasn't worth trying?"

"Sentinel, I agree with this man," said the woman on whom Olask laboured. "It may not have been by my choice that the uprising occurred, but knowing that by week's end I may again be in the bosom of my family—in *my* mind this vindicates *Voknor* and the rest of you in whatever skulduggery you employed."

Wagner cleared his throat indelicately. "Um, Tamek was nothing but honourable and indulgent and lightning-quick to act throughout this whole thing. The—um—'skulduggery' was pretty much all mine."

She looked sympathetically at Wagner. "I do not truly know you, *Voknor*, but for the many times that I have seen you in Balgor's company. I had no ken of your role in the uprising—only the Sentinel's and Bilahdu's and a handful of others on the palaestra. It was the *Sentinel*," she said, turning her eyes on Tamek, "who prompted me to rebellion. It was *he* who inspired all of us today. And it was the noblest, most gainful contrivance to which I have ever lent my skills."

"More 'contrivance' than you realise, daughter," said Tamek. "If I were to admit that we guided you by means more collusive than you know, would you still wish to sing our praises?"

She thought for a moment before answering. "I understand and accept that some manner of artifice would have been necessary to accomplish what you and *Voknor* and your complotters have achieved. Treachery in the camp was a pitfall that we all had reason to beware."

"If I may embellish?" spoke Olask.

Tamek sighed. "By all means—bring me to account. It seems that I have it coming."

"I cannot deny," Olask began, "that it upset me gravely when news of the uprising reached the infirmary. *What insanity!* I thought. *What unthinking peccancy!* Had I been a much different man, I surely would have sought out—and with my bare fists, recompensed—the short-sighted clods who devised and set in motion such ill-conceived recklessness. As we worked to gather the lame and the maimed for the uncompassable evacuation, I could little more than pity those who I knew would never survive the afternoon.

"My forecast of the final death toll was monumental. Many did in fact perish. My heart was torn from my chest one chamber at a time with each death that I witnessed, with each body that was left downpath, with each defending warrior who haplessly became this evening's hobbled. But, I am compelled to admit that *Voknor* is correct, Tamek. And Romina, here, as well. Healthy flesh must often be damaged along with ecchymosed tissue in order to extract an arrowhead. Mothers must sometimes die in the breech that their babes might breathe life. The casualties of today's grim triumph may offer some shred of meaning if we but let them. None of us need shed blood for a paying public's folly ever again."

The Sentinel gazed unbelieving at the physician.

"Old man, is this *you* speaking thusly?"

Olask shot him an expression that served as a shrug.

The Sentinel chuckled. "I am a stubborn, crusty traditionalist," he said, "and for this I apologise. I suppose that, at times, my views are so narrow and rigid that they become brittle if I do nothing to reinforce them with reasoning and logic and a peck of tolerance."

"Hear! Hear!" cried Olask, the only living being whom Tamek would ever allow to hamstring him with sarcasm in this measure. In immediate response, the Sentinel re-raised his guard and lit upbraidingly into his old nemesis, kicking off a new leg in their familiar duel of wits, with friendly criticism begetting not-so-friendly criticism until Olask finally had to beg off so that he could properly finish with Romina's sutures. It was here that Wagner took Tamek and steered him away, venturing a route along the outer hub of the resting wounded.

"I need to apologise, too," Wagner admitted after quelling Tamek's trenchancy. "Not for any action that I may have taken, but rather for the lack thereof. I didn't even think to lend my somewhat unusual services to these people earlier. Had I stayed sharp and defied my weary bones, I'm sure that I could have prevented a whole slew of amputations—even some deaths."

The Sentinel stared across the darkening, post-operative grounds. Spread out before him in uncomfortable and undignified succession lay the humanity he'd vowed to protect. Somewhere in the lonely umbrage just beyond the fore-copse, awaiting final unction and pyre, lay the bodies of those whom he had failed. Pining over *these* more than any other, he refrained from exhorting comment for the duration of his survey. Then, acquiescently, he managed a thoughtful reply.

"I cannot fault you, *Voknor*. When we first met in that filthy dungeon, I could hardly predict that your person would become the vessel of such miraculous wonders. You were, after all, only a heathen to me then, not the anachronistic viator who stands before me now, not the often insensate thaumaturge who acts by the seams of his pantaloons and whom the Fates cunningly tucked into mine own fold—where I would ne'er have thought to look for portent or prodigy."

"I'm no prodigy," Wagner insisted.

"If not, then I am not bumptious and overweening." He gave Wagner a moment to indagate his point. "We seldom see ourselves as others do, *Voknor*. I am the nonpareil transgressor of that rule, as you and Olask and many others so enjoy emphasising. But you must acknowledge the fact of your gift, e'en as you do not accept the source whence it comes to you. The Vorshalah is upon us. A Soork has been ungraved and defiled. The realm entire may become enlivened in the manner that has been denoted in sundry accounts of canonical scribblings. In time, it may be that magiks will be imparted by heavenly grace to many like yourself." He suddenly threw up his arms as if frustrated. "Or not. Verily, I do not know. The gods do not whisper their intentions in mine ear, nor can I say that they rain sweet revelation o'er my meditative extrados. Clarity and straightforwardness have ne'er been in their methodology. But that is not to say that the learned cannot interpret. As I now see it, both you and I, our comrades and our rescuers—we are all of us bound in duty to take back the realm. Yet, lacking the Soork's egregious might, we will need perseverance to do so—perseverance, courage, and I dare say a scintilla of madness."

Wagner lit up. "Not to worry—I can help you with at least *one* of those."

"I will depend on that help. For the nonce, howe'er, I would appreciate it in the form of comfort meted to some of my kinspeople."

Wagner consented. Accompanying the Sentinel, then, from invalid to invalid, he aided in the parcelling of cheer and sympathy and, when they both agreed it was essential, a careful and covert rejuvenation to the most critically suffering. On realising, however, that Wagner's physical robustness waned incrementally in the deploying of his sortilege, Tamek placed no demands on his heathen friend but to allow Wagner to dispense healing as he saw fit. It hinted at a bonding they'd not shared since the early days, since long before the growing suspicions, the subterfuges, and the alleged blasphemies. Unheralded, understated, and long overdue, it was a collaboration that truly honoured both men and seized each of them completely and utterly by surprise. Hostilities banished, distrust tabled, their camaraderie was born anew and sustained by the presence of the needy to whom they extended comfort. In thus broaching that terrible atmosphere of misery, and making it better for having done so, the restored vivacity radiated beyond the infirm alone, and left Wagner and Tamek with a tremendous uplift of optimism where only a trace had previously existed.

As night clasped its black grip about them, fires and torches were struck at the encampment perimeters in manner similar to what Wagner recalled while a captive of the NuRac caravan. Although their brilliance would travel for considerable distance in the extreme pitch of the Ergosian wilds—potentially betraying the rebels' position through even the thickest of thicketed terrain—it was unlikely that the pursuant NuRacs were desperate or vengeful enough to be willing to risk marching at night. Too great was the fear on either side of the roving predators whom Wagner had evidenced only in distant wails and by reliable hearsay. He had, however, received sufficient schooling to know that none but the foolhardy and the overbold took to strange woodlands between dusk and dawn, especially by the dark of the moon, when the night-hounds ran at their most aggressive. In all probability, wherever the NuRacs camped (if, indeed, they hadn't returned to QieLahr), then certainly they would have been forced to create fires of their own, and would therefore have been unable to see far enough beyond their own blazes to glean much clueing to the Ergosians' whereabouts.

As the scent of even the newly dead would provide too irresistible an incentive for night-hound brazenness, at roughly the midnight hour Tamek gathered to him a party of warriors and significant kin in order to usher the vessels of the recently lost back to their elemental origins. This would be Wagner's first funeral experience on Ergos, a quaint harkening to the ancient and third-world ceremonies of his home-world. Performing the ritual at this late hour not only facilitated the survivors' need to press on at dawn, but the added luminosity provided by the pyres made for additional insurance against the light-shunning hounds. While a number of unaccounted Ergosian dead may yet have lain kilometres back, at the point of the day's confrontation, they would not be forgotten in spirit. In lieu of retrieving and anointing and cremating these kinspeople, Tamek's eulogistic repertory was to include the proper requiescat to see said unreachable patriots into the next sphere with full honours.

By this time, a sleepy-eyed Balgor had made the scene, as had J'nea and Uthok and a considerable gathering of compassionate souls—rebels and refugees alike. The Bonecrusher and the former trusty both noshed on hardtack slathered with renderings (procured from who-knew-where), and neither one showed much receptivity to Wagner's suddenly ravenous entreaty to mooch a bite. Uthok, who creatively claimed that his given name translated from the ancient tongue as "he who does not share," pulled a war-axe on Wagner in feigned stinginess as he popped the last delightful biscuit into his maw in triumphant taunt. J'nea proved more kind-hearted—but just barely. Twice in tease she extended the cracker and retracted it before giving way and shoving the already nibbled end into Wagner's mouth. Crisp and pinguid and exquisite going down, Wagner finished it quickly while J'nea gobbled up a second biscuit even more hastily.

Not having obtained suitable nourishment since the morning meal, and now even more greatly spurred by the drain of the revivification process, Wagner was abruptly laden with the urgency of unconcealable appetite. Querying J'nea as to where he might acquire more of the same, she pointed him in the general direction of the concessionary shelter where she and Uthok had received the snacks. Yet, with some of their most proximate neighbours demonstrating unspoken disdain that he could think to indulge his empty belly when Tamek's elegy was about to commence, Wagner instead chose to remain humble—and in borborygmic want of sustenance—that he might share in something more meaningful and poignant than pangs and taste buds, no matter how devilishly he craved nourishment.

A single, comprehensive pyre had been erected for the sake of expediency out of twigs, faggots, and sere branches. In turn, the bodies, after receiving proper unction, had been respectfully placed upon the tinder. At the foot of the pile stood the Sentinel, mournful and solemn, ready to start with the eulogy. He had, in fact, been long ready, but had agreed to delay in order for Mirko of Vargath and his senior officers to join the assembly. These ranking men and women, apparently having made rounds earlier in the afternoon to greet the liberated and to garner the latest information, had spent the bulk of the early evening conferring in the command shelter with the day's reconnaissance teams, and had only now adjourned so that they could be courteously present for the ritual. Balgor, annoyed that he'd been absent and unconscious during the impromptu reception, now eagerly craned between the various onlookers' heads so that he might catch sight of the Vargathian and some of his old comrades among the higher rebel echelon. Wagner did the same, for he'd heard so much about this outfit during his forced tenure in QieLahr that he almost felt as if he were in the presence of extraordinary personage. In truth, it was a projection of reputed heroism that he and Balgor and many of the others bestowed upon these top brass of the freedom fighters, a deference and an exaltation that, though well-deserved, tended to downplay or shunt their *own* minor, yet nevertheless defiant, victories over the NuRacs during the difficult course of their incarceration. No matter, however, for everyone present was united now in common spirit, common dedication, common purpose. Aggrandised in their combined member-ships, they clearly had not yet the strength in number to confront SyKrahvo directly; but if spirit alone could ever win back a nation, they were certainly in the running.

The rebel officers proceeded through the assemblage, far fewer and less imposing than Wagner had imagined they'd be. Five in all, including Mirko, not one displayed the frippery or regalia of distinguished rank. As they typically fought independently of—and frequently unsanctioned by—the Ergosian army proper, such was understandable. In fact, nothing in their manner suggested undue haughtiness. Nothing in their mien distinguished them as anything but the soldiers that they were. Plain and austere, each could well have passed as just another of the loyally lusty ruck who followed them. Even Mirko, whom Wagner scrutinised from a lateral vantage, wore a loose, frock-like jerkin over his strapping trunk, presumably to check the mild chill that in the last hour had settled about the sylvan hideaway. Were he as under the weather as had been reported, by simply putting in this appearance he was making the grandest gesture of respect to those who weren't even around to appreciate it. The provision here, of course, was that he suffered from scourges of either viral or bacterial origins. If the source of his bane was incantational—as was popularly purported—then Wagner had no angle. Such concepts were as ungraspable, as unanswerable, as his own sundry enigmas.

As the quintet emerged at the face of the throng, something else began taking hold of Wagner that had little to do with quiet regard or awe. Praetersensual and prodigious, it started as but an intimation, an intuitive storm that glanced upon his mind's horizons. But how amain was it in gathering psychical momentum! An eddy awhirl and churning with redolent debris, it ushered with it an attrahent galvanisation for which Wagner couldn't quite account. There was something about the Vargathian, something in his bearing or his physiognomy that, fast outstripping the mystique of his great renown, prompted in Wagner an involuntary shudder of recognition, evoked a fuzzy, recollective engram of circuitous nostalgia that either reflected past experience or premonished a future that Wagner had already glimpsed in earthly visions of long ago. A previous encounter was unlikely; he knew no other Ergosians outside of QieLahr. Yet, if his other choice were true, there existed differentiae here that didn't fit the classic mind-trip archetypes. And Wagner appreciated the discrepancy at once.

With curiosity far too compelling to defy, he tacitly abandoned the company of his friends and embarked on a circumspectly inconspicuous migration along the edge of the gathering, furtively seeking a closer inspection of this man whose mere proximity seemed to flush some flurried ilk of revelation from his mental backwaters.

Before the pyre, the man known as Mirko came to face Tamek, greeted him, traded words; and although the Sentinel had ever been outspoken and up-front in his criticism of the Vargathian for, among other things, his impertinence and his unconventional methods, he now demonstrated uncommon self-restraint and cordiality in what was likely their second meeting of the day. Under most circumstances, taking refuge in the camp of his recidivist corrival would hardly have been enough to quash Tamek's guilelessness. But here, in the midst of such solemn purpose, the Sentinel remained as sober, genteel, and tolerant as he'd been with Wagner a few moments earlier. A dulcification of inner principles, it was as if he'd struck a spiritual compromise with his otherwise unsubduable, fundamentalist inclinations.

In the flickering torch-play, the visages of these two very diverse guardians were continuously consumed and restored by the variegation of shadow and sheen, and although Wagner sought to maintain a certain anonymity in his approach, he simply couldn't obtain an unencumbered study of Mirko without venturing conspicuously into the pair's presence. His gradual foray neither obvious nor intervenient, he remained just within the fold of spectators, slipping past one, then another, waiting for an occasion of vantage. How ironic it was, then, that when such opportunity presented itself, Wagner found himself completely unprepared.

By chance, the distant howl of a forest predator inclined the Vargathian's glance in a fortuitous direction, and for all of an instant each man's eyes fell upon the other's.

Wagner drew back aghast.

Yet, conversely, Mirko of Vargath turned unconcernedly back to his business with the Sentinel, the initial degree of his nonchalance challenged only by the lack of any notable impression that catching brief sight of Wagner might have effected. However, no sooner had he turned away then did he wheel about for what seemed a behindhand substantiation for what he, too, had just seen, almost as if in that trice he'd registered a phantasm.

To no avail; whatever, *whomever*, Mirko believed he had seen was there no longer. Only the bereaved stared back at him, and they, in unaffected ogle.

Raking raven hair from his eyes, the Vargathian took a backward step to gain himself a more generous perspective. Casting his glance across the composite of faces like a great fishnet of intrigue, he trawled for the telltale retreat of a lone figure slipping through the body of the crowd. His net would return unfilled.

"Is something amiss, brother?" the Sentinel asked.

Mirko held steady. His engraved stare had now taken on the makeweight of an introspection that prevailed for several of what seemed illimitable seconds. Finally, he relinquished.

"Nay, Sentinel. Just a... nay, proceed. By all means, proceed."

Tamek commenced with an archaic chant, thus initiating the final rite of the dead. Those present bowed their heads as he set into eulogising the brave souls lost, his beautifully articulated oration alternating between contemporary Ergosian and the more obscure idiom of the ancients. The latter, an ornate and melodious (and unwieldy) tongue, was one in which precious few people in the entire realm possessed any degree of proficiency, much less a basal comprehension—the exception being Wagner himself, whose inevitable fluency with any encountered language allowed him here a progressive access to this sacred acrolect of old. But Wagner took no interest in Tamek's dirges, nor did he find solace in the sanctity of the moment. He had so much more to ponder. Hidden but vicinal, his back pressed firmly against a shielding tree just beyond the cusp of mourners, he was still reticently assessing what he'd only seconds earlier discovered, namely that Mirko of Vargath—incorrigible rogue, upstart rebel leader, military strategist *sans pareil*—and the inscrutable tabloid shaman Wagner knew on earth as *Miracle* were one and the same!

This simply couldn't be. And yet, here was the man himself, on Ergos, just as Wagner was. A new and unexpected variable in his ever-readjusting fix on reality, it at once filled Wagner with excitement and reservation. The phenomenon of his own physical transference evidently no longer a freakish singularity, it appeared that an earthly kindred had joined him on this plane—and he now stood at odds with how to deal with it. This was a development that he could never have predicted, much less imagined. The fact that he'd been intuitively cautious in his approach suggested not so much any inherent shortcoming in how he handled knee-jerk reactions, but rather, it assured him of the soundness of his instincts, however ridiculous or excessively prudent they seemed. Seldom did he ever ignore his gut feeling, and as a result he'd managed to survive in strange and dangerous surroundings where the overly fearless or the unheedingly foolish may well have perished. Yet now, with his intellect gradually creeping back to switch out his shock, a decidedly intricate task lay before him.

Peering out from behind the tree, he carefully studied the alleged "Vargathian" to confirm his assumption, to verify this unbelievable discovery that suddenly set a thousand new hurdles before him. He hoped that this Mirko of Vargath simply bore a remarkable likeness to the earthly *Miracle*, hoped that his weary eyes had spun similarity from suggestion, hoped that the congruency he saw was no more than a trick of the night. He hoped vainly. Although there may have been minor nuances about the man that didn't perfectly match what little he'd read or seen of *Miracle*, at this stage he would bet his manhood that Mirko was a dead-on match.

Accepting the premise for the nonce, he juxtaposed Mirko's apparent history on Ergos against his own. A rich variance in fortune was instantly evident. Where, for weeks, Wagner in his introverted hesitancy had done little more than flounder in a muddle of pervasive uncertainty and callowness, here was this flamboyant Mirko/*Miracle* character who clearly had found his Ergosian footing right away, had adapted to this planet's archaic culture with astounding adroitness, had busied himself in the leading of armies, in combating tyranny, in conducting a multitude of followers so utterly devoted to him that their actions seemed as extensions of his own brashly authoritative intent. Wagner felt nothing less than absolute, unadulterated awe, especially since his own best efforts had proved him little more than a curiosity to his adoptive race.

One explanation may have had its origin in their personal creeds. Wagner believed that, through all of his trials, he had remained true to himself, true to his core being. But clearly, *Miracle* had made certain concessions in order to effectively embrace this new life, some of them noticeably at odds with the evangelical persona that the *Pursuer Weekly* had portrayed. For instance, *Miracle*, as Mirko, had come to acquire the ignominious reputation as a knave, a rounder, a scoundrel—terms that hardly jibed with his former earthly ministry, and which in fact were commensurate to complete apostasy. Still, where the mainstream opinion on earth had regarded him with the cynicism and the suspicion of too many gullible people fed too many lies on too many occasions—on Ergos he had forged for himself the reputation of hero and legend and lovable rogue; less resplendently put, he was a flawed man with bighearted principles. And truly, he'd accomplished so much. Oh, to have possessed enough charisma as to inspire so great a measure of humanity into surrendering its trust, its loyalty, its future, to a total outsider—what Wagner wouldn't have given to have osmosed even a scrap of this man's social talents. In fact, it came to his having to consciously repress his own envy and intimidation that he might respectfully pay homage to someone who'd availed himself of his planetary transference so much more efficiently.

The finest benefit, however, was that no longer was Wagner alone. Here, finally, was somebody with whom he shared common ground, a cosmic cousin who'd likewise become the unwary recipient of a mystic summons from beyond. The very means and meaning of said summoning as ungraspable as the mist at their feet, Wagner supposed that neither he nor *Miracle* might ever know the grander design. Nevertheless, he grappled with two theories: first, that the former prophet had either been drawn to Ergos in an incremental "phase'n'switch" manner, similar to his own experience, or second, that *Miracle* had been caught in the wake of his chanced proximity to Wagner at the moment that the spatial barrier was breached on Howsley's lawn. One way or the other—or neither—the Mirko/*Miracle* enigma stood mere metres away; and, in his Ergosian guise, he held influence over a people whose ignorance of his true self was such that it amused Wagner and at the same time infused him with a fervent curiosity to know the means by which he'd accomplished it. In retrospect, even his name was a blatant no-brainer, and Wagner might even have apprehended this had he taken the time to consider it on the many occasions that it was bantered about in the NuRac camp. Enunciated as it was, with the "r" rolled, "Mirko" actually rang so similar to its three-syllable earthly counterpart that Wagner felt foolish for not having at least noted it before. Yet, having met *Miracle* only as a brief flash of presence within a transient phasing, there'd never been an impetus to seek a correlation between the *Miracle* of earth and the Mirko of Ergos. But a correlation most definitely existed, and it was a germane discovery that begged investigation.

Tamek's ceremony was thoughtful and succinct. He delivered the last offices with warm solemnity, his final prayer followed in brief by an extempore musical piece piped out by one of the congregation. Blown on a simple reed instrument, the melody's gentle lilt evoked a haunting poignancy that swayed even Wagner into joining his neighbours in collective genuflection. Such ceremonies—and the demonstrative symbolism that they so often entailed—had always been awkward for him. He'd experienced only a handful in his life, usually for some relative of Sara's whom he'd never met, or for one or two of Howsley's *locals* whose illnesses had precluded Wagner from ever truly knowing the principal essences that lurked far within the rubble of their respective insanities. But here, now, in realising that his was a claim of partial ownership in these Ergosian deaths, Wagner suddenly felt the responsibility and the guilt that pressed like unwanted visitors at the stoop of his disconnectedness, so much that he was almost grateful when the flutist concluded his piece.

As was customary, those who had lost blood family to the day's carnage demonstrated respect by submitting on both knees, while friends and acquaintances and respectful strangers generally bent down on but one. Many mourners smeared a daub of earth across their foreheads as Tamek touched the torch to the pyre, and this "dust-to-dust" gesture Wagner had learned was representational of the fallen's inevitable reintegration with the elements by way of Eternity, Existence, and the Sacred Pool.

As the flames crackled voraciously, consuming kindling and kindred alike in the finality of offering, Wagner glanced once more at the figure that he alone knew as *Miracle*. For all of his quiet speculating, his inferences, his theories about the man and his earthly ministry, Wagner gradually came to sense a greater ensilage of ambiguity than originally suspected. Some assumption in his logic wasn't gelling to his satisfaction, some factor of precedence or of motivation or character—he wasn't sure which. He was torn between confronting *Miracle* directly and maintaining a cautious scrutiny from afar, for he could not hope to predict the man's reaction. Would he know Wagner? Would he embrace him? Or would he quickly seek to silence him before he could expose his sham? The more that Wagner thought about it, the more inclined he was to sidle towards wariness. He thus withdrew until he could be certain, until the time that he might identify and resolve the glitch in his reasoning.

Rejoining his friends at the rear of the concourse, he was questioned casually about his little pilgrimage, to where he had disappeared, and why. Shrugging evasively, he remained distant and disobliging of answer, although he gestured to Balgor in secret to accompany him away from the pack while the others began their saunter back to the heart of the camp.

Once sequestered, Wagner beset the realmson with all manner of inquiry.

"Tell me again—how long have you known this Mirko?" he asked.

Balgor pondered a moment. "Considerable years."

This puzzled Wagner. "How *many* years exactly?"

"A good ten, I would say. As I have told you, his rakish exploits were already popular fare in the alehouses long before I knew him, long before he and I ever caroused our way through lower Vargath. Ever the notorious figure, ever the most basely clever of strategists, when Vishkor fell that dark day, he reformed himself and began channelling his brilliance into the masterminding of many a successful martial campaign against the NuRacs. In the year beyond my injury, I left the army proper to again seek him out, and to join his self-formed militia. I fought alongside him for eight years before my capture."

Wagner muttered something to himself.

"I beg your pardon?"

"It just doesn't add up."

"What does not add up?"

Wagner made no reply. He had his answer, and it was far from a comfortable fit. In fact, like everything else in his life, it raised more questions than it squelched. Years versus weeks, rogue versus prophet—nothing about *Miracle* seemed to make sense. But that wasn't to say that Wagner stood bereft of hypotheses. The earthly *Miracle* had sought desperately to meet with Wagner, had travelled halfway across the continent to do so. Now, it was looking as if he may have journeyed considerably farther than that. Yet, with the exact nature of his Howsley sojourn pre-empted by Wagner's untimely limbo-launch, the purpose of *Miracle's* visit had never been made clear to Wagner; and whatever their connection was, it had remained as earthbound as a certain roll of tropical-flavoured candies. But also remaining was one very compelling theory. If this was indeed the man that Wagner believed him to be, then evidently *Miracle* had stumbled upon a means of existing in two worlds, either alternately or simultane-ously. If Wagner allowed for this, then perhaps, too, his alleged illness—that to which everyone so often alluded—may have stemmed not so much from malaise or malocchio, but rather from some incidental ilk of sphere-hopping dementia or trans-spatial jet lag. Nothing remained outside the realm of possibility, not anymore, and however creative Wagner's postulating, however fancifully optimis-tic his thinking, he thrilled to this single, pregnant prospect of a pilotable phasing. For, were such conjecture to actually pan out, it would bring with it the potential for opening the door for his own homecoming.

On the other hand, if the Vargathian turned out to be no more than *Miracle's* physical double, then Wagner's consolation would be forfeit to a quaint coincidence of nature, a freakish confluence of intersidereal ontogeny the cruel taunting of which would dangle like yet another loose thread on an already frayed veil of befuddlement. A foreseeably disappointed Wagner would then trudge on as before, braving this new existence, bracing for the next complication, continuing to carve a niche for himself within the primitive and turbulent society that the Fates themselves obviously deemed suited to his lubberly traversing.

Balgor and Wagner soon rejoined J'nea and Uthok in the greater refuge as the bulk of their compatriots began settling in for the night. At the edge of the encampment, the pyre would continue to burn long into the post-midnight hours, while the many torches in blaze around the safehold's perimeter were sure to be sustained by Mirko's most diligent sentries.

Wagner, beset anew by the harping of a long ignored belly, blundered serendipitously into a chance for satiation by way of one of the camp's considerate inhabitants, whose personal lodgement he practically trampled while zombied in thought. This benefactor, a wizened man with an ascetic's gentle demeanour, exchanged niceties with the war-torn foursome, and in the process he perceived a certain indigence about them—not only from their visages, but more so in the raucously audible demands emanating from Wagner's abdomen that, in truth, resounded nearly as loudly as had the day's battlefield. In the name of hospitality, he made available to them his own store of provisions as a late evening collation. Offering each of the group a few strips of jerky and a communal porringer of spiced and pickled kale, he additionally set before them a generous skin of water.

Then he rummaged about in his personal stowage until he produced a stomach-shaped flask that—presumably by its having endured the pass-around of many such conjoint partakings—appeared in general condition to be nearly as old as he. This vessel, uncorked with moderate effort, he wedged into Balgor's nimbly waiting fingers before swinging about to confront the source of a tremulous smacking suddenly assaulting his ears from behind. Clamping a hand to his mouth, he gazed in astonishment at the overzealous Wagner devouring his goods with an urgency uncommon for anyone save the most desperate starvelings of the wild. Such unbridled appetence the host found most astounding, and his attention remained riveted to this ultra-ravenous invitee who, in gorging himself on bite after ambitious bite, employed nary a chew, barely paused for breath, and summarily slaked his gullet with unrestrainably indulgent gulps from the fast-emptying waterskin. In the sum of all of the victualer's ample years, he'd witnessed scores of ravening and rapacious men, but none like this chestnut-haired, rusty-bearded, greedygut of a chap now before him.

Wagner, however—once glutted and his good sense restored to him—was immediately overtaken by embarrassment and horror for his blatant, orgiastic display of edacity. He apologised profusely, and insisted on replenishing the skin for his host even as Uthok and the others made comparable sots of themselves in the potation of the man's obviously palatable wine. Fortunately, the man, who called himself Jotal, was genial and happy to share, as he suspected that the four of them had been sorely deprived of such simple pleasures for far too long a time. But he wasn't a totally selfless individual; he did demand one manner of reciprocity from them for his philanthropy, that being the fierce insistence that they cloy a craving of his own—one for narrative, for stories about the toils of living in the gladiator camps of QieLahr. Not an inequitable request, once the grape had properly loosened the imbibers of a goodly heft of the day's encumbrances, they obliged with voluminous abandon, Uthok and Balgor clashing straightway over who should be the first to spin his tale, and J'nea squeaking past the ram-horns of their diatribe to beat both of them out, relaying to Jotal her take on prison life before either of her comrades had depleted his battery of expletives on the other.

Convinced that their host had bought himself enough squabbling entertainment to last a fortnight, the sated Wagner retreated from the gathering. Jotal's waterskin in hand, he headed for the east side of the encampment, where he'd earlier espied the rill that served as the rebels' water source. Fed by mountain snows, kilometres off, the delicate and unassuming rivulet wound a circuitous path through the woodland like a crystalline serpent, its mercurial body clear and pristine and, moreover, life-nurturing to the forest's indigenous denizens and to ambulant ones like himself. By night, the torchlight that reflected across its hurried rippling appeared stationary yet brokenly animated, and Wagner found it a very beautiful image to watch. Skimming the surface with the brush of a few fingers, he braced the water's cool fluidity, felt the sweep of its gently unceasing drive toward some greater, distant body. He likened it to himself, and to those ungraspable inner forces that impelled him to follow similar windings of an often visionally predicated destiny. Wagner knew that, in time, the rill would become one with the sea. But what he would find at *his* journey's end was anyone's guess.

Suddenly, a man's voice broke from close behind him. Three words, staidly delivered, they clipped the wings of Wagner's reverie, re-grounding him in the there and then.

"I know you."

Wagner tensed momentarily. The voice so impossibly familiar, so recognisably discrepant, he required no prompting to know the identity of its agent, even as he'd never consciously heard him utter a single syllable.

He answered the only way he could.

"Do you?"

Before Mirko could retort, Wagner submerged Jotal's vessel into the current. For the duration of the fill, both men stood and listened as the displaced air rapidly bubbled from out the narrow mouth, almost as if the skin was giving up secrets to the brook in order that neither man might need to divulge his own. But, once the gurgling subsided, once Wagner had refixed the cork and could forestall a confrontation no longer, he stood to face the familiar stranger who was himself displaced on this foreign sphere.

"How did you get here?" Wagner asked bluntly.

Mirko furrowed a brow. "A rather odd question," he remarked. Yet, in realising that Wagner was in absolute earnest, he forthrightly answered. "Doubtless, you must know—these are my compeers, my cohorts, my confidants. We travelled here together, on foot."

Now Wagner's brow scrunched. "No," he sighed, pointing in elucidation at the muddy bank. "How did you get *here*, to this world?"

No reply.

Wagner groaned. "To *Ergos!* How did you get to *Ergos?*"

Mirko stared, baffled. Then he erupted with a hearty, congenial laugh. "You, sir, battle on the brink of peril for the better portion of a day, and at its end you wish to engage in philosophising on the reintegrating of souls? By poor Juthac's flamebérge, you are a deeply thoughtful and mettlesome man!" He snorted merrily, demonstrating the same solicitousness that Wagner once used with the crazy soothsayers whom he'd occasionally encountered on the streets of Bishop.

However, once far enough beyond the aggregate of his amusement to see that Wagner was not pacified, he spoke again, catering to Wagner's original query. "Would it not be better to speak with Tamek about such matters? Do I truly look to be a man who exudes a wealth of esoteric credentials?"

Wagner stood mute. Something was amiss—this much was obvious—but it beggared his understanding. First of all, the man spoke to him not in English, as Wagner may have expected, but in the tongue of the Ergosians. In itself, there was nothing unusual about this; certainly, whatever force had been responsible for outfitting Wagner with his uncanny, universal fluency would likewise have predisposed *Miracle* to the same advantage. But, coupled with the fact that he had completely failed to comprehend Wagner's teleportation inference, it demon-strated that a bit of rework in the old "theorising department" appeared necessary. Of course, there always existed the possibility that *Miracle*, so immersed in his new identity, may merely have opted not to avouch Wagner's allusion for reasons of his own, reasons prudent or corroboratory or otherwise undetermined; if he was happier in this new life, it was conceivable that he saw no need, nor felt any desire, to reflect back on his old one. Still, another likelihood—albeit a farfetched notion at best—was that, due to some unidentified and overly convenient lapse in memory wrought of concussive or psychogenic trauma, he may honestly have had no recollection of his earthly life. After all, as Mirko of Vargath he was alleged to have been experiencing some menial ilk of mental fugue; the possibility therefore existed that his current behaviour had some as yet unseen tethering to this allegation, fabricated or genuine as it may have been.

Wagner gambled on a new tactic. "Okay, you say you know me. How then? And from where?"

This seemed to put the screws to Mirko. He stood befuddled, like an orator who'd lost his thought train. But then he just as quickly recomposed, offering up the one reply that Wagner hadn't banked on.

"I had rather hoped that you might be able to tell *me*," he said, somewhat sadly.

Wagner leaned inward, expecting elaboration. None was given.

"Then, you don't know me from *earth*." The statement was less an interrogative than a declaration of incredulity.

"Again with the earth?" Mirko was not only clueless, but easily as incredulous as Wagner. "Earth, soil, ground, marl—it is all the same. We issue from it. We return to it. What more is th—" His stare penetrated Wagner's like a bulldozer going through fence picket. "Do you suggest, friend, that mayhap you and I are bound by some telluric accouplement?"

Wagner laughed. "No, I'm sure I didn't say anything like that at all! What does that even *mean*?"

"Do you deny that we share some manner of kinship?"

Wagner shrugged. "I'm not convinced that we share anything other than the circumstances of timing and happenstance."

Even here, Wagner demonstrated reluctance to enter the domain of complete honesty. An outsider for so long, he actually found it quite trying to unburden himself of that status, even in the presence of someone who may have possessed the potential for understanding it—and complementing it—with a matchable array of personal experience. Granted, having found himself aligned earlier that day with Balgor and Uthok, J'nea and Tamek, Bilahdu, Graspa, even Skol, he'd experienced an unexpected, inward repletion of sorts, a sense that he may indeed have found a belonging within that battling ensemble. Warfare was ugly and horrid, but by having deemed the escape a just cause for warring, Wagner partook of its heinousness with all of the bloody abandon that his wilder persona could manufacture, the resultant jolt of exhilaration rocking the more civilised foundation upon which, for years, he'd been basing his self-knowledge. Rarely had he felt more vibrant or more at home than in those limbic moments when he and his inner savage shared control; for, in that trice, the innate pacifist and the newfound energumen coexisted, completing the missing—albeit not always desirable—component that the Wagner psyche alone had always lacked. And in a similar, yet unaccountably remote, manner, that same feeling existed here, in his proximity to Mirko.

"By what name are you called?" Mirko abruptly asked.

This surprised Wagner quite utterly, if only because he'd been told that the man in the lobby at the Howsley Centre had requested him by name. Barring the amnesia and subreption scenarios, the likelihood that *Miracle* would truly not know Wagner now lent itself more closely to impossibility than improbability; and it came to be that in Wagner's reply and the banter that ensued, his whole slew of preconceptions was forever altered.

Given the limited information that he'd culled from Balgor and Tamek and from various less informed sources, Wagner's mental construct of the pre-met Vargathian—and the qualities that apparently drove him—could hardly have taken into account his being anything but completely Ergosian. That he might have hailed from Wagner's world would never have been given credence by any who knew him best. Allowing this, within the scramble of conflicting data, Wagner could find only one supposition capable of reconciling the numerous discrepancies in Mirko of Vargath's recountable history—from that of boyhood rapscallion to military rogue to underground hero—with those of his clearly antipodal earthly double. Only one explanation fit without exception, although it required even more suspension of disbelief to embrace it. In this new assumption, Wagner was forced to accept that the broad figure standing beside him at the rill was definitely not the Colorado-based healer/holy man, he of the grass roots ministry who sought to create détente between a callously cynical American heartland and the time-honoured qualities of honour and probity and charity. He was not the reputed mystic who, in shunning most congregate venues, sought out the individually needy rather than beckon them to come to him. Nor was he the reportedly humble, often hermetic soul who had the pox of celebrity foisted upon him through endless streams of copy spewed from the *Pursuer Weekly* and its expository cousins.

No, Mirko was not that man.

Not yet.

But someday he would be. Somehow, someway, through some twisty-turny Möbius strip in the timeline, he would eventually become that man.

Of course, there was nothing empirical that inclined Wagner to make this conclusion. He simply knew it, knew it now with a conviction that grabbed hold of him like one of Skol's hammerlocks and wouldn't let go. Presumptuous, unsupported, permissive—yes, *yes* to the utmost degree—but as his instincts had seldom let him down, with this inspired and almost prescient connection Wagner felt absolutely Copernican in his enlightenment, and he would not be swayed. With nothing but unsubstantiated cognition, he construed a mirroring of his own predicament, one that bore the inconsonance of some quantum, calendric twist within the cosmic weave itself, a loopish, circulatory anomaly that would allow— and, in a sense, already *had* allowed—for Mirko to become earth's *Miracle*, just as Wagner had himself become Ergos's *Voknor*.

It was the one explanation, the *best* explanation, and Wagner was steadfast. By Ergosian chronology, Mirko had a much too documented history to have ever existed on earth in a timeframe that satisfied the skeins of conventional sequence. And as Wagner's conviction intrinsically held that Mirko and *Miracle* were indeed one and the same man, it only made sense that the "when" of their mutual world-traipsing would be equally as arbitrary as the "who," the "where," the "why," and so on. On earth, as on Ergos, time might have been a tool for event calibration; but moreover it was an abstraction. Like Tamek's similarly abstruse powers of Existence and Eternity, it encompassed realms far beyond the confines of human understanding. Until this moment, Wagner had regarded these underlying aspects of time as negligible to his own personal odyssey. But now, with Mirko's situation factored in, they appeared crucial, cryptic, and sublimely tortuous beyond Wagner's ken. Mysterious ingredients, whisked together and folded into the celestial stir-pot, they provided the completory integrant to a consummate, kismetic banquet of such extraordinary grandiosity that no mere mortal—and certainly not the disfranchised, comparably serfish Wagner—was allowed to sample except by means of the occasionally discarded table ort.

In his gentle supplications for any such illuminating morsels, Wagner gradually became awash in empathy at discovering that Mirko's episodic ailments—intimated to Wagner with less dissimulation than usual because of the uncommonly quick rapport that he and the Vargathian had forged—suspiciously sported all the classic symptomatology of the mind-trips of Wagner's pre-intangibility stage. Barring simple coincidence and all other interpretation, what this meant was that Wagner's was suddenly the seat of precedence whereby he might be afforded the opportunity to observe his once-ago ordeal from a purely extrinsic perspective. What it ostensibly boded for Mirko, however, was something entirely different: a descent into a pseudo-madness that required very little effort on Wagner's part to revisit.

Indeed, as the only resident veteran of that life-wrenching declension, as the only tutelary capable of counselling this troubled new ally through the chaos that would potentially come to overtake him, Wagner nevertheless refrained from tipping his cards prematurely. Despite the mortification and the tremendous angst that the good Vargathian tried burying beneath a rubble of bravado and good humour, Wagner held back on any reckless confessions for no other reason than that of timing. True, in the midst of physical battle he could be rash, live by flagrance, align himself with his inner hellion in defence of his life. But here, in the realm of rational thought, prudence and caution were his counsel, and revelation, a lamp to hide under a bushel until he was sure that Mirko could tolerate and accept its prophetic brilliance. To have come clean right there about their intertwining circumstances may indeed have alleviated some of Mirko's anxieties, perhaps even bestowed Wagner himself with additional insight; still, he felt it a complication unnecessary to broach so soon in their twenty minutes-old fellowship, however cruel or deceptive it may have been in the short term. For the nonce, he decided, he would restrict himself to observation, at least until he could find the means of proving or debunking his theory that Mirko was his cosmic reflection, a secretly tormented kindred who was destined to become cast away on earth. Only then would he commit to full disclosure. Only then would *Voknor* give Mirko the same heads-up that *Miracle* may have been belatedly striving to give Wagner.

This unique affiliation with Mirko presented Wagner with the first, truly meaty purpose to his Ergosian existence outside of simple survival. He wondered what his own last year on earth would have been like had he encountered someone who could claim to have endured the same malady and emerged from it with mental faculties intact. He tried rerunning in his mind how Mirko, as *Miracle*, had been depicted by Jon Mazzio in their last-ever conversation. Had *Miracle* been in as harried and hurried an urgency as Wagner had gathered? Had his visitor intuited the brevity of Wagner's remaining time before final phase-out? Was it mere coincidence? Extra-sensory perception? Providence?

If any of the above, Wagner had certainly drawn the short stick. Back on Howsley's grounds he'd only been meted a hazy glimpse, and no more, of his would-be ministrant. Here, in the rebel base, he anteceded this Mirko's imminent departure by calculable weeks, perhaps even months. Uncertain of the whys and wherefores—but determined to uncover something, *anything*—he carefully prodded the Vargathian for additional information, and dissected every connection and inconsistency, right up to the moment of one very unexpected intrusion.

"Can this be Mirko," Balgor's voice rang out from behind them, "lusty spawn of a krehak and a mountain nymph? Nay, surely not—the Mirko I knew was not so scrawny and demure!"

Mirko of Vargath closed his cerulean eyes and smiled with what could only be interpreted as fond annoyance. Then he turned to face the flamboyant realmson, who advanced amid the flickering torches, J'nea and Uthok in tow. Jotal, too, had tagged along for reasons of his own.

"If any man were to know about 'scrawny,' it would be you, brother Balgor—for I swear that you are the very model of it! What has happened to you, that your frame exemplifies only the bones and entrails that you are so fond of invoking?"

Of course, Wagner didn't buy this, for ever had he known his cohort to be the same strapping fellow who introduced him headfirst to the palaestra dirt, weeks back. That friends enjoyed a special prerogative when it came to deprecatory banter—and *old* friends, even more so—only the most obtuse of witnesses could fail to see that these two were as siblings under the skin.

"Prison rations," said Balgor. "No sausages, no forcemeat, no dumplings or torte to turn me soft like you self-indulgent freemen. But I have ingested enough gristle and strings in the past year to make me more than a match for the likes of you."

"Oh, hardly," countered Mirko, striding to meet Balgor's approach. "The only 'dumplings' or 'torte' that ever feel the tug of my gentle nibbling, *whore*-son, are not fashioned of potatoes or pastry, I assure you. But then, I would suppose that gaol has starved you of these delights as well—not that you ever had the good fortune to sample all that many. Not without proper coinage, anyway."

"Do not speak to me of good fortune, *whore-sire*," said Balgor, "when I have seen you plunk down a royal ransom to my meagre coinage. In fact, I seem to remember that any bawdyhouse that you ceased in frequenting was forced to put up shutters for loss of revenue!"

They embraced warmly, a sinewy grapple of pats and punches. It was an undeniable display of old comrades reunited, and although Mirko did not appear to be acquainted with either Uthok or J'nea, he was not remiss in extending an embosoming charm to them. The infectious smile beneath his double-pointed beard was as broad and as favourable and as welcoming as the forested refuge that he provided for his guests.

"By that familiar wine skin," he said, "I see that Jotal has not been sparing in his hospitality."

"By *your* law of hospitality, master," said Jotal.

"*Master?*" A suddenly curious Balgor looked the elder man up and down. "Of course!" he cried. "How is it that I did not recognise you by name? You are Jotal of the river country, Mirko's aide-de-camp from years ago!"

"*Many* years ago, I fear," said Jotal.

"Oho! Do not tell me that you still spend every waking hour wiping Mirko's nose and keeping him out of strife?"

Jotal glanced respectfully at the Vargathian. "Aye," he said. "And oft-times my sleeping hours as well."

"It seems to me, realmson" countered Mirko, "that I recall an instance or two when he generously held the bucket for *you* in the wee hours beyond your frequent excesses!"

If Balgor retorted—as he assuredly would have—Wagner didn't hear it. His thoughts were elsewhere. In fact, during the course of Jotal's reintroduction and history, he'd been carefully scrutinising his world-swapping counterpart with interest most generous, fascinated by Mirko's fizzy cordiality and by his gregariousness—neither one being traits that Wagner felt he himself exuded with all too much abundance. Even more, he found himself intrigued by Mirko's apparent inattentiveness to, and relative unconcern for, those secret and random episodes of psychical tumult that, by his own admission, heaved up with little warning to disengage him from the world he knew. Not while standing in the presence of his kinspeople did he exhibit his fears, anyway, and such was a tribute to his staunch, if not once disreputable, character. Wagner having himself been mired for years in nearly the same symptomatic predicament, he remembered demonstrating dramatically more broodiness and anxiety (indeed, petrifaction) in his own malady, not to mention the salvos of undeserved sarcasm that he'd customarily launched at every potentially helpful associate whom Jon Mazzio had been kind enough to bring around on his behalf. Too frustrated had he been, too jaded and mistrusting. In truth, no one but Sally Lemanski had ever succeeded in inspiring him to genuine hilarity as a form of escapism, and even then it had been a generic sort of induced hoopla, certainly not the boisterous and authentic jollity that Mirko entered into here with Wagner's gladiator pals. Such comportment was extraordinarily commanding and truly worthy of Wagner's respect; and Mirko—a veritable rock of a man—promoted a seemingly effortless air of gentle breeziness in the pocket calm of otherwise dark and weighty times.

More introductions and personal histories soon made the rounds, each amply embellished to maintain a suitable balance of social rivalry. It was all good fun, particularly in listening to Uthok, for his facts ever fell at odds, his deeds varying not only from previous tellings to the current version, but bogging in blatant self-contradiction from within the very same narrative. Too, now that Jotal's wine had sufficiently freed his tongue, the Bonecrusher was in the mode whereby he would not be dissuaded for hours from his braggadocio; for, even were this small huddle to disband for the night, he would undoubtedly rouse the first sleepy neighbour he stumbled across (or over) and go right on blathering till dawn.

In patiently obliging Uthok's "glory," Wagner shared a moment of mutual eye-rolling with J'nea. Her look of amusement gave him reason for pause; and she, catching him staring at her, signalled him into an impromptu aside, where opportunity permitted her offering up a personal take on their seat-of-their-galligaskins triumph risen from the day-long assault of absolutely direful obstacles. Despite the tragedies of suffering and hardship and loss—all of which she doubtlessly felt with immeasurable poignancy—the thrill of her newly earned freedom could not be contained, and her recap therefore burgeoned with uncommon enthusiasm. And Wagner, rarely seeing her so blithesome, stamped this endearing image into his memory, for as acquainted as he was with her whirligig mood swings, he suspected that such wonderful amiability would not last.

Confessing felicity and incredulity with the day's outcome, she admitted to having no idea how they could even have succeeded—barring one pertinent exception. Here, she referred him to the events of the arena substructure, and to how close he and Balgor had come to disaster but for her intervention. While she did magnanimously concede to Wagner's quirky resourcefulness, and to the unprecedented derring-do that salvaged the scheme from the doom of an equal number of strategic miscalculations and outright boners, J'nea all the while reminded him of how they would never, in an aeon, have been able to instigate the riot without her timely intercession and finely honed skills. And she did so with total ego.

While granting that her boasts were justified and deserved, Wagner knew that he couldn't agree with all that she'd stated without betraying his great debt to her. She had indeed been a godsend, maybe the most important one. But to actually *tell* her this? He would never hear the end of it.

So he scoffed. And he crafted a lie almost worthy of Uthok, insisting that she'd been part of his equation from the start. He claimed that he'd long factored her in as one of the predicates whose vital dispensation he'd gambled would manifest in precisely the manner that she'd provided it. He also added that, to ensure no incidental flak from her, he and Balgor had allowed her to maintain the illusion that her actions had been of her own accord.

Remarkably, he'd managed to maintain a straight face during the entirety of his revelation.

J'nea eyeballed him, her face unreadably beautiful and beautifully unreadable. And Wagner, thinking that he truly had her, permitted himself a wisp of a hint of a smirk. He would find his smugness far too precipitate.

Like a snake striking at an unwary field mouse, J'nea suddenly lashed out and tweaked Wagner's nose a good one. Relishing in his puppyish yelp, she asked him if this, too, had been anticipated in his master scheme.

Massaging his brutalised cartilage, Wagner answered in the negative. His wit, however, recovered more readily than his flesh.

"Do you know," he quickly spun, "that where *I* come from, the nose holds very phallic connotations? By my people's custom, you've just initiated aggressive sexual foreplay in the centre of a crowded rebel refuge."

Now it was her turn to scoff. By her expression, the earthly phrase of "you wish" came to mind. Had she been of earth, she likely would have blurted it. Instead, she gave up a snicker—but only one—and complimented him on his initiative. Then, shifting gears as he knew she must, she laid into him.

"You are such an ingrate! Would you even acknowledge the mother who bore you?"

Wagner looked at her, saw how important it was for her to not be written off, even in jest.

"You're right," he finally said. "You're *right*. We wouldn't be standing here tonight if it weren't for you. Thank you."

Surprised and triumphant, she lit up like a lamp. Her chin held high, her hand placed graciously upon her heart, she replied in overlavish, formal tone: "You are quite welcome."

Then Wagner flicked her nose.

Like a tigress in bristle, J'nea retaliated with wild, flailing fists. Though loosely clenched, they were wholly business-minded; and Wagner, utilising tactics gained under Bilahdu's tutelage, unaccommodatingly dodged them with a versatility that frustrated the woman tenfold. Availing himself of the careless heat of her swings, he shrank shy of them, waiting for an opening. Then, grabbing at her passing left wrist, he quickly clamped onto it, waited for her overcompensating right, and caught it, too.

So hampered, she would still prove far from helpless. An unprecedented tensility in her now-governed flailing, he contested her wiriness only through an anchoring of stance. But she, far more learned in combative kinetics, readily unbalanced him, booted him on the shin, and nearly bowled him over—all the while rattling off every synonym for "scoundrel" that she had at her muster.

He made a feeble attempt to calm her, stressing consideration for the weak and sick, the battle-weary, even the children, all of whom slept within earshot. J'nea, however, saw through his half-frantic/half-comic attempt to spare himself proper comeuppance. Chortling her disdain, she called him a coward and challenged him to take his lumps in manly fashion. He did less than this: he buckled under, with equal parts vehement apology and beseechful grovelling—enough, it ultimately seemed, to appease her to the point of dropping all and leaving him be. Of course, having spent far too many hours in the company of expert braggarts, Wagner stretched his credibility, over-carrying his emoting to limits beyond even Bilahdu's capabilities. He swore to J'nea that he'd been barely more than a milquetoast the whole day long, and that he'd fudged his way through the liberating of Skol, the abetting of the Vofspar, even through the grand battle itself, where he'd pitted himself "in the thick of a few hundred NuRac warriors merely so that my enemy, by its sheer numbers, might shield my shame and my plucklessness from the eyes of my peers."

By this time, Mirko and Balgor had ambled up for a better vantage, leaving Uthok behind with only the unenviable Jotal to brag to—Jotal and the moths and the chafers who danced a wild buzz about the nearby string of cressets.

Wagner and J'nea entrenched in bicker and skirmish, this had ever been one of Balgor's favourite cabarets, and he sought now to make of Mirko an equally appreciative aficionado. With fuel of his own for to feed the flames, from the sideline Balgor made audible wager on Wagner's defeat, hoping to route his friend into distraction long enough to incur a bonus lump or two, purely for the sport of it. And a fructiferous gambit it was, for as Wagner levelled an ire-filled glare at Balgor for his improvised allegiance-swapping, J'nea helped herself to Wagner's unguardedness by clobbering him.

Splashing clumsily into the reeds, the bested Wagner didn't even bother trying to recover his dignity. From his back he promptly yielded to the trusty, who, with hands slung proudly upon her hips, smiled queen-like down at his diminishment.

"I should have learned by now not to tangle with you," Wagner groaned, reaching up for her helpful hand but getting no offer. From behind her, Balgor moved up for a gander, peering past J'nea's shoulder to behold his friend's humiliation.

"Come, errant children," Mirko suddenly commanded from their rear, his manner more condoning than condemning (although both sentiments were clearly present). "Save your roguery for the morrow, when we may truly require it."

Sidestepping J'nea and Balgor, he edged down the bank and lent his accommodation to Wagner. Yet, with his reaching, the airspace between his fingertips and Wagner's arced with the crackle of incandescence. Like a meteoric bullwhip, it slapped both men rillside, and J'nea, backwards onto her rump. Dissipating, then, in almost the very moment that it occurred, it left nobody with serious injury—nor even in much distress beyond a general windedness from the tumble. Wagner and Mirko both suffering but a brief moment of refractory torpor, each regained himself with timeliness and made his own way up the bank.

Balgor having witnessed this phenomenon before, he naturally assumed that Wagner had emitted an inadvertent healing. Wagner, however, knew this wasn't the case. Nothing had been initiated by him, not intentionally and not indeliberately. But what then? What had it been? In its wake, it had produced no depletory after-effect—at least not anything that he could immediately sense. Neither did he perceive in himself, or in the Vargathian, any distinguishable invigoration that one party or the other might have exhibited. In fact, by anyone's reckoning, there had been no product of the incident at all. At end, Wagner's sole speculation was that he and Mirko had triggered some manner of disproportionate static backlash, influenced, perhaps, by whatever unseen beneficence made Wagner's body a vessel for its thaumaturgy.

To J'nea—who'd never witnessed Wagner's gift—it seemed eerily akin to the plasmatic energies that SyKrahvo had extorted from the Soork. Bereft, however, of the signature devastation wrought by said instrument, she remained as dumbfounded as the rest.

Mirko seemed by far the most surprised. He, too, provided no accounting for the phenomenon. Significantly, he likewise perceived no evidence of personal infliction delivered by the discharge. A benign, albeit provocative, happenstance, dismissing its symbolic implication would, for him, have been akin to denying his random hours spent in madness; and as his proximity to Wagner had preceded, perhaps even prompted, the kinetic exchange, personal semiotics were to become his unlikely resort of choice. In this, he rather stunned himself with his own presumptions, for they rafted him speedily toward the shores of irony. Never in his past had he assigned much import to boasts of prodigy and wonders in the accounts of others, despite the copious mysticism that pervaded all facets of his culture. But here was a portent, the first of its kind that he'd experienced personally; and in his desperation to attach meaning to the insanity that had slowly been consuming him, how comical it was that a view founded upon the unanswerable and the unknown sufficed best in bolstering his inexplicable psychical kinship with the man called *Voknor*. It would be his first glimpse of a far distant beacon within the ebon loom of the storm.

Amid the drowsy onlookers, most of whom couldn't be at all certain of what they may or may not have seen, strode Tamek of Vishkor, his work with the wounded and with the spiritually starved deferred for the night. An unexpected visitor, his issue came like a cloud that suddenly blocks the moon. Even Uthok's tongue had stilled at his passing. One evening, weeks ago, J'nea had jested to Wagner that whenever there was revelry to be enjoyed, Tamek would soon be along to quash it. The revelry this evening having given way to horseplay—and horseplay, to wonderworks—her observation, while not strictly vatic, nonetheless demonstrated how the Sentinel's personage often had the stigma of parental-like influence. By his presence alone could he cast a net of dourness upon the mood of any assemblage; such was the patriarchal boon and burthen.

Yet, Tamek wasn't unwelcome here. In fact, it seemed that the day's events had made him thoughtful and introspective, and thus less apt to be preachy. His eyes, agleam with a fieriness not entirely attributable to the perimeter torchlight, hinted at how his pyric ritual had stoked in him a restless resolve to extract justice from those who had so brutalised his people and offended his deities.

"Was that levin I espied a moment before?" he asked.

"Aye," said Balgor. "In a manner. But we are inclined to believe that its origin was not, in its nature, firmamental."

Tamek glanced at Wagner, who shrugged innocuously.

"A freakish spontaneity?" said the outworlder.

"Indeed," said the Sentinel. "Such 'scintillation' has become commonplace in these past weeks." Purposely ambiguous, he was unsure of who, other than Balgor, had knowledge of Wagner's abilities.

"The Vorshalah, perhaps," Balgor suggested with rather covinous concordance. "It is, after all, the harbinger of many a strange circumstance."

J'nea promptly humbugged the notion. When eyes turned her way, she elaborated: "No more than a feathery word," she grumped. "A sigil assigned to anything not easily explained."

"Then *you* can explain it?" asked Tamek, his disdain for blasphemy uncharacteristically in check.

J'nea, appreciating his effort, remained equally amicable, despite the hortatory fillip of Jotal's nonvintage still mingling with her blood.

"I cannot," she confessed. "But I will not stamp a seal of holiness on something simply because it is beyond my reckoning. I grant you that I am an arrow-maker and not a polyhistor, but I see no need to flippantly assign cause to every mystery in order to pander to humanity's insecurities."

Mirko nudged Wagner. "She has fire, this one," he whispered. "I do believe I like her already."

"I'll notify your next of kin," said Wagner.

Nothing propounded by debate would be settled this evening. With the clash of such powerful belief systems, battles equally as fierce as the one fought that afternoon could be fought on the Socratic plane—ideology versus ideology, faith against fact—with no clear victor, no distinguishable villain, and no self-declaring victim coming to light even long after throats went raw and verbal armouries gave way to depletion.

In watching his friends in their spirited interplay, Wagner came to a profoundly pervasive discovery. Engaged by their verve, by their impassionedness, and indeed by their soap-box sermonising, he experienced something that he'd never truly possessed on earth: a sense of family. Family in all of its wonderfully eclectic dissonance, family in its dysfunctional sedulity and its bullheadedness and its priority-bollixed upheavals, family in its often latent but basic camaraderies and loyalties that, like unseen rootage, kept the greater tree anchored through blustery gales and hardships—all this he sensed, and more.

It felt grand. It felt marvellously nuclear. It felt like home, the way that "home" was supposed to feel.

Granted, he had lived with a jejune facsimile of this before, when he'd embraced the squabbling fraternity of leather-clad, bandana-topped rowdies back in his Filthy Lucre days. He'd likewise dwelled alongside it with Howsley's rec room regulars, none of whom could ever remain agreeable long enough to properly conclude the simplest session of Chutes and Ladders without upsetting the board, the tokens, the table, and each other. But it was different for him now. For the first time since his planetary displacement, Wagner actually *wanted* to be here—not necessarily in his predicament, but with these people, even in the shadow of such ominous uncertainty. No matter the fact of how grim things looked for their side, he knew that adversity wouldn't hinder this bunch, no way, no how. Not satisfied with merely surviving the day, their outlook totalled far more than the residuum left by the decrement of their many misfortunes. Each of their souls blazed anew with desire, inspired by pure adamantness and by conviction that Wagner had encountered nowhere else. Balgor, J'nea, Mirko, Tamek—not one of them was at all like those bereft of purpose Filthy Lucre drones who'd choked down his greasy burgers, who'd complained through their sloppy-drunk jabber about every insignificant thing across the face of the earth, who'd never made even the most meagre effort personally to right the world's woes, and whose only fulfilling obligation at the time had been in lobbing their empty longnecks through the Lucre's kitchen fenestra like vintage German hand grenades. Through hardships far more bona fide did Wagner's Ergosian compeers claim their purpose and duty and commitment; and this, most of all, was what differentiated them from his disencumbered earthly rabble.

It differentiated him too. He'd discovered purpose of his own. He'd learned how to be tenacious. He'd rustled up some pretty righteous convictions. Perhaps most importantly, he had become one of this group, one of this proud assemblage—an Ergosian and a respected warrior. Adrift on chaotic tides for most of his life, it was only by the artifice of some still-unknown supernal force that he'd been psychically fly-fished into these cosmic waters, long before ever being diverted bodily. Still an impossible caprice to a reasonable man like himself, his feet nevertheless stood planted on soil that laid claim to him years before he knew it existed; and it seemed that, at least until he could solve all of the mysteries of his new existence, Ergos was where he was going to stay.

With questions too innumerable, and answers behindhand but incrementally forthcoming, he considered that any one moment might reveal some newer truth. Simply in encountering Mirko he had affixed a kind of completory cohesiveness to the collective riddle. Old dream symbolism that manifested here and now as the unearthly Soork had provided him limited insight into the complexity of his mind-trip allegory. His praeterhuman magiks, while neither fashionable nor commonplace, had been accepted without extreme overwroughtness by those who'd become privy to it, and in the prevenance of a war against SyKrahvo's newfound might it would be of no minor import to the downbeaten and the deprived. Yet, with its fleetingly degenerative effect on Wagner's physiology presenting an unforeseen bogey in an otherwise provident gift, he anticipated a time when he'd be forced to deal with the unbidden consequence, and he prayed that, when said moment arrived, he would possess the wherewithal and the apperception to handle such contingency.

Lastly, in conjunct with his own amok persona, he was apparently the patron saint of other such feral kindred: Skol and the Vofspar. Both now lost to him, both still indivisibly significant to his Ergosian itinerary, he could only wonder if another crossroads lay somewhere in their futures. In unexpected boon, through his unlikely connection to them he'd managed to wean some of his closest comrades of their misconceptions about said creatures, often at the risk of his own life. Skol no longer quite so unredeemably odious, the Vofspar not so unjustifiably virulent—Balgor and Tamek would henceforth need to sling their daemonic constructs onto other, less demystified entities.

There was so much ahead in which to immerse himself, so many weaves in the arras still to be explored, that Wagner felt puny and ill-equipped before the immensity of his challenge. Yet, no longer was he forced to confront existence as a solo act. A fosterling from his beginnings, *that* much had not truly changed; but this newest of families had become his own in a manner unlike any that had preceded it. No ready-made clan eager to bestow onto him its gifts of heart and hearth, this ensemble was one that he'd culled through circumstance. Their fellowship he'd earned gradually, through deeds and risk, chance and fortitude and—occasionally—by way of madness. The bond that he'd forged with these companions had come subsequent to his great effort and forbearance and curiosity (supplemented, of course, by a truckload of unattributable nutriture, compliments of some ever-anonymous, empyrean theurgy). Hammered truer with every new day, made roborant by the tempering of transpiration, these friendships—the recent, the established, even the yet to be—constituted the outermost edges of that fatidic jigsaw puzzle on which he'd laboured for so many years. Together, they provided framework for the search, the foundational borders from which to sleuth for deeper meaning. Already they had assisted him in piecing together a handful of historical relevancies and prophetic legends, enough to interlock with some of his precognitive impressions and to thus convince him that he may, in his muddle of hunches and theories, have actually been onto something premissable. The real eye-opener having come this very evening, mere moments ago, with the realisation that his Vargathian rescuer might well be facing an ordeal that mirrored his own in an inverted, yet undeniably ligamentous, similitude—if nothing else, it relieved Wagner's burden of being the sole instrument of cosmic hard knocks and circuitous paradoxes, and would undoubtedly compel his unanticipated recruitment as counsellor, guide, and mentor to this realm's most valiant hero—a man with his own lengthy list of travails in loom.

So much lay ahead, so much that was unknown and yet strangely prevenient. To dwell on it and to decipher it all was a grand task that Wagner had yet to complete, a task that perhaps had no satisfactory end. For the remainder of this night, however, it was a task that he would gladly abandon in favour of a little bit of earned frivolity. The threat of the Soork could wait for a few hours. The Vorshalah could greet them with its newest revelation on the morrow. And the *sigma*, what it represented and how it linked Wagner to AuwNiir—well, that would have to suffer an even longer delay. Wagner and his comrades had more immediate matters to ponder, namely what quantity of Jotal's wine yet remained in the skin, and how they might snatch it from Uthok's besotted grip long enough to toast the day and each other.

This night they were all free. And by Eternity's flowing tresses, they would act like it.

AFTERWORD

A few years back, when my muses grew so weary in their unfruitful attempts to inspire me that they finally changed their tactics to out and out threats, I got serious and set myself at organising the many scrawlings and character composites and brainstormed scribbles that I'd been amassing for over a decade, and embarked upon the literary undertaking that would eventually become *OF STAVES AND SIGMAS*. Squirrelling myself away for many a month, I went about said undertaking with verve most high, and with a happy and reasonable notion of where—among the sundry categories of genre fiction—my tale would ultimately find its niche and come to occupy shelf space in the formidably vast realm of printed matter. After all, with its mediaevalesque setting, its swords and its crossbows, its occasional mentions of mystical manifestations, it seemed pretty patent that I was scribing some manner of fantasy novel. And, no doubt, if you purchased your copy personally or checked it out of your local library branch, there's a fair surety that you found it tucked somewhere in the fantasy & sci-fi section, perhaps sandwiched quite humbly and respectfully between such estimable and prolific "V" authors as Vance and Verne. Not bad company to keep.

However, I must tell you that *OF STAVES AND SIGMAS* was a quite different animal at its conception. You see, I was a great deal younger when I first conceived it. My understanding of the world back then was more clearly—and erroneously—defined. Good and evil, love and hate, winning and losing—such distinctions seemed cut and dried to an inexperienced young fellow who still took so much of life at face value. And yet, interestingly, I must have intuited my callowness at some level, for I shelved my initial manuscript time and again for a number of years, tinkering with it only on occasion between jobs, between girlfriends, between therapy (ha-ha—only kidding—no, really), until Time had sufficiently taught me just how much I *didn't* know, and how truly varied are the gradations of grey that exist in thought, action, and argument.

With this new tempering of confidence and qualification, with "all systems go," I sat down—an older and a generally more learned being—and constructed an entirely new draft over the framework of the old, utilising all of the previously established elements, but updating and emending them with new vigour and complexity. And yet, although I was both proud of, and highly satisfied with, the results, at the end of said process I came to discover something that was both serendipitous and troubling: While the storyline had indeed grown rich and intricate through my more matured interpretational vantage, it had also become...

well...apparently very non-mainstream. No longer was it a single genre novel. In fact, it dragged a motley foot through a lot of different genres.

Truly, there's nothing wrong with this; for, as you ostensibly know by now (seeing as you're reading these few paragraphs at the *end* of the work), there are indeed smatterings of classic fantasy elements to be found within these pages. However, I do hope that along the way you also noted—and, hopefully, warmed to—just as many literary elements, just as many philosophical, theological, and sociological ones, and perhaps a few narrative devices and non-conformities that you didn't recognise, couldn't have anticipated, or never expected would have swept you in the direction that they did. If so, mission accomplished.

Still, the marketing end of my venture—though barely pushed beyond the gate at this point—has thus far hinted at a challenge. At the onset, my publisher, with its very best guess, classified *OF STAVES AND SIGMAS* as a fantasy & science fiction work. And, indeed, it's a pretty good fit. But I've since discovered that being slotted into so finite a category has arguably prevented it from being discovered by what I'm hoping will become a greater diversity of readers. Never intended to be a breezy read or a best-seller, never meant to be a huge pulse-pounder throughout, *OF STAVES AND SIGMAS* is basically an uncommon literary adventure that is introspective and character-driven—and which, on the whole, demands more than a simple once-over-lightly passivity from its audience. And while its expository chapters have recently drawn some comment as being all but insuperable for those who come at the book with more formalistic expectations, I must contend that the bulk of my critiquing readers claim to have found a most meaty and provocative body beyond.

And what of resolution? Well, as you surely know by now, resolution is meted only tightfistedly in Book One—and mostly only as it applies to the grander Ergosian immediacy. But even as I promise to deliver far greater insight into the Wagner/*Miracle* connection as I go on to craft Book Two, I am equally prepared to besiege you with a few more mysteries as well. In fact, for every riddle I answer, I may just present you with two more. Are you game? If so, stick with me. If you liked what's already been, you'll love what's coming next.

Geoffrey Verdegast

July 5, 2008

www.ingramcontent.com/pod-product-compliance
Lightning Source LLC
Chambersburg PA
CBHW020824030726
47496CB00001B/73